NEW WORLD ORDER

CRIMSON SHADOW BOOK SEVEN

NATHAN SQUIERS

ALSO AVAILABLE BY NATHAN SQUIERS:

CRIMSON SHADOW SERIES:

Noir

Sins of the Father

Forbidden Dance

Dance with the Devil

The Longest Night

Gods & Monsters

New World Order

OTHER WORKS:

Scarlet Night

(co-authored with Megan J. Parker)

Scarlet Dawn

(co-authored with Megan J. Parker)

Scarlet Dusk

(co-authored with Megan J. Parker)

A Howl at the Moon

Death, Death, and the Dying Day: A Weird West Story

Twisted Words & Melted Thoughts: A Poetry & Song Collection

The Winter Sun

(co-authored with Megan J. Parker)

New Moon: A Paranormal Reverse Harem Novel

(co-authored with Megan J. Parker)

Original Sin & Scarlet Rising: A Crimson Shadow & Behind the Vail

Story

(co-authored with Megan J. Parker)

Running on Empty: The Crows MC #1

(co-authored with Megan J. Parker)

Riding on Fumes: The Crows MC #2

(co-authored with Megan J. Parker)

Braking Down: The Crows MC #3

(co-authored with Megan J. Parker)

Journey to YOUR Story: A start-to-finish guide for your personal writing journey

(co-authored with Megan J. Parker)

Black Man White Man

(co-authored with Joe Janowicz)

Published by
Literary Dark Duo Publishing

This is a work of fiction. Names, characters, places, and incidents either are the product of the author's imagination or are used fictitiously. Any resemblance to actual persons living or dead, events, or locales is entirely coincidental.

Copyright © 2020 by Nathan Squiers
Cover Design by Bewitching Book Covers by Rebecca Frank

All rights reserved. No part of this book may be reproduced or transmitted in any form or by any means, electronic or mechanical, including photocopying, recording, or by any information storage and retrieval system, without the written permission of the Publisher, except where permitted by law.

PROLOGUE

LIKE A DREAM COME TRUE

Xander can't help but feel like he's in a dream; in a perfect dream.

It is so beautiful.

She *is so beautiful.*

Estella, skin like a flawless pearl and eyes glimmering like an exotic sea, approaches him; her steps slow, methodic. Perfect. A parted sea of friends and family sit on either side of her path, most of their eyes shimmering with the threat of tears as she passes. She draws nearer. Her smile grows as she does. It is hidden behind a veil the color of the sky reflected off a glittering snowcapped mountain, but Xander sees that smile all the same. Like it always does, it makes him smile back.

Seeing her son's lips draw upward in response to the sight of his soon-to-be bride, a sob that only half-disguises itself as a cry of joy slips past Emily Stryker's lips. Xander, in an impossible feat of strength, tears his gaze from Estella and catches sight of his mother—sad-eyed and lips parted in a smile of intense and impossible joy—just as his father, Joseph, drapes a comforting arm over his own wife's shoulder. As the two Stryker men's eyes meet, a silent moment of prideful exchanges pass:

You did good, son; found a real angel with her.

Thanks, Dad—for everything, *Xander says through the connection, then, to himself, he thinks,* It pays to have a psychic father.

Behind Joseph, grinning knowingly and patting him on the shoulder, is Depok. Beside him on his right is Marcus; Stan on his left, closest to the aisle. Most of this row—the groom's row—is nonhuman colleagues with the Odin Clan and a handful of Xander's closest friends, mythos and human alike. Compared to this row, however, the opposite set of seats—assigned to friends and family of the bride—is occupied by far more humans. There'd been an inside joke between Xander and his father earlier that the doorman could easily identify which side a newcomer would be seated at by checking what sort of teeth they had.

It was, admittedly, a lame joke, since both Xander and Joseph could easily pass for humans, as well.

As far as anybody who wasn't *a mythos was concerned, however, everyone in that room was one-and-the-same species: a "fact" that Xander, his father, and many of the others in attendance worked hard to maintain.*

That a second Stryker in just as many generations was marrying a human—that a second Stryker had exposed the truth to a human—is the reason for the two scowling faces in the back of the room. Though the Stryker family and the Odin Clan has assured The Council that such a step is unnecessary, the two hybrid vampires—armed with the assets of both sangs and aurics as well as a set of silenced Berettas and serrated blades—represent the closest thing to an agreement.

An agreement that almost everyone on the groom's side of the room shared an eye roll over.

Estella had been among the eye rollers, but now, stepping past Stan and still wearing the ever-growing smile, she shows no sign of irritation at the armed vampires overseeing the ceremony. Catching her once again in his gaze, Xander watches as his soon-to-be bride offers his sobbing mother a reassuring smile. Her chin dips in the slightest of nods, and Emily stifles another cry—the sad sounds never reaching her joyful expression—and, beaming a loving smile at her, brings the fingers of her right hand to her lips to blow her soon-to-be daughter-in-law a kiss. Estella, without breaking stride, makes no effort to hide the gesture as she mime-catches the airborne love and presses it to the modest dip where her chest disappears under her gown. Xander can't help himself, and he lingers on the sight of the bride's cleavage, a tantalizing view on any occasion. It's too perfect to not *appreciate at this moment.*

Estella catches him looking.

Seeing without seeing—thanks for the mind's eye, Dad—*Xander sees a dark eyebrow arch over sparkling blue eyes behind the mist of Estella's veil. There's no frown accompanying the gesture. Instead, Xander sees, with his eyes this time, the curvature of Estella's breasts swell beneath her gown as she puffs out her chest for him. Already past the final row of seats, the display goes unnoticed by all except Xander and Father Tennesen, whose aura shifts but remains otherwise silent about it.*

The old priest, who is standing before them not because of his role with the church but because of his friendship with the Strykers and, through them, his ongoing relationship with the Odin Clan. He calls himself an exorcist—off the record, of course—and, though he's accepted there's plenty he doesn't know, what he does know has proven useful more than enough in the past. Today, however, his knowledge and his power aren't what matters; he's here to lead the service and marry the two.

And, apparently, stealing an eyeful of Estella's cleavage as she presents it to her soon-to-be husband. Xander could roast a marshmallow on the flare of Father Tennesen's blush, which he needs neither his eyes nor his mind's eye to know is there. His grin widens, unable to even feel jealous at that moment.

Manipulative little minx, *he speaks without speaking, sending the taunt directly into her mind.*

But something in that doesn't sound right in his head...

A shrug so subtle that nobody else would notice—save for the minister, perhaps—tugs at the left edge of her gown, and her smile grows. A twinge of rapacious mischief presents itself behind her eyes; laced throughout her swimming aura.

*It's like she's put him under a spell—intoxicated him with some sort of enchantment—and Xander almost—*almost!*—forgets that his soon-to-be wife, this beautiful, glowing bride of his, does not know how to use magic. She'd always expressed an interest in his and his father's abilities after he'd confessed the truth to her; after he'd confessed that he was an auric vampire. His mother and father had both been present for that conversation, Joseph feeling it was only right that he oversee the exchange—it was a touchy matter, after all; opening up to a human—and Emily, a human who'd once been on the receiving end of that same conversation with her own husband, felt it only right that Estella have a kindred spirit present. When he'd finally told her, however, she'd surprised all three of them with two words:*

"I know."

She hadn't *known. Not really. She'd had suspicions, and with these she'd formed theories. And while none of these were necessarily on the mark—*"my boyfriend is a vampire who feeds on psychic energy,"* was, understandably, not an immediate go-to hypothesis in most cases—she was open-minded enough to bridge the possibilities she'd been working on to the eventual truth.*

With the family secret out, Estella became aware of one of the greatest secrets the world over: that of mythos, of nonhuman creatures that fed on the life-force of others, changed their shape, and wielded deadly powers of speed and strength and magic. Being aware did not mean being afraid, however, and Xander came to find that, while not interested in the gory, violent details of his and his father's outings, she was intrigued by the things he could do with his aura. Though not magic in the traditional sense, his ability to move things with his aura—the energy field he could manipulate as easily as any limb but unseen by her eyes—and read minds seemed no different to her than a show she might have seen on a stage or, as she preferred to say, the magnificent things that the wizards of her favorite books and movies could accomplish. She'd often tease him by calling him "Gan-

dalf" or "Dumbledore," stating that he should consider growing a long, gangly beard. He didn't bother to mention that such things would look foolish when he and his father went out to gun down rogues or investigate supernatural happenings. And while she never ceased to be amused by Xander's "magic," she never wanted to know how it was done or whether or not she could learn.

"The only reason I would ever want to do such things," she'd explained on one of the occasions he'd offered to teach her, "would be to help you." Then, framing him with her fingers, she'd added, "But between you and your father basically being superheroes, I think I'd be happier having my own private magic show and not having the tricks spoiled."

Admittedly, Xander didn't need any help when it came to being protected. Between the weapons and combat training he'd gone through with his father and the support of the mythos clan that Joseph had helped build, there were few threats that couldn't be faced. Despite all her interest, it appeared that, without an immediate threat to Xander to motivate her, Estella was fine with living her life never learning the arts.

Then why do I keep wanting to say 'witch'? *Xander thinks, catching himself as a frown begins to birth itself across his face.*

His chest aches, a deep, breath-robbing sense. Like his lungs...

Oh fuck! *he thinks.* They broke my ribs!

Then, as the pain subsides and his breath comes back to him, he suddenly wonders what he was thinking.

Who's 'they'? *he wonders,* And why can't I stop thinking 'witch'?

The two Council guards shift uncomfortably in the back, making no effort to hide the widening gate of their stances or, despite being in control of them, the aggressive flaring of their auras. Xander sees without seeing as one of them sets a rough, twitchy hand on the hard area over his suit jacket. He doesn't need his mind's eye to know there's a gun waiting there.

The other guard makes no move short of widening his stance, but Xander thinks he sees his aura snap out and—

"Hey," Estella's voice is more of a subtle breeze as she breathes out the word. She's made it to Xander's side while he was...

What had he been thinking?

Embarrassed, realizing he'd let his mind wander without having a single viable thought to show for it, he blushes, blinking—awestruck—at the beauty before him.

Estella.

His *Estella.*

Estella Edash...

Soon to be Estella Stryk—

"This... this isn't..." Xander's whisper trails off as he tries to decide how best to say that he's thought this before—done this before—and he's distantly aware that the guard's aura is—

Don't fight it.

The words come into his head so easily that Xander's almost positive they were his own thoughts, but why would he—

The guard...

"Hey," Estella's voice is more of a subtle breeze as she breathes out the word. She's made it to Xander's side while he was lost in thought.

Random thoughts.

Nothing important.

Xander shifts, discomforted by this. Letting his mind drift today *of all days? A part of him—a part he's not familiar with and, therefore, unprepared to mentally cope with—flares up with an intense fury. Plenty of times before, during clan missions and outings with his father, he's felt anger and, yes, even rage towards his enemies—enemies who meant great harm to others—and, channeling it, he had destroyed them.*

Now, however, thinking thoughts—random thoughts; unimportant thoughts; thoughts that make him feel... wrong—during his wedding day turns that rage inward.

How dare he spoil his and Estella's wedding, if even only in his mind!

Self-loathing is a foreign feeling to Xander, yet it carries with it a strange, almost comforting sense of déjà vu. *He can't be sure how or why, but hating himself for spoiling this perfect moment feels...*

Real.

Xander instantly wonders why that should be the first word that comes to him. Self-loathing is joined by confusion, and confusion urges him to—

Just stay up there and DIE!

Those aren't my thoughts! *Xander decides.* They're not my—

Both of The Council appointed guards' auras flare this time, and—

"Hey," Estella's voice is more of a subtle breeze as she breathes out—

Xander hates himself for it—a foreign-yet-familiar sensation—but he frowns at her.

"How long have you been standing there?" he asks.

No! Just play out the scene like a good boy; just go along with it and DIE!

"Hey," Estella's voice is more of a subtle breeze.

Man, Déjà vu is a hell of a thing! *Xander thinks, and he smiles and says "H-hey" back to her, flinching only slightly at his stammer.*

However, given the vision he's taking in, how can he not *stammer?*

"Good boy."

Xander blinks and almost asks Estella if she'd said something just now, but the guards begin to take a step and he remembers that's foolish.

"The bride and the groom have prepared their own vows," Father Tennesen says, and Xander can't help but feel that he's skipped something.

Isn't there supposed to be a 'dearly beloved'-part first? *he wonders.*

But that's just a random thought; nothing important.

You probably just drifted off into more random, stupid thoughts and missed it, *he thinks, then immediately wonders why he'd think of himself as—*

One of the guards fondles his Berretta; Xander wonders why he's...

You did good, son, *Joseph Stryker calls into Xander's mind, and he turns slightly to catch sight of his father giving him a loving, approving smile.* Found a real angel with her.

Something in the sight of his father there, happy and approving and alive, relaxes Xander, and he smiles back. Thanks, Dad—for everything.

There. Doesn't that feel better?

"I like to begin all journeys with the guidance of those wiser than me," Estella says, beginning her vows. Somewhere in the back of Xander's mind, he thinks he hears Stan's disembodied voice whisper —good advice—*but he can't quite make out the words.*

Random. Unimportant.

Estella's smile holds him, and something in that is so peaceful it almost seems wrong. "... a quote from one of my favorite philosophers, Aristotle:" she pauses to clear her throat, and the moment of broken eye contact has Xander wondering if he's heard this all before.

Love is composed of...

"'Love is composed of a single soul inhabiting two bodies,'" Estella says, and her smile holds him; her eyes trap him.

NO!

Estella's smile holds him, and something in that is so peaceful it almost seems...

Estella's smile holds him as she goes on:

"No greater sentiment can be said about my love for you or your love for me. Throughout these years, you have been everything for me —the strong arms to catch me when I fall, the shoulder to cry on for everything from stubbing my toe to watching my entire world getting ripped apart... but, most importantly, you have been a reliable..."

"...a reliable savior to you—well, to everyone, actually..." Xander finishes for her, beginning to take a step back.

Straight into one of The Council's guards.

When had he—

We'll behave or—

Why would I think of myself—

I'll behave or—

Why would I threaten—

I'll behave. I'll behave, and everything is alright. This. Is. *My.* Wedding day!

Xander feels a wave of nausea as he realizes he is letting his work as a mythos warrior carry over; his defenses and constant readiness for the worst on the battlefield are making him think crazy thoughts on his and Estella's big day. And, to make matters worse, all those crazy thoughts are...

That's right. Random and not important.

"... but, most importantly," Estella goes on, tears welling in her eyes, "you have been a reliable savior to me—well, to everyone, actually." She pauses then to let a momentary hum of agreement pass around the crowd then, then says, "No matter the circumstances, you make things better. Throughout all the good, the bad, and the ugly—and we all know there were a lot of ugly moments in the—

Wait... there *were* ugly moments. But what were—

"No matter the circumstances, you make things better. Throughout all the good and the bad, you stood strong beside me. I thank you for making every day special for me. I thank you for going out of your way day-in and day-out and I thank you for going out of your way in ways you think I don't notice just to make me smile. I thank you for not trying to become my confidence, but working with me to help build and mold my own. There's not a day that goes by that I don't realize just how lucky I am to have you in my life. I truly found my soul mate with you and I look forward to spending many more years growing with you and even creating a family together. I love you, Xander Stryker."

Wasn't there more? *Xander wonders.* I could've sworn there was—

Nope.

Didn't my vows come fir—

Nope.

But I thought—

"Xander," Father Tennesen's eyes are on him, knowing and... impatient? If not for the irritation bobbing like ugly clumps of mud in the priest's aura, Xander would pass the expression off as a trick of the light. But there it— "... your vows."

It feels more like a command.

Xander obeys:

*"Oh... uh, yeah—I mean 'yes,'" there is a soft round of chuckles from the audience as Xander shivers under the weight of the attention that falls upon him, and his shaky hands fight to pull out the numbered index cards that wore his scribbled handwriting. Getting his trembling fingers under control, he takes a moment to draw in a controlled breath and gazes into Estella's beaming blue eyes—they still have him trap... held in the serenity of the moment. There is a tremor on his nerves, but a tiny voice in the back of his mind reminds him it's all foolish—*random; not important—*and he calms soon after, a smile spreading across his face. "God damn, you're so beautiful—sorry," he glances at Father Tennesen long enough to get a passive wave for forgiveness. Something in the gesture seems wrong; like it was somebody else's body motioning for him to go on and Tennesen's head was only along for the ride. He shakes the thought away and says, "There are a lot of words that come to mind about marriage, and when you're a man, those words are sometimes...* inappropriate *for a ceremony."*

The crowd laughs, but it feels canned; the pre-recorded, forced laughter of a sitcom.

I'll take 'bullshit delusions' for three-hundred, Alex.

When did I ever watch—

ON WITH IT!

"I'm not that sort of man," Xander continues, ignoring his random, unimportant thoughts, "but I do find that the words that come to my mind are still inappropriate—words like 'shame' and 'failure' and 'disappointment.'"—Try "lost" and "oblivious" and "exposed!"—*"But these are words of worry that bounce around in my head already,"*—and rightfully so!—*"and I wanted to catch the word that best described this moment."*—Fake! Fake! Fake!—*"And*

now, before"—FAKE!—*"friends and"*—DEAD!—*"colleagues, I can say with certainty that the word is 'strength.'"*

Says the numb-nuts too dense to—

I've had about enough of...

He pauses a moment, taking in another breath and calming his tensing nerves.

Random and unimportant, *he reminds himself.* Random and unimportant.

That's right. Good. Good.

"I know that many of you were thinking that I was going to say 'love,'" Xander reads on, "and while we're certainly in love, I think there's more to this moment. This is about taking pride in the strength we've shown so far and preparing ourselves for the strength we'll need..." He catches sight of Estella's face, sees the love there in her face, but notices there's no tear.

There was a tear—a shimmering tear—the first time I... *he trembles.* Oh...

Don't. You don't want to do this. You *know* what happens if you go down that—

I know, *Xander's trying so hard not to cry now.* I know. I'll be good. Just give me—

Done.

He catches sight of Estella's face, sees the shimmering beginnings of a tear in her left eye and he feels his own throat knot...

Exactly like it did before.

Swallowing the tightening sensation, he pushes on, carefully slipping the topmost index card to the back of the pile to continue reading:

"Strength to grow."

"Afraid not, son," *his father's voice says sadly in the back of his mind.*

"Strength to stand together."

"BULLSHIT!" *Marcus' voice roars in his head.*

"Strength to overcome whatever dumb bastards might stand in our way."

"Not like this," Stan says aloud, and the room erupts into chaos as everyone turns on him, telling him to be silent. The Council guards are upon him, their auras snapping out and filling the room, flooding it, and—

"LADIES AND GENTLEMEN!" Father Tennesen's voice booms, and Xander can't remember the last time he'd ever heard the old priest sound so loud and boastful. "IT GIVES ME GREAT PLEASURE TO BE THE FIRST TO INTRODUCE YOU ALL TO MISTER AND MISSUS XANDER AND ESTELLA STRYKER!"

But I didn't finish, *he thinks, looking down at the unused note-cards containing his vows.*

You'll be finished soon enough.

Of course...

Married—finally *married!—and Xander had spent most of the wedding lost in thought and worrying about... what? He looks around, sees all his friends and family standing, applauding, and, in a few cases, crying. He can only hope, like with his mother, that they're tears of joy. He* hates *the sound of his mother's crying, has always hated it.*

He frowns, not sure when was the last time he legitimately heard her crying. It seems such a familiar sound—somehow even more familiar than her own face, though this seems impossible with her right in front of him—but he can't for the life of him remember why; can't remember the last time he'd heard her crying, or, if a memory can *be dredged up, it's certainly not recent or relevant enough to make it something that should be so familiar.*

"Perks of the job, eh son?"

Xander's eyes widen, and it's all he can do to keep from dropping to his knees. He sees it happening for the first time all over again, cast against the scene before him—a movie that's all projection and no screen—and, though it's an impossible vision (his mother is right there, *after all) he somehow remembers it all too well:*

*He watches, powerless, as Kyle—*How the hell do I know who that is? *Xander wonders as he watches the man... no, the* auric *—looks over his shoulder at his friends.*

"What do you say we have a little 'down time' with Emily here before we get to business?"

NO! *Xander's knees buckle, and he's certain that he* is *about to collapse in front of everyone. Nobody seems to notice the scene that's playing out all around them—the phantoms acting out a memory that he could have no way of having—and the confused faces occupying the pews are aimed solely at the groom.*

Son? *Joseph's voice distorts over the audio of the five year old, non-existent rape and murder of his wife. Xander can't bring himself to face him, can't begin to wonder how such a memory could exist if he's still alive.* What's the matter? What is it?

How could it have happened if you were...?

But Xander can't finish the question. The ghost of the auric rapist who, in another time and another place, was his stepfather is staring back at him, grinning.

"This is the life, ain't it?" *he calls to him, transcending time and space in a horrible, impossible way to reach him.*

"You never married her, you son of a bitch!" Xander growls at the vision, and he only realizes he's spoken aloud to the specter after he hears several of the more sensitive guests gasp at his outburst.

Father Tennesen clears his throat behind him. "Rest assured, Xander," he says, his voice sounding impatient; none of the shock the others seem to be showing present, "you are *married to her."*

You don't want to go down this path, Xander; you know where it leads. You know what you'll see.

He's already seeing a heap of men crawling over his mother, though; watching their leering, scrunched faces twist in glee as they lick at her face and begin to tear at her white gown.

But it wasn't white, *he thinks to himself, finally dropping to his knees as he remembers the red and purple dress that was destroyed on that day.*

A day that doesn't exist; that cannot exist. Not with all that's happening around him.

Dad... *he calls out to Joseph,* You need to help her; help Mo—

His eyes dart away from the phantoms crawling on his unsus-

pecting mother to his father, expecting the great Joseph Stryker to find a way to save his wife. He's the *Joseph Stryker, after all—world renowned auric warrior and, more than that even, Emily's husband. If anybody could save her it would be...*

The scream lodges in Xander's throat before it has a chance to be born.

The seat beside Emily—the seat that mere seconds earlier belonged to Xander's father—is now occupied by a gape-jawed corpse. The skin is dark, nearly black—the color of rotted fruit and spoiled meat. The receding, rancid layer of skin allows the sharp, angry bones beneath to stick out in grotesque clarity; a twisted skeleton wearing a damp sheet of decay sitting beside Emily Stryker, ignoring the assault on her and gaping back at Xander with cold, vacant eyes.

Eyes that had never even seen his son, let alone been available to watch his wedding.

God dammit, *the thoughts that are more than thoughts curse in Xander's mind.* You Strykers and your arrogance!

I... I don't want to see this. I want—

"Xander?"

He turns to face Estella, somehow certain that she can—

Not a witch; never a witch...

Then... how?

A shriek of pain shoots out, calling Xander back to the phantom rape of his mother. He watches as a clump of strawberry-blonde hair straight up like confetti from the writhing mound. The men—the memories—continue; twisting his beautiful, innocent mother to their whims, doing anything and everything they can to accommodate their perversions.

And he's powerless to stop it; powerless to fight.

For the first time, Xander can't fight.

Because you *didn't* fight; because you *couldn't* fight, *a familiar voice chimes in Xander's head.*

"Stan?" Xander calls out, too engrossed in the chaos of this moment to commit to thought-speak. "Wh-what's...?"

Stan, however, has no problem committing to it as he says, These dominos don't look right, do they?

The phantoms, still continuing to satiate their lust, begin beating on their unaware victim. Though Emily remains oblivious of their actions, her body wears the damage all the same. Her dress is all-but destroyed—hanging in tattered clumps here-and-there—and puddles of her attackers' semen and her blood roll in spiraling clumps down her bruised breasts. She stares, the tears of joy seeming a mockery now, with nothing but concern for her son, unaware of her nakedness or the wounds that continue to spread across her body. A weak smile curves upward, and the light catches on a fresh trail of spit that one of the phantom's tongues dragged across her cheek. A vase is raised, moved into position, and Xander finds himself reaching out towards her.

"MOM! LOOK OUT!"

Emily flinches at her son's warning, but the mass of painted ceramic falls upon her all the same; just the same as it had before. Her eyes cross—the concerned stare still locked on him; the bewildered half-smile still cocked his way—and the left dips downward, dead, as a thick, furious trail of red begins to burble down the side of her face. She does not fall. She does not cry out. She suffers all the damage of that horrible, non-existent day while staring back at her recently married son all the same.

"Xander," Estella calls to him, tugging his shoulder. "Stay with me."

You should stay with her, Xander, *Stan calls out to him again,* but I think you know that staying here isn't the way to do it.

ENOUGH OF THAT! *the thought that's not a thought roars,* YOU *WILL* STAY UP THERE, AND YOU *WILL* DIE! *The Council's guards are on the move again, their bodies and their auras alike seeming to have trouble navigating around the phantom vision that nobody else seems to even be able to see. As the thoughts that aren't thoughts continue to demand Xander's compliance, they're moving in to force it—the bodies enforcing the voice-without-a-voice—*

YOU'RE LITTLE MORE THAN A SCARECROW NOW, SO BE A SCARECROW AND—

Oh, be quiet, already! *Stan demands, and Xander more senses the flick of his wrist than sees it as his old friend casually casts aside both voice and guards.* You said it yourself: Strykers and their arrogance, right?

HOW IN THE HELL—

Another dismissive wave; another forced silence.

I said be quiet, *Stan repeats, and the voice and the guards are suddenly gone.*

Reality—this *reality—begins to fall away, the walls dimming and fading to a blackness that's far more vast than the room had been. The floor sinks away, leaving everyone and everything resting on a black abyss. The ceiling sails away into the same infinite void. One-by-one the guests begin to fade away, most dimming out of existence while a select few remain. Further back, an old, one-armed man who'd been silently watching from the rear of the room lingers, the thumb on his remaining arm extending in silent approval as he fades to black. Xander blinks at this, a tickling sense of familiarity making the back of his mind itch. Finally, the old man and any chance of remembering who he is vanishes, and Xander is forced to return his focus to the only things left in the otherwise vast, infinite blackness this world has become. His mother, unwavering despite her injuries, continues to stare back at him as the corpse of her husband, Xander's father, slumps forward and falls away after the vanishing floor. Behind her, Stan and Depok and Marcus remain. Though his back is to him, Xander knows that Father Tennesen is still with him, as well.*

And Estella.

Always, ALWAYS *Estella.*

These dominos don't look right, do they? *Stan repeats in his head.* I mean, they're prettier to look at, sure, but they're falling all wrong, don't you think? Granted, *anything* would be better than...

Though nothing is said or done to motivate the action, Xander looks back to his mother. The Kyle-phantom smiles down at her as he retrieves a serrated knife out of the darkness and spins it in his hand.

"Don't make me watch this..." Xander begs.

It can't be helped, *Stan explains.* You have to see it now, because you had to see it then. I wish it wasn't so, lord knows it's no picnic for me, either.

"But you're..."

Like them?

Xander's eyes are driven on their own once again, and he sees Depok erupt into flames—his body becoming a mound of fire that, oblivious to its fate, sits and stares back at him until it flakes away into ash and vanishes into the void. A moment later, Marcus' head leaps from his shoulders, a soft gasp of blood belching from the oozing, jagged stump of his neck before he, too, vanishes.

Behind him, Xander hears a series of grotesque pops and squelches, and he resists the urge to turn, knowing that he'd see Father Tennesen lying at his feet in a mutilated heap.

Yeah, *Stan says with a sigh,* I suppose I *am* like them. But that you know that now says a lot, doesn't it?

"What does it say, exactly?"

That you're more than a scarecrow, for one. And that you're not ready to die.

"Then what is all of this?" Xander asks, already knowing.

This, *Stan turns his head to look at Xander's mother,* is a convenient comfort. You've got a powerful enemy who's working to nurture this illusion.

"Enemy? Illusion? But I don't..." Xander blinks and shakes his head. "How are you even here like this? How can you break the illusion if you're dead, too?"

Stan's mouth parts to laugh, but no sound comes from it. Not outside of Xander's head, at least. Oh, Xander, *he speaks over the ongoing soundtrack of his own laughter in Xander's mind,* your naivety is still so charming.

The weight of awareness grows, and Xander's head sags from it. I'm talking to myself, aren't I?

Yes, but now that you have my (Stan's) powers, it's something you'll (I'll) have to get used to.

Sounds lonely.

It will be if you (I) don't let go of this comfortable illusion and wake up from this nightmare.

Xander whimpers and looks up at Estella, who stares back down at him with sadness and pity in her eyes. I just wanted Mom and Dad to see her—see *us*—like this. I just wanted...

I know, but that's not the way things happened. And more's at stake now; a lot more.

I don't—

But the memory of his mother's death decides to play out its remainder at that moment, and the Kyle-phantom, still grinning, holds the knife over Emily's heaving chest. Then, as if suddenly remembering his unwilling audience, he turns to look at Xander through both time and space with a smile.

"Perks of the job, eh son?"

And then the blade dropped.

And dropped.

And...

THE VOID SWALLOWED *all but the body of Emily Stryker as Xander clenched his eyes against the memory and screamed, a red-and-black storm raging around him in an ongoing effort to wash it away; all of it.*

Somehow, though, he still managed to hear them:

"Oh, God, it's still alive! Kill it! Somebody kill it!"

"What if he wakes up? Won't he kill us all?"

"Is that the same one from the internet?"

"What could have done that to him?"

Then...

"Xander? Oh my... Xander! XANDER!"

He drew in a breath at the sound of his mother's voice, bracing himself for the nightmare of what her face had been turned into. But when he looked up at her, he was delighted to find her just as untouched—every bit as beautiful—as she'd been at the beginning of this dream.

"Xan-Xander...?"

"Mom?" his voice was a whimper, and he felt a sharp, stabbing pain in his chest as he tried to speak the words. Knowing why but not prepared to accept the reality of it, he acknowledged that he couldn't quite see straight anymore. "M-mom?"

"Xander... baby, what'd they do to you?"

Xander wasn't sure what he was saying or why he was saying it. It didn't answer his mother's question, and it only served to birth more questions in his own aching head.

"My gun," he said, feeling a lifetime away from her as he struggled to wake up. "He had my gun."

"When the suicide arrived at the sky, the people there asked him: "Why?"

He replied: "Because no one admired me."

Stephen Crane (1871-1900)

"To live is to suffer,
to survive is to find some meaning in the suffering."
Friedrich Nietzsche (1844-1990)

It has begun,
But even the Great Machine is unsure where its cogs will fall;
Time—the grandest illusion—begins to fracture,
And they find themselves as one... but not.
A great loss;
Personal blame;
Nothing—utter blackness—a looming goal.
Pain... such pain.
They are as they were;
It was how it is;
The path, though jagged and forked,
Is set.
They are as they were...
She *is as* he *was.*
Their fate rests in the other.

And the Great Machine watches
As the dominos continue to fall...

"That wife of yours, Xander, has kept you alive at every turn."
Stan

CHAPTER 1
NOIR

"Mother, whose heart hung humble as a button
On the bright splendid shroud of your son,
Do not weep.
War is kind."
Stephen Crane (1871-1900)

"I need you to promise me that you won't die."
Estella Edash

Another night.

Another chance for Xander to die.

Long ago—long before their marriage, before becoming a vampire, and even long before reuniting and becoming Xander's lover—Estella had resented each night for what it represented to her childhood friend. It was a time of death, or, rather, of potential death; the gnarled and infectious roots of which stemmed from a single awful night tainted by a very specific, very significant death. Estella had been there, more or less, on that first night—watching via a magic spell through her old friend's eyes and experiencing every agonizing moment just as he'd experienced it. A short time later, worry and more than just a little curiosity driving her, she used that same spell again to check in on him. There, with the events of that first night echoing in his mind, she'd "watched" from the back of Xander's mind as he performed what he morbidly came to know as his ritual.

It was the most awful thing that Estella had ever known; the most terrible thing that Estella had ever experienced.

Until earlier that night, of course...

All those years earlier, however, she'd been *inside* Xander's mind, the Spell of Sight putting her essence inside of him and seeing—*living*—as he did; she'd smelled the blood and sweat and terror of that first night, and she'd felt the bitter chill of the gun's barrel and the searing self-hatred on the second. It had been personal, private, and, in a sick and awful way, intimate. Hours earlier, in a single moment that blasted all the fear and pain and torment of the past into oblivion, she'd been forced to watch Xander—her husband, her savior, *her* Xander—beaten, tortured, and possibly even killed. Worse yet, she'd been forced to watch it on her television along with the rest of the stunned and awed world.

So much for intimacy, even in a sick and awful sense.

The rest of the world, though, had other things to worry itself over. Fair or not, the wellbeing of the tired and anxious looking man proclaiming himself to be a vampire on a global transmission was of little concern. The savage, uncensored beating that followed the unorthodox confession served more as a driving point than a cause for worry. What many might have disregarded as some sort of elaborate prank suddenly became an uncomfortable possibility.

It seemed strange that a worldwide hijacking of both television and internet might have been totally disregarded had it not been for the "addition"—as some news networks were putting it—of the graphic and vulgar display that followed. A proclamation of vampires and werewolves and all breeds of what had once been passed off as myth could be swept aside as a hoax, it appeared, but utter a few "fuck"s and tear off a few limbs and suddenly the "what if"s start carrying a bit more weight.

The whole mess still might have lost momentum if left alone, however. Humans *were* a sick and creative lot, after all, and none of what had been seen was entirely impossible to fabricate in a day and age of hackers and what the internet savvy called "trolls"—*like they had any real idea what sort of reality that term held*, Estella thought, recalling a startling, yet not altogether awful, encounter with a tergoj some time ago. Reality *might* have settled back into the not-quite-real, where "trolls" were simply annoying, anonymous figures occupying a digital world and *not* ten-foot tall, eyeless behemoths with foliage roots laced throughout their flesh aside, though, if the humans had been left to disregard it all...

But panic was hardly a condition to which nonhumans were immune.

Before the broadcast of Xander Stryker was complete—even before the beating of Xander Stryker had commenced, and even before Estella Stryker had begun to unleash wave after wave of desperate magic to rip the mansion she and so many others had been trapped within to splinters—mythos the world over had begun to expose themselves in a blind panic. Certain that the secret that had been maintained for eons was out and that they'd be discovered soon enough—this, Estella figured, wasn't an entirely unfair conclusion to come to—all breeds of mythos began to worry less about being hidden. Some revealed inhuman traits or abilities in an effort protect themselves, others abandoned human disguises for stronger, more capable forms, and others decided that if the world was going to know that monsters existed then—"what the hell?"—they might as well just come out of hiding and be monsters.

The Trepis mansion was still being devoured by Estella's magic, many of their own members fleeing into the night and abandoning the clan the moment they were able, by the time the world had all the evidence it needed that the crazy man —*her* crazy man—on every screen the world over had been telling the truth.

It could have been just another night. It could have been a night like any other, with Xander, vampire or not, at risk of death; hurting and pushing on, loving Estella and fighting—always fighting—for nobody else if not just for her. It could have been. But in such a short time things had gone wrong—oh, so wrong!—and now...

"Folks," Serena Vailean had said shortly after they'd dragged themselves from the rubble of the decimated mansion, *"the shit has oh-ficially hit the fan."*

SERENA HATED BEING NOSY.

No, that wasn't necessarily true. Serena *loved* being nosy. She also loved being loud, vulgar, violent, outspoken, and, coupled with all those other things, she loved being horny (especially in situations when she was being naked and nasty with Zane). What Serena hated at that moment, however, was how much she hated what she normally loved. What she loved was, after all, more for the sake of feeling strong and stable—feeling *sassy*—for the sake of herself, her family, and her clan.

Fucking hell! she thought, stifling a shudder and swallowing a fresh well of worry, *How's the Clan of Vail handling all this?*

It had been some time since she'd left her home, leaving who-really-knew-who—how could she be expected to keep track of such things?—in charge. For all she knew their own headquarters were just as demolished as the late, great Trepis Clan.

...

Okay, maybe not *that* demolished. Serena had never seen anything like Missus Stryker and her special breed of "fuck everything and spunk it Peter North-style for good measure"-magic (Serena's own words for it; she was sure Estella didn't know the word "spunk" or who Peter North was). She'd seen, and been personally responsible for, any number of destructive moments. Explosions were practically a nightly affair, and if she didn't get Zane inside her at least four or five times a week she was prone to taking down a building or two just to relieve the tension.

That, she wasn't proud to admit to herself, was only a marginal exaggeration.

But nothing—fucking *NOTHING!*—in the wonderfully chaotic and morbidly lengthy resume of Serena's reckless and destructive history could have compared to what the Stryker couple had accomplished in a single night.

It would have been awesome if it wasn't so awful.

And Serena would have been scared to death of both Xander and Estella if she hadn't come to love them so much in the short time she'd known them.

Xander's reputation, like hers, had any on the outside either rolling their eyes or ducking for cover. And, like hers, Xander's reputation, while not entirely inaccurate, was an unfair representation of the truth. Like her, Xander Stryker had an ugly way of attracting bad luck—though she wasn't about to be entering any competitions for "Worst Day(s) Ever" against him; she'd be laughed out of that competition before judging had even begun—and, like her, he had loud and aggressive ways of dealing with bad luck. The entire world was going to shit around them, and Xander's name was the centermost point on an ever-widening spiral of dog shit that was smearing itself across anything and everything.

But the entire world knew even less about the true Xander Stryker than it knew of Serena, a self-proclaimed vampire badass who took the fact that her file with The Council contained the word "horny" in it as a personal achievement. The entire world could go screw itself for all she cared, because what they knew about Xander Stryker amounted to dick.

He *might* have threatened Serena, her husband, and her closest friends after she'd (ACCIDENTILY) smashed in the gates of his home and parked on—not near, but *on*—the front steps of his mansion. He *might* have beaten the shit out of her husband, destroyed a mythos safe house full of innocents, and been an all-around mysterious loner when the situation called for anything but those sorts of antics. He *might* have gone AWOL from his clan and, worse yet, his wife while a tropical shit-storm collided head-on with a clusterfuck of biblical proportions. And, sure, he might have hacked the entire world —*how in the shit is that even possible?*—to break the oldest and most crucial law their kind adhered to; a law that, as a warrior and a clan leader, he'd sworn to uphold and protect.

But Xander Stryker, like Serena Vailean, had his reasons, and Estella, though scaring the shit out of Serena at that moment, was doing exactly what she'd do if her own husband was in the sort of trouble Xander was in. And so, while the rest of the world went to shit and the name "Stryker" was at the root of it all, Serena couldn't bring herself to curse the name or to abandon Estella as she and the few remnants of the Trepis clan sought to find their leader.

But Serena, though she played the part exceedingly well, was not stupid. She was also loyal, empathetic, and worried-to-shit about her newest bestie-slash-fellow soon-to-be mommy.

Which brought her back to her original thought:

Serena *hated* the idea of being nosy and probing Estella Stryker's mind, but it was obvious that, in this circumstance, being loud, vulgar, violent, outspoken, horny, *or* naked and nasty wasn't going to help.

Estella wasn't talking.

She hadn't said a word since managing to gather the few warriors of the collapsed Trepis Clan and moving them and those too injured to decide whether or not they wanted to stick around or jump ship. Even then, her words had been few, far between and painfully distant; her eyes never seeming to see the people she was speaking to or the places she was navigating. Serena, holding her and Zane's sobbing little boy to her breast and doing all she could to keep from sobbing as well, followed along; staying uncharacteristically quiet while the others took the initiative to give the commands that Estella couldn't give with her limited voice. As soon as what remained of her and her husband's clan had been relocated to a storage facility neighboring a harbor—a burst of magic casting crates and cargo alike into the inky abyss of the night-bathed bay to make room for them—she'd turned away from them and started back out again.

Everyone had been too wrapped up in their own issues—most still reeling from the events while others, like an anapriektherion couple whose names escaped Serena at the time, busied themselves by helping the injured. Zane had just finished setting Ruby, a young, scrappy vampire who'd had a run of bad luck against the anti-mythos church Xander had set out to dismantle, onto a stack of crates that was supposed to serve as a medical gurney when they'd heard Sawyer call out to Estella. The Trepis Clan's head warrior (and one of the last people to speak to Xander before the incident) was starting at a jog that was ready to become a sprint at any instant, and it was then that Serena realized just how far she'd made it to leaving them all without detection. Catching her by the shoulder, she heard Sawyer asking where she was going and what she intended to do.

"I'm going to find Xander."

It was simultaneously the simplest and most impossible thing Serena had ever heard somebody aspire to accomplish.

She hadn't asked for the help or organized the search groups—all of that had been volunteered by everybody else—but nor did she argue against it. This, however, seemed less about accepting the assistance and more about being indifferent to it. Like before, her eyes weren't committed to the moment; the bright blue orbs wavering, staring out with vacant worry, and shimmering with so much moisture that Serena couldn't believe the tears hadn't begun streaming down her face.

Like magic... she'd thought as she watched Estella once again turn away from them and start away from the ramshackle shelter the remains of her husband's work had been crammed within.

Nodding to Zane, she'd moved to follow. Her own husband, needing no further prompting, was beside her a moment later with Zoey and Isaac in stride with them.

Estella's sisters and Xander's "bros" took to the night on the simple-yet-impossible mission. Three other search parties set out, as well, tracked and organized by Zoey and her auric prowess; among them, Sawyer and his human lover in one and a cat-like nejin who was cozied up beside another therion female (who looked too much like the one coupled with the anapriek medic to not be related) in another. Both of these groups were accompanied by a few of the clan's more loyal members, and several others, whose names Serena couldn't have been expected to remember, forming a fourth search party. With Estella and the rest of them starting out heading east, Serena watched Zoey's aura snake out and instruct the other groups to spread outward accordingly.

Serena wasn't sure how true to the direction Estella would stay, but there was no denying it was the best tactic given the circumstances.

Assuming that the worst hasn't already happened...

If Estella knew what was being orchestrated around her, she gave no sign of it. Her aura had long since been withdrawn into her body—a trait that only two things shared: auric vampires and corpses; Serena found herself shuddering at the correlation—and more and more she'd withdrawn into a darkness that Serena could feel like a winter chill.

"I'm going to find Xander."

It was the last thing that anybody had heard her say for hours. In that time, the four of them had tried to get her to say more, suggesting possible options or offering random reassurances, but, like the plans being orchestrated around her, she gave no sign of hearing them. Seeing her like that hurt Serena's heart. Though their friendship was still quite young—surprisingly only a few days old despite all they'd experienced in that time—there was a kinship that was shared between them that felt right. They were all like some sort of cosmic puzzle that had finally come together: Serena and Zane; Zoey and Isaac; Estella and Xander. But now Xander had gone and gotten himself... well, gone.

And, lo and behold, the world seemed to be ending because of it.

This, Serena figured, was more a thought conceived and birthed more because of her worry for her friend than any real belief. She'd never been the spiritual sort—never really been the "think deep on it"-sort, in fact—but Estella was a different story. Estella was magic, both figuratively and literally. After all, on top of casting some of the most incredible spells Serena had ever seen, the petite, raven-haired babe had somehow managed to not only find the deep-seeded warmth of Xander Stryker, but actually *share* it with the rest of them. All that magic and splendor had vanished from her eyes, though; the compassion and hope—hell, the sheer essence of Estella—was just as gone from her as Xander.

Serena was desperate to help.

Desperate!

But her normal fallback persona, vulgar and perverted and —*let's face it*—ditzy, didn't just seem pointless at breaking the depression Estella had fallen into, it felt like the sort of thing that might break what little hold Estella still had to the here-and-now.

So, feeling suddenly dirty for not being more sincere in the past and guilty for what she was about to do, Serena snuck a purple tendril of her aura into Estella's mind, probing for some insight to the torment her friend was silently suffering through:

... fault, all my... baby! He doesn't even know... be...

Xander...

... can't be... can't... DON'T

... Stryker

Where are you? Where...?

Xander...

NO! DON'T DIE!

... Stryker

... be! CAN'T BE! please... CAN'T...

Xander...

please... don't die... back to me, Xander; come...

... Stryker

Can't find him. Why can't I...? No... If he's gone, then—

Serena, I know you're there.

Serena yanked her aura back as fast as she could, but not before the sob was out and resonating through the vacant streets. Zoey had been doing a great job of keeping the mayhem of the rioters, the hunters (both new and preexisting), and the overall desperate masses clear, an easy enough trick for an auric of her caliber. Entering the minds of any in the surrounding area and steering them anywhere *but* across their path was a good way to avoid any unnecessary risks, but it made for very quiet streets...

Which apparently made for an excellent echo chamber for startled cries from the lips of those with prying minds.

Despite having been seemingly oblivious to everything else up until that moment, Estella stopped at the sound. Slowly, so slowly it made Serena's labored breathing drag within her aching chest, the raven-hair shifted and those bright blue eyes came to focus on her.

Her tears had finally begun to fall.

ESTELLA KNEW that the prying thread of Serena's aura was meant to be stealthy, just as she knew that the invasion was one committed out of concern. It neither eluded her nor reassured her. She had nothing against Serena. Hours earlier she'd have gone so far as to say she loved her like a sister. Hours earlier she'd have said she loved all of them. Hours earlier felt like an eternity ago, however, and she was feeling evermore certain that she'd never be able to say she loved anybody ever again.

Especially since...

She stopped herself in mid-thought and shook her head. This was a thought path she knew all too well, not because she'd traveled it before but because she'd watched Xander travel it over and over and over again. It was a cold and lonely journey, perilous and wrought with traps to snare even the most adept of mental wanderers and keep them held in that dark place. Possibly forever. It was on this path that Xander had set out each night for years to commit his ritual, journeying under his bed and into an old wooden box with a Yin-Yang carved onto its surface; trudging its winding depths in the hopes that one of eight trails might end in a sudden drop into nothingness. Depression was a dense forest filled with dead brier patches and wide-limbed, hollow trees disguised as shelter that blocked out all light, and it was in that shadowy place that her husband used to cling to hope that a loaded gun might make the pain go away.

And she'd been stumbling deeper and deeper into that dreaded thicket.

If Serena hadn't stolen into her mind and pulled her out...

Taking in the sight of the four, each wearing identical masks of concern, she was suddenly very aware of them; their own thoughts and even the thoughts of the panic-stricken masses scattered about the city floating about like the balloons hovering over the characters depicted in a comic book. She marveled at this, once again reminded of the pinhole view that depression condensed reality down to and how, so many times in the past, Xander had had to be reminded of the most basic truths.

Like how much he was loved, or how many were out there to support him.

How easy it is to be blinded in that forest, she mused to herself before offering a forced but in no way insincere smile to the others.

They were owed an explanation.

"I... I can't find him," she confessed.

The four heard these words and Estella, whose psychic awareness seemed amplified since being dragged back from the haze of depression, saw them coping with it in their own way. With Serena's jackhammering heart and labored breathing holding back her words and Zane and Isaac sharing uncertain glances, it was Zoey who said what they were all thinking:

"We haven't been looking for that long. I'm sure he's—"

Estella was already shaking her head, and the blue-haired auric trailed off in mid-sentence.

"Y-you..." Serena heaved in a fresh lungful of air, and her aura told Estella that she was thankful for the first solid inhale since the sob that had robbed her of her breath. Clarity and understanding rippled like beckoning waves of neon in the semitransparent purple mass surrounding her. "You don't mean finding him *out here*, do you?" she asked, and Estella could see her recalling the vacant look in her eyes and the ongoing chant—*Xander... Stryker... Xander... Stryker*—that she had seen woven throughout her thoughts. "If I didn't know any better—and, who knows, maybe I don't—I'd say that you're not out here because you're looking for him, but because you're not finding him."

"The fuck is *that* supposed to mean: 'not finding him'?" Zane demanded, making a face as though he'd bitten into something sour and folding his arms across his chest.

Serena, knowing that Zane had come to bond with Xander just as closely as she and Estella and, despite all pretenses, was just as eager to see him found and brought home, forgave his tone with a casual backhand to his chest. Estella, who understood this just as much as his wife but was less inclined to beat on him for it, offered him a solemn nod.

"In the past, though it hasn't always been pleasant, I've been able to... um, connect with Xander," she explained. "I'd focus on 'finding' him"—she punctuated the word "finding" with a light tap to her temple—"and, once I did, I'd be able to see through his eyes." Frowning, dissatisfied with the way that sounded, she shook her head and corrected, "More than just *seeing*; I'd... I'd *live* through him. His thoughts, his senses... *everything* would be mine, as well. In those instances, I *was* Xander." She felt her lip quiver and looked down, not wanting to see her friends' faces as they processed this information. Unlike with a comic book, however, removing the characters from sight did nothing to conceal the contents of the balloons that would normally hang over their heads; their thoughts—uncertainty from both of the non-psychic males and pity from both of the psychic females; neither pleasant as far as Estella was concerned—were still crystal clear. "I wound up sharing in some of his worst experiences *as him*," her voice broke and she shivered. "I... I could never really blame him for all the times he tried to kill himself—having lived through those few moments and knowing there was so much more I hadn't seen; hadn't experienced—b-but... but I had to be strong, right? Had to pretend *not* to understand so that he'd see how foolish it was to believe it was ever okay to..." she whimpered and clapped her hands over her eyes. "I hate thinking that I could ever understand that sort of thing, but that damned spell put me right there—*right fucking there!*—and made it impossible *not* to." Her arms seemed to grow heavy then, too heavy to hold up any longer, and they dropped to her sides. Then, feeling another strong pull but unable to do more than crawl her hands along her hips, she cupped the sides of her still-flat stomach—too early in her pregnancy to call it a bump but real enough to feel *something* beneath her palms all the same—and let her blurring gaze aim itself down at what her hands now framed. "But I can't... I could never think that—" She sighed, the exhale catching and coming out in a low croak, and she tried—failed—to focus on her friends. "I hate that spell for what it's forced me to feel, but I thought I could use it to connect with Xander again; see what he's seeing, feel what he's feeling—to hell with how much it might hurt—and then I'd be able to find him, go to him; save him. I could bring him home, tell him that everything will be alright and that he's going to be a father. I thought if I could just use the spell to do something for him rather than just make myself sick with how much shit the world keeps dropping on him, then maybe... maybe..."

But she couldn't figure out how to finish the thought, and she staggered forward as grief swept her legs out from under her.

Zane, though several paces away along with the others, was suddenly by her side and helping to keep her upright. The ordinarily gruff, tattooed vampire offered an understanding nod; his thick left arm tactfully cast across her upper chest, bridging across her collarbone and supporting the weight of her shoulders. Though, until that moment, Estella had thought of him as being the leap-before-looking type, she realized that, even in the blink-of-an-eye moment he'd crossed the distance to catch her, he'd been careful to do so in a way that was both effective *and* respectful. Granted, her fall would have been frozen in time as far as he was concerned while he moved in overdrive, but she was certain plenty of others would have either overlooked the courtesy or intentionally ignored it.

Then again, with his slap-happy wife already closing the distance between them, there was any number of reasons—his respect for her or his loyalty to Xander aside—that this was a wise move on his part.

Nodding her approval to her husband, Serena moved in and wrapped her arms around Estella, lightly cupping a palm behind her head and guiding her forehead comfortably into the hammock-like groove between her neck and shoulder. The gesture was every bit as tactful and effective as her husband's while carrying an unmistakably maternal quality; it was soothing and assuring, numbing away the heavy burden of the world.

It made Estella miss her own mother while reminding her that she was about to become a mother, herself.

The mother of Xander Stryker's child...

Free of the confines of that awful forest of the mind and overwhelmed by the reality of her situation, Estella cried freely.

"You said you couldn't find him," Zoey said, close now and fitting a hand on Estella's back. Warm, positive energies flowed from the auric's palm and Estella felt herself begin to calm; the effects not so much numbing her to her sorrow as much as making it bearable. This was as much an act of kindness as it was for the sake of making it easier for Estella to answer the next question: "What could that mean?"

Estella tilted her head to face Zoey, not drawing away from Serena but broadening the range of her vision. She dragged in a long breath, filling herself with the blonde vampire's scent —*like vanilla and oranges,* she thought—and said:

"He's out there. Not gone, not... not *gone,*" she couldn't bring herself to say the other word, "but he's not himself enough for me to find him."

Isaac, a therion of few words but great wisdom, seemed to be the only one to understand what she meant by this, his aura shifting like smoke in a sudden breeze. “Like if somebody’s scent suddenly changed?”

Estella’s lips curled slightly at this, the comparison somehow perfect despite how silly it sounded. “Yes, actually, only it’s more than just a smell. It’s... it’s *Xander*; everything that makes him who he is.”

“Has something like that ever happened before?” Zane asked.

There was a sharp pinch as Estella caught herself biting her lip and, finally withdrawing from Serena’s shoulder, she nodded. “Yes. Once,” she admitted. “It was after he’d reawakened as a vampire; after he’d been changed from who he was before.”

CHAPTER 2
SINS OF THE FATHER

"Do not weep, babe, for war is kind.
Because your father tumbled in the yellow trenches,
Raged at his breast, gulped and died,
Do not weep.
War is kind."
Stephen Crane (1871-1900)

"A wise man once said that
hating those who wrong you is like
consuming rat poison and expecting the rats to die."
Father Tennesen

Aleks.

He had presented himself as a low-profile vampire—a perfect if Estella had been forced to guess upon meeting him—and a truly annoying and pathetic one at that.

But who and what he *had* appeared to be meant little for what he'd turned out to be.

Estella had let herself believe, though not necessarily the best about him—he *had* presented himself as something of a creep upfront, though nothing more than flagrant flirting and arrogant assumptions—that he was harmless and, perhaps, even a hopeful warrior. When she'd first met him, dressed from head-to-toe in so much red, white, and blue that she should've known from the start not to trust his dense New York accent, he'd seemed (too) friendly; just a fresh-off-the-bus vampire awestruck by a new city and star-struck by the wife of *the* Xander Stryker.

Over and over again she and the others—though, strangely enough, never Xander—wound up crossing paths with Aleks, his hazel-green eyes framed under cap-tamed blond hair always burning with excitement each time he spotted her. Each time, despite all her warnings and outright threats, he'd start in with his "broad"-this and "doll"-that chatter. Estella's reactions, she remembered, actually seemed to encourage him. It was only because he'd helped save one of their clan's warriors, Ruby—who was still unconscious and still laid out with Zeek back at what was passing for their makeshift headquarters—from a murderous lot of magic-wielding, mythos-hating religious psychopaths calling themselves Cebourists that she'd allowed herself to feel like he could be trusted. Even then, though, she couldn't stop beating herself up for ever having believed he wasn't deserving of one of Xander's enchanted bullets to the head.

This thought, however—though constant in her mind—seemed outright uncharacteristic of her.

She had *never* been one to consider death—*killing*—to be a solution for anything; a personal philosophy she'd managed to keep from influencing Xander or the rest of the clan's business, but one that certainly kept her from ever carrying a gun or, moreover, taking lethal measures against an opponent.

More and more she was beginning to regret her nonviolent tendencies.

Her past was riddled with things she wished she'd done differently, but none more than the myriad of bloody fantasies she'd begun to harbor of every encounter she'd ever had with Aleks.

All the missed opportunities that had passed; opportunities when Estella could have just ended it all right then and there.

Opportunities like...

"I was wondering when I'd get to see you again!" Aleks cooed.

Estella winced at that, looking out across the bloodstained street. "Is that what this is? You trying to get my attention?"

"This?" Aleks motioned to all the dead bodies. "No, this is me saving your friend's life. The typical response to which, I might add, is 'thank you,' and, assuming that's what you meant, I'll go ahead and offer a 'you're welcome' before saying it again: I was wondering when I'd get to see you again, doll!"

"I was wondering the exact same thing," Estella offered with a grin of her own, disarming the smug asshole moments before she uttered a chant under her breath, sending out a kinetic blast that tore through his chest and had his insides spraying across the alley.

Or...

"Danger can be fun, doll," he winked and started to chuckle... but the sound was cut off after less than a second when Estella drove the blunt end of one of her tonfas through his throat.

Or, best of all, their very first encounter could've just played out as...

"Ya look like a broad with a load on her mind," a thick, nearly cartoony New York accent cut through the darkness and yanked Estella out of her own private world. The vampire stepped into pace beside her as she walked by the alley he'd been waiting in. He made no move to attack or advance beyond an arm's distance. He simply walked beside her. "Girl wit' that much on 'er mind can be a dangerous thing."

"A girl with this much on her mind and interrupted thoughts can

be an even more dangerous thing," Estella offered back before punching a hole through his chest and tearing out his heart.

Estella shivered at her own twisted fantasies. *Gaia's Green Earth,* she thought, *that fucker's actually making me think like Xander!*

It wasn't the first time she'd had that thought, the sense that she was becoming more and more like her wayward husband, and, though she didn't mind the idea, it was alarming just how different it made her feel. Part of her wondered if this change—this sense of carrying more and more of Xander within her—was some sort of subconscious response to her finding out that she was pregnant with his child; *literally* carrying a part of Xander as it grew and matured inside of her womb. But this, like a great deal of other thoughts she'd been having lately, felt more like a pretty fantasy, something akin to poetry or fine art, than anything factual. If nothing else, she figured, it was a simple truth of the nature of anger:

Xander Stryker had always had plenty of reasons to be angry, and he behaved accordingly; Estella, on the other hand, had never really allowed herself to be motivated by anger.

After all, somebody had to keep Xander and his own rage in check.

With him gone, however...

She was only distantly aware of her fists clenching at her sides as a repeating thought—*Gone because of* him!—exploded, burning away all other thoughts and clearing her mind for the cycle to refresh itself.

At the height of the chaos earlier that night, with the Trepis Clan working to take out the Cebourists, Estella and her band of "sisters" had encountered an unexpected threat and, at the center of it all, found Aleks. At the time, he'd been fleeing from the growing danger, begging and pleading for them to take him with them to the safety of the mansion. Serena, claiming to have never liked Aleks, was eager to kill him there in the street —*Gods above and below, I should have let her; I really should have!*

—but Estella, sympathetic and foolish, had stopped her and taken him in.

Everything past that moment was like a nightmare that she couldn't awake herself from.

The panic of realizing Xander was gone. Not just unaccounted for, no; he'd *intentionally* kept himself undetected. Then, in a moment of panic and sickness, discovering that the seemingly harmless Aleks was, in fact, much more than he'd ever let on.

Before arriving at the Trepis Clan's mansion, Serena and the others from the Clan of Vail—following up on a mission that Zoey and Isaac had been working—had been tracking their own loose end, an insane mythos rogue with an insatiable bloodlust and a penchant for butchering mythos and humans alike who dared to interact too closely with the other. Xander Stryker, even before he had become a global media phenomenon, and his once-human bride was a prime target for this creature. But, as it turned out—though his and his father's history for taking on human lovers was enough of a clue to steer the Vaileans and company to his front steps—there was a deeper seeded motive pushing the attack on Xander.

A motive that haunted the rogue's thoughts and pulled all his strings.

A motive calling itself "Messiah."

Though they'd begun to believe Messiah to be nothing more than a figment of an increasingly demented mind, the auric influence began to prove itself too real to ignore as more and more rogues began rising to *His* call.

By the time Estella and the others came to realize who *He* was, however, he'd already slaughtered several of Trepis' warriors and fled from the mansion, casting a familiar spell and locking everyone left within its walls.

Moments later, stunned to see her missing husband occupying the big screen TV in their bedroom, Estella watched as Aleks "introduced" himself to her husband. Gone was the New

York accent and the irritating playfulness, replaced by a syrupy foreign tone and a painfully direct savagery that the entire world got to watch firsthand:

"Hello, Xander. I believe it's time we got to know each other."

The beating and torture of the mysterious man—*vampire*—was every bit a subject of intrigue as the speech he'd given moments before. His words had cut deep, sure, but Aleks and a few of his followers—Messiah's followers!—had dug in and torn out what was inside...

Literally!

Estella had barely managed to stomach a few seconds of the assault on her husband before she destroyed the TV. Then, not willing to allow herself to be trapped a moment longer, she'd done the same to the mansion.

It seemed impossible to her then that the spell Aleks had cast to keep them locked within those reinforced walls should be dismantled—seemed impossible that the entire mansion, in just a few short minutes, should be just as dismantled—but it wasn't the first time that she'd managed to do the impossible.

After all, she'd brought Xander back from death enough times to defy even their own kind's scope of mortality.

It seemed that, provided Xander was the driving reason behind the effort, there was nothing Estella couldn't do.

But this, she knew, was a dangerous mindset to commit to.

Rage had a funny way of clouding judgement.

Is she okay?

Zoey didn't have to ask who Serena meant, and she didn't have to look to know that her friend, usually a wild and vivacious blonde bombshell of a vampire, was hugging herself as if against a violent chill and holding back tears. She didn't need to read her aura to know it, either; all of them were walking that way. All except Estella, of course, who walked as though she were eager to invite any sort of trouble.

And at that moment, there were all sorts of trouble to invite.

It was the sort of walk that Serena, herself, had used to carry her to-and-fro countless times before, and never with a murmur of "Is she okay?" following after her (unless the person asking was inquiring as to her mental health). It was even the sort of walk that Estella's husband, Xander, was known to employ before instigating some impressive breed of mayhem. Zane, Serena's husband, and Zoey's own lover, Isaac, could walk like that, as well, and rarely, if not never, with those in their company worrying about their wellbeing for it. That walk, however, did not seem right when carrying Estella Stryker.

It was wrong, wrong like this whole mess was wrong.

And that meant only one thing:

No, the word was a choked whisper even in the private psychic communication. *But what reason would she have to be okay?*

Zoey could almost see Serena's thoughts work like a slideshow as the events of the past few days played out again and again. It was only the past few hours that really mattered, though.

Yeah... Serena's psychic tone wasn't much different. *Watching your hubby shatter every Council law in a few short minutes and then get blindsided by some sucker-punching cock-suckers would certainly twist my tits in all the wrong ways.*

Giving a slow nod, Zoey stared after Estella and, like the others, worked to keep up without letting it be obvious that keeping up was no easy task. Stifling what wanted to be a sigh but would likely emerge as a sob, she moved to rub at the back of her neck. There, she felt a few young strands of not-blue hair tickle at her nape, and the discovery birthed in her a strange sort of dread. She was overdue for a touchup. An innocent enough observation, she supposed, but there was a crippling sense of uncertainty to be had with it. She was unsure when she'd ever get the chance. Scheduling a hair appointment would have been, only a few short hours earlier, an easy task. A quick phone call or, who knew, maybe even a few swipes of a finger on one of her phone's many apps and, *voila*, those unsightly roots would be hidden under a sheen of beautiful blue. The secret of her natural hair color concealed from prying eyes; disguised in plain sight. And none would be the wiser.

But several hours earlier the world had been a very different place. Several hours earlier there were all breeds of secrets—the least of which being Zoey's dull blonde hair—that were hidden away that had since been dragged out into the open. Several hours earlier a simple visit to a salon or an innocent walk down the street wouldn't have warranted any sort of concern or precautions (especially of the locked and loaded variety, as Serena had put it earlier). Several hours, as it turned out, was all it took to unravel... well, everything.

Riots, looting, violence; mythos and humans alike were behaving like it was the end of the world. A grim moment of deductive logic assured Zoey that, in this case, it very well could be. If every living thing on the planet locked in murderous panic wouldn't be enough to bring on the End, the spiteful, god-like vampire eager to kill all of them would happily move things along.

So... Serena finally chimed in again, *do you think she's* going *to be okay?*

I can't say for sure, Zoey answered, giving a subtle nod towards Zane that only Serena seemed to notice, *but he doesn't think so, and he seems ready to say so, too.*

Serena's purple eyes made a quick dart towards her husband, and Zoey noticed her lip tug back slightly. *I'll handle big, dumb, and beautiful,* she offered before giving her own slight nod back at Isaac, *and you handle dog-boy. Zane's a brash idiot, and idiots can only burp up so much truth. Your werewolf is like Winston Churchill, Gandhi, and that talkative president at the end of Independence Day. The sort of words he might say might destroy Estella while anything Zane says might just piss her off.*

Well, Zoey said, *let's hope neither happens.*

Isaac really didn't know what to make of all of this.

He came from two worlds: that of a therion pack leader and that of a clan warrior serving as a hand of justice for The Council. They were two very different lives, but, at the same time, not. Commitment and loyalty were crucial in both, as were dedication and the ability to make irreversible decisions for the betterment of himself and others. How things were handled might differ, and the role he held and the company he kept certainly were at polar opposites. Different, and yet the same. In this case, however, there was only one obvious path that his thoughts should take: Xander Stryker should be seen as an absolute and undeniable threat, one that warranted an immediate and lethal response.

As a therion pack, acting as their leader—their alpha—then Xander's actions would represent an immediate risk to his kin. Solution: rip out his throat and pass the carcass around to nourish the others to gain strength for what would come next.

As a clan warrior, taking orders and executing them without pause or question, then it would be clear that Xander's actions broke more laws than Isaac could admittedly remember, and any broken law—any *single* law—that represented even the possible threat of detection—of *suspicion!*—by even a single human was typically met with the death penalty. There were exceptions, of course—politics simply wouldn't be politics without exceptions, otherwise those highest in power would have to swallow the same fire they billowed at others—but the laws were there all the same. Xander Stryker hadn't hinted at anything. He hadn't risked exposure, hadn't bared his fangs at an enemy in a crowded street for human bystanders to witness or been caught in the middle of feeding (another no-no law, sure, but one that was more easily forgiven). He hadn't even confessed his secret—all of their secret—to a crowded auditorium. No, Xander Stryker, never one to just break the rules but outright decimate them and urinate on the remains, had exposed them all to the world.

As far as the law was concerned, there weren't enough death penalties one could serve to rectify such a thing. The Council had some pretty grim ways of punishing those that broke the major laws that governed their kind, Isaac knew first-hand that Serena's brother, who'd tried to play their system to his benefit and climb into a place of power by any means necessary, had faced a good long period of substantial torture for nearly making the mythos government look foolish. For all Isaac knew, he was *still* being tortured. He didn't like to dwell on the thought. But treason and conspiracy were nothing compared to this; by human standards it would be like comparing a serial killer to a jay-walker. But even that comparison felt too tame for Xander's crime.

Isaac was certain that if The Council could have their way they'd be harnessing Estella's prowess for dragging Xander back from the dead as a means of executing him over and over again, likely with extended intervals of torture the likes of which Isaac, who'd faced a fair share of torture somewhat recently, couldn't even begin to imagine. That was, of course, assuming that The Council figured out a way to fix what Xander had set into motion.

But Isaac knew there was no fixing this. There weren't enough aurics to sweep that many minds, and even if there were the footage of Xander's confession was out there. It was cycling through every news channel, echoing on every glowing screen, and had likely been backed-up and saved in countless formats by millions across the globe. It wouldn't surprise Isaac in the slightest if the confession of Xander Stryker existed on a stack of unmarked video cassettes by a paranoid and untrusting conspiracy nut just waiting for an opportunity to cash in on them.

The Council could rip the entire internet to bent and broken ones and zeroes, Isaac thought, *and the words would still exist somewhere for the world to find.*

But even The Council, with all their power and all their planning and contingencies, couldn't hope to fix this. Hell, they'd prepared for just about every possible scenario that posed a risk to their kind, and this had happened all the same. Xander Stryker, one single punk vampire who was still young by human standards, had actually found a way to dance around a system that likely predated human civilization. While their earliest ancestors were still grunting and slapping at rocks, Isaac was positive there were mythos ancestors—whatever sort of creatures they might have been—looking down on them and thinking, *They must not know that we exist.*

They MUST NOT know that we exist!

It had started as a means to maintain a food source. Back when feeding on their kind was simple, being nothing more than myth and superstition was a sure way to keep them from fleeing or finding a means to hide themselves. Cattle, after all, were much easier to butcher if they weren't given a reason to stampede. Then, as time passed and humans advanced, the need for secrecy grew with them. Over time, rocks had become swords, and swords became guns, and then the bullets started getting bigger and bigger, the BANG they produced that much more destructive. Suddenly it wasn't just calm prey they were keeping themselves secret for, it was to ensure that mythos kind—all those that humans knew from stories as dangerous monsters—didn't wind up getting themselves wiped out. If the cluster of human hunters out there and the still-thriving Cebourist church and its followers had proven nothing else, it was that mythos, with all their strength and powers, were just as killable as anything else that scampered about the planet.

THEY MUST NOT KNOW THAT WE EXIST!

Both the therion leader and the clan warrior in Isaac saw it as the perfect code; simply brilliant and brilliant in its simplicity. Seven words that, as a single law and the foundation for so many more, was a symphony in and of itself. In all the centuries that followed this was proven time and time again.

And in a few brief minutes it was all undone.

Such a thing had never even been conceived!

It shouldn't have been possible!

But Xander Stryker had done it. The entire world knew his name and, along with it, knew a secret that had put every nonhuman at risk. Both the therion leader and the clan warrior in Isaac knew *exactly* what sort of fate should befall a rogue move of such grand proportions...

And yet he wanted nothing more than to help Estella find him and, once they did, to stand by his side and fight any who would attempt to execute him.

Isaac might not have known what to make of all of this, but he most certainly didn't know what to make of *that* single fact: despite *everything* he was still committed to Xander Stryker and, for some strange reason, knew that what he'd done had been the right thing.

It's not that surprising really, Zoey's voice rang like an angel's song in his mind, and he turned to face his auric lover, finding her already smiling up at him.

He wasn't sure when he'd taken her hand into his own, but as their eyes met she gave it a gentle squeeze. Somehow it made him feel less conflicted.

He didn't need to ask to know what his lover meant.

You were in my head, he only had to think the words for her to "hear" them, a fact that both astounded and unnerved him and further reinforced his firm belief that Zoey was the single most incredible creature to walk the earth.

The upward curve of her lips was so slight that Isaac didn't think that anybody else would notice the smile. *Of course I was. It's almost as beautiful as the rest of you, after all.*

Almost? he asked, quirking a questioning brow that was just as subtle as her smile.

Yes, almost, she affirmed, turning to face forward with the rest of the group and lingering on Estella, who'd once again fallen into silence since confessing that Xander—or Xander's mind, who knew really—must have undergone some recent change that had rendered him untraceable on the magical plane. *To look at you,* Zoey went on in his mind, *is to look upon confidence. It's not uncommon for therions to look powerful, though —I can't say that you hold that over others of your kind, I'm afraid —but your mind...* the ghost-smile flared once again, threatening to make itself more obvious to any that might glance over. Nobody glanced over. *Your mind has none of the raw savagery or anger that other therion minds carry. It's precise and calculating; I've actually seen your aura grow calmer in cases where most other therions would lose all control.*

Isaac caught himself staring at Estella, as well. She didn't look like she was trying to find anything, her face down and her hands stuffed into the pockets of her silver jacket, but Isaac had learned enough in his time with Zoey to know that she didn't need her eyes to search for Xander. At that moment, he envied her for that clarity.

My mind's not a calm place right now, he confessed.

Nobody's is right now, Zoey offered. *But at least you're doing better than Zane.*

Isaac let his eyes shift to the side without turning his head to study his friend. Though his broad, tribal tattoo littered shoulders were pulled back and tense, he looked no more unhinged than the rest of them. This, however, was misleading. Though he was not without a sizable track record of flying off the handle and committing any number of bone-headed acts, he was not completely devoid of restraint. Zane, Isaac knew, was capable of a breed of rigid control that would impress even the most enlightened of holy minds. It was the sort of control that one learned *because* they were prone to being so absolutely out-of-control. It was the sort of control that would drive a berserk therion to chain himself up before a flare-up.

Not that even the most brutal of therions—or even an entire pack of them—could have compared to the raw monstrosity that was Maledictus. But, fortunately for them (and the rest of the world), Zane was rid of that curse and the monster it turned him into.

That bad? he asked, still trying to pinpoint any visible signs that his friend was as unstable as Zoey was implying.

There was none.

None that Isaac could see, at least.

Zoey nodded, obviously comfortable that nobody would notice. Nobody did. *This whole mess has taken the same sort of toll on him as the rest of us. His thoughts—and this is both surprising and unsurprising at the same time—aren't unlike yours: he knows what he* should *be thinking—what he* should *do in a situation like this—but he's already committed to defending the memory of Xander and what he's done.*

Isaac scowled at this and shifted his gaze, turning his head this time to look at Zoey again. *Defending... his memory?*

Another nod, Zoey's face twisted and, for an instant, Isaac thought she might start crying. *He and Serena both think that he might already be dead. Between that and the smell of blood in the air, he's on the verge of going "old school," as he's calling it, and joining the chaos.*

Isaac furrowed his brow at that. He could smell the blood, as well, and, if he focused, he could even hear the screams and cries in the neighboring streets. Humans, terrified at the revelation that vampires and werewolves and all manner of creatures of darkness were real, and mythos, terrified at the prospect that the safety and assurance of their lives had been compromised, were equally guilty parties in all of it. There were the humans chasing a "them or us"-mentality and taking up arms against anyone who even remotely seemed inhuman to them, those who'd accepted some morbid sense of fate—as though mythos had only just arrived and not been walking among them since the beginning—and, though not all outright killing themselves (though there was that, too), taking greater and greater risks under the assumption that fangs or claws would, eventually, be sinking into them. Then there were the mythos, who, following a similar mindset, were either ripping apart anything that could possibly pose a threat to them and theirs or dedicating themselves to a "Hail Mary"-approach, feeding freely under some twisted logic that the food source would suddenly exhaust itself or taking their own lives to avoid the inevitable moment when world leaders might push that all-powerful big, red button in the hopes of burning away anything that didn't have human blood pumping through it.

Isaac couldn't begin to catalogue all the things wrong with all of those various logics, but nor could he trick himself into believing that he at least didn't understand them.

And that's *why you're doing better than him,* Zoey chimed then. *Zane's not only convinced that Xander's already dead, but that* this *is the way of things now. He's prepared to shrug off his old life and go the ways of Mad Max. Even has a vision of himself as Mel Gibson with Serena in tattered leathers and decked out in ammo and little Gregori as some sort of feral beast-child who tears at would-be enemies and steals car parts.*

He would, Isaac rolled his eyes.

Zoey smirked at that, but the smile didn't reach her eyes. It barely even held at her lips. *All the same, it might sound funny, Isaac, but he genuinely believes that Xander's gone and that things aren't going to get better. Serena's doing what she can to keep him calm—keep him from saying anything to Estella, who I can guarantee wouldn't take any of that well—but...*

But there's no denying that there's some key points in that mindset that aren't exactly foolish, Isaac finished.

Zoey nodded, but offered no other reply.

Isaac looked back in Estella's direction as she turned a corner. There was no reason—none that he could discern, at least—to motivate the change in course, but the four of them followed it all the same. Beside him, though he couldn't see it or even fully understand it, Zoey was no doubt using her aura to enter the minds of all those taking to the streets—human and mythos alike—and redirecting them. Before long the stretch of road that they'd been occupying would grow loud with fresh chaos. Then, flooded by that chaos, it would be stained with the blood of those unfortunate enough to fall victim to others following the same futile thought paths as themselves. The urge to try to stop it, to help, tugged at him, working his logic centers to try to convince him it was the right thing or the honorable thing to do. He did not listen to that part of himself, though. Noble as it was, the urge was foolish. Sooner or later he'd be brought down, overpowered or maybe just exhausted, but dead all the same. Zane would fair no different, either; fantasies of dystopian heroism were fun, but the reality of those situations was that, in a world like that—a world where ninety-nine percent of the population was dead and buried beneath the fallen societies—the hope that any person could plan to be a part of the surviving one percent was either a product of idiocy or insanity.

Zane, unfortunately, was prone to bouts of both.

Like I said: Zoey broke her silence, obviously having seen Isaac's thoughts just then, *you're doing better than him, at least.*

Better or not, Isaac said back, actually finding himself trying to whisper in thought-speak, *I can't help but wonder if Xander* is *still alive.*

Zoey seemed genuinely injured by this statement. *But Estella said—*

How willing were you to count the loss and move on when you'd found out that Ezra and Jerrick had taken me?

She noticeably flinched at the names of the insane hybrid brothers who'd captured and tortured him months earlier during the mission that ultimately steered them to this moment.

That was...

Isaac didn't need to interrupt her this time; she trailed off and left enough silence between them for him to "say," *If you're about to say that it was different than I'd like to remind you who you're talking to. Calm and calculated, remember?* He sighed, and the sound was enough to make Zane glance his way. The moment was brief, however, and the vampire's mismatched brown-and-blue gaze shifted back soon after. *Serena's obviously ranting in his mind,* he thought.

The thought, just like speech, was "heard" by Zoey all the same. When they "spoke" like this, there was no real way to separate what was said to the other and what was thought to oneself. At least, that was the case for Isaac. What he "heard" from Zoey was entirely up to her.

Like I said, her own "voice" seemed hushed, and Isaac felt less embarrassed about his own efforts, *she's trying to keep him calm.*

Curious... he looked down, unsure if what he was "saying" was something he'd intended to be a private thought or an addition to his and his lover's conversation. *Is Zane really so wrong to feel how he feels right now? How logical is it to be calm right now, with everything that's going on?*

About as logical as it is to still believe in Xander Stryker despite all he's done. Going out there and being part of that mess makes about as much sense as seeking to find him and protect him; to find purpose in his choice. But you and I both know that, while those two options are equally logical—which is to say, of course, not at all—you and I both also know that there's only one right choice. You can't keep letting the word "noble" float about in your head if you're going to disregard nobility just because panic is easier.

It was Isaac's turn to look injured. Letting his own gaze fall to the street, following a similar blind-yet-knowing path as Estella Stryker, he considered all of these new developments.

So what if Zane's right? he finally asked. *What if Xander's already dead?*

Zoey managed to stomach this question better than before, but the disapproval was there all the same. *He can't be,* she said, the mind-whisper replaced with a mind-growl.

Startled by this, he asked, *Why do you say it like that?*

Two reasons... Zoey paused to take in a deep breath that, after the extended silence with nothing more than shared thoughts to serve as conversation, resounded in his ears like a trumpet blast. A part of him—the part that wanted to panic and fly off the handle like everyone else—was certain that all those Zoey had been holding back would hear it, override her influence in their heads, and flood the street to tear them apart. Obviously this didn't happen; Zoey was too strong and, truth be told, the inhale was only just an inhale. *Firstly:* she started, giving Isaac a knowing glance, *Xander did what he did for a reason. Whether or not it was a good reason remains to be seen, but it was* his *reason all the same. That means that, if there's any hope of making things right with the world, they rest squarely with him not only surviving all of this, but seeing his plan through to the end.*

Assuming he had a plan to begin with, Isaac thought to himself and then flinched when he saw Zoey give him a micro-glare in response to the thought. Eager to diffuse the tension and, admittedly, curious, he quickly added, *And the second reason you feel it's imperative that Xander still be alive?*

Zoey pulled her lower lip between her teeth and gave it a nervous chew, letting her eyes drift as a response to Estella.

All nobility, all logic, and all hope set aside... she began, and Isaac was surprised to find that a voice in his head could actually sound like it was crying, *I can't stand the idea of her baby growing up without a father.*

CHAPTER 3

FORBIDDEN DANCE

"The pain of parting is nothing to the joy of meeting again."
Charles Dickens (1812-1870)

"Ready or not, world..."
(from the journal of Xander Stryker)

T*his hurts.*

Merciful Earth Mother, this hurts so much!

Estella knew of all sorts of pain. There was the nagging, almost subconscious pain of the daily routine of being human; that, she believed, was the sensation of life moving, passing, and the driving urge to make something of the time that remained. It was an easy enough theory—poetic and nigh impossible to disprove, at least—until one died or became something *not* human. Then that nagging pain, though still present, was duller, buried much, much farther away in those subconscious regions. Humans, after all, got a few hearty decades, maybe a century to occupy, but vampires could easily multiply that longevity ten times over. Estella had even heard of others that saw their thousandth year come and pass.

Hard to imagine mortality stinging quite the same to a creature like that.

So she'd known the pain of humanity and its mortality. Then there was the pain of being reminded of that mortality, that of her parents' death. That was a different, more immediate and far more demanding sort of hurt. Sure, it hurt to lose a parent, more to lose both, that much more to lose them all at once—she'd have expected nothing less—but it wasn't a peaceful *knowing*, such as finding out after the fact, or even something abrupt and unexpected. It hadn't been a phone call or even a rude awakening with a flash of horrible memories—*"We were all together, happy as could be, and then... not"*—but, instead, several excruciating hours. In that time, a vengeful vampire, Lenix—the name still knotted up her guts and made her want to vomit, a reaction that only Aleks had recently come to parallel—had relished in the act of pinning her against her bedroom wall with his aura while he made a twisted, horrible show of the act. At the time she'd been unable to see the invisible "limb" that held her back, could only feel its immense weight and strength as she fought to pull free of it, but the rest was all-too-clear to her. In the moments when her tears shielded the scene or she'd dared to close her eyes against it, Lenix made certain to penetrate her mind and project his own view directly into her head. There was no blurring that out; no ignoring it. Not that anything could have blinded her to the smell of her parents' blood as it stained her carpet and caked over her floorboards, nor was there any way to shut off her ears against the sound of tormented cries and breaking bones. Being present to such a thing was, as Lenix had put it, "a feast for all senses."

And he'd even offered her a few unwanted tastes of their deaths, as well.

"You vill come to savor it, I promise," he'd said in that awful, heavily-accented voice.

Then he'd bitten her, an act which, on its own, represented any number of different pains, and she'd died knowing that all of it—everything she'd suffered through—had been orchestrated to hurt Xander. All the pain she'd gone through, in the end, had been for the sake of torturing him. After everything else, she'd slipped into the darkness of death feeling guilty for that fact.

Another sort of hurt, one that could never heal.

Pain, pain, pain-pain, pain. Life was full of it, death could come from it...

And then she'd been reborn into it.

The pain of reliving it all over again. The pain of realizing it wasn't over. The pain of accepting that, after all Xander's warnings and efforts to distance himself from her for her own protection, she'd practically *invited* her fate upon herself and her parents. The pain of blaming Xander, of *hating* him, and, inevitably, the pain of admitting to herself that she could do neither.

But then there were the pains she didn't mind so much. She wouldn't say she enjoyed these pains—though she was certain, in some way, that Xander did, perhaps relished in them as some sort of retributive sensation—but she certainly suffered through them with no regret. These were the pains earned in fighting alongside Xander, in stopping monsters who'd prey on innocence. Every time she took a bullet that was aimed for Xander or was injured while battling a creature like Lenix, she couldn't help but celebrate it for what it represented: love, purpose, justice. These were good things to hurt for, she believed.

Undeniably, Estella had known all sorts of pain. Some great, some small; some awful, some grand.

But this pain—the pain of losing Xander, a man who she'd loved before she could even understand what that word meant or represented—was by far the worst of all. It was a pain that dared to combine all the worst pains—those tied to mortality, death, hate, and guilt—and deny her the hope of the best pains—those tied to all the things that were right with her life. It left her doubtful and alone...

Painfully alone.

Aleks... that son of a bitch, she seethed inwardly, *has done to me what even Lenix couldn't!*

And, about that, she was right.

Lenix *had* taken much from her, but when she'd died she'd done so with a single empowering thought: *Xander. He's still out there.*

Now, trudging through the streets and trying again and again to find some hint of her husband's energy signature in the vastness of "out there," she found herself struggling to hold onto that belief; to refuse Aleks the glory of taking from her the only thing that Lenix left her:

Hope.

YOU LISTEN to me and you listen good, you grand, heaving cock-thumper, it was taking all of Serena's limited self-control to not let the psychic conversation she was having with her husband spill out into the open where all the world could hear. All the world, as far as she was concerned, could suck a sweaty nutsack, but, as Estella—whom Serena had begun to worship as some sort of goddess solely because she couldn't adore her as an earth-being quite enough—was still a part of her immediate surroundings it was worth it to keep things quiet. *That glorious woman is suffering enough right now, and I have zero—fucking ZERO!—problems with telling my son that I murdered his father if you feel the need to open that dumb gorilla mouth of yours.*

Zane glared at her, and Serena realized that their argument was slipping out of the realm of playful threats and beginning to spiral that great, cosmic, shit-and-puke-filled toilet bowl where all major marital arguments go to fester. Her husband wasn't a pussy—God, Buddha, and his holy hotness, Channing-"please eat my pussy"-Tatum, knew that to be the truth—and, if the subject was serious enough in his mind, Serena's feigned threats and love-tap slaps weren't about to sway him. That glare, she knew, meant that shit was serious—meant that Zane was serious—and she had to find a way to diffuse things in his head before a bad idea turned into a bad action, one that wouldn't be so easily diffused.

Estella Stryker was hanging on by a thread, one that only Serena and Zoey could see, and Zane's growing doubts, though concerns that they all shared, were like a pair of scissors in the hand of a scampering child.

Serena *really* didn't want an even greater clusterfuck dropped on them...

Why are you acting like I'm the asshole here? Zane's thought rang back in Serena's mind with such anger and resonance that she forgot in that instant that they'd gotten the Maledictus curse out of him. *We've been following her around for almost an hour! AN HOUR! And, in case you haven't realized, things aren't exactly awesome! Everyone wants to kill everyone else! It's 'Fear and Loathing EVERY-FUCKING-WHERE,' featuring every motherfucker and their dear-ol'-granny! I don't have to be psychic to know that either you or Zoe are keeping these streets clear of all the nutjobs out there—lord knows SHE certainly isn't thinking clearly enough to do it,* his eyes darted accusingly towards Estella—*but if you thought I didn't know they were out there then I'm insulted. The world's a dangerous place now; more dangerous than it was even a few hours ago, and then there was an entire church that could send Xander and me straight into the fires of Hell and turn Isaac into a snarling fuck-beast eager to snack on our throats! Us, Serena! His own friends! It was like he didn't even recognize us—hell, ask him now and he'll tell you he doesn't even remember it; he* DID NOT *recognize us!—and those crazy fuckers—*

crazy HUMAN *fuckers, mind you—put us all through the ringer! Even Xander's devil-friend was having trouble with them, and he's supposed to be, like, a fucking god! And that was THEN! Those motherfuckers are still out there—there's no fucking way that Xander and devil-man took 'em all out; I'm sure there's others like them all over the goddam planet, anyway—and now every human in existence is probably gonna start lining up for their fucked-up communion wafer just to know how to sling Hellfire at the big, bad monsters! Meanwhile, every mythos out there is scared shitless and raising their own hell because of it. And here we are, following somebody who just admitted she has no fucking idea where we're going, and looking for the single most hated son of a bitch in the entire world.*

There were any number of questions raised by Zane's rant that Serena wanted answered—*Hellfire? What the hell is that supposed to mean?*—but she knew better than to ask. Zane ranting in her head meant he wasn't running his mouth to Estella. That was good. But she had to keep him ranting, and she had to remind him who he was.

Do you hate him? she asked him, already knowing the answer.

Zane actually paused in mid-step. It only lasted a moment —if Estella noticed she didn't show any sign of caring—before he started back in stride, catching up so quickly that it was as though he hadn't stopped at all, but it told Serena a lot all the same.

You don't, right? she pressed, *The world's like* this *and everyone's scared, yourself included, but you still don't hate him, do you?*

Zane looked down. *I never said I hated him, I just—*

And you want him found, right? If you still see him as a friend—a 'bro,' or whatever—then you must—

He's fucking dead, Serena.

The conviction in the words nearly made Serena stop in mid-step. *You have no way of knowing that, Zane,* she was glad for the psychic connection, certain that her voice would have cracked if she'd tried to say the words aloud. *There's no way you could—*

How much of the footage did you watch? Zane asked, his voice in her head sounding more pitying than challenging.

I... Serena furrowed her brow, admitting to herself then that she hadn't been able to stomach more than thirty seconds. *Not very much,* she finally confessed.

Zane did nothing to hide the solemn nod that followed. Zoey and Isaac, she noticed, glanced over at the gesture.

There was something like a crackle of radio static in Serena's mind—like a mental draft of air from another door being opened—and Zoey's voice chimed with, *Everything alright?*

Yeah, Serena offered a brief answer, not wanting to give away to Zane that she was carrying on another conversation. Immediate guilt at the blatant lie, however, had her correcting herself soon after: *No. I... I don't know, Zoe.*

What do you mean? Zoey asked. *What's—*

Zane, having no way of knowing that he was interrupting Zoey in Serena's head, projected his thought over the word "wrong." *I forced myself to sit through every second of it. It didn't even stop,* he informed her. *The feed just died. Like somebody yanked a cable or something. Either way, it would've had to have happened on their end.*

Serena couldn't argue with that. The broadcast shouldn't have managed to go on for as long as it did. There were any number of systems and regulations set up on the humans' side alone that should have prevented it from happening. Beyond that, if somebody with ties to The Council had caught whiff of the broadcast, then any number of measures could've been taken to shut it down. And there was no chance that somebody with ties to The Council *hadn't* caught a whiff of it the moment it started. The second Stryker's face was occupying the airwaves, Serena knew that there was somebody in power trying to take it off. Before the words "vampire" could've been uttered, everything from step-A to failsafe option-Z-to-the-nth-power would have been taken. Stryker had probably even found a way to secure a private, unregistered power source, as any hack behind a keyboard on The Council's payroll would've likely sent everyone in that sector into a total blackout. As it was, the broadcast just kept on going; the entire confession rolling out across every channel and cycling like a virus over the internet.

It was even live-streaming on every porn site!

Shame for anybody out there who doesn't jerk off to gore-porn, Serena thought.

As if the uninterrupted words Xander had spoken weren't evidence enough that he'd taken every precaution to have his message be heard, there was more than three minutes of brutal torture and the sort of cursing that even Serena would have thought twice about uttering over the airwaves. Serena only hoped that some good came from the whole mess and that, somewhere out there, there were droves of FCC employees flinging themselves from the windows of their office building. That it had gone on for longer than ten seconds—let alone over three minutes!—was evidence that *nobody* who wasn't standing directly in that room with Stryker at the time had the power to end it.

And Zane, apparently, had watched every last second...

Why would you watch the whole thing? she asked, blocking out a wave of nervous questions from Zoey and feeling nauseous solely from the memory of half-a-minute's worth of the savagery.

Not because I wanted to, believe me, his fists were clenched and shaking at his sides. *I just... we were trapped. I was certain we weren't about to get out, and the only thing worse than what I was seeing at that moment was the idea of turning away and imagining the rest. I...* his shoulders slumped, *I couldn't have imagined worse.*

Then... Serena realized that there was a painful lump in her drying throat. She'd begun to cry. *Then you saw him die.*

Zane nodded again.

Tell me! she demanded, starting to reach out to grab his shoulders—to turn him to face her—but thought better of it and stopped, continuing the painful march after Estella. *Tell me what you saw!*

Zane's eyes darted from the back of Estella's head to Zoey and Isaac and then, finally, over to Serena. She saw tears in his eyes, as well.

No... she thought to herself, thankful that he couldn't "hear" her thoughts like she could with his. *Not you too, Zane. You... you never cry!*

I just did tell you, he answered flatly.

No! this time she really did grab his shoulder, but she managed not to do more than that. Realizing she was shivering, Serena forced herself to take a deep breath, glanced at Estella and dared another peek inside her mind—the words *"might recite"* cycling over and over again; *Oh, hun,* she thought, staring after her a moment longer, *just what are you doing to yourself in there?*—and then returned her focus to her husband. *Tell me* exactly *what you saw,* she demanded.

He did one better. Or, in this case, a billion worse...

He *showed* her the memory of the footage that nobody else had managed to watch.

"So while I address you," Xander Stryker concluded, staring out from the TV screen like a deer in the headlights pleading with an incoming truck, "people and mythos of the world over—whether I live or die after this—I suggest you choose peace over war... because I or others like me will stop at nothing to see this through. The line's been drawn, everyone, and I hope for your sake you choose the right..."

The exhausted, punk-rock reject looking vampire's words drifted off and his head turned to one side as a series of sharp, furious bangs sounded. Distant and funneled through whatever audio equipment

Xander was using to transmit his message, the impacts seemed hollow and artificial.

"What the hell?" Xander sounded more angry than startled, shifting his focus from the side to something just behind the camera he'd been talking at. "I thought you said that we wouldn't be—"

The next impact was more felt by the camera than heard by the microphone, the image jostling and feeling like a nod to a scene aboard the Starship Enterprise. Instead of watching William Shatner fake-stagger about, though, the view was occupied by a startled Xander as he threw up an arm to keep a gust of what Zane could only imagine was drywall dust from getting into his mouth and eyes. He failed. Through the thick veil of the dusty cloud Xander could be (barely) seen blinking and squinting against the haze, the obstructed microphone distorting his choked coughs and picking up on the sounds of a struggle off-screen.

Xander only had time to say "Who" and "in the" and finally "fuck are" before something crashed into him. At first Zane was certain he'd just watched a renegade NASCAR driver go full-on kamikaze into Stryker, but then he remembered that those racecars could only reach a few hundred miles-per-hour at best.

Whatever had hit him had hit the camera at the same time—or so human perception dictated.

Both camera and *Xander were on the floor, forcing any viewer to tilt their head for a decent angle at what was still being broadcast: a crooked, wide-angle view of what appeared to be a sound stage. Zane made out some extra microphones and coils of wires visible in the background and, just beside Xander, a capsized table that had spilled some computers that had seen happier days. Then, as Xander worked to pull himself up, something shifted in front of the camera, momentarily casting an all-encompassing darkness, and then moved away, approaching Xander, and revealing itself to be a pair of legs. Several other pairs of legs followed, moving further from the capsized camera until Zane could recognize the owner of the first pair of legs as the blond, femmy vampire that had locked them in the Trepis mansion.*

Suddenly he didn't seem so femmy, Zane noticed; suddenly he looked like the kind of guy even he would think twice before standing up against.

"Hello, Xander," he said in a voice that, like his physique, seemed familiar, but was very much different. There was no denying that he wasn't American at that point. "I believe it's time we got to know each other."

This time Xander only got "Who," "the," and "fuck" spoken before the Aleks-vamp's leg rocketed out to kick him in the face. Any human watching would've only seen Xander sail back another few feet and, if wielding a keen eye, a good spurt of blood spilling from a torn lip. The boot that connected with his jaw was otherwise moving too quickly to see—no amount of slo-mo would've caught the motion.

That camera could have been taking in thousands of frames per second and still not capture it. Kick like that could knock a bullet off course! *Zane caught himself thinking, suddenly feeling numb to what he was seeing.*

Something about seeing it on TV almost made it seem not real...

But it was *real!*

Powerful as the kick was, Xander was still in midair when he corkscrewed to his feet, recovering in a way that was eerily cat-like and, in a similar flash of too-quick-to-follow movement, seeming to exist in two places at once. In one instant he was at the "top" of the screen—occupying what should *have been the left side of the room if not for the poor fallen camera's perspective—and, in the next, he was in the bottom-center, seeming to glitch in the middle of a step and cross several meters worth of the sound stage. Some might have viewed it as a moment of "blink and you miss it," but the truth was they could've taped their eyes open Clockwork Orange-style and still missed the whole thing. Aleks didn't miss a thing, though. Xander's daring corkscrew-and-lunge—AKA Xander's glitch across a crooked screen—ended with the not-so-femmy vampire's hand holding him by the throat. A busted microphone offered a crackled hiss as Aleks said, "It's only just begun," and then he drove his free hand—flat and extended like a blade—straight through his belly.*

Xander gagged on what wanted to be a gasp but decided partway up to carry some extra blood with it. The mess sprayed out across Aleks and the three grinning mythos that accompanied him. They didn't mind the misting of blood; laughed at it, in fact. Aleks did something with his hidden hand that made Xander's legs go rigid and kick in a mockery of a docked fish. Zane distantly thought of the few times Serena had squeezed his balls too hard and wondered what was inside Xander's guts that could make him kick that way.

Then, looking like Gregori whenever he got bored with one of his toys, Aleks flung Xander aside. The gesture would've been more absently dismissive—open palmed and in a "what-everrr" sort of fashion—if it hadn't entailed Xander literally sliding off of it in the process. The busted microphone, thankfully, distorted the exiting squelch enough to spare Zane the HD quality.

*One of the others, maybe bored with watching or maybe following an unheard command, stooped over to pull Xander up by the hair, knotting his fingers at the base of his scalp to avoid letting it simply tear away, and four piston-like punches—*CRAC-CRACK... CRACK, CRACK*—drove a brick disguised as a fist into his face.*

Xander didn't have much to say under the onslaught, and it was then that Zane realized Aleks' initial kick must have broken his jaw.

Xander moved to raise an arm. Whether he intended to throw a punch or try to block a non-existent fifth attack to his face remained uncertain, as one of his attackers' aura stopped him before he had a chance. As far as the camera was concerned, Xander's extended arm just up and decided to break itself in two places and jut irregularly.

Xander's hand flopped against the pain of the broken arm, and the brick-fisted piston-puncher, who'd stood back to admire the aurally broken arm, stomped down on his wrist.

Xander found his voice as he screamed through a clenched jaw—yup, definitely broken. Blood seeped through bared teeth that looked prepared to shatter under the pressure.

Even from the distance and through the fading haze of dust, the world could see his fangs.

Zane could, at least.

But, then again, he knew to look.

This is bad... *he thought for the first time. It was a bit late for that response, he knew, but it wouldn't be the last time he'd think it, either.*

Without the benefit of Xander offering up his left arm, one of the other mythos stepped casually around his comrades and, kneeling over Xander with an almost delicate approach, set a foot over his shoulder before grabbing his arm and forcing it upward against the obstruction. The microphone offered little buffer against the familiar wet pop *of a joint hopping free of its socket.*

More stifled, clenched screams.

Xander's left arm fell over his head, the limb hanging all wrong and looking like a discarded tube sock.

Aleks' voice rose, but the audio pickup's suffering had grown bad enough to make whatever he said too garbled to make out to anybody still watching.

His goons, however, heard him just fine.

The beating of Xander Stryker continued. Two of the mythos began to trade blows nearer to Xander's head—seeming to argue over who'd get to focus on that choice piece of meat—but were soon disciplined by Aleks, who disappointed both of them by crouching over Xander and simply talking to him, seeming almost casual as he did so, as another began working on his ribs with a heavy-looking boot.

Aleks' lips moved, birthing more garbled, foreign-tinged hums. At one point, Zane thought he heard him say "mother" and remembered thinking absently, You shouldn't talk about the man's mother, *while replaying Estella's horrific story of rape and murder from Xander's childhood.*

"You just can't catch a break," he found himself saying absently, reaching out with trembling fingers to touch the television screen.

*As if to punctuate this in some cosmic sense of cruelty, Xander's body shifted, relieving whatever crippling effect had been stifling the microphone—*wherever that might be, *Zane wondered—and the* *sound of more of Xander's bones falling victim to the onslaught came through in perfect clarity.*

Finally, as though cued by some source that they were still broadcasting, Aleks turned to face the overturned camera and, smiling and exposing an entirely new set of fangs—one that occupied his entire mouth and not just his canines—he fetched Xander by the wrist, earning a clear-as-a-bell whimper in the process, and dragging him towards the viewing world.

Xander's bloodied face was slammed so violently against the lens that, for a long moment, the view was black once more.

Then it was red.

And red it stayed.

The audio crackled and shifted, bumped and hissed, and finally bellowed with a Euro-trash accent:

"Let this mark a new world order. My *order. Like the once-proud little clot-muncher said: prepare yourselves."*

The broadcast went on for another twenty-or-so seconds, the view unchanging, though occasionally shifting with unseen impacts, for most of that time. Then, with no response from Xander, something peeled him away from the lens—an unblinking, glassy hazel eye staring out at whoever was still watching—and then, with a faded crunch *and another jarring impact, the feed cut away to a pre-programmed image of a sad face looming over a cut cord and the words "TEMPORARILY EXPERIENCING TECHNICAL DIFFICULTIES."*

Zane could only assume that somebody had finally thought to kill the camera, too.

DAMMIT, Serena, answer me! Zoey was getting frantic, trying to think of a way of demanding answers without Estella finding out what they'd all secretly been discussing with their lovers behind her back. *What's wrong? What is Zane—*

He's dead, Zoe, Serena's voice was hollow and lifeless in her head; a whisper from a far off and deep down place. Zoey had never heard Serena, psychic or otherwise, sound like that. It scared her.

But not as much as the words she "spoke."

Xander, Serena's auric hold with Zoey's mind wavered around the name; the psychic equivalent of a voice cracking under the weight of a sob. *He... they killed him. Zane saw the whole thing.*

CHAPTER 4

DANCE WITH THE DEVIL

"What is madness but nobility of the soul at odds with circumstance."
Theodore Roethke (1908-1963

"Risky for **who?** *You're a* **god** *now!"*
The Power/Xander Stryker

Xander was missing, quite possibly dying.

And there was nothing Estella could do to stop it.

This was another of the ongoing and increasingly painful thoughts that plagued her mind as she navigated the streets. As she had so many times before, she found herself repeating his name to herself, hoping the chant would help to connect her to him:

Stryker...

Stryker.

The name had been cycling in her head for several hours, an intermittent dance that rang with pride or anger or terror. Other times, without prompt or warning, it stopped being a name and started being an action—a demand or an accusation; she couldn't be sure. By the time "Stryker" became "striker" and she'd caught on to the change, it had turned back again. Then pride and anger and terror blossomed anew with a fresh wave of confusion.

And confusion, she found, was close with doubt. They were practically lovers. When confusion nestled into the sheets of her mind, doubt wasn't far behind. Horny and impatient, it seized hold and took control; confusion could never say "no" to a lover like that.

Stryker...

Striker.

Stryker!

The lovers toiled and rolled. Over and over. The stink of their love fogged her mind and made the already hazy line between "Stryker" and "striker" nearly impossible to discern. It made her head ache. It made her body numb. It made the intermittent dance and the thrashing lovers that much more active.

And she just wanted peace and quiet; a solid moment for all of it to go still and silent so that she could think.

Estella...

Estella Stryker...

Stryker.

Striker!

She'd taken the name knowing full-well what it meant. It was a name that had gotten plenty of people—good people; mythos and human alike—killed. Then again, it was a name that carried with it an even greater death toll of the very real monsters who preyed on the weak and innocent. Once, not long before that moment, Estella would have never been able to fathom just how many had died, be they noble and just or selfish and evil. And, in that same close-yet-distant time of peaceful ignorance, she would have been hard pressed if asked to conceive of the sheer brutality and carnage those deaths had carried.

Those who didn't deserve to die perishing in the worst possible ways while those who'd earned their deaths seeming to blink out too soon.

All, however, sharing ties to that name:

Striker...

Stryker.

Stryker!

She'd taken the name all the same, though, believing (and accepting) that the risk would always hang over her head.

And woe be unto the self-destructive soul who threatened Estella Stryker, because Xander Stryker would make it better.

Xander would always make it better.

And if Estella were to perish, then the pain and anger would only make him that much more dangerous.

But Estella wasn't the one missing, and if Xander was...

NO!

No...

He's out there. He's out there, and he'll make it better.

Xander would always make it better.

It was a comfortable thought; a clean, tidy wrapping around the hefty package that was the very real, very awful risk that carrying the name "Stryker" represented. She'd always looked at it like holding the deadliest of guns, one that she'd gone and fallen head-over-heels in love with. She could hold it, she could care for it, she could admire how beautiful and lethal—how *sensual*—it was.

She could feel safe with it.

But guns didn't bleed. Guns didn't vanish into the night, turn the entire world upside-down and inside-out in an instant, and then...

Guns didn't bleed.

She'd always imagined that when the worst came to be, it'd

be her blood being spilled and Xander—her gun—that would *bang-bang* all the bad away.

And of the plans of mice and men... she recited in her mind, the rhythm of the poem's words acted as a waltz for the pride and anger and terror. A wince was suppressed as she flicked a wayward black bang from her angled gaze, and, casting poetry from her mind, she thought, *Confusion and doubt will be fucking in my head soon enough.*

An insane drive to laugh nearly toppled her in mid-step as she realized that the thought might have passed for the sort of morbid, vulgar "poetry" that Xander might recite. She caught herself in the middle of that thought—stopping it before the wavering fog of the words "might *have* recited" could congeal as a thought—and inwardly scolded herself, repeating "might recite, might recite, might recite," over and over again.

But this only gave Doubt a sturdier erection, and Confusion was wagging her sex in expectation, asking *"what if?"*

"What if?"

"What..."

Stryker...

Stryker.

Estella Stryker*!*

She'd taken the name certain that she was adopting a target on her head because of it, but the name had turned into something more. It was a calling. A responsibility. Several hours earlier, after watching her husband, the gun, fire a bullet of truth into the world that it might never recover from, Estella had to watch him beaten and tortured on the soulless window of an HD-TV. She'd had to watch the father of her unborn child beaten and tortured, sobbing and reaching to him, trying to tell him through the screen that he was going to be a father—something that, having just found out herself, he didn't know—because a part of her knew that she might never get the chance to tell him again. He couldn't hear, though; could only reply with blood and cries. She'd ripped the mansion, their home, apart in her grief; her magic ripping through the planks and beams and concrete like a box of tissue cast into the flames of Hell.

The Trepis Clan collapsed in an instant, the collapse of the hilltop mansion acting as a sort of birth to all breed of mythos —their members and warriors—as they spilled out into the night. Most, she knew, would never return—their leader having just broken the single greatest law; the law that so many hundreds of other laws were built upon. Most of the mythos executed throughout the ages had earned the death penalty because of some variation on this all-encompassing law that they'd tip-toed around.

But Xander Stryker did not tip-toe around anything. Like with everything else, he dropped in, feet planted and fists balled, in a flurry of blood and chaos and devil-may-care outlook for the consequences. Though, for some strange reason, Estella couldn't fully believe that last part, but even she, herself, was unaware of that thought and the weight that it carried.

Xander was *the sort to act without a plan, but that broadcast...*

No.

No, *that* had to have something more behind it; *that* he wouldn't have done if there wasn't a reason.

But what could that reason be...?

It was an important thought. It was the most crucial thought that the world should have been considering at that moment. Unfortunately, as far as Estella knew, she was the only one having it. And then, with the same bumbling haste that thought was born, it aged, withered, and died. Doubt was smirking at the thought-corpse, stroking a fresh erection, and Confusion couldn't be bothered to shed a tear for the loss. And Estella...

Estella couldn't think up a fresh thought to eulogize the most important thought in her head at that moment. Shambling through the city, there was only one true, driving thought that wouldn't die—a vampire amidst a cold, dark city of pitiful mortals.

Stryker...

Stryker.

Stryker!

Maybe she *had* married a deadly gun, one that the world saw as an even greater threat than ever before, and now that gun had been taken from her. She wanted it back; wanted *him* back. The dark, vulgar thoughts and curve of insanity growing ever sharper in her head might serve as reminders of the man she loved—she certainly *felt* like she was turning into him; carrying a piece that was growing and maturing with every step —but holding Stryker in her mind wasn't like holding him in her arms.

Maybe Xander was a gun, but he was *her* gun. And the ones that took him from her, and anybody who tried to keep him from her, would learn that there were far deadlier things in this world than guns. The world knew that much now thanks to her husband, and she had no reservations against proving it. She strode on, the four mythos behind her a distant-yet-comforting shadow of a thought, and relished in the realization that the hazy divide between "Stryker" and "striker" was growing even more uncertain. The word—content with existing simultaneously as a title and an action—danced with modest contentment within the depths of her gray matter, giving pause here-and-there to consider the empowering qualities that pride and anger and terror shared. And if, a short ways away from the emotional dance floor, confusion and doubt wanted to fuck on the dirty mattress of her mind then that was alright, too, so long as she could find Xander and have him back in their own bed where he belonged.

Zane! Zane, don't! Serena was beyond the point of joke-threats and playful beatings; was beyond the point of cursing up a storm or threatening to deny him sex—though, if she was being honest with herself, that would have to be filed away as a joke-threat, as well. Serena Vailean was desperate. *I don't care what you think you saw—I don't even care if it's true—you can't just—*

What I think *I saw? Serena, you just saw it, too; tell me I'm wrong,* Zane leveled a rock-like gaze on her. It was cold and unwavering. He'd made up his mind. After a long moment he repeated himself, *Tell me I'm wrong. Tell me that Estella shouldn't know the truth—that we should end this so-called search party and get back to the others—so that we can begin to take some genuinely productive steps towards what should happen next.*

Zane, I... Serena's efforts to hold back her tears was choking up even her ability to think. She couldn't even begin to imagine how to argue with him; couldn't even bring herself to disagree with him anymore. *Just... just do it right, okay? D-don't be an ass about it.*

A phantom exchange hung between them: him saying *"Look who you're talking to,"* and her giving him a look—*that* look—to which he'd reply *"Oh... right."* It was the funny sort of thing they did a lot; one of their things. But now wasn't the time for funny or for them to think about themselves.

Doubt and Confusion seemed to be taking a break.

Sore and raw, I'd imagine, Estella almost—*almost!*—made herself smile at the thought.

Strange...

Vulgarity, brashness, and wisps of insanity weren't usually her forte—were, in fact, Xander's; had been for as long as she'd known him—but she was surprised to see how well she was taking to them. Granted, she hadn't acted on any of those things just yet—*Thank Gaia for that much!*—so maybe it was a bit early to be staking claims to mannerisms that weren't typically her own, but something about it felt right. Like knowing she was pregnant with Xander's child, feeling like she was carrying a part of who he was—*Is! Is!* IS!—made her clichéd auric scans of the city and futile astral outreaches seem less cliché and futile.

The others might not believe it, but she *could* feel Xander out there somewhere. It just wasn't...

And that was where Estella kept finding herself stonewalled. There was *something* that was undeniably Xander out there, but his presence was so slight and fractured across such a vast space that it was like trying to pinpoint the first ray of morning light through a dense fog that consumed the entire horizon. There was simply too little of him refracted across too much of everything else to get a location. Moreover, there was something else—something far more powerful—that seemed to be riding on that small sliver of Xander's aura.

No, Estella chewed her lip as she was forced to admit something she didn't like to herself: *Whatever it is, it's not riding his aura—there's not enough of him left for that... No, he's being carried by it!*

This conclusion, however, amounted to nothing but an even greater headache and another mountain-high stack of questions to add to the range she already had. At first she'd hoped to use this finding to her advantage, to focus on targeting this new energy and follow it instead of Xander's. It was a good plan. After all, if whatever it was insisted on hanging onto his aura—*Enveloping his aura,* she corrected herself without meaning it—then it was a safe bet that wherever it was would be where Xander was. Plans, though—good or bad—had an ugly way of going wrong when Xander was involved. Estella could no more deny her love for him than she could deny herself air or deny the presence of magic, but it was a long-and-hard learned lesson that, if Xander was around, things were pretty much guaranteed to shoot off from any structured intentions and turn into something else entirely. Fortunately for her, though, this meant that boring nights had a way of becoming the most romantic outings she could ever dream of and that the well-laid plans of enemies were rendered a waste of time and a one-way ticket to a face-to-face meeting with one of Xander's guns.

Just thinking about it brought a smile to her face.

By the gods, but Estella loved him so much!

The smile sank and Estella felt her eyes set off towards a sliver of red—like a colored smoke hanging off in the distance—a moment before her body turned onto another street.

Xander's quirky way of turning plans inside-out was alive and well, and this was no more evident than each and every time that Estella tried to focus on tracking that mysterious energy enveloping the limited traces of his aura. It changed! Each and every time she felt she had a bead on the second source, it dropped out of existence and became something else. It was like trying to pick up an object that kept changing its shape.

Or like trying to track an animal that's always evolving... she mused with curiosity.

But it was there!

Dodgy and agitating, sure—words that Estella was certain his enemies had used against Xander before—but it was there, and it had Xander with him!

A part of him, at least...

Estella imagined herself looking for an hourglass and only finding a single grain of sand, and the thought made her shiver.

Doubt and Confusion decided they were good to go again.

No, no, no... Estella fought all the thoughts—all the reason and logic that she typically prided herself for—that pointed to one inevitable truth. *He's out there. He IS out there! And I will tear through anybody who—*

As if the universe wanted to challenge that last thought, Zane's aura shifted behind her—doubt already beginning to show on it—and, through her scanning mind's eye, she saw him open his mouth to speak.

Estella stopped in mid-step, waiting. She knew what he had to say.

Don't do it, she prayed on his behalf, already feeling her body beginning to prepare for something that neither she nor Zane would want. *Just... don't.*

She planned for her prayer to reach some point on a higher plane that would, in some cosmic way, understand that she had dealt with enough. She planned for Zane to think better of his actions. She planned on him and the others either continuing to follow her or even to give up and walk away. She wouldn't blame them for that, just as she didn't blame all those who'd renounced their ties to the Trepis Clan. Xander had not only broken The Council's single greatest law, he'd thrown the world into turmoil. Everyone had every right to fear and hate him.

Then again, everyone had always feared and hated Xander Stryker. He'd always been different, and he'd suffered for it. He'd just given them a reason to justify it this time.

But she would never abandon him. She could never hate him.

She planned to find Xander, to stay by his side and take on whoever tried to drive them apart. Even if that meant taking on the entire world.

But before she could follow through with that plan, she needed her plan—her prayer—for Zane to *not* say what he was about to say to come true.

"Maybe," Zane said the word as though it had five syllables, stretching out the last part into a long sigh.

Xander MUST still be alive, Estella thought with no real pleasure behind it, *because another plan just got fucked up.* Taking advantage of the two-yet-five syllable word that had birthed a most terrible silence between the five of them, she called over her shoulder, making sure to do it aloud this time.

"Don't."

Zane wouldn't listen to the cosmos—assuming the cosmos had heard Estella's prayer—and he certainly wouldn't listen to Estella. "I think it's time we start to consider the possibility that Xander might be—"

THAT WORD...

MUST NOT...

BE MADE REAL!

The ground vanished beneath Estella's feet. A moment later —or in the exact same moment, as time had ceased to function by traditional standards—Zane's did, too.

So much for not acting on vulgarity, brashness, and wisps of insanity, she thought, while, in the background of her mind, the words, *HE'S NOT! HE'S NOT! HE'S NOT!* cycled about in her head like an asteroid field, barreling and crashing into one another, demolishing all smaller thoughts as they did.

Confusion and Doubt were among them.

They fucked themselves to death! Estella thought and wanted to laugh at the sheer morbidity of the thought—the raw *Xanderness* of it...

But she and Zane were moving too fast.

The varcol blood that Estella had stolen was still alive and well in her, likely would be for the rest of her life. Through it, her body and her mind had been transcended in a way that evolution had robbed from modern vampires. Varcols, likely the oldest mythos in existence, were once perceived as gods, and when Xander and Estella had faced one of the few left—one with a spiteful history with Xander's father and an apocalyptic plan for the world—they'd seen firsthand why.

Her blood—Lenuta's blood—made Estella faster, stronger, and more powerful than Zane; made her more powerful than all four of them combined.

And this big, dumb, tattooed son-of-a-bitch just gave me a reason to prove it!

In an instant, she had Zane pinned against the grimy, graffiti-laced wall of an alley, the words "HE'S NOT! HE'S NOT!

HE'S NOT!" finally able to echo in open air, and doing so with an emotional range that started with enraged certainty and ended in pleading sobs. She slammed him, again and again, against the wall, his stunned face grimacing with each impact. Brick cracked and chipped away.

"HE'S NOT!"—*BAM!*—"HE'S NOT!"—*BAM! BAM! BAM!*—"YOU FUCKING LISTEN! YOU LISTEN TO ME!—*BAM! BAM! cah-RACK!*—"HE'S NOT!"

She threw him back against the cratered wall, letting red rock and chipped mortar crumble at his feet. He staggered, but Estella could see in his eyes it was more out of shock than pain. Somehow, despite the damage, she'd managed to hold back; managed to avoid truly hurting him.

A siren wailed in the distance, a sound that had become more and more constant over the past few hours, and Estella tensed. It was a shock to her system to hear any sign of life outside of the five of them occupying the various stretches of road that they'd been traversing.

Zoey... she thought, remembering a vague sense of seeing her aura at constant work over the past few hours.

Then, seeing Zane's stunned face taking her in, it was her turn to stagger.

"Zane..." she whimpered, shaking her head, "I'm so sorry. B-but he's... he's not..."

"You don't know what I saw," Zane's voice was a foreign croak, and it took Estella a moment to realize he was holding back a sob.

She nodded and looked away. "I do," she confessed. "I've seen it. I've been seeing it. Over and over again." She waved her hand around to indicate the city. "There doesn't seem to be a person around that didn't sit through every awful second," she explained. Then, tapping the side of her head, added, "I can't help but 'see' it. I know what you saw, Zane," she said, looking up and locking her gaze with his mismatched own. While others might have been deterred by the sight of a brown right eye and blue left eye occupying one face, she'd fallen in love with a man whose own beautiful hazel-green eye was paired with a deep, blood-red orb. In a weird way, it was a comfort to be looking into a pair of eyes like that. She even found herself smiling a little as she shook her head at him. "But you saw wrong. Everybody did. He's alive—Xander *is* alive—and I can prove it."

She touched the heel of her left palm against his forehead so that she could feed the "view" from her mind's eye into his head, and she scanned for what she'd been following all along.

There, like the first ray of morning light through a dense fog that consumed the entire horizon, they both saw him. Through Estella's view, Zane knew what he was seeing—though the more appropriate word for it would likely be "feeling"—but it all amounted to the same thing.

Xander *was* alive.

But only barely.

Zane blinked at the flood of reality that rushed back at him as Estella removed the connection. When he'd once again remembered how to work his eyes and understand what they were aimed at, he steered them back towards her. His chin was set. His muscles were tense. He looked ready to take on the world.

"Oh fuck! Oh fuck! Fuck!" Serena's panicked chant was coming out in breathy bursts as she sprinted through the streets, forcing herself to avoid overdrive—neither knowing where she'd go and knowing that Zoey and Isaac would be unable to keep up—as she tried to figure out where Estella and Zane had vanished to.

"Was that overdrive?" she heard Isaac ask Zoey behind her. While neither of them, not being sangs, could achieve what most called "overdrive," they were at least familiar enough with it to know that what Estella had just done seemed somehow different.

They weren't wrong.

Serena had seen Estella start to shift into what she'd assumed was overdrive. Being a perfect vampire—having both sang and auric abilities—allowed her not only to follow the superhuman movement with her eyes, but also witness the shift in others' auras when they were preparing to make the jump. Unfortunately for her, Estella was *also* like her—able to call upon the speed and strength and savagery of a sangsuiga while also having all the psychic and telekinetic powers of an auric—and there hadn't been much of an auric tell to warn Serena of Estella's intent. Ordinarily, like most aurics, Estella kept her aura inside of her body; offering nothing to gauge from. There *had* been a flash, though; an eruption of orange woven with black and red inlays. It had lasted less than a second, but that moment told Serena more than enough:

Firstly: Estella was about to do something intense, and, she'd figured, it would be a good idea to try following her into overdrive—even if only just to watch—to see what she had in mind.

And second: though still only a few weeks into her pregnancy, Estella was carrying a great deal more of Xander within her than she would have thought possible. That black-and-red streak woven through her own aura was, without a doubt, Xander's own, but it was too soon to be carrying *that* much...

Wasn't it?

The second observation, Serena decided, was too strange to dwell on for long. If she'd learned anything of the Strykers, Xander especially, it was that lingering on the troubling bits for too long was a surefire means of driving one totally batshit crazy. The first observation, however, was an easy enough process. Just allow her body to jump into overdrive, not much different than tensing a muscle once one got the hang of it, and let her eyes make the adjustment to follow the movement.

"Easy-peasy, lemon-squeezy," as she might have said to Gregori, who wasn't yet allowed to use overdrive but had been caught raiding Serena's stash of Snickers several times already in a blur of motion.

Except it *wasn't* that easy!

She *should* have been able to see Estella's movements clear as day once in overdrive. The rest of the world would become an eerie, frozen-in-time backdrop, a backdrop where the only things that moved were the things in overdrive. But she didn't see Estella. Okay, that was a lie, she did see *something*, but it was too...

Serena shivered.

Too fast.

In overdrive, bullets hung in the air like violent, death-seeking ornaments. A sang could dance circles around a fired bullet in overdrive; even go so far as to lick the side if they were so inclined. They *could*, but it'd burn like hell.

...

Not that Serena would know anything about that.

But, no, nothing—fucking *NOTHING!*—existed that was "too fast" for a sang in overdrive. Nothing *should* exist that was *that* fast. But...

But then there's fucking varcols in the world, aren't there? Serena inwardly cursed, solving the riddle and only serving to irritate and unnerve herself that much more in the process.

Estella had fed from that Lenuta varcol that she and Xander had encountered on their wedding night a few weeks earlier. The blood of a varcol flowed in the veins of that wonderful, goddess-like vamp-witch. And that meant that, while having the speed *and* auric control like Serena, Estella Stryker was nothing like Serena. She was the sleek, sexy Road Runner to Serena's blonde, big-tittied Wile E. Coyote—always a few hundred steps ahead, a lightyear away with the cunning wit, and a—*beep-beep*—way out of every conceivable trap.

If only...

But, for Serena at least, there was no following Missus Stryker's movements as she snatched Zane out of the street and vanished in a momentary blur, the words *"HE'S NOT"* left hanging like a dust cloud hovering in the wake of another of Wile E.'s botched schemes.

"No, Zoe," Serena called back, muttering a few more "oh fuck"s under her breath before throwing her hands up in resignation, giving up on the search, and turning back to her blue-haired auric bestie and her shapeshifting boy-toy. "That was most certainly not overdrive. Calling *that* overdrive would be like calling a burnt-out Chevy Malibu a Ferrari; like comparing Isaac's cock to—"

"Geez, Serena, I get it!" Zoey growled—actually growled!—and shook her head. "Is now really the time for those sorts of jokes? I don't even think now's the time for *any* sort of joke, but... I mean, you're married and Isaac's my..."

Serena rolled her eyes and shook her head. "I get it, Zoe! Okay! I'm sorry! I'm just..." she groaned and let her face fall into her open palms. "I'm just so nervous. Things are going to shit so quickly, and now... now I can't even—" Serena sniffled and looked up at Zoey with blurry vision, convincing herself it was just from rubbing her eyes. The wetness streaked across her face and palms she didn't have an excuse for. "I can't even sense them now," she explained. "Estella must be masking their auric signatures."

Isaac sighed and shook his head. "Now we know what she's been going through with Xander," he muttered.

Zoey shot him a look and said, "Now you're making jokes, too?"

"Not a joke," Isaac said with a shrug. "More of an observation. An ironic observation."

"People on my planet call those 'jokes,' Pogo-Dick," Serena called out, swinging her head back-and-forth in a futile effort to see with her eyes what her aura already knew wasn't there. "And they pay good money to see professionals make an hour's worth of ironic observations when their husbands aren't missing."

Isaac gave Serena a long, cold look. "Are you really about to lecture me on the nature of timing and etiquette in moments of social grace?"

"Yeah," she waved him off and turned away, starting up the street once again. She couldn't deny that, like Isaac had said, she did feel *a lot* like how Estella must have felt for the past few hours. "Another ironic observation. I'll look forward to your first stand-up circuit. We'll call it 'It's the Apocalypse, So You're Probably Not Here'-tour."

It'll be alright, Serena, Zoey called to her privately as the search resumed. *I'm sure Estella isn't going to hurt him.*

Serena sighed and fought the driving urge to let the tears come. She needed to get a grip; needed to remind herself who she was. Worrying wasn't for her! She was Serena-fucking-Vailean, after all; the stone-cold yet hotter-than-hell crazed bombshell with huge tits who could lay out a rogue with an auric bow and arrow or a right hook! She was leather and lace, for fuck's sake! She'd sent a dozen of her vibrators scattering down the hallway of her clan's headquarters and declared it a "DICK RACE" for all those in earshot to hear! Wife to a tattooed badass and mother to the most hardcore little punk to ever dart across the planet!

Serena Vailean *would not* let this get to her!

So what if Estella Stryker wanted to let off a little steam on her jackass husband? It'd serve him right for not listening to her.

Could you really blame her if she did?

Zoey didn't respond for a long moment, but then, *Zane is your husband. I'd imagine that you wouldn't want him to be hurt.*

Serena, not caring if Isaac knew that the two of them were having a conversation that he couldn't hear, glanced back at her. *Don't confuse my understanding for hope. I don't* want *Estella to hurt Zane, no, but that girl's got nothing else to hold onto right now* except *the hope of finding Xander. Maybe she knows that it's futile, maybe she's just trying to ignore how fucking pointless all of this is—being out here and meandering around with no real sense of direction—so that she can cope with the reality of it, or maybe she really believes that he's alive out there. Either's possible. Either way it's a fucked up and awful place for her to be, and we need to be here for her. That's why we're sticking around even though we know, Zoe; we haven't been tailing her around for the past hour-or-so actually believing that there might be a chance on finding Xander, we've been waiting for the moment when that poor girl comes to realize the truth. When that happens, she's going to need somebody to be there to catch her, and—dammit, Zoey—we're the best ones for that job, wouldn't you say so?*

And you'd be willing to let her hurt Zane so that she can cling to a delusion that her husband's still alive? Zoey demanded.

Serena shrugged. *Zane's a big boy. He's survived my beatings—loved them, in fact—so it's not like Estella's going to—*

Is it fair to compare a beating from her to one of your own if Estella can move faster than you? Zoey interrupted.

Serena stopped in mid-step, choking on a gasp of realization.

In the back of her mind, she imagined Zane rolling his eyes at being trampled by Wile E. Coyote while the Road Runner patiently waited its turn to plow over him.

She remembered that all that garbage about being hardcore and badass were all a front; they were a clever mask to keep her shielded against the very real fear and uncertainty lurking beneath.

Then Serena Vailean felt it all start to get to her.

"Oh fuck..." she whimpered.

"Come on," Estella turned away from Zane and started out of the alley. "I'm sure the others are worried."

She heard Zane's steps start up behind her, then he said, "Serena's probably thinking I deserve the ass-kicking they're probably all certain you're giving me." He quieted for a moment, his steps pausing, and Estella could see through her mind's eye that he was glancing back at the section of wall that had been cratered by his body not long before. "Not that I didn't get my ass kicked, I suppose," he chuckled and started after her again, "and not like I didn't deserve it."

"You thought you saw what you thought you saw," Estella said, not bothering to look back.

She didn't need to look back. Her auric senses were so alert that she could've navigated with her eyes closed; even "seen" every gesture and expression on others' faces. Thinking on it, Estella was certain that she'd actually "see" better if she wasn't using her eyes at all. Remembering the shield she'd put over herself and Zane shortly after taking him, she removed it and smirked as she sensed Serena's aura spike with recognition in the distance.

She chuckled. "And I'd think again about assuming that Serena wasn't worried."

"Oh?" Zane sounded curious but not surprised.

Serena's aura flared from several blocks away as she started to shift into overdrive. Estella knew she'd be face-to-face with her in less than a moment, which gave her just enough time to slow things down around her—from her perspective, at least—and get a look around.

There was a small gang of humans cloaked in hooded sweaters and wearing combat fatigues running at a diagonal towards them, a hand-written flag time-frozen in mid-billow from what had once been a mop handle that declared "THIS IS A HUMAN WORLD." A few of them carried handguns—small-caliber pieces that Estella easily disassembled with her aura in an instant—and another carried a small pocket knife that was slipped from his hoodie pocket and cast into a drainage pipe with the flick of an auric tendril. On the wall behind her and

Zane, just before the entrance to the alley they were emerging from, #THeRiOnLIveSmatTeR had been recently spray painted in large, irregular letters. There was something almost uplifting about the graffiti, something tragic and familiar that made her wonder if things might settle into a sort of chaotic calm.

After all, things weren't exactly perfect before all of this. The world was never without its excuses to hate and discriminate and throw itself into constant war with one another. It might not have been a beautiful, peaceful world, but it was what everyone only hours earlier would call "normal." Even now Estella could sense the minds of those in the city wishing things were as they were: *"I just wish everything could go back to normal,"* she sensed a nervous teen confessing to her boyfriend. And if *that* could have been seen as normal, then why couldn't the world rediscover that normalcy with the added tension between humans and mythos?

Estella sighed, depressed at the idea of hoping for such a thing, and turned her head in the direction of Serena. Her varcol-level speed and the perception of time it offered had slowed the fraction-of-a-second that it was going to take for her to cross the distance. In that time, she'd managed to survey the landscape, disarm some renegade, untrained mythos hunters, admire some pro-mythos wall art, and dwell on the notion of where the world might be (ideally) headed. But she could delay what was to come no longer. Easing back, time began to inch onward; the humans still frozen, but the definition of their forms beginning to solidify—everything around her beginning to feel more real. The tiny, insignificant-looking bits and pieces of the dismantled guns still floated about the humans' heads like a clustered hailstorm of springs and slides and bullets. But it was enough to unfreeze Serena from the moment, and Estella watched as she came around a building to her left. The blonde's body was pitched forward, pushing herself with all her might in an Olympic-level sprint—arms pumping and face pulled back in a desperate grimace. Her aura swam around her, a purple storm that sang with concern for Zane. Estella was very sure that, as far as Serena was concerned, she was breaking the very limits of overdrive to get to her husband.

But she still appeared to be moving in slow motion.

It was an awkward notion to see all that effort on Serena's face and to know that Estella was operating at a fraction of her body's new potential.

Not that it's doing me any good, huh, Xander?

But Xander didn't answer her. Instead, her mind was occupied by a frantic groan of slowed thought-speak:

E-sst-ell-ahhh! The time-stretched message sounded like a warped recording resounding in her mind, and Estella worked to shift further to meet with Serena's pace. *D-oon-nn't... h-uur-rt... my duummbass husband...* then, finally caught up, *Please!*

Overdrive didn't allow for speech. It barely allowed for a simple breath. When one was moving faster than sound waves, trying to speak was about as useful as using sign language in the dark. It didn't stop Estella from coughing out a laugh, knowing it wouldn't be heard by either of the two for a few moments.

He's fine, Estella assured Serena before dropping completely out of overdrive.

She was sure that Serena was going to use the opportunity to punch her for abducting Zane and putting her through some pretty obvious worry—though she wouldn't mention it, she could tell Serena had been crying—but, instead, she was surprised to find Serena hugging her as time returned to normal around them.

Bits of dismantled firearms scattered on the pavement like metal rain.

Confused and uncertain grunts echoed between the hooded humans.

A time-frozen laugh barked out of nowhere.

"I'm so sorry," Serena whispered to Estella. "I am so, so sorry. I wish it didn't have to be this—"

"HEY, FREAKS!" one of the bolder hood-wearers shouted, still standing at a distance in the middle of the otherwise deserted road. "WE DON'T WANT YOUR KIND AROUND—"

"Fuck off, trouser stains!" Serena growled, casting out her aura in a wide sweep that knocked the five humans back to the other side of the street.

Battered and startled but otherwise unharmed, the group made a show of dragging themselves back to their feet and reaching for their weapons. Realization dawned on them, and Estella sensed the original speaker's panic rise on his light-blue aura as his eyes caught the shimmer of moonlight on the scatter of gun parts where they'd been standing.

"What in the...?"

"How in the fuck did—"

Serena's lip curled and she turned away from Estella, making the motion of drawing back an invisible bowstring. As she did, however, her aura slipped free of her chest and formed itself into the shape of the weapon, suddenly occupying the gesture and giving it meaning. The auric arrow that she'd knocked into place swelled like an eager, living thing.

The humans, who couldn't see auras and, as such, only saw the crazed blonde holding her arms out as if to shoot them with a mimed weapon, laughed at her.

"Keep laughing, shit-wads, it'll make it all the more satisfying when I shoot all your dicks off at once!"

The threat, with no clear way of executing it, was met with more laughter.

"Serena," Estella sighed, though a part of her secretly pined to see the blonde follow through with the threat, and said, "don't."

Groaning in mock-defeat, Serena rolled her eyes and lowered her aim. Estella, assuming that the moment was over, let out a sigh of relief. Serena loosed the auric arrow.

"SERENA, NO!" Estella reached out to her, but, though she had the means to do so, was held back from using her own aura from stopping the auric projectile.

Just how much have I changed? she asked herself, mortified as she watched the bright purple bolt shoot across the street like a plum-colored streak of lightning.

It struck the pavement just shy of the closest human's feet. Concrete and litter exploded up in a violent burst. The gang was peppered with the fragments, a few earning some scratches and the beginnings of some healthy bruises. Their laughter turned to panicked cries, and before long they had the street to themselves.

"Peckerwoods," Serena sneered and shook her head. "You see that fat one? Fucker actually pissed him—" she cut herself off as she turned back to Estella, her normally playful, perked expression melting back to remorse the moment they were face-to-face again. "Oh, babe," her voice was once again worried and sympathetic, "are you going to be—"

"Spare her your piss-poor therapy session," Zane stopped her with a quick-yet-reassuring kiss to her cheek. "She was right."

Serena blinked at this, then turned to face her husband. "And just what the fuck do you mean by that?" she demanded.

Zane winced at the change in tone and rubbed the back of his neck. "Just that... uh, Estella showed me that... well, no, she didn't really *show* me, but... y'see, I saw-without-seeing that—"

Obviously having enough with the sang vampire's efforts at explaining his recent experience with auric perception, Serena turned back to Estella. "Did you break my husband?"

Estella felt her cheeks go red at the question, and, remembering the cratered wall, began stammering as well.

In the distance, Zoey and Isaac rounded the corner, the two looking weathered from their effort to keep up.

"Look," Zane held up his hands, eager to clarify, "I'm not sure how it all worked, but Estella shook me like a finicky newborn, used me as a man-shaped jackhammer, and then showed me Xander."

It was Serena's turn to stammer.

Estella's lip curled. "While I'm not thrilled with the newborn comment, I guess he's not wrong."

Serena's eyes lit up. "Then Xander's...?"

"Still alive, yes," Zane nodded. "But only barely. He's... there's not much of him, and what is there is, like, mostly something else."

Serena rolled her eyes again and looked to Estella for clarification, but Estella could only shrug.

"That's honestly the best explanation you're going to get from either of us. It's what I've been struggling with all this time."

"Oh..." Serena's brow furrowed and she went silent.

"Is everything alright?" Zoey asked as she and Isaac finally caught up.

Zane nodded. "Cliff Notes version: I saw wrong, Xander's alive—though probably not for long—and I'm apparently useful for breaking down walls. Now come on!" he ordered, nodding to Estella and starting back down the road. "We have to find him."

CHAPTER 5
THE LONGEST NIGHT

"A father is a man who expects his son to be as good a man as he meant to be."
Frank A. Clark (1860-1936)

"I wish I could have been there to see you in your prime, Xander. I bet you're a real sight. Now go save the world."
Joseph Stryker

Estella had always thought that vampires lived forever, and that was precisely why the questionable mortality of the vampire she loved seemed all the more a cruel taunt sent down from a higher power.

But, if this were the case, it wasn't the only cruel taunt it had in store:

"Hashtag 'Therion Lives Matter'?" Zane recited, passing another wall littered with fresh graffiti. "How 'bout 'Mythos Lives Matter'?"

"How 'bout you get a clue, Zane?" Isaac growled.

Zane held up his hands in a defensive gesture. "I'm just saying that—"

"And I'm just saying that you'd better not go there, dumb-ass!" Serena said with a sharp swat to Zane's chest with the back of her hand. "I'm not saying that I'm thrilled that the world is still seeing fit to communicate like everything's a damn social media post, but a point's being made all the same."

"And what point is that?" Zane grumbled, "That one species of mythos should get more sympathy than another while the word's aching to lynch us all up?"

"Coming from a guy who, simply because he was, quote-unquote, 'fortunate' enough to be turned into a vampire rather than being born a therion, got to enjoy the immediate luxuries of a mostly vampire-run mythos government and the honor of being taken in, cared for, and trained by a vampire clan leader who was a notorious therion hater?" Zoey, though able to maintain a level tone, was noticeably agitated by the topic; Estella saw without seeing that her hand had slipped to Isaac's and taken it in a tight, assuring grasp. "Have you already forgotten that, only a few short years ago, the Clan of Vail's stance of therions was just a hair above 'shoot on sight'?"

Zane was silent for a long, tense moment. Then, looking up at Isaac, he said, "Hey, man, you know I never had a problem with your kind, right?"

Isaac shrugged and grinned. "I chalk it up to penis envy, and, if we're being honest, I still think vampires are little more than leeches who managed to find legs. If it weren't for this one"—he gave Zoey a light nudge with his shoulder and smiled at her—"then I'd probably have ordered my pack to storm your clan's headquarters and put all your heads on sticks as a poetic homage to Vlad."

"Who?" Zane blinked.

Isaac rolled his eyes. "And to think we'd concern ourselves with your ignorance of other species."

"Least I don't lick my own crotch," Zane shot back.

Isaac smiled as he said, "Only because you can't reach."

Serena roared with laughter.

Zane growled.

Isaac, seeming proud with his comeback, stayed quiet.

Zoey sighed and shook her head. Though she said nothing, Estella "overheard" the thought, *As though things weren't tense enough already,* as it bobbed across her mind.

Estella realized, with only a minor note of guilt, that it was getting too easy to accidently pick up on others' thoughts. Ordinarily she could control it—focus on not letting the privacy of others' heads blossom like flowers in Spring and expose their secrets to her—but with her mind preoccupied and open to any and all hint of Xander's location, things were starting to slip past with a discomforting ease.

Still...

Estella found herself biting her lip at Zoey's thought—*"... tense enough..."*—and, with a healthy dose of resentment, found herself thinking not of just her husband and the mystery of his location—of his wellbeing—but of the past day. Of what the world had become in such a short time. Though it had been a few hours since Xander Stryker, son of the late auric prodigy Joseph Stryker and increasingly infamous leader of the freshly toppled Trepis Clan, had committed the largest crime of their kind, one would think from all the mayhem that more time would have elapsed since then.

"Tense enough" didn't even begin to cover it.

Xander Stryker's message couldn't have been more volatile if it had been written on rags, soaked in gas, and cast with reckless abandon into a burning building. Just a few short hours was all it took for an explosion of responses that ranged from (understandably) terror and hostility to (surprisingly enough) worship and praise. And everything in between.

While those proclaiming the "prophet" Xander and his

message as a holy action that surely was a sign of a rise of new gods were a breath a fresh air compared to the alternative, they were far outnumbered by those who were certain they'd just been told they were sharing the planet with monsters. These people, the latter, took to the news the same way Estella imagined one might if they'd suddenly discovered their home plagued by disease-riddled bats and rats, ones with large, bared teeth and claws caked in filth and ruin.

All of the first two, however, outnumbered the few who still clung to a desperate hope that it was all just a hoax. These, however, though a small hope for any seeking a return to "normalcy," were not convincing anybody else to abandon their panic, paranoia, or seething drive to exterminate. Even while their neighbors actively shed their human facades, these naïve few outright refused to the possibility of supernatural beings living amongst them.

Estella wasn't sure which was worse: those that believed and were ready to draw blood or those who refused to believe and seemed to pin what little veil still clung over this whole mess in place.

If only everyone could just get on the same page, she thought, *then we could begin to move forward.*

But there was no moving forward without Xander.

This she kept telling herself, as well.

It was his decision to announce their existence to the world, so whatever was supposed to happen next was something that only he likely knew.

Unless this was just the ultimate act in his traditional leap-without-looking approach to most things...

Estella didn't want to believe that, though; couldn't allow herself to believe that.

After all, Xander and the world... they were the same now: half human, half vampire; in a constant struggle with itself; self-hating, constantly punishing itself and others; but, most of all, both Xander and the world were just so full of love and beauty that, if only just for the benefit of confidence and trust, they might actually make something great of themselves.

Something great...

"Estella?"

She'd always seen something in Xander, even in the beginning—the very beginning—when they were still so young. Back then, before all the tragedies and before either of them knew what sort of potential thrummed within Xander's veins, she saw a beautiful mystery. Even then, people and their world felt like a waiting cemetery to Estella, everyone as cold and planted as a headstone; their name, their dates, and a sliver of wisdom borrowed and bared as something that defined them. Some headstones were bigger than others, sure, and some people were, indeed, more boastful of this-or-that, but it always reminded Estella of something she'd once overheard her father saying over the phone:

"We're all barreling towards a red light, sir. You can plant yourself in a Caddie, a Ford, or a shiny Rolls Royce—hell, you can join a bunch of other folks in a bus if it saves you the trouble—but we're all arriving at the same place eventually. Whether we file in nice and clean-like or get there in a pile-up is up to you and those you drive around, so if you feel comfortable driving stupid and with bad company then I'll take my leave of you and get to that red light on my own time and with a car that's seen better miles."

He'd been trying to talk his boss into offering him a promotion—partner, she thought—and was afraid that the job was going to be offered to somebody that he didn't have pleasant things to say about. In the end, he hadn't meant for the metaphor to be any kind of life lesson or bout of wisdom—he hadn't even meant for Estella to hear it—but it had resounded with her all the same, but not for the same reason. She, who'd always seen the world as a cemetery society full of flashy tombstones waiting their turn to become real ones, had always wanted something else. She wasn't sure what, and she wasn't even sure that there was something else worth wanting. In either case, Estella didn't want a cemetery life or a life headed for a red light with everyone else—she wanted a crimson rose that dared to grow among the gray stones; she wanted a car that steered away from that end-all traffic light and aimed its headlights at unexplored shadows.

And she'd seen it in Xander Stryker.

"Estella!"

Even then she'd seen in him...

... *something great.*

"YO! EARTH TO ESTELLA!"

A loud, demanding voice pulled Estella out of her thoughts and she looked back at the group. She realized then that she'd heard Serena's voice calling out to her, but was too distracted to reply. It was Zane's voice that finally did the job, however. Serena glared at him, her well trained hand raised and arched for one of her practiced backhand slaps to his chest. Zoey and Isaac, though obviously just as invested in getting Estella's attention as the Vaileans, looked just as disapproving with Zane's tactics as Serena. Likely sensing, he certainly didn't glance at the others for confirmation, the hostility surrounding him, Zane blanched and shrugged back. Perhaps, Estella wondered, he was responding to the suddenness and ferocity with which she'd turned at his call.

It was with this thought that Estella found herself wondering how aggressive she must have appeared. She realized that it had been some time since she'd considered her tone or posture, and, even then, she couldn't be sure what sort of expression she was wearing.

"I..." she began, frowning at her own voice and dragging a dry tongue across chapped lips. "I'm sorry," she tried again, still dissatisfied but knowing it was the best she could hope for. "I was..."

Serena nodded and offered one of her Serena smiles, something bright and perfect with just a trace of trickery. In this case, Estella knew, it was all just for show. There was nothing bright nor perfect to be smiling for, nor was there any need for trickery.

"It's almost dawn," Serena said.

Her voice was frosted like a cheap cake in sympathy and worry, but Estella could see from the wisps of aura that still stretched to both Zane and Zoey—carrying on dialogues that they likely thought Estella couldn't eavesdrop on—that the frosting was slathered over a mountain of panic. Being out there was a constant risk. They all knew this. A momentary detour from the safety of Zoey and her street-clearing aura had brought them face-to-face with a ragtag group of humans fancying themselves hunters. It was a simple enough process to disarm them and send them on their way, but it didn't change the reality of what it meant. Dawn and its encroaching sunlight would only add another layer of danger from the UV, not to mention amplifying the existing threats many times over. Daytime was the humans' time; they'd come out in greater numbers, empowered either by their beloved light or belief that the sun was lethal to vampires. It wasn't an untrue thing to believe, but exposure to the sun's rays was hardly the fireworks display that Hollywood and books had advertised. It was irritating (initially) and undeniably painful, and, if the enraged and agonized vampire didn't seek some sort of shelter it *would* eventually start to burn their skin. In the end, however, the deadliest thing about the exposure to UV radiation wasn't the burning, but the cancer-like reaction the vampire's body would begin to have after several hours. Four-fifths of their group were vampires. That rising sun was a whole new basket of snakes tossed into an already serpent-laden dungeon. And while Isaac might have been safe to prance around in the daylight, the growing masses of humans and their unobstructed eyesight made that immunity irrelevant. How safe would a therion truly be if a horde of bloodthirsty humans could easily catch sight of him standing among four slowly-cooking oddballs?

Like it or not, Serena had a point.

"Oh..." was all Estella could bring herself to say. Everyone's face sank, and Estella was certain that her own face looked as hurt as she felt at the idea of abandoning the search. "Well, I guess... I suppose we should head ba-*ah*—" a sob interrupted her and she clapped a palm over her traitorous mouth a moment before her eyes turned on her and went blurry with fresh tears.

A golden-haloed figure broke away from a dark mass blotted against the tombstone gray of the rest of the world, and Serena started to come into focus as she hurried to join Estella by her side. Thin, strong arms enveloped her. Once again Estella found herself crying into Serena's arms.

"I know this sucks the big one, 'Stell," Serena said, "but you *know* that he's out there. You changed Zane's mind about that, and, trust me, changing that man's mind about *anything* is like turning water into wine. So either you lied and mind-fucked my husband something incredible..." she held Estella by the shoulders at arms' length so she could show her a smile, "or we have every reason to believe that we're going to find him."

Zoey, nodding at this, approached from the side. "Now that I know what I'm looking for, I can sense it, too," she said. "It's faint, yes, and I can't seem to keep my focus on it once I find it, but it's definitely Xander."

"Exactly!" Serena chimed, "And that means he survived all of that!"

Isaac didn't approach, his aura mapped out that he believed it was better—more respectful—to leave the close-proximity assurances up to the ladies, but he said, "Suffice to say, we will find him. It's only a matter of 'when' at this point, but if we put ourselves in harm's way that 'when' may never come."

Zane stayed quiet, though his aura shifted in something that Estella compared to a nod.

Estella looked down, swallowed away a fresh batch of misery, and gave her own nod—something that was more a series of weak jerks of her chin.

Serena turned and hooked a gentle arm over her shoulder while Zoey started along at her opposite side, and the three began to walk back in the opposite direction.

"I sincerely hope one of you assholes was dropping bread crumbs or some shit like that," Serena groused back at Zane and Isaac. "'Cause my blonde ass has no fucking idea how we got here! I blame the pregnancy, personally," she announced, glancing at Estella. "Do you get that, too? That, like, pregnancy retardation?" She used her free hand to circle a pointer finger around her temple, "Can't remember shit or figure the simplest fucking thing out?"

"I... I wouldn't know," Estella admitted. "This is my first pregnancy, and I couldn't be certain what's hormonal and what's..."

"What's not?" Zoey finished, nodding. "Well, if it makes you feel any better—not that I expect it to—it's a little early for you to be... uh, 'retarded' from it. As Serena put it, at least."

"Says the one bitch in the bunch who ain't been knocked up," Serena said with a rolling of purple eyes that fell immediately on Isaac. "When you gonna remedy that, by the way, ya fertile fucker?"

Zane chuckled and nodded. "Given the weapon he's packing, I'm surprised Zoey's eyeballs haven't gotten pregnant."

Zoey opened her mouth to snap at them for once again joking about her lover, but she paused to sneer at Zane and shake her head. "What is that even supposed to mean?" she demanded.

Serena pursed her lips, thinking, and said, "I think it's supposed to be, like... 'cause, y'know, Isaac's so, like, fuckin' *deep* in there that..." she once again utilized her free hand to mock-measure from her lower belly to eye level. "I think it's a reaching joke, right?"

Zane rolled his own eyes. "And she's *blonde!* Not to mention suffering from pregnancy retardation."

Isaac shook his head. "Neither of which is a valid excuse. Zoey's a natural blonde, and if Serena gets like *this* because of being pregnant then when has she *not* been pregnant?"

Zane shot a glare his way. "You saying my wife's always retarded?"

"First of all," Isaac said flatly, showing no concern for Zane's threatening look, "I never said that word. Secondly: I'm saying that your wife is always Serena. Do I think that Serena's always like this? No. Frequently, but not always. Do I think it's more show than it is truth? Yes. Zoey's told me so, and she'd know. Moreover, I don't think—"

"Xander?" Estella heard herself say the name before she even fully came to grips with what she was seeing.

The others stopped talking.

Confused glances turned to awestruck staring.

Estella broke free from Serena's hold and knocked Zane's shoulder with her own. Nobody seemed to notice.

"I don't think that's..." Serena started.

But her voice was so distant, so unimportant. Like when she'd been calling to her before, Estella heard it but found herself unable to care enough to register it let alone react to it.

What was there left to think about, anyway?

He was right there!

"XANDER!"

His aura was so withdrawn that it seemed practically nonexistent, but Estella—who'd spent so many years thinking of that face, loving that face, and, after being reborn as a vampire, kissing and caressing that face; all without ever having seen a single aura—would know that face anywhere. It was beaten, bruised, and pulled up in a grimace of pain, but it was his. He approached her, slow—limping—an arm cradled against his ribs and the other dangling at his side. One side of his face was swollen, forcing his hazel eye shut. His blood-red right eye held her, though. He hobbled faster towards her.

He looked terrible, but there, coming out of the morning sunrise like some sort of crippled dream, Estella thought she'd never seen him look so beautiful.

If for no other reason than he was finally...

"Es...Tella?" his voice was hoarse, gravelly. It was the voice of a tortured man.

"Oh my... Xander, what did they—"

Xander gave one final lurch to bring himself to her, his limp, seemingly dead arm somehow finding fresh life and pulling her in, holding her tight. The impact of their union made Estella flinch. She was certain that it was too much for him; his broken body seemed too frail for such a thing. He didn't seem to mind. His other arm, which had been cradling ribs she knew to be broken, fell away so that he could pull her against his chest without it creating a barrier between them. He squeezed. She squealed, giggling at how quickly everything had taken a turn for the...

"Estella," he repeated her name into her ear, and she felt him inhale—drawing in her scent.

"Xander?" she moved to look up at him, "What happened? How did you—"

He kissed her, ending her questions with a crushing, dry force that felt...

Stifling.

Forced.

Wrong.

Estella wanted to enjoy it, had wanted nothing more than to kiss him again since she'd first seen him on their television back at the mansion, but couldn't bring herself to do so. She worked to draw away. He pulled her back in, holding tight and resuming the kiss. She began to pull, to whimper in protest. He didn't stop. For such a broken-looking body, not a single part of him seemed weaker for it. The kiss was beginning to feel less like a loving gesture and more like one of murderous intent. More and more Estella realized that she couldn't breathe, until she was certain that this was his intention. Her fists clenched, dread and panic pushing her to strike him so that she could get away. She couldn't bring herself to hit him, though; broken as he was.

And he was still...

He finally pulled back, and Estella was startled to see that his face was once again whole. The Xander that stared back at her was as immaculate and unmarred as the day they were married.

Exactly like the day they were married...

He smiled.

Estella saw none of Xander in that smile.

"I can still taste her on you," he said the words as casually and happily as one might if they were announcing a new purchase they were pleased with.

"H-her?" Estella blinked, confused. "Who?"

"My mother, of course," he said.

Estella blinked at this as visions of the night that she'd entered Xander's mind and watched with him as his mother was beaten and raped played out in her head...

Xander would never say such a thing after that night.

Not her Xander!

"Who are you?" she snarled under her breath, baring her fangs.

"Neat trick, huh?" he said in a forced, syrupy New York accent and smirking a familiar-yet-NOT-Xander-smirk. Then, his voice shifting once more to something more European, he said, "Would you like to see another?"

"You..." Estella's eyes widened as a white, hot rage—terrific and awful—washed over her. "I SHOULD HAVE KILLED YOU THE NIGHT YOU—"

"But you didn't, you leeching twat!" Aleks hissed at her as his face shifted back to his own.

Estella didn't like to admit that he didn't have to change much to look like himself once again.

How did I not realize how much like Xander...?

She wouldn't allow herself to finish that thought.

Xander was *nothing* like him!

Blond hair snaked downward until it was halfway down his back, the mismatched red-hazel eyes becoming green and exhilarated. In an instant, the man whose arms Estella occupied had become the single most loathsome creature in her world. Her body toiled with a violent conflict: whether she wanted to tear away from him or use the closeness to attack him; to try to end him then and there.

But what he'd said still haunted her...

"Xander's mother?" she growled. "Why did you—"

"When—oh, when—will the world cease its incessant obsessing over Joseph Stryker and his whore?" he spat, a vast, angry set of auras—billows of yellow, green, and red—flaring out like a spreading cobra's hood as he bared a mouthful of fangs the likes of which Estella had only seen once before. "What do I care of that meek, stinking piglet?"

The immense, multicolored aura.

The shapeshifting.

"Piglet."

"Oh gods..." Estella's rage was replaced with a nauseating realization that shook her just as violently. "Your mother... Lenuta!"

The smirk wavered, dropped, reconsidered, and then tugged back into a jagged mockery of itself. The effort didn't spread to his eyes, which narrowed into furious slits. "Once upon a time..." Aleks whispered, tightening his hold to Estella's back and pulling her in until she believed he would kiss her once again, "... the specks of greatness you now call mythos knew better than to call us by name."

"Your mother deserved—"

"ESTELLA!"

Serena's voice cut off what she realized was likely a life-ending statement. She couldn't bring herself to look away from Aleks—couldn't turn away from him even if she wanted to; his grip remained tight and unrelenting—but she saw his eyes flick up and over her shoulder to watch what she was certain was the others' approach.

A hiss that was more felt than heard started in his chest and began to work its way slowly up. What began like the rush of a distant stream channeled into something deep and heavy like a waterfall and came to flood Aleks' mouth. His still-smirking lips pursed and tightened, seeming to first taste, dislike, then clench in an effort to hold it in.

Though Estella was expecting something like a roar to emerge from his mouth, instead he said, "Ah, yes. The violet-headed harlot and her circus of bumbling buffoons. I'd say that you're involvement in all of this is unfortunate, but I've been too eager to see you turned into a stain beneath my boots to wait through all of this before finally hunting you down."

"You forget who was doing the hunting, Messiah," Zoey's voice was diplomatic and hard, and Estella could see her aura thrashing about her within her mind's eye.

She heard Isaac growl and sensed a swell of energy roll from him.

Aleks clucked his tongue and shook his head. "Nuh-uh-uh, mongrel. Best not to advertise ourselves out here," he chided before letting his voice take on a tone of phony concern. "I don't know if you've heard the rumors, but they say the humans know of our existence now."

He laughed.

Behind Estella, Zane's aura flared with violent intent; over-drive practically echoing on his mind. Along with it, a prepared statement: *How's this for advertising?*

How's this *for advertising?*

I got your advertising—

Estella wanted to call out to him, to warn him, that if she could hear his thoughts and see his intent then Aleks would be able to, as well.

Aleks grinned knowingly at her.

His free hand darted, becoming a blur as it did, as he reached behind him. When the arm went still, it did so with Zane's throat held in its grip. With a series of small, wet *pop*s, he turned his head nearly all the way around to face his newest captive. Estella could see his toothy grin stretch nearly to the base of his left ear.

"You Americans and your showmanship," he said, a rattling chuckle shaking past teeth that had to gap to occupy the new mouth. "Always advertising."

"***ENOUGH!***" Zoey's voice rumbled both inside and outside their heads as she cast her aura out, preparing to attack around Estella and free her and Zane from Aleks' grip.

A green section of Aleks' auras snaked beneath the street like an Olympian diving into a pool of water. Behind her, Estella's mind's eye saw it reemerge, birthing from the pavement like a transparent wall that first deflected and then ensnared Zoey's aura. Then, using its hold on the blue bolt, it began to weave throughout it, pulling and tightening its hold until it began to drag Zoey towards them. Isaac let out a startled yelp, and the arm that reached for her, Estella saw in her mind, was more beast than man. Though Isaac was quick, Aleks was quicker. Before he could get a hold of his lover, Isaac was forced to watch as Zoey was drawn into Aleks' trap—a trap that Isaac could not see—and yanked, kicking and screaming, into the air.

"I have wanted to do this since—"

"Put her down, cheese-dick!" Serena snarled, the hum of her auric bow and arrow resonating with her words. "Put them all down. Then you can drop trow, bend over, and spread your stinking ass so I can drive a truck-sized—GAH!"

Estella and Zane were granted a fraction of a fraction of a

fraction of a second's freedom as Aleks "stepped" away from them. She could only perceive of the action *after* it had been committed—had to watch through Aleks' memory once he'd returned to her and Zane, slamming them both onto the ground in twin chokeholds and stare, laughing, as Serena crashed to the ground.

Before either she or Zane could have celebrated their newfound freedom, Aleks was able to cross the distance, pop up behind Serena, kick her in the small of her back, and then return to his original spot to watch the aftermath.

His hold on Zoey, who was still crying out from Aleks' auric torture above their heads, hadn't wavered in the slightest.

It sickened Estella to admit that he'd done to Serena what Zane had intended to do to him.

"Do you see," he lowered himself to whisper in Zane's ear, "what can be done when one doesn't focus so much on advertising."

"Pffuchk yuu!" Zane growled into the street he was pinned against.

Aleks let out an impatient groan. "It's like watching a bunch of loud, annoying little mice run about a maze. You hate the sounds they make and know that there's better uses of your time—you could just take a hammer to each of their little mouse skulls and be done with it—but you find yourself compelled to reset the maze just to see how they'll scurry. Much as I want to *BASH YOUR CURSED BRAINS IN"*—his face shifted to something snarling and ravenous and then, just as quickly, returned to normal—"I simply can't get enough of how you scurry."

"Where's Xander?" Estella demanded.

Aleks regarded her as though she'd told a bad joke. For a long moment he stared, studying her, before he finally said, "Don't you watch the news? Or, in this case, don't you watch *anything?*"

Estella couldn't help but grin at that. "Then you don't know, either."

She hadn't said it as a question, and Aleks picked up that it wasn't intended to be one. This seemed to upset him. Both she, Zane, and Zoey all cried out at once as his respective holds on them tightened. A moment later, Serena and Isaac, finding themselves snagged in tendrils of his aura, let out their own cries.

"As your husband might say," Aleks growled, "'Do not *fuck* with me, bitch!'"

'... might say...,' Estella repeated to herself. *Present tense. He at least knows Xander's still—*

Do not make to keep secrets from me, girl, Aleks seethed in her head. *You should know better than that after what you did to my mother.*

Estella reeled as a fresh wave of that rage washed over her, and she decided to once again embrace that part of Xander that seemed to be rising within her.

Only wish I could have done this *to her!*

Pivoting just enough to get her legs angled beneath Aleks, she channeled her strength and focus into transcending overdrive and using her varcol speed.

Even on his best day, Zane would have been too slow to sneak up on Aleks.

Estella had no problem leveling the playing field.

Her foot connected between his legs at a speed that would turn most things into a puddle.

Aleks, however, having all the same speed and strength (as well as a personal interest in guarding such an attack), planted himself and clamped his thighs shut before any lasting damage could be inflicted. She *had* hurt him, though; that much she could see in his eyes.

She also saw enough of an opening to get him away from the others.

Using the weakened hold on her to her advantage, she

pushed off the street and into Aleks. Her own aura shot out, severing his hold to Zoey and Serena and Isaac. Then, focusing all her strength on the arm that still gripped Zane, she drove a bone-shattering attack with her elbow into his forearm. Aleks cried out and released the tattooed vampire. An instant later the bone was mended, and he brought both hands to Estella's throat. Ignoring the growing pressure on her windpipe, she ran with everything she had, gaining momentum and distance and letting the world go grainy and molecular as the very structure of reality began to lose its rigidity around them. The first time she'd traveled at this speed—locked in a similar battle with Aleks' mother—they'd crashed and flown through the interior of Lenuta's castle, passing through floors and walls as though they were curtains. At that speed, the wall one was barreling through didn't even show signs of being broken well after they were on the other side. Estella recalled all the times when, in what she now had to consider "normal" overdrive, she'd crashed through a window or door and seen the broken fragments float slowly through the air before being frozen by the laws of physics.

The difference was still staggering to her.

And, at that moment, enticing.

Neither the walls nor Aleks registered the immense damage being delivered to them as she veered off the street and started driving his back through every building she could put in their way. His face and aura told her that he felt nothing, but she knew all too well how pain liked to catch up all at once. Brick, concrete, steel beams, plumbing, electric wiring—she slammed Aleks through all of it and more. And every car that rested in between. After nearly a dozen blocks' worth of walls and vehicles, she slowed enough to bring tangibility back to a concrete mass that supported a jutting metal pillar that, in turn, served as one of many support beams for a monorail system that circled the city. Moving too slowly to outright pass through it, Estella managed to embed Aleks' back into the mass before dropping out of overdrive entirely. The impact sent a tremor up the length of metal, and the monorail track groaned a little.

Estella roared and punched him. Both his face and aura let her know that it hurt. She punched him again, then, still angry that he'd blocked her first kick, kneed him in the crotch.

He seethed. "Fucking Strykers!" he cursed, glaring into her. "None of you know when it's time to stop and die!"

"WHAT DID YOU DO TO HIM?" she shrieked, hitting him again.

"Not enough," he declared, moving to punch her.

Estella side-stepped, pocketed the attacking fist under her arm, trapping it, and drove a series of hammering punches into the strained shoulder, working to dislocate the arm.

Aleks yanked his arm back before she could.

Estella threw another knee.

Aleks rolled free, letting the knee pass through and lodge itself into the fractured concrete he'd been embedded within.

Not bothering to worry about her trapped leg, Estella improvised, snatching a large piece of broken concrete and driving it into the side of Aleks' head with enough force to confuse the shapeshifter's body and turn his face into a nightmarish flash of mayhem.

Teeth grew from his ear.

His eye ruptured and momentarily became a howling mouth.

His lips parted to reveal a mouth full of confused, blinking eyes that had replaced several of his teeth.

Finally, the sides of his neck splayed like a blossoming flower and transformed into a giant, gaping maw. The warping head lulled away, seeming to fall into Aleks' back, only to have an exact replica of itself be reborn out of the awful flower-maw.

He grinned at her.

"Wanna see another trick?" he said with a scoff.

"SHOVE IT UP YOUR ASS AND FUCKING DIE!" she roared, ripping free of the concrete and lunging at him.

Their battle was punctuated at that moment by a low, rumbling vibration that grew louder and more intense as the morning train howled above their heads along the track. Estella struggled to beat him, but he casually held her back with his aura as he let his gaze drift upward, fascinated, at the spectacle.

"What a world they've built," he whispered. "What a world I've come to claim."

"In your dreams!" Estella hissed, lunging at him again.

He moved to evade, but Estella's aura snapped out like a whip, snared him by the waist, and pulled him back. He threw a punch, hoping to use the momentum of her reeling him in against her. Estella ducked under the attack, pinned his legs in place with another auric tendril, and, focusing a concussive spell into her fist, drove an overdrive-fueled punch into the side of his left knee.

She relished in the grotesque sound that emanated from the destroyed joint and watched as he struggled to maintain his balance on only one good leg.

Content, she withdrew her aura into herself and tackled him to the street.

Their impact with the concrete seemed to daze Aleks, who was still noticeably working to will his body to mend the injury to his leg.

It'll be a bit before it'll be of any use to you, Estella warned him in thought-speak, her mind already working too fast to speak aloud.

Aleks shifted into overdrive to follow her movements, and by the time his eyes adjusted to see her she was already in the process of driving a superhuman punch directly towards his face.

Now. Now! FUCKING NOW! Serena's entire body was hurting from the demands she was putting on it. She was certain that, with all she was putting her unborn child through, they were going to be born incredibly badass or morbidly ass-bad. Frowning at that, she decided she was too focused to come up with good baby jokes and worked to focus her auric bow to work in overdrive.

It wasn't as easy as it should have been, but, then again, she had just had the shit royally beaten out of her.

Then again, so had Zane, and he was doing his part.

Assuming the dumb son-of-a-bitch could figure out what "now" meant!

Aleks would likely be expecting him—would be looking for him—to do the brash thing. Zoey had said varcols were smart—*like, scary-smart*—and could not only think independently in multiple layers, but use their aura the same way. Carrying on multiple conversations with large groups, performing dozens of auric tricks, and all while bench-pressing a small house at a single moment would be tops among a varcol's party tricks.

So give the sucker-punching fuck what he's looking for and then hit him with what he isn't, right? Serena thought.

Fair logic.

Except that "now" wasn't nearly NOW enough for Serena's liking.

Finally—fucking FINALLY!—Zane closed in on Aleks, and, sure enough, Serena could see the varcol beginning to shift to meet the attack.

This is gonna hurt, Zaney-poo, Serena called out to him. *Remind me I owe you one of those sloppy blowjobs you like when this is all over.*

She wasn't sure if Zane heard her.

In the next instant Serena's husband was time-frozen in midair, folded over at the midsection like a paper Zane-doll held in time on a collision course with an old Hyundai that had seen better days.

'Bout to see a far worse one, Serena thought with a grimace as

she loosed her auric arrow. *Come on,* she chanted to herself, *come on, come on, come on...*

The bolt pierced through the time-frozen streets as she continued to haul ass closer and closer to the varcol and Estella. They'd been fighting, for the most part, at a normal speed, which meant Estella was, for the most part, just as time-frozen as the rest of the world.

Except neither of them was.

Aleks turned his head towards Serena and her approaching auric arrow.

Estella tensed, her fist held in midair—inching closer and closer to Aleks' face. She had him pinned well enough, had a decent enough punch thrown, and, from the looks of it, it was poised to do some real damage.

Might even be able to give you an opening to truly fuck him up, sister; I gotta admire that, Serena thought, though she didn't bother to send it to Estella—she wouldn't take it as a compliment.

Not after all was said and done.

Though he wasn't about to be winning any races anytime soon and was undeniably pinned down and doomed to take the punch, Aleks had enough of a hold on Estella to yank her around and place her between himself and the incoming auric arrow.

He intended to use her as a shield!

Gasping, Serena focused all of her auric control on the rocketing bolt and steered her aching body onto a new course. If Aleks intended to let Estella receive the bolt, then Serena had to be sure it wasn't what it was originally meant to be when it reached her.

Which gave her about a millionth of a second to turn a bolt of death-seeking purple lightning into *anything* else.

But—fuck me!—no pressure, right?

The purple streak forked at the last second, bifurcating as though Estella's back was splitting it like a piece of firewood.

The now 'Y'-shaped auric tendril paused, lingered, and then closed around Estella, yanking her away from Aleks and dragging her after Serena as she fought to put distance between them and the crippled varcol.

The last thing Aleks saw before Serena vanished with Estella and her husband in tow was a giant, purple hand made of Serena's aura as it extended a five-foot tall middle finger back at him.

CHAPTER 6
GODS & MONSTERS

"In law, a man is guilty when he violates the rights of others.
In ethics, he is guilty if he only thinks of doing so."
Immanuel Kant (1724-1804

"My name is Xander Stryker, and I... am a vampire."
Xander Stryker

It felt like the worst of injustices at that moment.

And Estella Stryker had more than her fair share of experience in the realm of injustice. It was, after all, the very thing that had brought her into this world.

Still, being ripped away from Aleks mere moments before she'd been able to...

"WHY DID YOU DO THAT?" Estella demanded once she had air enough to fuel the words. She was glaring at Serena, but the anger in her eyes was muddied by the tears she knew were welling within them. "I *had* him! I *had* that monster broken and held down and—"

"And he had an auric tendril poised at your belly," Serena interrupted, refusing to slow down or look back at the enraged Missus Stryker. "You would've knocked that fuck-stain silly, sure, but you'd have done it at the cost of yours and Xander's baby, possibly even at the cost of both of your lives if he decided to start really dancing around in your guts once he was inside you."

Estella stared after her, awestruck. Reflexively, she reached up and cradled her stomach despite not yet having much to cradle in her hands. "My... my baby?"

Zane, still groaning and popping a series of joints in painful-sounding sequences, nodded. "Serena and I caught up in time to see you about to lay a most savage smack-down on that asshole," he explained, "but then she saw that his aura was, like, aiming itself at your... well, she tells me that he was definitely targeting your pregnancy." He scoffed and shook his head, saying, "Guess he doesn't want to bash in the little mice's heads, but he's got no problem with making damn sure they don't have any *littler* mousies."

"Gods..." Estella shivered, suddenly feeling cold and very, very tired. "I didn't even... I had no idea."

"You can't blame yourself," Zoey said, patting Estella's shoulder reassuringly. "He's a varcol, after all, he's—"

"No!" Estella pulled away, furious with herself and not wanting their reassurances. "No, I have varcol blood in me now, too. With the exception of the shapeshifting,"—something Estella would have no desire to use even if she could—"there's nothing he can do that I can't. He shouldn't have been able to just get the drop on me like that!" She stomped her foot on the road and shook her head. "I might as well have handed him my child on a silver platter with how sloppy I let myself get!"

The four stopped and stared at her. None of them appeared to believe what she was saying.

Isaac glanced towards Zoey for a moment, considered her, and then looked back at Estella. "You know what the problem with smart people is?" he asked.

Everyone stared at him.

Estella shook her head. She had plenty of guesses, but wasn't prepared to go randomly listing them or, worse yet, digging in his head for the answer he wanted.

"They might be smart," he answered, "but when they get stupid—and everyone always has their stupid moments—they get *really* stupid." He pointed back at Zane and Serena. "These two:" he went on, "almost always dumb as dirt. They don't care; don't mind it one little bit—ignorance being bliss and such. But then they have their moments of monumental wisdom or cleverness and you'd half expect them to hire a marching band for it."

Serena scoffed, not seeming offended by his words in the slightest, and said, "Tried to that one time, actually, but Zoey said it wasn't in the budget."

Zoey rolled her eyes. "It says a lot that you believed that, Serena," she chirped.

Serena seemed to consider this for a moment before her shoulders sagged and she muttered, "Fuck..."

Isaac shook his head, but couldn't manage to stifle a grin that came as a response. "Anyway, then there's Zoe and me. Now, I'm pretty much consistently a hot mess. I'll be the first to admit it. I don't like crowds, like groups of vampires even less, and generally get real uncomfortable whenever it's not just me and Zoey."

"Bow-chicka-wow-wow!" Zane sang.

Nobody said "shut up," but it echoed on enough auras around Estella for her to wonder if he might actually "hear" it.

"Now," Isaac went on, "I know my reaction isn't exactly reasonable. I'd even go so far as to call it 'dumb' when the anxiety hits. And then, to add insult to injury, I'll start beating myself up about it." He shook his head at his own confession before aiming a thumb towards Zoey. "Then there's this one. Smartest person I know. Real science-y and analytical about everything; created that synthetic blood you're all using and is always inventing new types of weapons and armors and such. Plus she's a brilliant tactician. All-around brilliant woman; smartest I know, like I said. Now, you're not exactly the science-y type—seem more earth-focused and centered on magic; stuff that's way over my... well, actually, all of our heads—so I guess that makes you and Zoe an awful lot alike; you might not be smart about the same stuff, but you're both the sorts to put your brains before everything else."

Serena sighed and glanced at a non-existent watch at her wrist. "There a point to all this, Donkey Dick?"

Isaac's eyes fluttered in mock-exhaustion and he shook his head, offering a wordless prayer towards the dawning sky before looking back at Estella and ignoring Serena entirely. "You've had a shitty night, Estella Stryker. I don't think even the dumbasses here can try to argue with that. You had that mess with the Cebourists, the stress of finding out you were pregnant and Aleks' assault on the mansion, and then"—he snapped his fingers—"all this drama with Xander, him getting attacked, and the impact he's had on the world since then. Nobody here is going to blame you for *not* being a genius after everything that's happened." He shrugged and took Zoey's hand. "So, yeah, you're right: you fucked up. You got sloppy, thought you had the upper-hand, found out it was the other way around. But things worked out this time, so—hey!—no harm, no foul. Accept that, if the dummies are allowed to celebrate when they have a glimmer of intelligence, we're allowed to slip up every now and again without pairing ourselves up with them. Now can we get back, already? Standing around here and waiting for either daylight or hate-mongering humans to come kill us is a fuck-up I, for one, am not willing to make."

With that, Isaac turned and, leading Zoey along with him, started up the street again.

Estella, smiling after Isaac and seeing him in a new light, was quick to follow.

Zane, glancing over at Serena, shook his head as they, too, started after. "I don't know which is worse:" he said, "that we basically sat there for an entire speech focusing on us as the poster children for dumbasses... or that I'm starting to wonder if that douche might be keeping a second brain in his dick."

Serena sighed and nodded, chuckling at the idea. "Lord knows there's room for it," she said, nudging her husband.

ESTELLA WASN'T happy to be going back empty handed. She was even less happy to see that, of the other groups that had gone out in search of Xander, none of them were fruitful, either. Though, in an ideal scenario, she would be the one to find him—though she couldn't begin to explain to even herself why, in any logical approach, that should be the case—she would have sooner seen her husband returned to her no matter the means. Not that that seemed to be happening anytime soon. That nobody else had even sensed Xander's auric scatterings across the city was in no way a good sign. But it was hardly the worst news that she received as they all returned to the seaside storage facility that had come to represent their current headquarters.

"Has anybody from their search party returned?" she asked, thinking at that moment of Ruby and Donald's outing a few days earlier.

Ruby had, more or less, gotten back to them a few days later.

Donald hadn't been so fortunate.

And now Sawyer, Diana, and the rest of their group were nowhere to be found, either.

Zeek shook his head, his long, pointed ears swaying as he did. While he and his therion lover, Karen, were manning the makeshift med-ward—what was really just a corner of the massive structure that had been hastily cleared to make room for the injured—they'd also become dispatchers for what remained of the clan.

Estella grimaced at the thought, reminding herself that, even if some of the members of Trepis remained, they were in no way a clan. The Council certainly wouldn't recognize them as such, nor would they let anyone considering themselves an ally, friend, or supporter of Xander Stryker live long enough to consider forming anything even resembling a clan. As far as the mythos government was concerned, everyone in that building was a fugitive awaiting execution.

And a group of them was still out there...

"It'd be asking a lot to expect me to recognize a lot of the faces that had been occupying the mansion a few days ago," Zeek groused as he used a rag to wipe some blood off his hands. At that moment he looked more like an anapriek posing as a car mechanic than one acting as a medic. "But Sawyer I'd be able to recognize in a crowd. And Dianna, while I'd appreciate you not repeating this to her, isn't exactly a face I'm going to forget anytime soon." He gave an apologetic shrug, though it occurred to Estella that he wasn't apologizing to her and, in fact, wasn't likely at fault for feeling the way he did about the reformed hunter. "I might not know if any of the others that left with them had gotten back, but I've gotta assume that, if any of them were going to come back alive, it would be Sawyer and Dianna first. Seems unlikely they'd get back, *not* check in, and slip away without Karen or myself noticing."

Estella nodded, staring past the anapriek and at the unconscious redhead that Karen was tending to, asking "How is she?" once the therion was finished checking her vitals.

Karen looked up, seeming startled by the raised voice directed her way. Then, offering a forced smile at Estella, she said, "She's doing better. Better than a lot of the others, at least."

This made Estella do a momentary sweep of the rest of the corner, taking in the various crates and pieces of abandoned furniture that had been used as makeshift beds. There weren't many—only those who'd already been in need of treatment and a few who'd been injured in the mansion's collapse—but, true to Karen's words, all the others were at least noticeably injured.

But then there was Ruby; Ruby, who for whatever reason hadn't woken up; Ruby who *should* have been fine—who *should* have been awake and who *should* have been with them—but, for whatever reason, wasn't.

For whatever reason...

To look at Ruby at that moment was like looking upon somebody in the throes of a deep sleep. She breathed evenly and without any sign of force. Her face was calm, serene even. Even then, after all she'd been through, Estella couldn't help but think that she looked beautiful and innocent.

Because she is *beautiful and innocent,* she reminded herself. Then, looking away from the unconscious sang and returning her focus to Zeek, she asked, "I don't suppose Sana has had any luck finding them?"

Zeek shrugged. "She might have," he said, "if somebody had thought to ask her."

Estella gave him a blank stare. "So you *didn't* ask her?"

Zeek returned the stare with an exaggerated one of his own. "There's a 'dammit, I'm a doctor' quote I've heard floating around a few times that I feel applies here. You and practically everyone else with a capable body left to find Xander. Not that I'm complaining, mind you—if Karen and I hadn't been told to stay here and help these poor souls then we would've been out there searching, as well—but there's only so much that we could do. Plus, and I hate to be a bother, but we're running low on the synthetic blood, and if I'm not mistaken I think I heard that one of the folks that came in with that loud blonde is able to make more?"

"Right, right. I'll ask Zoey if she can lend you a hand with that," Estella said with a sigh, already starting to turn away. Then, turning back, she asked, "Do you at least know where Sana is?"

Zeek's face reflected the blank stare once more.

Estella could all but hear him say *"Dammit, Stryker, I'm a doctor, not a babysitter!"*

This, she realized, was because he was *thinking* it for it to be heard.

Smartass, Estella "said" to him in thought-speak, once again turning away.

"You're more like your husband than you know," Zeek called after her with his best effort at an encouraging chuckle.

It came out like the forced laugh of a condemned man.

Estella didn't want to admit to the accuracy of that thought.

Estella continued on, but she could sense Karen's aura as it shifted and, a moment later, heard the therion's footsteps as they hurried to catch up to her. She slowed her pace, allowing her to catch up.

"How are you doing?" Karen asked.

The question was almost enough to make Estella stop.

It wasn't that it was an altogether unexpected question. It was a question, after all, that Estella had been hearing on the minds of everyone around her—*"Is she okay?"* and *"Will she be alright?"* and, of course, *"What'll happen if...?"*—but this was the first time that Estella had been in a place to ask it of herself.

How am I doing?

The immediate answer scared her, and she remembered all the moments she'd felt on the verge of cracking. Then there was the whole issue of...

"You're more like your husband than you know."

A notion that both elated and terrified her.

Xander Stryker: one of the strongest people Estella had ever met.

Also one of the most unstable.

But that, of course, was only a half-truth. Xander's "off the handle"-reputation was something of a myth, and, granted, they were in a world where myths weren't exactly untrue, but, like vampires, there was the myth and then there was the truth. Yes, Xander was a whirlwind of potential psychological bedlam; a short-tempered, rage-filled, and explosive personality with a low tolerance for authority and a brick wall that stood proudly between what he believed in and what the rest of the world expected.

But this didn't mean he was out of control.

Far, far from it, in fact.

Truthfully, and herein lay the divide where myth faded to reality, Xander was likely more stable than any other person—mythos or otherwise—could boast. Many times before, Estella had considered what she might have done—or, more to the point, what she might have become—if she'd been the one forced to deal with the life Xander Stryker had been born into. Abused, ignored, berated, scared and angry more often than not, and constantly being shuffled through a world that, on some level, he knew all along he was never truly a part of. Years of torment at the hands of his sadistic auric stepfather, Kyle; forced to witness the assault and murder of his mother; then all those years of self-loathing and loneliness. And all that *before* he'd lost his grandmother, watched what remained of his life burned to the ground, and turned into a vampire (only to watch it all burn away again).

And, through all of *that,* to somehow manage to come through it whole; to have the strength to fight *for* something rather than just *against* everything. That Xander Stryker, after all the trials he'd been forced to endure—after the dust finally came to settle—could step out of it, guns in hand and fangs bared against anything stupid enough to challenge him, and live and love as he did...

No, Estella couldn't call *that* unstable.

But if *she'd* been expected to endure all of that—if *anybody* else had—then what assurance did they have that they'd fare as well?

Most structures, if put under enough pressure, would simply collapse. Some, though, like the Roman arch, grew stronger and more sturdy from it; using all that negative force to strengthen it and keep it whole. Perhaps Xander was like a Roman arch in that regard, but Estella doubted that she was like that.

Sure, she was getting a heavy dose of all the negative forces that made Xander as angry and violent as he was, but when the dust finally came to settle what assurance did Estella have that she wouldn't be turned into one of the bad guys? How could she be sure that she'd come out of it fighting *for* something rather than simply *against* everything? And, the most nerve-wracking uncertainty of all, would she manage to come out of it living and loving as she had before?

"How are you doing?" the world was asking her.

About as well as a candle in a rainstorm, she finally admitted to herself; *Just one well-aimed drop away from snuffing out entirely.*

She didn't say that, though; didn't stop or even falter. What she did, however, was say, "Yeah. Fine. I'm doing fine."

She was certain that it was as convincing to Karen as it felt.

"Yes, well..." Karen started, already not sounding confident, "We all understand why you wouldn't be."

An awkward silence followed.

Estella dared a glance over at the therion, taking in the tense structure of her exotic, dark-skinned features.

Karen shifted her jaw. She sniffled, wiped her nose, and let out a heavy sigh. Her eyes drifted towards Estella.

They stared at one another, still walking through the building, and hoped that the other would say something.

Karen, clearing her throat, finally added, "That is, of course, if you *weren't.*" Then, averting her eyes and clearing her throat again, clarifying: "Fine, I mean."

"Right," was all Estella could think to offer, hoping it would be enough not to force any more. Then, realizing a change in subject would suit her just fine, she asked, "You wouldn't happen to know where Sana is, would you?"

Karen perked at the question, obviously just as eager for something to shift the tides of the conversation, and nodded. "Yes, I... uh, well, no. I'm not sure *where* she is exactly, but I do know that she and Timothy have been... um, well... getting off to—" her face went red and she shook her head, "No, no, no! That's not what I meant!"

Estella surprised both of them then by actually smiling. Seeing the flustered therion helped her to remember that, tough as things were, she wasn't suffering through them alone. Pausing and turning towards her, forcing her to do the same in the process, Estella gave her a smile, a real one; a genuine one.

"So you're saying if I find Tim then I'll find Sana, right?"

Karen, visibly relieved that her wording hadn't made things more awkward and even more relieved at the sight of Estella's smile, managed a sincere smile of her own and nodded. "Yes. And they're more than likely somewhere... hm, *private*. I mean, if that helps."

Estella's eyes shifted towards a small office that overlooked the rest of the facility. It waited at the end of a flight of stairs that cycled halfway up one wall, turned at the corner to complete the journey up its adjacent neighbor, and supported itself from the rafters and a few untrustworthy looking cross-beams jutting out beneath it and punching into the sidewall with ugly, uneven points that had been welded in place.

Except for ducking behind shipping crates or hiding inside a few pieces of heavy equipment that had once, long ago, hauled those shipping crates, that office was the only place she could think of that would offer anybody even a shred of privacy.

Sure enough, Timothy's aura was practically advertising itself within it.

Estella's smile widened and she nodded her thanks to

Karen, who followed her gaze to the office and turned a rather enchanting shade of red.

"Well," she nodded and took a nervous step back, "I guess I'll leave you be then."

Estella looked back to her, still smiling, and gave her a nod of thanks. "I appreciate you taking the time to talk to me. I know I haven't been the most approachable person tonight."

Karen's blush shifted, her aura flaring with a tremor of modesty. "Given the circumstances," she said, glancing back in Zeek's direction, "I wouldn't be, either." Then, looking back at Estella, she said, "I hope we find him."

There wasn't a shred of doubt in Estella as she said, "We will, Karen. I know we will."

"You'd better give me back my shirt."

"What? Why? Am I doing something wrong?"

Sana giggled and gave the nervous vampire across from her a kiss on his trembling lips. "No, silly, you're doing fine. Better than fine, even. It's just that..." she let her eyes move from his and point towards the door.

Tim's own eyes widened with realization and he vanished from the floor. Over the next few seconds, the nearly naked boy flitted in-and-out of sight, appearing at various points of the room. Each time he reappeared, he did so wearing one additional piece of clothing—first appearing behind the abandoned desk with a shirt, then again beside the couch on the other side with his socks—and tossing one of Sana's back in her direction. Sana didn't bother to look as he did this, didn't even bother to move, and easily caught each new article with her aura as she continued to monitor their approaching visitor's progress up the stairs.

"Damn, damn, fuck!" Tim cursed, appearing out of overdrive once again beside her still in his boxers. "Where are my pa—"

"Tangled inside my skirt," Sana said with a smirk, not looking away from the door.

Tim made an all-too-male show of looking everywhere *except* in the right direction. "And where's your—"

Sana pointed a dark finger sporting a manicured nail with a henna design on it towards the ceiling.

Tim glanced upward and gawked. "How in the hell...?"

"She's coming," Sana warned.

"She?" Tim parroted after an impressive jump that cleared the ten feet to the rafters to retrieve his pants.

Sana wasn't sure if it was pride or forgetfulness that kept him from just asking her to use her aura to retrieve their things, but smiled her appreciation nonetheless as he passed her skirt to the floating heap of clothes.

Then, seeming to realize who'd be coming their way at that moment, Tim's aura flared with panic and, in another flash of here-again-then-not, stood before her in his pants. Breathing heavily from all the flitting about, Sana wasn't surprised to see him sweating—though she knew very little of the perspiration had anything to do with exertion—and, despite this, accepted his offered hand to help her up. This, she was certain, was neither a matter of pride or forgetfulness. Tim might have dressed like Hollywood's depictions of vampires, but he was, in fact, a true gentleman.

"Shit!" Tim was practically vibrating with how quickly his sang body was shaking. "I can't let her see me like this!"

Sana began to dress, noticing that Estella had begun to take her time on the stairs for nobody else's sake but their own. She didn't bother to tell Tim that she already knew what was going on in there. "I'm sure she wouldn't think any less of you if she did."

"It's not that!" Tim assured her, "It's just... I mean... she's like... I don't know, like my sister or something! I've known her ever since I was a little kid!"

Sana nodded her understanding, pulling her shirt over her head and beginning to step into her skirt. "What if I shield you from her sight?" she offered. "She'll step in, see me in here—alone—and you can sneak out before she closes the door." She gave a shrug to pass the whole thing off as something simple. And it might have been simple if it weren't Estella Stryker they were talking about. But Tim didn't need to know that. "I can tell her I was up here working on tracking Xander."

Tim frowned at that. "Wouldn't it be mean to say you were looking for Xander when you weren't?"

Sana bit her lip. "It *would* be mean," she admitted, "if I *wasn't* looking for Xander."

Tim stared at her for a moment, seeming to forget all about Estella. Fortunately for him, she was actually waiting a few steps down, letting them finish. "You..." he blinked and shook his head, "You were looking for Xander *while* we were..." he didn't finish.

He didn't have to.

Sana started towards him. "You're not mad, are you?" she asked, not wanting to read his aura without his permission.

Tim smirked at the question. "Mad? Why would I be mad? My girlfriend can do something that cool *while* also fooling around? That's... I mean, it's..." his eyes widened. "W-wait, I can say you're my girlfriend, right?"

Sana let out a laugh that was more of a relieved sigh and nodded. "Yeah, Tim. I figured you already were. I've considered you my boyfriend for a while."

Seeming encouraged by this, Tim nodded and smiled, kissing her once more. Then, confident that his girlfriend would use her "awesome auric powers"—a phrase that practically flashed neon within his own aura—he backed away to the door and waited to sneak off.

Estella (finally) stepped through the door. Sana feigned an

innocent smile. Tim glanced, uncertain, between the two, realized that nobody was paying him any mind, and slipped through the door. As his footsteps started to clang down the stairs, Estella's aura snaked out and eased the door shut.

"He didn't realize that I followed his aura up here, did he?" Estella asked.

Sana shook her head, smiling. "I don't think he really understands how this whole aura-thing works. And he likely believes that being around me makes him invisible to auric detection by default."

Considering this for a moment, Estella walked over to the couch and started to sit down. At the last minute she paused, pointed back at the seat, and asked, "Is it safe?"

Sana blushed and nodded. "We only kiss," she assured her.

"Sure, that explains the race to get dressed," Estella said, but sat down all the same.

Still blushing, Sana thought, *I didn't say* where *we kiss.*

Estella stared at her.

Sana realized that her thoughts had been heard and blushed that much more. "I keep forgetting how powerful you are now," she admitted.

"Yeah," Estella sighed and nodded, cradling her face in her hands. Sana was startled by how tired she looked all of a sudden. "Sometimes I forget, too," she said, "Then I find myself hearing people talking and realize that they haven't said a word. It's getting to the point where it feels like I'm going crazy —so many damn voices in my head at once."

"It can be tough to handle at first," Sana said with a nod. "It helps if you think about ice cream."

"Ice cream?" Estella looked over, perplexed.

Sana shrugged. "Helps me, at least. You ever been eating ice cream and just realize the entire world seemed to slip away?"

Estella laughed and returned the shrug. "I mean, I *guess.* I just wasn't expecting you to say that."

"Just because I'm from India doesn't mean I don't eat—" Sana started.

Estella shook her head. "No, no," she defended, "It wasn't that. I guess it was just such an innocent answer to such an annoying problem."

Sana gave her a forbidden smirk. "If you can call ice cream 'innocent' then you're probably not eating it right." She realized Estella was still staring and looked away. "What I mean is you should focus on something that you can get lost in easily. Something that, when you have it, everything else slips away. For some it might be a book or a movie or—"

"Xander," Estella whispered, looking down.

Sana looked back at her, grimacing. "Well... yeah, or a person."

Estella sniffled and looked away, trying to hide her watering eyes.

Sana stared after her, trying to figure out what to say or do.

"I came up here to ask if you would try to find Sawyer, Dianna, and the others that they left with earlier. They haven't come back yet," Estella said, forcing her voice to be stern and deep.

Sana started to nod, realized Estella wouldn't see it, stopped, and then realized that Estella *had* seen it.

"Thank you," she said, already starting to stand up. "Sorry about interrupting you and Tim."

Sana watched as she took a few steps towards the door before she realized that Estella was actually planning on leaving. "You're not going to tell me that we're too young? Or bring up that he's younger than me?"

Estella looked back at her, staring as though she wanted to either cry or go out on a killing spree. Sana was too afraid to scan her mind for which was more likely.

"You're both horny kids," Estella said with a shrug. "You seem smart enough to know better than to let things get too far and Tim's too nervous about you liking him to let himself get carried away. Why should I care if you want to fool around?"

Sana bit her lip at that. "That's not what the rest of the world says about this sort of thing."

Estella shook her head. "Rest of the world wants to kill us, Sana. Don't know if you looked out there recently, but the whole human race pretty much wants us dead. Most of the mythos community wants *us*, in particular, dead, as well." She shrugged again, "All things considered, if Xander wasn't missing, I'd probably be doing the same thing with him."

Sana raised an eyebrow. "You mean instead of fighting?"

"There's always going to be fighting," Estella said, turning back to face her. "And, yeah, with all that's going on I'm sure there's going to be even more. But that doesn't mean that I don't want to, you know, 'get down' first," she finished with a bashful laugh.

Sana stared, wide-eyed and stunned.

"What?" Estella demanded, "I had to wait at the door while you two wrestled into your clothes and I'm supposed to pretend that I don't know what sex is just because you're a teenager?"

"Well... no, I suppose not. I guess I was just surprised about how willing you are to talk about it. You know, since Xander's so... *not*."

Estella folded her arms over her chest. "And why would you be asking my husband about sex?"

It was Sana's turn to defend her words. "I... no! It's not like that! I just meant that his mind's so... even when he thinks of you it's like... pure." She frowned, not seeming satisfied with that wording. "It's... it's hard to explain."

Estella's expression softened, seemed suddenly less suspicious and more interested, and she started back for the couch. "No. Please, try. I... I want to hear this."

Sana blushed. "You're not mad that I read his mind?"

Estella, now sitting once again, pulled her knees to her

chest and rested her chin between them. "I won't be if you tell me what you meant by that."

"Well..." Sana felt her heart skip, suddenly feeling even more on trial than before. "When I first came here—came to America to be a part of Xander's clan—it was because of what I'd seen in my dreams. I only knew of him from what those dreams showed me. It was all about his 'blessed vision' and the steps he'd take to unify us all. I really didn't know anything about *him* except for what the dreams showed me, and in the dreams he always came to me as a tiger."

Estella perked up at this, though Sana wasn't sure why. "A tiger, huh?"

Sana nodded, unsure why this should intrigue her so much. "A big red and black one. In my dream, he came into the city—I knew it was supposed to represent the world; just one of those dream-facts that seemed obvious at the time—and he, the Xander-tiger, roared. Then, just like that, the whole city—the whole world—knew that he'd arrived, and everyone just sort of knew that he was there to fight this big, terrible dragon. I hadn't seen the dragon in my dream—another of those 'you know because it's a dream'-facts—but I knew that we had to make a choice: the tiger or the dragon. I won't lie, Estella, I was terrified of the tiger; I saw him from my window, as big as the entire street—it's fiery sides scraping the sides of the buildings as it walked by—and burning hot as a sun. But..." she squinted her eyes, trying to summon the visions of the long-past dream back to her mind, "but I knew that, scary as that tiger was, he fought for us; all of us—the dragon only fought for itself, though; itself and other dragons. So the decision had to be made—tiger or dragon—and, having already made the decision, I began to run down the stairs to join the tiger." She trailed off, suddenly remembering more of the dream that had since been lost to her until that moment.

The octopus...

Estella leaned forward. "And then what happened?" she asked.

"I..." Sana shook her head, confused by her own thoughts, "I was taken."

"Taken?" Estella asked, frowning, "By who? What?"

The seven-armed octopus.

Sana shook her head. "Nothing. It... it seems silly now. Doesn't have anything to do with the rest of the dream or what I was saying before."

It stood between the great beasts, she thought, *wanting to strangle the life from both; it snatched up any it could reach, no matter which side they tried to flee to—it wanted them all dead.*

Estella stared at her, and Sana hoped that the bizarre dream-creature's involvement in her otherwise relevant dream wouldn't distract her from the point she was trying to make.

"A-anyway," Sana pushed on, shaken by the suddenly vivid memory of the dream, "when I awoke, I somehow knew that the tiger had represented Xander Stryker, who I'd only heard of in passing before that night. I decided then that I needed to join him—join *you*—and be a part of what he was doing. So I made all the arrangements, flew out here, and met him for the first time..."

"And?" Estella asked.

"And he was just as scary as he was in the dream," Sana said with a nervous laugh that made Estella smile and laugh, as well. "He wasn't mean or anything like that, but his aura..." Sana shook her head, still awestruck by the memory of her first encounter with him. "There was such rage and power and strength! He was just like the tiger, Estella, right down to his black-striped red aura! And I thought, *There must be something in him, something good and just and pure.* So, though it terrified me to do so, I searched; searched for some sign of what it was about this man that had called to me in my dream. But the deeper I went the more I saw a mind filled with pain and anger and hate and resentment and doubt and..." she sighed and shook her head, "I saw Xander for the tortured soul he truly is; saw how tortured he is. And there, in his own way, I saw the 'why'—saw that he fought so that others wouldn't have to suffer like he had. But this seemed wrong, too, because in many ways he was just as angry with the world as he was the people who'd wronged him. But then..." Sana smiled a wide, painful smile, "... I came across a part of him that wasn't burning—the heart of the tiger, I thought of it—and it was you."

Estella stared at her, tears welling in her eyes. "M-me?"

Sana nodded. "I saw that, as far as Xander was concerned, the entire world could burn in the fires of his hate... so long as he left a place for you to be happy and safe at the end of it." Sana watched as Estella cupped her face in her hands and let out a sob. She nodded, knowing how powerful this vision had been for her, as well. "So I decided that, to know for sure if I'd made the right choice with taking the tiger's side, I had to know who it was he was holding in his heart and away from all that fire."

"And what did you think after you met me?" Estella asked, still weeping.

Sana shrugged. "I'm still here, aren't I?"

Estella nodded slowly, beginning to shiver.

"There's a lot of anger and violence inside Xander, and, knowing him and his history better, I can't say I blame him for any of it. But whenever the subject of you comes up—in conversation or even just in his mind—he goes quiet and respectful. With any other guy, the thought of a significant other will conjure a lewd thought or visual, some degree of perversion along with all the other stuff. I figured that, this being the case, I'd be in store for some pretty dirty thoughts whenever you came up—I'd be prepared to think of ice cream and all other manner of distractions to escape those thought waves—but it was never like that. Everything else in him is so jagged and furious, but you, Estella... you're pure to him." She finally shrugged and wiped her face, feeling like she'd just signed her own death warrant with that confession. "So I... I don't know, I just figured you two were, like, celibate or something. That's all. That's why your"—she snapped her fingers—"immediate openness to the subject of sex just sort of clashed with what I'd come to expect."

ESTELLA WORKED to stifle her cries as she hurried out of the office in overdrive. Though she was sure the young auric prodigy could see just how her words had impacted her—was sure that anybody with a pair of working eyes could see that she'd been impacted—she didn't want another audience to watch her cry that night.

If she couldn't be alone with her Xander, she at least wanted to be alone with her sadness.

With no other place to go, she resigned to going to the roof. Despite the state of the world and despite being several weeks into winter, the sky above their city was blue and clear and the sun shone bright and proud and certain just over the eastern horizon.

"Fuck you, too," she half-sobbed, half-spat up at the shimmering orb.

She wasn't certain how much of this response was that growing "like Xander"-behavior she'd been noticing and how much of it was the immediate effects of the sunlight on her skin, but it felt good to curse at it either way.

Her hands moved out of instinct and shaded her belly. She wasn't sure if the sunlight could pierce the fabric of her shirt—the skin of her stomach didn't feel as itchy and irritated as the rest of her exposed flesh—and have any negative effects on the life growing within her, but she'd never been one to take careless risks before.

Still, in a weird way, it felt good to be out there.

The pain of the UV radiation assaulting her sensitive

vampire skin somehow seemed to offer validation to the agony she'd been feeling all night.

Yin... and Yang.

Estella blinked and looked away from the sun, then turned away from it entirely.

A thought...

Incomplete.

Finality seemed just out of her reach when she sensed an aura approaching and then—

CLANG! CLANG! CLANG!

"ESTELLA!" a muffled-yet-familiar voice shouted to her through the hatch that led to the roof from the inside of the building.

"What in the—Sawyer?" Estella started towards the voice.

"Yeah. Who else?" he called back. "Look, my ass got plenty tanned out there already, so I hope you'll pardon me for not hopping back out there, but we're back—yes, all of us; Zeek made sure to tell me to mention that for starters—and... well, there's something you've gotta see."

Estella opened the hatch and adjusted herself to block out the light as she saw Sawyer, looking, true to his word, burned and agitated, flinch at it. "Does it have something to do with Xander?" she asked.

Sawyer's frown said enough, but he added, "No, not in the long run, but you have to see it, anyway."

CHAPTER 7
NEW WORLD ORDER

God is dead. God remains dead. And we have killed him. Yet his shadow still looms.
How shall we comfort ourselves, the murderers of all murderers?
What was holiest and mightiest of all that the world
has yet owned has bled to death under our knives;
who will wipe this blood off us?
What water is there for us
to clean ourselves?"
Friedrich Nietzsche (1844-1900)

"Fuck! Fucking fuck with a dollop of freshly fucked fuck on top!"
Serena Vailean

"What is this?" Estella demanded, staring at the open laptop screen and the video that Sawyer and the others had paused and waiting for her.

"A response to Xander's message," Dianna said, folding her arms.

She didn't look happy about this, hadn't looked happy about anything since Xander's transmission, but Estella couldn't bring herself to think on that or even care.

She nodded to Sawyer to press play. He did so with a quick pass over the computer's spacebar:

Click

"—AFFRONT TO EVERYTHING WE AS A SPECIES HAVE EVER KNOWN. MANY THROUGHOUT HISTORY, MYSELF INCLUDED, HAVE TAKEN UP THE MANTLE OF FIGHTING THESE CREATURES—DEDICATED OUR LIVES TO LEARNING THEIR WAYS AND HOW TO—"

Estella sneered at the display and, hoping to once again pause it for the sake of establishing some context to what she was seeing, she mimicked the strike on the spacebar.

The video paused with the man held in mid-rant, his finger aimed back at them like a loaded gun. His eyes were grayish-blue but shone bright despite his later years. Everything about him—his posture, his hair, and his demeanor in the video—made Estella think that he was (or once was) military, and the six heavily-armed men standing ramrod straight behind him only supported this assumption.

"What did he say before this?" Estella asked, glancing back at the others.

Sawyer shook his head. "Nobody knows," he said. "That's exactly how the video starts. It was broadcast in much the same way as Xander's message, but it seems that he got to talking before the cameras were rolling."

Estella frowned back at the stilled image. "This was on all TVs and computers like Xander's broadcast?" she asked, wondering why she wouldn't have sensed something about it earlier.

"Sort of," Dianna cut in, still not sounding happy. "Most active networks have been spending the entire night working to avoid another hack like what Xander did, so this didn't interrupt anybody's *regularly scheduled programming,*" she half-whined the last three words like a network recording before adding, "but since all the news channels have been going crazy over the Xander footage they're just as eager to share this along with it."

Sawyer nodded. "Yeah, especially since it's riding on the popular side of 'gut anything that ain't human.'"

"So who is that awful man?" Estella asked.

"Oh, just watch," Sawyer said, moving to the spacebar once again. "He's not shy about introductions."

Click

"—DESTROY THEM! NOW WE KNOW THAT MANY OF YOU ARE SCARED—AND, I WON'T SUGARCOAT IT, YOU SHOULD BE—BUT WE ARE HERE TO TELL YOU THAT THESE CREATURES—THESE MYTHOS*—CAN BE KILLED! WE HAVE DONE IT! WE WILL CONTINUE TO DO IT! MY MEN AND I HAVE BEEN WAGING A SEVEN-MAN WAR ON THESE THINGS FOR THE PAST FEW DECADES, AND WE'RE NOT ABOUT TO STOP NOW!"*

Serena scoffed behind Estella and shook her head. "Somebody's cranky! Get him a fucking Cialis and some room-temp chicken soup!"

"Shush!" Zoey barked at her.

Surprisingly enough, Serena listened.

"... BELIEVE THIS TO BE A GLOBAL DECLARATION OF WAR! TALK OF CHOOSING SIDES AND ACTS OF PUBLIC VIOLENCE MAKE IT OBVIOUS WHAT THIS STRYKER-CREATURE IS SAYING, AND WE'RE HERE TO SAY THAT ***WE WILL NOT BE THREATENED!*** *BUT, MOST IMPORTANTLY, WE'RE HERE TO SAY THAT YOU, MY FELLOW HUMANS, ARE NOT*

ALONE! THE TRUTH HAS BEEN EXPOSED, AND WE'RE PROUD TO ANNOUNCE THAT THERE IS SOLACE AGAINST THESE TROUBLING TIMES: THE CEBOURISTS!

Zane growled and slammed the spacebar, pausing the video.

"Hey! Easy, man! The guy doesn't live in my keyboard!" Sawyer said with a glare.

Zane offered a half-hearted "sorry, man" before looking at Estella. "So I guess wiping out that Ariel bitch and her crew didn't slow down the rest of these Cebour-fucks everywhere else."

Zoey shook her head. "If anything it just gave the rest of them a martyr to mourn."

"Try a martyr *and* a smitten god," Sawyer said.

Everyone but Dianna gave him a confused look.

"The Cebourists were taking to the streets outside the church that they hijacked from that priest Xander knew," Dianna said.

"Father Tennesen..." Estella whimpered.

Dianna nodded. "Had Ariel's body up on this big pyre along with..." she shivered and hugged her arms across her chest, looking away.

Sawyer set a comforting hand on her shoulder.

"Along with...?" Zane pushed.

Serena nodded along with Zane's encouragement. "Yeah, toots, spit it out! We gotta play fucking Pictionary or something?"

Dianna glared at Serena. "My brother. My fucking good-for-nothing, psychopath brother!"

Estella's eyes widened. "Richard?"

Serena and Zane both grimaced at the realization of their blunder as a bunch of auras around the room—Zeek, Karen and Sasha, Satoru, and Tim's—flared with fear and hatred. None, however, flared with more fear or hatred than Dianna's.

Sawyer nodded. "Guess the Cebourists worshipped that

son-of-a-bitch as some kind of messiah. Probably why that word kept getting crossed connections earlier when we were dealing with those two cases," he sighed and shrugged. "Either way, between his less-than-wholesome tactics, his devil-may-care approach to what they've come to see as a holy mission, and his eagerness to use that serum that grants humans mythos abilities to give them a fighting edge, the Cebourists found in him a path to follow."

Dianna seethed, making a noise that Estella would have otherwise reserved for an enraged vampire. "Those sick bastards are treating my brother's insane vendetta like some sort of one-man holy war!"

Zoey sneered and shook her head. "And they took that vendetta to a whole new level by learning mythos-killing magic from an equally insane woman..."

"... and turned it into a new religion," Isaac finished.

Sawyer nodded to all of them. "He was trying to warn us all—mythos everywhere—of the Cebourists. With one of their founders dead and... and whatever they had planned for Richard's remains thwarted by Xander, they'd likely start a global mythos hunt. True to Xander's warning, the Cebourists are going public, doubling their efforts to recruit new followers and..."

"And it looks like cutting down that bitch Ariel has sprouted seven new cocksucking leaders," Zane growled.

"And such classy and charming cocksuckers, at that," Serena chimed, glaring at the paused video screen with the furious-looking man frozen thereon.

Estella, still shaking from all of this, reached out and gave the spacebar an uncertain tap.

Click

"MY NAME IS ROBERT DiANGELO, AND I HAVE A MESSAGE OF MY OWN:

"TO MY FELLOW HUMANS, THERE ARE TOUGH TIMES AHEAD—UGLY TIMES—BUT WE'RE HERE TO SEE AN END TO

THESE BLOODTHIRSTY MONSTERS ONCE AND FOR ALL! YOU CAN JOIN THE CAUSE—JOIN THE CEBOURISTS—AND HELP US TO FIGHT FOR A MYTHOS-FREE WORLD... OR YOU CAN STAY IN YOUR HOMES AND LET US DO OUR WORK!

"AND TO EVERYTHING ELSE, DON'T BOTHER RUNNING. WE'RE COMING FOR YOU!"

The man ended in what would have been a dynamic pose, once again pointing and sneering with an undeniably intimidating expression. In much the same fashion as the belated opening, however, the video rolled on for another few seconds, creating an awkward extension that ended with the man starting to turn back towards one of the six other men before it cut to black.

"You'd think such a charming scrotum of a man would be able to hire himself a capable video editor," Serena groused.

Dianna shook again and finally let out a heavy sob, her bottled emotions forcing their way out. The room went quiet as Sawyer took her into his arms and ushered her away, heading for the stairs that would lead them to the office.

Sana, who Estella could only assume had been watching in on everything with her aura from up there, conveniently slipped through the door and started down so that they'd have it to themselves.

As the young Indian girl started down the stairs, she and Estella caught one another's gaze and a shared thought, one that seemed irrelevant only a short time ago:

The seven-armed octopus.

Estella had "seen" the thought in Sana's head when she'd been talking about her dream, but, like Sana, she hadn't thought anything of the random element—just the sort of nonsense that dreams have a way of planting in the mind—that she'd disregarded it just as quickly as the gifted auric had.

But, as Sana worked her way down the stairs and hurried towards Estella, it became evident that there was more on the gifted auric's mind than just this new turn of events.

Her pink aura, which swirled and thrashed over her head, was practically screaming ***"XANDER!"***

It was quite possibly the most bittersweet of circumstances.

On the one hand, they'd found Xander.

On the other...

"Fuck!" Serena said with a gasp. It was one of the first times Estella had heard her say the word without a shred of humor or enthusiasm; the first time she seemed to take no enjoyment in the word. "Fucking fuck with a dollop of freshly fucked fuck on top!"

Sana had said they'd have company, all sorts of it, and she hadn't been wrong.

News vans were circled around the block.

Rioters were struggling to get past a line of police in SWAT gear who'd set up a perimeter around the unseen barrier set by Xander's aura. Though they held steady, Estella could see on most of their auras that, despite the job they were paid to do, they'd sooner be on the other side of it, clamoring and fighting for a chance at the monster they'd been tasked to guard.

How much of their effort is sincere and how much of it is because they already know there's no getting through? she wondered.

A way's away from the aggression, Estella spotted a select few who were kneeling in front of some low quality printouts of Xander's face from his broadcast and burning candles in his honor. Though it was, at first, a somewhat endearing sight, it also felt twisted and wrong; not at all the sort of thing Xander would have wanted. Still fixated on this, Estella watched as several of the further-back rioters, not content with poking glances over the heads of those in front of them, turned on the small group, kicking out their candles and then turning their rage on the people themselves.

Isaac, seeing this, as well, sneered in disgust. "God! What the hell's the matter with them?"

"Fear does ugly things to people," Zoey said in a flat-but-still-disgusted tone. "Makes them erratic and violent."

"So why attack one another?" Isaac asked, nodding towards the centerpiece of the mayhem.

Zane nodded, also confused. "Doesn't make sense. There's a few cops here and such, but that *nobody's* made a break for it and crossed the line to get to—"

"You can't see it," Estella said in a low tone, too sickened by the sight.

Serena and Zoey both nodded, staring.

"Well don't keep us in suspense, ladies," Zane growled.

"What are we not seeing?" Isaac asked Zoey as Estella broke away from the group and started on numb legs into the crowd.

"His aura," she heard Zoey mutter, sounding stunned. "Xander's aura is holding them all back."

The last thing Estella heard before she submerged herself into the crowd of hate was Zane's startled voice saying:

"How is he—"

The rest was swallowed by the cries of the people around her, but Estella could understand his shock. Given what she'd seen of Xander from a distance, it was a wonder that there was any aura left to shield himself with at all.

"Oh, God, it's still alive!" a woman wailed a short distance ahead, "Kill it! Somebody kill it!"

"What if he wakes up?" one young man asked another, "Won't he kill us all?"

"Is that the same one from the internet?" an onlooker muttered to no one in particular.

"What could have done that to him?"

The thing you should *be afraid of,* Estella thought as she shouldered past a cluster of onlookers. Then another. Then...

But the crowd only grew denser the further she went. Without exposing herself for what she was in the middle of the crowd, there was no way to move them; no way to get through to Xander.

Serena... Estella called back, uncertain and desperate. The sunlight was beginning to get to her, making her think crazy things. *I-I can't get through. What should I do?*

You're asking me? Serena's voice in her head rang with surprise. *No offense, darling, but if you're not going to Zoey for answers then I don't think it's answers you want; I think it's permission.*

Estella bit her lip, already beginning to see how right the crazy blonde was. Still, a part of her was holding back; yearned to be the controlled, subtle Stryker. *Permission... to do what?*

She could almost hear the wild cackles rising in the back of her mind as Serena said, *Whatever you have to, Goddess; whatever you have to.*

Estella gulped, nodded to herself, and clenched her fists at her side. *And you and the others?* she asked.

I'm rallying the troops as we speak. Zoey's getting on the horn with that stuffy Sawyer guy. I know you wanted to keep them out of the loop until we were certain, but—

Yeah, Estella cut her off, already regretting not telling the others about Sana's vision. *Make sure he brings his car, too... and lots of blood.*

You mean the synthetic stuff, right? Serena asked.

I mean whatever they can get to feed my husband as soon as we get him out of here. I don't care if you need to drag some of these assholes off their feet and open a vein to do it.

There was a long, unsteady silence in Estella's head.

Then Serena offered up only one word:

Damn...

Estella wasn't sure if it was in regards to her seriousness or her savagery. She didn't care.

Here I go... she announced.

Though Estella had grown up with a love of literature and, even as a young girl, classic tales of mythology, she'd always found the downtown statue to be a bit vapid. There was good intent there, sure—most bad ideas, she knew, started off as such—but it was nevertheless a vague, albeit boisterous, attempt at being empowering.

Somebody somewhere in Estella's distant past had said something to the tune of *"It's easy to pander to the masses when it's their own money that's paying for it,"* and, though she hadn't been sure what it meant at the time, she couldn't help but find it all-too-true in the here and now.

More than anything, however, was how appallingly ironic it seemed.

The statue, all in tax-paid bronze, was, at its tallest point, almost twenty feet, featuring an almost eight foot depiction of the Greek Titan, Atlas. The pose was a sloppy nod to Rodin's The Thinker—the figure showing none of the classic struggle with the burden but, instead, seeming strangely contemplative with his task—and holding a twelve-foot sphere over his head. This sphere, instead of representing the Earth, was perfectly flat across its entire surface, save for a winding banner that had been sculpted around its equator and boasting "ONE WORLD; ONE PEOPLE" around its entirety.

Estella recalled, during a class field trip that took them past the town's so-called "monument," some kids laughing at the absurdity of the message "PEOPLE ONE WORLD; ONE" and reciting it throughout the day in mock-idiot tones as "People! One world! One!"

As far as Estella was concerned, those responsible for the statue had managed to botch everything it was meant to represent.

Now, however, it was made all the more repugnant by being turned into a platform that held up the mangled body of Xander Stryker like some sort of centerpiece for the crazed onlookers to ogle as he slowly cooked in the early-morning sun.

No sooner had she made the announcement to the others than she cleared herself a path...

Estella's aura rocketed forward from her chest, weaving like a bright-orange snake around the onlookers and dividing the entire mass into those on the left and those on the right. Once the auric tendril had reached the surface of Xander's auric barrier—a gigantic red-and-black dome that encircled him and the awful statue—she acted. The divider swelled and pushed outward on either side, shoveling everyone away like a vulgar, hate-filled Red Sea before the mock-Moses, Estella. Angry, confused cries rose as people tried to figure out what was happening, some blaming the authorities and others claiming that there were divine forces at work.

Estella took a momentary indulgence in realizing that, in a twisted way, they were both right.

With the crowd parted and a clearing made, Estella hollowed out the auric block she'd constructed before herself and began to walk through it. Seeing this, several people began to catch on and, shrieking at the sight of the casual wanderer making her way towards the subject of their hate, attempted to lunge at her. Like the auric barrier surrounding Xander, however, Estella's makeshift "hallway" was every bit as unseen-yet-protective. Bodies slammed against its surface, their owners burping out pained and confused cries before finding themselves crushed by others behind them trying to do the same. Estella ignored them, too consumed by what she saw before her.

From a distance, Xander's body had looked dead as dead could be atop the statue's massive sphere. Drawing nearer, however, she found herself driven nearly to sickness by the damage he'd sustained.

He looked to be discarded on the surface on his back, the upper part of his body slanting over the arch and framing his bruised and battered face upside-down in a tangle of sweat-and-blood caked black hair. A hooped rope of intestines had fallen from his torn stomach and hung halfway over the edge, partially hiding the "L" in "WORLD" and caking the surrounding bronze in baked-brown blood. One arm splayed out over his head, hanging irregularly along the curve of the sphere and letting his twisted wrist dangle lamely. The other arm crossed over his chest, the shoulder worked over all wrong and a jagged length of bone poking at the sleeve of his shirt and creating an unsettling angle at the forearm.

Seeing this sent Estella into hysterics, and she broke out into a sprint towards the awful scene.

"Xander? Oh my... Xander! XANDER!"

ESTELLA! NO! Zoey's voice warned in her head, *THE BARRIER!*

Estella hit the surface of Xander's aura and kept on going; the shield that had held back hundreds of onlookers aching to express their hate and fear on the incapacitated body of the vampire they'd seen on their televisions and computers letting her pass as though it didn't even exist. Seeing this, the crowd began making a mad-dash for Xander once again, barreling through the SWAT members and sandwiching them between the still-active auric shield and a wave of unrelenting humans. Behind her, Estella could sense a riptide of fury, pain, and outrage from countless auras as the sweet scent of blood began to saturate the air.

Then she heard a therion's roar...

Though Estella still refused to turn away from Xander, she watched with her mind's eye as Isaac, now transformed, put on an intimidating show.

"JESUS FUCK! IT'S A GODDAM WEREWOLF!"

Screams echoed and grew, and the combined auric presence surrounding the crowd shifted from one of hate and aggression to one of fear. Rioting gave way to pandemonium as people who, only moments earlier, had aimed to work together to maim and murder a nearly dead monster before them disregarded one another to get as far away from the very near, very alive monster behind them. Some ran for their lives. Some found themselves trampled in the effort. Others, mostly those who hadn't come alone and had company they wanted to impress, found enough courage to linger and throw whatever they had on hand at the roaring beast.

When one dared to level a handgun in Isaac's direction, Zoey, posing as a startled onlooker, used her aura to tear it from their grip and strike them with the barrel. Witnessing this, somebody announced that the werewolf was in cohorts with a ghost and promptly wet themselves before running out into the street, where they were clipped by a speeding news van and left in a stained heap.

The van didn't stop.

And they call us the monsters... Zoey's voice rang out to all of them.

Though most of the news crews had decided that they'd gotten enough footage and made for a hasty retreat along with the rest of the onlookers, several others—more interested in ratings than self-preservation—took advantage of the growing clearing and started to rush in with their cameras.

"BREAKING NEWS, FUCKERS!" Serena cried out as she appeared in front of them, lifting her shirt and shaking her breasts at the closest of the cameras before using her aura to dismantle them.

The crews staggered, gawking in horror at the bits and pieces that had once been, Estella imagined, rather expensive recording equipment.

"Like what you see?" Zane growled at them.

Their faces turned and caught sight of the muscular, tattooed vampire as he made a show of extending his fangs and issuing an angry-sounding hiss at them. With ratings a distant concern, they took off in clumsy sprints to their respective vans.

"FREEZE, FREAKS!" one of the SWAT team screamed, still in the process of trying to retrieve his gun with shaky, unresponsive fingers.

The Vaileans shared a momentary glance of delight before jumping into overdrive.

Less than two seconds later the entire SWAT team had been disarmed and disrobed, standing naked and bewildered in front of Xander's auric dome. As these humans, too, began to make a run for it, Serena made a show of slapping the nearest on the rear, throwing a Boy Scout's salute, and telling him to "Keep up the good work," before offering Zane an apologetic shrug while still wearing a not-so-innocent grin.

On any other day Estella might have found the entire scene, which took only over a minute to pass, moderately amusing, if not a little crass. Now, however, she couldn't bring herself to feel one way or the other about any of it. She'd worked her way atop the should-be globe and knelt, sobbing, over Xander's body, taking in the full scope of all his injuries.

"Xan-Xander...?" Estella sobbed.

And, only adding that much more to the bittersweet moment, she saw him begin to stir in response to her voice. He worked to look up at her and Estella let out a cry at the sight...

He only had one eye, his bruised-yet-intact blood-red right.

"Mom?" he croaked and then whimpered, his effort to look around and speak clearly hurting him. As Estella worked to cradle his head in her arms she felt him finally drop the shield and let the others through. Despite all the pain she could see on him, he seemed to be taking some kind of comfort in her touch. "M-mom?"

Estella sobbed and began to stroke the top of his head, rocking herself against the horrors of this discovery.

"Xander... baby, what'd they do to you?"

"mhy guh'n," Xander croaked, trying to talk through a broken jaw. "'e 'ad mhy guh'n."

My gun, Estella heard in her mind. *He had my gun.*

She couldn't begin to understand what this meant, but Estella found herself nodding all the same. "That's okay, baby.

That's okay. We'll get it back. Just stay with me—just get better—and we'll make this all right."

She looked up as Sawyer's car wove through the street and tore across the lot, pulling up beside the awful, awful statue of the contemplative Titan and the twisted message of unity; coming to take Xander to what remained of his home.

"We'll make this all right."

[RESUME TRANSMISSION]

BRENT DIRKLEY:
Welcome back and, for those just tuning in, thanks for joining us.
We're discussing the recent footage—what some are calling an attack and what others are calling a hoax—of what appears to be a young man—a self-proclaimed vampire—issuing some sort of reveal for him and the rest of his kind.
Now it has been confirmed that this footage was broadcast on a global scale, and, understandably, it's created quite a stir the world over.
I've been joined by Colonel M.T. Howard and renowned biologist, Professor Ian Scott Thompson, and, before the break, we were shedding some light on the most obvious questions that people have:
Can such creatures exist?
And are they dangerous?
In just a moment we'll be joined with another guest who has some opinions of his own about all of this, but first:
Professor Thompson, to summarize our earlier discussion, can you explain to those just tuning in what you told us earlier?

PROFESSOR IAN SCOTT THOMPSON:
Of course, Brent.
Assuming, of course, that this isn't some sort of elaborate hoax,

and I feel it's worth noting that this is still under investigation regarding its validity, it's my scientific opinion that—

COLONEL MICHAEL TORRENCE HOWARD:
OF COURSE THEY EXIST! HAVEN'T YOU LOOKED OUTSIDE RECENTLY? THOSE DAMNED THINGS ARE—

BRENT DIRKLEY:
Colonel, please! I'll be getting to you in just a moment, but—please—let the professor have his say!

PROFESSOR IAN SCOTT THOMPSON:
Thank you, Brent.
As I was saying, the claims made by the individual in the broadcast were, to be fair, quite vague. There was no real explanation of what these words—"vampire" and "mythos" and such—really encompassed; no explanation, that is to say, of what they're capable of. That said, there are numerous accounts—documented and reasonably explained accounts, mind you—that describe conditions or abilities based on any number of conditions such as genetics and disease. Things like predominant teeth, enhanced strength, discoloration of the skin and eyes. All of these are, to be perfectly blunt, not anything new and, moreover, hardly a reason for the entire world to fly off the hinges as it seems to be.

BRENT DIRKLEY:
Noted, Professor, but, for the sake of argument:
Would you say it's possible that creatures like these mythos—creatures as they were depicted in the broadcast and as have been described in numerous reports—can truly exist and be walking among us?

PROFESSOR IAN SCOTT THOMPSON:
Well, Brent, I wouldn't go so far as to say that what we saw in

the footage or have heard from panic-driven masses can really be considered—

BRENT DIRKLEY:
Professor, answer the question please:
Can... they... exist?

PROFESSOR IAN SCOTT THOMPSON:
Well... I mean, sure. I suppose anything's possible if you want to go about it in such a black-and-white fashion. There's new species being discovered all the time with incredible abilities, so who's to say that these mythos cannot? But it's important to—

BRENT DIRKLEY:
Thank you, Professor. Absolutely fascinating!
Now, Colonel, if you'd offer us your insight on the second part of our earlier dialogue: are... mythos... dangerous?

COLONEL MICHAEL TORRENCE HOWARD:
Well I should say so, Dirkley! What we're dealing with here takes all the savagery, cunning, and stealth of the worst terrorists and hands them God-knows what sort of crazy abilities on top of it all. I've had men out there—good men, mind you—who've told us that these unholy mother[BEEP]ers can, I don't know, disappear and reappear at will—teleportation or whatever—and lift all sorts of things with their minds. I've got soldiers out there being put to sleep by the dozens with nothing more than a stare from one of these beasties. There's critters lookin' and talkin' every bit as sophisticated as any Tom, Dick, or Harry who can—BOOM!—turn themselves into something that looks like it jumped right off the screen of a big-picture horror show. Dirkley, you bet your ass these [BEEP]s are dangerous! You can't take the worst parts of humanity, give 'em teeth and claws and all manner of comic book super powers and expect them to be

harmless. These are monsters we're talking about, not a bag of puppies!

BRENT DIRKLEY:

Yes... well, I appreciate your honesty and openness with the matter, Colonel. And... uh, a follow-up question, if I may: Many have seen the videos that this... err, Robert Di-DiAngelo has shared in response to the initial broadcast. In it, he seems to speak of the same group—the... uh, the Saborists, I believe they're called—that Xander Stryker was addressing in his own message.

There's been some speculation about just who these Saborists are and what they might represent to all of this, but what I and my viewers would be interested to know is if there's any merit to the rumors that this DiAngelo-fellow has a military background, and, if so, what sort of—

COLONEL MICHAEL TORRENCE HOWARD:

Let me go ahead and polish off this little [BLEEP]-covered diamond so it [BEEP]ing sparkles and is crystal-[BEEP]ing-clear:

Robert DiAngelo is a madman. His crew are madmen. Now, the CIA, FBI... hell, everyone and anyone we got, we're all working to figure out who these Cebourist-[BEEP]s are and—and, by the way, say it right, Dirkly: CEBOURISTS! You don't so much report the news as much as you [BEEP] it out of your gaping maw—-but we are working tirelessly to understand who these Cebourist-[BEEP]s are and how they fit into everything. You ask me now and I'd say... no, no, I'm not slipping down that snake hole again; Colonel M.T. Howard isn't facing any more slander suits, that's for—

...

Anyway, Dirkley, the public record on DiAngelo is available for the world to see: he and his men were busted for war crimes, conspiracy, treason... hell, you name it. Unfortunately, given the shady nature of the sort of work they were doing for us back in the day—and this ain't how I'd've run things, you can bet your [BEEP]ing ass on that, Dirkley—everyone had to play nice; had to shake hands and promise that, in lieu of jail time or even execution, everyone would keep their mouths shut. The so-called "good" soldiers would get to walk off into their own private sunsets and the government would be able to avoid all manner of bad press for ever having worked with him in the first place.

PROFESSOR IAN SCOTT THOMPSON:
And you're saying that these supposed mythos are the dangerous ones?

COLONEL MICHAEL TORRENCE HOWARD:
Listen here, you bespectacled [BEEP], you might think that hiding away with all your dead critters and bleached cat skeletons and whispering sweet nothings to your aquariums of cock-a-roaches has offered you some insight to the world, but nothing—not all the heinous tweed jackets or all the tenure in the world—is going to offer you any real insight into what's going on out there. I've watched plenty of people dying and heard that much more in the throes of death detailing what these things can do; accounts coming in from the world over that prove, indefinitely, that these things aren't only real, Professor, but that they are dangerous. Now does that mean that we can't be dangerous, as well? Bull-[BEEP]ing-[BEEP], [BEEEEEP]! The United States military is very eager to show these mythos-[BEEP]s just how dangerous we can be; spill some monster blood in response to all the human blood they've been lapping off the [BEEP]ing streets! But I ain't about to blow sunshine up the skirts of the likes of you or Dirkley and say that there ain't dangerous bad people out there just as much as there's dangerous good people. And now that this big bag of [BEEP] has been spilled and everyone's [BEEP]ing smelling it,

it's only fair to say that, in my God's honest opinion, Robert DiAngelo and anybody associated with him should be considered just as dangerous as all these monsters we're seeing!

BRENT DIRKLEY:
Well that's... umm, quite an interesting view of things, Colonel.
Thank you...
Though I feel I should remind you that we are on the air.

COLONEL MICHAEL TORRENCE HOWARD:
That bloody-eyed demon was on the air, too, Dirkley. What's say we not be a total, [BEEP]damn, dumb-[BEEP], all things considered?

BRENT DIRKLEY:
Noted.
Anyway...
Thanks again for joining us this evening, Professor, Colonel; we hope you'll both consider joining us again as further developments reveal themselves.

PROFESSOR IAN SCOTT THOMPSON:
Don't bet on—

COLONEL MICHAEL TORRENCE HOWARD:
Fat cha—

BRENT DIRKLEY:
Joining us now is a young man who's rapidly making a name for himself. His online video in response to the Xander Stryker broadcast and resulting mythos scare went viral, and, since then, he's been called 'the human voice for nonhuman rights:' Mister Johnathan Erikson.
Now, John—can I call you 'John,' John?

JOHNATHAN ERIKSON:
Uhm... yeah, sure. Why not?

BRENT DIRKLEY:
Great! So in your video you argue that these monsters deserve—

JOHNATHAN ERIKSON:
If I can stop you there, Brent, I think it's unfair to call them "monsters."

BRENT DIRKLEY:
Yes. I bet you do. You were quite clear in your vlog about that. So you believe that these mythos deserve the same rights as people?

JOHNATHAN ERIKSON:
Yes. Of course.

BRENT DIRKLEY:
And that they're inhuman beasts puts no dent in that stance?

JOHNATHAN ERIKSON:
The same's been said about different types of people—different races, religions, sexualities...
It's not fair to take all the progress we've made as a collective species and turn back the clock on our morals simply because there's a new type of—

BRENT DIRKLEY:
I'm sorry, but you're referring to these things as though they're people. Do you expect anybody to accept that—

JOHNATHAN ERIKSON:

I don't want you or anybody to accept anything. I want you and everybody to consider the facts:

I want everyone to consider that our first real glimpse at the reality of mythos came not from an attack, but from a message, a connection. I want it considered that, prior to this connection, there's never been—in all of history—enough evidence for us as a whole to reveal their existence; they've managed to keep a lower profile than radical groups occupying small towns. I want it considered that the one who made this connection, this Xander Stryker, did so as a warning to his own people—it seems puzzling that so many have been impacted by this footage and yet nobody seemed to actually listen to its content —out of fear of the threat that others—humans at that—represented to them.

The colonel said it himself: there's good people and bad people; those who are dangerous for the rights of others and those who are dangerous against the rights of others.

Why can the same not be said of mythos?

Why can we so easily grasp that a cop with a gun is good while a psycho with a gun is bad, but then turn around and say that all mythos must, in turn, be evil solely because we're scared of them?

BRENT DIRKLEY:

Well, John, in all fairness, the colonel also said that people are being slaughtered by mythos even as we speak.

JOHNATHAN ERIKSON:

There are people being slaughtered by people as we speak, as well. We just won't talk about that because it doesn't help to support this anti-mythos argument. There's also mythos slaughtering mythos out there, too; there's entire support forums popping up every hour online for people who say they and their friends and family were saved from mythos attacks by other mythos. But you wouldn't know anything about that,

either, would you, Brent? Or how about the fact that a staggering number of the deaths of humans at the hands of mythos have been proven to be out of self-defense? You can't even scroll through Facebook right now without coming across phone-shot footage of nonhumans being beaten and tortured. And that footage isn't even censored, Brent! You can't view a video of a dog injured in a hit-and-run without accepting that there's violent imagery ahead, but I can scroll through my phone and get an eyeful of a so-called militia group yanking the entrails out of a still-screaming creature that's been tied to the bumper of a pickup truck.
Would you like to see how quickly I can find that footage, Brent? I'm sure your viewers would—

BRENT DIRKLEY:
I'll take your word for it, John.
You certainly speak with passion, I'll give you that, but I'm afraid that you're painting a rather liberal, sugar-coated view of all of this; it's easy to say these sorts of things when there's no real personal risk involved, wouldn't you say?

JOHNATHAN ERIKSON:
We were [BEEP]ed before the mythos scare started, Brent.

BRENT DIRKLEY:
Please, John! I won't tolerate—

JOHNATHAN ERIKSON:
You tolerated it just fine when it was the Colonel handing you your own ass on the air, didn't you? But it was easy to tolerate a [BEEP]-here and a [BEEP]-there when it at least strengthened the side you and your network have already taken.
And I understand. I do.
A little while ago I was staring down the barrel of a gun prepared to end it all. Then I heard Xander Stryker speaking on

the TV. We can convince ourselves that this moment is somehow a dark moment in human history. We can even convince ourselves that it's the end—a perfect time to stare down that proverbial gun barrel. But we are the ones who choose whether a moment strengthens us or destroys us. There's always a risk, sure—I'm not about to say that there won't be deadly mythos out there, no more than I wouldn't dare say that there's no deadly people out there—but we can follow your path, in which case we'd better just pull that collective trigger on ourselves now and save us the trouble of a horrible death, or we can open up to new possibilities and find a way to take the next step.

BRENT DIRKLEY:
Okay...
So, John, in your pretty little idealistic world, what's to be done about the mythos out there that are an undeniable threat? I mean, sure, a few people with automatic rifles or some bombs can represent a threat to a good number of innocent people, but we're talking about individual creatures here to whom guns and bombs and all conceivable means of defense seem to mean nothing; creatures who can wipe out—and who are wiping out —entire armies singlehandedly. Do you feel that polite language and understanding are going to convince them to change their ways, because such tactics haven't proven to work on violent humans.

JOHNATHAN ERIKSON:
I find it interesting that you're choosing this moment to compare violent mythos to violent humans, Brent.

BRENT DIRKLEY:
Answer the question, John.

JOHNATHAN ERIKSON:

Certainly.
In regards to the dangerous mythos—the ones who can't be reasoned with and the ones who we're powerless to stop—I suggest we take the same steps that we do when faced with dangerous humans who can't be reasoned with and with whom we're powerless to stop.

BRENT DIRKLEY:
And that would be?

JOHNATHAN ERIKSON:
We have faith that those with the power to stop them will rise up to protect us.

BRENT DIRKLEY:Y
es, well, let's hope that they do that quickly, then. Thank you for joining us, John, and good luck with your thesis.

Coming up next: could the Tide Pod challenge sweeping the nation be tied to ISIS? My next guest has some surprising insights that might make you a believer!
Stay tuned!

[END TRANSMISSION]

"And the light shineth in the darkness;
and the darkness comprehended it not."
John 1:5

"Religion is the recognition
of all our duties as divine commands."
Immanuel Kant (1724-1804)

The Great Machine moves;
The Great Machine is still.
It is as it was; it will never be the same.
The dominos fall, the* clack clack clack *of their namesake
Replaced by impacts made in blood and tears—
They are as the impacts of pebbles within a pond that has no surface,
No beginning; no end,
The ripples echo ever outward, spherical and unending.
The Great Machine, here now and never anywhere,
Witnesses the impacts—tastes the blood and tears—
And sees their path; knows it as something long-since past.
Knows it as something that will never come to be.

"What's happening?"

"Change."

"Will I wake up?"

"Uncertain."

"But Estella..."

"Yes. She needs you. Ruby, too. They all need you."

"Then I need to wake up! I need to—"

"Uncertain."

"Then what is certain?"

The Great Machine is as it was,
But it will never be the same.
It's moving; it is still.

Then, so close it births and so far it never was:

"Because he's Xander, dammit!"

"... without her, every step you've taken since your reawakening could have been your last!"

Stan

CHAPTER 8

GOOD AND TRULY FUCKED

A man said to the universe:
"Sir, I exist!"
"However," replied the universe.
"The fact has not created in me
A sense of obligation."
Stephen Crane (1871-1900)

"Is he... fucking shit, Estella! He's bleeding all over the—"

"I know."

"Well I'd goddam hope you knew!"

"Did you bring the blood?"

"I brought the *synthetic* stuff, yes; I'm not about to go making more of a—"

"Give it to me!"

"All of—"

"Yes! All of it!"

"Shit, Estella, I don't know if it's—"

"NOW!"

"Fine! Yes! Here! Take it! But I hope you realize you're fighting an uphill battle here. Jeez, you're wearing more of his insides on your outsides then he's got insides actually *inside* him! Sweet fucking... Is he missing an eye?"

"You still got two of yours, Sawyer, you tell me."

"How the hell is he still alive?"

"Because he's Xander, dammit! Now are you gonna keep running your fucking mouth or are you gonna drive?"

"'Stell?"

"What is it, Serena?"

"How long's it been since I said you're sexy when you talk like that?"

"Not long enough, Serena."

"Well, just in case: you're—"

"I appreciate what you're trying to do, Serena, I really do. But—please—just don't. Not now. Please."

Sawyer's car slipped into a shadowed pass between two tall, nearly identical buildings before turning once more into its destination. This turn, a calculated and gentle maneuver for the sake of the cargo, only served to irritate Estella, who'd been torn between the need for ease and the demand for speed. She didn't say anything about this, though, and started to open the back door before Sawyer could even bring the car to a stop. The handle pulled out with no give; the door did not open.

"Sorry, 'Stell," Sawyer called, stopping and beginning to shift into park. "I keep forgetting to take off the child safety—"

Estella didn't say anything.

Metal shrieked and wires wailed.

The rear, passenger-side door clattered to the concrete floor of the storage facility. Several of the remaining Trepis Clan members, standing close to the car for a chance to be among the first to see the return of their leader, had to jump back to avoid this. Everyone else, though standing at a safe distance, chose to move back, as well; knowing there were worse things than scraped shins.

"Or just take the damn door off," Sawyer sighed, standing in front of his car—as far as he'd managed to go in circling around before Estella made her own exit.

Serena remained still as she let Estella step out. The others—Zane, Isaac, and Zoey—agreed to stay behind; they'd wanted to keep an eye out for any signs of Xander's attackers as well as making sure that Sawyer's car wasn't followed. However, Estella had asked Serena to ride with them, knowing that, should they be attacked on the way back, it would be better to have another perfect vampire to defend Xander. Now, Estella could see that she felt out of place, awkward, and she traded glances between the two Strykers, weighing equal doses of sympathy and concern for both. Estella saw this on her aura; saw through her mind's eye as Serena trailed a long, thin finger across Xander's forehead, working a blood-soaked bang that had fallen over the gaping socket of his missing left eye. Xander's body shifted, making Serena gasp. Then she caught sight of Estella's gentle auric hold on her husband's body as she floated him free of the car.

A collective gasp swelled as Xander Stryker's body came into view; an aura that was actually many, at that moment, shared a myriad of emotions and carried a single thought:

How?

Estella wanted to kill them all.

No... she'd be satisfied with simply beating—

Estella wanted to...

She wanted to cry.

Estella Stryker needed so badly to cry that the pain from that need alone would have warranted a gallon's worth of tears.

She did not cry. She said nothing, and, instead, marched

forward; Xander held like the most fragile thing ever within her aura and trailing after her. Though she was prepared to use more of her aura to shovel the gawkers aside, it proved unnecessary as the others parted before her and offered a path to Zeek and Karen. She found Satoru and Karen's twin sister, Sasha, waiting with them. She offered nothing in the way of a greeting to them—barely acknowledged their presence save for a shared glance between them—before extending an auric tendril and dragging a long shipping crate loudly across the floor. Most of the other patients in Zeek and Karen's care jumped or shifted at the noise, but settled when they saw the "why" behind the "what." Xander's body was set with the utmost care atop it.

Ruby remained motionless throughout the entire process.

The crate came to rest beside her, close enough that, should she have decided to wake up at that moment, Ruby would be able to touch Xander's hand without leaving her own makeshift bed. For some reason, this thought brought Estella some sense of peace. It gave her the strength to hold back her body's demand to break down at that moment and finally bring herself to speak.

She didn't have the chance to, however.

"Fuck..." Zeek, an anapriek quick to anger but more selective with his angry words, said this word as though it were three syllables.

"He's alive," said Estella, hoping the words would sound encouraging, reassuring perhaps. They came out sounding argumentative.

Zeek only nodded.

Karen and Sasha, twins who almost seemed to make it a mission to look and act nothing like the other, held one another and began to cry.

Satoru's cat-like face sagged, ears drooping and whiskers dipping against his shoulders, and he set a paw-like hand on the small of Sasha's back.

Estella said it again—"He *is* alive!"—this time making no

effort to keep the challenging tone from her voice. Then, narrowing her gaze at Zeek, she said, “Save him!”

Zeek blinked down at the leader of his demolished and diminished clan. Estella saw thoughts float over him as easily as she would have if they were written there for all the world to read:

Could this *truly be alive?*

How in the world are we going to...?

... whoever did this to him suffers the worst kind of...

... a symbol of what we've...

They swirled faster and faster, no longer having beginnings or ends, but throughout the scattered half-linked chains of thought there was one that loomed larger and more constant than all the others; a question that made Estella rethink her kill-or-cry options:

What can be done?

“Please...” something deep within her whispered. It was the part of her that she'd been burying, the part that she normally got to indulge in; the part that was still her—Estella.

As she realized this—thought it and felt it with a genuine swell of acknowledgement—Xander's lips parted and, as if to assert the life that still echoed within him, drew in a ragged, painful-sounding breath.

It was enough to make the four hold their own.

It was enough to make Estella finally cry.

Fortunately, Serena was waiting behind her to catch her as her knees gave out.

“WELL, he's good and truly fucked,” Zeek said after a long, excruciating silence wherein he examined and catalogued the extent of Xander's injuries, “but—yes, Estella—he *is* alive.”

“So he's going to make it?” Sasha asked, beating Estella to the same question.

Estella glanced at the normally sultry but now just sulky therion, endeared by her concern and, noting this, looked around. While the corner was not big enough for everyone to occupy, everyone was, in their own way, listening in; everyone was just as concerned.

Endearing as this was, it also gave Estella a gut-wrenching moment of self-reflection. She'd been so focused on tracking down Xander—so on edge about everything that had happened—that she'd started to slip into a dark place where she didn't recognize herself.

A dark place she'd had to help Xander out of so many times before.

That must be Hell... she thought absently.

Zeek made a noise that was both uncertain and uncomfortable. On its own it answered the question, but he still said, "I can't say just yet. He's been through... well, it's no secret what he's been through. Honestly, I'm not sure how he's made it this far, and I'm even less sure what's keeping him alive right now."

Karen had been busying herself with cleaning Xander, mopping away blood with dampened towels they'd found in a supplies closet and casting them aside when they'd soaked up too much to be of any use. The pile was nearly tall enough to reach her waist. Hearing Zeek say this, however, she paused and looked up at him, narrowing her eyes.

"What do you mean by that?" she asked.

Zeek looked over at her, confused. "Mean by what?"

Karen tossed aside another blood-soaked towel. She'd been working her way up and had finally gotten to Xander's head. She'd easily doubled the size of the pile since.

"You said 'what's keeping him alive.' You could've said 'how he's staying alive' or even 'what he's staying alive for,' but you didn't. You specifically worded it as though there's some other force doing it for him; you said it like a doctor who's referring to a machine or a drug that's shouldering the process. Why?"

Zeek blushed at the question and looked back down at

Xander for a long moment. It looked to Estella like he was either reanalyzing his process or meditating on some profound moment of spirituality.

As far as his aura was concerned, it was both.

"I guess I didn't realize I'd said it that way," he confessed, though he nodded his head as though agreeing nonetheless. "But, now that you mention it, I suppose it feels right to say that he's *not* doing it himself. I guess, if I didn't know any better, I'd have to say that he *was* being kept alive by... well, I don't know; being kept alive by *something*."

A long, confused silence passed.

"How bad is he?" Serena asked, though it felt like the question was more asked just so that she wouldn't have to suffer the silence any longer.

Though Estella had come to find the blonde vampire's urge to avoid silence somewhat off-putting at times, she was relieved for this particular effort.

Everyone else seemed to be, as well.

Still nodding, though now with a bit more vigor and purpose than before, Zeek turned back to Xander's body. His shirt had been cut away, exposing a torso littered in a visceral sort of graffiti that made Estella feel a wave of sickness with each look. Though there was still some blood drying inside his left ear and the blackened well that had once been his left eye had been left untouched—demanding more care and precision than anything some hand towels could offer—the rest of him had been cleaned well enough to make out the bulk of the various messages and symbols that had been carved into him.

"I could go on for days about all of the torn muscle fibers and internal bleeding," Zeek started. "He's got a break in his left ankle and a decent crack in his right femur. Neither of which are bad enough to demand attention over the rest of him. Pardon me for saying so, but whoever did this obviously wasn't interested in working much on his legs."

Estella took in the sight of the name "STRYKER" carved

lengthwise on his left side, rolling and dipping with each of his ribs. Surrounding the big, bloody letters, peppered in smaller, fairer ones, the word "die" had been carved several dozen times.

"They went to town on his ribs," Zeek went on, indicating with his pointer finger without making contact with Xander's midsection as he did. "Every single one's broken, most in more than one place. Same with his collarbone: broken and cracked; two total breaks on the right and one on the left."

The word "WEAK" was gouged in a long, shallow arch over Xander's stomach. In sloppy, uneven letters, "how many deaths will yo" was carved, unfinished, into the meat of Xander's left shoulder, starting a short distance from the side of his neck and curving around onto the top of his arm. Estella had to suppress the urge to trace her fingers across this, reminding herself that the horrible wounds wouldn't heal from her touch alone.

"He's got a pair of arms that will, best case scenario, never work right again. Right arm's broken in more places I feel comfortable counting without an X-Ray machine or an auric; wrist's dislocated, but that's hardly a concern. Same sentiment for the dislocated left shoulder, but not so much for the compound fracture he suffered here," Zeek held out his hand, palm up, towards where the skin was broken by a bone he'd since set back into place.

Estella forced herself to take in the multitude of crude eyes that had been carved all over his body. The almond-shaped symbols—sporting a hollow circle and, within this, another carved-out circle that served as a pupil—were scattered about in various sizes. The one at his throat was wide enough to arch around the sides of his neck and nearly merge with the 'h' in "how" that began the message that traveled to his shoulder. More eyes, some large and some quite small, were decorated around the wounds in his stomach; a trail of medium-sized ones seemed to travel up his right side. Another, carved vertically so that it would fit, took up his right bicep. Then, across each of his palms, was a pair of eyes that stared out from behind the thick bangs of his curled fingers. The words "ALWAYS" and "WATCHING" had been carved on the backs of his right and left hands accordingly.

"And," Zeek sighed, taking in the sight of Xander's hands, "as if those sick fucks weren't thorough enough already..." He carefully drew attention to Xander's left pointer finger while also nodding towards his right, "They broke both his trigger fingers, too." Shaking his head at this, Zeek straightened and gave Estella an apologetic look. "Could you help me turn him around?"

Estella bit her lip and nodded, extending her aura and lifting him as she had before so that Zeek could show them Xander's back. It was all she could do to not cry out at the question that waited in thick, bloody letters for them there: **"WHERE IS TREPIS NOW?"**

The spiral burn scar that Xander had grown up with since Kyle had held him against the stovetop as a child was now "highlighted" with a variety of jagged designs that stemmed from it. Estella thought these looked like something a child might do with chalk to an old runic symbol cast in concrete.

"The bruising here"—Zeek gestured to an area that was so purple it might as well have been black—"is a part of that internal bleeding I mentioned earlier; potential organ failure. Then there's his spine, which... well, let's just say his arms and trigger fingers will be the last of his concerns if he pulls out of this." He flinched at his own words, gave Estella an apologetic look, and then nodded for her to set him back down.

She did so. There, on his chest—the largest of the violent messages scrawled across her husband's flesh—the word "**ODIN**" stared back at her; each jagged line making up the letters the thickness of a finger.

"Meanwhile, to state the obvious: he's missing an eye," Zeek started to finish, "he's got a broken jaw and a busted nose, he's concuss, there's substantial trauma to his lungs—one's more than likely deflated from all the broken ribs—and, along with all the other love letters I'm sure you've been noticing carved all over him, somebody also decided to declare him a 'traitor' along the calf of his left leg." He groaned and shook his head, then wiped his face. He looked suddenly exhausted from the summary alone, and Estella began to wonder what the workload would do to him. His hand paused on his face to scratch absently at his cheek, and then he finished with, "Then there's the gash at the base of his belly," Zeek indicated the still furious-looking wound that he'd worked to return Xander's intestines back into. It still hung open like a stunned man's mouth. "I'm pretty sure whoever did this was hoping it would be the killing blow: disembowel him and leave him out in the sun for all the world to see."

Estella heard Sawyer growl "Bastards!" under his breath.

Dianna, who looked ready to cry, moved to hold him, but only got as far as his arm before a sob loosened itself from her throat; she muffled its followers into his shoulder.

Estella glanced back at Serena, who didn't seem to notice her looking. She just stared, her purple eyes transfixed on Xander's body, as her head swayed with slow, trembling passes from side-to-side. Estella wasn't sure if she knew she was shaking her head or if she was just having trouble keeping everything upright.

All around her, Estella saw everyone in some state of shock. The auric density of their combined sorrow was heavy enough that even those with no sense of how to perceive them seemed weighed down by it. Nobody spoke above a mumble, and what was said was neither surprising nor assisting in nature. Nobody knew what to do; nobody knew what to say.

Until...

"GET THE FUCK OUT OF MY WAY! THIS AIN'T A FUCKING FUNERAL! MOVE! I SAID MOVE IT, ASSHOLES!"

Serena's aura spiked and twisted before receding back into her body. "Son a whore! SETTLE THE FUCK DOWN, ZANE!"

"FUCK!" the small-yet-deafening voice of the Vaileans' first child, Gregori, chimed from the open office door—Sana and Tim working to reel the small vampire back inside with them.

Serena rolled her eyes and looked apologetically to Estella. "I'm sorry, Goddess," she said in a near-whisper—the closest Serena could get to a real whisper—"That kid's getting to be more like Zane every day."

"It's fine," Estella whispered back. She couldn't help but smirk, but her mind's eye told her she was the only one. "I'm sure this won't surprise you, but that particular word is making a constant appearance on the minds of just about everyone in here."

"I bet," Serena nodded, though it was a solemn and joyless nod, and gave one last, quick look towards Xander before turning to meet her husband. "And I doubt there's any pussy to go along with that otherwise beautiful, pussy-laden word."

"STAY UP THERE, LITTLE BUDDY!" Zane called up to Gregori before turning back to the task at hand and shouldering his way through the crowd, working his way towards Estella and the others. "The fuck you looking so goddam sad about?" he demanded when he'd finally reached them. He spared a glance at each of the others with a rapidity that bordered overdrive before locking eyes with Estella and taking Serena's hand into his own. "He's alive. He'll make it."

It wasn't a question.

Nothing about how he said it sounded uncertain.

A sang, bearing no ties to his aura save the natural connection he'd been born with, *knew* that Xander would be alright. The absurdity of it was a distant concern to Estella as she found herself smiling—*beaming!*—at this. She nodded. A heavy whimper on its way to being a sob slipped past her stretched lips. She kept nodding.

Behind them, she sensed Zoey and Isaac working their way more delicately through the crowd towards them.

"I understand that you weren't here for my breakdown of his injuries," Zeek began, "but—"

"He breathing?" asked Zane.

Zeek's aura shifted, almost seeming to recoil from the question. "Yes, but only bare—"

"His heart beating?" asked Zane.

Another auric twitch, this time a sag like impatient shoulders. "Yes, but, again, just—"

Zane nodded, seeming bored. "And we're still talking about Xander Stryker, right?"

This time Zeek visibly reacted, holding up his hands like he was about to lecture a child. It was the sort of gesture that Estella could imagine Zane using when trying to explain to Gregori why he was being unreasonable. "Yes. Yes, of course," the anapriek said, the "but" echoing-yet-unspoken on every word, but never getting the chance to be uttered.

"Good. I was beginning to get nervous," Zane spat. It felt more like an accusation—an attorney jabbing some obvious piece of evidence at a particularly dense opposition—and he let that linger a moment before offering a winning grin. Estella was sure it was that sort of grin that first got Serena under his arm. "Then work your anapriek magic—I hear your kind's pretty good with healing and such—and dump a few buckets of that ass-flavored synth blood into him. As luck would have it, the co-creator of the stuff is here"—he pointed a thumb back to Zoey as she slipped into view, and Estella had to wonder if there wasn't an auric trace to him—"and I'm certain you won't even have to ask to get her to help."

He moved to turn away, steering Serena with him and motioning for Estella to follow. She made no effort to resist; needing Zane's confidence that Xander would be alright at that moment.

"And, while it ain't gonna happen, I feel it's worth mentioning that, if Xander *does* die, I'm gonna feed your elfy ass to my not-always-furry buddy here," he added with a hearty pat to Isaac's shoulder as they passed him.

Estella sensed an angry spike at the threat to Zeek from Karen, but nothing more.

Everyone watched as the Vaileans retreated with Missus Stryker to the office at the top of the stairs. Zoey stayed behind with Zeek, already planning on helping with the care and healing of Xander; Isaac stayed with Zoey, feeling there was no other place in the world for him.

Estella felt the tears begin to fall, but much of the sorrow had left her at that moment.

BEHIND THEM, though nobody would have seen it otherwise, Xander and Ruby made a connection. It was, while not with their hands as Estella had imagined it, felt by both sides, and if anybody had been looking at that moment they might have seen the two of them give the slightest of twitches as it happened.

CHAPTER 9

ALL PATHS LEAD TO RUBY

"Time flies over us,
But leaves its shadow behind."
Nathaniel Hawthorne (1804-1864)

It shows him the 'what if's.

It shows him the 'never was.'

It shows different channels; paths.

It shows everything... and nothing.

Xander does not like what he is seeing.

Xander does not know what he is seeing.

Xander does not believe what he is seeing.

Xander does not understand what he is seeing.

But, most of all, Xander does not know how to stop seeing what he is seeing.

They are not dreams—Xander has dreamed quite a bit and is beginning to know the difference without being sure how *he knows the difference—but they were things he experiences in his prolonged, extended unconsciousness.*

He watches as time winds back, dialing itself to before he was born. His father and a team he'd specially chosen for an important mission cross a foggy barrier as they ascend a particularly terrible mountain in Romania. They are not successful, but, then again, they never had been. However, time has not wound back for a rerun. No. And this run's failure is in no way a repeat of the one their time had known. In this run, Xander sees the failure that his father suffered extend further; the failure that motivated his father and Stan to lock away their target within her castle is not enough. The sliver of success to come from that mission, in this new run, is an all-out failure. In this alternate path, Lenuta breaks free. Xander watches through eyes that are everywhere and nowhere—all-seeing as only a god could be, he imagines—and sees the murderous varcol's horde stop them at the door, keeping them away from the freedom and opportunity that waited just beyond. Watching and unable to do anything more, Xander sees what remains of his father's team as they are dispatched one-by-one; the mythos subduing Joseph and Stan—the auras of many holding their own at bay while the arms of many others keep their bodies pinned and immobile—baring their teeth and hate. Lenuta comes, all purrs and impurity, boasting a new heart and a vendetta ripe and ready for harvest. Xander watches, screaming from a mouth that is not there with air that did not exist, as he is shown an alternate timeline where Lenuta wins—Joseph Stryker torn down, fed from, raped in every way a person could be, and thrown off the mountain for the wolves to scavenge upon. Then, free to do so, Lenuta sets upon the world; sets her sights on the Stryker line first and foremost.

In this time—with the dominos falling as they would had a single domino not fallen to the left, but, rather, to the right—Xander's mother never makes it to childbirth; in this time Xander never was.

The pain of nonexistence hurts more than he ever imagined.

It steers him back, sets the single domino right and travels forward. Time rights, and Xander sees himself born. He cries, small and frail and uncertain, and his mother cries, also small and also frail and, yes, also uncertain. Xander sees this through his own eyes but with a mind that is wiser than it was; wiser than it ever will be. He hears, in a mind that is both his own and is not, a voice, familiar and strange all at once; it sounds like life and death made one:

"I gave it all I had, son, but I'll stay as long as I can."

Xander cries, both a baby and a man, and isn't sure any longer where one stops and the other begins.

Time moves again.

It shows him more.

It shows him the day that Kyle first found his mother. Time and its dominos reset, Lenuta is, as she had been and as she should have been, locked away in her tower; a fairy tale villain the likes of which were commonplace in the storybooks Xander's mother used to read him. With Lenuta locked away, Kyle—her lapdog; her lover; his loathsome bane—has been sent, as he was and as he should have been, to target them, the wife and son of Joseph Stryker. But in this new time—in a new path wherein a single domino sets forth a path that never was—Kyle is found; the predator, so engrossed in stalking its prey, is caught unaware by an even greater predator. In this new time, on this new path, a humble warrior of the Odin Clan—an auric armed with nothing more than a semi-automatic and the hopes of living up to the late, great Joseph Stryker—sees a particularly shady-looking auric stalking the surviving Stryker family. Just a loving mother and her innocent son: a doe and its fawn. And Kyle, neither hungry nor sporting, is only a hunter acting on orders and a sadist's hunger for pain and misery. In this time, the fortuitous Odin warrior catches sight of his intentions and, considering Joseph Stryker as he did so, ended Kyle's personal line of dominos then and there.

Xander and his mother never know the pain and torment he'd inflict on them, and—oh!—how Xander, watches this and knowing the alternative, celebrates. He gets to watch himself grow, gets to see himself smile through years he'd never smiled through, gets to see himself grow certain and strong, grow close to new friends and, best of all, grow close to Estella. He gets to watch himself slip into his teen years never having known a beating so severe he'd miss school. He gets to see himself ride bikes and play video games; he gets to learn that, if left unobstructed, he'd take an interest in acting and go on to star in the school play alongside Estella. He sees them share their first kiss in rehearsals, and he sees them never stop kissing since.

Xander cries without tears from eyes that aren't there. He mourns the nonexistence of this timeline; one that is so perfect that it seems a cruel joke that things will happen as they do.

He watches on; his all-seeing non-eyes unobstructed by his tearless weeping.

He watches himself grow, celebrating birthdays that his mother helped plan that, in actuality, she will never get to see. He watches as...

He watches as she grows sick.

He watches as life and vigor bleed from her body. Learns of the cancer in her bones—a vampiric force feasting on her very essence—that has gone unnoticed too long. He watches himself, grief-stricken, fall, and, having never fallen so hard before, watches how badly it breaks him. He only acts for the masses now, pretending to care when, in fact, he can't bring himself to feel a thing for any of it. Xander sees himself in this new timeline, turning his back on the masks of comedy and tragedy and wearing one of bitter indifference. He watches as this alternate Xander grows cold to all, especially himself and the voice in his head that has been with him all along. This Xander has never known pain; has never known loss or what it meant to hate—truly hate—how things turned out. Now—in this new "now"—he is too old, too ill-equipped to handle a loss that is not yet a loss, a loss that he watches slowly decay what had, on a day long ago and by the hands of a humble auric warrior he'd never know or get to thank, been gifted to him. Xander watches as, on the night his mother finally slips away, he sneaks into Estella's room, climbing with a body made strong with years of play and activity, into her bedroom window.

Xander watches himself say goodbye to this new timeline's Estella. He does not kiss her as he always had before; he can barely bring himself to even look at her.

He only says "goodbye."

Then Xander watches as this other him, running home and listening to the voice in his head crying "NO! DON'T!" over and over, take a nine-inch length of painful familiarity from his dead mother's knife block and retreats to a hot shower and a cold end.

Xander sees this timeline fade to black—curtain's down—*and he bobs, nonexistent, in an ethereal void that is neither white nor black—neither light nor dark—because such things exist solely for minds, living minds, that can perceive of such things.*

And in this timeline, Xander Stryker is dead and unable to perceive of anything.

But still he is somehow able to perceive of the Estella of that alternate reality; able to hear her cries and feel the impact of every tear like the collisions of a world-ending meteor shower.

I get it, *he speaks through cold, dead lips to the thing showing him these things.* I don't need to see any more. I don't want to see any more.

It shows him more.

The domino representing Kyle is reset, and in a flash that was more sensation than light Xander goes from being dead to being miserable.

The dominos dance in a flurry of taunts:

The Odin Clan survives the attack? Lenix's efforts against them during Xander's transformation is thwarted and he is defeated? Xander awakes, unaware and goes on untold, and exists as he would: as a warrior, beloved and accepted, but never anything more. A year later, when the murder of Marcus and the attack on Estella should *have happened, all seems well.*

Xander and Marcus were as brothers, brothers with a great secret between them: that of the figure who'd stepped out of the Stryker history for revenge.

Xander and Estella were as lovers, lovers with a great divide between them: that of strength and power and longevity; one doomed to forever play the role of prey to a world of predators starved for her blood.

The toll of not knowing and the burden of constantly protecting...

This timeline is saturated with potential tragedies; the catastrophic outcomes growing greater and closer together with each fall of a domino until every waking second represents a spider's web of potential disaster.

Xander watches the Odin Clan perish a thousand times.

He watches Estella murdered in a million different ways.

He is shown each and every possible failure he commits—too many for even a force as great as this to illustrate.

And he experiences all of it—every agonizing possibility—in the blink of a nonexistent eye.

GOD DAMN YOU! *Xander swears without voice at the force that shows him such things.* GOD FUCKING DAMN YOU! WHAT DO YOU WANT? WHY ARE YOU SHOWING ME—

It grows tired of his curses and his inquiries.

Once more time rewinds. Once more time resets.

And on again time moves.

Xander hurts. He doesn't think it's possible to hurt so badly with no body to know pain, but, as he is quickly learning, pain is like sunlight; a body like a house. A house can have many windows or very few, perhaps even none, and the amount of light—the amount of pain—it let in was limited and entirely up to the mind occupying the home.

Now Xander knows what it was to be scalded by pain.

True pain.

Estella...

Xander does not know how he says it—does not even know if he says it—but the name gives him strength. Then Xander says something—and this time he is certain that he has—that he does not understand:

Ruby!

It, however, knows; it understands. It says it will show him.

I don't want to see any more!

YOU MUST SEE!

And it shows him.

It shows him the 'what if's.

It shows him the 'never was.'

It shows different channels; paths.

It shows everything... and nothing.

Xander does not like what he is seeing.

Xander does not know what he is seeing.

Xander does not believe what he is seeing.

Xander does not understand what he is seeing.

But, most of all, Xander does not know how to stop seeing what he is seeing.

As a vampire, Xander Stryker has suffered the sun—has suffered the pain of the sun—every time he's allowed its rays to touch his skin. Now, as nothing—as everything—he suffers pain as he is certain the lingering cells of his flesh know it: overwhelming, relentless, and glorious.

Time does not need to move back to show him this sequence.

It shows him the here, the now.

And then it moves forward; a snowflake hitting a hill and rolling, rolling, and rolling still—gaining mass and momentum and, finally, becoming something great and unstoppable.

Estella is...

Oh my—

The fate of the world shifts to one of sudden greatness; Xander suddenly can't remember why.

It means nothing if you do not see!

But Xander isn't sure he wants to see. Doubt floods him, and he closes eyes that do not exist, daring to peek through only at bits and pieces.

Why? *he wonders,* Why again is the fate of the world more important?

RUBY!

What about her?

SEE!

But time does not stop—time never stops—and he's already missed so much.

Another domino falls, and Xander sees himself with Zane and Isaac and Sawyer and...

No... Oh god, Sawyer. I'm so—

Xander clenches his eyes; Xander forgets.

SEE!

I WON'T!

YOU MUST!

Xander dares a glance.

Another domino falls, and Xander stands before a small army of mythos—all banded and sided with him against the world; against...

The Cebourists!

The murderous, mythos-hating worshipers have found new leaders, powerful leaders, but they and their magic stands little chance against Xander, because Xander has...

Their magic? Why would I...?

SEE!

Tragedy. Death. Tragedy. Death. Pain, pain, pain. Flesh and eyes.

Xander doesn't want to see; he's had enough of tragedy and death and pain.

He forgets as fast as he is shown.

Then he spots something he can't block out:

Estella!

Running! Running so fast and so hard that his body is tearing at the seams. He is—yes, he is*—on course to her, but time...*

Oh, time moves back-and-forth so easily in this place of unconsciousness; so fluidly from side-to-side and back again...

But Xander sees, in that instant, that he'll never make it in time.

Estella...

*Estella's life and so much more—*Why the fuck can't I remember what else there could be? What could mean more than Estella?*—was on the line...*

But Xander will never be fast enough.

FUCK YOU! RESET THE DAMN DOMINOS! DO IT AGAIN!

AGAIN! AS MANY TIMES AS IT TAKES! THERE'S GOT TO BE A REALITY WHERE I—

There isn't.

In no reality—in no possible scenario—will Xander Stryker ever make it to Estella and that which he's blinded himself to in time.

He will fail.

Aleks will...

NO! *Xander closes his nonexistent eyes, turns his nonexistent body, and blocks out that nonexistent force as it tries again and again to show him.*

The nonexistent voice rages on: **SEE!**

But he's made up his mind.

He will see no more.

He's been shown an inescapable future where he is unable to save Estella and something that made his success that much more imperative. Such a failure isn't worth watching.

He will sooner die than go through a future without Estella.

It'd be better to never wake up... *he resigns and reaches out across the abyss of unconsciousness for any hope.*

Ruby...

What about her? *Xander demands, but then he sees her.*

She is close to him. So close that it seems impossible he hasn't seen her there before. So close that, even without moving, he can practically reach out his hand and take hers.

His hand does not move.

Nor does Ruby's.

But a connection is made all the same.

Xander?

Estella?

Hey, Ruby.

Just... just stay with me, okay? It'll—

How are you...?

SEE!

I'm not sure. Sort of taking everything as it comes. It's hard to explain.

I'm so sorry.

I bet. Nothing's ever easy for people like us, is it?

E-Estella... I love Xander; I always have.

No. I suppose it isn't.

Estella, I'm sorry.

I'm sorry, Xander.

SEE!

I'm tired of seeing, *Xander declares to the force.* Leave me alone!

It does.

Xander blinks—not with real eyes, but with a familiar sense of being that he welcomes all the same—and looks up, seeing Ruby standing there across from him. He recognizes this, welcomes it, as existing in the mind of another with his aura.

And he understands.

Estella, you wonderful woman! You found me! *he thinks, forgetting that thoughts are as good as words in the minds of others.*

Huh? *Ruby stares back at him, looking confused for a number of reasons.* How... how are you here? And where is here? *she asks.*

We're in your mind, *Xander explains.* We're together in your mind, and that means that we—our bodies, I mean—are likely still unconscious back at the mansion.

Oh, *Ruby says, looking around with a new appreciation for her surroundings.* That's good to know, I guess.

Xander isn't sure he can agree that knowing things are good at that moment, but he feels better knowing that much, at least.

CHAPTER 10

OF WHAT'S TO COME

"It is during our darkest moments that we must focus to see the light."
Aristotle (384-322 BC)

"Estella—honey, doll, Goddess, and all-around gothic babe!—I don't think you're truly considering the big picture here," Serena prattled as she, in a single fluid motion that undoubtedly carried with it many hours of repeated practice, used her teeth to simultaneously tear open and retrieve one of the many individually wrapped miniature Snickers bars laid out before them. Then, with her mouth full: "You're pregnant!" This she said in mid-chew while pushing another half-sized candy bar across the table to Estella while, with the opposite hand, retrieving another for herself. "You got a bun in the oven! Your eggers is preggers! This getting through to you? You're eating for two, a baby-momma, and, in no other words, a fleshy sperm-sock for the congealing jism of Xander-fucking-Stryker!"

Estella stared at Serena as she retrieved the candy, opened

it, and took a bite. "I think there's quite a lot of other words for it, actually. But, yes, I know I'm pregnant."

"Well no-shit you *know*, 'Stell; you might not be showing, but it's pretty fucking obvious for anyone with half a brain to see it." She smirked and repeated the tear-and-stuff process with another mini-Snickers. "And I should know, 'cause I'm a blonde—I've only naturally got half a brain, and I was the first to see it."

Zoey sighed and rolled her eyes. "You're an inspiration to blondes everywhere to follow my example and dye both fully and frequently."

Estella misheard "dye" as "die" and felt her insides knot. A moment later she found herself wondering why and reached for another Snickers. Both Serena and Zoey paused to watch her, and she wondered how much of her thoughts might have been broadcast on her aura. After a moment she decided that her mind was still closed off and they were, in fact, more startled that she'd taken another candy bar on her own.

"That's my girl," Serena beamed before sending yet another Snickers across the table and taking another for herself.

There were over a dozen bags of the things—where Serena had been keeping them seemed to be one of the blonde's most coveted secrets—and they'd made an appearance mere seconds after the small group had retreated to the office. Forty minutes later, which amounted to two bags and plenty of bad dirty jokes, Estella was beginning to feel a bit better. Around that time, Zoey and Isaac stepped inside. After explaining that she and Zeek had exhausted their reserves for the synth blood and they would have to go out to get the supplies to make more in the near-future, she'd taken a seat at the table, stared down at all the candies littered across its surface, and asked if she could have one.

"Nope!" Serena barked with a mouthful of peanuts and chocolate. "These here're prego-candies."

Frowning at that, Estella had begun to argue in Zoey's defense.

This had been the catalyst for Serena's pregnancy rant.

"And because of that Zoey can't have a candy bar?" Estella demanded.

Zoey shook her head. "It's fine, Estella. Really. I know better than to argue with Serena, *especially* when she's pregnant!"

Serena rolled her eyes and rolled a balled fist under her left eye while she used her free hand to feed herself another candy. "Oh boo-fucking-hoo, ya bitchy, blue-haired baby! I said you couldn't have one of my pregnancy Snickers! Never said nothin' 'bout not being allowed to have a candy bar!" With that she retrieved a king-sized Three Musketeers bar from her stash and worked it between the limited-yet-available opening of Zoey's cleavage. "There ya go, champ!"

Zoey smirked at the gesture, shook her head, and motioned to Isaac, who was seated with Zane on the couch at the other side of the office. "You want half?" she offered.

Before Isaac could answer, Serena jumped to her feet and slammed her palms on the table's surface hard enough to make the candies jump; a few of the wrappers caught the updraft of air and flew away like startled birds.

"NO!" she roared, pointing an accusatory finger at Zoey. "That's YOUR candy! YOURS! Isaac gets..." she trailed off and sat back down, beginning to once again rummage through her stash. "Ah! Here!"

A moment later two Almond Joys flew across the room, thudding lamely against Isaac's chest and falling into his lap.

Isaac stared back at her, unimpressed.

"Get it?" Serena demanded. "GET IT? A pair of nuts! PAIR... OF... NUTS! As in bust a nut in poor Zoey so she can get in on these pregnancy Snickers!"

"Serena!" Zoey was trying to sound shocked, maybe even offended, but the effort was lost with the giggles that slipped through.

Estella looked around a bit, then shook her head. “Seems like a lot of thought went into this.”

“Damn right,” said Serena, already chewing on a fresh bar.

Estella hadn’t even seen her open a new one.

“She’s pregnant,” Zane said as though it explained everything.

Strangely enough, Estella realized that it did.

“So does Zane get a candy bar?” asked Estella.

Serena looked up at her, swallowing the wad of pulpy sweetness she’d been working on and making no move to replace it with another. “Why would he get a candy bar?” she demanded, sounding almost irate at the notion.

Estella shrugged. “He helped you get pregnant. Feels like it should count for something.”

Serena folded her arms across her chest, shot Zane a look, and then looked back at Estella. “And what, pray tell,” she drawled, “do you think Zane should get for all his grinding and thrusting?”

Blushing at that, Estella shrugged again. “I don’t know. Maybe, like, a peanut butter cup or something.”

The rest of the room, save for little Gregori, stared at her. Cheeks burning at the attention, Estella tried to pretend to focus on Gregori’s antics, and saw that he was busy overseeing the heated battle between an armless action figure with long black hair and a red jacket and a Transformers figure that, from the looks of it, turned from a giant dragon to something infinitely more hideous.

Though she hadn’t intended for the distraction to actually become distracting, something about the sight seemed relevant.

But the weight of those expectant stares wouldn’t let her dwell on it.

“A peanut butter cup?” Serena pressed, sounding far too diplomatic for the subject at hand.

Sighing, Estella looked back up at her and said, “I guess,

yeah. Because, you know, they've got, like, mushed-up peanuts inside the chocolate—Daddy—and Mommy's bar is all lumpy and full of almost fully intact peanuts and all sorts of goopy caramel and such inside." She shrugged and hurried to get another Snickers bar into her mouth, finding comfort in not having to make sense around a full mouth. "Sort of like the whole pregnancy process, right?"

Serena stared at her for a long moment. Then she shared a look with Zoey before looking back at Zane, who, in turn, shared a look with Isaac.

They all started laughing. It was a good laugh. It was the sort of laugh that served as one of only two potential outcomes for the sort of day they'd been through. And, as nobody was being killed or maimed, it was undeniably the better of the two potential outcomes.

Estella blushed, wishing she could laugh like that, but only managed a weak-yet-sincere chuckle.

"HO—*ack-hock!*—HOLY FUCKING SHIT!" Serena cried out, nearly choking on residual Snicker juice. "Did..." she gasped and slapped the table in hysterics, belting out another bout of laughter before finally saying, "Did you just tell a jizz joke, Missus Stryker?"

"I... I guess I did," Estella confessed.

Then she found herself laughing a bit more heartily.

Gregori looked up from his toys at the sound of the laughing, spotted the candies littered across the table for the first time, and jumped to his feet. The one-armed action figure was thrown aside, vanishing somewhere under the couch, and he clutched the transforming dragon toy while reaching towards Serena with his now-free hand.

"Mommy, can I have a chocolate?"

The laughter died down as everyone, having just seen Serena's rigid policy regarding candy and its assigned placement, waited to see where her son fit into things.

Serena cocked her head, fed another mini-Snickers bar into

her mouth, and said, "I don't know, kiddo. You know how you get when you've had sugar."

Gregori gave her a look that, as far as Estella was concerned, was the perfect blend of Serena's "fuck you"-vulgarity and Zane's "I will end you"-aggression. But there was something more there, as well; a sort of cold wisdom that seemed almost terrifying on such a young face. "You're giving *that* baby chocolate!" he accused her while jabbing a small finger towards her belly. "And he doesn't even know how to 'preciate it!" He stomped his foot and Estella watched as his aura flared up with a startling accuracy towards the table before stopping in mid-reach; a child defiantly reaching for the cookie jar but deciding at the last minute to try asking once more. "And besides," he thrust his balled fists against his hips, "you get worst than anybody when you get sugar, and you already ate more than anybody else!"

Isaac and Zane worked to stifle their laughter at the sight of the child scolding Serena.

Zoey looked like she wanted to applaud him.

Estella stared, awestruck at the sheer display of power she'd witnessed from the boy.

Serena just glared.

"You're a little shit when you want something, you know that, kiddo?" she finally asked.

Gregori beamed at this as though it was the greatest of compliments. "'Course, Mommy. 'Cause you are, too!"

"That's fair," Serena laughed at this and nodded, ushering her son over with an open arm. "Come on, then; come get sugar-high with Momma and your baby brother."

Gregori squealed with delight and vanished from the center of the room—the transforming dragon toy dropping to the floor where he'd stood—and suddenly occupying the space under his mother's arm, a Snickers bar already unwrapped and half-buried in his chewing mouth.

Overdrive, too? Estella marveled.

"This mean I'm gonna get that peanut butter cup?" Zane called over.

Without looking up from Gregori, Serena shook her head. "Nope. You'd just get fat."

This earned a few chuckles around the room, but nothing like before.

The energy, Estella could really think of no other word for it in this case, had dried up.

Though it seemed mean to her, Estella noticed that Serena's comment (or refusal to share candy) hadn't had much of an impact on her husband. Like before—like nothing had happened—he sat, leaning back on the couch with his legs spread and arms draped out. Isaac sat beside him, upright and all clean angled—a confident-yet-reserved posture. If Xander were sitting there with them, Estella imagined, he'd be knit-up; knees pressed together, leaning forward—almost folding himself—and resting his arms across his legs. He'd stare off—wearing neither Zane's all-inclusive gaze of a world that was his plaything nor the skeptical-yet-optimistic view that Isaac adopted—and only two things would be obvious: he was thinking and he was sorry about something.

It hurt Estella to imagine her husband that way, but it was like trying to imagine a summer sky without thinking of the color blue.

This, in turn, got her to thinking about Serena's hormone-driven rant—*"You're pregnant!"*—and she began to wonder...

"Zane, what was it like for you when you found out Serena was pregnant with Gregori?"

The question birthed itself with only a marginal conception within her mind. Details like how different Zane and Xander were—details that would have otherwise made Estella think twice about asking him such a question for a frame of reference—didn't have a chance to come into being let alone become variables to determine whether she was asking the right person.

This, however, would have been an irrelevant concern, as it wasn't the person she asked that came to answer:

Serena, in a display that seemed almost impossible, cackled, smiled reassuringly, scoffed, and swooned all at once. Then, feeding herself another mini-Snickers and sliding two more in Estella's direction, she said, "He cried like a baby—no shitting you, 'Stell, just like a baby—and started swinging me around like you see guys doing in those cheesy commercials."

Zane scowled at his wife's unflattering description, but he did nothing to argue against it. Estella noticed his knees draw closer together as he sat more upright; his arms came down, one coming to occupy the armrest and the other folded casually across his lap.

Suddenly he and Isaac seemed to be a lot more alike.

Estella considered this, wasn't sure what to make of it, and looked back to Serena, wondering how she might steer this response back to the vicinity of what she wanted—*needed*—to hear. Unsure of what to say, she didn't speak. Embarrassed, she felt both Serena and Zane looking at her, analyzing her in their own ways.

Through her mind's eye, she saw Zane make a subtle gesture in Isaac's direction, then, looking to Zoey, she sensed a spike in his aura that had the blue-haired auric glancing back at him. Estella, making no move to show that she'd noticed this, wondered if he understood what he'd done to create that auric "call"—whether it was a certain thought or emotion that he'd learned to use as a sort of psychic bell to get his friend's attention—but, in either case, it worked. The threads of communication passed between them, and a moment later Zane and Zoey rose to their feet and, as though rehearsed, switched places, Zoey settling in beside Isaac on the couch while he took his place beside her and Serena.

While this went on, Serena's face had shifted from one of perverse good humor and near-diabetes inducing levels of sugar highness to one of stern assessment. It was an alien look for her, but, in a strange way, also a fitting one. Without a word —not a spoken one, at least—Serena grabbed the open bag of Snickers, which still had what looked to be ten or so candies left inside, passed it off to her son, and nodded for him to return to his play.

Eyes flashing electric at the sugar-laden bribe, Gregori just as wordlessly retreated back to the center of the room, his aura absently reaching out to retrieve his other toy from under the couch.

"Be honest, hun," Serena said, drawing Estella's attention back to the table and sliding over another Snickers to join with the untouched others and setting her hand over top Estella's, "you don't give a rat's friction-burned nutsack about how Zane felt about being a daddy, do you?"

Estella blinked at the question, a part of her curious how somebody could word it in such a way and still look so straight-faced—even moreso that she'd actually managed to pull it off as a serious question—while the other felt a twinge of embarrassment. She hadn't fooled anybody. Feeling the heat intensify in her cheeks, Estella pulled her hand away and retrieved the Snickers bars. Working to mimic Serena's movements, she worked two of the bars into her mouth, chewed furiously, swallowed half the syrupy-sweet wad of nutty chocolate, and then crammed in the third.

Zane and Serena stayed quiet, letting her work out her thoughts and emotions on the bars.

Finally, choking down the last of the candy in her mouth, Estella slipped her hand back under Serena's. It felt right there. Serena offered a smile, not seeming to care that there was still chocolate smeared on the fingers she now massaged with her thumb.

"I was wondering how Xander would react..." Estella finally said.

Neither of the two seemed surprised.

They shared a look, swapping no judgement in the process.

Estella imagined two athletes mapping out a particularly complicated play, considering all number of factors and conditions. She wondered what she'd gotten herself into.

Serena gave a single nod, giving away that there'd been some sort of conversation going on—Estella found herself simultaneously relieved that her mind was back to filtering her psychic abilities and nervous that she had no idea what to expect from them any longer—and looked past her towards Zoey and Isaac.

Estella followed the path of her gaze and caught Zoey staring back at Serena with an intensity that told her that there was another psychic conversation going on around her. A few seconds later, Zoey nodded, gave Isaac an extended, not-just-a-look look, and the two rose from the couch and started for the door.

Save for the dramatic exhalations from Gregori as he went back to playing, the room was silent as the door *click*ed shut, leaving the Vaileans alone with Estella.

Biting her lip, she turned back to face the rest of the table.

She asked, "So where did you send them?"

Zane shrugged. "Zoey said they needed supplies to make more synth blood. Figured there was no time like the present," he explained as though it was the real reason they'd left.

"Plus they need to fuck," Serena added, still straight-faced. "We need to fuck, too. And you—I'm sure you and Xander are going to break down some walls once he's up and running again."

Though this seemed like a more acceptable reason—other than the truth: to give the three of them some privacy—Estella caught herself glancing back towards Gregori, wondering what sort of reaction she'd see from him regarding Serena's statement.

If the little boy had heard, he didn't seem to care one way or the other.

The one-armed action figure seemed to have come back

around and was beginning a relentless assault on the transforming dragon.

"I don't suppose we can open another—" Estella started to ask as she turned back, only to discover that Serena was setting a fresh bag of Fun-Sized Snickers between them.

"Fun-sized" my pregnant ass! Estella thought, and immediately caught herself in yet another uncharacteristic moment of vulgar cynicism. She began to wonder if it was Xander or Serena to blame, but decided it wasn't worth it to decide and tore into the bag of candy.

"What do you think of Zane?" Serena asked after Estella had finished her first bar from the new bag.

Estella stared back at her, confused, and then looked at Zane, gauging his expression, in the hopes of gaining an understanding of where this was going.

He stared back, indifferent. His mismatched eyes took her in with the same patience as Serena, and Estella became painfully aware of Xander's missing eye.

She looked away; looked down. She didn't want the Vaileans to see her cry.

"I... I don't understand what you're asking," she said, ignoring the cracks in her voice as she did.

Serena's hand returned to hers.

Estella began to feel a wisp of dizziness that passed and made way for a strange sort of calm. Her breathing slowed, and she got to genuinely appreciate the next flood of air—cooling and calming—as it flooded her nostrils and filled her chest.

Estella realized with no real feelings one way or the other that it was Serena's left hand resting on hers. She was calling upon her auric abilities and draining some of her pain away, offering a bit of clarity as she did.

"What do you think of Zane, sweetie?" Serena repeated, slower and sweeter this time.

Estella thought on this a moment—thought distantly that

Serena was a lot like a Snickers bar, nutty and sweet; a forbidden indulgence—and felt herself smiling.

"I think he's who Xander might have been if he'd been allowed to live the life that was meant for him," she said, her voice airy. She could hear the smile on that voice.

It sounded nice.

She wished Xander could hear it.

A tear welled in her left eye, and a drop of sadness rose within her. A blink loosed the tear, sent it rolling away—salty clarity—and the sadness evaporated. Serena inhaled, seemed to breathe in the steam of her sadness. She made a face that had Estella thinking about lemons and bad medicine. Then she was smiling again.

"I like that," Serena said in a mother's voice. "And I like that Zane and Xander found each other, don't you? I like that they get to balance one another out."

"Yes," Estella's smile crept upward, and she felt it tighten her cheeks, brighten her eyes. "They're good friends. They're good balance. Like Yin and Yang."

Estella remembered something Xander had said, something distressing that seemed suddenly clear, obvious. Serena's thumb caressed her hand, seeming to wipe away the bad thoughts.

Estella could not remember what had seemed obvious. She did not mind.

"Yin and yang," Serena repeated, smiling and nodding. "Yes, that's a good way to look at it. Different, but also the same, right?"

"Right," Estella agreed, lulling her head to the side to look at Zane. A sort of sadness that did not make her feel sad came, and Serena's auric touch left this for her. Tears came, but they were not the bad kind. No. She stared at Zane, and he, seeming to know what she needed, stared back, quiet and understanding. "How..." Estella tilted her head, thinking she could almost see the answer just beyond the gruff features if she looked hard enough. They were there—like the words on the opposite page of a dampened text—but it felt like too much work to read them there. Finally she asked, "How did you feel... in here"—she dragged her free hand, which felt long and heavy, across the table and set it over Zane's heart—"when you found out?"

"I knew"—Zane spoke like God; spoke like scripture; spoke like Xander—"that I had a lot more to fight for. I knew that my life had taken on new meaning; that I was suddenly more important and, at the same time, so much less significant. I was scared, Estella, and I'd never been happier."

Estella hadn't realized how tired she'd gotten, and it occurred to her that she hadn't slept in over twenty-four hours. In that time her world had inflated, crumbled, burned, shriveled, and scattered. Now she had Xander.

She had Xander.

She had her family.

And she had her answer.

"Xander..." she whispered, still smiling, and she felt Zane's arms wrap around her and lift her from her chair—Serena's hand never leaving hers—and carry her to the couch.

"He'll be with us soon, Goddess," a golden angel's voice chimed from far, far above her. "And then you'll get to fuck, too."

CHAPTER 11

"HOW MANY PEOPLE WANNA KICK SOME ASS?"

"We are twice armed if we fight with faith."
Plato (427-347 BC)

"Damn looters! It's impossible to find anyplace that hasn't been completely ransacked!" Zoey groused as Isaac maneuvered the rusted VW Bug that might, at one time, have been orange around another corner.

This block, like every block before it, featured a stretch of broken windows, rolling smoke plumes, and wailing alarms that weren't likely to be soon answered. Isaac took in the scenery with passive interest, the unobservant eye of a man who didn't know what he was looking for but yearned to appear useful in the search, and let his thoughts drift to simpler times.

When he'd been the leader of a therion pack, living out in the woods and thriving on what the land had to offer, it had all been so different. Granted, even then Isaac had some exotic interests—what his pack might have called "unconventional" if they'd cared enough to put a word to it (which they didn't)—and, with these interests, a slightly more complicated set of processes to indulge in them. A love of music and a drive to play the violin, for one, had posed him with an interesting challenge: how to get one. His other interests, such as literature and art, were simple enough to pursue—there was never a shortage of discarded or easy-to-steal books, and there were always plenty of street artists for a patient eye to appreciate—and a trip out of the woods and into the city was never stingy with those needs. But music was an entirely different sort of challenge. One such challenge presented itself in a way he'd since started taking for granted: simply *listening* to music. This, though solved with a bit of luck when he happened upon a discarded Walkman and a stack of classical CDs inside the dumpster of an old record shop, paled against the challenge of *playing* music, however. Musical instruments, as it turned out, weren't the sort of thing people simply threw out—not without good reason, of course. What he did find was damaged beyond use, though these proved useful in at least learning some basic lessons in the mechanics of the instruments. And one particular violin, bowless and suffering from some awful trauma stemming from one of the f-holes and networking across the upper and lower bouts, still had a meticulous set of color-coded tape laid out across the fingerboard that had helped him practice his placement for a time. All of this, however, did nothing to allow him to play; to have a genuine moment with a working instrument and apply what he'd only experienced in bits and pieces from pilfered books on music or humming along to his Walkman.

Until he'd finally come up with a diabolical idea of how to fulfill his needs.

Isaac nearly slammed on the brakes as this memory led him back to the present with a solution to their current problem.

"What about the college?"

"What?" Zoey looked over at him, squinting through her confusion.

"The college," he repeated, nodding to himself. "It wasn't one of my proudest moments, but I stole one of my first violins from the music department of one of the local colleges back at home. It's relatively easy to get into—people are always coming and going at all hours—and, provided you look like you're meant to be there and not up to anything wrong, you could pretty much walk out with anything without anybody saying anything. One of the security guards even asked if I smoked during his break *while* I was walking out with the violin case. I don't think they're paid enough to really care, and they weren't about to think that something like an instrument represented a theft in progress. I'm guessing that whatever we need would be available there—chemistry and medicine stuff and all—and, since most of that stuff is locked up anyway, the fact that you were even able to get to the stuff would make most security guards assume you had a key or something. Besides, even *if* somebody tries to stop us, you could just"—he snapped his fingers—"and they'd leave us alone."

Zoey thought about this for a moment. "But what about the students? The faculty?"

Isaac shrugged. "So what? Assuming any of them actually went in with the crisis and all, what would it matter? Look:" he nodded towards the empty street ahead of them, "I'm guessing that these cleared streets are *your* doing, right?"

Zoey's blush was answer enough.

Isaac nodded. "Exactly! And even *if* there was somebody on this street, how hard would it be for you to enter their heads and make them think we weren't here? Or even to make them think we were Godzilla or something and send them running?"

"Not hard at all," Zoey said with a chuckle.

Another nod. "Exactly!" Isaac smirked.

"But what if somebody else already thought to raid their supplies?" she asked, motioning out towards a set of broken windows in front of a pharmacy. "Pretty much any place that *could* be robbed *has* been robbed."

"Funny thing about criminals:" Isaac said, "they tend to avoid prisons and they tend to ignore schools. Damnedest thing, I know."

Zoey giggled. "How'd I get lucky enough to fall for a genius like you?"

Isaac grinned and turned the Bug around. "We'll save the debate for who lucked out for another time," he said. Then, remembering his train of thought from earlier, he added, "I hope you won't mind if I steal myself a new violin, as well."

"ARE YOU PIG-FUCKS *REALLY* GOING TO CHASE ME ALL DAY WHEN THERE'S *ANYTHING-FUCKING-ELSE* YOU COULD BE PUTTING YOUR AUTHORITATIVE DUTIES TOWARDS?" Serena screamed at the half-dozen blazing sirens that screamed after her and her stolen BMW i8 Coupe.

The blood-red gem of German engineering in all its glory roared around a corner, handling like a wet dream on wheels—Serena tried to ignore the tiny bursts of orgasm-like delight that rippled through her as she and the car made sweet, dirty love with the road—and she made a note of hanging her left arm out the window and wagging her middle finger for every one of the limp-dick cops to ogle as they struggled to keep up. She cackled as they failed.

Failed *miserably!*

Two of the cop cars collided in mid-turn. Another botched the hairpin entirely, jumped the curb, and lodged its ass-end in the already busted window of a raided bakery. Of the last three, only one managed to not lose all momentum in the turn and actually managed to keep the needle around sixty as it did.

"That's cute," Serena cooed, clutching and shifting, then, wetting her lips, tickling the gear shift with her index finger and imagining it was Zane.

Gonna let him do me on the hood of this baby, I swear, she promised herself.

The cop car drew up behind her, growing larger in the rearview mirror, and she rolled her eyes.

She'd been courteous in leaving half the speedometer untouched, and she'd been outright saintly to not simply mind-fuck the cops into moseying on by and leaving her to her business. But a kind gesture in the world rarely went unpunished, and in this new, lawless world, a girl with morals was just a victim painting a target on her own backside. Considering this, Serena weighed the pros and cons of trying to flash her ass at the pursuing officer, decided it wasn't worth the effort—and she certainly wasn't about to make his life all the better by letting him get a glimpse of her money-maker—and she decided to settle with flipping him another bird.

He responded by creeping that much closer in her rearview mirror.

"Motherfucker," she hissed, "if you put a dent in my new baby's fender I'm going to send you home to a family that won't fucking recognize you!"

Another shift—another absent tickle—and she gained a few more yards on the wailing car. Then, with a fresh thought occurring to her, she yanked the emergency brake while cranking the wheel, let the car swirl deliciously around in the most beautiful one-eighty of her life. She and the car came to face the oncoming cop head-on. Her lip curled as she teased the accelerator, letting it purr a warning.

The cop car slowed.

"Damn right, bitch!" Serena muttered, working the gas as she let her aura snake out of her body, through the Coupe, and into the oncoming cop's car.

He damn near pissed himself when his window started to go down.

He started to piss himself when the wheel in his grip swerved to the right.

He'd just started to get a grip on his bladder by the time his brakes activated, and he found himself wondering if it was worth holding it as he looked out the window to see the stolen car careening towards him.

Serena was still cackling as she worked the Coupe around the parked cop car—guns and handcuffs and all other manner of potentially useful supplies sailing through his open window and through hers like a violent rendition out of Fantasia—and worked her way back to the others. She repeated the process, using her aura to "dance" all their gear into the passenger seat of her new car.

One of them had even been kind enough to buy her a King Sized Snickers.

As she took the corner that had caused all the trouble once more, she reached back and wiped their minds for a little bit of extra security.

She left them with only the sound of her laughter.

"Bullshit! BULLSHIT! BULL-FUCKING-SHIT!" Zane drove a fist down on the hood of Sawyer's car, which had become an impromptu desk for the maps and files regarding the matter at hand.

The fist withdrew from a crater; crumpled metal whimpering in the final throes of agony.

Sawyer stared at the dent as one might a leaky faucet in a flooding room. "You wanna tell us how you really feel, big guy?" he asked, scratching his chin. "Or would you rather piss in my gas tank? No, really, have at it! This is, if I'm not mistaken, the only car we've got left—rest got buried when the mansion came down—and, oh yeah, almost all our weapons are in the trunk, too. Not to mention the few computers and hard drives I was able to gather while running for my life. So, in short, basically everything of our practically demolished clan is in this car. And, though Missus Stryker saw fit to tear the door off—and while I understand that your kid might like using it as a toboggan to ride down the staircase—I was holding out some hope of maybe getting it fixed. But, really, if it makes you feel better then, please, Mister Vailean, take it out on the car. Hell, why not set it on fire? Everything else of the Trepis Clan has been destroyed—even its damn leader would be lucky to ever walk again—so why not just make it official?"

Dianna set a hand on her increasingly angry vampire lover's back. "Sweetie," she whispered, "I don't think he meant to do it. Relax."

Zane stared down at the dent, pursed his lips, and finally nodded. "I might have overreacted."

Sawyer stared at him, started grinding his teeth. "When's your handler going to come get you and return you to the zoo?"

"My wife's stealing us some new gear," Zane answered.

This succeeded in making Sawyer smile. "Don't suppose she'd be willing to steal me a new car?"

"This is my wife we're talking about," said Zane, smirking and rapping a knuckle on the dented hood. "Probably roll in here in something that'd make this piece of shit look like one of my kid's toys."

Sawyer beamed at this and gave a nod, looking down at the map and the many scribbles thereupon resting on the hood. "Here's hoping. And, in all fairness, if I were small enough I'd be taking turns on that door-toboggan with your kid."

Zane nodded. "Wouldn't we all?"

Dianna, satisfied that the two weren't about to become violent, leaned in to kiss Sawyer's cheek and started away. She wanted to check in with Zeek on Xander's progress.

XANDER THINKS he sees Estella in the distance. She's too far to make her out clearly, but she's too close to easily turn away.

He wants to call to her.

Wants to go to her.

Wants her.

He can't.

He doesn't like that he can't, doesn't take to knowing it well—not well, at all—but there's nothing for him to break here. Nothing for him to express a damned thing.

Worst of all, he knows that's exactly what he's here for.

Before him, aggressively set between him and the high, far place that Estella rests, is a decagonal table. He finds himself wondering how he knows that word.

"I was *a teacher, you know," Stan's voice announces.*

And, just like that—as if the table needed nothing more than a voice to reveal its hosts—they are there.

Ten corners; nine dead faces.

Stan, seated at the corner closest to Xander, is facing away from him, looking out towards the others. Despite this, Xander feels that he is somehow watching him. His eyes move, and in the back of his mind Xander imagines they were the quivering second-hand of some sort of strange clock.

His father.

His mother.

His grandmother.

Depok.

Marcus.

The Gamer.

Osehr.

Father Tennesen.

And back to Stan.

The tenth seat, waiting in front of Xander and resting between Stan and Xander's father, waits in front of Xander. Unprompted, he sits. The cycle completed, the chairs push in—guided by phantom hands—and Xander realizes that they are no longer alone. Though he cannot see him, Xander can sense a familiar energy radiating from under the table. He is certain that, were he to crouch down and explore beneath it, he would see the shimmering, feline eyes of a strong and graceful creature waiting there. Around the table—around him—and traveling on and on and on are many others. He cannot see them, cannot make out their faces, but he knows them.

He shakes his head.

He knew *them.*

Looking up to where he'd seen Estella, Xander now sees only darkness. Feels only darkness.

Turning his head to Stan, he tells him that he wants to leave this table; that he wants to go to Estella. Now.

"That's not up to me," Stan tells him.

"Not up to me," the eight others at the table announce in unison.

Xander says a bad word that Estella had always hated.

Estella yawned and worked to chase the grogginess from her sleep-numbed body with a series of deep breaths. Eyes still blurry, she worked her fists against them and then, opening her palms, wiped her face. She realized then how tired she must have been, and then, considering herself at that moment, revised that thought. She was still tired. Looking down at the couch—*It really is more comfortable than it looks,* she thought—she came to the conclusion that no sleep, no matter how deep or fulfilling, would make her feel rested until she would be able to sleep beside Xander again. This, in turn, made her think of Xander down in the corner section of the storage facility, lying side-by-side next to Ruby.

She surprised herself then by realizing that, instead of feeling jealous, she hoped that there was some sort of comfort granted to one or the other—*preferably both*—for this.

She felt like she dreamt of them, standing in some warm, bright place, and talking of pleasant things. It was a good sort of talk, or so she wanted to believe; the sort of talk that good friends get to share after coming together after a long time apart. At times in her dream, though, Estella remembered that Ruby had stopped looking like herself, and that Xander had begun looking like his father. She had only seen a few pictures of the late Joseph Stryker, not enough, she thought, to have committed the face to memory. But there he'd been in her dream, anyway.

Sometimes Xander and Ruby.

Sometimes Joseph and...

Who was that? she thought absently, her right hand moving from her face to scratch the top of her head while her left hand moved, as though prompted by another force, to her—

"Bullshit! BULLSHIT! BULL-FUCKING-SHIT!"

The cursing was followed by a loud, metallic impact that helped to chase some of the last remnants of sleep from within Estella's muscles. It was Zane's voice, distant-yet-unmistakable. Worried that Serena's husband might be ready to kill one of the last few members of her own husband's clan, Estella pushed herself to stand and see what was the matter. Before she could make it across the room, however, she became aware of two facts:

First, she could "see" through her mind's eye that two very different types of cars were approaching them.

And second, she had absolutely no idea what time it was; almost felt as though she'd lost all concept of time, in fact.

The first of these facts should have been the most worrisome—after all, most of the human race wanted their kind dead, and most of the mythos community wanted everyone tied to Xander dead—but along with the knowledge of the cars came the knowledge of their occupants. It was, in actuality, the second thought that truly gave Estella a moment of deep and genuine dread, a sort of dread that seemed immediately after foolish. And then, just like that, she had no idea why she'd felt it at all. Blinking, she felt her left palm throb and looked down, discovered that it was laid flat against her stomach.

She half-expected a kick or some sign of life, then remembered that her pregnancy was only weeks old.

Usually have to wait a month just to suspect... she thought with a grin.

Then, spotting a few Snickers wrappers that *weren't* torn open, she liberated two more of Serena's pregnancy candies from the table and started for the door.

SERENA WAS BACK and arguing with Zane as Estella made it down the stairs. Though the Vaileans seemed to make a routine out of arguing, Estella had come to recognize most of it as a sort of vocal dance that the two engaged in more as a twisted romantic gesture than to settle an actual disagreement. There'd be a bunch of cursing, some truly ugly (and, to any other relationship, potentially relationship ending) insults—Estella had never heard the C-word thrown around as much as she had since meeting the Vaileans, and that usually came from Serena—and then a mutual spark would light up in the two's eyes and they'd "resolve" the matter privately. Then there were the real arguments; the arguments where somebody had to shuffle Gregori, who'd usually be shouting the word "fuck" like it was the punchline to any joke, out of the room.

This was one of those arguments.

Dianna hurried from Zeek's corner—Estella frowned that she couldn't see Xander from her current angle—and collected Gregori. The boy, seeming not to notice the rising tension between his parents, was hanging through the open window of a rather showy red sports car that, even parked, looked like it was going dangerously fast. It was this car, Estella realized as she approached, that seemed to be the subject of the argument.

Dianna got ahold of Gregori's legs and pulled him from the

window, then gasped when she realized that he was clutching a pump-action shotgun in his arms like a new, beloved pet.

"No, Gregori! No! Drop it!"

Serena paused long enough to glance over, shake her head, and wave off the concern. "No worries, doll, it ain't loaded."

Estella could see with her mind's eye that, yes, it was quite loaded.

Serena—knowing this, as well, but knowing that Dianna didn't—made a show of pulling the shotgun away from her son with her aura. As the weapon hovered through the air, the butt knocked against the back of Zane's head.

At the sound of the *clunk,* Dianna hurried away with a still-giggling Gregori.

"Whoops," Serena said in a voice that held no real remorse.

Zane growled and took his wife by the throat with one hand.

Concern flared up in Estella's chest.

Serena only laughed.

"Where the fuck do you think we are, Zaney-poo? The bedroom?" she swiped her arm around, knocked her husband's grip away—Estella realized he hadn't really committed to the choke, after all—and kicked him in the shin. "Don't be starting what you ain't got the fucking balls to finish, bitch! And don't be promising my shit to other—"

"The fuck are you gonna do with it, anyway, you crazy cunt?" Zane hissed, working to not show how badly his shin was hurting him. "The whole damn world's out hunting us and you wanna make yourself an easy target driving around in *this?*"

"Fucking-A right, I do!" she countered. "I dare any motherfucker to try some shit after seeing me scream by in this thing. You ever try to fight with a hard-on? Oh, wait, look who I'm talking to! OF COURSE YOU HAVE! With *me!* And you *lost* those fights. Every... single... one! And, lemme shed some truth on you, baby-cakes: it's no easier to fight as a woman with a pair of flooded panties. Like fighting in a swamp, Zane; A FUCKING

SWAMP! This baby"—she patted the car's hood—"is *insurance!*"

"You're fucking crazy," Zane said, shaking his head and turning away. "And you're giving the car to Sawyer. End of story."

"End of...? FUCK YOUR MOTHER WITH A WEED-WHACKER, YOU RUPTURED RECTAL WART!" she spun around and glared at Sawyer. "Why the fuck is he telling me you get my trophy ride, anyway? Huh? You nuzzle his balls while I was out or something?"

Sawyer sneered, looked at Zane, shuddered, and then opened his mouth to speak.

Serena recoiled. "Holy shit, Sawyer! Nobody ever tell you to brush your teeth after gulping a load?" she asked, glaring once more at her husband. "The car's *mine,* bitch! I had to go through a lot to score this thing, I'm already in love with it, and—"

"I sort of punched through the hood of his..." Zane confessed, suddenly looking embarrassed.

Serena stared at him in disbelief. Then she looked back at Sawyer. Groaning, she passed along the keys and shook her head, shooting Zane an accusatory look.

"Given the nature of this trade," she said calmly, "he probably *should* suck your dick."

Sawyer's aura sparked with disgust behind her.

She turned and leveled a look at him, smirking. "And I'd insist on watching, Princess. Dianna can join, too. We'd have popcorn. Make a whole show of it."

"You're disgusting," Sawyer said flatly.

Serena shrugged. "Opinions are like assholes, and assholes like you got shitty opinions. I'll worry about how disgusting I am when my hubs stops sticking it to me."

Then, with that, Serena pulled Zane over to her and kissed him. Hard.

The spark erupted in the two's eyes; their auras melding.

At that moment, despite the raw intensity of it, Estella realized that it *had* been one of their normal types of arguments, after all. It was all like a dance, this particular one was just far more aggressive than usual. She "heard" Serena connect with Zane and mention something about making a promise about the hood of the car in question. Then she saw Zane offer the quickest of glances at first Sawyer and then at his new car.

Later, he thought back to her.

Estella rubbed at her temples, not glad to see that she was once again receiving others' auric transmissions so easily.

"So," Estella called out as she cleared the staircase and came to join the others, "there's been an awful lot of shouting going on down here. Hope it's all been *for* something."

Serena turned to look at her, her face pulling back apologetically. "Sorry, 'Stell," she started. "Hope we didn't wake you."

Estella shook her head. "No. I mean, it *might* have, but I..." she started to remember how she'd wound up asleep on the couch in the first place and couldn't help but smile at Serena. "I woke up on my own."

"Pleasant dreams?" asked Zane.

Estella thought of Xander and Ruby; she thought of his father and...

She caught her left hand traveling to her stomach again and redirected it to brushing some stray hairs from her face.

She nodded.

The Vaileans smiled at this.

"So why *was* everyone shouting?" Estella asked again, then shrugged towards the car. "Other than *that,* I mean."

At that moment, the second car Estella had sensed—*not* a luxurious speed-mobile—hobbled through the open shipping gate and, belching out a cloud of black, oily exhaust, died behind the first.

As Zoey and Isaac climbed out of the small, ugly thing, Serena looked at Sawyer and nodded back towards it. "You sure you don't want *that* car?"

In flagrant disregard for the otherwise awful turn of bad luck they'd all been having, both outings had proved fruitful. Zoey and Isaac's hunt for the materials necessary to synthesize more of the enchanted blood substitute was, in Zoey's own words, "better than we'd hoped for." Estella noticed Isaac clutching a small case after they'd delivered the materials to Zeek, and, judging from the look on his face, he agreed. And while the car —a dark-red vehicle that, in Estella's opinion, looked like a bullet on wheels—had wound up switching hands upon arrival, Serena's quest for weapons had *also* proved a success. Along with a bunch of police-issue firearms, she'd also managed to fill almost every available bit of open space within the car with all manner of weaponry.

"Where on earth did you find all of this stuff?" asked Zane as he inspected some rather dull-looking throwing knives.

"Drug den," Serena said with a casual shrug. Estella couldn't help but feel that warranted a whole list's worth of new questions, but the blonde only added, "Crazy fuckers stockpile all sorts of awesome shit."

"You left the drugs, I'm hoping," said Zane.

Serena rolled her eyes. "Don't you know anything? In a post-apocalyptic world water is more valuable than anything else." She paused then, slapped her forehead, and said, "Damn! I forgot to steal bottled water!"

Estella stared, unsure if she was joking or not.

"Moving right along," Sawyer said after clearing his throat.

Estella turned her attention to him, eager to know what he and Zane had been arguing about in the first place.

The Vaileans, in a true twist, went quiet.

"Obviously the shit has hit the fan," the vampire warrior started, "and it's made prioritizing our next steps sort of... hmm," he glanced up at Zane and smirked before saying, "debatable."

Serena leaned in close to Estella and whispered, "Master-debatable."

Estella giggled and shushed her. She both loved and hated how the blonde could lighten a mood and even cultivate a smile where one would be thought impossible to flourish.

"We've got three major issues," Sawyer continued, "and very little manpower to address even a single one of them. In no real order: this Aleks guy, who I've been told is a varcol—obviously this makes him a sizable concern, especially since he seems to be amassing a following." Sawyer paused to reach for a stack of papers and files he had waiting nearby. "Then there's the Cebourists. Now, we knew that they'd continue to be a problem with or without that Ariel-woman, but this new guy, DiAngelo, and his team seem to be taking it to a new level. He might not be a... um," he cleared his throat, "well, like that Stan fellow," he paused and looked to Estella, "there's still been no word on him, by the way."

Estella nodded solemnly, feeling like she already knew why they hadn't heard from Stan.

"But," Sawyer pushed forward with his summary, "god-like or not, DiAngelo and his team *were* military—that much has been made public—and *bad* military at that. Moreover, with the intel we've managed to gather so far, it would appear that they've acquired and begun using the same sort of serum that... uh, well..." he stammered and stopped as Dianna approached.

Seeing her, Estella scanned the storage facility for Gregori's location and spotted Sana and Tim escorting him back up to the office, the promise of pilfered candy on all their minds. She considered for a moment warning Serena about the fate of her stash, but decided it would be better to just let things happen and help re-stock the candy reserves later.

"It's alright," Dianna said with a "it's not alright"-sigh. When Sawyer still said nothing, she finished for him: "The serum that my asshole brother and I worked to develop; the one that imbues the users with mythos abilities." She stared off, not looking at anything but, instead, trying very hard to look at nothing. Sighing again, she gave a single nod. "The Cebourists have perfected it—weeded out the imperfections that allowed us to kill Richard in the first place—and now DiAngelo and his men have started taking it."

"And how can we know that?" Zane asked, folding his arms across his chest.

Sawyer set a hand on top of his closed laptop and tapped it with his index finger. "Because the assholes are advertising," he said.

Serena sneered and looked like she was going to spit, then didn't. "So what's the third problem?" she demanded, seeming more intent on changing the subject.

They all knew what the third problem was, anyway.

Everyone glanced back towards Zeek's medical corner; towards Xander.

She winced and looked away first.

"Right..." Serena said, unsurprised, as her hand found her shoulder.

"Okay," Zane more growled than said, turning back to Sawyer. "So can we finally agree that Aleks needs to be our main priority?"

Sawyer gave him a look. "You going to scream 'bullshit' and put your fist through my new car if I don't agree?"

Estella realized then that that had been the argument they'd been having: which threat they should be focusing on. Out of the three issues, though, she felt like they were focusing on the wrong ones.

Serena shook her head. "I don't think you're fully appreciating just how dangerous Aleks is if you don't feel like he deserves all of our attention right now. Forgetting entirely that he's a cunning and manipulative fuck-wad," she went on, seamlessly merging her skills as a tactician and a leader with her prowess to weave filth and vulgarity into every sentence, "there's the simple fact that—HELLO!—he's a varcol! Those fucking things aren't exactly a daily experience for any of us, and it's safe to say that we've all faced off against some pretty fucked up powerhouses in the past. I mean, fuck, with the exception of Estella and... well, with the exception of the Strykers, I'd say it's safe to say that almost nobody else—in this room or on this planet for that matter—has recently tangled with one of them. The fact that one of them is out, about, and building up clout should, on its own, motivate us to make him concern *numero uno.*"

"Anybody else find it the least bit suspicious that this Aleks motherfucker showed up, like—what?—right after that cunt in Romania?" Zane asked. "I mean, what are the odds that there's an encounter with one of the oldest species of mythos—a species, let's not forget, that has either mostly died out or has since been playing the greatest game of hide-and-don't-seek *ever*—and, immediately after, another one pops up? And staking after the exact ones who aced the first, at that."

Sawyer sighed and nodded. "It's safe to say that Aleks had some connection to Lenuta," he admitted. "And, yes, varcols are powerful and dangerous. I'm not denying any of this."

"Here comes a lunch lady 'but' of immense proportions," Serena muttered.

"*But,*" Sawyer shot Serena a glare but continued on anyway, "he's still only *one* threat. Even amassing a following he's still only a *local* threat. The Cebourists are *worldwide,* however, and they're actively recruiting; growing faster on a scale that Aleks has no hope of achieving."

Oh, how that one underestimates me! a slimy, familiar voice oozed through Estella's head.

She jumped, looked around; saw that nobody else had seemed to receive Aleks' message. They had, however, noticed her reaction to it.

"You alright?" Sawyer asked her.

Estella's mind began to work in overdrive as she considered her options.

She could tell them. She could be honest that she'd just received a message from Aleks, that he'd made a connection—likely knew where they were at that moment—and challenged Sawyer's claims.

But what sort of reaction would that get? Panic? A rushed, perhaps suicidal response? Could telling them motivate a series of actions that might put everything at risk?

Or she could lie...

She caught herself looking back towards Zeek's corner—towards Xander—and she caught herself touching her stomach again.

"I just..." she started, stopped; Aleks was laughing in her head. "I feel like—" she was looking back towards where Xander was laid out again.

"About that third issue?" Serena cut in, raising her hand like an eager schoolchild and drawing the attention off Estella.

By the Earth Mother, Estella privately said to her, *you are a saint!*

Anybody ever tell you that you pronounce 'slut' funny? Serena said back in her mind. Out loud, however, she said, "I mean, no offense to all you remaining Trepis folks, y'all seem lovely to me and such, but we seem to be forgetting that Xander's the one that shafted the Cebourists with that broadcast. Granted," she shrugged, "he sort of shafted all of us with that, but he's a cutie, so we'll cut him some slack there. Plus, it was him and the goddess here"—she nudged Estella—"who smoked the other varcol. And like Zane said, they're pretty much the only ones anywhere who can boast that. Shit, if anybody else could've boasted something like poaching a varcol you'd think we'd have heard it by now—shit would've been on Facebook in an instant."

"What's your point?" Sawyer asked.

"My point, boy scout," said Serena, "is you're talking about Aleks and the Cebourists as though we got a single dick between us decent enough to fuck either of them, when the reality is that there's only two people who can really do what we're talking about trying:" she motioned with both hands, one towards Estella and the other back towards Zeek's medical corner. "And, like the Wonder Twins, I don't think we'll like the results of trying a full-scale assault on one or the other without *both* of the Strykers leading the mayhem."

"I don't know if you've noticed," Dianna chided, "but Xander's not exactly in fighting condition."

"And I don't know if you've noticed," Serena shot back, "but between a beaten-to-shit Xander and a reformed mythos hunter who, in any other circumstances, could just as easily be on her knees for that DiAngelo douchebag, I'd still side with Xander on my worst of rag-days!"

"HEY!" Sawyer snarled, baring his fangs and taking a step towards her.

"One more step," Zane flexed and stepped in front of him, "and I'll be pouring what's left of you in your new car's gas tank."

Dianna's aura shifted, spiked, and then sagged, defeated. "How dare you..." she whimpered, turning away.

Estella stared, dumbfounded, after her friend as she retreated away. She realized, with no small amount of shock, that she was heading to Zeek's corner; heading straight to Xander.

"Serena..." Estella felt hollow, Dianna's pain quickly becoming her own. "That... you... no."

"Do you think I'm going to let her get away with saying that?" Sawyer growled at Zane. "What would you do to me if I'd said something like that to *her?*" he demanded, jabbing a finger back towards Serena.

Serena stared after Dianna, her shoulders sagging. *So much for being a saint, huh?* she asked in Estella's head.

Need... Cebourists'... ma-gic...

Estella nearly sobbed at the sound of Xander's voice in her mind. Her hands clapped over her mouth and she trembled, overwhelmed by the immediate reactions she wanted to succumb to and the right ones. Much as she wanted solely to cling to the fact that her husband was somehow communicating with her—somehow understanding everything going on around him—she knew she had to focus on his words.

She knew she'd be doing a disservice to all of them, Xander especially, if she didn't.

Focusing on the laughter that still echoed in her head, Estella welled up all the auric control she could muster and put up a shield against Aleks.

She didn't need him eavesdropping on what she had in mind.

The Cebourists magic...? she thought to herself. Then, to Zane and Sawyer: "The Cebourists' magic. Do you think it would work against Aleks and his followers?"

They all stopped and looked at her.

"Estella?" Serena began, obviously unsure of where the question was coming from.

Estella ignored her. "You saw firsthand what the Cebourists' magic could do. You said it turned Isaac into a feral monster and burned you and Xander both," she said to Zane.

Zane sneered. "Didn't just burn us," he argued. "Sent us to our own private Hell, is what they did."

Estella nodded. "Right. *Exactly!* They have magic that hurts mythos."

Sawyer scowled. "And you want to harness that to fight Aleks? Isn't that kind of sick?"

"Isn't all of this kind of sick?" Estella demanded. "At least then we'd have an upper hand against him and his followers. Plus," she grinned at both Zane and Sawyer, "wouldn't hunting down the Cebourists for the sake of arming ourselves against Aleks serve *both* your purposes?"

The two sangs paused and glanced at one another, unable to argue that last point.

Serena offered an approving smile and a nod before starting

after Dianna, looking like she was prepared to try for an apology.

Estella could only hope she'd follow through with it.

"OKAY," Zane shouted loud enough to be heard throughout the building as he drove a fist into his opposite palm, "HOW MANY PEOPLE WANNA KICK SOME ASS?"

CHAPTER 12
MISSIONS

"It was not well to drive men into final corners;
at those moments they could all develop teeth and claws."
Stephen Crane (1871-1900)

If there is anything more annoying than being trapped in a cosmic, kaleidoscopic lecture, Xander decides, it is somehow being able to hear the Vaileans' incessant bickering even through the heavy veil of...

What?

Death? Near-death? A goddam coma?

He feels like if this was just some sort of deep sleep—and why shouldn't he be tired after everything he'd been through?—then hearing those two carry on with their porno catchphrases and their "I just bought the complete curse-word encyclopedia set!"-swear-offs would have been enough to wake him up by now.

If for no other reason, *he thinks,* than just to tell them to shut the fuck up!

But Xander does not wake up. Instead, he is so deep in whatever state of being he is in that he is existing in multiple planes of it—*whatever* it *is—at the same time.*

Now, at this very moment, he finds himself committed to any number of simultaneous moments:

He's at the table, looking out at all those who, in some way or another, he'd been responsible for killing.

He's walking and talking with Ruby in her mind, distantly aware at various moments that she is no longer Ruby... and yet, at the same time, is.

He's dragged and pushed through all number of various timelines, shown all manner of "what if"s—how but a single change to one past event would change everything—and, slipping forward to times that had yet to pass, seeing potential outcomes to things he hadn't even done yet.

And, through it all, he is in a dingy building neighboring the harbor—not his rebuilt mansion, he realizes with a heavy heart—and, at the same time, everywhere else...

And nowhere else.

In these instances, Xander finds himself wishing that he felt more attached to his head so that he could at least commit to the headache he's sure this is all causing him.

Worst of all, in all these many planes of being that Xander is divided between, he can't help but feel that it is all, at the same time, a single happening; one event happening in different ways; the fractals of one image, scattered and distorted through a broken viewfinder.

"Or a fixed one," Stan offers from beside him.

Xander tells him that he's not helping.

Back in Ruby's mind, she asks him if they're going to be alright; if he believes that something good can really come of all this. He's afraid to tell her that, of the many potential outcomes he's witnessed so far, only a few of them work out in a way that Ruby would call "good."

Then again, there's a lot that he wants to tell Ruby.

He wants to tell her that she should fight to wake up faster, but he also wonders if he should tell her to wait to wake up, to maybe commit to unconsciousness until all of this is over.

But... no, that won't work. Not for Ruby, no, but for Ruby, yes.

This confuses Xander, and the force that's been trying to show him that single line of dominos—the one line of dominos he outright refuses to watch fall—howls at him.

Xander lies to Ruby, then changes the subject. He tells her to listen to Onyx.

"Who's Onyx?" asks Ruby.

"Careful," Stan whispers at the table. "Those dominos don't cross paths."

And then Xander can't remember who Onyx is, either.

The force ushers him away from the confusion, his father and mother tell him to take his time—"It's not real time, anyway," Joseph Stryker points out—and Xander once again decides to watch the fight between him and Aleks; between his people and their people.

Good and evil seems a weird way to look at it...

But he has no problem seeing it as black and white.

"Do you think," Ruby says to him, and she's reaching for his hand—they're on a beach now; a beach in Ruby's mind—"that you and I, in another lifetime..."

Xander watches as he and Aleks struggle in one potential reality. A familiar gun barrel is leveling close—too close—and a decision is made. Xander flinches without a body as he watches his head explode from the impact of an enchanted bullet. In this vision, Aleks looks just as surprised as Xander feels; both realizing at that instant that Xander chose to shoot himself.

"No, Ruby," Xander says, but he allows her to hold his hand anyway—it's her first day at the beach, after all. "All possible roads for me are with Estella."

"Oh."

Xander restacks a few of the dominos, traveling back as though rewinding a movie, and sets them back into motion, curious how things would turn out if—

His head explodes again.

Again.

Again.

And, yes, again.

Strange, *he thinks.* I thought I was past that...

He feels unsettled with how passively he thinks this, feeling like he's not really thinking it at all.

"If not you then whom?" Stan asks, and Xander can't help but feel that this is the sort of question that a teacher asks a student, not the sort of question a therapist asks their patient.

Fucking tests... *he thinks, and he's confident this time that he is the thinker now.*

"I don't know if you've noticed," *he hears a familiar voice break through the planes of existence and draw his attention to the world beyond his body—sees Estella struggling with growing tensions among the others. Dianna continues, saying,* "but Xander's not exactly in fighting condition."

Astute as always, *Xander thinks.* But, no, this won't do. They need...

He stops watching his head explode in a loop and travels back again, isolates the final conflict—the one where any of them stand a chance—and begins to cycle through their strengths there. What gave them... ah, yes.

*He sees a few possible scenarios where the Cebourists' magic is utilized against Aleks and his army—*Holy shit! It really is an... stop! Focus!*—and, yes, it seems that in most of these cases it pushes things in their favor. Still more failing scenarios than winning ones, but...*

But we take what chances we can get, right?

He lingers, seeing a possible path where one of the strongest of the Cebourists actually takes sides with them. Intrigued, he follows this particular man—this Allen Carrey—and his line of dominos to see what changes his mind so...

Oh god! *Xander recoils from the vision,* No! That's not—

But he's already forgotten that path; forgotten it like he's forgotten why he has so much more to fight for; why his life has suddenly taken on new meaning. He's too afraid to know why he's suddenly more important and, at the same time, so much less significant. Most of all, though, he's scared about how happy that mysterious turn makes him. And so he's forgotten it; forgotten it like he's already forgotten millions and millions of other realities that hurt too much to remember.

But at least he remembers that, yes, the Cebourists' magic can help them, and, most important to him at that moment, he can see that it will help Estella.

Despite every other effort—moving time and walking freely in Ruby's mind and even talking to a bunch of dead people—being so simple, he's surprised to find connecting and communicating with Estella quite difficult.

Like trying to grab a fish out of the water while wearing a blindfold... *he thinks.*

But, because he's been doing the impossible all day anyway, he finally does this.

Then, exhausted, he moves the dominos back to watch his father's raid on Lenuta's castle; he settles onto a tree branch with Ruby in a vast forest; he sets his head down on the ten-sided table.

He rests.

THE NEXT FEW hours were almost—*almost!*—enough to distract Estella. In that time, planning and organizing with others and assigning roles and giving orders, it began to feel like it had been.

While Xander had been the formal leader of the Trepis Clan, there'd been none in the mansion who challenged or doubted Estella when she lived up to the undesired title of "Queen." While she had her suspicions that it was Xander's late therion colleague, Osehr, who'd put that term into circulation, it stopped mattering who started it when everyone else started using it. Xander had hated the title of "leader"—he'd lived up to it marvelously, no matter what he tried to convince himself —but he at least tolerated it. Nobody, but *nobody*, however, was brave enough to call him "King Stryker." This courtesy, whether it was fear or respect or something else entirely, was not extended to Estella; something that became a sort of playful routine around the mansion until even Xander had taken to calling her "Queen Stryker."

It had never occurred to Estella back then that she'd ever come to be endeared by this.

But then...

"You got it, m'queen," one of the remaining warriors said with a smirk and a salute as she finished assigning him one of the quadrants of the city with another group.

Hearing that helped Estella slip back into the role. Everything after that, though it didn't come to fully distract her from her concerns about Xander, fell into a familiar rhythm that was at least not hindered by her worry.

She eavesdropped—intentionally this time—as Serena and Dianna came to a shaky truce, the two agreeing that tensions were riding high and ugly things were bound to be said as a result.

Zoey and Isaac worked to help Zeek and Karen make more synth blood, which was immediately put to use—almost all of it being strung up in medical-grade bags from any available source to feed into Xander.

Satoru and Sasha, along with all the other available warriors, began to arm themselves and take their places with the teams they were assigned with. Sawyer and Dianna, once Sawyer was satisfied that things between his fiancé and Serena were patched up, took their own assignments, but stayed with Estella, assuming their original roles as head warriors to the clan, and helped to engineer what Sawyer loosely called an "attack plan."

It all sounded like it could actually work out. Dianna had figured out a way to track down their location, and Sawyer had begun to map out a means of getting the drop on them—a sizable task in and of itself with DiAngelo and his men likely having any number of mythos abilities to sense incoming dangers.

As they deliberated over the plan, Estella couldn't help that she'd heard that name before—DiAngelo—but, for the life of her, couldn't begin to recall from where. She certainly hadn't encountered that awful man before, and she didn't think that she'd ever encountered him during her and the others' time tracking and fighting the Cebourists. Understanding that she'd plagued her mind with enough that day—and recalling Isaac's speech about smart people—she decided it was better not to distract herself with it for the time being.

She knew she'd figure it out eventually.

In either case, the plan was underway, it had Zane and Sawyer working together rather than arguing over priorities, and it was giving direction and purpose to all those who might otherwise find themselves succumbing to the same tension and resulting ugliness that had erupted between Serena and Dianna.

Simply put, it was a good a place to start. Best of all, though Estella had taken to her new abilities—practically becoming a varcol overnight—with alarming ease, her true strength and passion was and always had been magic. To simultaneously rob the Cebourists of their greatest strength as well as gain a new weapon against Aleks and his followers was a chance too great for Estella to pass up!

And then Zane and the others came to tell her that she wouldn't be going.

General DiAngelo was fed up of failures and fuckups; he'd lost patience with losers and letdowns; he was sick of all the shit-for-brains. And—god-fucking-damn!—they were EVERYWHERE!

Did every competent mind with a committed sense of integrity just up and swallow a bullet when he wasn't watching?

He'd taken a promising contract with that Ariel-bitch, and she'd proven to be nothing but a bunch of cryptic BS and cloak-and-dagger chatter. He'd trusted his daughter—his own damn blood!—with his secrets and training, turned her into a weapon...

Only to have her run off with some boy, only a kid!

(He wasn't about to even entertain the rumors disguising themselves as solid intel that that boy just so happened to be a therion piece-of-shit; *that* he simply couldn't bring himself to dwell on. People—lots of people; lots of *innocent* people—would be dead if he had to imagine his only child bedding it up with some fucking mythos trash.)

His own government before that—reigns snatched up by a bunch of flower-power faggots and limp-dick peace peddlers—marking him and his men as monsters. He'd been publicly shamed, humiliated, and ripped out of the life he was best at all for the sake of PR; a country that used to mean something, used to stand for something, suddenly being run overnight like a goddam television show: suddenly everything was about approval ratings.

If anybody ever stopped to ask Robert DiAngelo, he'd tell them that napalm and torture made for the best ratings of all. And if a few of his boys wanted to get their dicks wet at the expense of a few brown babies then—what the hell?—they should be allowed. They were there for their country, about as far away from their wives and families as a man could get. Screw Vegas, what happened in those countries *stayed* in those countries.

That was the deal!

That's what they were sent in for: to get shit done.

DiAngelo and his men got shit done. Got it done about as well as it could get done. And what was the heroes' welcome they were rewarded with? Well... they'd been out of a job, right?

But their time in those countries had been good for something else. America was a good place for monsters to hide—the liberal freakshow offered up all number of ways for nonhuman filth to parade around under the guise of goths or punks or whatever foreign-loving, cosplay trend was sweeping the masses—but vampires and the rest of their ilk couldn't make that shit work nearly as well in places where the best you got to hide yourself was a turban and a brown-god prayer. No, no, no. DiAngelo and his boys discovered the truth of their kind *real* quick in those places, and they learned all about them. Oh, hell yes, they learned; they studied, tracked, and, when they were confident that they were able, they killed, dissected, and learned some more.

As satisfying as it was to hook a car battery up to an Islamic extremist or repeatedly drown some pesky native leader who didn't like to listen, Robert DiAngelo had never felt anything quite as good as cutting open something that couldn't even call itself human while it was still alive.

It was a good hobby while it lasted, and when the United States military decided to crucify him and his men it was an even better fallback career.

Best of all: it paid under the table.

Uncle Sam never saw a cut.

It felt good to screw it to those who'd screwed it to him, but when the Cebourist-job popped up he'd seen a glimmer of hope. To him, it looked like a chance to change things; to reshape the world; take it back, make it theirs. Make it right. Then Ariel, for all her big talk and mystical mumbo-jumbo, screwed the pooch and got herself dead. Worst of all: she'd allowed one of those vein-tapping, goth-fag wannabe monsters to be the one to change things; to reshape the world. Ariel's fuckup had singlehandedly given that Xander

Stryker vampire a chance to take the world and make it theirs.

Moreover, he'd gone and crucified the Cebourists—put them out in the spotlight as the monsters—and threatened DiAngelo's best shot at a second chance.

Well fuck that!

And fuck Xander Stryker.

Much as he hated rooting for a monster, he couldn't help but watch and re-watch the footage of that Anne Rice worshipping, Marilyn Manson fetishizing cocksucker getting the ass-kicking of a lifetime. And, no, the erection it gave him didn't make him queer, at all. It was the same hard-on he'd get watching some spicks in the ghetto gun one another down —*doing us a favor,* he'd think one way or the other—or the lower-belly tickle he'd get imagining some desperate wetbacks drowning one another in a panic while trying to cross the border.

So, yeah, it had become a mission—a personal one, but a mission was a mission all the same—to get the Cebourists back on their feet, make them a powerhouse for the ages, and make use of their mumbo-jumbo—it was incredible, mythos scrapping mumbo-jumbo, but mumbo-jumbo all the same—to really put the hurt on those monsters. Sure, they were a church, and DiAngelo wasn't exactly a follower of their faith—this Cebour-thing wasn't the one, true God, so why would he be?—but they didn't need to know that. Surely not every warrior in the Crusades was all Christy, right?

Sometimes you just had to nod your head to the preachy crap so that you could be sure you were on the winning side.

But now all he was getting for his trouble were rednecks and assholes! Beer-bellied, slack-jawed, inbred, untrained and undisciplined trash! There was maybe—*maybe*—a decent potential for every fifty initiates they saw! And the numbers...

They should have been galloping in by the thousands—by the millions!—but instead they were getting little bursts of incomers, all of them shuffling in with hats pulled low and collars pulled high. Hiding. The flower-power faggots and limp-dick peace peddlers still had their claws enough in the fabric of society to make those with at least their senses about them *cowering* upon arrival at what should have been a great and powerful beacon at this point!

The Cebourist recruiting centers should have been bustling with the eager, untamed masses of hardened, capable humans in their prime, aching to take up arms against the monsters who threatened their way of life. Wasn't that the dream? Wasn't that what every red-blooded human secretly pined for? A chance to fight evil—true evil; not just what boundaries and ideas defined it as—and be a hero?

Yes, General DiAngelo was fed up of failures and fuckups. He'd lost patience with losers and letdowns, and, indeed, he was sick of all the shit-for-brains.

What had humanity allowed itself to become?

Grousing at this thought, DiAngelo drank down another vial of serum, plucked another syringe from the labeled rack in front of him, and buried another needle into his already inflamed thigh. Around him, his men went about their own business. Most, like him, drank their own serums and shot up with their own syringes. They were free to choose which traits they desired—which of the monsters' abilities they most wanted for their own—and, taking advantage of one of the Cebourists' greatest resources, they dosed freely. Already DiAngelo was feeling stronger than he had in...

Well, ever.

Even pushing into his fifties, Robert DiAngelo was certain nobody had felt like this. He could move like lightning, lift a car, and, soon, he'd be able to turn his body into a weapon that would strike fear into even monsters.

Robert DiAngelo wasn't sure what humanity had allowed itself to become, but he'd sure-as-hell show them what they could be.

"Excuse me?" Estella said, genuinely feeling she'd misheard Serena's husband.

He looked uncomfortable then, glancing back at Sawyer and Dianna, who flanked him on his right. Zoey and Isaac stood to his left, but the two of them were focused more on Serena, who was Estella's only real backup at that moment. Sawyer gave Zane a nod—his face giving away that he wasn't entirely over what Zane had said to Serena earlier—while Dianna reached across her chest and gave her arm an absent rub. She seemed to be working on itemizing everything around her, looking everywhere—anywhere—except at Estella.

Estella was about to say something to her, to try to get her to agree to let her go—surely if she could get Dianna to change her mind then Sawyer's mind would be changed, and then the rest wouldn't have the support to fall back on—but then Serena's hand came to rest on her shoulder from behind.

The breath dried up in Estella's mouth and she realized that the blonde behind her *wasn't* her only backup. She started to turn, the word "don't" beginning to form on her tongue. She beat Estella to it:

"Don't," whispered Serena, her purple eyes focused on hers, reading her. "Don't fight this; don't go."

"But..." It was all Estella could bring herself to say.

There was so much more to be said, sure: the fact that the mission was one of learning magic—something she knew better than any of the others—being the most pressing. There was also the fact that it was her mission; her idea. And then, buried beneath any number of other reasons she had to offer, there was the fact that to not go, to stay, was to stay with Xander; to have to see him like that. At that moment, Estella felt that this was like asking her to be buried in a box with his corpse—too much to bear.

"It'll be alright," Zane nodded slowly, seeming to understand, and nodded back towards Serena. "You'll have Serena here to keep you company."

A violet aura ignited like a forest fire behind Estella. "Excuse me?" Serena growled.

The others flinched again, and Estella saw Sawyer and Dianna shoot a glare at the back of his head that seemed almost practiced. Isaac and Zoey didn't look the least bit surprised by this reaction.

"The fuck you mean I'll be here? When in the shit was that decided?" the blonde vampire demanded.

Zane stared at her, dumbfounded. "You... uh," he rubbed at his temples and shook his head, groaning. "Dammit, Serena! *You* decided it, remember?"

Serena let out something that was part laugh and part scoff. "Horseshit! When did I—"

"... think that Estella should sit this one out," Serena's voice chimed up, and everyone turned, startled, to see that Zoey was holding a cell phone over her head, the recorded voice emanating from this. *"This has all been hard on her, and to be forced into the shit this soon after everything—y'know, with Xander still laid-out and such—it... it just wouldn't be right. 'Sides, she's pregnant! Pregnant girl has no business being out there, right?"*

"Serena!" Estella whipped around to face her.

"Whoa!" Serena held up her hands defensively, "Hold up, doll! To be fair—*to... be... fair*—it's not like anything I said back there was out of line, right? And—" she frowned and glared over Estella's shoulder at Zoey, "AND FUCK YOU, BLUE-BUSH! FUCKING RECORDING ME WITHOUT MY CONSENT? SHIT'S *ILL-E-GAL!*" she stretched the last word into something with too many syllables and more Jersey-girl twang than any word should be saturated in. Then her lips curled and she confessed, "I knew I still loved your tight, dyed ass for a reason." Then, seeming to remember why she'd been upset in the first place, she growled, "And I *DO NOT* see where in that I *agreed* to stay behind."

Zoey slid the timer dial on the phone back and pressed the play key.

"... be right. 'Sides, she's pregnant! Pregnant girl has no business being out there—"

Serena stared, expectant.

Zoey repeated the action.

"—e's pregnant! Pregnant girl has no business being—"

Then, in an almost comedic repeat:

"—ant! Pregnant girl has no business—"

To Estella's amazement, Serena still looked like she was waiting for a reason as to why she wasn't being allowed to go.

"Oh sweet fucking Jesus, our son's gonna be a window licker, for sure," Zane groaned into his palm before finally yelling, "YOU'RE PREGNANT, SERENA! 'Pregnant girl has no business...' for fuck's sake am I really doing this?" He shook his head at her. "I figured when you said that you were *acknowledging* that you should be staying behind as well!"

Serena opened her mouth, twitched with a thought that stopped the words from coming—*First time I've seen that,* Estella thought—and then glared down at her somewhat rounded belly.

"You're more trouble than you're worth, you know that?" Serena snarled at her own torso.

SERENA HAD COMMITTED her fair share of fuckups, sure, but in trying to keep Estella safe and using her pregnancy as an excuse to bar her from the mission, all but forgetting their shared condition, she'd basically shot herself in the foot. The only fuckup that even nearly compared was the one time that she'd very nearly shot herself in the foot while suiting up for a mission several years earlier. Fortunately, the rogue shot found another warrior's foot by chance.

Lucky her.

Suffice to say, Serena was pissed. She was pissed at herself, pissed at Zane for actually following through, pissed at Zoey for being so sneaky and awesome as to record her for just that purpose, and, most of all, she was pissed at little Onyx. Not even out in the world and breathing air, and already the little asshole was causing her all sorts of grief.

You're grounded, she thought, glaring down at her stomach. *Grounded 'til you're, like, fifteen or something, you hear me?*

"Serena, I—" Zane began, still trying to get her to talk to them after the embarrassing episode.

Serena, not looking up from her stomach, held up a finger to silence him.

It was not her "hold on a second"-finger.

"Oh come on!" Zane growled. "How in the hell was I supposed to swing that sort of conversation to all the others, huh? What, something like, 'Hey, guys, we totally can't let Estella tag along, even though she's way stronger and—holy shit!—this is all about finding out about the Cebourists' magic and she's actually, y'know, a fucking *witch!* Why? Well, 'cause, like, she's pregnant and, well, mentally distraught from her husband being mutilated and laid out at the moment. What's that? My wife? Oh yeah, you mean the pregnant one who's basically made it a life mission to prove to everyone, her darling husband included, that she's totally batshit crazy? No, no! She's *totally* fit to tag along with us!'" He scoffed and shook his head, "Yeah, I can see that conversation gaining some major leverage with all of those uptight assholes." Groaning, he took the liberty to close the distance between them and sit down beside her, absently draping a thick, tattooed arm around her shoulders. "It wasn't for a lack of trying, babe. You and I both know that, pregnant or not, you'd kick more ass out there than any of them. Hell, we could probably say the same of Estella."

Serena gave him a look that melded the scornful, analytical eyes of jealousy and the coy, knowing smile of agreement. "You seem awful admirable of Missus Stryker, Zane. Should I be worried?"

Zane smirked at that and nodded. "Yeah, probably," he said, working a hand over the back of his head and wincing. "Assuming I piss her off again—and we know how I can be—I'd say it's worth worrying that she might kill me. But the sort of worry you're talking about?" he shook his head, "No, not likely. She's cute, I'll give her that—Stryker might dress like a Black Veil Brides-meets-Michael Jackson concert tour, but he definitely scored himself a good one with her—but, no, I can't see myself trying anything with her, honestly. No more than I can imagine Stryker trying to get with you."

Serena's eyes widened and her expression shifted to an all-out glare. "And what makes you think it's so outlandish that Xander Stryker could ever want me?"

Zane gave her a vacant stare.

"What?" she demanded, "Suddenly I'm not hot enough for *the* Xander Stryker?"

Her husband actually laughed at that. "How come you never ask if I want to fuck Zoey? Or, how 'bout this: how come we've never had this same conversation about whether or not Isaac wants to fuck you?"

Serena sneered at the ideas and shook her head. "No. No! Ew! Fuck! What's the matter with you? That's so—"

"Wrong?" Zane nodded and smirked. "Yeah, I'd say so. And, if you asked me, I'd say that Zoey's a good looking gal in her own right, too. And I'm sure you don't find Isaac as beastly as his species implies." He shrugged again and looked down, contemplative. "Zoey's my friend, has been for a long time. I can't see past that to other possibilities; I'm sure there might have been a time that it was possible—one of those "take this path and *blah* or take that path and *blah*"-sort of deals—but it simply never came to be, and I can't begin to imagine it now. And I have to imagine that you don't point that horny radar of yours in Isaac's direction because he and

Zoey are just so... I mean, they're perfect for each other, Serena. The same way that, in our own fucked up way, you and I are perfect for each other. The same way that Xander and Estella..." he trailed off, still staring at nothing in particular.

Serena watched him for a moment, considering his words. She smiled and leaned against his shoulder. "My big, dumb gorilla-man," she whispered longingly against him, taking in the scent of him and falling in love with him all over again. "How come you're only such a beautiful, romantic specimen when we're alone?"

She felt his body rumble with a chuckle; the arm he had around her tightened, making her feel secure and warm. "Because then it wouldn't be something that's exclusively yours, babe. You've shown me parts of yourself that nobody else gets to see—and, since this *is* you we're talking about, that doesn't leave much."

"Hey!" she smacked him. "You *told* me to post those pussy pics online!"

"No," Zane corrected, wagging a finger at her. "I *dared* you to post them online. And, yes, I said it'd be hot and, admittedly, I still think it's hot," he emphasized this point with a kiss to her forehead. "But that's hardly the point. See, much as I might joke otherwise, I don't mind if guys wanna ogle your body—it'd be a full-time job trying to break every face that dared to follow you with its eyes—but it's what's up here:" he lightly gave a few taps against the side of her head, "that I consider *mine.* You've shown me the Serena behind all the protective layers, and I know what those layers mean to you; it's a big deal that *anybody's* gotten to see the real you, let alone me, a big, dumb gorilla." He smirked at her again. "There's plenty that can make a person good for any number of other people, and, sure, Estella Stryker is severely fuckable—the same way that Zoey's severely fuckable or Scarlet Johanson is severely fuckable or Bonnie Rotten—"

"I get it, Zane," Serena cut him off, giggling and nuzzling against him. "You don't believe in soul mates."

Zane shrugged. "Maybe not quite in those words, no, but I believe that being severely fuckable in the eyes of somebody is hardly enough to make something of substance. Being severely fuckable might make you *good* for somebody, but Zoey and Isaac, Estella and Xander, you and me..." he looked off again, his aura swelling with pride, "There's substance there. True substance. And you don't fuck with that."

Serena smiled at that and nuzzled further against him. "You should write R-rated greeting cards."

"And you should direct pornos," Zane offered with a laugh.

Serena said "Speaking of Bonnie Rotten..." and then shared in the laugh with him.

Eventually the laughter trailed off and left them in a sweet, palpable silence that Serena felt perfect in.

"You know you're the only one I can feel comfortable in silence around," she whispered to him after a long moment in that perfection.

Zane smiled and nodded. "Yeah. I know. That's exactly what I was talking about."

Another long, sweet silence passed.

Zane asked, "So are you still mad at me?"

"Very," Serena said, though her voice was soft and loving. "But I'll still eat your asshole tonight."

They shared another laugh at that, then another long silence.

Finally, Serena pulled herself up and off of her husband and, taking a moment to adjust to the empty chill of *not* being against him, let out a heavy sigh. "I need you to do something for me," she finally said.

"Anything," he said, and she knew he meant it.

"I need you to go talk to Estella," she said. "And I mean *talk* to Estella—like... like *this* sort of talk; the real-Zane sort of talk."

Zane frowned at that. "But what about all that stuff about it being just yours?"

Serena shrugged. "It made me feel better, and if it can make her feel even a little bit better than I've got no right to keep something like that to myself."

He stared at her, a long and deep stare that penetrated her in ways she couldn't even begin to joke about. A wisp of a smile crossed his features, kept a ghost by the sheer awe that he wore. "I'd say that the world deserves to see the sort of person you really are... but I'm too selfish to share," he whispered. Then, nodding, he smiled a full smile, leaned in, and kissed her. "I'll do what I can for Estella. Just try to not be mad at me or our unborn, kay? We're doing our best."

"Assholes always do," Serena teased, but, like so much that she said, she didn't believe a word of it.

"Estella?" Zane knocked against one of the stacks of crates that served as the divide that separated the rest of the storage facility from the makeshift medical center.

She barely looked up from Xander, but Zane caught a shift in her shoulder that told him she'd heard.

He stepped across the imagined threshold, stood a few paces in.

"How's he doing?" he asked.

Estella finally looked up. Zane saw tears in her eyes. He wondered if she could see them in his, too.

Her shoulder tensed as though she were about to shrug, then she stopped, thought, opened her mouth to speak, paused, closed it, and finally settled on a shrug with the opposite shoulder.

Zane nodded and took a few more steps towards the Strykers. "That good, huh?"

Estella looked back down at Xander. Zane saw a few tears

fall from her cheeks onto her husband's bare torso. He imagined one of the movies that he always wound up watching with Serena and Gregori—those Disney nightmares *Tangled* and *Frozen* hanging in the forefront in this case—of such a symbolic event suddenly awakening the seemingly dead hero to a chorus of church bells, angel songs, and the excited fornication of woodland creatures across the landscape. Xander Stryker did not awaken.

Fuck you, too, Walt, Zane thought.

Zane looked down at Xander Stryker, the legend, himself. He looked dead. He was littered in stitched-up lacerations, his arms wore thrown-together slings composed of crate planks and torn fabric, and he had three bags of synth blood hanging over his head and feeding a steady source of the rancid stuff through feeding tubes that traveled past his wired jaw and into the darkness of his insides.

He thought absently that, with that much of the awful-tasting stuff not even earning a gag from the punk, it only reinforced the "already dead"-theory.

Estella flinched, and he wondered if she was holding back a sob or if she'd seen inside his head.

"I'm sorry," he said, assuming that, one way or the other, it was the best thing to say.

She shrugged again.

Zane thought for a moment, remembered what Serena had said, and took a deep breath.

"Xander told me he was bi earlier," he blurted out.

This made Estella look up at him. "What?" she asked, her voice husky from a lengthy silence.

"Bi," Zane repeated. "Like 'bisexual.'"

Estella rolled her eyes. "I know what 'bi' means, Zane. I meant 'what does that have to do with anything?'"

"Oh, right," Zane knocked his forehead in a "doi"-fashion and, taking a few more steps and finally getting close enough to do so, leaned against some unoccupied crates and folded his arms across his chest. "Well..." he stretched out the word so that he could map out the path of his words. "I just remember it sort of taking me off guard at the time."

"What are you telling me, Zane?" Estella sneered and folded her own arms across her chest. Somehow she seemed more intimidating for it than Zane ever felt doing it. "You some sort of homophobe?"

Zane blinked and shook his head violently, unfolding his arms to wave his hands in front of him. "Whoa! No! No, no, no! Nothing like that! I, uh, I even joked that I'd wished I was batting for the other team so I could..." he caught Estella raising an eyebrow at him and decided there was no saving that sentence. "Nevermind." He groaned, sighed, and let his head fall back. "God! This is so much easier with Serena..."

"What is?" Estella asked.

Zane frowned, wishing he hadn't said that aloud, and blew out another gust of air. "I... uh," he shrugged, "I was talking to Serena a moment ago, and, when I'm alone with her and get to talking about, you know, important shit and whatnot, I can tap into this... this... I dunno, like, this pool of 'rightness'—the right shit to say and the right way to say it, you know?" He shrugged again and looked up at her. "She calls it my R-rated greeting card talk. How cute is that, huh?" he asked, then blushed, wondering why he was saying that and why it mattered to the point.

But he had Estella listening, and—holy fucking shit!—he had her *almost* smiling.

Don't stop now, Zaney-boy! he heard himself say in his head, though it sounded suspiciously like Serena.

"Anyway," he went on, "I guess I just said the right shit the right way, 'cause she didn't seem so mad at me. Even said that I should come over here and say the right shit the right way for you. Only..." he shrugged a shoulder, "I don't seem to be so good at saying the right shit the right way when it ain't my wife I'm saying it to."

"Maybe," said Estella. "Then again, maybe not."

Zane studied her for a moment, so used to sarcasm and insincerity that he had to be sure there wasn't a delayed punchline waiting to crack down on him. There wasn't.

Estella leaned back against the crates holding Xander, absently taking his hand into her own as though it were the most delicate thing on the planet. Zane wondered, for the time being, if it wasn't.

"So," she said, her voice suddenly challenging, "you were mentioning my husband's sexuality?"

Zane nearly choked on the intake of a gasp and needed a moment to collect himself. "Y-yeah," he admitted. "Maybe not the best opening line ever."

"Guess we'll have to see where you go with it to find out," Estella offered.

Zane blinked, realizing that she was actually humoring his efforts—his *failing* efforts—and still giving him the benefit of the doubt.

"Right, well... I brought it up because it sort of stuck out as this moment when I saw him for more than what he is." He sighed and shook his head, "That sounds so stupid."

"Don't change cords in the middle of a song, Zane," Estella warned.

Agitated at himself, Zane drew in a deep breath and said, "It's like this: I'd always thought that bisexuals were, like, all *out there*. It seems stupid, I know, but I'd never really put too much thought on it before that moment. It just seemed that the key reason somebody would be willing to get down with both guys and girls would be because they *do* get down with both guys and girls—sort of a means of keeping the playing field open and available. It never really occurred to me that somebody could be bisexual *and* settle down with just one person, because to do so would—"

"Would make them out to be either straight or gay based on who they settled down with, right?" Estella finished for him.

Zane nodded. "Exactly. Exactly! So, like, what would be the point, right? Why say you're bisexual if you're shackled—pardon the term—with a single person. If a bi-guy settles down with a guy, then he's gay; if he settles down with a girl, then he's straight. End of story. But... but that's not the case."

"No," Estella agreed. "No, it's not."

Another nod. "And it just sort of opened my eyes up to a bigger picture, 'cause I got it at that moment: pardon the example, but if that same bi-guy settled with a chick, then he could still be watching gay porn and the other way around, right?"

Estella shrugged dismissively.

"It just occurred to me that... that there's the part that the world sees—dude's with a dude: gay; dude's with a chick: straight—and that's the reality they know. Xander Stryker..." Zane caught his eyes drifting towards Xander as he said his name, "he's got all sorts of bullshit reality tacked to his name by a world that just saw a convenient outer layer. Before we got here, we, like everyone else, just assumed Xander was some off-the-rails, spoiled brat with an ugly knack of blowing shit up and getting a free pass for it; obviously we know him better now. Sort of like going a long time talking about how so-and-so is queer as a three-dollar bill for marrying a guy, then walking in and catching him jerking off to Bonnie Rotten."

Estella sneered and said, "Who's... you know what? I don't want to know."

"Sorry," Zane nodded. "Got a little carried away there."

"Just a little," Estella said in a "way more than a little"-sort of tone.

"Moving right along," Zane said, clearing his throat nervously, "when Xander told me—well, told *us*—all this, it came around that none of it mattered one way or the other, 'cause he was with you. Case closed. There was this major complexity to the man that nobody would have ever considered, and he didn't even seem to care about it himself... because it rooted back to you. See, *that* was what got me to thinking more on it; the man..." he was now staring down at Xander, and Zane couldn't convince himself that he wasn't also talking to him at that moment, "he's just got so much shit going on at once. You know that more than anybody, I'm sure; I look at him and see a hundred-and-fifty pound guy with about three-tons of bullshit stacked on his shoulders, and, truth be told, I can only perceive, like, half-a-ton of it. I just don't get the rest of it. Probably never will. Just like his sexuality and how passive he was about it, I know there's even more layers to the guy that he's just, like, 'fuck it' over. World's gonna end? Fuck it! Everybody hates me? Fuck it! That badass Zane just called me Paris Hilton? Fu—well, no... he pretty thoroughly beat my ass after that, but you get my point."

"I'm not sure I do," Estella said, grinning, "but I like hearing it, anyway."

Zane couldn't help but smile, as well. "It's like this, Estella: there's an awful lot of 'fuck it' to be had with Xander Stryker—his sexuality, his status in the eyes of others," he shrugged, "*anything*, really—but *you*, Estella..." Zane blew out a breath for emphasis and shook his head, "Everything—EVERYTHING!—with that guy that even remotely stems back to you is, like," he held two fists together and yanked them apart, mimicking an explosion sound as he did and opening his palms as he separated them. He let the gesture linger a moment, dropped his hands, shrugged, and settled back against the crates. "Others might be stumped, might not know *how* that goth-loving son-of-a-bitch managed to stay alive through all that, but I think I've figured it out. They, like me, saw the beating; watched what that motherfucker and his team of sucker-punching douchebags did to your husband, and, like me, they were convinced that that was it! Lights out! Just like how they'd look at the two of you and—that's it!—assume he's straight. Case closed." Zane cocked his head to look at Xander from an angle, "But there's more to him. There's always more to him." Zane, still staring, realized he'd started nodding.

Estella stared at him, and Zane couldn't be sure if she was stunned out of admiration or disgust. "What have you figured out?" she finally asked.

Zane looked up at her. "Hmm?"

"Before," she clarified, "after you said that others are stumped about how he could've lived through that. You said that you think you'd figured it out. What have you figured out?"

"Oh," Zane nodded and shrugged, feeling like it was obvious at that point. "Same as everything else that he's not 'fuck it' over, 'Stell: you. Anybody who knows that boy enough to look past a convenient reality like 'gay' or 'straight' knows that the deciding factor is always you. Simply put, I don't think there's much of anything Xander couldn't do—or wouldn't try to do, at least—if he knew he was doing it for you."

CHAPTER 13
"LET ME OUT"

"Let me into the darkness again."
Stephen Crane (1871-1900)

Xander can feel Estella's hand on his; can hear the tears in her voice. His forms in all the planes of existence he hangs within tremble with rage, and he bellows the demand. He has had enough with visions, has had enough with wandering Ruby's mind, and he has most certainly had enough with this god damned table and all the dead faces.

"It's not that easy, Xander," Stan tells him.

Joseph Stryker nods, though he seems just as upset as Xander for this fact. "It never is, son."

Xander demands to know why; he goes around the table, asking them all what else there could possibly be. He might not know where he is, he admits, but he knows that he's not dead; not yet. This place—this moment—must exist as some sort of choice, and if that choice is whether or not he leaves Estella to face the outcome of his decision then he's already made it.

Xander makes the demand again.

"It is not that easy!" Stan repeats.

"It's not enough to simply make a decision, sweetheart," Xander's mother says, "you have to know why.*"*

Xander roars at that, pounding the table and cursing. None of the dead faces so much as blink at the display. He recites, over and over and over, about his love and his sacrifices and his efforts, through all of it, to do what he knew was right for Estella.

"You have to know that there's more to it than that," says his grandmother.

The Gamer wheezes and nods. "Side mission's not yet completed."

Xander whimpers, explaining that he doesn't understand what they want from him.

"My boy," Osehr says with a scoff, "why do you always think it's what the rest of the world wants from you?"

Father Tennesen nods and adds, "Have you not given enough of yourself, Xander?"

Xander says that it won't ever be enough; not so long as Estella is out there *and he's...*

"Still a numb-nuts!" Marcus throws his hands in the air and shakes his head. "The kid's always, always, always *gonna be a know-nothing numb-nuts!"*

"And you weren't?" Joseph Stryker says with a grin.

"Give him a chance," Xander's mother says.

Xander stares at them, makes the demand again.

"IT'S NOT THAT EASY," all nine of them say at once this time.

Xander, taken aback by the aggression in this, finds himself thinking for the first time on their words. Breathing in something he can't even be sure is air, he asks them all why they're there.

"Because you're still here," they all respond, once again.

SERENA WAS on the verge of tears by the time Zane finally stepped out of the corner. She had, and she knew that he knew, been not far off and eavesdropping the entire time. She'd tried her best to "sound" like him in his head, to give him the push he'd needed with that "*Don't stop now*"-line, but she knew—

"Zaney-boy?" he groused at her as he walked by, shaking his head. "You actually think I'd call myself that in my own thoughts?"

Serena shrugged and followed. "It was either that or 'dip-shit,'" she said, "It was a gamble, I know, and I'm willing to admit when I bet wrong."

Zane sighed and nodded, turning to face her. "How'd I do otherwise?" he asked.

"You did good," she admitted, giving him a hug that carried the sincerity she knew he'd be doubting. "Bit of a checkered start with that 'your hubby's a homo'-talk—super-hot to know that, by the way—but, yeah," she nodded against him, "you made it work."

"I didn't call him a homo," Zane defended.

Serena shrugged. "I know. And you also didn't picture the two of you locked in some vampiric rendition of *Brokeback Mountain*, either; but..." she gave another shrug.

Zane groaned and shook his head. "And what would you think if I joked about you and Estella all oiled up and buried face-first in each other's—"

"Oh, Zane," Serena smirked up at him, "do you *honestly* believe I haven't slapped my meat wallet at least a dozen times to *that* thought?" Her husband noticeably reeled back at this, and Serena saw his aura shift in a flurry of activity. She had to stifle the urge to cackle at that moment. Wondering how far she could take the joke, she put her mouth to his ear and whispered, "Now ask me what sort of fantasies I have about Zoey."

"Whoa!" Zane shook his head and pulled away, half laughing and half retching. "No! Nope! *Nuuuupe!* There it is! I know you're fucking with me!"

Unable to hold it any longer, Serena laughed. It was a good, folding-over-til-the-baby-kicks sort of laugh. She needed that laugh at that moment.

Zane shook his head and groaned. "I'm not going to survive you like this," he muttered. "I'd nearly forgotten how... how *crazy* you get when you're knocked-up."

"Yeah? Well," Serena shrugged, "you marry crazy, you get crazy."

"Fair enough," Zane was walking past her and heading towards where the two cars were parked.

Though he'd already gotten suited up for the mission, he'd waited on arming himself. Dipping into the remaining armory in the trunk of Sawyer's destroyed car, he began to pick-and-choose from what was left. A few automatic pistols found their way under each of his arms, some extra magazines in a hip-mounted leather bag, and, as his hands traced over a few mid-sized blades, Serena caught his gaze lock onto a small-yet-vicious-looking hatchet that had been all but buried in the back corner of the trunk. It was somewhere between something a Viking and a native warrior might have carried, but dulled by rust and years of misuse. Serena thought it had become more hammer than axe in that time, but this, from the look on his face, was not a deterrent.

Smash a lot of skulls with something like this, she "heard" her husband think as he hoisted it and gave a slow, calculating test swing with it.

"So what do you want me to knit you?" Serena asked. "Maybe a pair of ball-warmers?"

"Huh?" Zane looked back at her.

Serena shrugged. "Y'know, kinda like mittens, but just one of 'em, and it goes over your balls to—"

"Not the—*fuck!* What's wrong with you? I just don't know what you're talking about!"

Another shrug, this time paired with a pout. "Well, I figure since you're leaving us useless pregnant ladies behind we might as well do something wifey, right? I don't know shit about baking apple pie, 'cept that that one movie made it obvious you're not supposed to fuck them."

Zane rolled his eyes. "You don't know shit about knitting, either," he pointed out. "And, for the record, I'd never, never-*ever* put my balls in *anything* you made. Knowing my luck there'd be a mouse trap or something waiting in there."

Serena mock-pouted at that. "Was hoping you wouldn't figure it out."

"Not such a dumb gorilla, huh?" he said.

"You still sore about that?" she asked.

He shrugged and strapped a sleek-looking silver revolver to his side. "Why not? You still seem sore about having to stay behind."

He had her there.

"Besides," he went on, "I thought we were past all this? You and I had our moment—you even making that licking my asshole remark, which I don't want, by the way—and I even did what you asked with Estella."

Serena rolled her eyes. "In order of appearance: just because it was clarified that I adore you with everything that I am *does not* mean that I'm suddenly ecstatic about you going out there without me. You're the father to my children and the love of my life, Zane; I don't like the idea of letting that just slip out into certain danger with a hug, a kiss, and a 'love ya, babe.' In case you haven't noticed, husbands facing near-death experiences sort of seems to be a theme right now, and with how competitive you've been with Stryker in the past I worry that 'near-death' won't be good enough for you." She looked away and sniffled, shaking her head.

She knew that Zane knew that she was shaking her head at herself. Before he could say anything, though—before he could even try to stop her train of thought—she took off with it again:

"I don't have to like the idea of *not* being there to keep your ass from doing something stupid!" She sniffled, forced a cough, then locked her eyes on his, forcing her "I'm a horny bitch who jokes about testicular mittens"-face back into play. "And—oh yeah!—fuck you for knocking a rimjob from yours truly." She smacked him and shook her head. "Honestly! I let you fuck my ass *constantly*, but the minute it's your asshole getting a little play I gotta put up with the macho-man, 'exit only!'-crap? Spare me! Don't knock it 'til you try it, Zaney-boy!" She caught him about to argue, saw on his aura that he was about to use the "let you fuck my ass"-line against her, and, before he could get the chance, interjected with, "And before you go pointing out that I *ask* you to fuck my ass, I'd like to point out that, when I'm done with you, you'll be *asking* me to strap on a mile-long dildo and fuck yours, as well!"

Zane blinked, blushed, and, realizing that a few people had overheard their conversation, shook his head. "Look, whatever, okay? Just, *please,* stop being pissy and moany and..." he sighed, "fine! Whatever you want! Just don't make me go out there thinking you're upset."

Serena smiled, though not for the reason he likely thought. She felt lucky to have a husband like him at that moment; felt good to have a man who, despite everything the world was going through, could make her feel like things *weren't* changing.

Then she remembered Estella; remembered Xander. The smile slipped from her face, and she looked back towards the corner.

Zane had done right for Estella.

Maybe it was time somebody did right for Xander.

"I'm not mad at you, Zane," she offered, turning back with a warm, sincere smile, one that he likely didn't get to see as often as she felt he deserved. She made a mental note to let him see it more often. "You go kick some ass, baby," she said. "And give one of 'em a kick to the nards for your baby-mama, kay?"

Though he could tell that she was up to something—his aura kept no secrets—he only nodded.

And then, after a few minutes' worth of chatter, orchestrated almost entirely by Sawyer and Dianna, they were gone.

Serena watched them head out, on foot—not nearly enough cars to carry even the modest number of warriors—and waited until they were out of sight before heading back towards Xander.

XANDER DOESN'T UNDERSTAND what the dead faces meant by "Because you're still here." This, to him, seems like a weird reason for the dead to stick around. Unless, of course, they were waiting on him to die. He says this, making sure they can hear the repulsion in the theory.

His father shakes his head at him. "You're right to think that you're neither alive nor dead, son. But you're not here because of us. You've trapped yourself here, and we're here because you're here."

Xander asks why he'd do that.

"Because your dumb ass is still blaming yourself for my death," Marcus says.

"Mine too," The Gamer offers

Osehr, nodding, says, "And for mine."

Father Tennesen only nods.

"In some way, shape, or form, Xander, you blame yourself for all of our deaths," Stan summarizes, shrugging, "in some way or another."

"And still many more have died, and even more will go on to die," his grandmother goes on, nodding back to all the many other faceless forms that surround them.

*Xander still believes he can almost—*almost!*—recognize some of them, but he can't place names to any. Looking away, he asks if any of them, with the exception of his father, believed he wasn't somehow responsible for their deaths. His father, he admits, he can't begin to take blame for, having not been born yet, but the others...*

He points out that Kyle pursued his mother to get to him; that his grandmother died protecting him when his budding powers began attracting hostiles; that Depok and the entire Odin Clan, for that matter, died for bringing him into their ranks. Marcus, he goes on, died because of a vendetta against the Stryker family—was even given a chance to walk away and leave Xander to Lenix—and Osehr, after sacrificing an arm to the same cause, died when he sacrificed his auric hold on him in the middle of a plane crash to focus on saving Estella. Shaking his head, feeling like he was making a series of solid points, he nodded towards The Gamer and then Father Tennesen, pointing out that they'd died because he ignored obvious threats—missed every opportunity to save them when he had a chance—and points out that even one of the newbies in his clan would have had sense enough to pick up on those threats. Then, leveling his eyes at Stan, he says that he'd only hours ago watched him die solely *because he wasn't fast enough or smart enough to take down Ariel when he had the chance.*

Father Tennesen shakes his head at all of that and says, "Such blind guilt; such reckless shame. When—oh, when—will you stop hating yourself, Xander Stryker?"

Xander's mother whimpers and says to Joseph, "He was always such a happy boy before..." then, unable to finish, she stifles a sob into her hands.

Xander's father frowns at that, saying, "You can't keep blaming yourself for Kyle."

His mother bites her lip at that and shakes her head, replying, "I do... because he *does."*

Xander's eyes widen at that, but he's unable to deny her words or defend her from their meaning at that moment. He's realizing that, though bits of their auras have remained with him—stayed with him in their own way—they're almost entirely reflecting his own ideas of what they must think; what they must feel. Looking at his mother, he wonders how much is her, *and how much is bits of his own guilt holding the rest together. He wonders then, feeling sickened by it, that his mother is blaming herself for Kyle because, somewhere deep down, if he still blames her for Kyle.*

He hears Stan sigh beside him. "Still playing that blame game, Xander? Haven't you learned anything?" he chides him.

Marcus scoffs at that and says, "Take it from me, numb-nuts here won't learn a damn thing unless you beat it into him over and over again. Kid's a bigger masochist than that Vailean-babe probably is."

Xander shudders, wondering, if his theory has any merit to it, if ghost-Marcus' attraction to Serena means that he has some subconscious attraction to her.

Somewhere on the outskirts of his subconscious, the words "severely fuckable" *echo.*

"Oh my!" Xander's mother gasps, and Xander isn't sure if it's a response to Marcus' "masochist"-line or if she's somehow hearing his most distant thoughts. Then, as a secondary thought that sweeps away the first, he realizes that her "oh my!" sounded more like something Estella might have said; the response seeming familiar for all the wrong reasons. He realizes then that he has no memories of his mother and her outlook on the subject of sex—she'd died when he was still too young for the subject to come up with any real substance—and so, with no frame of reference, she seems to be getting patched together with a convenient substitute: the most perfect woman in Xander's mind.

It doesn't exactly prove his theory—for all he knew his mother was *like that—but it's making him think.*

"Listen," Marcus goes on, "the kid needs guidance. Why else do you think he brought us here? Why else do you think he's stuck himself here? He's got a game plan, he's got the know-how, he's even got Stan's fucking powers, but here we are! Here... we... are! What does that tell you?"

"Tells me that he lacks faith," Father Tennesen says with no small amount of sympathy riding on his voice.

Depok shakes his head. "Tells me that he's scared, and with good reason!"

Osehr laughs at that. "Xander? Afraid? There are only two things that scare Xander Stryker, friend: himself and his wife!"

"And with good reason!" Depok repeats.

"It tells me," Stan says with a heavy sigh, "that he never took the gun barrel out of his mouth."

Xander's mother lets out a sob.

Xander tells Stan to shut the fuck up.

"Then take the gun barrel out of your mouth," Stan says.

Xander blinks at this, realizes that he can't find his voice—that, in fact, he'd never had his voice; he wonders how he's said everything so far without actually saying a damn thing—and, shivering with a sudden dread, he pulls his hand away, feeling a cold, metallic weight slip free from his open mouth.

He sets Yang down in front of him. The eight-chambered, bone-white revolver contrasts with violent crispness against the dark table and the black backdrop that everything here is set against.

Xander stretches his jaw and shivers. "Thought I was doing better with that..."

His mother's eyes shine wetly as she says, "You are, sweetheart, it's just not—"

"I'm obviously not *when I just pulled a fucking gun out of my—" Xander moves to yank up the gun—to illustrate a point—but, where it rested moments ago, a familiar tatter of red and purple material looks up at him.*

"What the...?"

He blinks, and a pitcher of iced tea is sweating on the table in front of him.

He looks up, startled. Nobody else mirrors his confusion at the phenomena.

"What's...?" he begins, looking back down. A yellowed page torn from an old, dusty book has taken the pitcher's place. Xander jumps to his feet, and in the interval between sitting and standing the switch has happened again and he's staring at a kukri, it's boomerang-like blade shimmering under a nonexistent light.

Xander weeps, covering his eyes. "Why are you...?"

"They're not doing anything, Xander," Stan explains. "Now open your eyes; face your loaded gun."

Xander, trembling, takes his hands away. There's a case of enchanted bullets waiting for him. Shivering at the sight, he looks up at The Gamer, who gives him a casual shrug in response.

It's only a moment between glances, but when Xander's eyes return to the table's surface, The Gamer's bullets have been replaced by a severed arm, blood pooling out of the hacked end while the other, clawed and bestial, clenches blindly. It's practically dragging itself across the table to Osehr.

Xander cries out and falls back, lands hard; he spots Trepis staring out at him from beneath it, the tiger's eyes luminous and sad.

"Oh god..." Xander groans, shaking his head. He wants nothing more than to crawl under that table with his tiger, to nuzzle in his fur and forget all about what's waiting for him on the table's surface. It seems such a cozy idea: just to hide under it all with Trepis.

"Stand up, Xander," Stan says.

Somewhere far off—feeling almost like a completely different lifetime away—Xander feels something warm and perfect push up beside him; feels Estella against him, asleep and happy with him. And then, just like that, he doesn't feel like hiding.

He remembers that Stan had told him to stand.

He does.

Father Tennesen's rosary is waiting where Osehr's arm had been.

Letting out a slow breath, Xander keeps his eyes focused on the beaded necklace, the cross hanging at a lopsided angle on one end. Though he'd never been a religious person, it's a peaceful relic to stare at for the time being; better than the severed therion arm, at least.

"Some have given more than others," Stan says beside him, "but you need to remember that none of them—none of us*—ever resented giving these things for you."*

Xander thinks about this for a moment, then, taking in a deep breath, prepares to blink. He knows that Stan's relic is next, and he's certain that it won't be as pleasant as the rosary.

"Quite a shit-show, isn't it, hot-stuff?"

He blinks.

Xander is staring down at a white revolver.

He frowns and looks at Stan. "What about your...?"

Stan chuckles and shakes his head. "You can't fit what I've given you on this table, buddy; can't even fit in in this place. It is *this table, it* is *this place, and it* is *what's trying to get you to see."*

"The Great Machine," Xander whispers.

Stan shrugs. "It calls itself lots of things. Like us—like you—it has a flair for dramatics. Hopefully you two get along this time, maybe learn to play nice. Then again," he gives another shrug, this one less passive and more possessive, "it was never you and it *that had a problem getting along, was it?"*

Xander remembers arguing with his reflection; remembers cursing himself and the awful places parts of his mind went with the freedom that Stan's power offered.

Begrudgingly, he realizes it was never really the power's fault.

"There you go playing the blame-game again."

*Xander stares down at his late father's gun—*his *gun—and shivers at the faint metallic taste lingering in his mouth.*

Xander wants to ask them all why they're there once again, but this time the question comes out "Why am I here?"

ESTELLA WAS ASLEEP. She'd somehow managed to wedge herself beside Xander on what little space remained on the crates so that his body went undisturbed. It looked uncomfortable and sad and awful, but Estella's face was the most peaceful Serena had seen since all this had begun.

Certain as she was that Missus Stryker would be waking up sore, she opted to leave her be. Scooping up Estella's jacket, she used it to cover her and Xander—believing true love slept under the same covers—and planted a rose-petal soft kiss on Estella's forehead before whispering "it'll be alright, Goddess."

Estella let out a soft hum at this, smiled an angel's smile, and cozied herself closer against Xander.

Battered as he was, Xander didn't seem to mind.

Serena wanted to believe this was because he wanted her there, but she couldn't deny it was likely because he was too gone to even know she was there. She sighed, shook her head, and then buried her face in her palms. For a moment, maybe a minute—who the fuck can really keep track of shit like that?—Serena toiled with the idea of letting herself cry. Then, resigning to certain inescapable quirks of her inner self, she admitted that she could never let herself do that so long as there was a chance that Estella might wake up needing a dry shoulder to cry on.

Instead, she looked at Xander, seeing where they'd taped some gauze over where his left eye should have been, and said, "Quite a shit-show, isn't it, hot-stuff?"

Xander Stryker said nothing, but Serena thought she saw a shift in his aura. For the briefest of moments, she had herself convinced that he'd responded to her, but then she realized that his aura was still *inside* him—concealed within his battered body—and that what she'd seen was—what?—a shift of the light, or maybe some dust that caught a soft air current at just the right moment?

All the same, Serena decided to keep talking.

She told Xander that she was thinking of making a call back to her clan, that she wanted to check in on things at home. Then she said that she had some friends—Nikki and Raith—who might be able, though perhaps not so willing, to help.

"In either case," she said with a sigh, "it's worth a shot. Every little bit helps, right?"

Xander Stryker said nothing.

Serena found it easier and easier to talk to Xander, though she was distantly aware that what she was doing was better described as talking *at* Xander. It was as safe as talking to herself with the added comfort of having a face to confide to, one that wore enough pain and suffering that Serena didn't feel the need to sugarcoat the painful and sufferable. She didn't have to be a mommy at that moment. She didn't have to be the crazy, erratic blonde that helped convince everyone else that things weren't so bad. At that moment, talking to Xander, she didn't have to pretend.

It wasn't long before Serena realized she was crying, and this, she decided, was okay, because the Strykers were asleep and she could be strong for either one of them once they were awake.

Eased, weightless, Serena talked to Xander Stryker.

And still Xander Stryker said nothing.

Serena talked about Zane—about what a wonderfully brilliant and shining fuckwit he was and how, no, she could never love anybody the way she loved that man—and she talked about how she hoped little Gregori would be a good brother once she'd gotten through this hormonal hell known as pregnancy. Inspired, but not about to spill the beans, she told him that Estella missed him terribly, and that, when he finally got his stubborn, tight little ass out of his coma—"or whatever it is"—she had some wonderful news for him. Serena told Xander that, though he shouldn't be worried, she'd fallen head-over-heels in love with his wife, that she knew they'd be friends forever, and, dammit, he'd better be okay with her taking Estella off to Vegas and Paris and Tokyo and—why not?—even Channing Tatum's backyard on what she decided then would be "weekly weekend girl getaways."

"But don't worry," she assured him, "because Zoey's gonna come with us, too, and she's good at making sure I behave... most of the time."

She tried to giggle at her own joke, but it erupted into a choking sob that had her bawling so heavily that she found herself leaning against the crate.

Xander Stryker said nothing.

But Serena heard his heartrate double and sensed his aura, undeniable this time, as it shifted like somebody might shift in their sleep.

Gasping, she moved to look up.

Xander Stryker said nothing...

But he stared at her through a heavily-lidded blood-red eye.

"H-hey..." Serena stammered, not sure what else to say or do at that moment.

Xander blinked, looked like he wanted to move, and then caught sight of Estella at his side. His body went still, as though he was dead set on not interrupting her rest, and Serena saw his body seem to melt with happiness at the sight of her. The sheer, radiating happiness that exuded from his body—not just his aura, but *him*—put Serena in a time not long ago, standing in the most wonderful rain shower, caught in Zane's arms, and knowing—*KNOWING!*—that he was the one.

Then, blinking away tears of happiness, Serena saw that Xander was looking at her. He looked sad, sorry even, as though catching her in the middle of some terrible tragedy. Somehow, Serena realized, he was. He wasn't *here*, she saw—not with her in some ramshackle storage facility neighboring the harbor, at least—but somewhere terrible and tragic. She could see that he wanted to say something, but he was working to choose his words carefully.

She wanted to warn him that his jaw was broken; that his jaw was wired. She wanted to tell him that he wouldn't be able to—

His jaw remained locked, but his lips moved around his feeding tubes. No words came out, none that she could hear, but he spoke to her anyway:

I'm sorry you couldn't save him, but, in the end, he saved us all.

"I'll take 'Philosophical Questions for the Ages,' Alex," Osehr jokes, and Xander tenses at the name for a brief moment before realizing that the old therion is talking about a gameshow host.

"I get it," Xander groans, not getting it at all. "I need to go back. Estella needs me. Please," he says, repeating himself: "let me out."

"It's not that easy," Stan says again.

"Look," Xander growls, slamming his fist down on the table. The white revolver thumps *from the impact, "while I'm in here talking to you—talking to myself; whatever* this *is—people are dying out there. My friends..." Xander blinks and shakes his head, fighting the urge to cry, "E-Estella... I can't leave them to face this on their own! It's not fair to do that to them!"*

"IT IS NOT FAIR TO DO THIS TO YOURSELF!" Joseph Stryker roars at him.

Xander staggers back, staring, wide-eyed, at his father.

"You..." Joseph shakes his head, "You've come all this way, done so much for so many, and you still, still, STILL work to destroy yourself! How far have you come, truly, since the nights of squatting in the room your grandmother gave to you, carelessly gambling with the life your mother died to protect with one of my *guns? What great epiphany, what glorious revelation, have you triumphed since those days? Huh? HUH?" Joseph spits and shakes his head at Xander, "As far as I'm concerned, that camera you were staring into was no different than the gun barrel you insisted on swallowing."*

Xander flinches at this, his lip trembling. "I... I thought I was doing something—"

"Something what, numb-nuts? Something bold, brave, revolutionary?" Marcus asks, shaking his own head. "Ha! If you thought it was such a wonderful idea then why didn't you tell that pretty wife of yours what you were planning? I'm gonna go ahead and guess it wasn't for her protection—not really, dipshit—no, I'd say it was because you knew *that she'd be the voice of reason. You* knew *that she'd say that you were on to something—and, oh yeah, you were, no argument here—but that your idea sucked major ass."*

Depok sighs and nods. "I'm inclined to agree, Xander. You went rogue with that one; took a lot of steps to basically ensure you wouldn't survive the night. And if Stan hadn't given you his powers..." he finishes with a shrug.

"Great! Fine! Whatever! I was stupid! But you can't honestly expect me to say that I wanted this,*" Xander argues. "Taking reckless chances is not the same as sticking a gun in your mouth!"*

Stan shrugs at that. "A one-in-eight chance with a gun versus—what?—you against the entire mythos world?"

Joseph glares at Xander, shaking his head. "Your chances were better with the gun, son. And you knew that."

"Can't we at least agree that, as a symbol, it's—"

"LISTEN TO THE HIGH-SCHOOL DROPOUT SPOUTING ABOUT SYMBOLS NOW!" Marcus roars with laughter.

"There is a vast journey between not *sticking a gun in your mouth and loving yourself," Osehr says.*

Xander growls, thinking, Maybe I'm tired of the journey!

"We can hear your thoughts in this place, dipshit," Marcus scoffs. "But at least we're getting somewhere; at least now you're being honest with yourself. You're here—say it with me class:—BECAUSE YOUR DUMB ASS ISN'T SURE IT WANTS *TO WAKE UP!"*

Stan sighs and nods. "It's true, Xander. I know you think you made the decision after the fight with Ariel for the sake of protecting mythos—for the sake of protecting Estella—but, and I need you to understand this as the truth, you made the decision after the fight with Ariel because I died in that fight."

"The straw that broke the camel's back," Xander's grandmother says with a nod.

"Not enough hit points left for the beating you're always giving yourself," The Gamer chimes in.

Xander's mother whimpers. "Xander, you've just kept adding more and more blame—taking on more and more guilt—and it's dragged you down all over again."

"And now that part of you is refusing to go back," Osehr explains. "You've convinced yourself that you'll just get everyone killed."

"Nobody can blame you for hurting like this, Xander," his mother goes on, tears still streaming down her face, "but, sweetheart, you can't keep doing this to yourself!"

Father Tennesen nods. "Cleanse yourself of the past, Xander; have faith."

Joseph Stryker nods, frowning. "You won't be any good in the coming war if you're in your own head warring with yourself."

"The war..." Xander repeats, and he once again sees a flash of an inescapable future where Estella's life hangs in the balance...

And he doesn't make it in time.

Xander shakes his head so violently it feels like it might fall from his shoulders. He hopes it will. Then, just like that, he's forgotten that path and every domino leading up to it.

"See what I mean?" Marcus says. "Stubborn asshole's gotta fight us every step of the way."

"Why don't you want to see?" Xander's mother asks him.

Xander shakes and looks away. "I can't watch her die," he confesses.

"She has to die, son," Joseph Stryker says.

"Does he know who—" Marcus begins, but Stan shakes his head at him.

"If he can't bring himself to see," Stan explains to him, "then who are we to think that we can bring him to see?"

"I can't watch..." Xander whimpers, swaying in his chair. "I can't watch... I can't watch... I can't—"

SEE! *a booming voice trumpets without sound over them, and everyone at the table jumps. Everyone except Stan, who only shakes his head.*

"Your tenacity, though admirable, is far from helpful."

Xander shivers, forgets what he's shivering about, and looks up. He sees nine faces that he still believes he's failed sitting with him at a ten-sided table. They're surrounded by countless others he's put there; countless others who died in some way or another because of him.

Exhausted, he lets his head fall back so he can stare up at a sky of nothing. He feels a tiger he loved deeply, one whose likeness was magically branded into his arm, nuzzle his left leg. Somehow, unsure how he could possibly know such a thing, he knows the word "TRAITOR" has been carved into his flesh in that spot. Seeming to know this, as well, Trepis drags a sandpaper tongue across it, but the spot the tiger licks and the flesh bearing the wound are a lifetime apart.

He's too tired to make sense of that; too tired to understand what all these dead people want from him—or what they suspect he wants from them, if their riddles are any indicator of what this is all about —and he's definitely *too fucking tired to make sense of why he can hear somebody who* sounds *like Serena Vailean but talks like a regular person telling him things that Serena would* never *tell him.*

This is the part where I smell burning feathers, *he thinks.* I'll taste pennies, see some flashing lights, and then, if there's any justice—any justice, at all—I will be dead and all this will be gone from me.

"Stupid motherfucker!" Marcus growls.

Xander's mother whimpers at the outburst... or Xander's thoughts. They can *be heard, after all.*

Xander sighs and lets his head drop back so he can see them once again.

"Let me hit him!" Marcus demands from Stan. "Just one good shot across his jaw ought to—"

"You get up from that chair and there won't be enough of you to swing a punch," Stan says with all the annoyed boredom of a teacher who's already taught this lesson.

"I've asked for you to let me out of here," Xander accuses those at the table, "and you've all said it's not that easy. 'Not that easy,'" he mocks, "'not that easy,' 'not that easy!' Fine, then! Give me easy! Is the other way easier? You want me to just give up? This some sort of revenge mission for all of you? I got you all dead and now you're here to trap me in a corner where the only way out is me willingly checking out? Fine! FINE! I give up, then! You can get your way, I'll go the way of the dodo, and maybe, with my pathetic ass dead and gone, Estella can find herself somebody worth a damn!"

"It's not that easy," Xander's mother, grandmother, and Stan all say at once.

"MOTHERFUCKER!" Xander roars, scooping up the revolver. "I'll show you easy!"

He moves to jam the gun into his mouth, but what slips between his teeth is flat and tastes bitter and chemical-laced.

Drawing it away so he can see what the gun has become this time, he finds himself staring at an old photo of himself and Estella as children. The photo that Estella had kept of them, even during the worst of times.

It was the picture that, through her magic, she used to connect herself to him.

"Estella...?" Xander sighs and shakes his head. "Why show me this if wanting to wake up for her isn't enough?"

"You keep showing him," Marcus grouses, "and he keeps forcing *himself to forget!"*

Joseph glares across the table at him. "Dammit, man, how would you take knowing that sort of thing?"

Xander's mother nods, sympathetic. "It's a very complicated thing to try to cope with," she says, "without the weight of everything else."

Behind him, Xander hears Ruby call to him. She says it's time, that they're going to be late.

Damn birthday parties, *Xander thinks, rolling his eyes—*eye? *he wonders, then wonders why he's wondering and confirms, yes,* eyes!*—and follows Ruby. They're all there, but it's Serena Vailean that, for whatever reason, he's drawn to at that moment. She's sad—so sad—and who could blame her?*

Wait... why? *Xander knows he knows, but doesn't know what he knows.*

He travels back. Hops the dominos of time leading to that moment until he reaches... yes, this is—

"NO!" Xander cries and moves to look away.

SEE!

Xander has no eyelids in this place. No front or back to turn away, but he can *forget and fight every new replay to keep on forgetting.*

Keep on forgetting!

Keep on...

He forgets what he's working to forget; forgets the why and the what. Now all he sees are shadows of a past of a future. He's lost in time—lost in the dominos—and there are nine dead faces sitting at a ten-sided table telling him he has to SEE! SEE! SEE!

But all Xander sees is the shadow of a woman—platinum blonde and crazy as life itself—as she wails the wail of loss, clinging to a male—strong and certain and as close to the blonde as a man can get to a woman—who's just died in her arms. This death, Xander sees, will haunt the blonde forevermore—she's sad, and who could blame her?—*but, in dying, he paved the way for great things.*

But how do you tell somebody something like that...?

It hurts Xander to imagine—it's a heavy burden to bear—but, yes, Estella is there with him. She's sleeping, beautiful; wonderful.

Sleep, baby, *he thinks to her, wondering why he cannot touch her at that moment,* you've done plenty.

But having her there gives him strength enough...

Then he's back at the party—Damn birthday parties—*and he's drawn to Serena Vailean at that moment. She's sad—so sad—and who could blame her? But Xander knows just what to say:*

"I'm sorry you couldn't save him, but, in the end, he saved us all."

Serena Vailean cries then, but they're tears of appreciation. She hugs him—a friendly hug, and why not, they've been friends for so long—and the party carries on around them.

Xander falls back into his seat at the table, still feeling Serena's arms around him, still tasting her tears. He is crying with her, but it's not yet time to cry—will not be time to cry for some time.

"I'm sorry."

"Sorry."

It feels right—or, rather, it will feel right—to Xander, apologizing for a death; sharing in that pain.

"I... I'm sorry that you all died," Xander says to the table.

"Swing and a miss!" Marcus laughs at him.

His parents and his grandmother regard him as only parents can regard a child who's just not quite understanding a simple lesson.

The Gamer groans, looking bored.

Depok and Osehr and Stan wipe at their faces, a pair of enlight-

ened minds trying to figure out how to connect with one that just doesn't get it.

Xander groans and shakes his head, annoyed. He remembers that he'd been onto something, but then he was dragged away and shown...

Something...

Something else.

Driven, Xander strains, pushes his mind to remember the conversation that he'd been having with them seconds *ago...*

Only it was really nearly a decade now, wasn't it?

But it was about Estella, yes. Estella...

Right?

"Estella..." he says, speaking more to himself.

"Xander, brother," Marcus says, pleading with him now, "not everything is about her now, man! Don't you get that! There's more now! MORE! You just won't allow yourself to see her!"

"See... who?" Xander asks.

He hears Ruby calling to him, and, just like that, he's walking with her in her mind again. She's apologizing, saying she didn't have any other choice. Then she's not her, and she says she loves him and asks if he'll hold her until she falls asleep.

And, damn him, he says he will.

Estella...

"Ruby!"

Estella...

"RUBY!"

"At some point, Xander," Stan's speaking softly to him, "you're going to have to accept that you can't save everyone. And sometimes that's just the way it has to be."

Xander sees a future where Estella's life hangs in the balance...

And no matter how he moves the dominos he cannot ever make it to her.

"Ruby..." a voice calls from somewhere at the table, but Xander isn't sure who says it.

Another whispers, "Estella..."

"You can't save her, Xander," Stan says again, "and you can't go into that moment without understanding that she needs *to die."*

Xander shivers. "You expect me to wake up... knowing that?"

And, damn them all, they did.

ESTELLA GASPED AND SHOT UPRIGHT, overbalanced on the thin section of crate she'd balanced herself on, and threw out her aura to catch herself before she fell. Then, on her feet but still gasping—not from the sense of falling upon waking, but something that she carried with her out of sleep—she began to calm her breathing, focusing with each new breath on evening them out. Her heartrate settled, the jackhammer pounding subsiding until it no longer thundered in her ears. Then, finally, she took in a healthy, normal breath and blew it out.

Without her heart or her labored breaths to block it out, it became so easy to hear the panicked sobs that Estella found herself wondering how she'd ever missed them.

"Serena?" she called.

The crying did not stop, didn't even stutter at the sound of Estella's voice.

Worried for her friend, Estella hurried towards her, pausing only briefly to look back at Xander. Then, tearing herself away once more and following the sound, she spotted Serena, sitting in the middle of the stairs. She'd made it as far as the first landing, where the steps on the north-facing wall met and started up along the east-facing wall. Serena was sitting with her back against the corner, her legs splayed out across the platform so that Estella had to step over one just to get to her. Her eyes were wide, staring out towards the ceiling but, Estella knew, not at the ceiling, and she heaved, fighting for air to fuel the sobs. She was hyperventilating.

Overwhelmed by the scene, it took Estella a moment to hear

the second set of cries, which, stifled, sounded more like whimpers.

"Oh god, Serena! SERENA! You've gotta let him go! Too tight; you're... dammit, Serena, you're holding him too tight! Gregori! Come here, sweetie! It's okay! Your mommy's gonna be okay! Just... oh god, Serena, what—upstairs! Go on upstairs, Gregori. I'm going to help Mommy, okay? Just go on upstairs; we'll be right up, okay?"

Estella had to draw out almost all of Serena's strength to pry her suffocating son from her arms. The moment Gregori was free from Serena's panic-driven grip, the blonde vampire shrieked in agony—shrieked as though somebody had just murdered Gregori rather than simply freed him from her arms —and her sobs began anew as she pulled Estella against her, cradling her as she had her son. Gregori sniffled, worried for his mother, but scampered up the stairs and slunk away into the office.

"Serena! Serena, please!" Estella had to struggle to keep Serena from dragging her into the same suffocating hold. She looked up, unable to get Serena to return to the here-and-now. She gripped her arm, drew more energy—now needing to weaken her not just for clarity, but for the sake of not being strangled—and, finally, managed to reach a point where they could sit together, holding one another. Estella stroked Serena's hair then, mimicking the soothing process she'd shown her earlier in the streets—trying her best to be like a mother to Serena at that moment—and said, "Please, Serena, tell me what happened."

"Xan—oh god! Oh fuck! Oh fuck! Oh god, no!" Serena gasped and heaved, threw herself forward like she might be sick, gagged, then threw back her head and wailed, screaming like she wanted to bring down the roof. When she'd exhausted her air supply—exhausted everything, it appeared—she slumped back, panting, and buried herself against Estella. "I...

I'm sorry, 'Stell. I'm sorry... I-I didn't mean to wake him up. I didn't mean to, but—"

Estella stared down at her, dumbfounded. "Wake him... You mean Xander? He woke up?"

Serena whimpered, terrified, and buried herself further into Estella, hiding her face in her shirt. "Mmhm," she hummed, her voice muffled. "I... I was just talking to him. I wound up saying a lot, I'll admit, but... but nothing bad. Nothing bad, Estella; nothing bad, I swear! B-b-but I... I got sad. I try to stay strong, dammit; I fucking try. I do. I try. But I was talking, and I just kept talking, and I looked away, Estella—looked away for, like, a fucking second! Honest—and when I looked back, he was l-l-looking at me. He was looking at me, he was with me, 'Stell, I felt it—he was *with me...*" she shook her head, whimpering, "B-but he wasn't with me here. It was like he saw me somewhere else... and he was sad. And that made me sadder. A-and he... he said..."

Estella was listening, awestruck, unable to fully process most of what her friend was saying. "What?" she asked. "What did he say?"

Serena told her. She told her, and, once she had, she started crying all over again, finding new energy—new misery and terror—to fuel the crying.

"Oh, Serena," Estella held her tight and shook her head, "No. No, Serena. It's alright. He must have had some awful nightmare and come out of it delirious and said something he saw in the dream. Serena. Serena! Listen," she held the crying blonde by the shoulders, looking into her eyes. "Stan used to say it all the time: the future can't be told like that. They're pages of a book that haven't been written. I promise you—Serena, I *promise* you!—Zane will be fine!"

Serena whimpered, clenched her eyes against a fresh wave of tears, and shook her head.

"Estella..." she cried, burying her face back between Estella's breasts. "I don't think he was talking about Zane!"

*"*CAN *you at least tell me how Estella's doing right now?" Xander asks. "Out there, I mean—in the world."*

"Better than you," his mother replies, "but worse than she would if you were there for her."

Xander wants to jump to his feet at that, but something won't let him. "Then let me wake up," he demands. "Let me out and let me be there for her. I don't know why I can't—"

"You do *know why, boy!" his grandmother scolds him and nods downward, seeming at that moment to see through the table, towards the tiger lying below.*

"Faith isn't as easy as the false worshippers would have you think," Father Tennesen says.

"What does that have to do with anything?" Xander growls.

"Only everything," Marcus says with a condescending shrug. "But don't worry about it; just forget that, too."

Xander's mother looks down, seeming disappointed.

Joseph Stryker takes his wife's hand and says, "Let me ask you something, Xander: what would you be doing if Estella was where you were now?"

Xander shakes with a familiar rage at the question. "I'd kill, Dad, and I wouldn't stop killing until there was enough blood to bring her back!"

"Blood healing, huh?" Joseph muses and gives a half-nod. "A bit old-school, I'll admit, but—sure—why not? Just bleed any and all in your way until you had an ocean to bring her back, right?"

"And that *would be easy, wouldn't it?" Depok asks him. "To just rip and tear and mutilate until enough blood was spilled to awake the dead; to awake one or all of them a thousand times over? Okay, that's a noble, albeit savage, effort, but I can respect passion when it's sincere. But let me remind you, in this little 'what if' of ours, that it would be* her *at this little crossroads; it would be* Estella *here, making this choice wouldn't it? You could go and bleed the entire world dry in her name, but if she chose death—if she didn't drink*

that life-giving blood you stole for her—then what? What would you truly *do if it was her facing this challenge?"*

Xander doesn't answer; can't answer.

"It's easier to take steps with a game controller than your feet, Stryker; easier to bury a few arrows in some NPCs' knees than worry about whether or not you should just unplug the console."

"Please..." Xander begs. "I was wrong. I know that. Just, please, let me wake up... please!"

"What would you want Estella to do if she was in this very situation," Depok asked.

"She wouldn't be in this situation," Xander admitted, "because she'd never turn her back on life."

"You're wrong, sweetheart," Xander's mother says. "She's dangerously close to turning her back on life now; now, when it's most important that she not.*"*

Xander gapes at that, shaking his head slowly. "N-no..." he whispers. "She wouldn't..."

"Why not?" Marcus asks. "You would if the tides were turned. If she was in here and you were out there and there wasn't a damn thing you could do about it. You're in here all wishy-washy about life, but you expect us to believe you'd be Mister Grounded in that situation? And she's got more to fight for than you; she's at least willing to see!"

"I'll figure it out once I'm awake!" Xander declares, frantic. "I always do! Sure, I'm too frazzled right now to get it, and I'm sorry for that—I'M SORRY!—but—"

"It's not us you need to convince," they all say at once.

Xander thinks he hears Stan's voice whisper "It's not that easy" in his mind.

"And yet," Stan sighs, "it's each and every one of us you need to convince."

"But I know you can, Xander," Joseph says, giving Emily's hand a squeeze and nodding towards Xander, "because you are a Stryker; you're our son."—all the others chant "our son" in unison at that,

and Xander can't bring himself to disagree—"and that," Joseph goes on, "means that you will succeed."

Xander glares at him. "Being a Stryker means I'll succeed? Is that what this damned name means, Dad? Like how you succeeded with Lenuta? Or how you at least succeeded to stop Kyle back at her castle before all this could happen? How about how you succeeded for Mom; how you managed to keep yourself alive for her; for us? Are you kidding me with that crap? Being a Stryker means I'll succeed? 'Cause from where I'm sitting, old man, being a Stryker means I'm more likely to fail!"

Then, just like that, Joseph Stryker was gone from the table.

Emily Stryker cries at the disappearance of her husband. She screams "NOT AGAIN!" and then, like him, is gone.

"M-mom? Dad?" Xander's eyes widen, panicking. His mouth feels cold and clammy and... and he demands to know what's happening.

"They need faith—your faith—to stay strong, Xander," Father Tennesen says with a sigh, "just as we all do. Just as you do."

Burning with rage, Xander demands to know what Tennesen thinks of faith and strength after allowing Ariel to use his church as a breeding ground for the Cebourists. He points out that Tennesen doesn't have to struggle with the decision to wake up for anybody now that his decisions have freed him from any more responsibility.

Then, like Joseph and Emily Stryker, Tennesen is gone from the table.

Xander looks away, hoping his shame doesn't show to the others but knowing it does.

His grandmother sniffles, a sound of defiance and not sadness, and she draws in a ragged breath. She, too, is already gone from the table, but Xander hears her whisper "power and grace" even without her there to say it.

"Xander..." Depok begins, but says nothing more. He's already gone.

"You really are a dumbass, Crimson Shadow," Marcus says sadly.

Before Xander can even think the words of their old back-and-forth, the seat where his late mentor sits is empty.

"The quarters are in your pocket," The Gamer says, his body nothing more than a shadow in his seat. "This doesn't have to be Game Over!"

Osehr and Stan remain, looking back at Xander.

"Old dogs can be taught new tricks," Osehr points out, "but can the son of Joseph Stryker learn a single lesson before it's too late?"

Xander points out that learning a few psychic tricks isn't exactly the same thing as...

But Osehr is already gone, so Xander doesn't bother to finish.

Though he wasn't sure when the warm caress of the tiger's muzzle on his leg had stopped, he is suddenly aware that Trepis is no longer curled up at his feet.

Only Stan remains.

Xander marvels that he is still there when the others were so quick to vanish.

"There's a difference between leaving and being thrown out," Stan says. "And I think you'll find it a bit harder to cast me away."

Xander asks why that is.

"Because," Stan explains, "the things you hold are easy to let go of—whether or not you should*—but you can never let go of your hands."*

Xander tells him that's a corny metaphor.

"Seems fitting, though," Stan offers, "since it's what I gave you that's allowing you to hold on. Though I wonder if I made the right decision, since all you've done with my power so far is land yourself here *so that you could scare yourself, chase away people whose only crimes were giving a damn about you, and put that fucking gun in your mouth all over again!"*

Xander blinks at that and, sure enough, discovers that he's once again put the bone-white revolver between his teeth.

Yanking it free, he discovers his voice again and shakes his head, wondering when the struggle with himself will be over.

"Never," *he hears someone call out in the ocean of nothing beyond the table.*

He ignores this—forgets it soon after—because he has to.

"You talk about it like you died on purpose," Xander growls, surprising himself with his own voice all over again. "Was giving me your power a part of some great plan, because—NEWS FLASH!—locking it away like you did nearly got me killed."

"No, Xander," Stan counters, "not using the key that I also gave you is what nearly got you killed."

"What key?" Xander demands.

Stan shakes his head. "You ask as though you didn't already know."

"If I knew about a key to unlock those powers, smartass, then why wouldn't I use it?"

"Same reason anybody with a key doesn't use it."

The words "because they choose not to" *echo in the distance like... like something Xander has forgotten, and it's a moment until he realizes that the source of the voice isn't* out there*—isn't even somewhere else.*

Xander realizes that he and Stan are speaking the words at the same time.

"Why would I choose such a thing?" Xander asks.

"With so much at stake," Stan muses and gives a playful shrug. "That's what I'd like to know. Unless, of course..."

Xander bites his lip and looks down, sighing. "I thought it'd be easier to die after... after what I did; let the world handle the next step without me around to fuck it up."

Stan scoffs at that. "If only it were that easy, right? If only the part you played in all this could be so small, so insignificant. Tough titty, kid; you got the lead—you and that wife of yours."

That wife of yours...

"But you saw different pretty damn quick, didn't you," Stan goes on. "Saw just how much you're truly needed? And being shown a fuckup of that *magnitude—being shown something as heavy and inescapable as* EVERYTHING *when you just committed the biggest*

'WHOOPSIE-DAISY' in mythos history—well, that'd scare the wits out of just about anybody. I don't blame you for wanting to forget; none of them do. Not really. It's just... we all have high hopes for you; had an unfair advantage—like you—to see what you'll be capable of, and it's discouraging to see you struggling so early. Still..." he shrugs.

"Still?" Xander presses.

"Do you at least understand the reason to see what you're seeing?" Stan asks.

"I'm not even sure what it is I'm seeing, Stan... or how," Xander whispers.

Stan nods and sets a hand on Xander's shoulder. "You've got the key in the lock, son. Now you just need to turn it."

"How?" Xander asks, looking up, and though the pressure of Stan's hand remains on his shoulder, he finds himself alone.

Even the table is gone now.

Xander sighs, knowing that there never was a table or anybody sitting at it—knowing that he suddenly misses it and all its occupants terribly—and, feeling he owes it to Serena, turns away from the nothingness and begins to search for Zane.

CHAPTER 14

OF SUNBLOCK, FLU CELLS, & UNWRITTEN TEXTBOOKS

"Whosoever is delighted in solitude is either a wild beast or a god."
Aristotle (384-322 BC)

"So what do we know about this douche-nozzle?" Zane asked, scratching the back of his neck for possibly the twelve time in under a minute. Then he thought, *Fucker's got me* Reservoir Doggen *with these tight-asses in the middle of the day when I could be cashing in on that sloppy blowjob from Serena...*

He caught a few of the nearest warriors giving him a look and, though he was certain he'd only thought it, he started to wonder if he wound up saying it aloud.

Or maybe they were aurics. Had he actually forgotten about them for a moment?

It was an easy enough mistake to make, he supposed. Isaac and Zoey had fallen back to the rear of their laughable-yet-not-insubstantial group, and with no way of knowing—with the exception of Sawyer and Dianna—who or what the others surrounding him were it became easy to stop thinking of them as varying races and begin thinking of them simply as "them."

Still, it bothered him that his mind was beginning to feel so slippery.

"Fucking sunlight," he growled, deciding to say it out loud just to avoid confusing himself.

Something impacted with his chest and, for the briefest of moments, he wondered when they'd let Serena tag along. Then he realized it was a plastic bottle full of...

"Sunblock, Princess," Sawyer told him. "Now SP-shut-the-F up."

Zane stared after him, conflicted between the simultaneous urges to kiss him and kill him. Resigning to neither, he peeled off his shirt—at that point not much caring about the added exposure to the sun—and began liberally applying heaping globs of the stuff. Not caring what it looked like or how much might have been considered "too much," he worked to cover his entire upper body. Then, as he started working a gloopy palm over his neck and the bottom of his chin, he caught one of the former Trepis Clan's more loyal recruits—a younger-looking brunette with piercing green eyes and a row of rings adorning her left ear—taking in an eyeful. Frowning at this, he finished the task and yanked his shirt back on.

"Put your tongue back in your skull, hun," he scolded her. "I'm married."

The color that flooded the girl's face was dark and deep enough that Zane had no qualms about passing the bottle of sunblock over to her as he walked by, telling her that she looked like she needed it. When he'd finally caught up to Sawyer again, he said, "Thanks." Then, practically in the same breath, he said, again, "So what do we know about this douche-nozzle?"

It was Sawyer's human squeeze, the Dianna-chick, who answered with, "I take it you mean DiAngelo."

Zane looked past Sawyer to her. At a glance, she had the delicate features, the studious expression, and the "leave no detail undocumented"-eyes that could mean trouble for any guy too dumb to read that she did, in fact, mean trouble. It was all the beauty and poetry-inspiring femininity that existed in every mind's symbol of a rose until the owner of that mind learned the hard way that, yup, those fuckers still got thorns. Moreover, she looked pissed; like, next-level pissed. Zane had seen that degree of POed in the past from Serena—okay, so he'd seen it from *a lot* of chicks, many he wasn't proud to admit that he'd had to pay for back in his not-so-good days—and, completely disregarding the fact that Dianna was a human, it scared the shit out of him.

He could practically hear Serena saying *"Watch yourself, Zaney-poo."*

And, whether it was his wife or just the thought of something his wife might say, he listened.

"Uh..." he scratched at the back of his neck, felt a wad of sunblock cake up and collect under his fingernails. "Yeah. Him."

Dianna looked him over, sizing him up. With no effort to hide it, her eyes traveled the full length of his body, taking in each weapon and anything else that could conceivably be used as a weapon. It held none of the intrigue or want that the other ogling vampire had shown. She might have been a reformed hunter—might be fighting with them and off to face off against her own species—but, as Zane had said before, you could take the dog out of the fight... but you couldn't take the fight out of the dog.

He allowed Dianna to finish what felt like a Terminator-level scan of him—let her finish thinking of all the ways she could kill him—with no interruption.

"Your axe is dull," she finally said without much commitment to the statement.

"That's one way to look at it," Zane said with a coy smirk, knowing he'd have only one chance to make a decent impression with her with all the tension that had been raised back at the storage facility. "Another would be to say that my hammer is sharp."

Dianna raised an eyebrow, considered this, and then laughed.

Zane's shoulders relaxed. He hadn't even realized he'd been tensing them.

Seeing his lover laugh, Sawyer's own demeanor shifted, became eased and satisfied. Zane fought the urge to smirk. It was nice to see what that looked like from the other side.

"So," Zane pressed, rubbing the thick wad of sunblock from his neck between his fingers with all the nervous absence of a man-child who'd wandered too far from his wife—*When did I get so utterly pussy-whipped?* he asked himself—"about this DiAngelo-guy?"

Dianna scoffed and shook her head. "You were better off calling him a 'douche-nozzle,'" she said, and Zane decided that, yes, she could run with their crew anytime she liked. "A lot of the key points he hasn't exactly been shy about sharing: ex-military; he and his team—all, from the sounds of it, just as unhinged and sadistic as he is—were considered the best-of-the-best back when being the best at the worst kind of killing was something to boast. These are the sorts of guys who lost *a lot* of glory and business when terms like 'war crimes' stopped being a joke."

"Were terms like 'war crimes' ever considered a joke?" a younger recruit who was walking nearby cut in.

The three of them regarded him with genuine intrigue, and Zane realized he must have been recently turned. If his looks were any indicator, he still fit comfortably in both the human and mythos worlds' dual definitions of "young." Zane couldn't imagine he was even out of his teenage years, and he was sure most of those years were spent on chatrooms of the "Make Peace, Not War"-variety. It was, in a bizarre impact of conflicting emotions, both wildly funny and terribly depressing.

The Trepis Clan was certainly bringing in all sorts, it seems, he thought.

"Still are," Zane finally said when nobody else spoke up after a few seconds, then he shrugged and added, "with the winning sides, at least."

The young vampire frowned at that, looking like he'd had an unpleasant brunch or something, and fell back a few paces.

Zane gave both Sawyer and Dianna a look.

"He's actually a very skilled hand-to-hand combatant," Sawyer defended.

"Means jack-and-shit when I've got a dull axe-slash-sharp hammer," said Zane.

Nobody laughed at the joke this time around.

"Okay," Zane sighed, "so DiAngelo was a nutcase who led a nutcase team for our boys in uniform back in the day. The world changes, his breed become seen as savage monsters—ironic—and the military career ends. So—what?—he just came home and took up mythos hunting"—he snapped his fingers; the sunblock kept it from making much of a sound—"just like that?" He shook his head. "I mean, I can't imagine he was minoring in the tracking and killing of mythological beings when he was in training to kill his own kind, right? So how did that all come about?"

Dianna looked down, frowning and seeming more personally invested all of a sudden at what she was about to say. "Most hunters come from some sort of military background, actually, and not for the reasons you'd suspect."

"I'd suspect it was because they got a taste for killing but hated killing their own kind," Zane said. "And I'd suspect that it was also because it's harder for mythos to hide in other countries that aren't so loosey-goosey about how people look on the streets. They discover monsters, see a new challenge with a target they don't have to feel guilty about wasting with extreme prejudice, and they take their new hobby home where they can pursue the proverbial American dream."

Sawyer and Dianna both looked at him as though he were a chimpanzee that'd just recited Newton's Second Law of Thermodynamics.

Zane suddenly wanted to look at himself in that same way.

How in the fuck do I even know there's a 'Newton's Second Law of—SON OF A... damn you, Isaac!

"Yes, actually," Dianna said, nodding her approval. "That's exactly how it usually happens."

"And," Sawyer added, "in this case, it's *exactly* how it happened."

Dianna nodded as she led their team into a parking garage on the outskirts of the business district. It wasn't as packed as Zane figured it usually was—world coming to an end and all—but there was still a decent number of expensive, hoity-toity cars parked here-and-there.

Zane was just glad to be out of the sun.

The three of them held back, letting the others through, Zane feeling like a shepherd lazily watching a bleating flock meander into its pen. Finally, when Isaac and Zoey had closed the gap and stepped into the shade of the concrete structure, Sawyer asked if Isaac could stand watch at the entrance.

"I wouldn't ask you to stay in range of the sunlight while we do this," he said to Zoey before nodding back to Isaac, "but I figure between the two of you—your tolerance to sunlight and your connection with him and outreach to the rest of us—we can manage to do what needs doing without worrying about somebody wandering in on us."

"If that's what you need," Isaac said with a shrug.

Zoey, staying quiet, gave Zane a look and made like she was going to laugh at him. *You have a huge glob of lotion on your neck,* she informed him.

Yeah? he thought back with a smirk, *Does it remind you of date night with Isaac?*

Zoey's jaw tightened, and Zane wasn't sure if she was fighting against the urge to yell or laugh.

Before the exchange could go any further, though, Dianna was already starting further into the garage with Sawyer close behind.

Zane had no choice but to chase after.

"So how exactly can you be so intimately aware of this DiAngelo fuck-trumpet's personal harrowing tale?" Zane asked once he'd caught up to them again.

Dianna shrugged as she selected a black BMW with heavily tinted windows and began to fish about in a sleek black bag at her side. "I hacked his personal computer before we left," she said nonchalantly as she pulled out a tightly rolled satchel.

Zane swapped glances between her and Sawyer, who smirked proudly back at him. "You can do that?" he asked, impressed.

"Yeah," Dianna said as she began to work a hooked length of wire into the driver's side door through the window divide. Without seeming to focus on what she was doing, she grinned back at Zane. "Yeah," she repeated, "I can do that."

As if to punctuate her point, the lock on the door popped as she gave the wire a slight yank.

Zane rolled his eyes at the display. "You know you could just punch through the window, right?"

Dianna rolled her eyes right back, opened the door, and crept under the steering console to begin hotwiring the BMW. "I could," she said, not trying to keep the sass out of her tone, "but it'd sort of defeat the purpose of protecting your delicate skin if I did something so brash and stupid, wouldn't it?"

Once again punctuating her point, the car roared to life at that moment.

Sawyer's prideful grin grew.

Zane nodded to him, unable to mask his own grin. "Yeah," he admitted, "she kicks ass!"

XANDER IGNORES *the many calls beckoning him to return to... whatever all* that is.

He still can't be sure if it's some sort of personal, fucked-up limbo, his own head—he knows this, however, to be its own kind of personal, fucked-up limbo—or if it's all some sort of cosmic intervention.

The Talking Down of Xander Stryker: The Asshole Who Destroyed the World (a Great Machine production).

Trying to scold me for wanting on some level to die, *he grouses as he distances himself further,* and, in the process, driving me to want to die on *every* level. Christ, who knew it'd be such a fucking ordeal just to wake up.

You did, *Stan's voice follows him.*

Xander knows that his late mentor and longtime friend isn't really following him. Not physically, not metaphysically, not even metaphorically. Stan's dead. But, all the same, he's there, not "following," sure, but only in the same way that Xander's name doesn't follow him everywhere he goes.

This, Xander realizes with no small sense of irony, is a concept that he'll have no trouble coping with. After all, he'd spent the first eighteen years of his life with his dead father "following" him in his head, offering advice, insight, and, yes, even insults when needed, and also offering so much more.

Xander understands this sort of thing all too well. He is certain that, for however long he's stuck like this, he will never get used to the dead faces at the ten-sided, nonexistent table, the scenic trips through Ruby's mind with Ruby and Ruby(?), and even the time-traveling, domino-shifting "trips" through reality and all its many intangible branches. But having a dead man "living" in his head? Shit, that was practically a rerun.

I'll take 'Been There; Done That' for six-hundred, Alex, *he thinks to himself as he slips through the veil of reality as easy as he would a shower curtain.*

His mind splits for the briefest of eternities to replay every moment that he'd known Osehr, and with the bits of extra time between existing nowhere and then everywhere Xander plays through a few alternate possibilities. He's saddened to realize that, even if Osehr had lived through the plane crash in Romania, there were only seven possible scenarios where he'd live through the night that followed. Five of those possibilities involved him keeping watch outside of the castle—several hundred other possibilities of him making it that far end when the therions in Lenuta's employ ambush him after Xander and the others have gone inside—and another leaves him more crippled than he'd started. The only other possible path, one where Estella manages to save him from an initial attack and then, using her recently acquired varcol strengths, masks his presence so that he can hide, ends with Xander losing parts of himself. In that domino path, they all get to go home, yes, but only so Osehr could die several days later at the hands of the Cebourists.

That *path, Xander discovers, is irreversible and unnegotiable. To try to save Osehr in that single possible timeline would be to sacrifice countless others and* still *lose the old therion in the end.*

The brief eternity passes, and Xander is now free from nowhere and floating through everywhere like a sentient beam of light. He knows he shouldn't be able to see at this speed, that the world should be a nonsensical blur that offers nothing of clarity. He hasn't even got eyes to see the world with, after all! But, eyes or no, he does more than see—he can feel, smell, hear, and sense everything on its most simple and complex levels at once. He is intimately aware of the brief-yet-infinite lifetime of a single flu cell as it's loosed unto the world through a muscle-seizing sneeze of a mother of seven whose husband has, unbeknownst to her, fathered another three with his receptionist, her mother, and their eldest daughter. It's a beautifully tragic and wonderfully complex flash of everything about the complex system that has constructed into this single being that thinks so little of herself—this once-proud high school cheerleader who once called herself "Tiff" but has since been self-demoted to Tiffany—and Xander sees as he cycles by that the flu will start in her lungs what the impending depression will finish. Tiffany Belle Willows, fighting through sickness to gather supplies for her family to sit through this mythos scare, will die in eight days, fifteen hours, forty-eight minutes, and twelve-point-six-two-nine seconds, less than three short hours after her husband's receptionist sends a lewd, poorly-lit photograph to his cell phone while he's masturbating to pirated kiddy porn in his office.

His children—all of them—will hate him; they will all testify at his court hearing in eleven years. He will be sodomized for several weeks in prison before a former member of the Hells Angels buries a sharpened toothbrush into his carotid artery.

Only his sister attends his funeral, provided she does not take the eastbound train in several days. If she does take that train, she will die when the stress of the crash triggers an aneurism. There are no possible timelines—no dominos that can be rearranged—wherein Xander can save her if she boards that train.

It takes a million-trillionths of a nanosecond for Xander to process this, and in that time he finds himself curious how that flu cell will fair against the elements.

There's a cruel crosswind coming.

Zane, *Stan's voice reminds him.* If you're going AWOL from the other side, do so with focus and purpose. And try to remember that people matter more than cells—it gets tricky when you're this separated from life, the universe, and everything.

Right, *Xander acknowledges, remembering to mourn the woman* —You still have time to be "Tiff," *he whispers in her mind—as he hones in on Zane's auric signature and, with no lapse in time whatsoever, arrives at his side.*

Less than fifteen minutes after the ragtag remains of the Trepis Clan entered the parking garage, they were leaving again. This time, however, they were leaving in nine "borrowed" cars of varying makes, models, and years. Both the variety and the term—*"borrowed,"* Zane found himself scoffing at it again—

were Dianna's decisions; the reformed hunter operating on a worst-case-scenario thought path wherein authorities gave a damn about car theft anymore.

Zane mentioned this once—*once!*—as they were in the process of jacking the fourth car, a fully-loaded silver Tribeca that he outright refused to set foot inside. In response to this, Dianna had reminded him of the story surrounding Sawyer's new car and Serena's daring escape with all of the pursuing officers' guns and equipment.

As an added gesture, she made certain that Zane not only set a foot inside the Tribeca, she put him in charge of driving it.

Grumbling that he'd managed to avoid the minivan life that long despite having a kid and another on the way, he followed Sawyer's car, the BMW that Dianna had first hotwired, out of the parking garage.

"I don't think this is a minivan," the "Make Peace, Not War"-vamp chimed from the backseat.

It took everything in Zane's power not to brake test the kid.

Just as they'd planned before, Dianna steered her stolen—*"borrowed"*—Jeep left onto the first intersection they came across. Sawyer's BMW kept straight, and Zane followed at a distance for two more intersections—the Zeek-anapriek and a few others turning off behind them—before he finally turned right onto the next street and hit a thicker dose of traffic that was being blocked by a haphazard group of self-entitled "militia."

Or so their hand-painted banner declared them.

Rolling his eyes, Zane threw the Tribeca in reverse, cut the wheel to avoid rear-ending the car that had turned in behind him, and steered into a side alley adorned with an official-looking sign that declared "DELIVERIES ONLY."

Zane muttered something about "deliveries in rear," and the brunette he'd caught ogling him earlier, who'd insisted on riding with him, forced a giggle from the passenger seat.

He rolled his eyes again and imagined what sort of witty response Serena might have offered.

The Tribeca's passenger-side mirror was torn off as Zane miscalculated the turn and brought it in too close to the building coming in at the right. The ogling brunette's forced giggle lurched into a bark of surprise as she watched the building pass mere inches from her window, then, blushing again, looked down sadly, embarrassed. Catching sight of this in his periphery and cursing himself for giving a damn—already knowing he was going to regret his decision—he asked if she was okay.

The blush remained, but the shame slipped away from her face and she gave a meek nod.

Then, thinking himself a genius for coming up with the idea while still navigating the hideous vehicle through the narrow pass, he passed his cell phone, which had the GPS app opened and showing them the "recalculating" path to the site that Sawyer and Dianna had preset into each driver's phone, over to her.

"You two," he said, calling the attention of his passenger and the peace-loving kid behind her and pointing both of them to the glowing screen. "Navigate."

"Why do you need two of us to—" the kid started, but clammed up when Zane shot him a brief-yet-effective look over his shoulder. Then, either catching on to Zane's efforts or simply deciding he didn't want to push his luck with him, he nodded and stammered, "R-right."

The two of them began deliberating over the phone, working together to decide on the best alternate route. Being young and dumb, they both figured they knew everything better than everyone else and, sure enough, were soon convinced that through the power of teamwork and positive thinking they'd outsmarted even the app and come up with a faster, more "stealthy" course.

Zane fought the urge to hum the Scooby Doo anthem or

throw a G.I. Joe-style thumbs-up at the two. The kid was no longer focused on Zane and waiting for an opportunity to inject his half-formed insights, and, sure enough, the brunette's eyes had begun to wander Zane's way less and less.

Show you a poster-child for dumbasses, donkey dick, he inwardly taunted Isaac, wishing that he'd been paired with him and Zoey rather than a couple of dopey youngblood recruits who must have thought they were the mythos equivalent of social justice warriors for having stuck around with the Trepis Clan after their leader went and broke the world.

Feeling content with himself, Zane took a right onto a new road, swerved an oncoming car and took to the opposite lane. A machete-waving human wearing tan fatigues and green camo face paint had to dive out of the street to keep from being crushed and, in the process, propelled himself face-first into a lamp post.

Zane's contentment swelled another ten times over.

The brunette cleared her throat and said, "Next left."

Zane took the turn and, as he did, felt a strange tickle over his chest. He had the strangest impression that they'd suddenly taken on another passenger, but convinced himself this was just a bizarre reaction to his swelling pride.

"I AM NOT SICK! I *am not* sick! I—" Tiffany sneezed again, her aching muscles bunching in a tangled mess and nearly making her drop the twenty-four pack of bottled water she had wedged under her arm. The effort saved the waters, but the tension caught up with her and she flinched as all the plastic bags she was carrying dug a little further into the soft meat of her palms. She wondered how Josh made his single trip "kamikaze" missions look so easy, then chalked it up to the prowess of a wonderful husband as she continued reciting, "I *am not* sick! I *am not* sick!"

The threat of another sneeze tickled her senses and she paused, hoping to avoid a repeat of the painful mess she'd just gone through. Unintentionally, she held her breath at that instant, and a wave of crippling depression the likes of which she hadn't felt since her postmortem days after Ally's birth struck her all at once. It was the sort of unexpected, spectacular bouts of absolute misery that sync up with everything all at once to tell her that everything—absolutely everything!—was a waste of time.

After all, the depression says to her, *you're expected to keep your family safe in a world of monsters now. What possible hope do you have?*

At that moment, Tiffany was certain that, one way or the other, she was going to die and that nothing was worth its lick of salt.

You still have time to be "Tiff."

Her held breath caught, and Tiffany took in the sweetest lungful of air she could remember in a long time. It was like the voice of an angel. This she was certain of. Still feeling a looming sense of limited mortality, Tiffany... she stopped and smiled to herself; no, *Tiff* decided that, if she and her family were going to be hiding in the house for as long as they likely were, she might as well get to work on that home theater she'd been promising them.

Then they could all just binge-watch Disney movies until fate decided what should come next.

"Movement, sir," Carlos Sanders drawled, staring off at the wall. He wetted his lips, punctuating the simple statement with a wet sound before grinning like he used to before cutting the lips off of a prisoner.

DiAngelo quirked a brow and turned his focus to Mike McNeel with an uncertain scowl. Both he and Carlos had bonded with the blood of psychic vampires and, for the most part, seemed to be catching on to how to use it with relative ease. Between the seven of them, they were the only two who'd both opted to add the mind-feeders to their list of serums and, more importantly, managed to make it work right for them. DiAngelo had a bit of psychic in him now, too, though his came from a hybrid vamp, what their kind called "perfects"—what a laugh!—and, though he'd gotten pretty good at floating things around the room and seeing what color various peoples' energies shone, it had done squat in regards to reading minds. Allen Carrey, meanwhile, had *specifically* sought the blood of multiple mind-feeders, and had since only admitted to "sort of" being able to see those same energies surrounding everyone. He couldn't even tell DiAngelo the color of a single one of them.

Though he couldn't figure out *why* Allen's body wouldn't be accepting the formula as well as himself and the others, his first instinct was, as it had always been, to blame the man and not the method.

He just wasn't sure *how* Allen could be blamed for such a thing.

This, however, bothered him less than Tim Mason's "bad," seemingly allergic reaction to his own werewolf serum, and even *that* bothered him less than William Barnes' outright refusal to use any serum, at all. Tim and William were both good soldiers, and watching one tweak out like a junkie while the other opted for weakness made DiAngelo want to throw both of them through basic training all over again.

"Get with the program or get off the air!" as he used to say.

And so it was that, out of the seven of them, only four of them *should* have been able to sense monster activity. Out of those four, though, one was taking to the serum like a bird to the sea, and the other like a bird with only one wing. It disgusted DiAngelo to have to admit that he was among the "broken" two, but there was no denying reality when it reared its ugly head. This left the responsibility on Carlos "Colonel"

Sanders, who only wanted the mind-feeders' abilities so that he could torture folks from the inside, and Mike "Eel" McNeel, who'd opted to go full-on vamp and use from both the blood-drinkers and the mind-feeders.

DiAngelo was worried that Mike's decision reflected some sort of closeted hope to someday become one of the monsters, but, since Carlos was a sick fuck and not entirely trustworthy in this regard, he had nobody else to turn to. This, he resigned, explained the uncertain scowl.

Mike shifted with obvious discomfort, not facing DiAngelo but obviously sensing the weight of his disapproval.

"McNeel?" DiAngelo called, knowing the soldier knew what he was asking.

Mike only nodded at first. Then, seeming to remember his place, said, "Confirmed, sir. Got a couple of them inbound, they seem to be—" he stopped, tensed with focus, then said, "Two more, sir."

"Two more *what?*" DiAngelo demanded. "Vamps? Wolves? Flyers? Swimmers? *What?*"

Mike shifted again, getting more uncomfortable. "Cars, sir. Two more *cars.*"

"Details," DiAngelo said, closing the distance between the two of them.

Carlos wet his lips again and snickered, twisting the thumb and pointer finger of his left hand in a clockwise cycle. DiAngelo wasn't sure if the sick bastard was playing with invisible tits or trying to tune the imaginary dial of a radio, but, after a few more twists, he finally said, "The Stryker-vamp's pals are on a field trip!"

DiAngelo's eyes widened with excitement, and his own blue energy field did a dance. A few maps and loose supplies kicked up, spiraling around and then falling as if blown by a sudden gust of wind. There was no wind, though, and DiAngelo was getting sick of not being able to discipline his own energy when he'd worked so hard to discipline everything else in his life.

Except for Abigail, of course, something that felt like a thought flared in his head, and this time it was a filing cabinet that crashed down as a result.

Six soldiers jumped, tensed, and worked to find a way to pass it off as nothing.

DiAngelo didn't want to believe that he'd thought that, but reality *was* reality, and who-the-hell-else's thoughts could they be?

Both Carlos and Mike were trying very hard not to look back in his direction despite the silence everything had fallen into.

Eager to get things moving, DiAngelo said, "Is Stryker with them?"

"No, sir," Mike said, obviously just as eager.

"Mind, blood, wolf," Carlos recited, his eyes twitching as he did, "blood, blood, blood, elf, wolf, wolf, cat—"

"What in the hell is he saying?" DiAngelo demanded.

Mike tensed again and, trembling, finally looked up at him. "He's listing off the species in the oncoming caravan. 'Mind' is auric, 'blood' is sang, 'wolf' is—"

"I can figure out the code, idiot," DiAngelo growled, baring his teeth and suddenly wondering why. He kept on forgetting that he didn't have fangs. "I'm asking *why* he's listing them off like that!"

Mike stared up at him as though he was afraid to answer; as though it was so obvious and DiAngelo might berate him or even strike him if he dared to say it like he didn't know.

DiAngelo glowered down at him, demanding a response.

Mike gave a slow nod, seeming to assure himself of something, then said, "That's who's coming, sir. Or, at least, what's coming."

DiAngelo felt the breath stick in his throat. "That many?"

"Three more cars," Carlos announced.

A chair resting a few feet from DiAngelo flipped itself. "Three more...?" he couldn't keep the gasp from his voice. "How many?"

"Seven," said Carlos.

Mike shook his head and corrected, "Eight."

"EIGHT?" DiAngelo growled and moved to grab Mike by the scruff of his shirt.

At that moment he felt like it was somehow his fault that there were *eight* vehicles carrying comrades of the monster that had incited this wild, global circus headed their way.

Then Carlos gave a nervous giggle and said, "Nine."

DiAngelo roared, toppling some more furniture with his renegade energy, and snapped Mike "Eel" McNeel's neck.

Five pairs of eyes watched, horrified into a stunned silence, as one of their comrades collapsed to the floor.

"Arm up, boys!" DiAngelo ordered, turning away from the corpse at his feet and using his energy to "sweep" it under a nearby desk. "The hunt's on!"

TRAFFIC WAS an utter pain-in-the-balls up until the point when Zane's Tribeca—he *hated* thinking of it that way—reconvened with Isaac's Subaru hatchback. It was, admittedly, just as much of a ball-and-chain sort of car as the Tribeca, but Zane still found himself jealous for some odd reason. Isaac, who wouldn't have taken the wheel if Zoey wasn't sitting shotgun with him, didn't have to ask to get his way, and having the pixie-headed auric as a passenger offered the lucky bastard with an option that no car on the market came equipped with:

Instantaneous traffic control.

Zoey and her mind tricks were obvious the moment Zane had swerved out of the way of a pickup truck with a pile of flaming bodies stacked in the bed and onto a totally vacant street. Stunned by the sudden calmness, he spotted the hatchback as it steered in beside him. The street they'd come from, though already filling with cars and people, had obviously been just as clear during their brief moment on it. Absently, Zane wondered how many streets ahead of them had already been cleared by Zoey and her immaculate auric precision.

More than you can count, Zoey joked in his head.

Bitch, he shot back.

There was a titter of psychic laughter in his head, then, *I'm going to tell Isaac you called me that.*

No, don't! Zane hoped the fake whine carried through his thoughts. *He might strangle me with his—*

Suddenly his head was occupied with an unshakable view of his naked grandmother swooning over him with a rectal thermometer in one hand and a copy of *Playgirl* in the other.

Zane nearly swerved off the road with the eruption of disgust that flooded his entire body.

Sweet fucking hell, Zoe! he begged. *Don't do that! God... damn! I won't be able to get it up for a month! What am I supposed to tell Serena?*

Another titter. *Tell her that Zoey's had enough with the penis jokes,* she announced.

Fine! Fine! Whatever! then, grinning—though the others in the car would think it was only to himself—he added, *Bitch.*

The tittering was harder and, though Zane didn't understand the *how* behind this, at a deeper frequency.

Though there were more winding roads to take from that point than they'd already traveled, it took less time with Zoey clearing the path than it had prior to meeting up. More and more of the caravan reconvened as the various paths brought the nine cars back together in front of an eight story building labeled simply "HOTEL."

Well if that *doesn't advertise a Hitchcockian shower-stabbing then nothing does!* Zane thought, throwing the Tribeca into park.

As he stepped out, Zoey was already joining with Dianna a few paces away.

"You're sure they're here?" she asked.

Dianna studied her for a moment, then asked, "You can't sense them?"

Zoey shook her head, looking at the building as though one of the curtained windows facing them might advertise something she hadn't noticed before. "No," she admitted, "but I *know* that you can't, either."

Dianna smirked at that and nodded. "True, but I can trace an IP address to its source," she explained. Then, nodding towards the hotel, she said, "And DiAngelo's internet searches and video uploads were sent out from here."

Sawyer, walking over from his own car, kissed Dianna on the cheek. "Gotta love a sexy geek," he boasted.

"Nice way of saying 'nerd,'" Zane said with no real conviction to the joke, realizing with a growing mountain of aggravation that the sunblock had already started to wear off.

You ever think that maybe the sunblock's working just fine and your reaction's just psychosomatic? Zoey asked in private, genuine concern coming through the psychic channel.

Don't know what 'psycho some addict' means, Zane thought back, *but the sunblock's definitely wearing off.*

Zane took the following silence to mean that Zoey trusted his judgement in the matter.

The twin sister of the therion who was shacking up with the Zeek-anapriek—Zane promised himself that he'd remember their names eventually—shambled over and whispered something to Dianna. Dianna, looking around for a moment after listening, gave her a shrug and then turned to Zoey.

"They're asking if the streets are safe?" she explained.

Zane had the urge to tell the therion to take a look around, maybe take a fucking dose of reality. The streets hadn't been safe all day, might never be safe again for their kind.

He *had* this urge, but, in a moment where he startled himself, he didn't act on it.

If a Vailean was defined by anything, he thought, *it was the certainty that they'd act on their urges.*

Period.

But then...

Don't do it, Zane.

He spun around, certain he'd heard a voice.

There was nobody there. Nobody who would have whispered to him, at least; just a few of the straggling remains of the Trepis Clan—nobody who would...

He startled himself again then.

He whispered, "Xander?"

He had no idea why.

There was no answer, but he *did* feel something—a tickle—and it made him start to brush at his shoulder. Then he stopped, feeling nothing there, but, still confused as to *why*, looked there.

Zane shook his head at himself and thought, *What are you expecting to find, Zane? A bird? A little red bird with a black cap of feathers and a blood-red eye? One that hops about for a moment, opens its beak, and says—*

Incoming, Zane. Warn the others to keep an eye on the rooftops and the fourth floor windows. Seventeen seconds.

Zane's eyes widened and he glanced back at the hotel, saw nothing on either the roof or at any of the windows—fourth floor or otherwise. But, still uncertain about everything, he said:

"Uh... guys? I think we should brace ourselves. Something's gonna be coming from the roof and... uhm, the fourth floor windows in a few seconds."

Everyone within earshot stared at him like they'd been expecting him to lose his mind and he finally had.

Eight seconds, Zane.

"You gonna fucking gawk at me or you gonna fucking listen, dipshits?" Zane growled. "Rooftop and windows in five... four... three..."

The countdown seemed to strengthen the point, and everyone began to brace themselves behind the closest cars they could find.

Zoey, looking nervous, connected with Zane's mind to ask

how he could possibly know such a thing when she couldn't sense anything.

Above him, Zane thought he heard the flutter of wings and, glancing up, caught sight of a small red body and a black cap of feathers. Then, though it hadn't gone anywhere, it was gone.

"A little bird told me..." Zane whispered aloud, thoroughly confused.

Then the hotel's parking lot turned into a warzone.

~Two minutes earlier~

"YOU MAGGOTS KEEP GAWKING AT ME AND YOU'LL BE JOINING THE EEL UNDER THE DESK, YOU GOT ME?"

Five pairs of eyes stared at DiAngelo, still dumbfounded; still unbelieving.

"I SAID *DO YOU GOT ME,* SOLDIERS?"

Life returned to those eyes and instinct took over. Their bodies went rigid, their arms locked at their sides; just like that they were ready to kill for DiAngelo again.

"SIR," five voices rose in trained harmony, "YES, SIR!"

"ATTA'BOYS!" DiAngelo clapped. "At your stations! Attack formation: 'Loch Lomond.'"

Carlos Sanders giggled perversely, twitched, and sang a few bars—"You take the high road, and I'll take the..."—before he flinched and paused as DiAngelo swung his full attention around on him.

"Where they gonna land, soldier?" DiAngelo demanded.

Carlos belched out a nervous whimper of a chuckle, his eyes giving a darting glance under the desk where DiAngelo had crammed Mike's body, and his fingers twitched as though he was working the world's most uneven typewriter.

"SOLDIER!" DiAngelo roared, "RESPOND!"

"G-gah! Ah-haha! Aaahh!" Carlos' eyes fluttered and his head twitched twice to the left and then once to the right. His fingers typed more furiously, then his right hand swung inward and he slapped himself square in the chest. "E-east! Y-yeah... yeah, east!" his eyes widened and he slapped himself again, this time in the face with his left hand. "NO!" he corrected, "The north, sir! They're gonna be in the north-facing lot i-in..." more twitching, more typing, and another slap to the face. Then, as though a switch on his insanity had been flipped, Carlos "Colonel" Sanders' body jerked, went upright, and he looked back at DiAngelo with absolute clarity. "North-facing lot in just under two-minutes, sir."

DiAngelo stared at him, not sure if he deserved a round of applause or a straightjacket. "You got your shit together, soldier?" he asked.

"Sir," Carlos nodded, "Yes, sir!"

"You good to go then?" he demanded, "You gonna do me proud?"

The murderous grin that spread across Carlos' face reminded DiAngelo of his days in the bush, back when he painted himself in the blood of dead soldiers and wore a necklace of labium strung along on a fishing line. This, DiAngelo remembered, he called his "pussy wire," and he was never shy about taking it off each night and publicly masturbating with it until the shaft of his penis bled.

Grinning back at Carlos, DiAngelo gave the man a nod of approval. "Good to have you back, Colonel."

"Good to be back, sir," said Carlos.

"Think you're up to blocking our energies from the psychics in that incoming monster entourage?" DiAngelo asked. "I don't want them getting the drop on us before we can get the drop on them."

Carlos' sadistic grin was answer enough, but he still answered, "Sir. Yes, sir."

"YOU HEARD THE CRAZY SON-OF-A-BITCH!" DiAngelo called back to the others. "I WANT A HIGH-LOW STRIKE PREPARED AGAINST THE NORTH-FACING WALL *YESTERDAY!* IF YOUR ASSES, YOUR GEAR, AND YOUR HEADS AREN'T IN THE RIGHT PLACE IN T-MINUS *THIRTY* SECONDS THEN I WILL PERSONALLY TURN YOU INSIDE-OUT FROM YOUR ASSHOLES, DO YOU HEAR ME?"

The song of "Sir! Yes, sir!" was muffled around a flurry of activity as five bodies went to work.

Though he'd always fancied the M16A1 along with his standard sidearms, DiAngelo, wanting his arsenal to match his new, super-powered body, had decided to upgrade. After holstering his Sig under his left arm and a pair of Glocks at his waist—*I'll always be a cowboy at heart,* he thought with a smirk—he hoisted his new baby and marveled at how it felt in his hands.

The M242 Bushmaster was over two-hundred-and-fifty pounds and more than eight-feet of chain-fed "FUCK YOU." He'd fallen in love with the autocannon back in the seventies, when he'd gotten to use one of the bad boys to mow down an unresponsive village from atop a Hummer parked nearly two-thousand meters away. Trees, wildlife, and every soggy hut within range had been turned into confetti in a matter of seconds.

It was love at first shot.

And, now that DiAngelo was strong enough to handle one without mounting it to anything, he could *really* have some fun.

It'd taken a few modifications, but William Barnes was a genius with that sort of work. He hadn't disappointed. And, as DiAngelo swept up his new baby, he marveled at how light it felt in his new arms. Grinning, he tucked it under his arm—unable to rest it across his shoulder without punching a hole in the ceiling—and started to march towards the door.

He caught sight of Tim Mason hooking the marked sling of his M79 over one shoulder, a belt stocked with fresh grenades for the launcher, each one bearing the corny, hand-painted symbol of the Cebourists on its surface, already looped over the other. The sight of the old weapon made DiAngelo nostalgic; made him horny. He didn't pay much mind to Mason's red, inflamed face or the way he scratched incessantly at his forearms.

James Chan already had his assortment of blades sheathed and hidden across the entirety of his body, and as DiAngelo passed he fed the last three slugs into his Mossberg 500 before resting the angry-looking black shotgun against his shoulder, still holding it by the pistol grip and already teasing the trigger.

A distance ahead, DiAngelo found himself racing a small fuse line as it snaked across the floor, jumped into the air, and slithered into a medium-sized pack. The opposite end of this, he saw, was being pulled through a side pocket by William Barnes, who twisted the opposite end into place with a patch of exposed wires that waited on the bottom-side of the pack. Once he'd done this, William slipped the pack on—wearing it like a suicide vest across his chest—and pulled on a pair of modified, tech-laden, and wide-rimmed sunglasses that, in DiAngelo's opinion, made him look like a cross between a sci-fi villain and John Lennon (during his bearded years).

Can't wait to see what that *does,* DiAngelo thought with a grin.

Then there was Carrey. Allen-fucking-Carrey. DiAngelo *wanted* to be mad at the man for not gaining the psychic powers from the serum. Granted, he couldn't be nearly as mad at Carrey as he was at William Barnes, who wouldn't take the serum at all—it was, after all, one thing if a child wasn't getting better after taking their medicine and an entirely different thing if the child refused to take it in the first place—but it angered him, nevertheless. From the beginning—the very fucking beginning!—Carrey had been DiAngelo's best—his go-to!—and he'd specifically asked him to take the auric vampire serum so that his go-to could be an even greater source of information. All the same, however...

Carrey had been the first to catch wind of mythos way back in the good ol' days, and he'd been the first one to bag one of the nonhuman fuckers. DiAngelo remembered that hot-as-hell, gloomy-as-shit twilight all those decades ago, ankle-deep in sewage and dragging a hollering native declaring himself a shaman back to camp for questioning. The grunts and clicks had grown tiresome, and when Carrey had wheeled around, rifle drawn and muscles bulging with fresh intent, DiAngelo was certain that he'd grown tired of the man's babbling and was about to shoot him in the face for it. Instead, the barrel of Carrey's gun rose skyward—*Are you watching, God,* DiAngelo had thought back then, and the thought had stuck with him ever since—and he'd taken four shots. The tracking and spacing had been nearly superhuman even then, but the target had been swift enough to dodge the first three rounds. But Carrey had found his mark. Carrey *always* found his mark, and he'd shot the shrieking, hissing shit-sucker right off a tree branch and right into the history books.

Those history books haven't been written yet, DiAngelo mused. *But when the world's ours and the great war of humans versus mythos is behind us, the pages that tell the next generation all about it will know all about it.*

After they'd gotten back—after the United States government had royally fucked all of them—it had been Carrey who'd found other hunters, reaching out and making connections that would secure him, DiAngelo, and the rest of his crew with the gig they'd come to fall back on since then. In many ways, Allen Carrey was like the son that Robert DiAngelo had never had; was wishing he'd had. He wanted to tell Carrey he was proud of him. He wanted to tell Carrey that he was still his number one; his go-to. He wanted to give him some words of praise and encouragement. But Carrey's body wasn't accepting the serum, and it had been Carrey who'd told DiAngelo that his daughter had run off with a therion. The only reason Carrey was alive was because he was DiAngelo's go-to; his number one. The only thing keeping Carrey alive at that point was that DiAngelo *had* been proud of him up until the moment he'd failed him and told him he'd fathered a mythos fucker.

Instead of words of encouragement, he said, "I'll take the roof. That puts you at the low ground—fourth floor in this case. Think you can do that without fucking up?"

Carrey didn't flinch like the others at DiAngelo's harsh tone —never had—but he did look up at him with leery eyes before giving a single nod.

"Nice gun," he said, pointing with his eyes at the Bushmaster tucked under DiAngelo's arm. Then, giving a smirk with absolutely zero humor in it, he added, "Recoil's gonna be a cunt, though."

"I can handle it," DiAngelo said, opening the door with his free hand and starting through. "Just make sure you can handle yourself out there." Then, stopping just on the other side and looking back in—looking at his men as they prepared for war—he gave Carrey his "my will be done"-look and said, "I want you to call in for backup."

Carrey looked up at that, frowning. "Backup? What backup?"

DiAngelo felt his anger flare at that, more felt than saw a corner of the door frame chip away under the force of his thrashing energy. "The recruits, Carrey," he forced himself to say in a calm, level voice. "I want as many of the church's newest enlisters as we can get here A-S-A-P," he explained, stretching out the four letters until he began to wonder why he'd bothered abbreviating at all. "And tell Tim I want him recording everything with those cheesy specs of his."

CHAPTER 15
WHERE DOES THE DREAMING END?

"Hold fast to dreams,
for if dreams die, life is a broken-
winged bird that cannot fly."
Langston Hughes (1902-1967)

Xander likes being a bird.

He liked *being a bird.*

He is simultaneously aware that he will forever be a bird and that he never was a bird.

Only because Zane wanted to see one, *he thinks, but he knows it is not he who thinks this.*

"'I dreamed I was a butterfly, flitting around in the sky;'" Xander hears Stan's voice reciting somewhere both far off and quite, quite near, "'then I awoke. Now I wonder: am I a man who dreamt of being a butterfly... or am I a butterfly dreaming that I am a man?'"

"Assuming that's where the dreaming ends," Xander says, wishing he had a pair of eyes to roll.

"Now you're getting it."

"Getting what?" Xander might have no mouth—might have no

voice—but he feels like he's scoffing just fine all the same. "I get to play Jiminy Cricket to Zane Vailean—telling him when not *to act on bad urges and where to look for an ambush—and get turned into a bird for—what?—half-a-fucking-second just because it's what he* thinks *he's going to see? What I'm getting is impatient, Stan! They're going to die out there!"*

"Not all of them."

Xander wishes he could growl. "I know not all of them! I KNOW! *And I fucking hate knowing that, by the way! You're supposed to be my friend—all of you are supposed to give a shit about me!—and now I'm stuck here and forced to watch while—"*

"Then wake up."

"I'VE WANTED TO WAKE UP! YOU WON'T—"

"I'm not me, Xander," Stan's voice says, then, taking on all the voices of the others, they say, "None of us are. And yet—"

"'And yet we are,'" Xander finishes for him, for them, for himself. "Yeah, yeah. I know. Funny thing about existing everywhere and nowhere all at once: I've heard this all already; I've watched *this all already—hundreds upon hundreds and even hundreds more times! I don't want to see which reality this turns out to be! I don't want to see which row of dominos get to fall! I want—"*

"You want to awaken without knowing why, *" Stan's voice is once more his own, "and we cannot allow you to do that."*

"You mean I can't allow myself to do that," Xander corrects.

One and the same, *something—not Stan, not even a voice —announces.*

"Oh, you?" Xander would be laughing if he had a mouth and a voice, "Right. What do I call you now? The Great Machine? The Power? Nega-Xander? I didn't like you the first time, and I like you even less now. At least the first time you helped me kick some ass rather than locking me away inside my own head."

"Do you still believe you're in your mind, Xander?" Stan's voice asks him.

Xander is beginning to wonder how much of Stan's voice is actually Stan and how much of it is...

You must see *why* you have gone on this far. You must see *why* it is so important. You must *see* that—

"I've seen enough!" Xander declares. "A future where I can't save Estella? A future where she dies? What sort of place am I waking up to if that's all that's in store for me?"

You demand to be awake so that you can do something... *the non-voice condemns.*

"... and yet you admit there's nothing to awaken to if you can do nothing?" Stan's voice finished.

"It's not about her, son," Xander hears his father's voice call out to him. "I didn't die for myself, and I didn't die for your mother."

"THEN YOU DIED FOR NOTHING!" Xander's screams ripple through the world like a ripple through a river.

The ethereal plane shimmers with the silence that follows, and Xander looks out at the parking lot that his friends and colleagues have come to occupy. From his vantage point, he can see the access door to the roof begin to open. On the fourth floor, three men with death on their minds, hate in their hearts, and serum in their veins take their places in three different rooms.

"Bang, bang, Zane," he chirps into the shimmering silence.

There is more at stake than you know, *Xander hears without hearing.* And if you do not see, then there is no way that you can succeed.

"Success is relative," Xander says, but he no longer feels it is him thinking the words he is saying—it is, however, what he means in his heart. "You've shown me a certain reality where I cannot save Estella and a near-certain reality where I turn my head into a Jackson Pollock painting." He is not at all surprised that he's able to reference an artist he'd never put much thought into at that moment. Stan is with him. Still arguing with the non-voice, Xander makes up his mind to not *be a spectator any longer. "If that's the sort of shit you want me to see—if there's a* why *in any of it—then, fuck you, I'm not watching. I'm done tuning in. And I'm done being held back."*

Then, doing the impossible—but he's been doing the impossible all day, hasn't he?—he slips through yet another barrier, one that should not be so easily slipped through, and takes to the battlefield that the parking lot's become.

He hears "Now you're getting it" again, but he wonders if it isn't, in fact, the first time he's heard it.

Just where does the dreaming end? *he thinks.*

EVERYONE WAS STARING at Zane as though he'd finally lost his mind. Then he'd spotted a bird that, for a single instant, had existed first inside his head, and then, for less than an instant, above his head. Zane was very sure that he *had* finally lost his mind.

Then, exactly seventeen seconds after he'd heard the little bird, all hell broke loose.

It started, as all things started, with a big bang. There was light, then vibration, and then—

BOOM!

Zane remembered stumbling into the Cebourists' trap during their mission with Xander to take the bastards out. Nothing more than a bit of paint on the wall—the religious nuts' symbol of three spirals trapped inside a triangle—and he and Xander had suddenly been trapped in a world of fire and suffering the likes of which shouldn't have been possible. It was as though Zane, in a single instant that lasted forever, existed inside a million bodies and all of them were burning at once. Swords of fire scored his flesh as beings made of pure flame took turns fucking his very pores.

By the time Zane had come back from that place—a place, apparently, that existed on the street he and Xander had collapsed upon—he was certain that he'd never recognize himself again beneath all the charred flesh.

Imagine his surprise when he realized he was still pretty.

The big bang that came exactly seventeen seconds after the bird he'd seen first in his mind and then for half-a-second in the sky made the brief eternity in his own personal hell feel like a day trip to the tanning booths.

I died, he thought, feeling a searing pain so intense that he couldn't even bring himself to rationalize the suffering it brought him. *I never even saw it coming—never even suspected—and I just died...*

THEN YOU DIED FOR NOTHING!

Zane wasn't sure where the voice was coming from, but he decided that it was right. Deciding—not knowing, but just setting his mind to an absolute certainty—that he *was not* dead, Zane roared.

He thought that he heard himself call out to Serena, but that was already in the past and he needed to move forward.

The parking lot came back into view as his eyes decided to start working—*Not dead,* he repeated to himself, *not dead, not dead, NOT DEAD!*—and he darted out from behind the Tribeca that he'd managed to hide behind. Zoey had been knocked back in the blast—*grenade,* Zane thought, spotting the smoldering portion of pavement that had been blown nearer to the SUV she'd ducked under—and he could see that, dazed and disoriented, she was an open target.

Bang, bang, Zane.

The little bird's warning told him all he needed to know. Jumping into overdrive, he glanced skyward towards the hotel's roof. A man stood, braced on the ledge like a waiting suicide, with a gun nearly half as long as the Tribeca. The muzzle burned bright as the sun, and Zane found himself wondering what sort of impact he had to look forward to from a beast-gun like that.

Gonna stick that monster up your asshole and pull the trigger 'til the last round's been spent, he promised the man, hoping beyond hope it was the DiAngelo-douche.

But first...

Zane closed in on Zoey, then, cradling her into his arms in an awkward stoop-and-scoop maneuver that had his footing slipping out from under him, dove to the side, bracing himself for a series of ugly impacts.

The first impact: slamming into the pavement and slipping out of overdrive. This he took with his shoulder, guarding Zoey's body with his own and letting the momentum roll him into a ball around her frail form. Behind him, where Zoey had been lying a split-second earlier, the first of the beast-gun's rounds hit, then, after a tense-yet-brief pause, another. Then another. Only three rounds, and well enough—though not nearly well enough—away from Zane and his cargo, but the sheer force of each concussive blast had him reliving the grenade all over again. He felt the heat of each one at his back, felt the force rattle his bones, and, between them and the shot out of overdrive, he was thrown into...

The second impact: crashing into the door of the SUV. As pain flooded his system, Zane was aware of Isaac, already in his bestial form and squatting beside him, as he barked in surprise.

There was no question about what had shocked him.

Much as Zane exploding out of nowhere with Zoey in his arms and colliding with monumental force mere inches from where he was huddled was the sort of thing that would startle him on any other occasion, it was the second trio of beast-bullets that came down, clapping thunder across the parking lot and biting chunks out of concrete.

Barely even registering Zane's "arrival," he saw Isaac preparing to dash into the point of fire, no doubt intending to either pull Zoey out of it or go down with her.

Zane grabbed the therion by the shoulder, the simple act of moving his aching shoulder a small torture in and of itself. Isaac growled, whipped around—intent on eviscerating whatever dared to keep him from his lover—and stopped, eyes wide and ears drooped, when he saw that she was safe in Zane's arms.

There was nothing witty that Zane had to offer in response, so he simply nodded and let Isaac pull the gasping auric against his chest.

She didn't realize she'd been saved yet, Zane saw. She'd seen her own death coming and then...

Feeling Isaac's powerful, fur-covered arms around her—something Zane figured she was quite familiar with—her next gasp came out a cry and she scrambled to hold him, whimpering.

"Zoey! ZOE! Come back to us, girl! We need you with us!" Zane called out to her, relieved when the automatic barrage had finished tearing a fresh hole into the street. He leaned in, gave the blue-haired auric's face a few gentle slaps and then shot Isaac a "don't start" look when he dared to bare his teeth at the effort. Slowly, he saw clarity come back to her. "There you are," he said with a smile.

"Z-Zane?" she stammered, shaking her head. Her eyes darted back to where she'd been knocked by the grenade blast, spotted the smoking crater left there, and then frantically began checking her body for any sign of injury.

"Fine; you're fine!" Zane assured her. "You were—"

"How? How could you have... and you were—" Zoey's lip trembled and she shook her head. "I couldn't sense a... they must be—it's just not possi—H-how? How did you..."

"Long story short:" Zane said, cutting off her nerve-wracked ramblings, "Xander. He's here. Somehow. I don't know. Just know that—" Zane was suddenly overtaken by that tickle from earlier, but it now existed everywhere within him. He felt his body droop slightly, his shoulders slouching; he was suddenly aware that he was thinking more than he was used to and he felt...

What a novel concept.

Zane, realizing that was not one of his own thoughts, thinks, *What the fu—*

"Zoey," he heard himself say—felt his mouth move, his lungs pushing out the air to birth the words in his own voice—but was very sure that he was not the one speaking at that moment. "You need to listen carefully and broadcast what I'm about to tell you to everyone else. Do you understand?"

Obviously just as surprised by Zane's shift in tone as Zane, himself, Zoey's lingering panic dried up and she nodded.

Zane's runaway speech went on: "We got three on the roof and three on the fourth floor. DiAngelo's on the roof with the automatic cannon along with a man wielding the grenade launcher that did *that,*" his head cocked on its own in the direction of the first blast impact. "That man is Tim Mason, he's an epileptic who's been dosing with therion DNA; it's not reacting well—new therion eyes and old epileptic brain. You do the math. Use that to your advantage. The last man on the roof is Carlos Sanders, and he has auric powers. He's the one blocking your scans. You got this so far? Are you sending this to the others?"

Zoey gave him a look—one that Zane wanted to give to himself—but she nodded.

"Good. On the fourth floor, from left to right: James Chan, second window in room four-oh-two, dosed with anapriek and nejin DNA—they call him the 'ninja;' I'm sure you can imagine why—he's got a shotgun up there, but if he had his way he'd be down here and engaging hand-to-hand. Don't let him. Whoever can get a shot on him: take it and take it quick." Zane paused and looked off. He felt his brain buzz, begin to ache, then go quiet and calm. "Tell Lawrence he'll have a clear shot in about twenty seconds, but let him know the shot's gonna want to go left. Did he get that?"

Zoey nodded.

Zane wondered who the hell Lawrence was and how he knew to tell him such a thing.

"The middle man is William Barnes, fifth window from the left—room four-oh-eight—and he's strapped with what could either be a bomb that will decimate this entire parking lot *or* a suicide vest that will bring down that entire building and all the men inside. We can allow neither to happen. We must..." Zane felt his body tense, shiver, and distantly thought he heard the words "No! No, I can't let that—" chime in his mind before they were overwhelmed by something that neither resounded as sound nor thought but, instead, as total silence; all it left was certainty. His jaw tightened and, though unsure why, Zane agreed with his body's gesture in this case. He didn't know what decision had been made, but he recognized it as a tough one. "We must make certain that the last man on the fourth floor—room four-fourteen; last window on the right—is left alive..." Zane was suddenly aware that he was trembling, and then his vision went wet and cloudy with tears. "He will help us after... after—"

Zane gasped and shook, his body feeling at that moment as though he'd been hit by another grenade blast, but he realized this was just his body suddenly becoming his own again.

"Oh, sweet fucking hell," he groaned, doubling over and puking all over the pavement. "I feel like Isaac just fucked my guts with a spiked condom!"

He puked again.

"Oh my..." Zoey jumped back, then started towards Zane once she was certain he was done being sick. "What just happened? How did you—why were you talking like that?"

Zane retched and gagged, shaking his head. "I think... I think Xander just fucking possessed me or something!" he said.

"Zane," Zoey's voice was all sympathy and no belief, "Xander isn't—"

Isaac let out a confused whimper, and both Zane and Zoey followed his line of sight.

A short way's away, an uncertain-looking sang dove up from behind the trunk of the car he'd been hiding behind and, taking a moment to line up a shot and then another to shift it a hair to the right, fired a single round at the second window of the fourth floor. The shot sent a spider-web of cracks through the still-intact glass, distorting the momentarily visible man-shaped silhouette coming into view behind it. The shifting silhouette and the broken window became one, and then became neither as the glass burst outward and a man in a long, black turtleneck and camo cargo pants plummeted through; a black pump-action shotgun tumbling away from him and clattering beside his body a moment later on the street.

Then, starting as an enraged roar and ending with a series of jackhammer claps of the beast-gun's firing, a fresh trio of beast-bullets came down, forcing the daring vampire to take cover once more. The impact of just one of those shots, Zane saw, was enough to shift the car's position on the street. A hole that would have easily fit one of his fingers had been punched cleanly through the metal siding of the roof.

Zane thought he heard the shooter screaming something in their direction, but what could be heard in between deafening blasts was reduced to:

"—OOD ENOU—" ***BANG!*** "—OUR DEL—" ***BANG!*** "—LATES, MON—" ***BANG!***

Another trio of shots fired, this one uninterrupted by the shooter's voice. Then a pair of angry double-bursts against the trunk that forced the vampire to roll free and squat behind the driver's side door.

"I'm gonna guess that *that's* Lawrence," Zane said, nodding towards the noticeably shaken vampire behind the decimated shell that had started as a decent car, served momentarily as a fair shield, and now existed solely as scrap. "And I think that should speak for itself. We can debate about how I did it later, but in the meantime just take everything I just said to heart and do as I say."

Zoey stared back towards Lawrence for a moment longer before daring a glance towards the now broken window. Then, nodding, she said, "Guess I'm about to give Tim Mason a seizure."

XANDER ONCE DREAMED that he was a human, but humans hated and rejected him. They were driven by baser instincts and sensed in him, without knowing or understanding how or why, that he was different, dangerous. It was the uncertain-yet-certain restlessness of sheep sensing a wolf among their flock—in this case a wolf that didn't know that he was not a sheep; a wolf that didn't yet know he was a wolf.

Then Xander dreamed that he was a vampire—they were his people after all; it was his rightful place—but, much as both sides hated to see it, they were no different than the humans; the dream didn't change.

Just where does the dreaming end? *he thinks again for the first time.*

Xander had dreamed he could be a protector, but he'd allowed others to come to harm.

He'd dreamed that he could be lover, but he could not even manage to love himself.

And he'd dreamed that he and Estella...

What? What had it been? Why couldn't he remember? And why was he too scared to try; too scared to—

SEE!

"Anyone ever tell you that you're a real pain in the ass?" asks Xander.

He is distantly aware that the source is saying—without actually saying anything—that the same can be said of him.

This, he figures, is fair. And, more to the point, yes—plenty have said that to him.

Got nine dead faces waiting for me back at a table that doesn't exist to keep on telling me, too, *he thinks.*

Fortunately for Xander, he has a distraction:

He spots DiAngelo, toting a gun that no man has any earthly business toting, along with two others who are, though carrying their own weapons, armed more modestly. Xander knows that he needs to know as much as he can about them—about everything—and so, just like that, he does.

He is light itself as he moves: existing everywhere at once and knowing all he touches in that instant.

He is the darkness: looming in all corners, seeing all secrets, and creeping—always creeping—about for a chance to swallow the light.

He is the blood, the auras, and the Power; he experiences life passionately on the molecular level and, in the same instant, sees this all as a speck of dust grazing a single gear-tooth in the never-ending whirr of the Great Machine. Everything sheds all pretenses of complexity and relevance as it all breaks down into its simplest forms for him—all positive and negative charges; all ones and zeroes; all 'yes's and 'no's—and, just beyond a barrier that's more imagined in the eyes of life, the universe, and everything, there is nothingness.

It seems better, cleaner, to just let it all slip into that nothingness.

He can even help it along if he so desired it. Just a thought and...

The Power makes it happen.

"You really are a pain in the ass," Xander says again. "Not even awake and in our body and you're starting in with that shit."

He says nothing.

Xander wishes he had eyes, if only to roll them at himself.

"Come on," he says, turning their attention away from the allure of how, once everything is stripped away to 'yes' or 'no,' it's easy —too *easy—to cast it all away.*

He puts the layers back into place. He needs them there to see the 'why' behind saving it.

And he will *save it.*

He has to.

For...

He hears Ruby call out to him, but he can't bring himself to answer at that moment.

He is the light; he is the darkness; he is the blood, aura, and the Power.

And, at that moment, he is God.

Xander Stryker, of the battle that's about to unfold here at this hotel, knows all that was, all that is, and all that could ever come to be.

And he HATES *knowing.*

Brace yourself, Zane, *he thinks,* because this will probably suck.

All at once, a single vampire's body becomes the host to light, dark, and everything in between.

All at once, Xander Stryker is painfully aware of what it is to be alive again—the weight of it; the feel of air inflating lungs, of blood coursing through veins, and the wonderful-yet-awful hum of a brain that's actually attached *to one's thoughts.*

What a novel concept, *Xander thinks, cozying up to existing.*

But there's no time to bask...

"Zoey, you need to listen carefully and broadcast what I'm about to tell you to everyone else. Do you understand?"

Zoey's aura swirls, unsettled and uncertain, and she tries to reach into him with it; Xander does not allow her to—knowing it will force him out. This only unsettles her that much more.

"We got three on the roof and three on the fourth floor. DiAngelo's on the roof with the automatic cannon along with a man wielding the grenade launcher that did *that,*" *Xander nods Zane's head towards the impact crater.*

His explanation stretches on. He remembers to leave out the Carrey-hunter's name—knowing that it will only complicate things if Dianna knows he is there too early—and with each new word he dreads the moment that's coming, seeing the dominos that need to play out and feeling his resolve breaking bit-by-bit as he does. Xander remembers the flu cell; remembers it and how its fate concerned him more than that of a woman with a family.

"... try to remember that people matter more than cells—it gets tricky when you're this separated from life, the universe, and everything."

Not the case when you *know* the person—*know* the cluster of cells—that's about to be killed, *Xander thinks.*

And then, too soon, he's arrived at the first domino that will lead to Dianna's death:

I'm so sorry, Dianna... *he thinks, then,* Sawyer, oh god...

"The middle man," *Xander speaks on through Zane,* "is William Barnes, and he's strapped with what could either be a bomb that will decimate this entire parking lot *or* a suicide vest that will bring down that entire building and all the men inside. We can allow neither to happen. We must..."

Xander remembers all that Dianna has suffered; remembers what she means to so many—what she means to him and Estella—and, of course, what she means to Sawyer. He considers all of this, and realizes what sort of trade he's putting into motion...

"No!" he protests, suddenly wanting to take it back—he wants to forget this line of dominos like he's forgotten so many others—but it has already begun. "No, I can't let that—"

It is this, *the not-voice tells him,* or absolute failure!

Xander sees the only paths that lead to any chance for any of them, feels Zane's body lurching with sickness in response to his thoughts, and, before he slips—his sorrow too great to hold on any longer—from the tattooed vampire's mind, he finishes what he has to do.

DIANGELO ROARED as he watched James Chan's body crash to the street. He was certain that he was about to watch any number of the monsters scatter out from behind the cover of their cars to feed on him, but they didn't. This, he thought, almost seemed worse.

"NOT GOOD ENOUGH FOR YOUR DELICATE PALATES, MONSTERS?" he screamed as he once again focused a series of short bursts from the Bushmaster.

The car that Chan's murderer had ducked behind began to crumple and fold in on itself. DiAngelo reset his weight bearing leg—*The recoil really is a cunt,* he groused to himself—and ignored the growing throb in his supporting shoulder. He honed the Bushmaster on the car's trunk, where he'd last seen the leech lurking. The car shuddered under each impact, actually beginning to hop as the downward force started slamming it repeatedly against the concrete.

Then, realizing that he no longer had a decent target to shoot at (and secretly needing an excuse to stop shooting before the Bushmaster ripped his arms from his shoulders), he stopped. His breathing was coming out in labored, raspy gusts, his eyes sweeping the parking lot for any sign of...

"Where's my fodder?" he demanded.

Carlos looked up at him from the scope of his M4A1, twitched, gave a chuckle that slipped into a barking giggle, and then went totally straight-faced once more.

DiAngelo was beginning to worry about Carlos.

"Your fodder, sir?" he said.

Growling, wondering if Carrey had even made the call for the Cebourist recruits, DiAngelo contemplated hoisting the Bushmaster again, wanting to see more of its destructive prowess, even if only on the hotel's parking lot and the cars that the monsters insisted on ducking behind.

Just what the hell do they intend to do, anyway? I've got the high ground two times over, he thought. *So why aren't they running yet?*

"Sir?" Carlos called to him.

Several floors below him, DiAngelo heard an M16 rattle off a few tight bursts. With James dead and Carrey practically married to his S&W .44 629 Special—*What sort of man commits solely to a revolver in this day and age?* he thought with a scoff, *And that's coming from a true-blue cowboy!*—there was no doubt in his mind that what he was hearing was William doing his damn job. This, DiAngelo decided, was a good sign that Carrey *wasn't* doing his.

DiAngelo jumped, startled, and the Bushmaster rattled under a fresh tug from his energy. He stared at it a moment, curious, but then turned away and ducked behind the roof, not about to let himself get picked off like James had.

"I gave Carrey an order, Carlos," he explained, "and I'm waiting for it to be obeyed."

Carlos nodded, but he didn't look like he understood. "Orders, sir?" he said, his voice slipping a few octaves from sane to not.

DiAngelo nodded back towards the door. "Get down there. Find Carrey. Ask him where the backup is. If he says *anything* that isn't 'on their way' or, better yet, 'already here,' then I want you to shoot him."

Carlos stared at him, his face, which was normally mad as a hatter when DiAngelo gave him a kill order, was stunned and maybe even a little disgusted. "Sir?" he asked, pressing DiAngelo to change his mind.

DiAngelo did not change his mind.

"Movement, sir," Tim announced.

Neither DiAngelo nor Carlos paid him any mind.

"Listen close, soldier," he kept his voice low and bordering a growl despite Tim shooting off another of the magic-infused Cebourist grenades—the blast in the distance was music to his ears—"I'm beginning to doubt Carrey's loyalty, just like I'd begun to doubt Mike's. Now, I *will* be putting a new body under that desk by the end of this; it's up to you to decide if it's Carrey's... or your own."

William's M16 barked to life a few floors down. It was as if DiAngelo and Carlos didn't hear it. They simply stared at one another, each one waiting for the other to start making sense.

Carlos' body shook, and he looked like he might slip into insanity again. "But, I-I thought..." he stammered, shook his head, slapped himself, and then said, "Aren't I just shooting him if he *hasn't* called for the backup?"

DiAngelo didn't answer him. He reached over, unclipped the madman's sidearm, and slipped it free of its holster. Then, after racking the slide, he gently flipped off the safety, turned the gun in his hand, and set it into Carlos' already sweaty palm.

"Find out about my backup," DiAngelo told him, his voice sounding like it used to when he'd tell Abigail to take out the garbage, "and then put two bullets in the back of Carrey's head.

If those bullets don't find their way into his head, then I shall personally see to it that they find their way into yours. Is that order in any way unclear, soldier?"

Carlos gulped, closed his hand around the gun, and then shook his head. "Sir..." his voice seemed pained by its own sanity, "No, sir."

CEBOURISTS ARE ON THEIR WAY, *Zane,* Xander's voice, reminding Zane of the psychic messages from his wife or Zoey but seeming, at the same time, vastly different, called to him. *And Carrey's lifeline just shifted; if you don't get up there and save him he's going to die.*

"Get up there?" Zane scoffed, shaking his head as a storm of automatic gunfire peppered the parking lot. "Sorry, Strykerbird, but I don't see that—"

Carrey is about to die! Xander repeated.

"And I missed the part where I should give a fuck about any of those choad-munchers," he growled, ducking his head as a ricocheting bullet clanged against the headlight of the SUV.

Isaac and Zoey stared at him, their faces showing growing levels of concern.

Zane ignored them as he said, "We've got bigger problems than—"

Carrey is why you're here. He dies: you've failed. All of this will have been for nothing.

Zane considered this, groaned, and punched the side of the car.

Both Isaac and Zoey jumped at the outburst. Zoey set a hand on his shoulder, and he felt a wave of dizziness as she started to drain out some of his anger.

He pulled away, shaking his head. "Don't do that," he said, shaking with fear and trying not to admit that fact to himself. "I need my wits about me."

"Why, Zane?" Zoey asked. "What's happening? Who are you talking to?"

"I already told you," Zane wiped his face. His eyes burned, and he couldn't tell if it was the sunblock riding on his sweat or the tears he felt welling up. "Xander's—"

"Zane," Zoey cut him off, "Xander *is not*—"

"I don't have time to argue," Zane muttered, starting to get his feet planted under him. "I need to do something stupid."

"Why?" Zoey demanded.

Zane shrugged. "I don't know."

"Then why...?"

"BECAUSE IF I DON'T THEN WE'VE FAILED," Zane hissed at her. "And..." he shook his head, "And all of this will have been for nothing!"

"That doesn't make any sense," Zoey argued, reaching out for him again. "Zane, just—"

Zane was on his feet and sprinting at a human pace—an Olympic-level pace, sure, but still only a human one—away from the SUV. With the exception of the Lawrence-vampire, the men stationed at the hotel didn't have much in the way of known targets. Zane, though not exactly in a mood to die, knew that giving them—all of them—a single target was the best way to draw their random, sporadic fire.

Who knew when that random, sporadic fire might actually find one of theirs?

He remembered what Serena had said to him before he left —*"... with how competitive you've been with Stryker in the past I worry that 'near-death' won't be good enough for you"*—and he stifled a cringe that could have likely made it come true.

Please don't choose now to be right, babe, he prayed back to his wife. *Please!*

The automatic gunfire started following him, slapping at the concrete behind him. The sound followed him like a serpent. He darted to the left, starting in the direction of the hotel.

They're expecting you to make for the door.

"You're pretty chatty for a bird," Zane panted as he faked to the left as though he were going to make a dash for the door and then turned right.

And you're pretty bald for a gorilla.

If there'd been any doubt in Zane's mind who he'd been talking to, it was gone now.

"Care to tell me why you're not here in person to help us? Back at that shit-shack fucking your wife?" he demanded.

I wish. Still can't wake up.

Zane wanted to laugh at that, but a grenade blast a few meters ahead of him had him scrambling out of the range of the enchanted blast and the bullet storm that had resumed following him. "H-how... how could I ever question your man-card, Stryker? Here the world's... going to shit... and you're *napping!*"

Figured you could handle my mess. With all your big talk I sort of figured I could take a snooze and trust the job to be done before I got up.

Zane wanted to laugh at that, too, but really it just made him sad.

"We... we miss you, buddy," he confessed.

I know. I'm working on it. But you have to get in there and save—

"The fuck... do you think... I'm trying to do? Th-the door's... back there! How am I—" Zane stopped, cursed at himself, and yanked out one of his pistols.

Two shots later, he'd made his own entrance through one of the first floor windows and dove through into an unlit hotel room.

"Status?" he asked, landing on a queen-sized bed, knocking a partially melted chocolate mint off of one of the pillows, and rolling to his feet and clipping his shoulder on the outer wall that fed into the short hallway.

Slick, Xander taunted him.

"Come on, ghost-boy! Bust my balls later!" Zane demanded as he yanked the door open and stepped out into a corridor of numbered doors.

Fourth floor, Xander reminded him. *If you could jump straight up and two rooms over you'd be there by now, but—*

"Yeah, yeah," Zane was already running for a nearby stairwell. "I ain't a ghost-boy like you."

No, you're not, Xander agreed. *But I'm not a ghost. Case in point:*

Zane's body lurched just as he started up the stairs and, though his next step was still on a set of stairs, he suddenly found himself facing the wrong way and only a few feet from a sign telling him he was staring at the doorway to the fourth floor.

"How in the hell?" Zane gasped, looking back and seeing more stairs behind him on that landing alone than he'd taken in the entire trip.

He thought he heard *"the Power makes it happen,"* as though muttered by somebody back on the first floor and letting the echo chamber of a stairwell deliver the message, but...

But nothing's that easy, he thought.

Nothing ever is, Xander agreed.

Zane threw the door open and ran into the hall as he said, "You're creepy, Stryker."

Been called worse by better, Vailean.

"Funny. Becoming a ghost has made you funny," he sighed, looking around. "Fuck! What room nu—"

Four-fourteen, Xander told him.

Seeing that he was a few paces from four-fourteen, Zane started for the door.

DON'T! Xander screamed in his head, and Zane yanked his hand back like the handle might bite him.

"But you said—"

I said Carrey's in four-fourteen, but if you go in there he'll shoot you in the face and this all ends here.

"Then what am I supposed to—"

Kill the nutcase on your right.

Zane jumped, startled by this, and leveled his gun to the right, taking fierce aim at...

An empty hallway.

"Fucking hell, Stryker, there's nobody—"

An elevator *ding*ed at the end of the hall, and a twitchy man, muttering and cursing to himself stepped out and into Zane's sights. Turning in his direction, the man continued his insane ramblings for several seconds before finally catching sight of Zane and stopping in mid-step and mid-ramble.

The two stared at one another, confused.

Stunned to the point of shaking his head—seeming to actually refuse the possibility of Zane standing before him—the man broke the silence and then said, "How did I not—"

Zane, not at all curious what he was about to say, tightened his grip on the trigger.

Two shots, Xander told him.

Not caring why that should be important, he squeezed the trigger of the semiautomatic two times.

The bullets were practically traveling side-by-side by the time they found their mark.

Then, marginally curious, Zane asked, "What was he saying?"

He wanted to know how he didn't sense you down here, Xander explained.

Zane was about to ask how he didn't, paused, and then said, "You shielded my aura, didn't you?"

Lift you up four flights of stairs in the blink of an eye: nothing, Xander said with a chitter of laughter over Zane's ear. *Block your aura from detection: shock and awe.*

"Was kind of hoping to forget about the stairs, actually," Zane said. "Whole fiasco actually made me pee a little."

Yeah, Xander said. *I know.*

DiAngelo heard the two shots he'd been waiting for.

And faster than I expected, too, he thought with a growing smile.

He wondered if this meant that Carrey had told Carlos that there *hadn't* been a call for backup—which he'd made clear warranted an immediate response—or if Carlos, being as squirrely and nervous as he was about the whole thing, had just figured it'd be better to just kill Carrey and "to hell" with asking about the backup.

DiAngelo didn't care one way or the other. Carrey was dead and gone, Carlos was redeemed in his eyes...

And—*Looky, looky!*—he could see a bunch of Cebourist fodder storming towards the parking lot.

"I'll be damned," he said aloud with a chuckle. "Carrey actually managed to do something right."

CHAPTER 16

When Heroes Fall

"If I am going to be drowned—if I am going to be drowned—
If I am going to be drowned, why, in the name of
the seven mad gods, who rule the sea,
was I allowed to come thus far and
contemplate sand and trees?"
Stephen Crane (1871-1900)

Q*uick! The room across from you!* Xander's voice in Zane's head was one part "set too loud"-transmission and one part "which one of us is thinking?" It was, simply put, giving Zane a headache. *They're coming, Zane!*

If Xander had been decent enough to be with them in person, Zane might have hit him at that moment.

"Motherfu—" Zane stopped himself and forced a deep breath, knowing that it was better to listen to the disembodied voice than suffer the alternative. "The rooms are locked, Stryker! And *who* are 'they'? Ours? Theirs?"

Theirs, Xander told him, answering out of order. *Lots more of them. Ours have been warned already.*

"And the door?" Zane pressed, already moving to test the handle.

It opened.

Zane paused and moved to retrieve the body from the hall. Though he couldn't be sure—not sure like Stryker, at least—he felt that leaving it might advertise his presence.

The body was gone. Even the bloodstains on the hall and carpet had somehow magically vanished.

Zane scanned the corridor, sweeping his head in both directions twice to be sure. Though he knew it was impossible, he thought the only explanation was that the man had just gotten up when he wasn't looking.

Nothing.

"What in the...?"

There was that chitter above Zane's ear, and then Xander said, *How long until you realize I'm not just a voice?*

"Hasn't anybody told you? I'm not such a fast learner!" he scoffed as he ducked into the room, shutting the door behind him.

No sooner had the latch to his room *click*ed into place than he heard the door across from his open with a soft, wooden whine. A few seconds later, another door opened—this one, from the sounds of it, further down the hall—and then:

"You heard that, too?"

"I thought I heard... something. Maybe sound carries funny in this place."

"You think so?"

"Maybe. Old building. All sorts of old ducts and such. Maybe Carlos' was cracking off a few rounds and the shots echoed through the air intake."

"Yeah," the first voice said, the one closest to the door —*Gotta be Carrey,* Zane thought. He didn't sound convinced, but he didn't say anything to disagree. "That was probably it then," he finally said.

Zane had an uncomfortable feeling that, during that silence, Carrey had been staring at the door he'd just slipped behind. He stayed quiet, even went so far as to hold his breath. If the psychotic lot of them were dosing with mythos DNA, then there was a chance that they'd be able to hear a fly fart.

Finally, though, the further door *click*ed shut, followed immediately after by the closest. This, Zane assumed, was a good sign that Carrey didn't suspect anything.

As if reading his mind—and who's to say that he wasn't, right?—Xander said, *It's safe. They've gone back to their posts.*

Zane nodded and took a moment to catch his breath. "So where'd you send the body, anyway?" he asked.

Don't worry about it, was the only answer Xander offered.

"INCOMING!" somebody a few cars over shouted, and Isaac turned his head in time to see what looked to be a poorly-funded and worse-planned parade.

Instead of an exuberant marching band toting freshly polished instruments, they came bearing any number of means of killing. And instead of dazzling and matching outfits, the crowd looked to be wearing whatever each one had been wearing during their otherwise normal day-to-day routine before being called upon to participate. Most looked to be wearing street clothes, but a good number of them were still wearing the ridiculous hues and pairings that reeked of the human's pseudo-comical commercial enterprise system. Bright oranges layered on grayed blacks, neon greens and deep purples, and—were it not for his transformed body Isaac might have actually laughed—even a few caps and name tags bearing the wearer's place of work.

Considering this, Isaac assumed it was more like *former* place of work.

He wasn't sure what McDonald's stance on the mythos scare was, but he was certain the pockmarked, grease-laden young man with a pump-action shotgun and an apron hand-scrawled with "GOD HATES MONSTERS" was not the face of their newest ad-campaign.

I'm guessing they're not here to protest in our favor, he thought with an audible groan that sounded more like a growl.

Zoey shook her head. "Cebourist recruits," she said.

Couldn't even bother to get changed, huh?

"I doubt most of them knew they'd be here when they were getting ready for the day."

Isaac couldn't argue with this. He certainly wouldn't have guessed that he'd be in this situation if asked to guess twenty-four hours earlier. If he'd been a human and keeping human hours, he'd have set his alarm and gone to bed just like any other day; maybe he'd even manage to sleep through Xander's broadcast and the resulting mayhem and, with luck, wake up and start the day with no inkling of what was in store. He wondered if this was the case for the folks still wearing their work uniforms—*How far into the morning did they make it,* he thought, *before learning that nothing would ever be the same?*—and when, in the midst of it all, they'd decided to mosey over to the Cebourists' recruiting center.

Not that any of them looked *nearly* as dedicated or ideological as the Cebourists he and the others had faced the day before. Though Isaac hated to give any of them any semblance of credit, at least their people looked dedicated to something *other* than presenting themselves as an angry mob. He wondered how many of them truly believed in the Cebour-god and how many were just swayed by DiAngelo's "this way to kill monsters"-propaganda.

Though Isaac had no way of knowing for sure, he was positive that DiAngelo didn't even believe in Cebour.

Shame, he thought, and if he could have smirked in that form he would have, *because faith is what gives the strongest Cebourists their power.*

Overhearing this thought, Zoey shook her head. "Don't let your guard down," she warned. "They might not all have the faith to power their magic, but some of them do. And the others..." she nodded towards a small cluster who wielded automatic rifles with a trained rigidity that told Isaac that they, too, were once military.

Yeah... he agreed with a dog-like huff, *Enough mice can bring down even the mightiest wolf, right?*

"At least the lot of them being down here will slow down the gunfire coming from up there," Zoey said.

I'd wait on that theory, Isaac warned, glancing back towards the roof of the hotel. *I'm not sure I like the idea of trusting DiAngelo's sense of brotherly love with these folks.*

DIANNA HAD AN UNEASY FEELING. She was not afraid, though. Fear, she'd learned long ago, could be managed; it was an ugly little creature with a long, probing neck that, when one stopped fleeing from it and actually turned to face it, was convenient for a stranglehold. There was nothing wrong with being afraid—something that her brother had both taught her and neglected to learn—as it was the first and best response to a dangerous situation. And Dianna, between the "family business" of hunting mythos and the cruel cosmic joke that was being born with a brother like Richard, had grown up facing any number of dangerous situations. Learning to wrangle her fear at an early age had given her an edge; rather than being trampled by it she discovered that she could, instead, ride it out of (or even into) the danger that birthed it. She was a stronger warrior because of her fear in much the same way a knight was stronger upon a horse.

But Dianna was not afraid.

She could not take this crippling sense by its metaphorical neck, wring it, make it hers, and then ride it; could not even identify the nature of this particular feeling. It held all the grim certainty and adrenaline-pumping panic that fear did, but there was a blanket of serenity that covered it all, muting it all and turning it into something completely different. She would not even humor the delusion of the voice, though. *That*, she knew, was neither real nor a creature of her mind that she could tame and harness.

It hadn't even been an actual voice!

Voices spoke; voices made clear, to-the-point statements; hell, voices *belonged* to someone, *anyone*!

This voice had not spoken; it had made nothing clear, made no point; and, congealing her theory into something that quivered and threatened to come undone but still remained solid, the voice had seemed to belong to her gun.

Guns... do not... speak! Dianna thought to herself, working to prove this point by squeezing off a few roaring shots into the crowd of approaching Cebourists.

Sawyer was already gone from her side, jumping into overdrive the moment the call of "INCOMING" had warned them of the ambush—*Just who in the hell gave that warning, anyway,* she absently thought, not really caring in the long run—and appearing in the center of the group. From there, with shock and panic working in his favor, he'd been able to start cutting them down from the inside-out. Whenever the horde thought they had a bead on him, he'd—*POOF!*—suddenly be somewhere else in their midst; a few more of their own taken down at the knees in the process.

"God, but I love that brilliant vampire!" she'd heard herself boast as she put a bullet in the back of a Cebourist who was in the process of trying to struggle against the current of the crowd to get to her fiancé.

And that was when her gun had spoken to her.

It spoke without words or clarity—offering no real point—and, once again, it had come from a gun, which all logic dictated could not speak.

But if it *had* spoken—if guns had somehow, in this horrible, mixed-up world, managed such a feat—she was certain that this gun, *her* gun, had conveyed a myriad of wordless thoughts and neutral emotions that all boiled down to a single word that was more a product of her own interpretation:

Sorry.

It was definitive. It was unquestioning. It was sorrowful.

It was decided.

Dianna stared out at the crowd of Cebourists as more of her team followed Sawyer into action. The Isaac-therion, already transformed and moving like a jungle cat into the fray, was all teeth and fury while his auric lover, the blue-haired genius who Dianna wished she'd gotten to know better, lay down a round of suppressive fire. Nearer to the front of the horde, a dozen Cebourists were swept off their feet and careened back into more of their own—no doubt falling victim to more of Zoey's efforts. A pair of snarls, twins in their own right, rang out, followed by a pair of savage grunts and, in a scene that was nothing short of inspired and hilarious, the car that Zeek had driven to the scene was careening through the air.

The therion sisters, Karen and Sasha, had transformed and turned the vehicle into a makeshift projectile.

Because who needs bullets, Dianna thought, trying her best to shed some humor on her own personal sea of not-fear.

It didn't work.

To add insult to injury, she saw, Zeek and Satoru had actually climbed atop the car before letting their lovers hurl it into the crowd of scattering Cebourists. Uttering a pair of war cries—one a deep, yodeling hum that would have been better set in a snow-capped mountain and another that, on any other occasion, would have most certainly come from a lion or a tiger—the two warriors rolled free of the car's roof as it collided with the ground. Sparks shot off the concrete in a wave. Metal shrieked and folded. Zeek's staff and Satoru's katana swung out in blurs as the two rolled to their feet like synchronized dancers. Behind them, Karen and Sasha took to the air like a pair of identical furry missiles. Cebourist eyes couldn't grow wide enough to take in the full scope of the incoming threat, and the ones who weren't taken out by staff or blade were eviscerated from behind by tooth and claw. As this onslaught befell the front-end of the Cebourist horde, Isaac hacked a zig-zag path through their center, convening with Sawyer and several of the others who'd already made it to him. The chaos had the swarm of magic-wielding worshippers blindly throwing attacks, most of their spells falling without effect on their fellow humans while a few wound up shooting or stabbing their own in the confusion.

It was a beautiful thing.

But Dianna still had an uneasy feeling...

"THOUGHT YOU SAID that you'd warned the others about these guys," Zane whined as, with one hand, he slammed the barrel of one of his pistols against the chest of a Cebourist and fired a shot that had one of their ribs making a surprise visit to their spine. With the other hand, he retrieved his rusty axe, driving the blunt back end into an incoming attacker's forehead before forcing the crusty blade into the meat of another's shoulder.

Judging from the effort it took and the volume of the scream it earned, he imagined the victim was becoming increasingly aware of just how badly the weapon was in need of sharpening.

Zane made a note—but knew already that he'd forget in a matter of seconds—of trying to shed a tear for the man. He snapped his neck to hurry things along.

The split second it took for him to complete the task while

releasing the axe was enough for Xander to "say," *I warned them about the group that was coming in from the* front *of the hotel.*

"How'd you do that?" asked Zane, curious if Xander was being just as chatty with others out in the street.

They're all convinced they heard somebody else call out a warning.

"Right..." Zane drawled, wondering what made him lucky enough to be hearing Xander with this degree of clarity.

I can communicate with you—do everything I can with you—because you believe I'm going to make it.

Not bothering to wonder how Xander could have known what he was thinking, Zane asked, "Why should that make any difference?"

Why should you be able to hear a radio station that you're not dialed into?

"So what about the people who *sort of* believe that you're going to make it?"

They're sort of *picking up on my static, I suppose. Dianna is...* Xander's voice stopped there.

Zane didn't believe for a moment that he'd lost him.

"What's going to happen to Dianna?" he asked, slamming the axe into the chest of a nearby Cebourist, dragging him side-by-side with another, and executing the both of them with a well-placed single shot to one's head.

Xander remained silent.

Zane still knew that he was with him. Growling, he jumped into overdrive and repositioned himself behind a Cebourist who'd been trying to get the drop on him from a nearby fire door. He paused long enough to break the time-frozen human's outstretched arm before dropping back out of overdrive and letting his would-be attacker stumble in a pained heap between him and a pair of pursuers. Three shots later the hallway was three Cebourists deader.

Not nearly 'deader' enough, Xander mused.

"Thought you mind-fuckers had some policy about not

reading thoughts," Zane groused after shooting another three Cebourists and hurling his axe into the stomach of a fourth.

I'm more-or-less occupying your head right now, Zane, Xander explained as Zane went about retrieving his weapon and putting a round in the still-squirming human's chest. *Your thoughts sound just as clear as your words.*

Zane paused at that. "So you're, like, all up in my business right now?"

In a manner of speaking.

Zane cleared his throat and then immediately wondered why. "I... uh, might've said some stuff about Estella to Serena that I don't exactly want you taking out of context?"

You referring to "severely fuckable?"

Zane stayed quiet but nodded.

He immediately wondered why.

Well... Xander began, and Zane wondered just what sort of damage an ethereal Stryker "living" in his head could do up there. *I suppose you're not wrong.*

Zane could have toppled over at that moment.

After composing himself, he said, "Really? You're not, like, gonna blow a blood vessel up there or read me some riot act about what I said? Besides, aren't you Mister 'Too Good to Like Sex'?"

I can see more of the conversation than just the "severely fuckable"-part, Zane. I can see all of it: everything you said to Serena and *to Estella.*

Zane felt himself blush. "And?" he pressed.

And I appreciate it.

Zane was almost too stunned to react in time as a Cebourist charged from the stairwell with a shotgun leveled at him. *Almost.*

"Guess you're not Mister 'Too Good to Like Sex' anymore, huh?" he offered with a chuckle.

You'd be surprised what nearly dying and being forced to float around without a body for this long does to a crazy thing like bashfulness.

"'Bashful' doesn't begin to cover it," Zane said, "I was actually beginning to think they called you 'Crimson Shadow' because you dressed in black and blushed whenever someone mentioned tits."

What I wouldn't give to have a set of hands to feel a pair of tits right now, Xander replied, actually sounding sad.

"Almost enough to make a dead man wake up, aren't they?" said Zane.

If only.

"Well," Zane smirked, "since you're not POed at me for talking about how sexy your wife is, I guess it'd only be fair for you to say the same about mine."

The chitter of Xander's chuckle tickled at Zane's ear. *I might,* he said, *if I didn't find her so fucking annoying.*

Zane almost hated himself for laughing at that.

Enough of the Cebourist horde had been thinned out for Sawyer to slip free and return to Dianna's side. She didn't actually see him leave the battle—didn't actually *see* him coming at all—but was just suddenly aware that she was no longer alone. Between his and the others' efforts, several hundred armed foot "soldiers" had been reduced to only several dozen. Though Dianna had no way of checking, she was sure that it hadn't even taken them half-a-minute.

Thirty seconds later, and close to two-hundred Cebourist corpses littered the street outside the hotel.

DiAngelo had obviously been hoping for better results, because Dianna didn't need to be psychic to know that the roar that rose from the roof of the building was one of raw disappointment.

Then the shooting started up again.

Somewhere in the distance, the same voice from before rose, calling "FALL BACK."

None of the humans seemed to hear it, and so it was that none of them were spared in the events that followed.

As every member of the ragtag remains of the Trepis Clan darted free—all seeming to know what area to avoid at that moment—the first shot struck directly in the thickest part of the remaining Cebourists. Both the living and the dead were ripped apart in an instant that sent a red mist billowing into the air. Two seconds later, another shot landed. The cannon firing the rounds was an automatic, this Dianna knew, but a weapon like that could feed in a fresh round only so quickly without jamming. The resulting impacts felt like the tremors of sprinting giants. Though most of the vampires managed to vanish from the scene at the first call of danger, those unable to jump into overdrive—among them were Zeek, Karen, Satoru, Sasha, and Isaac—were forced to run. With bodies littering the street and little immediate cover, this forced them to begin a serpentine dash with periodic hurdles back towards the parking lot.

And the sprinting giants gave chase.

The majority of Cebourists who were still alive gave up their mission—in that instant likely gave up their affiliation with everything Cebour-related—as their so-called leader's automatic cannon became every bit their own problem as their enemies'. The few who tried to hold onto their "death to all mythos"-mentality were too blinded by hate to see the arm-length bullets that rained down on them. In a few short seconds, the entire street was awash in screams, panic, and blood.

And the sprinting giants' steps were drawing ever nearer to Dianna's friends...

Then her gun told her that she and Sawyer needed to go to room four-oh-eight.

"Why in the fuck am I in here dealing with these queef-nuggets if our guys outside are being kept busy by them?" Zane demanded.

They thought they'd be clever to send in two teams, Xander explained.

He'd finally gotten to the sixth floor only to find it just as congested with Cebourists as the fifth.

"Lucky us," Zane growled, yanking his axe free as the now-dead body collapsed at his feet. He kicked it with relative ease into three incoming Cebourists. "Can't you just, y'know, zap me up to the roof like you did with the staircase?" he demanded.

The magic doesn't work like that, Xander explained. *I could move you between those two points because there was nothing blocking the path from one side to the other. If I tried to do it now you'd come out of it with every person and obstacle between here-and-there fused to you on the molecular level.*

Zane sneered. "So I'd come out of it inside-out?"

"Inside-out" doesn't even begin to describe how you'd come out of it, Xander said. *You ever see* 'The Fly?'

"Ain't that a bit before your time, young'n?" asked Zane with a chuckle.

Jeff Goldblum version, Xander clarified, *it was on cable. You'd be surprised how many movies I got to catch up on after my stepfather laid me out for a few months. Anyway... remember the man-fly fusion?*

"Unfortunately," Zane admitted, recalling David Cronenberg's slime fetishizing, mid-eighties, sex-and-insects alike masterpiece.

You'd be Goldblum and everything *that exists between* here *and* there *would be the fly.*

The two were silent as Zane worked through a few more Cebourists; this information conjuring a number of mental images that had Zane thankful that Xander wasn't about to try teleporting him again anytime soon.

"Gonna be honest, Stryker," he finally said. "Knowing that now kinda makes me wish you hadn't done it at all in the first place."

Touch your shoulder with your left ear.

"Huh?"

NOW!

Zane almost forgot what Xander had said, but somehow managed to tilt his head at a sharp enough angle to *try* to bring his left ear to the side of his shoulder.

A gunshot echoed behind him.

The heat from the bullet nearly scalded his right cheek.

A Cebourist in front of him lost the upper portion of his skull and let out a barking scream-laugh as what remained of his brains tried to make sense of the impact. Before sense could be made of anything, he was dead and his body was sprawled on the floor in front of Zane.

Maybe time to start trusting my judgement. If you'd have taken the stairs you would've either been delayed and caught or, *if you'd used overdrive, you'd be too winded to live through what's coming.*

"And what's coming?" Zane demanded, shooting the gun-toting Cebourist behind him first in the belly and then again in the chest. He fired another three shots into whatever surface his bullets could find in the interval between standing and dead just to be sure there wouldn't be any more surprises from him.

Can't tell you that, Xander answered.

Zane growled. "Why the hell not?"

Because things need to happen as they're meant to happen.

Zane felt his eye twitch. "That..." he said through clenched teeth as he took the opening to sprint up the stairs to the next floor, "is a *really* infuriating answer."

I know, Xander said. *And you don't get used to it, either. I'm not exactly thrilled to finally be understanding it.*

Zane let out a roar as he kicked through the door to the

seventh floor. He'd have been content heading straight for the roof after his business on the fourth floor, but he'd discovered the stairwell between the fifth and sixth floors blocked off with rubble and been forced to cut across the hall for the staircase on the opposite side. Now, however, he was forced into the next hall not out of interference but, rather, out of safety regulations.

The stairs leading to the roof weren't accessible from there.

While he understood the thought process behind this—*Wouldn't want people staying at the hotel to have easy access to the roof, after all*—he nevertheless managed to place all sorts of blame on architects, hotel management, and a few more gods than he actually believed in for the inconvenience.

The door swung open under the force of the kick, fracturing the skull of a daring Cebourist who probably thought he was getting the drop on him. A short distance away, the noise drew the attention of others, and they turned, readying their own attack. Still cursing—now somehow pairing the Hindu Shiva with the legend of the Flying Spaghetti Monster—he opened fire on the group, one of which was in the process of trying to cast a spell on him with a small, triangular medallion.

"SWEAR TO FUCK," he growled in their direction as the corpse bowled them over, "THE FIRST ONE OF YOU COCK-KNOCKERS TO BURN ME IS GETTING YOUR BALLS STUFFED IN YOUR OCULAR CAVITIES!"

Is that even possible? Xander asked.

Zane plowed forward, gun firing and axe making repeating swings at victims who quickly realized they would have preferred the gun. "Maledictus made it work a few times. Actually made a local coroner quit his job."

How the hell could you know that?

"Zoey helped cover up a lot of the shit that monster did when he was rampaging around in my body back then."

I'd feel worse for you and your history if I hadn't just watched you prolapse a man's asshole with your boot.

"Like you wouldn't have done the same."

I wouldn't have, actually. I like my boots.

Zane actually laughed at that.

"TELL me again why we're doing this," Sawyer said as he tailed after Dianna, who was giving his vampire speed and reflexes a run for their money at that moment.

Dianna wasn't sure how to answer him—somehow "My gun told me to" didn't seem like a good way to motivate him—and so she said, "Zoey said we had to deal with the potential suicide bomber on the fourth floor. She said she'd help the others."

The truth was Zoey hadn't said anything. Not to Dianna, at least. Dianna had seen a shot from the auto-cannon that *should* have been the end of Isaac and the others erupt in midair, staggering the group but leaving them otherwise unharmed. Guessing this was the blue-haired auric's doing, Dianna was, though lying through her teeth about the details surrounding it, confident that she wasn't exactly lying about the facts:

Zoey had things covered in the parking lot, and a voice *had* told her to go to the room with the bomb-wielding Cebourist.

She wasn't thrilled with the idea of lying to her fiancé, but Dianna had a driving need to get to room four-oh-eight and time, though she had no reason to believe this, was of the essence. There was no countdown—none that she was aware of, anyway—and, near as she could tell, they were taking more risks in rushing in like this than if they'd adopted a bit of stealth.

But all of that felt like the wrong path.

And still she refused to believe that her gun was telling her all of this.

All the same, she refused to holster it. She also refused to explain to herself that the reason behind this was because it might muffle more of her gun's words.

God, she thought, *I've finally lost my mind. I kept it together for* years *with Richard beating and threatening me and* now *I'm starting to crack!*

Sawyer scooped her up in a fluid movement, hurdled through the broken window that Zane Vailean had made earlier in his similar mad-dash into the hotel, and, just as fluidly, he set her back down once they were inside.

"I could've done that on my own," she chastised, giving him a "I'm mad but not really mad"-look for carrying her through.

Sawyer rolled his eyes and started ahead of her. "I won't challenge your skillset, baby," he said, keeping his voice low, "but I'm not about to let you gouge your palms trying to vault through broken glass. Get your vertical leap up to thirty feet and I'll let you do it yourself."

"Or I could just throw your body over the glass and walk in like royalty," she offered with a grin.

Sawyer grinned back. "Nothing says true love like a belly full of window shards. Let's go."

The subject of the window had her looking back towards the makeshift entrance that Zane had created in his own (seemingly) insanity-driven dash to get into the hotel. Even then, moments earlier, she'd watched him commit to the effort along with everyone else, and, like everyone else, attributed a hearty amount of the act to insanity.

After all, she'd thought, *any man who's willing to settle down with* that *woman* must *already be a bit touched in the head, right?*

But there seemed to be an eternity in the few minutes that divided *then* from *now,* and Dianna, with her uneasy feeling and her increasingly chatty gun, was beginning to wonder if maybe she and Zane Vailean shared insanity as a common trait.

It certainly wasn't the only trait that they shared...

She had a scattered understanding of Zane's past—a few free moments spent scanning his file, which, she had to admit, likely deserved more time and focus—but the part that stuck out most to her was a term that she knew all too well: taroe.

Few, even within the mythos community, knew of them; few knew they even existed. For most, to mention the word "taroe" was to conjure thoughts of beautifully illustrated cards offering cosmic foretelling of life, love, and all other breed of mystery. That was just fine as far as Dianna was concerned. Her memories of the taroe were not pleasant ones, and, from what she'd gathered from Zane's file, his own memories of them would likely be even less pleasant.

The taroe, who were *technically* human, were a tribal people. They were scattered across the globe, never favoring one region over another provided they were isolated and had access to what they needed. And, as far as Dianna was concerned, they were a peaceful and innocent people. Zane would likely say otherwise, she was certain, but Zane wasn't exactly an innocent in his circumstance.

What made the taroe special—what both set them outside of their own species, made them of interest to Dianna's brother, and made for so much trouble for Zane—was their magic. More specifically: their magic tattoos. The already powerful magic-users, as a rite of passage, were given their first tattoos as teenagers using a specially-made enchanted ink that was then intricately etched into the flesh with ceremonial wooden barbs. It allowed them to channel and focus their already sizable abilities into something that was, with the exception of Estella Stryker, beyond any sort of spellcasting that Dianna had ever seen. The tribal designs, beautiful in their own right, would glow like unobstructed moonlight when the user was preparing to cast, and the results would be spectacular.

Spectacularly grand, Dianna thought, *or spectacularly awful...*

Dianna's brother had wanted the tattoos to be a grand weapon in their fight against mythos, and he'd tracked down, tortured, and eventually destroyed an entire tribe of taroe to get his way. As usual, he'd forced Dianna to follow along, to help him, and together they'd been tattooed by the elders of the tribe—held at gunpoint and certain that Richard would leave them all in peace once they gave the homicidal humans what they wanted—and imbued with the magical abilities they offered. Richard had not let a single one of them live after the act was finished.

Where Dianna's taroe tattoos represented something that Richard had forced the taroe into giving, and, in turn, forced Dianna into accepting, Zane had simply been forced, punished for sneaking into a tribe's territory with the intent to steal a sacred—and cursed—relic. Driven mad by the very relic Zane and his friend were there to steal, the act motivated the tribe to punish the two. The details in the report were hazy, checkered, and, ultimately, quite awful, but it all boiled down to Zane being forced, over several days, to endure a full-body tattooing. The end result, however, did not offer him any powers or amplify any magical abilities; they acted as a power source for a curse that had been meant to destroy Zane and anybody who ever dared to get too close to him.

Since Richard's death, Dianna had made a note to never use the magic of her taroe tattoos; she'd even gone so far as to work on keeping them covered whenever possible. Near as she could tell, the only people who even knew she had the tattoos were those who'd personally known her in her previous life—a life she'd been working hard to put behind her and forget.

Zane, who'd never gotten any benefit from his own tattoos, however, seemed content with flaunting them—or perhaps he was just content flaunting the gigantic slabs of meat that the tattoos rested upon. Dianna couldn't be sure, and, quite frankly, Dianna didn't care; she'd never been one for overly muscled men, and she cared very little for tattoos on their own. When the tattoos were of taroe origin, however, she couldn't help but feel a familiar and incredibly painful burn in her chest.

Though Dianna harbored no real ill-will towards Zane or, with their shaky truce, his wife, there was an inescapable sense of repulsion towards the Vaileans at that moment. She did not want any shared traits with either of them, but it seemed that the moment she'd found herself living in was forcing her to recognize any number of them.

Dianna and Zane shared a painful history with the taroe.

Dianna and Serena shared an arrogant pride.

And now, Dianna realized, she shared both of the Vaileans affinity for insanity.

Great... she thought as she followed after Sawyer. *While I sink into Vailean-levels of insanity—taking my cues from a gun—and lead the love of my life into certain peril for no reason, he's willing to lie on broken glass for me. Dianna, just what in the hell are you doing?*

What you need to, her gun told her.

Dianna wondered if the Vailean's insanity was so reassuring.

The door to the staircase nearest the room they'd entered through was barricaded, the small window offering a view of the other side blocked off by what looked like chunks of concrete and steel. Near as either of them could tell, the stairs had collapsed on the other side.

"Elevator's by the front desk," Sawyer said, glancing down the hall, "but I'm not sure I like the idea of being trapped in a metal box with everything that's going on."

"That leaves the other set of stairs on the other side of the hall," Dianna felt a well of dread at the delay they were being forced into. "And no real assurance that those stairs aren't just as inaccessible."

"Guess that leaves the metal box of death," Sawyer said grimly.

Dianna shook her head, thinking. "Unless they thought to destroy that, too."

"I doubt they would," Sawyer argued. "Otherwise they'd have trapped themselves on the upper floor with no way of getting out."

"Here's hoping they weren't just planning on jumping off

the roof when all this was over, then," she groaned, starting for the elevator.

Xander had become more and more silent as Zane finished shooting, hacking, hammering—though those two were practically one and the same given the state of his axe—and otherwise bare-hand brawling his way through the remaining Cebourists. The struggle wasn't exactly a tolling one for him. These worshipers, unlike the ones he and Xander and Isaac had faced earlier when first squaring off against the homicidal, mythos-hating church, were obviously fresh out of the recruiting office and barely worth the wood they were going to be buried in. Out of the dozens he'd killed, only five had actually tried to cast any sort of magic on him. And, out of those five, only two had connected a magical attack. The first had singed Zane's hand—or so it had felt like it—and forced him to drop one of his guns. The other had made him puke up another sizable portion of the synth-blood he'd forced himself to choke down for the outing.

The first spell he'd been pissed about, and he'd taken a bit of pleasure from punching through that spell-caster's stomach before putting him through a nearby wall.

The second spell he'd actually thought was pretty funny. He'd always had a hard time keeping the synthetic stuff down, anyway. He'd still punched the Cebourist's nose to the back of his skull, but he'd done it with a smile on his face and a "nice one" muttered under his breath.

Between those two and the few who'd managed to land some kind of blow on Zane, he found himself ascending the stairs behind the "AUTHORIZED PERSONELL ONLY" door with a decent number of aches to show for it. The humble trail of blood dribbling across the stairs in his wake were really more for show, in his opinion.

But it was Xander's silence that was really beginning to drag at him, he found. Not because he missed Xander (he did), or because having his voice there to help carry him through the battle took the edge off (it did), but because Xander, silent or not, *was* still there in his head. His silence was a result of some deep sense of mourning, perhaps even regret; he was sorrowful and angry and hurting. And Zane knew all of this because, with Xander still "living" in his head the way he was, Zane was feeling it, too.

But damned if he could figure out *why*.

"What's going to happen?" he whispered.

Xander said nothing.

"Stryker," Zane pressed on. "Your vibes up there are bumming me out. The fuck's going to happen?"

What has to happen, Xander finally whispered back, though he had no reason to.

"That ain't a good thing?" asked Zane.

"Good" is a relative term, Zane, Xander said, his voice suddenly distant; Zane was somehow aware that Xander was leaving him then. Before he felt the connection cut out completely, he "heard" Xander say, *The world's worst tattoo removal will be a "good" thing, too; doesn't mean you're going to like it...*

"The fuck is that supposed to—" Zane stopped in mid-question.

He'd reached the door to the roof, the DiAngelo-douche was on the other side with his beast-gun, and he was officially alone.

Zoey was exhausted, but Zoey was also, as Serena would have put it, pissed-the-fuck-off. She'd been in enough battles to know that concussive impacts on her aura could, though not exactly "hurt," be uncomfortable. Enough of them, moreover, made her body's demand for psychic nourishment nearly unbearable. It was easy to forget that aurics were still vampires, and, like their blood-drinking counterparts, they could be drained of their resources.

It was a severe misconception that the blood-drinking vampires were the scarier of the two. People had a tendency to fall into a mindset that, since blood was the tangible symbol of vitality—not to mention the central focus in all those dreadful horror films—then any creature that freely fed on blood *must*, by some sort of default, be far more terrifying than something that simply drank in one's mental energy.

People were idiots.

Idiots who could keep their blood.

Zoey, exhausted and pissed-the-fuck-off, was coming for everything else.

She had deflected over a dozen shots aimed squarely for her Isaac and her friends, shots that would have proven a problem for a tank or a helicopter. She had swept *hundreds* of dead bodies out of their path to make for a clear route back to safety. And, on top of all of that, she had been forced to shield herself and fork out her aura to fight off a few of the bolder surviving Cebourists who'd managed to get too close for comfort.

Zoey Hartnett made a note of proving to every Cebourist with even a shred of aura left in them that a starving auric vampire was up to the challenge for competing against the traditional horror icon. Though fear and pain tasted foul—"taste" not being the right word for it, but also being the only word for it—it was a better source of quick sustenance than any alternative. She made them afraid; she made them hurt. And when she felt the least bit guilty for it, she dug around in their heads for any sign of what they'd intended to do to Isaac—*her* Isaac!—and, yup, she started feeling just fine with it all over again.

That's it, Zoe! she heard her inner-Serena—the bit of her self-confidence that still wasn't quite confident enough to make itself sound like herself—praise her. *Be the badass we all know you can be!*

Zoey's aura drained all the surviving Cebourists in the parking lot in just under two seconds, those who'd managed to come out of it standing collapsing over their dead comrades as their already weakened bodies gave up the fight. Then her aura moved to the hotel. There were plenty of Cebourists in there, as well, most dead, but plenty still in the process of dying. These she fed from, too.

Until she reached the fourth floor.

Until she reached rooms four-oh-eight and four-fourteen.

Not these ones! the thought struck her with such ferocity and certainty that it startled her.

It *had* been her own thought...

Hadn't it?

Still not positive but not about to question it further or even begin to challenge it, Zoey skipped over the Cebourists occupying those two rooms—both of whom were still trying to get in shots on her and their team—and, remembering Tim Mason, focused her efforts on the hotel's roof.

She'd made a promise about a certain epileptic that she'd yet to keep.

DiAngelo had run out of mythos targets, but he'd yet to run out of ammo.

And he was far, *far* from running out of rage.

General DiAngelo was fed up of failures and fuckups; he'd lost patience with losers and letdowns; he was sick of all the shit-for-brains. And—god-fucking-damn!—they were EVERYWHERE!

And so he just kept on shooting that Bushmaster, ignoring the growing pain in his shoulders and the thrumming, throbbing ache in his thighs. His new body could handle the automatic cannon's weight, and he could even manage to remain standing with the recoil, but it appeared there was a big difference between what a monster's body was capable of doing and what it was willing to *continue* doing.

DiAngelo found himself feeling evermore drained and, with this sensation, evermore thirsty, though the thought of water or any other beverage that had quenched his thirst in the past seemed far from appetizing at that moment.

Doesn't make any goddam...

DiAngelo felt something tickling at the back of his mind. He was reminded of the pests that buzzed around his head during his time in the bush and, arms still preoccupied with the hammering Bushmaster, he used his energy to sweep it away. It did the trick just fine. He sensed the tickle withdraw, linger, and then finally leave.

In the back of his mind he had the strangest thought of blue, but the Bushmaster bucked in his arms, pinching a nerve in his back, and he decided he didn't give a wetback's sundried nutsack about it.

Three more rounds burst out of the Bushmaster, and a few more of the useless turds who'd burdened the Cebourists' recruiting offices erupted into baser components.

Then...

"S-sir...?" Tim Mason called behind him, sounding whiney.

DiAngelo remembered Abigail, age four, whining like that at him whenever she'd made pee-pee in her jammies.

He wasn't about to entertain a soldier who sounded like a baby who'd just pissed on himself.

"S-s-ssssiii-iii-r-r-r-r-r-r-!" Mason suddenly sounded like he was calling from atop the world's most agitated mechanical bull.

"What's the matter with you, Mason?" DiAngelo growled, finally letting up on the Bushmaster. "You sound like you've crammed one of your momma's vibrators up your—"

He was struggling to turn to face the man, the weight of the gun he'd taken such pride in a moment ago now every bit the burden everyone said it would be, and when he finally set eyes on him he found him thrashing on his back, eyes rolling behind his lids, and frothing at the mouth like a crazed dog.

Tim Mason, General DiAngelo realized, was having a seizure...

And, to make matters worse, he was pointing back towards the access door that led back into the hotel.

A tank of a monster stared back at him from it.

ALLEN CARREY HAD BEEN on edge ever since hearing something in the hall a moment earlier. He'd known better than to voice the concern to Barnes, who, like DiAngelo, took any form of caution and tact as a sign of either weakness or treachery, and likely would have been distracted by any claims that there could've been *something* going on in the halls. Allen, however, had known what he'd heard, and when he heard the gentle *ping* of the elevator—something he was certain Barnes would neither be listening for nor keen enough to pick up on—he moved to the door to investigate.

Knowing better than to try opening the door and announcing his presence to whoever might be entering onto their floor, he dropped down in front of the door and slipped a small length of reflective metal from his cargo pants. Though there wasn't much space between the floor and the bottom of the door frame, there was enough for him to work the mirror-like length out into the hall and tilt it so that he could get a somewhat unobstructed view of the newcomers.

At first the man and woman who glanced about the hall just outside the elevator looked to be nothing special. *Then again,* he thought, *a lot of these monsters don't appear to be anything special on the surface.* No sooner had the thought come and gone, however, than he found himself pausing on the woman.

Not a woman, he had to correct himself, but a girl...

A little girl. Barely into her teenage years and already with a furious edge that made him certain she would be a brilliant hunter someday.

At least that's how Allen remembered Dianna. That's how she'd been the last time he'd seen her.

Dianna...

Her parents had been among the first hunters that Allen had managed to get in touch with—among the first who'd allowed him and the rest of DiAngelo's crew to get a foothold in their world; get started in the business of hunting monsters—and, from what he'd heard, she and her brother hadn't been heard from ever since they'd faced off against a nest of monsters in this area. More recently, the Cebourist founder, Ariel, had claimed to have found the body of their son, Richard, and had some demented plans at using that body to boost their war against the mythos. With all that information, Allen had assumed that Dianna had also been killed.

But there she stood, alive, well, armed, and standing surprisingly close and cozy with a vampire...

Allen felt his mouth go dry and his mind go blank. He didn't know what to make of this sight, and so he just stared at the small strip of reflective metal; just watched as the two newcomers started towards the door to William Barnes' room. He did nothing as they drew their weapons, preparing to ambush his colleague; did nothing as they nodded to one another, preparing to get the drop on one of his own.

Little Dianna...

Fighting with the mythos.

Allen was still trying to figure out what it was he was thinking when he heard DiAngelo's voice, both roaring inhumanly loud as well as resonating within his mind like a psychic call:

. . .

"MONSTER?! MONSTER?! YOU TALK TO ME OF MONSTERS, VAMPIRE? THE WORLD KNOWS OF YOUR KIND NOW, HAS TAKEN ITS SIDE, AND IT DOESN'T TAKE A GENIUS OR A KEEN EYE TO KNOW WHAT SIDE IT'S CHOSEN. I'VE KILLED MANY, YES—TODAY ALONE I'VE TAKEN MORE LIVES THAN SOME WARS CAN CLAIM; EVEN PERSONALLY SEEN AN END TO TWO OF MY OWN MEN—"

ALLEN FELT himself tense at that, thinking he knew exactly who that second death was *supposed* to be referring to.

"AND I JUST GAVE MYSELF A PAINFUL ERECTION BLOWING A BUNCH OF MY OWN MEN TO PIECES! BUT THEY WERE USELESS AND, MORE TO THE FUCKING POINT, YOU BLOODSUCKING CURR, I'M STILL WHO GOD FAVORS IN THE WEB! YOU CAN'T CALL ME THE 'MONSTER' WHEN YOU'RE THE ONE WITH BLOOD STILL DRYING ON YOUR CHIN!"

ALLEN COULDN'T BRING himself to calculate how much blood had stained DiAngelo over the years. On his face or otherwise...

"DO YOUR WORST, VAMPIRE. SEE ME OFF TO THE PEARLY GATES SO I CAN GET ANOTHER MEDAL FOR THE *HUNDREDS* OF YOUR KIND I'VE PUT IN THE GROUND ALREADY. DO IT! DO IT! DOOOO IIIII—"

ALLEN JUMPED as he heard DiAngelo's gun fire off another of its insane rounds. He didn't hear another word from General DiAngelo. Realizing what he'd just heard and thinking back on what he'd just seen in the hall, Allen Carrey made a decision.

Standing, he stepped quietly out into the hall and headed after Dianna, all grown up now, and her vampire companion to Barnes' room.

~Thirty seconds earlier~

ZANE WASN'T sure how it was possible, but the DiAngelo-douche looked even douche-ier in person. One of his men—Tim Mason, Zane guessed—was thrashing about as if in the throes of the world's greatest blowjob from the Invisible Woman. Neither Zane nor DiAngelo showed any real concern for the man, and, though Zane didn't think he was in a position to think or feel much, he wondered if the soldier felt at all betrayed or lonely at that moment.

"JUST GONNA WATCH HIM DIE LIKE THAT?" Zane called across the distance.

DiAngelo smiled—actually smiled!—at the question and said, "You obviously haven't been paying attention."

Zane took a step out onto the roof and let his eyes fall on the giant gun in DiAngelo's hands. His arms were bulging from the weight, veins raised against the skin and throbbing from the exertion of holding onto it. Just the sight made Zane's own arms ache, and he was certain he could out-lift the old man even on his worst of days.

He called out again, working to be heard across the distance with the wind howling around the rooftop. "I HAVE TO IMAGINE THE RECOIL ON THAT—"

"Yeah, yeah!" DiAngelo groused, not bothering to speak up. "It's a real cunt."

"Not the word I would've chosen," Zane offered with a shrug, figuring it wasn't worth it to shout if DiAngelo wasn't going to extend the same courtesy. He had a feeling the DNA-doping asshole could hear him just fine, anyway. "Which is funny, considering this is me we're talking about."

"I'm sure that's supposed to mean something," DiAngelo's face twisted with hatred as he worked to level the massive weapon, "but I've got no desire to get to know you to figure out what!"

Zane saw him prepare to fire the weapon and, remembering what Xander had said about preserving enough energy for one burst of overdrive, decided to act.

He was across the rooftop and standing beside DiAngelo before the old man could blink. The strain on his shoulders and back were even more obvious up close, the joints looking tortured and ready to give up. Zane gave them a helping nudge. Two overdrive-driven punches and a kick to the side of DiAngelo's knee had him confident enough to drop out of overdrive, keeping himself to DiAngelo's left in the off chance he still managed to get a round off before things went the way they were about to.

He didn't get a round off.

DiAngelo's shoulders dislocated at once with a pair of squelches that nearly had Zane puking up the rest of his synth-blood. The weight of the giant gun dragged his arms halfway down his torso, a set of ripping sounds issuing as more damage spread through his chest, before his hands gave up the fight and the gun dropped onto his right foot. Crying out at the series of injuries, the old man's busted left knee gave out and started to sink him to the ground, forcing him into an excruciating-looking kneel; the weight of the beast-gun actually keeping him upright and forcing the weight of his body down onto his shattered kneecap.

"Yeesh..." Zane mock-grimaced. "That... uh, that wasn't exactly how I planned that going down," he admitted. Then, shrugging, he offered the DiAngelo-douche a content grin, "Then again, a monster like you deserves only the best, right?"

"MONSTER?!" DiAngelo's roar actually managed to kick up an auric storm, and Zane could feel his budding psychic powers projecting his words as he spoke them. It all would have been rather impressive if it wasn't also pathetic. **"MON-STER?!"** he said again, working to try to lift the gun off his foot before realizing his arms no longer were working. **"YOU TALK TO ME OF MONSTERS, VAMPIRE? THE WORLD KNOWS OF YOUR KIND NOW, HAS TAKEN ITS SIDE, AND IT DOESN'T TAKE A GENIUS OR A KEEN EYE TO KNOW WHAT SIDE IT'S CHOSEN. I'VE KILLED MANY, YES—TODAY ALONE I'VE TAKEN MORE LIVES THAN SOME WARS CAN CLAIM; EVEN PERSONALLY SEEN AN END TO TWO OF MY OWN MEN—AND I JUST GAVE MYSELF A PAINFUL ERECTION BLOWING A BUNCH OF MY OWN MEN TO PIECES!"**

Zane sneered at this confession and actually averted his eyes skyward to avoid even accidently seeing if he was telling the truth.

"BUT THEY WERE USELESS AND, MORE TO THE FUCKING POINT, YOU BLOODSUCKING CURR, I'M STILL WHO GOD FAVORS IN THE WEB! YOU CAN'T CALL ME THE 'MONSTER' WHEN YOU'RE THE ONE WITH BLOOD STILL DRYING ON YOUR CHIN!"

Not feeling like pointing out that the blood on his chin was the synthetic crap that the Cebourist spell-caster had made him puke on himself, Zane decided that he'd heard enough and hoisted the beast-gun off the old man's foot, testing the grip and handle for himself. He could hold it and, sure, if circumstances called for it even carry it, but he could already tell he wouldn't be happily firing the thing without something to brace the bulk of it. DiAngelo was obviously some sort of psychotic striving to compensate for *something* with a weapon like this.

Still, he figured it'd do the trick. Maybe he wouldn't go so far as to empty the rest of the belt—there were still *a lot* of big fucking bullets on that thing, after all—but he'd made a promise about that gun and DiAngelo's fate back on the parking lot.

Seeing him working the beast-gun around on him, DiAngelo sneered and continued his rant: **"DO YOUR WORST, VAMPIRE. SEE ME OFF TO THE PEARLY GATES SO I CAN GET ANOTHER MEDAL FOR THE *HUNDREDS* OF YOUR KIND I'VE PUT IN THE GROUND ALREADY. DO IT! DO IT! *DOOOO IIIII—*"**

Zane didn't bother to put the barrel up DiAngelo's ass, but the bullet he put through him did a decent enough job dragging most of his bowels out across the rooftop.

ALLEN CARREY ROUNDED the door to the room Barnes' was stationed inside in time to see his colleague level a pistol in Dianna's direction. A swell of panic grew in his chest at the sight of the familiar face getting fixed in the crosshairs, but he was still too far away to do anything about it.

And he couldn't be sure what calling out to Barnes *not* to shoot her might make the crazy, bomb-wearing bastard resort to.

Then the gun went off.

The vampire Dianna had entered with was an even greater blur than the bullet as he moved to intercept its trajectory. In less time than Allen had to suck in a gasp of surprise, the vampire was at his feet, a fresh blossom of gore opened up on his shoulder. It took Barnes a moment to register what had happened, but it wasn't long enough for anybody else to act before he decided he was okay with the way things had turned out. Grinning, he leveled the barrel on the chivalrous vampire and squeezed off another two rounds before Dianna, shrieking like a woman possessed, barreled into him and knocked him into the full-length window at the end of the room. A spider-web crack formed where the corner of his suicide vest knocked the glass, but it otherwise held as he pushed his ravenous attacker off of him.

Allen glanced down at the vampire, seeing that he'd taken the last two bullets in his stomach and right thigh. He was sure they were painful as hell, and he couldn't imagine the guy darting around like his kind had a way of doing, but, if treated, he didn't see this representing a fatal set of injuries.

And if Dianna cared for him then...

Then *what?*

What was Allen thinking?

He was a vampire! He was the enemy! He was...

A monster?

DiAngelo's words echoed in his head, and Allen found himself wondering what could turn a promising little hunter like Dianna against her own kind and not just onto the side of the mythos, but into the arms of one.

Obviously she had to redefine what a monster is.

Allen spun, sure there was somebody behind him whispering things in his ear. There was no one; no one but himself standing in the doorway.

Suddenly it felt more like he was standing at a crossroads.

Barnes had regained his footing, gotten a hold on Dianna's throat, pinning her against the adjacent wall, and was beginning to aim for the vampire once again.

Allen surprised all of them by stepping in his path.

"Put the gun down, Barnes," he commanded.

Barnes stared at him, bewildered. "Carrey?" he said his name as though he didn't believe it was really him. "What's this—"

"I said put the gun down," Allen repeated. He could feel the eyes of both the vampire and Dianna staring at him in shock and awe as they realized what was happening; realized what he was doing.

It took him a moment to realize what he was doing, too.

Barnes figured it out slightly faster.

"You switching sides now, Carrey?" he asked, giving his classic "all's I need's a reason"-grin.

Allen didn't reply; didn't move.

Barnes started to reach for the trigger on his suicide vest.

A series of winding patterns began to give off a bright glow beneath the layers of Dianna's clothes; something that felt like a warm gust of wind kicked up in the room as her hair began to whip about her head.

And then things started to move strangely slow in the eyes of Allen Carrey.

He almost thought he heard that non-existent voice say something...

It sounded like, *I'm sorry...*

GUILT TASTED ALMOST as bad in Zoey's heart as the fear and pain that she'd just gorged herself on, but, awful as it all was, she felt stronger for it.

And, better yet, she was in the arms of Isaac, who was comforting her through the guilt as well as the fear of losing him that had motivated her in the first place.

Then she heard something that made her think of Zane and his little bird...

She heard Xander.

"Wh-what?"

Isaac looked up at the sound of her voice, letting out a confused whimper.

She wanted to respond to him, but her eyes were already starting back towards the hotel, honing in on the windows of the fourth floor. Honing in on...

"Xander said I have to contain it..." she heard herself say, not quite sure what she was saying.

Then, just as her eyes trained on the window she was being guided towards, the glass exploded outward and a pair tumbled through, beginning to spiral towards the ground.

Zoey could hear a pain-filled shriek—*"NOOOOOO!"*—echoing from inside the room.

Contain it, Xander said again. *Or we all die here and now.*

Seeing exactly what was about to happen, Zoey wailed along with Sawyer, seeing what it was she had to do and how awful it was.

She threw her aura out, wrapping it around Dianna and the Cebourist wearing the activated suicide vest. The reformed hunter had the man in a chokehold, her face twisted in rage and concentration; Zoey could sense a swell of magical energy working to delay the blast—struggling to get the impending explosion as far away from Sawyer as possible—but it was too little, too late. Zoey tried to convince herself that she could separate the two and still manage to contain the blast, but even as her aura extended towards the scene she knew it would only set it off early. Shaking, she focused, using every bit of the energy she'd felt compelled to rob from the fallen Cebourists—more energy than she would have had otherwise—and let out a body-wracking sob as she felt the blast go off within the protective orb of her aura.

Dianna's aura was snuffed out within her own instantly.

Even around her own cries, Zoey could hear Xander, wailing and crying with her, screaming his apologies.

CHAPTER 17
BACK INTO THE FRAY

"The only thing stronger than my drive to die
is my will to live."
Xander Stryker

Time is an illusion, and time is an asshole.

Xander knows these things to be true because, though not very much time has passed since he'd sent a worldwide message to mythos to be ready for the rising Cebourist threat, he has witnessed an infinite number of eternities. Less than twenty-four hours, apparently, amounted to—what?—billions-upon-billions of generations; eons; millennia in the "eyes"(?) of the Great Machine. Or is it still "The Power?" Xander can't be certain that it has a preference, so long as it gets the center of the stage and biggest, brightest spotlight.

It wasn't its fault that it had nearly turned him into a genocidal "god" a few years back—that was simply where Xander's mind, tortured and unraveling as it was, had taken things. He is not proud to admit this—especially given that he'd been driven to attack Estella as a result of that growing insanity; it was much easier to blame an external force than his own head for that, *after all—but the truth stood there: center stage and beneath the biggest, brightest spotlight.*

Time is an illusion and an asshole.

Xander, always one for managing the impossible, ripped free of whatever realm his mind was being bottled in and existed—there was really no other way to describe being both everywhere and nowhere at once, he supposes—and worked to shape the outcome of a seemingly unimportant and random battle that would, in fact, define the outcome of what had yet come to pass.

He'd looked upon it like a chess master.

He'd examined each piece—recalling his love for some pieces, growing fonder of others, and decidedly loathing the rest—and considered their roles in the moves to come.

He'd looked past the moves made and the moves yet to be made, looked at the checkered board: at its shape, at its history, at the very atoms that it was built from.

And then he'd looked beyond that, too; looked at the table the board was set upon, the room the table occupied, and, within this, the windows and doors that offered glimpses and even passage to rooms and even worlds that lay beyond.

It had been through one of these doors that Stan, long ago and yet not very long ago at all, had traveled so that he could obtain The Power.

Had that been the birth of the Great Machine? *Xander wonders.* Did he have any idea what would truly come of that journey?

Would any of this be possible without...

Ruby?

Xander blinks, remembers that he does not have eyes—realizes that he has instead "winked" back into a sort of non-existence—and finds himself tumbling through a familiar ether of simultaneous darkness and light.

I am all; I am nothing.

"Estella is..."

***YES! YES!! SEE! SEE!* SEE!**

Xander slips through a wall that has become a ceiling, is passing in slow motion through a room—The teachers' lounge!—*at a sideways slant. He sees himself, young and miserable and unknowing*—human!—*and he sees Stan. Though seen as a trickle of time, he "hears" the conversation as it took place:*

"Maybe Yin will take me tonight," *he hears himself whine, and the urge to roll nonexistent eyes almost*—ALMOST!—*rings with irony within him.* "Then I won't have to worry about where I'm going, right?"

Then, in a moment that catches Xander off guard, he sees Stan look at him—at him *in the here-and-now; at the him that should not be seen—and... and, yes, Stan actually* grins *at him and, returning back to the way things had gone, rolls his eyes on the "now"-Xander's behalf.*

"I doubt you're going to find your escape tonight," *he says, and Xander feels that he's talking to* both *of the hims in the room at that moment.* "Or tomorrow, or even the day after that." *There's a knowing chuckle then that warms Xander's non-heart,* "I mean, if I *seriously* thought you were in any danger I'd have had you put away long ago."

"So why haven't you?" *the unknowing Xander asks.*

"Because I don't think you really want to die," *Stan says, and now Xander is certain that he is addressing him, as well,* "and I don't think you realize what that means just yet."—*"I DO! I DO! DAMMIT, I DO!"*—"However, and this goes back to that whole potential thing I was talking about, I do know that you're not worth much to the world in a padded cell."

"Wouldn't say I'm worth much to the world *at all*!"

Xander sees the fate of things if he can't bring himself to awaken, and the thought that he'd ever believed he mattered so little staggers him in ways he no longer thought possible.

How could I have been so blind?

You think you're not still blind? *Stan's voice chimes, and Xander sees that he is looking at him again as he continues to fall*—

so slowly it's almost painful—sideways through the room. He thinks *this to the now-Xander, but to the then-Xander he says,* "There's a lot more to the world than you'll ever know. You just haven't seen enough of it to know where your potential fits,"

"All these riddles sound pretty concrete, Stan," *Xander's past-self says, his untrained aura shifting almost towards something enlightened.* "Is there something you're not telling me?"

This would make Xander laugh if he had any of the necessary components.

Once again acting on his behalf, Stan laughs then. "There's plenty I'm not telling you, and for damned good reasons, too."

Xander sees the same tension, the same aggravation, in his past-self towards Stan that he felt from Zane towards him back at the hotel.

It never stops being a pain-in-the-ass, *he thinks.*

"Then can you at least tell me what's going to happen?" *past-Xander asks.*

"I've told you before:" *Stan's eyes shift to follow the now-Xander as his journey through the room has nearly carried him through the opposite wall,* "the future can't be seen. It hasn't been written yet."

Xander wants *to shout "BULLSHIT" back at the memory—back at the still-living Stan that's somehow wrinkling space and time to speak to him—but he knows that, no, it's not bullshit. He cannot be sure if it is him, Stan, or the Great Machine that holds this truth out to the others, but nor can he be sure that he is not, in fact, all three —now one.*

The future can't *be seen. That much is true. But, with The Power —with eyes and a mind that can perceive the complex workings of the Great Machine—there is nothing keeping one from calculating outcomes.*

Time is not a series of curtains hiding the next moment from view until one has stepped through. Time is an equation that one can read in sequence or take in all at once; an equation that, should eyes be capable of reading it and a mind be keen enough to solve it, can be simplified, reduced, and even solved.

Xander remembers how much he hated math.

Stan remembers how much he loved teaching.

The Great Machine can't care less about such things.

Still falling, Xander passes through bubbles of time. Each orb, only slightly larger than the non-existent space he is occupying, blips in and out of perception—in and out of existence—and is, for that instant, a new reality to him.

He is a warrior of the Odin Clan.

He is a rogue on the run from his own father.

He is head of The Council, hunting Estella for crimes against their people.

He is a god seated atop a pyramid of corpses before a sea of blood; the world burns.

He is a tiger prowling in the jungle.

He is a human wanted for the murder of an abusive stepfather.

He is...

He is a father.

YES! YES! **SEE!**

*This bubble, Xander realizes, feels right—*is *right!—and he fights to return to it. Gravity, nonexistent and intangible in this place, allows him to swim nearer to it, even lets him graze it with a tendril of thought that* might *be considered a fingertip—*Oh my god! *he thinks,* She's so beautiful!*—but then he's falling again.*

This time, however, with a purpose.

Xander Stryker, beginning to see—beginning to remember—is not falling...

Xander Stryker is flying.

And Xander Stryker is seeing!

He bursts through a wall—no, the floor—of a private room in the back of a plane, sees himself from a time not-long-ago as he and Estella, now his wife, christen their marriage. She is riding him, their bodies working together—fitting together—like a great machine; moving and operating as though they were made for one another.

He has no reason to believe that they weren't.

Xander watches, unashamed, at the perfection that the two of them—he and Estella—represent, and he watches, now unsurprised, at the perfection they're unknowingly creating.

Oh my god! She's so...

"Xander?"

YES! YES! YOU'RE SEEING! GO! GO ON!

Was I always this bossy? *Xander wonders, but he does as he's told.*

He turns away—flies away—and leaves he and his wife to their devices.

They've got a long night ahead of them.

Then he's standing there, in a place that is not a place before a ten-sided table that does not exist with nine dead faces staring back at him.

...

Nine dead faces... and Ruby.

"Oh..." Xander cringes, asks himself if he wants to forget all over again—start all of this over—but decides that, yes, it's time.

"Back into the fray, eh, son?" Joseph Stryker says, looking proud and holding his wife's hand.

Marcus grins and gives a slow clap. "You did it, numb-nuts!"

Xander bites his lip and sighs, nodding. "Still can't believe I thought you all expected an apology from me," he scoffs.

"I wouldn't mind an apology for how long I was made to wait," says Osehr, barking out a laugh.

"Amen," offers Father Tennesen.

"Funny," Xander says.

And, smiling with nonexistent lips, he means it.

"So...?" his mother asks, expectant.

Xander nods, knowing she deserves what's coming most of all:

"I forgive you," Xander tells the nine dead faces, taking in each one in order:

His father: "I forgive you for not being there the way you wanted to be."

His mother: "I forgive you for not protecting me the way you expected yourself to."

His grandmother: "I forgive you for not being as strong as you wanted to fight what was coming."

Depok: "I forgive you for all that you feel you left unfinished and unsaid."

Marcus: "I forgive you for failing when I needed you most."

The Gamer: "I forgive you for letting your pride get in the way of your success."

Osehr: "I forgive you for not being the father you promised yourself you'd be to me."

Father Tennesen: "I forgive you for letting faith overshadow fact; for not seeing good for good and evil for evil."

Stan: "And I forgive you for everything you've done since the start. I... I understand now what a burden it is."

The nine nod to him, looking content—at peace.

"And do you forgive yourself?" they ask.

Xander looks down at his hand, knowing what he'll see there now, and nods. He lets out a deep, heavy breath and fills his lungs anew with a satisfied inhale—feeling like it's the first he's taken in his entire life—and steps up to the table.

He sets the revolver down on its surface.

"Yes," he confesses. "I think I'm finally ready to do that, too."

Stan smiles at this and nods. His hand moves, reaching as if to take the gun, but it only scoops up a swirling light—a glowing mass of black and white—that shrinks down to a glow no larger than a spark.

Xander sees within that spark everything he'd come to define his life by.

But no longer.

Still smiling, Stan finally stands up from his seat. As he does, Xander knows without seeing that the other eight are no longer seated at the table. He also knows, however, that they are not gone.

"Shit's about to get real," Stan says.

"'Bout fucking time it did," Xander responds.

The glowing spark hovers over Stan's thumb, and he pushes this against Xander's forehead, just between his eyes.

Xander sees, and with eyes that aren't there he knows he's crying.

"I'm so sorry, Xander," Ruby says. She's close, but now very, very far away. "I tried."

"You did great, Ruby," *he hears himself say.* "You did great."

Then he hears himself saying the words to Ruby as he hears Stan saying the words to himself:

"We're allowed to fail, so long as we don't allow those failures to define us. I won't let this one define you."

And he knows that they're both telling the truth.

Only time would tell, for certain, but Xander knows that time, though an illusion and an asshole, is not a liar.

Xander, for the first time since he's begun this shit-show, knows exactly where the Great Machine is taking him. He'd made a decision —a bad decision, granted—and he had to understand it and what it meant to what was coming:

Once again and for the first time, he is standing in the studio, staring past the camera he's been talking at—he couldn't bring himself to feel like he was talking to *anybody—and, for a brief moment that he didn't understand the first time around, he can only stare at newcomer and his entourage as they approach.*

Aleks! *he practically hears the hiss of hatred in his own thoughts.*

But neither the camera nor his soon-to-be attacker hold his focus right now. No. That belongs to a distant auric blip that he's just picked up on.

Estella!

His Estella.

She needed him. Truly and desperately needed him. So badly that he could feel that desperation—that demand—spanning across the city and drawing all of his focus even in that instant of certain, encroaching death.

Stupid! *he thought.* So selfish; so... fucking... stupid!

He'd thought he was doing right by everyone, Estella included, in doing what he was doing. Sacrifice himself so that they could all arm themselves against what was coming. Sound thought, sure; all ideas look great up until the moment they're put into action, after all. But he'd ignored the big picture, ignored the small picture, and ignored every possibility in between.

Knowing the rising Cebourist threat...

Seeing Aleks coming at him—knowing in that instant exactly *who and what he was...*

And then, in that instant, seeing something he could have never anticipated on Estella's aura.

She...

SEE!

... was...

SEE!

... pregnant!

YES!

At that moment, all at once, there was more to fight for, more to live for, and a whole lot of things that could go wrong.

He was *about to die, after all.*

At that moment, Xander Stryker, knowing that he was going to be a father and seeing a possible future where Estella and his child would be left unprotected, could not forgive himself for being so prepared to die only seconds earlier.

And so he didn't.

The Power—Stan's final gift to him—though still dormant, did what it did best:

It made the impossible possible. It kept him alive.

Barely.

He watched himself get beaten and maimed, watched bones get broken and his eye get gouged out after Aleks had made a note of beating him with the very camera he'd used to broadcast his message. And then, seeing Aleks and the few followers he'd gathered for the event circle around him, Xander saw himself begin to float away. He saw Aleks and company stare, confused—a few of them able to perceive that it was not Xander's own aura doing the lifting—and then he saw his beaten, mangled body tear through the studio rooftop and take to the sky.

Far, far from where any could reach him; far from where he could even reach himself.

Oh, though Aleks certainly tried *to reach...*

There, floating and riding the curvature of the new world's ozone—seemingly one with both the planet and everything beyond it at that moment—Xander dreamed sweet dreams of Estella. And Aleks, unable to swing in the killing blow, tried and tried and tried to push Xander's unconscious mind to slip off into death; tried and tried and tried *to twist his dreams into something that would sedate and lull him off.*

But Xander, even though he was ashamed of the truth he'd overlooked and forced himself to forget that truth, could not shake the knowledge that there was something more worth living for now.

He might have forgotten about Estella's pregnancy—about the new life growing within her that now mattered more than both of them—but he could not forget that he had chosen life in a moment when he was so ready for death.

Forgetting the "WHY" drove him to a place where he and his budding powers demanded to unravel the mystery...

*But—*god-fucking-damn!*—what a painful revelation!*

Round and round. Xander watches the scene, remembering it all as it plays out before him. Round and round the new, chaos-filled world; round and round inside his head.

He really had been so... fucking... stupid!

But...

BUT!

We're allowed to fail, so long as we don't allow those failures to define us.

Xander sees the sunrise on that morning, sees his beaten body bathed in the new day, and, knowing it was either a matter of staying up there and cooking in the UV radiation or hoping that Estella found him first, he'd let himself fall.

And he just kept on falling, he sees, until he finally found rest beside Ruby.

Ruby...

Sighing without breath, Xander "turns" from the memory—forgiving himself all over again for what very well might have been the single greatest fuckup of his entire life—and finds himself staring at the ten-sided table.

Ruby is its sole occupant.

Her, and his gun.

"It's time to wake up," he tells her.

She nods, looking scared. "Will you be there when I do?"

He offers her a smile.

She really is a pretty girl. It might never have worked between them, he knows, but she might've found true love at some point.

Under any other circumstance.

"Yeah," he promises her. "You might get there first, but I'll be right behind you."

She looks at him lovingly.

Then she's gone.

ESTELLA HAD *FINALLY* MANAGED to calm down Serena. It had taken nearly an hour-and-a-half and several rounds of draining the auric overflow of pain and panic and terror, but she'd done it. Then, in much the same way she and Zane had done for her, Estella helped guide her up to the office to let her rest. Gregori, though still shaken from the ordeal, hurried to his mother's side as they entered, whimpering and hugging her with a tightness that, Estella could see, hurt Serena's hips.

It hurt her, but Estella could also see that it did more to comfort her.

"I'm so sorry, sweetheart," Serena whispered to her son

after scooping him up and carrying him with her to the couch. "Mommy... Mommy had a really bad nightmare."

"Was it Xander?" Gregori asked. "Did Xander give you the nightmare?"

Estella wanted to believe that maybe he'd overheard Serena say Xander's name in her ramblings, but the face that the blonde made in response to the question made her wonder.

"No," Serena answered, and Estella could see on her aura that she wasn't lying—she did not blame Xander for whatever she had seen. "No," she repeated, "he just... I think he accidentally showed me something I wasn't supposed to see."

"What?" Gregori asked. "What did Xander show you?"

Serena thought for a moment, looking more and more confused as she did, and then finally shrugged. "You know... it's the damn-dest thing, kiddo, but I can't remember."

"Maybe you made yourself forget," Gregori said with a passive shrug.

"Yeah," Serena agreed with a grin as she carried him, with Estella's help, to the couch. "Maybe I did. You up for taking a nap with me? Mommy's pooped."

Gregori giggled at his mother's choice of words and gave a nod, punctuating his agreement with a well-timed yawn.

Smiling at the exchange, Estella helped the two onto the couch and covered them with the blanket that she'd found draped over her earlier that morning.

"Thanks, Goddess," Serena whispered, already half-asleep.

"Anytime," Estella whispered back.

"Time?" Serena giggled a little in her sleep. "Time's an illusion... and a fucking asshole."

Gregori, nuzzling up against the pillow of his mother's breast, cooed happily and muttered "fuck" in his sleep.

The two, finding comfort with one another in their sleep, held the other tighter as their gentle snores began to sync with one another.

Estella watched this a moment, endeared by the sight, and

found herself wondering if two sleeping bodies so close together might also offer comfort in one another's dreams.

Estella liked to believe that they could.

Then, turning away, she'd started out of the office and down the stairs.

With the scene finally behind her, Estella had a moment to relax. She focused on her breathing—recited her "peace" mantra; "peace of mind; peace of heart; peace of soul"—and meditated on pleasant thoughts. Thoughts of Xander. Thoughts of their growing family. Thoughts of the future.

Halfway down the second flight of steps, she felt Ruby's aura spike and, immediately after, heard her gasp and cry out:

"X-Xander?"

The future, Estella decided at that moment, was now. She was down the stairs and beside the heaving redhead in a span of time that likely couldn't be measured by any conventional means.

XANDER STARES *down at the black revolver on the table. He remembers all the times he'd turned it on himself, remembers hating himself and, yes, even hating his father and his mother; remembers wanting to escape that hate. He remembers choosing life time and time again, then remembers the pull of death luring him back down dark paths—he'd promised himself and others time and time again that he'd never think like that again—and he sees beyond what's remembered to know that, no, such times cannot be predicted or prevented.*

One could no more promise to elude the drive to die than they could read the pages of a book that had yet to be written. But he knows now, with capable eyes and a keen mind, those moments might be predicted with an accuracy that might—MIGHT!—seem precognitive.

Having a better understanding of... well, everything, Xander picks up the symbol. What was a gun on the table becomes a photograph in his hands, a familiar one of him and Estella as kids. Even then, a capable eye and a keen mind can see the perfection that was shared between the two; a balance so perfect it seems almost as if by design.

"So we can trust you to do what needs to be done without going off the deep end again," a voice calls out from the darkness.

"I can't make any promises," Xander says, tracing a finger over the face of little Estella and working to make a connection across the divide. "But I can say that the only thing stronger than my drive to die is my will to live."

"No mortal mind has ever put it better."

The picture became a ribbon—a familiar red ribbon that would have looked better tied in a bow atop a head of raven-black hair on the first day in a new school—and Xander followed it home.

DESPITE THE PANIC in Ruby's voice upon awakening, Estella was surprised at just how calm she seemed after a few deep breaths. Though it was clear that being unconscious for as long as she had been was taking a toll on her equilibrium—even just sitting up on the edge of her crate-bed had her swaying a little—there didn't seem to be any real lasting damage.

And Estella was relieved to see that Ruby had come back whole.

Her encounter with the Cebourists had left her exhausted, badly burned from extended exposure to the sun, and, with everything else weighing against her vampiric anatomy, nearly starved to death. All of those problems, though, were commonplace for their kind, especially for warriors acting on behalf of The Council. What *wasn't* commonplace, however, was having one's vampire strength and speed stripped from their body with a degree of faith-fueled magic that hadn't been utilized to such a degree since the Dark Ages. The research it had taken to know that had certainly offered up some intriguing details for Estella, who'd always liked learning new things, but it was hard to take a genuine interest in subject matter when the subject in question was a close friend. The facts were fascinating, sure—and it had certainly given Estella a glimmer of hope when the concept of utilizing that same magic against Aleks and his followers arose—but she'd have traded all that knowledge if it meant Ruby would awaken with all of her powers.

As it turned out, though, she didn't have to.

Ruby was dizzy and a little disoriented, sure, but she was otherwise fine.

Even being able to see this for herself on the drooping aura of her friend, Estella found herself asking the question again.

And, again, Ruby answered, "I'm fine, Estella. I... I promise. I'm just... I'm thirsty."

Blushing at this response, realizing that it made perfect sense, Estella nodded and started to turn towards Zeek and Karen's stash of medical supplies. "R-right," she stammered, beginning to look around. "I think there's some synth-blood left around here somewhere. Most of it's been used on Xander, though. I'm not sure—"

"N-no..." Ruby called, the blush showing on her aura even with Estella facing away from her. "I just meant, like, *thirsty*-thirsty. I need water."

Estella looked back, saw the embarrassment on Ruby's face, and felt herself smile at this. After everything everyone had been through, for her to wake up and have such a simple request felt like a small miracle in and of itself.

"You're the miracle, 'Stell."

Estella's body went rigid at the sound of his voice. She trembled, suddenly unable to move; afraid to even look. Some distant part of her was terrified that to move, to look, would be to negate those words from existence. Ruby glanced past her, looking over Estella's shoulder and smiling. She didn't seem surprised by what she saw, and Estella felt that she somehow owed a great deal to the beautiful redhead at that moment.

"Took ya long enough," she whispered.

Estella nearly began weeping with joy as she realized that Ruby wasn't talking to her.

That could only mean...

"Had a long way to go," he answered, and Estella heard him move—could imagine him sitting up behind her.

With how broken he'd been when they'd found him, everyone was certain he'd never move again, but...

"I've been doing the impossible all day," he whispered to her as he moved his arms over her shoulders and gently led her back against him.

She finally let out a sob of pure joy.

It *was* him! It *was* Xander!

She didn't even have to look to know it, and then...

And then they were moving.

Estella, too serene in Xander's arms at that moment, was only distantly aware of him asking Ruby to keep an eye on their ramshackle little headquarters.

ESTELLA...

Her lips were Heaven because he'd waited so damn long for them and Hell because he knew that it wouldn't last forever. They were soft and smooth. They were warm and inviting.

And, at that moment, they were his.

They were, once again and forevermore, his!

He held her—body and mind—and refused to let her go. He felt her arms as they wrapped around his neck and rested on his shoulders, claiming him as savagely and relentlessly as he was claiming her. As they worked in mutual desperation to hold the other tighter against themselves, he was aware of the new heights they were reaching. On an emotional level, sure—he wasn't above admitting to such a thing—but on a literal one, as well.

As weightless as he felt with Estella finally—*FINALLY!*—back in his arms, it was made all the moreso as they rose higher and higher into the sky, rising above everything and anything. He'd rode that very horizon earlier that morning, though it had been in circumstances he'd have sooner avoided. He wanted a new memory up there, one with *her* in his arms as a lover rather than in his guilt-ridden mind as a regret. He shielded them—from the sun, from sight, from harm—and maintained their own personal atmosphere within an auric bubble that was all theirs at that moment.

It was all they needed to have their own private paradise in a world that seemed to be going to hell. There they were safe. The rest could wait.

He kissed her again, whispering words of love and praise and worship against her lips; thanking her and begging her forgiveness. And she whispered right on back; whispered the same words in an all new sequence—thanking and begging just the same. She felt she'd done wrong in destroying their life—mansion and clan alike—and casting aside all else in an effort to find him. She said she'd felt herself slipping away, realized she wasn't strong enough to survive her own darkness the way Xander could. She begged his forgiveness for allowing herself to slip into a dark place that she'd so often forbade him to dwell.

She kissed him again and again as she said this, and Xander promised her it was alright. He tried to tell her what he knew; tried to imbue the essence of what it was to apologize for such things—to try to control such a wildly irrational creature as one's own thoughts—but only succeeded in kissing her right back. This, however, seemed to get the message across.

"I..." she panted, nearly crying around bouts of laughter as Xander's aura began to tear away the layers of clothing dividing them. Her own aura snaked out, helping things along, and began to strip him, as well. "I have to tell you something."

“Please,” Xander whispered into her mouth as the last of their clothes melted away and he slid inside her in a single, fluid motion. He gasped at the feel of her, she gasped right back. “Tell me,” he said as he began a slow, even tempo.

Estella moaned. Tears carrying the flavors of too many emotions to count streamed down her face—Xander kissed these away one-by-one—and she undulated her hips against him with every instroke. “I’m... I’m pregnant.”

The sound of the words said aloud felt like new lifeblood in Xander’s renewed existence.

“Say it again,” he pleaded.

She did. Again and again.

PAGE 22 – 4 PANELS

PANEL 1 – ~~XAVIER STEELER~~, dynamically posed in midair, levels his TWIN PISTOLS, Fang & Claw*, at a GANG OF ROBED MEN**. The closest, holding up a TRIANGULAR AMULET, is chanting in a foreign language while another holds a CEREMONIAL DAGGER (shaped like a lightning bolt).

~~XAVIER STEELER~~
(screaming)
DIE!

ROBED MAN #1
(chanting)
Buweh-ha'enya ooru d'cha el'i

PANEL 2 – CLOSE-UP of FANG & CLAW'S barrels, the muzzles flashing with gunfire.

SFX
(guns firing)
BANG! BANG!
BANG!

PANEL 3 – POV aerial view of the GANG OF ROBED MEN, their faces scared. Two of the nearest, AMULET-holder & DAGGER-wielder, have bullet holes in their chests where ~~XAVIER STEELER's~~ shots have landed.

SHOT ROBED MEN
(screaming)
AAHHHHH!!

PANEL 4 – Dynamic panel, ~~XAVIER STEELER~~ has landed in a classic SUPERHERO POSE; GUNS raised, RED LEATHER JACKET blowing in the wind, and looking totally badass with his new EYEPATCH*** and BRAIDED BLACK HAIR.

~~XAVIER STEELER~~
Actually thought you'd
seen the last of me, huh?

Editor's Note:
Replace all mentions of Xavier Steeler
with "Xander Stryker"
(No point in keeping the secret now)
Joseph Wilson

*There's GOTTA be a better name for the
guns (lol)

**What are they called? Why can't I see what
the religious guys call themselves?

***Can't see how Xander lost his eye, either.
Are the powers wearing off?

"He is a man of courage who does not run away,
but remains at his post and fights against the enemy."
Socrates (469-399 BC)

"Life is only a long and bitter suicide,
and faith alone can transform this suicide
into a sacrifice."
Franz Liszt (1811-1886)

The Great Machine thrives,
And yet...
And yet the Great Machine still sleeps.
It is infuriating; it is relaxing;
It is time; it is yet still too early.
The Great Machine is ready, willing—
He, however, is not.
He sees, but he is blind.
He achieves, but still he does nothing.
So crippling, this business of love and worry...
Oh! But the vastness of understanding—
All that could be done, learned, and achieved—
Should one be so brave to forego the ties that bind.
And yet...
And yet...
And yet...
Through her—through her and, of course, through she—
Perhaps more...
Perhaps more than even the Great Machine—
With all Its infinite scope and insight; with all Its power—
Could ever hope to perceive.

"I think he accidentally showed me something
I wasn't supposed to see."
Serena Vailean

CHAPTER 18

WHISPERS FROM THE CORNERS

"And when it came night, the white waves paced to and fro in the moonlight,
and the wind brought the sound of the great sea's voice to the men on shore,
and they felt that they could then be interpreters."
Stephen Crane (1871-1900)

"Yo! Tony! Wait up, dawg! Where you headin' to in such a muthafuckin' hurry?"

"Ty? Fuck, man! I don't wanna deal with your mangy ass right now, nigga. Shit's stirred up bad 'nough without your fucked breed of influence comin' 'round an' makin' it worse!"

"Fuck's wrong with you, 'Two-Ton Tone'? Wake up next to a Doberman again? HA-HA-H—"

"The fuck I jus' say to you? Huh? You not hearin' me; NOT... HEARIN'... ME! I need to get gone, an' I need to do it fast, kay?"

"Whoa! Shit's *that* serious?"

"Nigga... what the hell I been sayin' to your ass, huh? Ya got dicks in your ears or some shit?"

"Homes, talk to me. I know shit's been fucked since the world found out about us, but we're still the top-dogs, Tone; humans ain't got shit on—"

"Cut the crap! And quit calling me 'Tone,' *Tyler;* no more of this 'Two-Ton' or 'Tons-o'-Tone' or whatever other bullshit-fuckin' nicknames you come up with, kay? And quit fuckin' acting like we ain't got shit to worry 'bout, ya dumb fuck! I just... I gotta get gone! I gotta get out of here! That's all! I gotta get outta here right... fuckin'... *now!*"

"The fuck, man? The fuck happened? You look like you seen—"

"Don't you dare fuckin' say it, Ty; just... just *don't,* kay?"

"Tony...?"

"DON'T!"

"The fuck, man? Who the fuck you think you're talking to? I ain't some fuckin' side-bark brother or one of them niggas from San-Fran, man; this is *me,* man! Talk to me! What happened?"

"..."

"Dog! What the—"

"...!"

"Whoa! Okay! *Okay!* My bad. Quit glaring, Tony. Old habits, you know? Now—*please!*—just talk to me. You're scaring the shit out of me!"

"I... I—fuck! Tyler, I nearly just died!"

"What? The fuck... *how?* What happened?"

"What happe—Jee-zus-'fuck me'-Chree-ighst, Ty—what *didn't* just fuckin' happen to me? I... well—*well!*—for fuckin' starters: those humans you think we can manage so damn simple-like ain't so fuckin' manageable, my man! Those fuckers are... they're crazy, Ty; fucking certi-fucking-fiably *insane!* You know one of those assholes had a fuckin' RPG pointed at me?"

"A what?"

"A... the fuck, man? For all the tough-talk you spout day-n'-

night your ass don't know shit! A fuckin' *rocket launcher,* dumb-ass! One of the humans had a *rocket launcher* leveled at my ass!"

"Oh shit! What did you... I mean, was it just the one?"

"One? No. No, no, no, Ty; try a dozen. Maybe more. Fuck if I know. Fuckers were like roaches when they got moving—couldn't keep a lead on any one of 'em. And they're all armed to the teeth! Not all RPGs, I'll be honest there—only one mother-fucker *that* crazy—but nothing to laugh at, either. One minute all's well an' the next there's a fuckin' bullet-storm comin' down on my ass!"

"How the fuck they make you, man? Don't tell me you was out there runnin' around in your fur suit!"

"You think I'm fuckin' stupid? *No!* Course I wasn't! Shit like that was fuckin' suicide *before* all this noise! I... no, man; no! I was just, I dunno, I'm not 'bout to say I was 'mindin' my own bid-ness'—shit's cliché, and, honestly, prob'ly bullshit—but I didn't think I was callin' any attention my way!"

"Then how—"

"Fuckin' *listen,* Tyler: *I... DON'T... KNOW!"*

"Okay. Okay, that's fair. So what happened?"

"Right. So.... So I see the fuckers comin' my way—can see the devil in their eyes; I just *know* they're comin' to kill my ass —and then, yeah—I'll admit it—*then* I made with the fur suit. But that was *after* I just barely got free of the first round of bullets. So I duck into an alley—I mean, I'm kneeling in fuckin' garbage an' hugging the side of a damn trash can like it was my momma—an' I'm hearing 'werewolf'-this an' 'lycan'-that along with all manner of ugly talk—I swear, Ty, these bastards were comin' up with slang I ain't never even heard before—an' I'm thinkin', 'Shit! I'm 'bout to get my furry ass blown to shit by a bunch of fuckin' hairless monkeys!' So then I think, 'Not without a fight,' right? An' I wolf-out—still duckin' all those fuckin' bullets; waitin' for an opening—and I peek around the corner of my cover, an'—an' *that's* when I see the fucker with the RPG, by the way—an' I see this... this, like... like this shadow or some shit comin' in from the alley *behind* the humans."

"What you talkin'... What? Like, something *worse* than the rocket-launching, crazy-as-hell humans?"

"Y-yeah—*ha-ha!*—I'd say 'worse.' 'Worse' is a good word for what was comin' out of that alley."

"The fuck could be worse than—"

"Stryker."

"'Scuse me?"

"You fuckin' heard me, Ty. Stryker; Xander-fuckin'-Stryker! He was—"

"Tony. Tony! You're not making sense! You fuckin' saw what happened on the TV—*everyone* saw that shit!—and what happened was Xander Stryker getting' hisself killed! There ain't no comin' back from—"

"Motherfu—WHY THE FUCK YOU THINK I'M SO DEADSET ON GETTING OUT OF HERE?"

"...?"

"...!"

"You... you're fuckin' serious? Fuckin' Xander Stryker's still alive?"

"Yes, man; yes! Xander Stryker is still alive! Fucker's got an eyepatch—doin' this whole Johnny Depp-pirate thang now—but I'd know that pasty goth-boy's face anywhere!"

"Oh fuck. That's not... Wait. So what happened next?"

"The fuck you think happened? Stryker wasted them! Came in like a fucking bloody hurricane! All they guns fell apart in their hands—shit was like a magic trick or something—an' a few of 'em just, like, dropped to the ground. They was still breathing an' shit—Stryker, like, knocked 'em over or some shit while runnin' 'round like them bloodsuckers do—an' he appears, standin' 'tween them an' me, and makes with the scary fang-face; hissin' like a pissed off cat or some shit. But these humans—crazy as hell, remember?—they ain't getting' scared off that easy. So's they move like they're gonna try to hit him—fuckin' *hit* Xander Stryker; ain't many who got balls to try that shit if they know what's good for them—an' he... well, he wasn't havin' it. Simple as that."

"And, what, he jus' let you walk away after all that? He smokes the humans but let's you walk?"

"Yeah, Ty. That's pretty much exactly what happened."

"Shit, dude..."

"Yeah. 'Shit' 'bout sums it up. So there it is. I can't stay here. Shit's getting' too weird. I... You know I was actually hired to try to kill him, Ty? Back before they even turned him? Fuckers put down hard cash—good cash, too—to shoot him back when he was just a human kid."

"No shit? So what happened?"

"What? Back then? Obviously I didn't get him. It was... well, it was a shit-show. Couple of big-league vamps fucked up, too; brought all sorts of hell down on the hospital and Stryker bee-lined down the fire escape while I got chased halfway around town by a damn police chopper."

"Shit. So Stryker was a slippery little fuck even before he was a leech, huh?"

"Guess so. And, even after all that, he let me live. He survived that crazy shit, and then he saves my ass from crazy asshole humans and lets me walk. I'm just... I can't handle that shit, Ty; I can't stay here."

"Oh come on, Tony! If Stryker saved your ass then he probably didn't even realize who you were! I mean, he might've started all his shit, but he *was* a warrior; it was his job to kill folks like us. It's not like he's gonna go and change *that* much! If he let you live then that means—"

"Ty... he looked right at me—right... fuckin'... at me!—and said, 'Almost didn't recognize you without a sniper rifle. Too bad I can see you remembered me,' an' then turned his back on me. Just said *that* and turned around and walked away—like he *knew* I wasn't gonna try something."

"Was you gonna try something?"

"No, dumbass. That's what makes it *knowing!*"

"..."

"..."

"Fuck. So Stryker's alive an' still doin' his shit?"

"Stryker's alive an' doin' his shit. Yeah, dog."

"..."

"..."

"Maybe I should think about getting' my ass outta here, too."

"OH MY... Did you see that? Did you see—"

"Of course I saw it, Terri! I was right there with you, wasn't I?"

"I... I know, I know! But... but that couldn't have been... I just can't believe—"

"What's not to believe? We've known things like that have existed for *weeks!* Did you think you'd never see one?"

"I... I... Damn, I don't know. I guess I never really thought that I'd actually be *attacked* by—"

"And why the hell not? What makes you so special that you think monsters would never consider you a food source? Adam's stepdad is still in the hospital, they're not sure they can save his leg. My grandmother's neighbor was bitten—*bitten!*—and, after three days at the morgue, they lost the body. Rumors say that's how long it takes before you come back from a bite, but... well, I guess that's as good as proof. Whether or not anyone can actually find him is another story—sort of funny to think of a seventy year-old man being turned into a vampire, but... Well, that's not the point. Adam's stepdad, Grannie's neighbor, and who-knows how many others each and every day. Why would you think that we'd *never* come across something like this? I mean, do you realize the likelihood that we're going to die before the end of the month?"

"..."

"...?"

"Why are you being such a bitch, Brittany? Can't you see I'm scared? You don't have to treat me like I'm stupid!"

"I'll stop treating you like you're stupid when you stop acting stupid. If that makes me a bitch then, oh well, I guess I'm a bitch."

"... wasn't that stupid when I got us out of there, was I?"

"What was that? Stop mumbling!"

"I SAID I SAVED YOUR LIFE, BRITT! HOW ABOUT SHOWING A LITTLE THANKS?"

"'Thanks'? You think I should be *thanking* you? You asked me if I saw all that, but I'm beginning to wonder just what you think you saw. We were attacked by a monster, yeah, but if you think we got away because of you then you clearly didn't see what really happened. For starters: there's no way that either of us was going to get away from that thing on our own. Doesn't matter that you grabbed me. Wouldn't have mattered any more if I'd grabbed you or if we'd both been running with all we had on our own. Wouldn't have mattered if we were the fastest girls on the planet... we'd still only be the fastest *human* girls."

"And yet here we are! So explain that!"

"We weren't alone."

"'Weren't alone'? What do you mean by—"

"It was that monster from the internet. *He* was there, and *he* saved us!"

"What are you talking about? There was only the one: the one that was attacking us! I heard you gasp, I turned to see what you were—"

"How did you not see him?"

"Because there was no other 'him' to see *except* the 'him' that was attacking us! I saw him, he came down on us—all fangs and drool and wicked-bad BO—and that's when I grabbed your hand and started running."

"And that's really how you remember it? You don't

remember him playing cat-and-mouse with us for an entire city block?"

"Well, I mean, *of course* I remember—"

"Or when you tripped and started going down like a cheesy scream queen in a bad horror movie?"

"I wouldn't have fallen..."

"No, you *didn't* fall, because I caught you! And it was in the moment I stopped to catch you that the monster—the only one you noticed, apparently—caught up to us."

"So maybe he gave up! Sometimes the cat gets tired and lets the mouse get away."

"...?"

"..."

"You can't possibly believe that, can you?"

"It makes more sense than—"

"Than *what?* Us being saved? You said it yourself: you'd fallen. I can understand missing something like that in the blink of an eye—I would *hope* that you'd seen it, too, but I can accept it if you didn't—but I won't accept you telling me that you'd sooner believe a monster would just give up the chase after one block."

"There was nothing else; nobody else!"

"There was! And while you were too busy collecting yourself from your near-fall, I spotted the other monster standing at the end of the street. He was staring right at us. Then you grabbed my hand and—"

"End of the street? How could he have saved us right when I'd grabbed your hand if he was *that* far away only a second before—"

"There's monsters in the world and one of them just chased us through the streets and you want to ask me where the logic—"

"You questioned my logic first! Coming in like I was out of my mind for not seeing something you're claiming you saw here-and-there, when I'm telling you I didn't see him *anywhere!*

Yes, there was more to it than 'see, grab, run,' but it all happened—details and specifics set aside—just as I said: we encountered *one* monster, we ran. Next thing I know I'm having this conversation with you. Where, in all of that, was there room for anything else, let alone the monster from the internet, who, by the way—in case you hadn't known—was killed on the air!"

"Then... then you really didn't see? He *was* there! Right after you grabbed my hand, I looked back, sure he was going to come after us, and I saw the other one—*not* dead, *by the way*—standing behind the other. Why... why is this so hard to believe?"

"..."

"...?"

"I... I might be willing to believe this if you were just telling me it was another monster—any other monster—choosing to pick a fight with the one that was after us. I can accept the idea of a cat challenging another cat for the mouse that it's chasing. But... but you're asking me to believe that the first monster any of us saw—the monster that the entire world watched die—just arrived and saved our lives? I... I can't believe that!"

"Why? Why the hell not? He seemed to care enough in his broadcast. Why can't he care enough to want to help us?"

"BECAUSE HE'S DEAD! WE... We all watched him die!"

"So he survived it? So what?"

"So what? If he could survive something like *that*—if the monsters can live through all of *that*—then what the hell can stop them?"

"...!"

"...?"

"I... I know what I saw. I know... and scary as what that might mean, I couldn't feel scared seeing it: him crossing the block in an instant like that, getting ahold of that monster like he was catching a disobedient child, and then... he was gripping his throat and holding this big, white gun to the side of his head. And he looked at us—well, at me, at least—and just sort of nodded. Then you dragged me away."

"See? Now I *know* you're making this up. Gun? There was no shot! In fact, with the exception of your gasp, I didn't hear anything!"

"I didn't say there was a gunshot. I said there was a gun!"

"What good is pulling out a gun on a monster if you're not going to—"

BANG!

"Oh shit! Oh shit! That was, like, *really* close! Run! RUN!"

"Oh God! I'm sorry I didn't listen! I'm sorry I didn't believe you! I'm so sorry!"

"Apologize later, girlfriend, those things are going to kill one another, and I don't feel like being caught standing around when they level this entire street!"

"Should we be taking sides? Maybe helping the one with the gun?"

"Help him HOW? They're monsters, we're not! If that thing could survive the sort of beating we saw on the internet then how do you expect to help him when we can't even stay on our own feet long enough to run for our lives?"

"Well somebody should do *something!*"

"I think somebody is..."

"Can't believe it. Barely even half-a-month and it's like a warzone everywhere you go."

"It's the world we live in now. Get used to it."

"You know I actually watched two gangs of humans fighting—killing one another, no lie—over who'd get to shoot a watsuke? The thing was cuffed-up, damn-near crucified with chains between two light posts—I could see its webbed feet still kicking around, trying to stand up on its own. It couldn't. It just... it couldn't—couldn't reach the ground, not really, but if it had I'm pretty sure it wouldn't have been able to hold itself up anyway. Chains did that for it. It was all dried up, too; scales were flaking off like dying leaves. Not even enough moisture left on it to make a sound, so it just kept with these airy gasps. Everything about it made me think of a fish that had gone and gotten itself docked on a hot day. Made me sick, 'cause the first time I saw a watsuke was when I was a kid. The hippies had done a good job of tie-dying just about everything, so I thought—"

"Hippies? I thought you were only, like, in your twenties or something. How old are you?"

"Old enough, I guess. Anyway, like I was saying, I thought I'd seen colors in just about any way they could be presented, all patterns and pairs and such. But my brother—my older brother, Jakey, I mean, not Neil—he comes to me and says, 'You want to see something?' and, of course, I say 'sure!' Next thing I know we're heading off to the beach. Now I'm starting to get a little nervous, it's nearly sunrise and we're heading off towards the Cape—I mean, we are literally heading off to stare out at a watery horizon where the sun's about to be born. There's no shading yourself from something like that. But my brother, he just smiled and kept telling me it'd be worth it. Finally we get there, the sun's creeping up over the edges of the water. Now everything's bright-as-hell, and at its brightest that means that everything else looks real dark, so at first I don't see them. Jakey keeps saying 'Will you look at that!' and all I'm seeing is this massive, orange-and-red glare growing in front of me, water's turning all sorts of crazy colors and such—all of it's beautiful in its own right, sure, but I'm just not seeing it and the UV was starting to get me edgy."

"As it has a way of doing for your kind."

"Yeah, well, least I can go for a walk in the woods without marking trees and coming back with ticks. Anyway... so Jakey's going on-and-on about what I should be seeing, and all I'm seeing is the sunrise and all these crazy colors—and I mean *insane* colors!—reflecting off the water; dancing and shimmering around. It was like starlight decided to take acid and go out to a rave or something. Just the absolute most crazy sort of colors coming off the water of the Atlantic, right? 'Look at that! Just look at that!' Jakey keeps saying, right, and I'm about to read him the riot act for cooking my bacon just to show me a sunrise and some crazy colors over the water. Then I realize the colors aren't coming from the water anymore; they're coming *out* of the water. Like, literally coming out of the water. These shimmering, flowing reflections of blue and green and red and purple... it was like they grew arms and legs and just climbed right up out of the ocean. I was watching the ocean give birth to living colors, and Jakey says 'You see them?' and I... I just nodded."

"And those were the watsuke?"

"Yeah. They'd come out each morning to sunbathe and try to score an easy meal on hermit crabs who were doing the same. After the sun broke over the horizon it got easier to see them in detail, but they were no less amazing for it."

"Surprised you didn't marry a watsuke, with the way you talk about them. Maybe chase some sort of *Little Mermaid* fantasy or something."

"Funny, but I can appreciate art without wanting to date it. So... yeah, I always thought they were beautiful, and I had to see one of them strung-up, looking like all sorts of death at the fish market, while some crazy humans went to war with one another just to have the 'honor'—that's what they called it: the 'honor'—to kill something that you could have just as easily convinced me was dead already."

"So what'd you do?"

"What I could do: nothing. They would have killed me, too, and there was no saving the thing at that point."

"Why are you telling me this? You're not sharing this sob-story just because you wanted a moment of silence for a watsuke, awful as it all must have been. But that's not what... come on, what's really on your mind?"

"..."

"...?"

"Do you think we did the right thing?"

"I'm not sure what's 'right' anymore, so... no, I don't."

"But Xander *did* break the law. *The* law! Granted, our kind have a lot of laws, and I'll even admit that some of them are bogus. But *this* law—the law that was supposed to protect our secrecy—never even had to be taught! Kids know it! Everyone knows it! Even the worst-of-the-worst never dared do what Xander did. But then why..."

"Then why do you feel guilty for bailing on the Trepis Clan?"

"Don't say it like we didn't both bail, but... yeah."

"Well, I think the fact that he survived is a good start. None of us thought he was alive after that. Standing with Stryker's clan when there's no Stryker is a good way to put a target on your back. Anybody burned by the idea of not being able to go after him would set their sights on the rest of the clan. I can't speak for others, but I just sort of figured it was the safest move."

"That doesn't exactly make me feel better. They took us in —not just Xander, the entire clan came together in a way I'd never seen before—and, like, the moment things got rough we just up-and-ran."

"I'd say the entire planet becoming aware of our kind is more than just 'getting rough.' There are mythos out there being slaughtered by the dozens. Clans or not. There's no more certainty in the world. When I first joined with the Trepis Clan, it was a big deal; it simply hadn't been done before. Hell, there are actually laws prohibiting interspecies interactions—superstition and bigotry and 'superior race'-nonsense. I swear, for all our advancements, we're no different than the humans. So when I heard about Xander and the Trepis Clan and everything they stood for I saw it as a chance to be a part of something big. But I let my excitement get the better of me, I forgot all the old stories. Joseph Stryker stood for the same thing, also pushed for similar changes in structure and, sure, he even made some progress that stuck. None of that mattered for him either, though. Joseph Stryker was killed for believing differently—for acting differently—and the same sort of thing is happening again with his son. Alive? Dead? It doesn't matter. The Trepis Clan is basically nonexistent and any of them, Stryker included, might not last much longer."

"That all may be the case, but you're wrong about one thing."

"And what's that?"

"There's one certainty left: Stryker."

"What about him?"

"He's alive! And he's back on the streets, fighting for both sides now. With no more secrecy, there's nothing holding him back. So I guess what I'm saying is..."

"You're thinking that, with Stryker alive and kicking, we should go back to them? Even after everything I just said?"

"Well... yeah."

"Forgetting all the obvious arguments I could bring up, I gotta know: do you think they'd let us back in just like that?"

"I don't know. Probably."

"...?"

"Don't give me that look! Just think about it: you said yourself that they're all under a pretty big gun. Humans want all of us dead, any clan that hasn't fallen apart is, along with The Council, aching for a piece of Xander or anybody siding with him, and—"

"And you think that makes it was a good idea to join them again?"

"I'm saying it was never a good idea to leave! I think that Stryker and the few that stuck around aren't going to be enough to take on the entire world, and I'd rather take the side of change than the side of ignorance or mayhem. Isn't that why you said you'd joined in the first place?"

"And the fact that you'd still be putting a target on yourself isn't turning you off to the idea?"

"I know it should... but no."

"So suddenly you're okay with Stryker blowing our cover like he did?"

"I don't know. I can't say I agree with what he did... but a lot of others didn't agree with what he was doing with the Trepis Clan in the first place."

"There's a big difference between starting a clan that takes in all breeds of mythos and spilling the beans about all breeds of mythos to the entire human race."

"Well, sure. Yeah. That's a given. But Xander was thinking on a whole 'nother level with the Trepis Clan. Maybe this is just a level of thinking that we're still not considering."

"I don't think Stryker was ever much of the thinking sort."

"How could you say that?"

"I'm just repeating what he always used to say."

"Still..."

"THAT WAS STRYKER, RIGHT? XANDER STRYKER?"

"It... it certainly *looked* like him, but... but, I don't know, maybe it was somebody just dressing up like him. Maybe some fanatic trying to keep the so-called Stryker legacy alive by—"

"Bullshit! BULLSHIT! That *was* Stryker! He was minus an eye and a bit more cleaned-up than the last time I saw him in action, but—"

"Now *that's* bullshit! You've *never* seen Xander Stryker before!"

"Sure did. Not too long ago, either. Before the world went to hell—well, obviously—but still pretty recently."

"When? Where?"

"You heard about Renfield's Corner, right? The safe house that tried to shadow itself as a bistro or some fancy nonsense like that?"

"Yeah. I heard Stryker and Zane Vailean tore the place down. Why?"

"Well, I can't say who the other guy was—he was big, that's all I know—but, yes, that's what happened. And I was there. It was my sister's birthday, and she could never get enough of their desserts. I stuck around for a whole fifteen seconds while he and that big sang threw each other around the place like a pair of wrecking balls."

"Yeah? Well... good for you, I guess. Doesn't change the fact that *that* wasn't Xander Stryker. It couldn't have been."

"HA! If you'd have seen the sort of beating that guy could take you'd be singing a different tune. Plus, it's no secret that he's not a fan of those Cebour-guys."

"And you think that's evidence enough that the vamp that just saved our asses from those Cebourists is Xander Stryker? I challenge you to find *one* mythos in the entire world that *wouldn't* like to rip a Cebourist's throat out."

"Okay. Okay! *That's* fair. But that *was* his aura!"

"Well, I can't see auras, so pardon me for not just swallowing that pill dry."

"Okay, Mister Know-It-All, who else would it be?"

"..."

"Heh! Thought so!"

"Silence is hardly a sign of forfeit."

"It's a good first step towards forfeit, though, and, in this case, forfeit would be a good step, because that *was* Xander Stryker!"

"If that was really Stryker—hell, if he was really a mythos—then how come the Cebourists' magic didn't work on him? They barely even looked at me and I felt like I'd been trapped in a burning box for *years!* I was on fire in there, feeling a kind of pain I didn't even know was possible, and, near as I can tell, they did the same thing to you. But they seemed to be pushing everything they had at that *maybe*-Stryker and... and nothing was happening to him! How could that be possible? Maybe he was really some human who's figured out his own magic—maybe like that DiAngelo-nut with his serum and whatnot—and he's using all that as a means of posing as Stryker without having the weakness of being one of us."

"I can't say *how* he'd be impervious to the Cebourists' magic, but that *was* Stryker!"

"Okay! Fine! Whatever! It was Stryker! Why's it matter to you so much? Isn't it enough that we're still alive?"

"No, man; no! That's not enough! Not now! If Xander's still alive—and, yes, he most certainly is!—and he's figured out a way to fight back against those sons-of-bitches—which he most certainly has!—then I'm gonna join him!"

"Join him? Are you insane? If Xander Stryker is alive then there's going to be *a lot* of people that are going to start working to make him dead! You want to just join with the most hated individual on Earth?"

"Well, I don't hate him, so... yes."

"Son-of-a... And there's nothing I can do to talk you out of it?"

"Nope. You gonna tag along and make sure I don't get myself killed?"

"Isn't that the whole reason that the Cebourists caught us both out here in the first place?"

"Something bothering you, Stephen?"

"Oh jeez—"

"Sorry. Didn't mean to startle you."

"For God's... Dean, you can't just sneak up on a guy like that!"

"Sneak up...? By Cebour's all-seeing eye, Stephen, I've been in here for nearly twenty minutes. This mythos blood doesn't wash itself off the walls, you know."

"Oh… I-I guess I just sort of…"

"…?"

"…"

"Drifted off? Like just now?"

"Yes. I guess so."

"So…?"

"Hmm?"

"So, is something bothering you? No offense, Stephen, but usually you're so with it; you're one of the strongest among us, certainly one of the most powerful in our chapter, and you're typically so honed in on anything and everything that we'd all started taking bets that you were some kind of robot."

"…?"

"Okay, so *that's* an exaggeration, but all the same. So what's on your mind?"

"I… well, this isn't easy to say."

"The things most in need of saying rarely are… Hey! Don't roll your eyes at me! I'm being serious!"

"I know you are, Dean, and that's part of the problem. I'm starting to feel like some things are better left unsaid, like maybe… like maybe we've made a mistake."

"'We'? 'We,' as in…?"

"I think I'm going to leave, Dean."

"Well I should hope so! It's after hours, after all, and you've already been pushing yourself for nearly twenty hours. It'd be good to—"

"I don't just mean to leave for the night; not just leave here, Dean, but to leave *here*—to leave *this,* all of it."

"…?"

"…"

"…!"

"…"

"Ste-Stephen? No! You can't be—You mean to leave *us?* To

leave your fellow Cebourists? What, do you plan to leave Cebour, as well; do you intend to abandon your god?"

"I've abandoned three gods in my lifetime already, Dean. I got tired of being bullied for being Jewish when I was eleven—said 'no more,' and abandoned that god. I attended Bible camp when I was sixteen in the hopes of catching the eye of a girl who told me I should find Christ. That summer, after seven weeks of the Lord's Prayer and nonstop preaching in between kickball and celibacy lectures, I caught her trying to find Christ in the pants of a boy who'd once flushed my kippah down the toilet in grade school. I went home early from camp that summer, and I went home abandoning another god. Then, a few years after that, I had to accept Jehovah once more at the request of my grandfather after he fell ill. I did so, believing that maybe *his* god would rid his bones of the cancer if I started praying to Him once more. He did not. My grandfather died, and my renewed faith—artificial as it was—died with him. Dean, the only reason I ever believed in Cebour was because I'd been attacked by a monster—a winged demon-like creature; still haven't seen anything like it since then—and it was Father Tennesen, the priest that Ariel had us murder, who saved my life."

"I... I had no idea. How did you... I-I mean, what...?"

"What happened? Ariel—she's what happened. Tennesen told me that I would be safe at his church while he went after the monster. He said it didn't matter what I believed—or, more specifically, what I *didn't* believe—and that a shelter was a shelter all the same. Too shaken to challenge the offer, I went, and Ariel was there. She still whispered Cebour's words back then, I don't know that they were anything more than words then—perhaps there wasn't even a name to put behind them—but, after what I'd seen, those words made more sense than any others. Cebour became a security blanket, and saying the name, *empowering* the name, gave us a means to fight the monsters. What reason would anybody in my place have *not* to go along with it? But what does it amount to? If the KKK or

Westboro could set fire to the objects of their hate as easily as we can would that make their ideas or their god any more real?"

"So—what?—you're gonna run off and sing songs with the niggers and faggots now? Why not just invite the entire mythos world to climb into your bed, maybe drink from your veins and even take your body however they saw fit? What you're talking about isn't just heresy, Stephen, it's *madness!*"

"Madness? Madne—Dean? Have you looked outside? *We* did this! It's all madness, and we're to blame!"

"Us? It was that Stryker-devil who told the world the truth of their existence. Even we weren't so brash."

"The Cebourists are many things, Dean, but they have never been prudent."

"*We*, Stephen! *We!* You *are* one of—"

"No, Dean. I already told you that I can't do this anymore. I might not have any love for the mythos, but nor can I say that I have any left for humans, either. Ariel forced Stryker into action, of that I'm certain—he wasn't exactly discreet in explaining to the world that he was warning other mythos of our existence. None of this happened by accident; none of it purely the fault of one side or the other. Our outspoken hate for their kind motivated Stryker, and now the whole world's a cesspool of hate. And, no, I'm not about to say that I'm not still filled with hate: I hate the bullies, I hate the hypocritical Christian girl and the jerk she was fooling around with that night so many years ago, I hate the demon-monster that first introduced me to this world, and I hate Tennesen for making me believe that things might actually get better. And now, after all this, I've come to hate Ariel for not having sense enough to know that sharing wisdom makes for wiser masses, but sharing hate makes for more hateful masses. And what has all that hate gotten us, Dean? Answer me that! Is the world a better place for it? Are we safer for it? We've spent all this time spouting what we thought—what we *felt*—as though it were fact, and now we're too damn wrapped up in this Cebour-nonsense to even know what's true anymore!"

"Hold your tongue, Stephen! Cebour will deem you unclean and you'll be nothing more in his eyes than—"

"You don't know what you're saying, Dean. You only believe it."

"My belief is knowledge enough! It gives me the power to—"

"The power? The *power?* The power that got Ariel killed? The power that got her precious dead hunter even more dead? How is any of that any different than the power that some mythos have used to kill? And there's whispers in the corners that say that the Stryker-devil is back—that he's still alive!—and, what's more, that he's using our own magic against other mythos! Now if there's even a shred of truth to those whispers, Dean—even a single iota—than what does that say of Cebour, of the magic that supposedly *he* grants us with, or the so-called truths of their kind that we preach? Belief may be enough to motivate action, but stop spouting your beliefs like they, or the actions they motivate, are any indicator of truth. And don't for one more second try to tell me that any of it makes the Cebourists any more right than any other extremist cult."

"You can't honestly expect me to let you just walk out of here after hearing you say all of this, can you, Stephen?"

"..."

"...?"

"I... I *was* hoping you might, Dean. You said it yourself: I'm stronger and more powerful. And, more importantly, I've had a lot of time to think about this."

"And you think that having time to think has given you some advantage?"

"I do, Dean; I really do. Because if I've learned any real lesson—one that's tangible and real; one that's *true*—it's that sometimes it's better to keep quiet and think on things rather than be loud and outspoken."

"Oh? And what has silence and thought granted you that makes you think I'll let you just walk out of here?"

"That I don't need to believe in Cebour to use the magic, Dean, and that the magic isn't just limited to mythos if you know how to use it properly."

"...!"

"Elder Luis?"

"Yes, Anton, come in. I've been expecting you."

"Y-yes. Yes, of course you have."

"That a problem? I certainly hope you wouldn't think that something like secrets would be easy to keep around here."

"No, sir. I wouldn't be so daring as to accept a position with one of The Council's most renowned aurics and expect to keep any secrets."

"It wouldn't take an auric to sense the 'but' here, Anton."

"Yes... *but* I can't help but wonder why I'm even here. If it's so simple to sense that I'd be coming here, can't you just as easily sense what it is I'm coming here to say?"

"Let me answer your question with another one: how many others did you need to speak to in order to have all the information you're here to deliver? Actually, let me make this easier: how many *elders* did you speak to for all the details?"

"A-all of them, sir."

"Right. All of them. Now, excluding myself, there's *seven* immediate elders with auric abilities and *two* sangsuigas who, in their own rights, are quite clever with how they deliver information. That means that, while I knew that you were coming with news of the utmost importance, a good portion of that information has been shielded in your own head from outward detection, and more of it exists as a series of phrasings that, if an outside auric mind were to try to read you, would offer up nothing more than a nonsensical stream of consciousness. For example, if I try to read too far into your mind right now, I can practically hear the opening lines of Sir Elton John's 'Tiny Dancer.' I'm guessing Darien was singing casually at his desk when you went into his office, right? And you probably thought nothing of it?"

"Well, now that you mention it..."

"This is the protocol for business of this nature: split the intel between the elders so that no single one of us ever knows enough to compromise a situation before we're ready to act. Even now—even knowing everything you know and are about to tell me—the information is incomplete without what I already know. Rest assured, Anton, you might be working for one of the most renowned aurics, but you're still very much an asset. Now, if you will, please: sit and divulge."

"Y-yes... *ehem*, of course, sir. Well, I suppose I understand now why all of the others referred to the subject of this conversation as 'the subject.'"

"Yes. I'm imagining by this point you're curious who 'the subject' is, correct?"

"I have my guesses, sir."

"I'm sure you do. Care to share your guesses?"

"I'm... not sure that I should, sir."

"And why's that?"

"Council protocol operates to break up information and then funnel it into a neutral channel—in this case, me—so that none of that information is compromised."

"That is the gist of what I just explained to you, yes. And?"

"And if that neutral channel proved himself to be... well, adept enough to be not-so-neutral, one could go so far as to say that they'd no longer be of service to The Council, sir; one could go so far as to say they were no longer an asset."

"You're afraid that your guess would somehow jeopardize your position with us?"

"There's that, sure, but also my life."

"Your life, Anton?"

"You're The Council, and it's not like things around here—well, anywhere actually—have been easy for any of you. Moreover, it's not exactly a secret that The Council has other protocols. What sort of protocol is in place for an asset that can figure things out for itself? What sort of protocol is in place if that asset could ascertain key secrets and present itself as a threat? There might be 'Tiny Dancer' lyrics in my head, sir, but between what else I've been told and my own intuition there'd likely be enough to start a small war. Or possibly a very big one. Yes, sir, I'm worried about my position with The Council, but mostly because I'm guessing you wouldn't exactly let me leave here with my life."

"Do you truly believe your peoples' government to be so savage, Anton?"

"I believe my peoples' government is smart—they'd have to be to survive this long, longer than any single human government in history—and I don't believe that a smart government would allow a potential risk to their security, especially in such dire times, to go about unchecked. If it weren't me we were talking about, sir, I'd say you'd be foolish *not* to destroy such a non-asset."

"So I imagine it would be in such an asset's best interest to *not* make those sorts of guesses, am I right?"

"Yes, sir."

"Then why tell me you have guesses in the first place?"

"Because you're one of the most renowned aurics on the planet, sir; you might not know all of what the other elders had to say of 'the subject,' but I'd be foolish to try to keep secrets. Remember?"

"Heh. Yes. Yes, of course. I like you, Anton. I can tell you that you didn't guess wrong, but I can also tell you that, being a smart government, we're prepared for things like... astute assets. In either case, you're safe. You're not going anywhere, occupationally or mortally. Now... what do you have to say about our dear Xander Stryker?"

"..."

"...?"

"I... uh, well, sir, he *is* alive—'the subject is active'—and, according to a number of sources, operating against threats."

"Locally?"

"Sir?"

"Is the subject operating solely within his immediate area?"

"I... uh, well... that's where the details start getting a little strange, sir. Sources, and logic, state that, yes, the subject would only be active in—"

"I'm already sensing a 'but' here, again."

"Well, sir... there's a few reports from, uh, not-so-local regions claiming to have spotted Stry—the subject. Regions with heavy Cebourist activity as well as regions with increases in the psychic 'Messiah' phenomenon."

"I see. Are the sources for those reports reliable?"

"With all due fairness, sir, they're as reliable as a source can be claiming that a subject managed to travel hundreds of miles for an event that amounted to, at most, five minutes of activity."

"Then you don't believe the reports?"

"What I believe has nothing to do with the intel the other elders provided."

"Nobody's saying it does. I want to hear it anyway."

"I... uh, I believe *something* happened in those areas, but I don't necessarily believe that... uh, the subject was there in person."

"Explain."

"Sir, the reports only say that the... uh, sir, permission to use subject's name?"

"Granted."

"The reports only say that Stryker was seen for a brief period. All the reports were from witnesses."

"And you think this is evidence that he wasn't there in person?"

"I think it's odd that none of the sources were aurics; that every source that claims to have *seen* Stryker couldn't support an auric presence, as well."

"Your logic seems backwards, Anton."

"It *would.* A body can be present without an auric signature to validate it, and any other sort of presence, astral or otherwise, would exist solely on the auric spectrum and not be seen at all. The former would be visible to anybody with working eyes, while the latter would only be visible to psychics and aurics. So, logically, a set of reports *solely* from eyewitnesses would lead one to believe that he was physically there. However, if he *was* physically there, why would auric sources not be able to provide reports of him as an auric presence, as well?"

"What other possibilities are there?"

"If Stryker *wanted* to be seen in those areas for whatever reason, he could project himself as a physical body into the memories of those who have since provided the reports."

"You're suggesting that Stryker intentionally planted a vision of himself in the minds of sources who'd go on to say that they'd seen him there? Sources who, according to you, were hundreds of miles away from him? Do you understand what sort of power that would take? Do you understand that Stryker, despite his noteworthy lineage, could not possibly possess that sort of power?"

"I understand all of that, sir, and I understand how it sounds. I can't begin to offer any potential reasons, and I certainly can't say that I believe that to be the case, but I will say that makes more sense than any other possibility."

"And why's that?"

"If somebody wanted to project an image of themselves into your head—into any trained auric's head—how likely would it be that their efforts would go unnoticed?"

"Interesting. You're implying that the only reason there were no auric witnesses was because he was certain not to try to plant himself in their minds."

"Exactly, sir."

"That still doesn't explain the 'why,' though. And it almost seems to imply that Stryker would be doing all of this intentionally; that he *knew* we'd be having this conversation right now."

"I think any mythos with a working brain would *know* that we'd be having this conversation sooner or later, sir. And, again, all I'm saying is that it makes more sense than anything else."

"Interesting. And you say that these eyewitness reports are cited in areas with heavy Cebourist or 'Messiah' activity?"

"Yes, sir."

"Any further word on just what this 'Messiah' business entails?"

"None, sir. It's been hard enough for everyone to track Stryker, to be perfectly honest."

"Understood. So Stryker's alive, active, and committing some rather... curious acts. Would you say his actions represent a threat?"

"You mean any further threat, sir?"

"Of course."

"No. His methods are unconventional, but they always were. And he's not taking any measures to guard against detection, but one would wonder why he'd bother. The only real curiosity, sir, is that he's not selective about who he's protecting. We have documentation of him rescuing both human and nonhuman victims from both human and nonhuman assailants."

"Quite the Good Samaritan, wouldn't you say?"

"It would appear that way, sir."

"But we can agree that this does not excuse what he did, correct? Stryker must still answer for doing what he's done to us; to the world, wouldn't you agree?"

"Not that it's up to me, but, yes, sir, I would agree."

"What's the news on the others? On his wife and on what's left of his clan?"

"There's nothing of the Trepis Clan to speak of, sir. Stryker has a following—including Missus Stryker—and, while some of that following were prior members of the Trepis Clan, they are not operating as they had. Not that this is surprising, sir—after all, what good would such an effort prove without our resources?—but the way they're operating is outside the system; more rogue than anything else. They still have ample resources, ones that we have no way of cutting off, and they're using them however they see fit."

"Well I'd say that's all the more reason to pay Stryker a visit."

"All of the other elders seemed to be in agreement about that, though obviously the details weren't all there. I also have news on the Vaileans and their colleagues—more of their clan were reported to be en route in that general direction—and I know that Damiano Moratti has already set out on an undisclosed mission, though he hinted that he planned on seeing you soon."

"He was right about that. Thank you, Anton. That will be all for now."

CHAPTER 19
THE MYSTERIOUS, NEW XANDER STRYKER

*"I mean, you got this celebrity warrior daddy—
co-founder of one of the most influential clans the
world has ever known and world-celebrated badass—
who wracked up, like,* crazy *street cred, right?
Them's some* big *fucking shoes to fill,
and you're... well,* not *very big."*
Zane Vailean

"This is crazy, you know," Allen Carrey muttered into the palms of his hands. A cup of coffee, his seventh in less than an hour, sat, untouched, beside an overflowing ashtray with a still-smoking cigarette threatening to teeter over its edge.

Estella didn't need her aura to know that he was overwhelmed. And she certainly didn't need Xander's powers to know he likely wasn't going to make it through all of this. He'd come back with the others after their battle at the hotel—a battle that, though nobody was sure *how,* many claimed that Xander directly helped them win—and, since then, he'd been a vital source of information. Not only was he able to teach them how to guard themselves against the Cebourists' magic, but, as they'd been hoping, he was managing to teach them how to utilize it, as well.

Unsurprisingly, Xander and Estella took to these teachings the fastest; Zeek a close second to the two of them.

What *was* surprising, however, was the number of "students" Allen found himself training. Each and every day since his arrival—since the day that Xander had awakened—more and more new recruits began to arrive. Estella wasn't sure just *how* they were all tracking them down, something that Xander's many enemies—Aleks included—seemed unable to accomplish, but she had her suspicions. As powerful as everyone was becoming, after all, none could compete in that arena with Xander. She supposed that, given this fact, it should be no surprise that he'd have no trouble tracking down anybody willing to support him and his cause; have no trouble showing them, one way or the other, *exactly* how to find him.

And what was most surprising—though at this point it seemed pointless to be surprised by anything anymore—was the nature of the support that was arriving. Many of the members and recruits that had fled the Trepis Clan at the first sign of danger began to shuffle in, shame and uncertainty masking their features and riding their auras up until Xander welcomed them back with every bit of willingness and certainty as the first day they'd arrived on the steps of their high-priced mansion. Then came the rogues, mythos of all shapes, sizes, and backgrounds who, on any other occasion, would have looked upon Xander as a certain threat. They came, some as families and some as gangs, and Xander took them in, too; gave them shelter, gave them training, and, most importantly, gave them hope. And then—like Xander, himself, seeming to challenge the very ways of the world—came the humans. Terrified and skeptical, those that Xander had inspired and those that he had saved since his awakening began to arrive. Some, Estella marveled, confessed that they had left the Cebourists and were hoping to find retribution with Xander and his people.

And, by that point, Xander's people were many!

More and more of the surrounding property was utilized, turning the entire pier—a once bustling port of business and activity since reduced to an abandoned cluster of buildings that served only to store things indefinitely—into a sort of dormitory for what became loosely known as "Stryker's Vagrants." It was in no way a flattering title, but the sheer ridiculousness of it seemed to motivate its members and advertise to others.

And Xander, somehow, just kept on going.

The collective auric mass of combined fear and hatred that hung like a heavy fog over the city had begun to thin. The Cebourists' numbers were beginning to dwindle; many abandoning the new church while the rest began to migrate out of the city. With the threat of empowered haters thinning out, tensions with mythos began to ease. This, in turn, led to fewer mythos attacks; the "get them before they get me"-mentality that had driven many for those first few days began to die out as a sort of phantom confidence was restored to the city.

Many had been saved by Xander since he'd awakened. More had heard of his return. And even more yet, those who refused to believe he could be alive, could not deny that *something* was happening to make things safer.

Xander just kept on going, and "Stryker's Vagrants" just kept on growing.

Sometimes he left with others. Zane was always quick to join on the missions that Xander didn't specifically express a need to go on alone, and, with him, Isaac and Zoey were often not far behind. With their growing numbers, however, the normal "crowd" became nothing short of a small army. Many, however, were left behind. Whether this was due to inexperience, direct orders, or, in Estella and Serena's cases, pregnancy mattered little, as those who stayed did so with their own mission: train.

Though he'd been vague and continued to be vague ever since, Xander made it clear to all of them that there was a war coming, and that it would demand much from all of them. Fortunately, despite many of their initiates' inexperience, Allen Carrey was able to call upon his time as both a soldier, a mythos hunter, *and* a Cebourist in order to fulfill a sizable role as a trainer. For the inexperienced vampire recruits, Estella was proud to see Sana and Timothy taking on the task of combat training—the two teenage lovers proving surprisingly adept at teaching mythos even five times their age how to utilize their natural abilities in a fight. For the other species, Zeek, Satoru, and the therion twins were willing to step in, the four already having experience from their time in the Trepis Clan.

With little else to do but work on her new Cebour-magic lessons, which never took long to master, Estella found herself watching these things pass with a sort of distant wonder. It all became a sort of bizarre time-lapse, one that began each night when Xander left and ended upon his return right before dawn; one that showed a scene of desolation and uncertainty blossoming into...

What?

Was it fair to be optimistic? Was it logical or reasonable to assume that, just because Xander had made a difference in their city, that somehow there could be hope for the entire world? Like the phantom hope that had crept over the city, a sort of secondary optimism had begun to haunt the back of her mind. Though she could not bring herself to feel any great hope for the fate of the world—and she did not feel she was being unreasonable in that sense—she *could* feel hopeful that someday, perhaps, she might. It was an optimism that allowed her to believe she might come to feel optimistic, and, after watching Xander silently struggle for years for any reason to go on day-by-day, Estella saw no reason to see this as anything less than good.

Any kind of optimism, after all, even of the secondary or ghostly variety, was better than the alternative, right?

Then Allen Carrey—fresh off another round of teaching new recruits how to fight, handle weapons, and, of course, the wonderful-yet-awful art of conjuring and guarding against anti-mythos magic—pointed out that it was all crazy.

And, honestly, who could blame him? Estella thought.

Allen Carrey hadn't seen Xander in action over the years. He hadn't even seen Xander in action over the past few weeks. Allen Carrey only saw Xander—now sporting an eyepatch and braiding his hair with a long, brown leather cord—strap a few guns to himself before slipping out into the night. What could that sight alone mean to him? And how could that sight possibly translate into any sense of hope? No matter how many fresh faces showed up on that pier with each passing day, how could Allen Carrey possibly link that one, single mythos with the breed of unrelenting hope that was growing all around him?

Allen Carrey had a mind like Estella's: one driven by reason and logic. There was nothing reasonable in assuming that a scarred, one-eyed, gun-toting vampire would change the damaged world for the better; nothing logical in looking for something more beneath the easy-to-read surface.

Estella's own mind wanted to think the same way. But then she remembered all the things she'd seen Xander accomplish before, remembered that Stan had done *something* to him before dying—left him with a power that still worried her greatly—and remembered all that she'd seen from Xander since his awakening:

She remembered how, in a single instant, Xander had seemingly come back from the dead. A body that shouldn't have been able to move did just that. Arms and hands that shouldn't have been able to hold her did just that. A broken jaw that should have never been able to kiss her did just that. And, along with everything else he'd done with her—to her—in that beautiful, perfect moment, Xander Stryker had defied the very laws of gravity. Then, though still missing an eye and unable to rid himself of the awful graffiti-like scars, he'd reclaimed his city. He'd come back from what many were certain was the end stronger and more confident.

And a great deal more mysterious.

Mysterious, Estella thought, and sometimes a bit scary. Since his awakening, it was not uncommon for her to catch him drifting—his gaze staring out at nothing but seeming to see so much more while his face bent and twisted, reacting to things that nobody else could see. She'd caught him crying or laughing when he thought he was alone; heard him whispering words she, even with her superhuman senses and psychic powers, couldn't follow. Once, during a meal, his eye had gone vacant while he was staring at Isaac and, with a dip in the constant hum of the dining hall, he'd said,

"Who knew you could see so little and so much all at once?"

It had, with good reason, given both Isaac and Zoey a good scare, and when they asked him what he'd meant, Estella had watched his eye regain its focus—its light; its hold on the here-and-now—and blink, confused.

He could not remember what he'd said, and when reminded he was just as confused as the rest of them.

It was all very nerve-wracking, but none of it quite came to compare to the times that Estella heard him crying out to her in his sleep; screaming her name, his face sweat-drenched and red with determination, and then, immediately after, calling out to Ruby.

Allen Carrey and Estella might have shared a similar sort of mind, but Xander had a funny way of blowing reason and logic away in much the same way he blew the heads off of his enemies with his enchanted bullets. Estella remembered all of these things—the good, the bad, and the ugly—and she could not bring herself to think so simply; could not allow herself to be confined by barriers of reason and logic.

Then Zane's bizarre-yet-brilliant speech about Xander being bisexual ran through her mind again—*"I look at him and see a hundred-and-fifty pound guy with about three-tons of bullshit stacked on his shoulders, and, truth be told, I can only perceive, like, half-a-ton of it"*—and she couldn't help but smile.

Allen Carrey, seeing this, said, "Not sure what there is to smile about."

Then Estella, suddenly sounding an awful lot like Xander had been more recently, said, "I'm sure you will, Allen."

EARLY ON IN XANDER'S "CAREER," Estella had used the Spell of Sight to watch him on enough of his outings to see him in action. Then, after being turned, she'd had the chance to watch him fight firsthand—even used her magic to replicate his skills in herself so that she could join him. Since then, she'd worked to hone her abilities, working her magical abilities into her combat training to create something new, branching off and creating a fighting style that was all her own. But she'd never stopped being fascinated by Xander and his methods.

Crude as he was—with all the risks and what seemed to be a personal challenge to spill as much blood as possible—she couldn't get enough of the raw confidence Xander exhibited when he fought. As a human, he'd always carried himself with his head lowered and shoulders slumped—a sad and desperate effort to make himself as easy to miss and even easier to forget as possible. He was not a fighter then. He'd had all the hate, sure, but that he reserved solely for himself. His introduction to the world of mythos and learning of his place within it, Estella knew, was what gave him a much-needed outlet. Suddenly, all that trained and polished anger had a new place to go, and with a bit of formal training he became something spectacular, indeed.

In fact, it seemed that the only time Xander Stryker *wasn't* the super-confident vampire warrior that many either feared or revered was when the person he was standing in front of was her. The moment all the danger and threats and mayhem were behind him and Estella was standing in front of him, the red-faced, stammering, uncertain Xander slipped back into being. And while Estella had never minded the bashfulness—finding it endearing and even empowering, in fact—she'd always seen a sort of irony in their duality: his limitless confidence blazing like the sun itself in the face of unspeakable violence and danger and then burning out in the presence of undying love and attraction, and her unsteady-yet-somehow-effective tactics on the battlefield weighed against her absolute certainty and strength in regards to passion and lust.

They were like Yin and Yang when it came to war and love; one flourishing while the other seemed convinced they were getting by solely on luck.

If anybody asked Estella how she fared so well in a fight, she'd almost certainly tell them it was *anything* except skill. And if anybody dared to inquire from Xander how he managed to keep Estella, she was sure that he'd turn a shade of red that would shame his own aura, shrug, and say something along the lines of "she's just really patient, I guess."

Ask the other the same questions of their partner, however, and they'd surely have nothing but the utmost praise to offer.

Estella certainly *knew* that Xander was a capable lover (more-than-capable if she had to rank performance), and she was sure that he would have said the same of her in regards to her skills as a combatant. But if Xander and Estella shared one common flaw above all others, it was that they both let their confidence wane where they likely shouldn't.

That, however, had not been the case lately.

Though it wasn't for a lack of trying, Estella's involvement with much of anything, with the exception of training and working with Allen Carrey to perfect the Cebourists' magic, was essentially nonexistent. She *wanted* to feel useful, but there was only so much a pregnant woman—vampire or otherwise—could do. Not even having the benefit of the magic to fall back on, Serena was vocal about this fact to a repetitious point that seemed almost surreal.

But, eventually, Xander would return each night, and the loneliness and doubt would fall away. Because, though Xander *had* lacked confidence as a lover, and, though he *had*, as Sana had pointed out several weeks before, always been shy and reserved regarding the subject, his confidence was far from lacking in any department, it seemed.

He arrived while Estella was still cycling through her conversation with Allen Carrey, and all of her worries about craziness and anti-mythos magic were swept away as he scooped her up and kissed her (again) like it was the very first time.

This had become the norm, and Estella, with the exception of having to stay behind each night and feeling useless, couldn't be happier about it.

"You're here!" she cooed as the kiss broke, and she nuzzled her face against the juncture between his neck and shoulder.

He smiled at this and gave a dismissive shrug. "You say that every night as though you suspected I wouldn't be," he teased.

It was an innocent tease, even a practiced one at that point. It was, at its surface, a totally harmless statement. But Estella didn't want to say aloud that the night that he *wasn't* there—the night that he *didn't* just come home—was still not that far off in the past. Instead, she smiled at him and pulled herself deeper into him, inhaling the air of him. He smelled like death and fear, the stink of smoke, stale sea water, sweat, and lots and lots of blood clinging to the more obscure scents and validating them several times over. He smelled like work, but, beneath it all, she could still smell the natural collection of pheromones, adrenaline, and the tinge of gun oil and leather that had come to define Xander. *Her* Xander. But there, along with the rest of it, was a new smell—not unpleasant, though.

It just...

It's not Xander... Estella thought.

It was exotic. Peppery, but not carrying any sort of tickle to her nostrils—a spice from someplace far off—and also earthy, reminding her of new plants growing in an old forest. But there was more there, too: something that, for whatever reason, made Estella think of starlight, options, and ticking clocks.

How one could *smell* any of those things, however, was beyond her.

But much of the Xander Stryker that had awakened after that horrible night—the night that he *hadn't* come back—seemed to be carrying more than what had been there before. This, much as she wanted to celebrate his return and simply move on, had Estella thinking.

She'd been crushed to hear about what had happened to Stan. He'd been one of her favorite grown-ups, and, though not technically a teacher, she'd often talk about him as such when reciting to her parents what had made a particular day at school better than others. It was, after all, almost always Stan who managed to make a day better. Especially the days when Xander didn't come into school. She'd loved Stan, and his ties to magic made him all the more spectacular in her eyes. And then there was all that he'd done for her and Xander...

But now he was gone.

Xander was back, Stan was gone, and that, Estella kept telling herself, was that. Except that that *wasn't* that. Xander was different—she'd never say worse, and many might go so far as to say better, but he was undeniably different—and she couldn't shake the feeling that Stan, dead or not, had something to do with this.

She shivered as she realized that Allen Carrey's words weren't as dead to her upon Xander's arrival as she'd thought.

And Xander, being Xander, caught onto it immediately.

"What is it?" he asked, holding her at an arm's length but, thankfully, still holding her. "What's the matter?"

It felt wrong to lie. It had always felt wrong to lie to Xander—they'd always adhered to an unspoken oath to always be honest with one another—and this moment was no different.

"It's just..." Estella began, then stopped. She needed to collect her thoughts, make sure that she said this right. Finally, wetting her lips, she said, "I feel like something's different about you now."

Xander's blood-red eye studied her a moment. She could almost imagine how his now-missing hazel eye might match the expression and slight movements, but now there was only a black strip of material covering that side of his face. Seeming to hear what she was thinking—and he very well could have, she supposed—he dipped his face down and to the left, hiding that side from her view. The remaining, visible eye shifted, contemplative and sad, and then looked back at her.

"You're thinking about Stan?" he asked, though she didn't doubt that he'd at least seen enough of her thoughts to deduce that much.

She nodded.

He drew in a deep breath and shrugged out of his red leather jacket, tossing it to the corner of their room and beginning to undo the leather tie in his hair. The room that they'd come to occupy, now in an office building that overlooked their initial storage facility, was larger and, in many ways, more accommodating than the lone office. This building and many of the other surrounding buildings their growing group had come to occupy, though unavailable when Estella and the others had been looking for a place to stay that first night, had begun to empty out soon after Xander's awakening. Whether this was his direct doing or an outcome of rumors of nearby mythos activity was another of the mysteries that Estella had been too nervous to address until that moment. What had once been a private corner office was now a makeshift bedroom that allowed the Strykers to look out over the small cluster of buildings that had come to be called the "dorms." At night, the view of the water beyond the pier was infinite and ominous; intimidating if stared into for too long. During the day, however...

Estella remembered waking up in the early afternoon a few days earlier and spotting Xander, out of bed and staring out from those windows. He'd been floating. His legs had been folded tightly over one another, and his arms had been resting across his thighs so that his hands could come together, his fingers bent and steeped to create a strange geometric form that was silhouetted against the sunlight from Estella's angle. Noticing that the curtains they normally kept up had been pulled down and nervous that he'd be burned by the exposed sun's rays, Estella jumped from the bed to check on him. That was when she noticed the wide auric shield he had cast out in front of him, looking like a giant lens across the glass, that seemed to be filtering out any potentially hazardous radiation. She'd checked him anyway. Not noticing her, he'd continued to float a foot-or-so over the floor, his body motionless save for the occasional shift in the pattern made by his fingers. He'd almost seemed to be sleeping, Estella thought, except that he'd been whispering—low and nearly inaudible even to her sensitive hearing—to himself. Finally, she'd managed to realize that he was whispering the same two words over and over:

"... course... On course... On course... On..."

Unnerved by this finding but unafraid—it was still Xander, after all—Estella had set a hand on his shoulder and given him a gentle tug. It was the same sort of gesture that she'd used before to guide him back from other times he'd been lost in thought. That he was doing so while defying gravity, she figured, should make no difference. It didn't. Feeling the familiar pressure, Xander had stopped his mumbling, and then his legs had unfolded and lowered, coming to rest on the floor so that he was standing. Then, still seeming asleep but smiling at Estella's arrival, he'd allowed her to turn him away from the window and followed her back to bed. It had been her intention to lie him down and then fix the fallen curtains, but as they'd shambled sleepily back to the bed, she'd heard a faint rustling and saw the room fall into a familiar darkness as Xander's aura did the job for her. Once in bed, he'd pulled her to him—setting an open palm on her stomach—and whispered *"Just keep going. You're almost there"* into her ear.

Strangely settled by this, she'd rested herself against him, draping an arm over his chest, and fallen back to sleep.

"The Padmasana," Xander whispered, pulling Estella from the memory.

She could see that he was nodding, though he was still working to keep his missing eye hidden from her. His hair, now free of the strip of leather he'd been using to tie it back most nights, hung freely, wildly, around his face and curled out around the base of his neck and shoulders. At that moment, she thought, he looked like something rugged and divine; in a strange way, he was finally starting to look like the person she'd always felt he was.

"The what?" she asked.

Xander shrugged, a guilty-looking gesture, and he let himself fall back. Estella nearly called out that he was about to fall, but his aura snaked out and forked off into a rudimentary shape that, as Xander "fell" into it, supported his weight and allowed him to sit before her. He smiled at her—a pleasant, familiar smile—and he motioned for her to sit. Though there was nothing behind her to rely on, she had no doubts as she, too, allowed herself to fall back into a sitting position.

Xander's aura was there to hold her, just as she knew it would be.

"I owe you a lot of explanations," Xander said, biting his lip as he gave her an apologetic look. "It'll be easier if you let me scan your mind for the exact questions so I can be sure I tell you everything I can."

"Everything... you can?" Estella asked, finding this a strange thing to say.

Xander's lips tugged back in a momentary scowl as he

nodded. "Some things I can't really..." he sighed and wiped his face, leaning forward in his auric chair. "Imagine a person—a mother—is very, very sick, alright? Now, she can get through it. The medicine's all there, it's working and such, and there is every possibility that she'll live through it..." he paused to take in a deep breath and, as he did, gave a single shake of his head. "But she still very well might die. Let's for the sake of argument say that there's only a few factors that will decide whether she lives or dies, but one of the biggest factors is her will to fight this sickness. Right? She needs to have all her focus and drive on the sickness inside her—no outside distractions or concerns; nothing like that—in order to have *any* chance of beating this and living through it. Now imagine you're her doctor; you know this to be the truth—she needs to be focused and unstressed in order to fight. And then there's her family—husband, siblings, kids... the whole lot of them—and they're all looking at you to fix her; to *cure* her. But they're *also* looking at you for each and every detail: 'Is she okay?', 'Will she be okay?', 'Is there anything I can do?', and so on and so forth. If you tell *them* too much—if you tell them the truth, for example—there's a strong likelihood that their reaction will inadvertently become the distraction and stress that winds up killing the mother. And, on the other hand, if you tell them nothing, then they might go straight to her with their efforts and offers. Noble and beautiful as those might be, however, they'd still be risking her life. The same can be said for what you say to her: to tell her that her family's worried will distract her from the goal of getting better, but to say nothing of them might let her forget what she's fighting to stay for." Xander sighed, shaking his head again. "I'm like the doctor now, 'Stell. I'm not happy about it—I outright hated it when I had to hear it all from Stan, and now I'm stuck holding the Power for myself—but I've got to do what I can to keep the world on course while also keeping the people and mythos occupying it from flying off the handle and doing something we'll all regret."

Estella considered this for a moment and then, matching her husband's posture, sat forward. "Are you telling me that you can see the future?" she asked, "And that you have to be careful what things you tell people to ensure that things happen the way they're supposed to?"

Xander shrugged, paused to think, and then shook his head. "No. No, not necessarily like that, I'm afraid. You see, even in that example, the doctor doesn't *know* whether his patient will live or die—only that the best way to ensure that she *does* live would be to say the right things, lies included, to keep the family from interfering while telling her *exactly* what she needed to hear to focus on fighting the sickness. I don't so much see the future as much as I have an *annoyingly* keen sense of how everything that's happened works into everything that's happening and, based on that pattern, where things *might* go. A lot of the time that means I'm looking at, like, a few hundred possible outcomes to me deciding whether to shoot my gun to the left or to the right."

This, Estella decided, sounded more like a burden than a gift. She found herself resenting Stan at that moment. "This has to do with Stan's power, doesn't it?" she asked. "You can see these things now because Stan gave them to you again, right?"

"More or less," said Xander. "I felt like I was getting glimpses even before Stan gave me his powers—and it's worth pointing out that, though I can do *a lot* with it right now, most of those powers are still locked away inside me; not sure *why* that is or *how* I'm supposed to get to the rest of them."

Estella remembered how the powers had impacted Xander the last time he'd acquired Stan's powers and felt a wave of guilt as she thought she'd sooner never see him unlock them if that was the case.

Xander, looking sympathetic, nodded. "I'm not exactly in a hurry to have them back, either," he told her, confessing in that statement that he was still reading her thoughts. "But," he continued, "at the same time, I'm kind of scared of what will happen if I don't get them soon."

Shivering, Estella asked, "Why is that?"

Xander glanced off for a time. "Imagine—in that same doctor-patient example I gave earlier—that the sick mother focusing on fighting the sickness *wasn't* enough to save her life. But the amount of time that her fighting to survive *would* be enough to keep her alive while the doctor got a shipment of medicine that she needed to make a full recovery."

"Okay..." Estella said, not sure she understood.

"But you, the doctor, don't really know if the medicine's coming... or when," Xander went on. "You're just trying to stall everyone else and keep your patient alive and her family calm in the hopes that it'll come in time."

"Oh..." Estella looked down.

Xander nodded and leaned back again. "So I've been doing all I can to handicap the Cebourists, track Aleks and his followers, *and* get all the pieces in the right places to prepare for..." he trailed off and looked down, suddenly looking like he might cry.

"For what?" Estella pressed.

Xander looked up at her for a moment, his eye shifting in tiny bursts of movement as though he was watching a movie playing out on Estella's face. Then, seeming satisfied by the outcome of what he saw, he said, "I guess it won't hurt anything to tell you there's a war coming. And I'm pretty sure I don't have to tell you who it'll be against."

Though Estella knew that there'd been more encounters with the Cebourists over the past few weeks, she wasn't surprised to hear herself whisper, "Aleks."

Xander nodded.

"Where is he now?" Estella asked.

Xander shook his head. "I don't know," he admitted. "He's been moving around a lot. His 'Messiah'-bullshit is ringing in a lot of minds around here, sure, but it's beginning to chime more and more all over this region. Each day it spreads a little further.

I can't say that he's left the city, but he's certainly working his way across the country in some form or another."

Estella sneered at the idea and asked, "Why?"

Xander actually laughed at the question. "From the looks of things," he said between chuckles, "he's doing it because you scared the shit out of him in your last encounter."

"I... uh, what?" Estella squinted at this for a moment, confused, before playing out their last battle the morning of Xander's disappearance. She remembered breaking his leg and then nearly landing a killing blow on him, one that would have risked her and Xander's baby. Sneering, she offered a chuckle of her own. "Serves him right for kissing me, I guess," she spat.

Xander didn't look surprised by this—he *was* looking inside her head, she figured—but nor did he look happy about it, either. "He wants numbers," Xander explained after a silent moment of disgust was shared. "It was always his intention to challenge me, if for no other reason other than to avenge his parents. But things have changed since then; the world found out about our kind after I went on the air to warn our kind about the Cebourists, so now he views fighting me as a sort of grudge match to see which side gets to take control of the world."

"Why?" asked Estella, "How does fighting you determine the fate of... well, everything?"

"I didn't say it does," Xander said with a shrug. "But my father was always sort of working towards a unified world. The idea of humans and mythos coexisting was sort of the grand fantasy of Joseph Stryker—it *was* why so many hated him and wanted him dead—and it was always Lenuta's vision to... well, just take it all. She wanted to turn the planet into a blood-stained playground for fellow mythos sadists; a sort of apocalypse where most people are dead, a few are around to worship Lenuta—or, in this case, Aleks—and offer themselves as servants, while whatever remaining humans basically serve the purpose of cattle. It's two sides of one coin: one side where we all try to make it work and another where we're all basically dead or kneeling to a psychotic mythos with a god complex."

Estella gave a slow nod. "I guess it sort of does make sense that he'd want a war, then; things are more or less in the perfect place to go in either direction."

"Exactly," Xander nodded. "So I've been trying to ensure that, when that war comes, we've got the best possible chance of being on the winning side."

"And how good are our chances at this point?" asked Estella.

Xander looked away. He didn't answer.

Estella's heart sank. "That bad?" she asked.

"'Good' and 'bad' are terms that are getting tougher and tougher for me to invest in," he said with a heavy sigh, sounding almost like a growl. "What's good for our chances is absolute shit for..." he sighed and looked up at her. "How's Sawyer doing?"

"Sawyer?" Estella repeated the name, confused to why Xander would bring him up at that moment. "I... Well, I haven't really seen much of him lately. He's been..." she sighed sadly, shrugging, "I guess he hasn't really been too interested in, you know, talking to anybody. But who could blame him?" she defended, "He *did* lose—" She felt the air vanish from her lungs, croaked on what was going to be Dianna's name. She remembered hearing the stories from those who'd been on the battlefield at the hotel the day that Dianna had died; the same day that Xander had awakened. An awful possibility dawned on her and her vision blurred as she looked up at Xander. "O-oh... oh gods, no. Xander... D-don't tell me..."

Xander looked down, wiping his remaining eye of a tear that had begun to betray him. "I didn't want to let it happen, 'Stell," he whispered, "but Dianna's death put certain things into motion that we needed to have happen in order to even have a chance to—"

"Does Sawyer know?" Estella demanded.

Xander blinked at the question, his mouth hanging open as if he was already about to answer. He said nothing for a long moment, though. Finally, closing his mouth long enough to wipe at his face again, he shook his head and said, “No. No, Sawyer doesn’t know. And it’s better that he...”

He didn’t finish.

He didn’t need to.

Estella nodded and swallowed a sob. “It’s... I think it *would* be better if we don’t let anybody know,” she admitted. Estella felt awful saying that, but she knew it was nothing when compared to how Xander must have felt. “Just tell me it was worth it,” she finally said.

Xander sighed and nodded, a half-hearted shrug lifting one of his shoulders. “We’re on a better path than we would have been otherwise,” he explained. “Allen Carrey wouldn’t have joined if he hadn’t seen the daughter of one of his late comrades sacrifice herself for the mythos she loved, and Carrey’s military expertise and intel on the Cebourists and their magic will give us an undeniable edge against Aleks and his followers when they make their move.”

Estella nodded at this, still holding back her tears, and looked down for the question that was coming next. “Will Sawyer be okay?” she finally blurted.

Xander stared at her for a long, hard period of time.

Estella looked up at him. “Xander?” she pressed.

“You don’t want me to answer these questions,” he said.

“No,” she admitted, “but I need you to answer the ones that you can.”

His eyes moved across her face again—*watching another movie that I can’t see,* she thought—and, finally, he answered, “No.”

He didn’t answer any further.

“Is there anything we can do to help him?” she asked.

Xander shook his head. “Not without possibly hurting our cause in the long run.”

Estella scowled at that. "What does that mean?"

Xander looked down. He looked tortured by his own silence.

Estella nodded slowly, sympathizing with the massive burden he was struggling with. She lifted herself from the auric chair she'd been sitting in and closed the distance between them. She knelt down before him, cupping her hands around his, and setting her cheek against their combined hands.

"I'm sorry you have to go through this," she whispered to him.

Xander shivered at that. "Please don't apologize for any of this, 'Stell," he said, sounding genuinely wounded by what she'd said. "Things are... they're moving. And possibly even in the right direction—'right' for us, at least—and I'd be lying if I said that it's not the thoughts of you and our baby that are keeping me on track to get it done."

Estella gave a weak smile at that. "So can you tell me what's going to happen next?" she asked.

She closed her eyes, still resting against her husband, and "saw" Xander give a slight nod in her mind's eye. "The Council's going to be arriving soon," he said, his tone calm about that revelation. "And they'll be eager to kill me and everyone else here to prove a point."

Estella's eyes snapped open and she jumped to her feet. The suddenness of the movement seemed to startle her more than it did Xander, who regarded her with a face that was every bit as calm as his tone had been.

"What?" she demanded. "The... The *Council* is coming *here?*"

"Yes," Xander said, still calm.

She reeled. "Coming to kill you? Coming to kill all of us?" she repeated, hoping to see a reaction from him this time around that made sense.

He only nodded again.

"And you're not worried about that?" she demanded.

Xander smirked—actually smirked!—and shook his head. It was a beautifully familiar gesture, rolling with all the confidence and arrogance that she knew Xander to exhibit in regards to combat and threats on his life, but in no way the sort of reaction *anyone*, himself included, would have extended when threatened with the wrath of the mythos Council.

"Why should I be?" he asked. "I've been working for nearly nine days to make sure they'd get here sooner rather than later."

Estella nearly felt faint at that confession. "Wh-what? Why?" she asked.

"Let's just say—getting back to that doctor-patient metaphor earlier—that this particular patient is going to need more than just one dose of medicine."

Estella studied him for a moment. "And The Council is going to represent a dose of medicine in this case?"

Xander nodded.

"But people are going to die!" she pressed.

"Of course people are going to die," he sighed, "it *is* going to be a war, after all. But they're not going to kill any of us. With any luck, in fact, we won't have to hurt them, but you don't have to worry about killing any of them."

"You can tell me that with absolute certainty?" asked Estella, who, since Xander's return, was glad to see the violent streak that had been growing within her subside.

Xander shrugged. "Provided somebody named Elder Luis isn't with the group," he said. "Most of the rest are pretty modern. They'd rather open with negotiations and escalate into the intended execution. So long as we can get a dialogue going with them we have, for the most part, good chances of not having a fight break out."

"And if a fight *does* break out?" Estella asked, still concerned.

Xander shrugged again. "Like I said: none of ours are going to be at risk one way or the other. If it comes down to a fight, most scenarios lead to a negotiation after we incapacitate their forces. That negotiation will serve the same outcome as it would if we hadn't fought at all."

"How is it possible that, with all the possible outcomes, our side can't suffer any losses and theirs can?" Estella asked.

Xander shrugged. "In any circumstance wherein a fight begins, they send in all of theirs and we only send in four of ours: me, you, Serena, and Zane."

"You and Zane would let me and Serena fight The Council? Even though we're pregnant?" she asked, not believing that explanation.

Xander shook his head. "Zane and I don't *let* anything happen in any of those situations. In all *natural* cases, I volunteer to fight on my own. Zane, being Zane, refuses to let me fight alone. Serena, being Serena, decides to get in on it, and once she bullies her way in you see an opportunity and take it."

"And there isn't any negative impact in telling me this?" asked Estella.

Xander shook his head. "If and when a fight breaks out with The Council—and there's no guarantee that it will; like I said, much of it relies on whether or not Elder Luis is among them—I will go through the motions of volunteering to fight alone. Whether or not you know what's happening at that point doesn't change anything, because you'll join one way or the other. If I told Serena or Zane, however, they *might* be eager to see the fight take place and push it to happen in a situation that would otherwise go without needing it to happen in the first place." He sighed and shook his head, rubbing over the patch-side temple. "There's actually a lot that I *can* tell you without really negatively impacting the path of things," he finally said, then mumbled, "... and plenty that I *can't*."

"Oh?" Estella blushed at this, though she wasn't really sure why—it didn't sound like the sort of thing one would traditionally be flattered by. "Why do you think that is? The part where you *can* tell me things, I mean. I can understand the other part just fine—makes more sense to me, actually."

Xander grinned a little and shook his head, saying, "Because this has never been my story."

Estella frowned at that, not sure she heard right—not sure she *wanted* to hear it right—and asked, "What do you mean?"

"It's just something Stan said after we got back from our honeymoon," he explained, waving a dismissive hand. "Don't worry about it."

This only made Estella want to worry about it more.

Xander's aura slithered out, a lazy tentacle from a deep, cavernous place exploring brighter terrain, and moved towards her. She let it in. Immediately, she felt the warmth and calmness that Xander often brought begin to amplify, growing and swelling within her—becoming a part of her. She remembered those awful moments a few weeks before when she'd felt like all the angry, self-destructive parts of him were growing within her; being carried within her. This, she decided, was exactly like that...

Only the complete opposite.

"I feel like you're avoiding the question," she tried to scold him, but her voice came out too airy and content, almost giggly. It was impossible to take herself seriously with that voice.

Xander, however, seemed to understand that her words were sincere. He moved towards her, his feet falling without sound against the floor—everything about him had become a display of grace and power; *so beautiful,* Estella thought—and he took her into his arms. "You've been like a key for me for so long," he said, his words gentle and loving, but the weight of their meaning crashing down like the end of days. "Without you, I wouldn't have lived this long, fought this hard, or pushed so far. Without you, none of this could have come to pass."

"W-wouldn't that be a good thing?" she asked, stammering.

Xander shook his head. "Stan saw to it that things moved the way they should. What's happened was meant to happen, much as it might seem unlikely now. He thought it was me for a long time—keeping me alive, withholding the information from me that might throw things out of balance, and focusing on making sure that I was ready for the next step when it came

—but there was an oversight. It scared me at first, 'Stell," he chuckled and shook his head, "I actually thought Stan had lost his mind when he had the revelation... but I see it now, too."

Estella shivered, still feeling the reassuring warmth of Xander's aura but unable to ignore the looming darkness riding the edges of his words. "What? What do you see?"

"It's like I said—like Stan said—" he paused to sigh and shrug, "it was never my story. I'm not the hero; I'm just the gun in the hands of the hero."

Estella's breath caught at that, feeling a strange sense of familiarity to the metaphor. Before she could dwell on it for long, though, Xander went on:

"There's a great deal that I can tell you without impacting the timeline," he explained, "because you trust your gun; you trust me. Most of what I could tell you of what I've seen you'd simply accept because you know that, no matter what sort of trouble comes our way, your gun is loaded and will always find its mark."

"And..." Estella gulped, pressing herself against him further, "what about the things you *can't* tell me?"

"A person can find themselves in a bad place if they know their gun might fail them," Xander said in a low voice. "And they might put themselves in even worse places if they remember that their gun is more than a gun..."

Estella felt a moment of understanding flare up within her, a painful stab of *knowing* that had her aura rejecting the warmth and comfort of Xander's own. "NO!" she snapped, working to turn on him and demand to know what sort of danger he was in; to know what he foresaw in his future. "What's going to—"

Xander's aura seized her, slipping past her defenses and enveloping her in the serenity once again. Estella struggled to maintain her worry—fought to stay angry at him for hiding whatever it was he was hiding—but she felt him inside her, making everything better; making her...

Making her forget...

"Shh," he whispered, running his hands over her hair. "It'll be alright. That was too much—I said too much," he confessed, sadness echoing on his words.

Estella whimpered, still certain there was something she had to do for him.

Xander...

He needed her help...

Didn't he?

She looked up at him, saw a tear growing in his eye, and wondered what she'd been thinking. She blinked, confused, and he was smiling back at her—dry-eyed and filled with that confident warmth.

How could she ever believe that Xander—this new, mysterious, power-and-grace filled creature—could ever be so frail as to have to cry?

"Whether or not you know what's happening at that point doesn't change anything," Xander was saying, and Estella blinked, wondering how she'd managed to get distracted from his explanation, "because you'll join one way or the other. If I told Serena or Zane, however, they *might* be eager to see the fight take place and push it to happen in a situation that would otherwise go without needing it to happen in the first place." He sighed and shook his head, and Estella wasn't surprised to see him rubbing at his temple—she was having the strangest sense of déjà vu all of a sudden. "There's actually a lot that I *can* tell you without really negatively impacting the path of things."

Estella waited, feeling like he was about to say something else. He didn't.

She felt that she was supposed to ask him *why,* and so she did.

Xander just smiled and said, "Probably because you trust me," and gave a shrug with a single shoulder.

She almost thought she saw his face betray a hint of

sadness, but it was gone before she could be sure. "This all sounds really complicated," she said with a frown.

"Like I said:" Xander sighed, "I'm not thrilled about having this ability. I don't like..." he paused, looking skeptical for a long moment. Then, stiffening and pulling back his shoulders—something Estella had seen him do whenever he had to make a compromise he wasn't happy about—he finally said, "I don't like having to keep secrets and feel like I'm manipulating people, especially..." he sighed, "Especially when you're among those I have to lie to and manipulate."

"I can't imagine," Estella offered, running her hand over the top of his head. "But, it's like you said: I trust you. I have always trusted you, and I will continue to trust you, Xander. I don't envy the decisions you have to make right now—it's an awful burden that nobody should have to bear—but I know you're working to do the right thing." She smiled and kissed his cheek. "You do whatever you feel is best, and do so knowing that I support your decisions... even if I can't understand them or even know about them. Honestly, I feel safer knowing that you have this power."

Though she couldn't be sure, Estella thought she saw Xander flinch at that. Ignoring this, trusting that Xander would be honest about the bits that he *could* be honest about, she took his hand and started to lead him towards their private bathroom.

"Come on," she said to him, smiling for his benefit and feeling the effort it took to hold it lessen at the sight of the smile she earned in return. "It looks, and smells, like you've had a rough day. Let's go take a shower and you can tell me all about it."

Xander chuckled at this offer and, squeezing her hand, said, "I was wondering when you'd get along to mentioning the smell."

CHAPTER 20
NEW THREADS

"The individual has always had to struggle to keep from being overwhelmed by the tribe."
Friedrich Nietzsche (1844-1900)

Xander was feeling fresh.

Freshly showered.

Freshly rested.

And, yes, even freshly laid.

True to what he'd said during his out-of-body encounter with Zane back at the hotel, finding himself formless and alone had left him with a new appreciation for private time with Estella. This was not to say that he hadn't appreciated private time with Estella before, but facing down a very possible eternity of nothingness had a funny way of inspiring a guy to take in all of life's pleasures with a renewed sense of value. In this case, the simplest mound of flesh—*"a pair of tits"* as he and Zane had referred to them—was elevated to divine levels when somebody was certain that things like sight and taste and touch were lost to them forever. Moreover, when that certain somebody could experience those simple mounds on a whole new level—when they could *see* how their transfixed gaze influenced the physical response of their partner, when they could *taste* the shift in body chemistry as their lips worked over the pink flesh, and when they could *feel* the responses spark within their partner's body like jolts of electricity beneath their fingers—"a pair of tits" could, to the right somebody, be something of a religious experience.

Shame the Cebourists are too obsessed with burning mythos to discover tits, Xander thought.

The night had fallen over the makeshift dorms of "Stryker's Vagrants"—a new "day" starting for the ragtag group of mythos—and many were beginning to migrate to-and-fro. Xander was pleased to say that he recognized some as members of the Trepis Clan who'd since returned to them. Among these, some had come back upon hearing that he hadn't been killed while others had been convinced to return once again after seeing what a difference his efforts were making. Then there were the other mythos that had joined, many of whom had no training or expertise to offer as fighters but who otherwise had no other safe options. Xander, deciding that he would sooner build a community than a second-rate clan, accepted them all without question. But this, he knew, was hardly the most bizarre addition to their growing group. This he was reminded of as he walked by a small, nervous-looking cluster of humans. Though none of the others paid them any mind, it was obvious that they were still adjusting to being surrounded by creatures that, only a short time ago, lived only in the realms of fiction. It was an understandable reaction, but it was a fear that was wasted there—Xander made it clear to newcomers that intolerance either to other mythos *or* to humans wouldn't be tolerated, and should that intolerance escalate to the realm of violence...

Well, Xander Stryker *was* still Xander Stryker.

"You look tired," Xander said to them, trying to sound as

pleasant and nonthreatening as possible. "Just because they're all used to a nocturnal schedule doesn't mean that you have to be."

"But that Carrey-guy only teaches at night, right?" one of the humans, a young woman with shoulder-length, curly black hair, asked. She seemed nervous to ask this, and Xander could see on her aura that she was worried that he might think she was planning to learn the Cebourists' magic so that she could use it against him and the rest of their group.

Xander offered a reassuring smile, knowing it would only unnerve her that much further to explain that he was now impervious to the effects of that magic. *It pays to have a wife with such strong ties to the arts,* he thought to himself, but, out loud to the humans, he said, "I'll see if I can't convince Allen to take a few morning shifts for you and any others who'd rather sleep at night, okay?"

The humans all smiled sheepishly at this, going so far as to bow their thanks to him. Xander watched this, perplexed, but offered a smile in return and nodded them towards one of the buildings furthest from the bustling activity, assuring them that the noise shouldn't carry out that far. He turned away almost as soon as they did, not wanting them to catch him watching their retreat. Though that exchange had noticeably eased much of their concern, he knew it would be a while before they'd trust nonhumans to the degree he needed for a sense of community to blossom.

"I know we just got done talking about this," Estella's voice called out to him from behind, "but you've changed a great deal in such a short time."

Xander barely had to stop and turn to face her for her to catch up to him. He smiled at her as they fell into a comfortable pace beside one another and headed for the storage facility.

"This is the part where you tell me what you mean instead of forcing me to read your thoughts again?" he pushed.

She smirked up at him. "Like you didn't like being inside my head last night," she said, nudging him.

"Not as much as I liked being inside other parts of you," he replied, nudging her back.

Estella stopped in mid-step, staring after him with her jaw nearly hanging open.

Xander stopped and stared back at her, smirking knowingly.

"What did you just say?" she demanded, the strained shock in her voice betrayed by stifled laughter.

"My, my," Xander said with a chuckle. "Did I just make you blush? That was way too easy. I thought I'd have to visit Ruby and ask for one of those little vibrating thingies to *really* get the red in you cheeks."

"Oh my..." Estella hurried forward to clap a hand over his mouth, looking around to check if anybody had overheard them. "Jeez! Who are you and what have you done with my bashful husband?"

"I ate him," Xander joked, then, smirking even wider, started to say, "If you want I can eat you—"

Estella, unable to keep from giggling, clapped her hand back over his mouth. *Later tonight, definitely. Now behave!*

You're cute when you're red like this, Xander thought-spoke back. *I can see why you did this to me for so long.*

Estella beamed at that and, removing her hand from his mouth, paused to replace it with her lips.

Xander made no move to hide the kiss or hurry it for the sake of not being seen. This, he knew, would *also* come as a shock to Estella.

He was right.

Giggling again, she pried herself free and issued another nudge. "Come on, you beast!" she said. "The others will be waiting."

TRUE TO ESTELLA'S WORDS, the others *were* waiting.

Though, it would appear, none of them were very patient.

Serena and Zane were already chattering with one another, though, much to Xander's surprise, the subject matter was focused neither on their sexual escapades nor which of them was being a "dick" or a "bitch" at that moment. Without prying too far, it seemed that they were discussing the arrival of some friends from the Clan of Vail. This, however, was enough for Xander to know... well, everything.

Though the ability was far, *far* from precognitive, it was easy for even him to forget that. Knowing that Nikki and Raith would be joining their ranks—though still uncertain whether they'd live long enough to prove useful—was something of a relief. The paths of reality where the two of them *didn't* join them meant more deaths of key players that, in some way or another, were crucial to the outcome of the battle.

Nikki needs to reinforce the monorail support... he reminded himself, then immediately wondered why.

Before he could trace the dominos to see what this meant, however, he felt Estella's hand on his shoulder, pulling him back into both the here and now—as opposed to the here and forty minutes ago, where Zoey and Isaac nearly walked in on the Vaileans... *Oh geez!* Xander recoiled and forced himself to focus—and they started towards the table where everyone else was sitting.

Zoey and Isaac were quiet, their hands clasped under the table (but Xander didn't need any sort of extrasensory powers to know that) and a large, neon-orange tote bin set atop the table before them.

Zeek and Karen sat beside Satoru and Sasha, the Vaileans seated to the former's right while Zoey and Isaac waited to the latter's left. This left an opening for Xander at Zoey's left and Estella at Zane's right. These were the only two spots left at the...

Xander stumbled and felt his heart skip a beat at the sight of a familiar-looking ten-sided table.

Estella stopped and looked back, sensing his pause. "Everything alright?" she asked.

The question motivated the others to look over, and Xander, feeling the combined weight of their gazes, couldn't bring himself to look away from the table.

"Where did this come from?" Xander asked, running his palm over the surface to make certain it was real.

Zane gave one of his "who gives a shit"-shrugs and said, "Found it with some of the other office junk. Why? You like it?"

"I hate it, actually," Xander muttered.

"Didn't peg you for the interior decorating sort," Serena said with a laugh.

Xander didn't reply.

"Baby?" Estella said, setting her hand atop his own.

The added weight pressed his palm further against the polished wood and he shivered, suddenly sure that if he looked up he'd see Depok sitting at the corner across from him. Forcing himself to look away from his and Estella's hands on its surface, he caught sight of Zeek, looking with grave uncertainty back at him.

"Something the matter?" the anapriek asked.

Xander shook his head, his mouth too dry to form a response, and looked around the table.

Ten spaces... ten of them.

But how could that...?

"Wh-where is..." he paused, took a deep breath and worked to stave off the growing cottonmouth, and dared another look around the table. "Where's Sawyer?" he finally asked.

Everyone at the table grimaced and looked away, none eager to answer.

It was Karen who finally cleared her throat and said, "He couldn't make it."

"More like *wouldn't*," Sasha corrected, though there was

none of the usual playfulness that typically rode with her jabs against her sister.

Though the others remained silent, all seemed to agree with this general summary.

Xander looked down, stifling the urge to drive his fists through the table. For one sick, awful moment, he worried that doing so might hurt the tiger lying beneath its surface. The confusion from seeing the table and the guilt surrounding Sawyer and how he'd been taking Dianna's death started to take their toll, and he forced himself to sit down at the seat beside Zoey.

Seeing this, Estella took her own seat beside him.

The room seemed to spin to Xander, the surrounding room obscuring and hazing into blackness, and he could practically see the nine dead faces looking back at him. Knowing that they weren't really there, he worked to stifle his frenzied nerves, drag in a deep breath, and wipe the haze from his vision.

You were shown a great deal, he reminded himself. *The Great Machine—'great asshole,' more like—forced you to choke down so many visions... You obviously saw this table—possibly this moment —at some point when you were lost in your head and constructed that 'meeting' with the others using* this *vision. Get ahold of yourself!*

This, he was relieved to find, helped ease most of the tension. All the same, however, he couldn't help but realize that Estella was now sitting where he'd been seated during the "meeting" in his mind.

Which meant he was sitting in Stan's seat...

He shivered.

"Xander?" Zoey's voice beside him was low, full of concern.

"You need a puke bag or something, bro?" Zane called, not at all low but carrying the same concern.

Zeek started to stand, his aura shifting as it often did when his instincts to heal took over.

Xander raised a hand to stop him and forced himself to shake his head.

"It's fine," he told them, though his voice was raspy and low. He cleared his throat, suddenly remembering all the times Stan had seemed to falter from his "higher-than-high"-stature. Had he ever gone through something like this? Clearing his thoughts of this—knowing that questions like that would do him no good—he exhaled again, imagining all the negative energies riding the air out on the "bad breath." Surprisingly—though, somehow, not surprisingly at all—this worked. *It is what it is,* a thought—but not *his* thought—chimed in his head, and, strangely satisfied by this, he offered the group a reassuring nod and finally said, with a clear voice, "I'm fine. Just had a freaky moment of déjà vu."

"Hate that," Sasha offered, though her aura gave away that she was only saying it to make him feel better.

The others all agreed in their own way, all for the same reason.

Though they were all confused and in no way capable of understanding what it was Xander was going through, their efforts *did* work to ease his mind.

"It *is* an ugly fucking table," Zane muttered after the sympathetic agreements died down, scratching at a patch on its surface where something had scratched it.

Serena rolled her eyes. "Whatever. Maybe you two can start one of those gay 'fix my home' shows after all this is over with."

"Assuming we get to the actual meeting so that we can get this over with," Zeek spat with impatience.

Seeing this as an opportunity to steer things in the intended direction, Xander spoke the words that he knew would get everyone focused:

"The Council is coming."

Eight sets of breath seized in unsuspecting lungs. Estella, already knowing this, kept her gaze fixed on Xander as he waited for the news to sink in for the others.

Zane's body tensed, but he otherwise offered no response.

Zeek and Karen shared a nervous glance.

Sasha shifted closer to Satoru, her aura matching the lean in a subconscious effort to take comfort from him. The cat-like mythos, without having to look, extended a striped and furry hand and set it on her thigh.

Zoey and Isaac, seeming conflicted, gave each other questioning glances. Xander could see on their auras that they were uncertain about viewing their peoples' government in a negative light, but also knew that they were, through association with him, fugitives to that government.

"Welp..." Serena finally said, adding a sharp *pop* at the end of the word as she drummed her fingernails on the table. "That's... I mean, it's bad, right?" She stared at Xander, obviously trying to gauge the severity of the situation.

Soon everyone was looking at him in the same way.

Xander stared off for a moment, trying to decide which sequence of words would serve their cause the best. Too lax, he saw, would make them all feel that there was no need for concern. This, despite everything, would motivate suspicion from The Council, suspicion that could divert from the natural path and set an entirely new sequence of events into motion. They could wind up going to war with them rather than gaining their support, which would leave all of them weak and vulnerable to attack when Aleks made his move. Worse yet, if Xander couldn't get The Council to come to his side, they'd almost certainly target Allen Carrey and the rest of the humans they'd managed to recruit, and even if Xander and the others managed to escape with their lives they'd be doing so without one of their most effective weapons. Without Carrey, the only other person with a strong handle on the Cebourists' magic was Estella, who...

Estella!

Running! Running so fast and so hard that his body is tearing at the seams. He is—yes, he is*—on course to her, but Xander sees, in that instant, that he'll never make it in time.*

He will never make it to Estella before...

No!

Xander jolted out of the memory that he knew was not a memory. He felt tears in his eye and cast his aura up in a shield that hid his reddened, panic-strewn face from the others. They'd only see him staring back at them as he had been—as he should be—until he managed to calm down again. He didn't need them seeing him like that; didn't need them worrying about him or doubting him.

To lose Carrey was to lose a powerful weapon in the war on Aleks, a weapon—a role—that only Estella could occupy. And to put Estella on that battlefield was...

On course... On course... On course!

It was not an option.

The Council could not be allowed to destroy Carrey, which meant The Council needed to feel confident in Xander and his group. And if some of the strongest members of Xander's group—namely those sitting around the table—seemed too relaxed upon their arrival, they would have no reason to feel confident in putting their trust in them. Edgy as The Council already was, being received with anything *except* the reaction they'd be expecting would give them any number of reasons to feel suspicious.

And, when The Council was involved, suspicion was a good way to motivate unwanted deaths.

At the same time, however, if Xander made them all think that The Council outright intended to kill them, there were any number of reactions that could end poorly, not the least of which being an attempted preemptive attack.

And with all the high-level aurics The Council had at their disposal, Xander knew that a sneak attack was nothing more than an elaborate suicide.

"It's not great," he finally said, deciding it was best to instill just enough uncertainty to maintain appearances while still offering a glimmer of hope.

With any luck, Serena and Zane would...

Serena and Zane?

Xander studied them a moment, noticed a direct line tethering their mutual history back to...

Yes! They had ties to a high-ranking Council member!

Aren't we lucky that Damiano Moratti will be among those paying us a visit, he thought.

"Earth-to-Stryker!" Serena called out through cupped palms. "Where do you keep drifting off to?" she demanded once his eye were focused on her once again.

"Everywhere," he answered.

There were a few nervous chuckles that cycled around the table, but when Xander's face gave no hint of humor—and it wouldn't behind the shield he was still hiding behind—these died down.

"Oh..." Serena said, looking unnerved. "Gotta be racking up those travel points, huh?"

"Like you wouldn't believe," Xander offered. Then, addressing the rest of the table, he said, "I'm not going to lie to you all and say that they've got good intentions in coming here. They don't. Right now, the main focus on all of their minds is killing me, and most of them believe that anybody in league with me should die, as well."

The others all looked nervous about this, but none of them gave any sign that they wanted to leave. Even their auras remained fixed, certain of where they stood.

"However..." Xander went on, needing them all to have faith enough to carry them through what was about come. Without meaning to, he glanced towards Zoey—remembering how Tennesen had occupied that spot in his mind "meeting"—before realizing that the old priest was not there. "I'm confident that I can change their minds about... well, all of this. Perhaps even get them to agree to help us. It won't exactly change *every-*

one's mind if we regain their support—there'll be plenty willing to believe that I'd simply corrupted The Council just to maintain that I'm the enemy—but it *will* bring many to our side."

"And that will give us the edge against Messi—" Zoey began before catching herself and finishing with, "—against Aleks, right?"

Xander regarded her again, remembering that she and Isaac had been the first to catch on to Aleks' earliest schemes back when he was still brainwashing rogues under the title of "Messiah." Obviously it was still a bitter subject for her.

Nodding, he said, "It will give us *an* edge against him, yes. There are a few other things that have helped to lean the outcome of the battle in our favor, but..."

"But this *is* a varcol we're talking about," Zane finished for him. "A psychotic, dick-weed of a varcol who's been actively recruiting followers of his own."

Xander nodded.

"Any progress on his whereabouts?" Isaac asked.

Xander looked his way, not surprised to see him glancing at Zoey. His aura was a flashing sign with her name written across it in varying tones and intents. He was certain that, if his own aura shone so simply, it would show the same for Estella. He considered this for a moment, then considered Isaac, remembering Estella telling him how, during a blackout, Xander had said something about seeing and *not* seeing to the therion. He still couldn't remember exactly what he'd said or, moreover, what it was supposed to mean. There were just too many rows of dominos to go blindly chasing one. In either case, both he and Zoey were intent on being a part of the fight against Aleks.

Nevermind the fact that he could see that *neither* of them knew what they'd do once they had the chance. Nobody did.

Hell, even Xander—with the Great Machine pumping future possibilities into his head and a mind unwillingly calculating pinpoint outcomes—couldn't even begin to hold onto any semblance of certainty regarding what he was going to do when the big event finally befell them.

Hopefully I'll have unlocked the rest of Stan's powers by then, he thought.

So turn the key, that familiar-yet-mysterious voice called back to him.

Realizing that Isaac was still waiting on an answer, Xander said, "No."

Then he realized that Isaac hadn't even finished his sentence—wasn't even a syllable into the word "whereabouts" before he'd answered him—and that, not only had time *not* been passing while he'd been thinking, he'd actually been seeing things a few seconds ahead of time.

Blushing at what had come off as a brazen interruption and realizing he was thankful that his calm-and-composed illusion was still masking his red, teary-eyed face, Xander sighed and apologized.

"No," he repeated again. "Aleks is... well, he's very good at hiding himself and his intentions."

"Even from you?" Zoey asked, furrowing her brow. "With how powerful you are now?"

Xander sighed and set his hands on the table. "Look, about what I can do now," he started, "I... I know how it all must look, but it's all more confusing than it is liberating. I'm not seeing and hearing things before they happen, you see, I'm... I can just *know* how things will happen based on certain patterns. You see a ball rolling in a general direction, you can guess where it's going to go; maybe even know what it might hit. Put a dog in that room, and it's not hard to guess that it might chase the ball. Add a flimsy table with an expensive vase in the ball's path with an excited dog chasing it, and... well, it's like that. Just on a much, much, *much* larger scale. Things fall into a pattern on a cosmic level. For me it becomes obvious—just guessing various outcomes that fall within those patterns—but, to everybody else, I'm predicting lottery numbers."

"Oh shit! Can you predict lottery numbers?" Serena asked.

Xander gave her a face that reflected itself through his illusion.

Serena didn't seem to be phased by the look. "Well," she pressed, "can you?"

"Does that really matter?" Zoey demanded.

"It does if we want to be rich!" Serena argued.

"You're already rich," Isaac pointed out.

Serena shrugged. "Well, yeah, sure. But not from winning the lottery!"

"I could tell you whether a quarter dropped forty-seven years in the future by a man who hasn't been born yet lands heads-up or heads-down and you're going to ask me about lottery numbers?" Xander challenged.

Serena stared at him, contemplative.

The rest of the table settled, certain that the subject was done.

"So..." the blonde vampire drawled, "You *can* predict the lottery?"

"Yeah. Sure," Xander rolled his eye as he dropped his face into his left palm. "I can predict the lottery, but how 'bout I just give you the three-million dollars and we leave it at that?"

"Only three-mill?" Serena frowned.

Zeek scoffed. "Don't watch the news, do you, Blondie? Economy's not doing so good since people started assuming they'd be dead within weeks due to monster attacks."

Zane sighed and nodded. "Not enough people dreaming of being rich when the new dream is staying alive. No dreamers means no lottery tickets."

"Well fuck that noise!" Serena growled.

"Anyway!" Estella said with a sigh, "Back to the *important* stuff!"

Zeek leaned back in his chair and wiped his face. "Well... we've got The Council coming to kill us, but Xander seems pretty certain that *that* shouldn't be throwing us into a panic.

Personally, I think we'd have a better chance of Satoru announcing the winning lottery numbers, and since he doesn't talk I hope everyone understands I'm of sound mind that we're all going to be royally screwed when they get here."

Xander, realizing this was a better frame of mind for them to commit to than one of blind optimism, did nothing to argue with the anapriek.

Considering their leader's silence, the table's thoughts regarding The Council shifted further towards worry.

This, Xander realized, helped align the right rows of dominos...

He hoped.

"Then," Zeek pushed on with a groan, "assuming that our all-powerful government hasn't exterminated every memory of us, there's the little problem of a god-like mythos with, near as I can tell, a whole hell of a lot of reasons to have a personal vendetta against our fearless leader." He held up a fist and started by lifting his index finger. "First offense: offing his daddy."

Xander thought back on that night in Maine. Visions of blood-stained snow and a skeletal forest strewn with dead bodies. The familiar face of Kyle, the man—the monster—who'd tormented him as a child and finally killed his mother.

"Second offense:" Zeek held up his middle finger to join the pointer, "blowing up not only his castle, but also his mother."

Though he couldn't say he regretted killing the death-mongering varcol, Lenuta, Xander *had* found himself wishing that he hadn't gone so far as to remove Stan and his father's spell from the castle. Even with the mountaintop structure *trying* to collapse, the spell *would* have been enough to keep it intact and, in doing so, would have kept Aleks trapped within those tortured walls. Then again, neither Xander nor Estella had any way of knowing that there was a second varcol hiding away within those walls when they'd made their escape at the end of that night.

"And finally:" Zeek held up a third finger, "while I can't say that I know much about this Aleks-guy, I have to imagine that he would've rather taken the world by surprise when he put his plans for global takeover into effect. You bombarding the airwaves with the truth of our kind," he nodded a pointed chin towards Xander, "likely stole *a lot* of wind from his no-doubt puffed-up sails. From now-on and forevermore, the world will *always* remember *you,* Xander Stryker, as the vampire that moved us all into the next chapter of this planet's history."

Zane scoffed and nodded. "Yeah! Sort of Christ-like when you think about it, huh? Maybe we'll start knowing this as the year One AX: the first year 'After Xander.'"

Xander was about to say something about crucifixion, but before he could a familiar vision of a firing revolver turning his head into a bloody puddle made him decide to stay quiet.

Estella's hand moved to his knee and gave it a gentle squeeze. Xander glanced at her, wondering if she could read his thoughts. Still uncertain, he doubled his auric shields, not wanting her to see.

"History can only tell what history will make of these moments," Zeek said with a sigh, "but the point is this: there's loads of trouble headed our way with very little reason to feel confident about any of it. If we totally ignore the subject of The Council, there's still the matter of Aleks and his following. Most of us don't have the means to take on somebody like him. To be blunt, only Xander and Estella can even *hope* to stand toe-to-toe with the likes of him. And as both a friend and the closest thing this group's got to a doctor, I don't want to see Estella anywhere near any of this when it happens."

Xander gave him a nod of agreement, ignoring the swirl of conflicting thoughts rolling off of Estella's aura.

"And what worries me most," Zeek continued, letting his raised hand drop under the table then, "is how quiet he's been lately. With the exception of the out-of-state intel Xander's brought us regarding his mass recruitment, which in and of itself is terribly unnerving if you ask me, nobody's seen or heard anything from him in—what?—the past few weeks. A creature like that is a threat *without* the benefit of a plan or an army."

Xander could practically watch the reality of these words sink into the others like an airborne toxin; their auras seeming to grow sick as they breathed it in.

"He's likely thinking the same of me right now, though," Xander finally said, breaking the silence. The others looked up at that, the proverbial sickness seeming to subside within their auras as new hope was offered. Xander nodded in response to their unspoken skepticism. "It wouldn't have done any good to panic you all at the time," he explained, "but, before I came back, Estella said that Aleks had tried to make a connection with her shortly after you all came here."

Eight pairs of eyes widened in Estella's direction. She looked down, guilt and embarrassment beginning to rise with a flush across her cheeks.

"She did the right thing in not telling you," Xander defended, realizing his voice had come out a bit harsher than he'd meant it to. "With how bad things were, there was no good that could have come from it."

"So what'd you do?" Serena asked, taking Estella's free hand.

"I... uh, I shielded us. All of us. I... well, I didn't want him finding Xander, and I figured if I kept the minds of *everyone* shielded against him..."

Serena beamed proudly and nodded. "You really are a goddess, Goddess," she praised.

Estella's blush deepened, but this time for the right reasons.

Xander nodded, glad to see the pressure falling away from his wife. "Anyway, after I woke up I worked to reinforce the shielding. Obviously it's needed to expand since then, and I've even managed to plant psychic shields in the minds of those I've encountered during my outings. To put it simply: Aleks can't sense us, either; he might have heard that we're growing or that I've been active, but he can't trace any of it."

"So if all this psychic-stuff was like a radar," Isaac chimed in, "then his is just as blank as ours?"

Xander gave a slight nod. "More or less, yeah," he admitted. "Not that you should get too excited by it, but his 'radar'—so to speak—is actually seeing *less* than ours."

"How do you mean?" Karen asked.

"Because I can still 'see' where he's recruiting," Xander explained. "The name 'Messiah' has become a sort of beacon for the areas he's trying to gain followers, so wherever that psychic presence is most dense I know to target it."

Sasha quirked an eyebrow at that. "Target it for what?" she asked.

"Well, I can't travel out that far," Xander explained, "not physically, anyhow. But I *can* project my aura further than before."

"What good is your aura at fighting Aleks or his recruits if he's too far out for you to travel?" asked Isaac.

Xander smirked. "Who said anything about fighting? Haven't you heard? Xander Stryker came back from the dead, and he's come back as some sort of one-eyed demigod." He chuckled and shrugged. "At least that's how the stories have been spreading. Humans and mythos alike no longer consider what they might have known about me *before;* they're motivated entirely by the impact of those stories. For most of the mythos who are considering joining Aleks, they're *afraid* of what opposing this symbol of me might mean for them."

"So you're just playing off their fear?" Zane challenged. "Just taking the Batman route and hoping it's enough?"

"It's more like the Devil route if you think about it," Xander said, earning nine confused faces in response. "Think about it: you've got an entire planet of people who *fear* the idea of Xander Stryker but are still considering joining Aleks *solely* because he's a more immediate threat. They don't know what to expect from *me*, because all they've got to go on are rumors and stories, but Aleks... he's *there*, going around and simply proving that, yes, he *is* a varcol and, yes, he *does* intend to snatch control of the entire world. Even *we're* sitting around shivering at what he's going to do, and at least we know what a varcol is capable of!"

"So how does that make you the devil in this shit-show?" Serena asked. "I mean, *except* for the whole 'tempting me to gamble'-part, of course."

"Better the devil you know..." Isaac chimed in.

Xander smiled at him and nodded. "Exactly. Exactly right! So when I find out that Aleks' influence has begun to inflate in a particular area, I project my aura into the minds of a few of the more talkative mythos, the ones most likely to take what they *think* they saw—which is *anything* I want to show them—and go on a rumor-spreading rampage about how Xander Stryker showed up and—"

"And proved that he's a bigger, badder ass-kicker than that tampon-sucking fist-fucker Aleks could ever hope to be!" Serena finished for him.

Xander shrugged. "Not how I would have put it, but... yeah, exactly."

"So how's that been working out?" Zane asked.

"A lot of possible recruits that Aleks was hoping for have gone into hiding the world over," Xander explained.

"But not all of them?" asked Isaac.

Xander shook his head. "No, not all of them. Though *some* of them..." he smirked and shrugged, "Well, you didn't think that *all* of our new arrivals have been people I *saved,* did you?"

Serena slapped her palms down on the table. "Shut... up! Shut the fuck up, Stryker! No!" she gasped out as she began laughing. "Are you telling me that you've actually managed to gank some of Aleks' intended recruits and steer them our way by mind-fucking them?"

Xander grinned. "Again: not how I would have put it, but yes."

Zane started a slow clap at that.

"That's all well and great," Zeek interrupted, seeming less tense but still far from relaxed, "but shouldn't we at least work on knowing where Aleks is? Maybe trying to figure out how far along he is in whatever plan he's devising?"

Once again the table went silent.

Considering this, Xander sighed and gave a slow nod. "I *could* lower enough of my personal shielding that he'd be able to make a direct connection with me. It wouldn't be enough for him to pinpoint this location or even learn of what we've been doing, but it would allow for enough of a connection to..."

"Xander, no!" Estella whimpered. "He could still hurt you that way!"

Xander took her hand and gave it a reassuring squeeze. "He could say hurtful things, sure, maybe even project an upsetting image, but, no, he wouldn't be able to do much more than that."

Zane gave a dismissive shrug at that. "So—what?—he'd call you an 'asshole' or show you some visions of your grandpa in a Speedo? Big whoop, right?"

Xander caught Estella giving him a look that practically screamed "YOU HAVE NO IDEA," but she remained otherwise silent.

"So how hard would it be to lower your shields that specifically?" Sasha asked.

Xander drew in a deep breath, preparing for the worst, and made a single shift to his aura's outreach across the area.

"That hard..." he said.

"Then... it's done?" Karen asked, showing more concern than her sister.

Xander nodded, still bracing for whatever Aleks might want to say or show inside his mind.

Nothing happened.

THE MEETING WRAPPED up soon after. There was a bittersweet sense to it, nobody outright seeming upset that Aleks hadn't instantly taken advantage of Xander's lowered shields but everybody obviously disappointed that it hadn't motivated some kind of response. None, however, more than Xander, whose entire body was beginning to ache from the tension of being mentally braced for something that didn't come.

Estella's concern hadn't been for nothing. Despite how little the opening would allow through, there were any number of things Aleks could do to strike at Xander. Even before they'd identified who Messiah was, he'd managed to hook Xander with threats against Estella and auric probes regarding his past. Those subjects alone were enough for Xander to hurt himself. Though he didn't want to confess this to the others, he was essentially granting Aleks access to the one part of him that was now most vulnerable.

But a point had been made: information was needed. Not simply for the benefit of Xander and his team, but for The Council, as well. They were on their way, coming to deal with a threat; a goal-oriented powerhouse of some of the strongest, most influential mythos the world over. Xander could work with goal-oriented; "goal-oriented" meant that, provided a new, more demanding goal was offered up, he could have an easier time motivating them to overlook their original goal of killing him. He hadn't considered it as an option in his negotiations, but the others' urging had inspired him to "investigate" what such a path might offer should he manage to collect enough evidence of Aleks' intentions. All he'd need is a tangible thought from Aleks—some sort of psychic boast of what was to come—that one of The Council's aurics would be able to read.

It was a perfectly feasible plan, one that even justified the risk that Xander was taking to his mental wellbeing.

Figures that Aleks would find a way to fuck it up, though, Xander groused to himself.

He and Estella had remained seated at the table after the meeting had been wrapped up. Assignments had been passed around, though these were, for the most part, orders to continue what everyone had already been doing.

With that, Zeek and Karen returned to the medical center, which had seen a sizable upgrade since the storage facility was no longer serving as both that *and* the living quarters. The lone office in that building now served as the pair's private quarters, overlooking what had since become a small hospital in its own right. They still struggled to keep the area supplied, but, with fewer and fewer patients to tend to, that problem wasn't nearly as tolling as it had been. The bulk of unused space, much to Zeek's annoyance, had more recently become a sort of garage, where Zane had decided to begin teaching little Gregori, at high volume, how to "tinker" with cars.

Satoru and Sasha left with Zeek and Karen, though Xander knew that they'd be heading towards the auditorium that neighbored the office buildings that had since been renovated into living quarters for the growing community. Though it forced the spectators to be seated during lessons, this auditorium had become the site for the various training sessions that took place. This was where Allen Carrey "lectured" the recruits on how to utilize the magic that he'd learned during his time with the Cebourists, and also where the former Trepis Clan's warriors put on combat demonstrations. Though it did very little for the trainees in the long run, giving them no space or freedom to practice what they were being shown until *after* they'd left the auditorium and the confining seats therein, it was, as Zeek had begrudgingly put it, "better than nothing."

Though he hadn't said or done anything to give the others any reason to stay, Xander still found himself in the company of Zoey and Isaac and the Vaileans. The first two he wasn't surprised to see waiting behind—the large tote that had been waiting on the table in front of them had yet to be brought up, after all—but when neither Zane nor Serena made a move to leave he decided that they must have been in on whatever it entailed, as well.

"For starters," Zane said, nodding towards Zoey and Isaac's tote once the others had gone.

Taking this as a cue, Isaac reached into the bin and pulled out a dark red bundle that had been folded into a perfect square. He passed this along to Zoey, who, in turn, set it in front of Xander, a wide smile beginning to spread across her face.

"What's this?" Xander asked.

"Consider it what you will," Zoey said with a dismissive shrug, though her tone gave away that she wanted him to like it. "A tool, a prop, a... I don't know, a gift?" she said the last word with such a flippant inflection that it was obvious that was *exactly* what she intended it to be.

Xander had already decided that was exactly what he'd consider it to be.

"Either way," Zoey went on, starting to turn red with embarrassment, "it's something I've been working on for a while."

"Something you *inspired* her to work on," Serena cooed with a laugh.

Zoey's aura flashed from her body like a wild blaze. Then, a moment later, she regained enough control to reel it back inside herself before shooting Serena an angry glare.

"Oh come off it, sister!" Serena said, sticking out her tongue at the blue-haired auric. "I've been ranting on-and-on about my crush on Stryker in front of him *and* his wife since we crashed into their lives, would it kill you to confess you've got a crush, too?"

Zoey's eyes darted about between Xander and Isaac, her mouth working to protest the claim but only succeeding in stammering out nonsensical noises.

Smiling, Xander set a hand on her shoulder and nodded. *It's okay,* he said to her in private. *Isaac and I both know where your heart is. And I appreciate the gesture all the same.*

Zoey's stammering calmed, her blush subsiding.

Serena frowned and she shot a glare at Xander. "What did you say to her?" she demanded.

Xander shrugged as he began to unwrap the bundle. "I told her you only said all of that because you have lesbian fantasies about her," he quipped.

Serena glanced between the two of them, trying to gauge whether or not this was the truth. Finally, she shrugged and scoffed. "Well *that's* hardly a secret!" she said with a laugh.

Xander was about to roll his eye at the crazy blonde when his efforts with the bundle finally allowed it to fall open and he found himself staring at an ankle-length jacket. Gaping at the garment, he studied the lightweight-yet-thick material, which looked to be some sort of leather but felt more like silk. Testing this, he flicked his wrists to get a ripple moving through the jacket and watched it take for only a few inches before falling still once again.

Zoey beamed with pride. "It's a synthetic fiber that I enchanted," she explained. "More durable than leather, but light enough to let you move with absolute freedom. This is the crowning achievement, however:" she said as she reached out and gave one of the sleeves a gentle tap, earning only a single sway. Then, as though it had never happened, the sleeve fell flat once more, seeming to defy the laws of physics. "I'm still not sure *how* you manage to fly," she said in a voice that sounded almost defeated, "but I figured it couldn't be easy to do so with a jacket that would be whipping about and catching any and all stray air currents that pass its way. I wanted to make sure that, durable and light as it was, you could fly, run, and even swim without once feeling a single tug of resistance from your armor."

"Armor?" Xander asked, glancing up.

Serena laughed and nodded. "Oh yeah, Stryker. Zoe doesn't

just make sexy and fashionable costumes. Her shit's built to take a beating so that you don't have to!"

Zoey smiled at that and nodded. "Mm-hmm. It won't do much against direct shots or straight-on blade attacks—so, you know, it'd be best to still try not to get shot or stabbed—but it'll guard against blunt impacts that might otherwise break bones as well as extreme heat and cold. Provided you keep your face covered you could probably walk out of an explosion without much injury to show for it."

"It's magnificent!" Xander beamed, standing up long enough to slip it on and marvel at the perfect fit. Beside him, Estella's eyes lit up and she reached out to run her hand along the length, cooing at the feel of it. Though it wasn't a priority to him, even Xander had to admit that it felt wonderful. "Thank you," he finally said when he could admire himself in it no longer.

"You're very welcome," Zoey said, obviously elated at the response.

"Yes, yes! Very nice!" Serena purred, "Be sure to vogue it up later. In the meantime, though, there's other business to attend to!"

Xander sighed and rolled his eye. "If you're going to ask me about lottery numbers again then you can—" he began.

"I'm going to guess that you've already keyed in on the fact that we've got friends coming," Serena interrupted him, catching him off guard with an unnaturally professional tone.

Raising an eyebrow at the shift, Xander leaned forward again and folded his hands in front of him on the table. "Yeah," he admitted. "I thought I heard something about that when I was coming in."

"'Heard,' huh?" Serena's lip curled up in a coy smirk. "Surprised you didn't 'watch' it in a crystal ball, maybe even go so far as to get their blood types."

Xander pursed his lips, unable to tell without being invasive whether or not she was being serious. "It doesn't exactly work that—"

"Stow it, Cyclops," she said, rolling her eyes. "It was a joke."

"Not a good one," Xander rebutted.

Zane nodded. "Her material gets a great deal dryer when her audience is smaller. I'd say it was a curse, but..." he lifted a shoulder and held it in a frozen shrug that put his taroe tattoos in view.

Serena swatted his raised shoulder, earning a yelp. "Any-hoo..." she drawled, brushing a blonde bang behind her ear before resting her elbows on the table so she could frame her chin within her palms. "Our friends—names are Nikki and Raith if it makes any difference—agreed to come out here, but it's worth noting that they're not exactly thrilled about it."

"Because they're not fans of mine?" Xander guessed.

Serena gave him a "tut-tut"-look and shook her head. "All that 'dog chasing the ball'-talk and you can't get a single guess right, Stryker."

Xander crossed his arms over his chest and narrowed his eye at the leering blonde. "Maybe because I'm trying to be polite and *not* know everything you're about to say. You'd be surprised how quickly this conversation would be ended if I decided to be creepy with it."

Serena considered this and then cast a questioning look towards Estella, who gave a nod that, yes, Xander could do what he claimed.

"Fair enough, Long-John Stryker," she resigned.

Zane gave her a look and repeated, "'Long-John Stryker'?" before yelping from another smack.

"Because of the eyepatch," Isaac said in a flat tone.

"So I'd gathered," Xander sighed. Then, turning back to Serena, he asked, "So why are your friends not thrilled about coming out here if it's *not* because of my reputation."

"Because they're aware of the situation," Serena explained,

"and they're pretty sure that coming out here and joining you is going to get them killed."

Zane sighed and nodded. "Look, Xander, Raith is..." he trailed off and sighed, glancing back at Serena for a moment.

Serena didn't seem to notice; she kept her eyes fixed on Xander.

Xander stared back at the two of them. Realizing that neither of them was certain how to explain the situation, he decided to prove that he *wasn't* as blind as Serena thought.

"Raith was with you when you went into that taroe village," he said. "And Raith was in a secret relationship with one of them—with Nikki—and was asked by her to steal the relic that got the two of you cursed with the Maledictus. That curse is what got that particular taroe tribe demolished by The Council, who needed to make an example out of them for using that sort of magic, magic that risked exposing not only the existence of magic but the existence of mythos to the world. Meanwhile, you and Raith were forced to occupy one body—*your* body—so that his therion shifter abilities could be channeled into forcing you to transform whenever the curse took hold. For all the years that you had that curse, Nikki was on her own—everyone she'd ever known and loved slaughtered in the name of preserving a secrecy that I've gone and thrown away—and Raith was little more than a twinkle in the back of your eye, forced to suffer as a sentient non-being whose only real purpose was to make his best friend suffer. And now, after all's been said and done and Nikki's rediscovered her lost lover and Raith's been granted the gift of his very own body, the idea of just hopping into certain death is sort of a sucky notion. That about sum it up?"

Both Zane and Serena stared back at him.

"I'm guessing you didn't read that from a file," Zane grumbled.

Xander shrugged. "I caught a few of the earlier bits and pieces when I was reading up on you two, but—no—the bulk of that was me being uncomfortably invasive."

"And whose mind did you read it from, exactly?" Serena asked, looking nervous.

"All of yours," Xander confessed. "Yours, Zane's, and even Nikki and Raith's."

Zane blinked at that, shaking his head. "They... they're not here yet, are they? No, they couldn't be. We only just talked to them a few—"

"They're still a few days' out," Xander explained. "They're thinking two or three, but it'll be closer to four with all the road blocks and interference they'll come across."

The staring continued.

"Want me to check their blood type now?" Xander asked with a smirk.

Zane laughed and nudged Serena. "See, babe?" he said around chuckles, "*That's* a joke!"

Serena smacked him again, but did nothing to hide her own chuckle. "That really is creepy-as-fuck," she said.

"Yeah. You're telling me," Xander offered, glad that the tension was bleeding away from the conversation.

"So they're still *days* away," Serena speculated, "and you could still pinpoint them *and* read their thoughts? Just like that?"

"And that impresses you?" Xander asked, raising the eyebrow that wasn't hidden under the patch. "I *did* just explain that I've been projecting false memories of myself into the minds of people much, *much* farther away."

Shrugging, Serena said, "I guess you've got a point there. There's just a big difference between hearing you say 'I put memories in far-off folks,' and having you clearly recite the thoughts of people we *know* are several time zones away. I mean—shit, Stryker!—you even *sounded* like Nikki a few times. Didn't he, Zane? Didn't he sound like—"

"Unfortunately," Zane said with a sigh.

Xander cleared his throat and traded one-eyed glances between the Vaileans. "So what was this all about? I feel like there's a question waiting to be asked regarding your friends' agreeing to come out this way."

Serena and Zane shared an uncertain glance. The glance became a long, silent stare. Xander finally realized that they were holding back, hoping that the other would give in and be the one to say what had to be said.

"Well?" Xander pushed.

Serena growled and slapped Zane again. "God-fucking-damn, Zane! See if I let you fuck my shit-chute again after putting me on the spot like this!"

Estella sneered and shivered, mouthing "shit-chute" to herself.

Xander had to resist the urge to laugh.

"I... well, *we*—the Dickless Wonder and I—" Serena started, giving Zane another smack to punctuate the insult, "were wondering what sort of risk Nikki and Raith are facing. We were thinking it might be easier to get them to help if we could promise them they wouldn't..."

Xander frowned and gave Estella a pained glance. "You're asking me"—he sighed and looked down at the table's surface —"if I can tell you whether or not they live or die?"

Neither of the Vaileans said a word.

Xander scratched at his chin and groaned, letting his head fall back so he was staring up at the ceiling. "This, of course, is part of a larger question," he said, not taking his gaze off the ceiling. "That question being whether or not I can tell you whether or not you live or die, whether or not any of us lives or dies. You can deny it. Hell, you can even *mean it* when you deny it. What you think you're thinking and what you're truly thinking are two *very* different things." He sniffled and let his head drop forward so that he could look at the Vaileans once again. "I can't answer that question. Not because I don't want to—god! Do I ever *want* to be able to just *know!*—but because I've seen so many possible paths that I can't even say with any real certainty that *I'll*—" He stopped as he felt Estella's aura spike with concern and looked away. "I'm sorry, guys," he said sincerely. "But I've watched all of us die and I've watched all of us live so many times—over and over and fucking over again!—that I just can't give any one answer for *anybody* that doesn't have about a million '*if*'s attached it. Every outcome is relying on a set of circumstances that I can't even begin to explain. The... shit! The fucking direction the wind's blowing that day *alone* can impact over a thousand outcomes! That, what day it happens, what time of day, the temperature, whether or not Isaac decides to lead with his left foot or his right as we head into battle..." Xander sensed Isaac's aura twitch at that and he considered telling the therion that it was another joke, but then he realized that, no, it wasn't really. "I can't make any promises for you or your friends. Can I say that we could really use their help? Yes, absolutely. Do I want to be an asshole and *lie* so that you'll tell them what they want to hear so we can be certain to get that help? So fucking badly! And how easy would it be for me to just wipe all your minds of everything I've just said and paint a happy fucking illusion of certainty so that any risks I've put into motion with this lunatic rant would vanish in an instant? As easy as one... two—"

Xander stopped in mid-sentence. His heart racing, his breath coming out jagged, his fists clenched...

And his skin burning.

He'd felt this way before.

Something was wrong...

"Xander? Honey?" Estella was reaching out to him, but her hand looked wrong.

Black, bony fingers with putrid ribbons of rotting flesh clinging to the ligaments, the stretching fibers threatening to snap at any moment. The hand wavered, seeming to clench blindly for any possible victim, and Xander spotted an old, familiar ring clinging lazily to the exposed knuckle of the third finger.

He jumped back, crying out.

"WHOA!" he heard Zane call out, heard the legs of his chair slide back as he moved to stand.

"N-no!" Xander trembled and tried to look past the horrible, decaying vision; fought to see Estella—*his* Estella—beyond the grotesque sight. But the skeleton...

The skeleton, sitting where Estella had been moments before, was wearing a red and purple dress.

Xander clenched his eye shut against the horror of what he was seeing.

"No..."

A scream issued, sounding too far away to be coming from inside the room and yet somehow emanating from where Serena was sitting. Except it wasn't just where Serena was sitting, he realized with a rising shudder of sickness; somebody else had been occupying that seat when he'd been at that table in his mind.

Somewhere not far from that he heard a deep, rolling laugh that he didn't want to recognize.

"No..."

"XANDER!" the masculine voice was loud, screaming, but buried under everything else—too little and too far to matter—"SNAP OUT OF IT, MAN! WHAT'S GOTTEN—I"

"XANDER! XANDER, PLEASE HELP! DON'T LET IT HAPPEN TO ME AGAIN!"

That voice...

Don't look... don't look... don't—

Xander let his eye open in Serena Vailean's direction and saw his blood-drenched and sobbing mother crying out to him.

"OH GOD... MOM? NO!"

CHAPTER 21
INSTIGATIONS

"All great things must first wear terrifying and monstrous masks in order to inscribe themselves on the hearts of humanity."
Friedrich Nietzsche (1844-1990)

"WHAT THE FUCK?" Zane said for possibly the hundredth time in under a minute. "WHAT THE FUCK? WHAT THE FUCK? WHAT... THE ACTUAL... FUCK?"

Serena, like her husband, was spewing a singular stream of obscenities, but with no rational beginning or end between the thought patterns it all rolled out as one long trashy sentence filled with anger and confusion and the occasional demand for a Snickers bar. She stood, auric bow and arrow drawn and glowing brightly, and swinging her aim at anything and everything that posed as a potential target.

"Where...?" it was the first time Isaac had spoken, and this was following a lengthy moment of silence on his part wherein he seemed unable to cope with what had happened.

Zoey and Estella, however, couldn't bring themselves to say a word as their auras worked to scan first the immediate area and then, finding no threat within their territory, reaching out further...

Trying to find Xander.

"SERIOUSLY!" Zane roared, "WHAT... THE—"

"Shut the fuck up, already!" Serena hissed at him. "If something just attacked Xander then it's hardly a good idea to act as a beacon to your loud-fucking-mouth!"

"Nothing attacked Xander," Estella assured them. "Not his body, anyway."

"Then what did *that?*" Serena demanded, aiming her auric bow and arrow up towards a gaping hole that had been torn through the ceiling, exposing the night sky above them. The five stared up at the bewildering spectacle, watching as some lingering bits of debris fell free and crashed down on the table, which had been split into three almost equal parts.

"Xander," Estella said, still shaking from the event. "Xander did that."

She watched as Isaac stepped carefully up to the corner of the table where Xander had been seated. Moments before he'd exploded from the room, he had moved as though he meant to jump onto the table. The last thing any of them had seen was him landing on the wooden surface and taking a single step towards the table's center.

Then, in a deafening burst and a tremor that had knocked all but Zane from their seats, the table had been smashed and the ceiling had been blown out. Zane, who'd only remained standing because he'd been standing at the time, was left blinded and coughing under the wave of dust that rained down over him.

After the outburst they'd witnessed from Xander, all of them were certain that they were under attack. Three sets of auras went about clearing the haze, already able to see they were still alone in the room, while Zane and Isaac, coughing and staggering in bewilderment, braced for anything.

"Xander?" Serena asked, shaking her head. "Xander did *that?* He flipped shit at you, called me 'Mom,' and then did *that*" —she pointed at the table and then up at the ceiling—"and *that?*"

Estella didn't take her eyes off the hole in the ceiling as she nodded.

"Why?" Isaac asked.

Estella opened her mouth to answer, but it was Zoey who said, "Aleks. He must have gotten into Xander's head."

Zane shook his head, growling. "Why the fuck would Xander do *that* just because—"

"He said 'Mom,' Zane," Estella hissed at him. "Consider what I told you about his mother and then think *real* carefully about whether or not you want to question how a varcol with untold psychic potential could motivate a response like *that!*"

Zane stared back up at the ceiling and, body beginning to shake and hands working themselves into fists, finally drew back his leg and kicked the portion of shattered table closest to him.

"FUCKING PIECE-OF-SHIT VARCOL ASSHOLE!" he bellowed as the slab of jagged, polished wood crashed against the far wall. "I'LL FUCKING KILL HIM!"

Serena's auric bow and arrow dissipated and withdrew back into her chest as she moved to rub her heaving husband's back. "I'm sure you want to, sweetie," she said in a soothing voice, "but this is a bit much for any of us to handle, I'm afraid."

"Not me," Estella said, still staring up at the hole in the ceiling. "I can fight—"

"You can bottle up that thought and line it up with most of Zane's 'good' ideas on the 'bullshit' shelf, Goddess," Serena said, closing the distance between them and planting a firm grip on her shoulder. "Because you're not going anywhere!"

Estella startled both of them by baring her fangs at Serena then. "And you're going to stop me?"

Serena shivered but did not move away or let go of Estella's shoulder as she said, "N-no... but your baby should."

Estella's knees buckled at that and she forced herself to look back up at the hole in the ceiling. She could barely make out the view around the growing haze of tears.

"Merciful Earth Mother..." she whimpered. "If somebody doesn't get to him and pull him out of his own head there won't be anything to stop Aleks from killing him."

Zane took a step towards the two of them, clearing his throat. "Where can I find him?" he demanded.

Estella turned to face the sound of his voice, unable to see clearly around the tears. "I... Zane, you can't—"

"Don't tell me what I can't do, Estella," Zane growled. "I'm the only one here who isn't pregnant and can cross any kind of distance without turning it into a full-scale hike. So unless you want Bulldog-the-Thundercock and the psychic Sailor Mercury to try hoofing it after your hubby for the next few hours I suggest you tell me where I can find him."

You buried her, Stryker, the oily voice oozed throughout Xander's mind as he raced through the city. *You butchered her and then you buried her beneath the rubble of our home. You should have seen this coming; you really should have.* The laughter that had started inside his head back in the room—back with Estella and the others, now so far behind him it was all barely a memory—cackled on. Broken. Jagged. Heinous. It looped, overlapped, and came in waves, some so slight they seemed almost to have silenced and some so heavy they threatened to throw Xander to his knees. And, ringing over the laughter as though it was nothing more than the backing tune for some awful, taunting chorus, came Aleks' psychic call:

You buried my mother, Stryker, so do not seem so surprised that I've seen fit to dig up yours!

Xander was aware that he was screaming, roaring with such ferocity that he tasted blood in the back of his throat, but he was moving too fast to hear it. Legs pumping, he streaked across rooftops, the tails of his new jacket streaking out behind him and making him look like a right-red comet tearing through the night. He hadn't so much flown out of the room as he'd allowed his aura to shoot him from it like a bullet from a gun barrel. The force had left that accursed table split and the ceiling gaping like a flesh wound. Cutting across the skyline in a wide, shrieking arc, he'd crossed two miles before realizing that he'd even left.

It was another few miles before he managed to convince himself that he *hadn't* really been looking at his mother's corpse occupying Serena's seat; that it *hadn't* really been her cold, dead hand flexing towards him from Estella's arm.

Something deep—too deep to matter—inside of him told him that logic was not a sound replacement for sanity; that many logical decisions were made during unforgivable moments of insanity.

That deep, *deep* voice tried to remind him that he hadn't unlocked the potential within him yet, and that *this* was no way to go about it; it reminded him what happened the last time he'd mixed crazy with power.

Shut... up... Stan! Xander clenched his eye shut—let his aura guide him—and worked to silence that deep, damned voice that insisted on making sense. *Shut the fuck up! I'm going to kill him! KILL HIM!* ***KILL HIM!***

There's much to be said for the tenacity running through your veins, Stryker, Aleks taunted him within his mind. *But it would appear that idiocy is the most dominant gene.*

I'M GOING TO RIP YOU APART! Xander roared back through the connection.

At first, the only response was the laughter. Then, so minute in Xander's mind that he nearly missed it, Aleks said, *Perhaps there's still enough meat left for me to continue what my father started...*

Xander howled in fury.

His aura burst beneath his feet, shooting him into the air again. He flew—as best he could without the focus needed to maintain flight without Stan's full powers unlocked—and used an auric tendril to hook a skyscraper's scaffold. Using this as a tether, he pulled himself towards it, aiming his feet on the building's outer wall. He was already in overdrive once again by the time his boots met the glass. Landing sideways at a full sprint, he cut across the reflective surface, leaving fractured echoes of moonlight behind each footstep, until he felt the ghostly, time-bogged pull of gravity begin to make demands. A part of him wanted to laugh at that, wanted to cackle right along with Aleks.

Nobody made demands of Xander Stryker!

Not even the laws of physics.

That deep voice called to him, told him this wasn't the way.

Xander howled again, this time aiming his rage inward.

Control...

Xander shoved off the skyscraper, leaving what would soon be a series of glass-strewn rooms in his wake. For now, however, with time hanging in an eternal instant, all that broken glass just hung there, miming the shape of the windows they'd once been a part of.

Your mind is like that glass, Stryker, Aleks giggled to him. *Eventually all this momentum's going to die down, and, when it does...*

Won't make a difference if I take you out before that happens, Xander shot back.

Dropping out of overdrive, he let himself slip into a freefall through the night. Though flying was proving difficult with limited focus, he *could* do a decent job of gliding, he discovered. Physics might not want to be defied by one with a broken mind, it seemed, but it didn't mind bending a little for one. Angling himself, Xander used an auric tendril as a rudder while adjusting currents of air around him to steer. Bursts of heat pockets and willed cyclones—things he'd used in the past during combat—became makeshift means of generating lift and thrust. True to Zoey's claims, though his new coat *should* have been tugging and pulling with every new shift, Xander tore through the air totally unobstructed. Moreover, though the crosswinds and currents would have been enough to batter his body as he barreled through the air, he found that the material let all of the potential pressure glide off of him. The same, however, could not be said for his face. His leather-tied ponytail had begun a vicious windmill cycle that slapped his shoulders and tugged at his scalp with each rotation, and his cheeks and eye had begun to burn from the relentless stream of air.

The tears in his eye, however, he wasn't so certain he could blame on his high speeds through the night sky.

Oh my... Aleks cooed in his head. *I seem to have found something shiny!*

This was enough to shatter the small bits of focus keeping Xander aloft, and he slipped in the middle of trying to steer himself and wound up in a midair spiral that drove him into an angled rooftop. A series of solar panels tore free, upturned, and clattered with mad fury along with Xander's body. Glass and metal peppered his back, but he more heard than felt the bombardment as Zoey's jacket held against the onslaught. Without the distraction of what was happening behind him, Xander spotted the ledge where this new building's roof dropped out into a vertical fall. Beneath, over forty stories below, the once bustling city streets waited, dark and foreboding and hiding more predators than ever before. Leaping free and directing his fall to a neighboring rooftop, Xander let the debris spill over, seeing in a flash that the resulting hailstorm of busted solar paneling would scare off a cluster of Cebourist-wannabe militants.

If left unchecked, they'd find a pair of fresh victims in just under ten minutes.

Xander landed, rolled to his feet, and jumped back into overdrive as he aimed himself for the cemetery on the outskirts of the city.

He wouldn't get to hear the militants fleeing in terror.

ZANE WAS THANKFUL THAT, after all of his boasting and assurances to Estella, there was nobody around to see him. He was winded, and he was lost. Worst of all, he was...

Not as alone as your dumb ass would like to think! Serena's voice roared in his head.

At first he was mortified that his wife was laughing at him, but after a sharp static whine that had him flinching in the same way a smack to the chest had him cringing he realized that, nope, she was pissed at him.

Please don't, Serena, he thought, sure she was still in his head to "hear" it. *I got... I got turned around, that's all. Please don't tell Estella. Oh... oh fuck, she's not in my head, too, is she? Please tell me she's not—*

She's not, Zoey's psychic voice rang in his head, *but I am.*

Fuck... Zane thought.

"Fuck" is right, ya fucking fucker! Serena barked at him, *You made some big, tough-guy show about how you were gonna go get that sweet goddess' husband back and now you're standing in the middle of the street with your fucking thumb up your ass! What is it with dipshit gorilla men and not being able to follow directions? Huh? I mean—fuck!—you'd think with you dick-swingers being so adamant about* not *asking for directions that you'd at least have brains enough to fucking* follow *them in the first place! You dumb fucking sack of—*

Serena? Zane had to struggle to get the thought to the surface of his mind around the psychic onslaught from his wife.

Yes, dear? Serena said, sounding a little too much like something out of the Stepford Wives for his liking.

Kindly shut the fuck up. For once in your ceaseless, chatter-riddled existence, just stop talking. If you're not going to start being helpful, then strain real, real *hard and work on not saying anything. Kay? I don't care how many muscles you have to pull or how gray your hair goes from the effort—just shut the fuck up.*

An uncomfortable silence followed as Zane tried to determine which way was North. Starlight was practically nonexistent with all the ambient lighting of the city and, with all the looming buildings surrounding him, he couldn't even get a bead on the moon. He'd left with a relatively sound notion of direction and, after Estella pointed out the cemetery on a map of the area, he was certain it wouldn't be hard to make it there in a zig-zagging bee-line.

What he *hadn't* considered was that the harbor their little community was being built on occupied a good chunk of what should have been that simple bee-line, which forced him to horseshoe around nearly half of the coastline before getting back on course. That was when he discovered that, while it all looked so crisp and simple on an overhead view of the city, a vast inky body of water to his right and block-after-block of what appeared to be the exact same buildings to his left had an eerie way of creating a monotonous sense of being nowhere and everywhere at the exact same time. Over and over he had to convince himself that there was no way he'd managed to circle the entire body of water—*it has to open up to the sea* somewhere, *doesn't it?* he reminded himself—and, with that being the case, he couldn't have gone as far as he felt he had.

And yet he felt like he'd already overshot the path and gotten himself pointed in the wrong direction.

Zoe, he thought-projected, *you still there?*

More or less, she called back. *Serena's talking Estella's ear off—thankfully keeping her preoccupied and feeling confident that everything will be okay—but she keeps clenching her fists and shaking whenever she's not looking. I think you might have really pissed her—*

"Pissed"? "PISSED"? Serena's voice roared in Zane's head, and he realized that he'd become a sort of psychic bridge for the two's chatter. *Did you hear what he fucking said to me? Did you hear* how *he said it to me?* Zane cringed, certain he was in for an ass-kicking when he got back. *HOLY SHIT, ZOE! That was so fucking hot! He sounded, like, totally fucking rugged and fierce! So badass and, y'know,* grr*-like! Like a big, fuckable bear or some hot-as-balls lion or something! By Channing Tatum's cum-drenched danglers, I hope he comes home and fucks me* hard *after that! Maybe he'll even spank me with his belt and pull my hair! FUCK! Maybe I can get him to fist my—*

JESUS FUCKING CHRIST, SERENA! Zane wasn't sure which was worse: the fact that Serena was back to distracting him during this dire moment or that she was giving him an erection in the street. *Can somebody* please *help get me back on the right path?*

THE CEMETERY.

Xander had avoided going there for a long time because of the guilt he felt whenever he looked upon his mother's gravestone. (Granted, the guilt was there all the same without the benefit of visiting the cemetery in the first place.) Then, as years passed, the guilt was joined by a heavy, crippling loneliness. The cemetery—and, as far as Xander was concerned, any cemetery, for that matter—was a painfully lonely place. Encased in a box and cast into the dirt, it was a place for those permanently occupying it to be just as permanently alone. And for those visiting, momentary though it may be be, it only ever served as a reminder of loss. It was impossible to look upon those markers and not feel a sense of emptiness that no stone, no matter how beautifully its poetry might resound, could fill.

Xander could remember the face of his mother's tombstone better than he could remember her own face; could describe the feel of its cold, course surface better than any memory would let him remember the feel of her touch.

All those embraces, all those goodnight kisses, each and every time she'd held his hand on one of their walks...

All overwhelmed by the texture of cold, lifeless stone.

The cemetery...

Xander had only visited here a handful of times since the night he'd killed Kyle. On that night, kneeling before her gravestone, he'd talked to her, he'd cried, and he'd ceremoniously buried the ruby pendant—*her* ruby pendant—after years of carrying it with him.

He'd hoped that, in doing so, he was serving some dual purpose: returning it to its rightful owner while also casting away something that had become a personal symbol of his self-loathing.

That his self-loathing had insisted on relentlessly clinging to him since that night was proof enough that at least *half* of his good intentions had been for nothing.

It was only a matter of time, he supposed, before the second half came around to bite him in the ass. The pendant hadn't switched hands—it hadn't been in the possession of a new owner, let alone a rightful owner—it had only been cast into the dirt a few feet above somebody who was every bit the property of that cemetery as the rest of the cadavers planted beneath its soil.

This thought only served to cement Xander's convictions as he jumped over the chained-up gate in much the same way he had the night of Kyle's death. His feet left the ground in a place of life and potential and landed in a place of guilt and loneliness.

And, sure enough, he was met by all sorts of reasons to feel guilty and lonely...

His mother's gravestone, familiar as it had become, was

nearly unrecognizable. Like the awful table he'd left behind, it had been shattered; fragments of varying sizes littering the upturned earth around where it had once stood. A set of deep, savage claw marks tore across two of the segments, carving out the name.

"Emily Stryker..." Xander whispered aloud in its written absence, the sight conjuring a new sort of guilt within him.

"I have to imagine," a familiar voice spoke in a casual, nearly friendly tone to his left, "that she was quite a looker in life."

Trembling with rage, Xander turned to face Aleks. He was seated atop one of the taller gravestones, a large, marble cross, in a near-squat, using either side of the horizontal stone as footholds while he rested his bottom on its squared peak. Around his neck, Xander could see the ruby of his mother's pendant flickering as it wavered against his chest. The elbow of his left arm rested on his knee, the palm upturned to cup his bored-looking face. His right hand, hanging lazily in front of him, was still holding...

Xander's eyes widened.

"I'll admit it's hard to tell now," Aleks mused, raising his hand to bounce the skull with a casual playfulness in his palm. A few lifeless patches of wiry hair skirted about; waving in the first breaths of open air they'd felt in over a decade. "But she managed to get your daddy's attention, right? And mine, of course," he chuckled at this as though it was a simple, innocent joke. "And if my mother's stories were any indicator," he went on, pausing to look the skull in the face, "she got the blood pumping in quite a few other gentlemen just before my father—"

Xander roared and lunged into overdrive at the varcol.

His mother's skull exploded against his face, knocking him off his feet, out of overdrive, and into a new layer of guilt and loneliness. He coughed, hacking on bone dust and dead hair, and worked to stand.

SERENA FLINCHED as Estella loosed a shriek that had her convinced they were all about to die. Any aspect of "how" they were about to die or "why" they were about to die was irrelevant—gone the way of the dodo, the Macarena, and UGG boots (if Serena had her way, at least)—because, with a scream *that* blood-curdling and awful, there was no fucking way that absolute and certain demise wasn't coming.

Death didn't come.

And the screaming didn't stop.

"WHAT THE BALLS?" Serena, still in mid-duck from what she was sure was an incoming attack, had to scream to be heard over Estella's howls.

Terror.

What she was hearing, Serena realized, was terror.

Zoey, always a step ahead with tact (if not a few steps behind with sass), reached Estella's side a moment before Serena. Clapping a left hand over the hysterical vampire's back, she began to draw in energy—working to calm some of... well, whatever the hell it was that was doing *that* to her.

"Fucking hell!" Serena's body was on high-alert, the sound of her friend's screams triggering her empathy and working her into a panic without even knowing *why*. "What's happening to—"

Estella's back pitched as she moved to push Zoey away. Zoey, however, having her fair share of experience with this sort of process didn't budge, holding fast and continuing her efforts.

If she can stay planted on Isaac's cock then not a bull on earth could shake her, Serena thought.

In a flash of orange that was *nothing* like what any bull or Isaac could accomplish, Estella's aura rocketed out. Both Zoey and Serena were knocked back and sent tumbling. Serena, lucky enough to *not* be the first to Estella, had been granted enough of a warning from the impact against Zoey to brace herself using her own aura. It was enough to keep her (mostly) upright—if not entirely planted on her ass—and allowed her to catch Zoey before the force threw her into the wall.

"XANDER!" Estella cried out, scrambling to pull herself from the chair she'd been sitting in.

She only managed to kick the furniture out from under her, sending her toppling in a crooked heap to the floor. Her palms slapped the floorboard, stopping her forehead from doing the same. Her blue eyes blinked, taking in what Serena was certain was an old, scuffed floor, and the shrieks began once again.

"What in the hell...?" Serena narrowed her eyes at the sight. Whipping around to face Zoey, she demanded, "What the fuck did you see in the short moment you were in her head?"

"I..." Zoey was panting, dazed from the impact of Estella's aura, "I'm not sure. It was... *most* of it was a blur, but I *did* see Mess— *Aleks!*" she shook her head and quickly corrected. "I saw Aleks in a graveyard and..." she squinted, shaking her head. "I'm not sure past that. It all seemed shaky, and everything was blurred with... with..."

"Fucking shit, Zoe!" Serena growled, "This ain't suspense-hour, where we circle 'round and lick Stephen King's puckered rectal-ring! OUT WITH IT!"

"Dammit, Serena," Zoey's voice was strained, frantic; her face flush and tight with concentration. "I... DON'T... KNOW! Everything seemed... red."

Serena blinked and looked back at Estella, cursing under her breath. "Shit!" she hissed, hurrying towards her. "I *knew* she seemed distant when I was talking to her."

What? Zoey called after her in thought-speak, knowing that Serena would already be focusing her ears on trying to communicate aloud with Estella. *What do you mean?*

It's that fucking spell, Zoe, Serena explained as she dropped to her knees in front of Estella and worked to pull her into a tight embrace. "Shh, shh! Come back to us, Goddess; come back to us. You can't do this to yourself!" she whispered aloud. Back to

Zoey she projected, *She's been watching everything through Xander's eyes again. Whatever's happening on his end must have been* really *fucked up.*

Then why couldn't I see whatever it was? Zoey demanded.

Serena continued to try to soothe her friend. *You spent much time poking around in Xander's head?* she asked.

Zoey's aura noticeably tensed from across the room. *N-no...*

Even though you have a tendency to build a psychic profile on everyone *you meet?* Serena pressed, beginning to stroke Estella's hair. Again she whispered to her to come back to them; to leave Xander to handle the bad things like he always did.

The screams had begun to die down to high-pitched whimpers that exploded out in random intervals around labored panting.

I tried a few times, sure, Zoey admitted.

But... Serena challenged, already knowing the answer.

Zoey's aura sagged in defeat behind her.

Too fucked-up in there to linger, I bet. Assuming that you can even snake an auric probe in there in the first place, right? Have an easier time working a greased-up pinky up a nun's stink-tunnel.

Zoey's aura flinched. Ignoring the subject of her vulgarity, Zoey "said," *That still doesn't explain why I shouldn't have been able to* see *whatever it was that Estella saw!*

Fuckin' A, yes it goddam does, Zoey, Serena shot a stern glance over her shoulder. *We can barely stomach taking a peek through the tinted windows into that boy's mind. Estella was just* living *in his head—seeing his sights, thinking his thoughts, feeling his... Fuck, Zoe, don't you get it? She* is *Xander when she casts that spell. She experiences firsthand and fully immersed in what we can't even bare to squint at from a fucking distance.* Serena paused to tighten her hold as Estella began to squirm, groaning and repeating Xander's name over and over again. "No, no, Goddess," she warned, pulling Estella's face to her breasts to try to stifle the chant, certain she was trying to return to her husband's mind. "You gotta stay here with us. Don't go back there. Don't!"

Oh my... Zoey trailed off, considering the impact of the spell. A moment later, Serena felt her kneel down beside her, then her own arms worked their way around Estella.

"I'm so sorry, Estella," she whispered. "Whatever it is you saw... I'm sorry you did."

Estella's voice was a tortured rasp as she struggled to look up at the two of them. Her face was damp from a smearing of sweat and tears and snot. Serena wasn't sure how, but she still looked beautiful.

"H-h-his m-mo..." her mouth drew open in a silent scream, held a moment as though her jaw had locked, and then trembled with a new series of rattling sobs. "Oh gods..." she wheezed, "Aleks... h-he got to his mother!"

For the first time in Serena's life, she found herself without a stream of vulgarity to reflect what she'd just heard.

The unprecedented moment of silence, unfortunately, was short lived.

There was a knock at the door.

Three sets of eyes—wearing masks of chaos, confusion, and sorrow—drifted to it as it opened and a slender, young Indian girl poked her head inside. Though Serena was certain there was no way she could understand what sort of fucked up shit-show she'd just politely entered into, her morose expression and compressed pink aura said otherwise.

Serena worked to hide Estella from the newcomer's view, but a small, pale hand caught her and kept her efforts.

Estella, still looking like a Catholic prom queen wearing a two-ton tiara made of dog shit, forced herself to ask, "What is it, Sana?"

"I..." stammered the Indian girl—Sana, as it turned out; *Man!* Serena thought, *My dumb, blonde ass has gotta start learning these folks' names!*—"I-it's The Council. They... they just landed on a private airstrip outside of town."

"I see..." Estella's voice sounded hollow, distant. Serena wondered if she even cared about them or the threat they presented at that moment. "How long until they arrive?" she finally asked.

"Two... maybe three hours," Sana answered.

Estella nodded.

Sana lingered in the doorway, glancing between the three inhabitants in the demolished room. Finally she locked her gaze on Serena.

Is there anything I can do to help her? her voice rang with startling clarity in Serena's head.

How old are you, kid? Serena asked her, then immediately realized the question came off rude. *It's just... this is some heavy shit, and I don't think it's right to drop a clusterfuck on a kid's lap if it can be avoided.*

I'm old enough, Sana told her, and while there was no edge to the response Serena was pleasantly surprised by the edge of sass it carried.

Kid's got potential, she thought privately.

More than you know, Sana responded, proving that she'd managed to slip Serena's defenses and "overhear" a private thought with no effort.

Despite everything, Serena smirked at her and nodded. *You wanna help?* she asked, then, without waiting for an answer, said, *Stall those Council-fucks.*

Sana nodded and closed the door. Soon after the *click* of the latch, Serena heard her voice announce, *I can stretch that two or three hours into a solid three if you want me to be subtle about it.*

And if I couldn't give a rat's piss-stained nutsack about subtlety? Serena called back.

Sana's response actually earned a smile from Serena.

"What?" Estella croaked up at her. "What did she say?"

Because *of course* the wife of Xander-fucking-Stryker wouldn't be so naïve as to think that Serena and the Indian auric were just making faces at each other. Serena, still smiling, rolled her eyes at herself.

"Kid says she can stall The Council 'til daybreak," she told her.

Zoey frowned at that. "They're not going to like being interfered with," she warned.

Serena scoffed and shook her head. "We're talking about a group of stuffed-shirts so full of themselves that they actually capitalize the fucking word 'the' in 'The Council,' Zoe. They probably kick the dog if their pencils aren't sharpened evenly. Fuck, I'm sure even their hemorrhoids take Xanax." She waved a dismissive hand at the matter and began lightly rubbing Estella's back. "I'm not about to have us walking on eggshells about whether or not the people coming to kill us are cozy with their drive when the one who knows how to keep them from killing us is facing who-knows-what. With any luck they'll stroke out before they get here and we'll be off the hook. In the meantime, make sure my idiot husband finds that cemetery while I help the goddess here, alright?"

A NEON-BLUE AURA, every bit as annoying and painful on the eyes —*eye!*—as the lights of an insisting city, slammed into Xander like a truck. It tore him off the ground, where he'd been kneeling and working to cope with more pain and rage than he knew what to do with, and began carrying him with all the delicacy of a rampaging wild animal. Tombstones and skeletal trees exploded against his back as he was driven through them, but his new jacket dulled the impacts. What would have likely begun tearing muscle and breaking vertebrae instead only knocked the breath from his lungs. This, however, didn't bother Xander much, as he'd been working to hold his breath since he'd first realized he was hacking on bone dust.

His *mother's* bone dust...

Another roar burst from his tortured chest. Through his mind's eye, he saw the old, jagged stretch of the cemetery's barred fence racing up behind him. The series of tall, time-warped iron rods would not give as easy as old tombstones, he knew; would not uproot and splinter like seasonally weakened trees. Not wanting to see how well Zoey's gift held up against being slammed into the iron bars by the stampeding auric force, Xander used his own aura to right himself in midair—twisting his body and planting his feet beneath him. Earth and stone exploded in twin bursts from the toes of his boots as he worked to secure a foothold on the ground; the relentless force not waning in the least. Xander slapped his palms together before his chest, creating a physical point to focus his aura, and pushed out with both his hands; a bolt of red-and-black emerged, wicked and moving with murderous intent. His aura lanced the obnoxious blue wall, splitting it and sending it splaying out on either side of him. Behind him—uncomfortably close for his liking—he heard the iron bars whine and shriek as the bifurcated auric wall crashed into them.

Xander had less than two seconds to celebrate his freedom from what had felt like a vengeful wall of Vegas lights before a therion the size of a small truck tackled him from the side. Jaws snapped inches from his face, and he found himself thankful for his missing eye and the lack of periphery. The last thing he wanted to see was the inside of the snarling mythos' gullet—listening to it was bad enough. Razor sharp claws tried to sink into the meat of his torso, but Xander's new jacket refused to let them pass through. As the two of them crashed to the ground, the therion's lack of grip forced him to slip away. It growled, irritated, and moved to spin back around to face him. Xander darted to the side, following its turn to keep himself in its blind spot, and drove the heel of one of his dirt-caked boots up between the hulking monster's thighs.

The kick connected.

The therion howled, the pitch higher than before, and faltered to one of its massive knees. Xander threw an overdrive-fueled punch through the creature's back, digging through meat and bone. He'd wanted to tear out the therion's heart, but he realized he'd missed his mark when his fingers grazed the inner length of one of its ribs. Not about to be deterred, Xander took hold of this and yanked his arm back. He didn't draw his arm back with the therion's heart, but he did draw his arm back after embedding a pointy length of bone through that heart. It took a bit of awkward maneuvering, sure, but after being caught off guard and getting an earful of snarls and slobber he was willing to put forth the extra effort.

Why in the hell didn't I see that—

As if to punctuate his curiosity, Xander's insight failed him yet again as the familiar, neon blue aura ensnared him and hurled him straight up into the air. Unsure of *how* both his mind's eye and his more recent "cosmically keen" powers of insight weren't alerting him to all of these threats, he focused instead on *why* the auric had worked to catch him off guard only to throw him harmlessly a few meters into the...

Something caught his ankles, yanking him back down with enough force to make his head snap back as he careened back towards the ground. A pair of sangs—one built like a bullet and the other like a sledgehammer—were waiting for him there. The sledgehammer-vamp, who still had a firm grip on his ankles, began to spin him in a wide, whipping circle. Xander didn't need his powers to know that the bullet-vamp would likely be waiting at the end of that circle. Prepared for this, Xander jumped into overdrive. All at once the blurred world froze in his eyes—*eye!*—and, sure enough, he caught sight of the second vampire waiting, a pointed fist already hanging, frozen, in mid-punch. Not even one second (in real-time, at least) away from having the side of his head caved in. Retrieving Yang—thankful that he'd been mindful enough to carry at least his revolver on him at all times; a lesson that had, unfortunately, taken him a long time to learn—Xander planted the bone-white barrel against the waiting fist and pulled the trigger.

Being frozen in time, nothing happened.

This, however, was part of the plan.

Releasing the revolver's grip and letting it hang in midair and mid-fire, Xander considered the bullet-vamp, in the instant to follow, more-or-less dealt with. Turning his hyper-sped focus on the sledgehammer-vamp swinging him from his ankles, Xander focused a narrow tendril of his aura to act.

Once satisfied, he twisted his ankles free of the time-frozen grip and braced for what was certain to be a bloody mess.

Easing out of overdrive, letting time begin to creep back into being rather than simply exploding into existence, he heard the strained groan of the gunshot beginning a short distance from his face. Catching Yang's grip, he let the enchanted hollow point crawl out of the barrel and tear into the other vampire's steadily creeping fist.

Though it all happened in slow-motion for Xander, the two vampires' auras flashed with alarm as, in what should have been an insubstantial instant that *should* have ended with the infamous Xander Stryker's brains caked on a set of knuckles, a deadly fist became a gushing stump. The sledgehammer-vamp, beginning to realize that he'd lost his grip on his quarry, tried to gasp as his comrade began wailing. No sound came. Instead, a spurt of blood burst from his throat through the narrow hole that Xander had put there with his aura.

Panic flooded the sledgehammer-vamp's aura as the reality of his fate slammed down on him, and more bursts of blood arced out from his throat as he fought to breathe. The bullet-vamp, too wrapped up in his own problems, watched as his forearm was steadily consumed by the enchantment from the bullet that had already blown off his hand. Flesh and muscle sizzled away, reminding Xander of a cigarette burning away to nothing, as bone crumbled shortly after it.

To his right, through the periphery he still possessed, Xander caught a flash of neon blue. Though something—*Or someone!* he considered—was still hindering the Great

Machine's visions, his common sense was still strong. Roping both of the panicking vampires in a pair of auric tendrils, Xander yanked them into the incoming aura's path. The two's already pained cries and gurgles were laced with confusion as something they couldn't see began to crush them.

Realizing that their attack had fallen upon two of their own, the mystery auric withdrew their aura; the headache-inducing neon glare flashing out of existence as it was withdrawn back to its source. Grinning, Xander followed its path and spotted a coattail vanish behind a large gravestone.

There you are! he thought, casting out his own aura in much the same "runaway truck"-fashion in their direction.

The gravestone exploded into pebbles as the auric was flung off their—*her!*—feet. Watching the black-clad body tumble through the air against the wall of semitransparent red-and-black, Xander willed his aura to fold over around her. He imagined a housefly being crushed between the pages of a book as it was slammed shut. And then, just like that, it was done.

Withdrawing his own aura back into his chest, Xander saw Aleks casually strolling his way, tapping the fingertips of his right hand against the open palm of his left in a condescending mock-applause.

"Fabulous," he said with no hint of pride nor despair on his voice. He didn't care that Xander had just slain some of his followers, and he certainly didn't seem to have taken any real enjoyment from watching him fight. Instead, Xander realized, he seemed to be considering what he'd seen in much the same way he imagined a scientist scrutinizing over a test subject. "I'll admit, Stryker, I was disappointed when I thought I'd killed you after that little stunt you pulled. Well, maybe not so little," he grinned, "you *did,* after all, manage to throw the entire world into a frenzy in just a few short minutes. I almost wish I'd thought of it, but I prefer to do things the smart way. In either case—"

Xander roared and jumped into overdrive, poised to drive his fist into Aleks' face.

The varcol, however, had vanished.

"*In either case,*" Aleks repeated from behind him, sounding impatient, "I *was* disappointed that I didn't get to see more of what you had to offer. My entire life I've known *nothing* but hate for you—hate for all Strykers, honestly."

Xander lunged again, and again Aleks effortlessly moved to a new location only a few paces away.

"My mother raised me on a steady diet: fed entirely from her breasts and from her scorn for your father. *My* father," he paused to let out an angry sigh, shaking his head, "never has a boy been so close and yet so far from a parent. He could stand at the castle gates or beneath one of our windows, yes, and we could even communicate. It was all up here, of course," he knocked at the side of his head and sneered. "I can't say that I ever heard my father's voice. That's something I—"

Another attempted strike. Another failure.

"*That,*" he groaned, "is bothersome."

"Stop... talking!" Xander growled around labored breaths.

"And I suppose this is your attempt at enforcing that demand? Look at you! You can barely stand at this point! Meanwhile, if I so desired, I could *walk* right through you—twist your insides and rearrange everything holding you together until not even the best of us could recognize you as meat."

"Then why don't you?" Xander demanded.

Aleks rolled his eyes. "Let me tell you something about myself, Stryker: I prefer the chase. All predators do. You're no different, and don't bore me by trying to claim otherwise. Luring you into my traps has been more fun than the few times now that I've nearly ended your life."

Xander remembered Aleks, then known only as "Messiah," goading him into a one-on-too-many-to-count battle against a horde of mind-enslaved humans. Shortly after, in a flash of movement that not even Xander's overdrive could follow, he'd been beaten nearly to death. Then, adding insult to sizable injury, Aleks had healed Xander so that he could lure him into yet another trap.

Aleks nodded, and Xander knew that he was seeing into his head, watching the memories, and telling him that, yes, that was the motivation all along.

"You see," he said, making a note of leaning against a tombstone and folding his arms across his chest, "you were supposed to be my favorite toy. My entire life had been spent in that castle. I knew nothing but starvation! I was starved from nourishment *and* from an identity! My mother..." he shivered, "She loved no one but herself, Stryker. By the time I'd been born, she'd eaten all the others; everybody else that your father and that devil-man had trapped inside that castle had been killed, consumed, and turned to shit before I was even born!" Aleks bared a set of teeth that should have been in a shark's mouth. "Even that shit had known more purpose than me, Stryker."

"You're breaking my heart," Xander growled at him. "Why don't you let me put you out of that misery?"

"Charitable, but no," Aleks dismissed with a smile, now showing teeth that appeared perfectly normal. "You see, my kind are not without our own burdens. I won't call them weaknesses—no, no, no; we're delightfully free of those, as your wife has proven with her stolen blood—but they are... hmm, inconvenient. For starters, as you already know, we're *dreadfully* resilient. That means that, born into an empty castle that wouldn't even allow vermin to pass, the only blood I ever got to taste was my own. If I'd ever been so reckless as a babe to *bite* the breast my mother fed me from, I'm sure she'd have thrown me down the stone steps to her bath hall. And, even as a babe, I'd have lived," he beamed at that and said, "Resilient, like I said." Then, cocking his head, he offered a perverse leer and rubbed his palms together. "You remember my mother's bath hall, yes? Where you first laid eyes on her; *all* of her," he groaned around the word "all" and finished by dragging a sickeningly elongated tongue over his lips.

Xander sneered.

Aleks glared at him. "She offered herself to you, Stryker, despite her hate for you and everything you are; offered you her flesh as a trade to release us."

"I still got her flesh," Xander growled back at him. "I was picking chunks of it out—"

Xander wasn't sure when Aleks had taken him by the throat and hoisted him into the air, but he vaguely recalled the words "it" and "out" feeling a bit strained before his sentence was interrupted entirely.

"For a sniveling little punk who gets red-faced and roar-happy at the first mention of his pathetic piglet of a mother," a deep, bellowing voice emanated from the too-wide, fanged maw that Aleks' face had become, "you're quite careless with your words regarding others'."

Xander gurgled around the grip on his throat. Realizing he couldn't speak, he simply thought, *Must have* really *pissed you and Mommy off that your auric turd of a father was taking a Stryker's sloppy seconds, huh?*

The howl that bellowed from Aleks resonated on a personal level with Xander. Then he was airborne, careening through the cemetery.

This time, he couldn't stop himself from crashing into the time-warped iron gate.

Aleks was already crouched there, waiting over his slumped body.

"Why did I not kill you just now?" he demanded.

"Uhhng..." Xander groaned, half-whimpering with his face pressed to the cold, acrid earth. "B-because... you're not done playing?" he tested.

Aleks kicked him, but not hard enough to injure him. The jacket, taking a fair share of the impact, actually reduced it to nothing more than a sharp ache.

Obviously sensing this, Aleks kicked him again. This time harder.

"At least you know how to listen, Stryker," Aleks heaved, taking three heavy steps away before turning back to face him. "As I was saying: my kind have their flaws. They don't die easily, meaning I had the pleasure of surviving over twenty years without ever knowing a full meal. Yes, I got to drain the auras of an occasional wanderer—a lost traveler or perhaps one of my mother's less-than-useful servants who'd decided to pay an untimely visit to the castle walls—but even you, a weak offshoot of our glory, know such a thing would be insufficient. And all the while I heard nothing but my mother's tireless rants of *you*—of your bloodline, of your father, and of how we needed *you*; early on: of how my father would deliver *you,* then of how my father *failed* us by *not* delivering *you,* and, finally, of how my father had been slain by *you!* You, you, you! Some pitiful half-breed who's only true hold to glory was a watered-down evolutionary accident. Joseph Stryker... *BAH!* On and on and on! Because, Stryker, along with our resilience, varcols are *painfully* driven and independent. You take my mother—a proud, powerful, insightful varcol with aspirations to assume her rightful role as a goddess and rule this world as she saw fit—and trap her with a child, and you can be certain that child will know of nothing else but what her hearts desired. Her goals became my goals, her hate became my hate; I knew nothing else! And the only pause to her vendetta that I was offered in all that time was when her physical demands grew too great and she took from me what she wanted—my blood, my energy, my body—" he glared at Xander, "because we both know that she *needed* none of it—not to survive, no—but she knew that being her food when she hungered and her flesh when she lusted was a surefire way to ensure that I'd be her minion when she finally got her claws into you and we were free. And then, Stryker, you and your pretty little wife showed up... and killed her."

"Sounds like I did you a favor," Xander groaned, rolling onto his back. "Your mother fed from you, raped you, let you starve, and all the while tormented you with her obsession? So why hate me for freeing you from that?"

Aleks appeared over him again, kicking him repeatedly. "BECAUSE THAT WAS ALL THE LIFE I'D EVER KNOWN!" he roared. Then, pausing, he knelt down, carefully brushed a bang from Xander's face, and planted a long, soft kiss on his still-gasping lips. "Except, Stryker—*EXCEPT*—for the obsession, *her* obsession, that she passed on to me. Because, in killing her—in taking the life from the one who used me as little more than an extension of herself—you gave me the opportunity to take her dream—take her *hate*... and make it—and you—mine; conquering you will almost be a greater victory than conquering this world!" He gave Xander's face a few harsh, stinging slaps. "I am your opposite, Xander Stryker; the Yin to your Yang," as he said this, he reached under his knee-length, black dress jacket and pulled out a familiar black revolver.

Yin...

Xander had had a preference for it years earlier, in his former life, when his thoughts were as dark and foreboding as the gun's sheen. After he'd been reborn, however, he'd come to wield both with the balance of their namesake. He liked to think he was doing right by his father's memory—his legacy—and, once again, rogue mythos looked in horror at the eight-chambered, black-and-white duo with fear. Then, too soon, he'd lost Yin—supposedly crushed under however-many-tons of debris—leaving him with its pearly-white sibling. At the time, this had seemed symbolic in its own right.

Goodbye, dark thoughts...

Right?

But denial only went so far in the realm of symbolism, and when the original point of the actual symbol was balance—light and dark; right and wrong; love and hate—there was no denying what the loss represented. Whether or not it was only symbolism, though—they *were* just guns at the end of the day, after all—Xander *had* felt imbalanced. The revolver's weight under his left arm was a constant reminder that there was none under his right, and that very real imbalance echoed in his mind not as a cosmic punishment, but as a sign that he'd already failed to live up to his father's legacy.

But symbols never died, it appeared.

And neither, as it turned out, did coal-black revolvers.

It wasn't up to Xander to decide if there was some sort of cosmic merit to the symbolism. He certainly didn't believe that there was. But, then again, Xander had gone most of his life not believing in vampires, werewolves, or that he'd ever find a purpose in life. So maybe there was something to all that symbol business, or maybe he was just looking too deeply into things when he *should* have been more worried about the reality of the loaded gun staring him right in the face.

I thought I'd lost that... Xander thought absently.

You did lose it, Aleks replied in his head as he thumbed back the hammer. Then, out loud, he said, "Where you gave in to despair, I was strengthened by it. Where you blinded yourself to potential, I taught myself to know nothing else. And where you failed to live up to the legacy of your bloodline... I snatched it at the first chance and made it mine." He stood, leveling the barrel of the long-lost Yin at Xander's head.

Seeing the coal-black, eight-chambered weapon left Xander with mixed emotions.

He was elated to see that his father's old gun *hadn't* been destroyed as he'd thought; that, in fact, the famed revolver set Yin and Yang had *not* been rendered halved and incomplete years earlier...

But he wasn't exactly thrilled to be looking down the barrel.

As far as familiar sights went, this one wasn't a welcome one.

Glancing beyond the gun aimed at his face, Xander could see his mother's stolen pendant, its ruby catching the needles of moonlight and shining like fresh blood, and, beyond that, the determined face of the varcol who meant to destroy the world.

The Great Machine sputtered and coughed as the chokehold that Aleks unknowingly had on It began to wane. Now that it was no longer a priority, he was beginning to release his auric binding, what had been concealing his lackeys' presence and intentions from Xander's mind's eye.

Suddenly *seeing* wasn't a problem for him.

And then, beginning to work his own concealment binding, Xander Stryker started to laugh.

ZANE HAD ALWAYS KNOWN that Xander was a bit... off.

And—for fuck's sake—who could blame the little punker? Zane was a bit off his rocker, too, and he wasn't sporting the sort of history Xander was. Hell, if Campbell's wanted to start an ad campaign that targeted traumatized orphans with histories of mental and physical abuse for a new line of "It'll Get Better... *Maybe*"-alphabet soup, then Stryker would have been their perfect spokesperson—his face, rocking a chicken broth teardrop hanging from one blood-red eye, would be emblazoned on the cans; and surely any heartbroken folks who'd managed to stay alive up 'til that point would be clamoring to fill their shopping carts.

But this wasn't an audition for Campbell's "Cup-o'-Tears."

This looked more like an execution.

And Xander-fucking-Stryker was *laughing* in the face of the varcol holding the gun!

What the fuck, Xander? Zane thought, working to climb the rest of the way over the cemetery gate without giving himself away. *You finally gone and lost what little of your mind you had left?*

What's happening? Zoey asked, still maintaining the connection she'd held with him to guide him that far.

Zane paused to focus on the sight, creating a mental snapshot of it for Zoey to see as a thought.

Oh no...

Zane slipped inside the cemetery and darted behind one of the nearest tombstones large enough to hide his bulk. *"Oh no" is right, Zoe. What the fuck am I going to do? I can't fight that guy—I can't even sneak up on...* his thoughts trailed off as another thought occurred to him. *Why hasn't he noticed me yet?*

There was a crackle of mental static, the psychic equivalent of an awkward silence, and Zoey finally asked, *You mean Aleks* doesn't *know you're there?*

Zane shook his head, then wondered why. *Not that I know of. Cocksucker would have at least glanced my way or something, right? That or just crushed me with his aura before I was even over the fence.*

More mental static. *Zane,* Zoey sounded confused but, at the same time, hopeful, *Aleks can maintain connections with multiple subjects from hundreds... no,* thousands *of miles away! There's no way that you just slipped under his radar. Either he knows you're there and you haven't been paying attention, or...*

Zane smirked. *Or Xander's keeping me hidden.*

And, Zoey added, *judging from his behavior, he's keeping him distracted.*

Great! Zane's optimism was only halfhearted... at best. He decided he could suddenly go for a steaming bowl of It'll Get Better... *Maybe*"-alphabet soup. *So what the fuck am I supposed to do?*

XANDER MIGHT NOT HAVE BEEN as strong as Aleks. He might not have been motivated solely by a single obsession or empowered by a god complex. He might not have had the upper hand, the higher ground, or even decent footing.

But Xander did have tricks.

He'd failed enough to know what worked and what didn't. He'd lost more sources of motivation than Aleks would likely ever know in his lifetime. And while he wasn't empowered by a god complex, Xander *did* have the powers of a complex, god-like being.

If only he could unlock their full potential...

In either case, a few turns of the proverbial gears within the Great Machine were enough to "see" Zane coming before Aleks and his high-powered aura could sense him. It was, after all, the difference between knowing that a rolling ball would soon enter one's field of vision and having to wait to actually see the damned thing. And while he might not have been strong enough to hide *everything* he was thinking from Aleks, he could shield enough of his mind to keep his knowledge of Zane's arrival a secret.

Provided, of course, the surface thoughts were interesting enough to keep him from digging further.

And what could be more interesting than laughing in the face of the most powerful mythos species on the planet?

It was certainly making Xander's night more interesting.

Aleks kicked him again, snarling, and, though he didn't mean for it to, the pain actually made Xander laugh harder. It was a sign that it was working; that he was getting to the so-called superior being. Knowing that he still had some power over Aleks was worth a chuckle, but there was a little something extra to sweeten the punchline and make the laughter roll that much harder.

"Just what do you find so amusing, Stryker?" he hissed down at him, kicking him again.

"Y-you..." Xander belched out a fresh cackle, rolling on his back as he folded himself around his aching sides. He wasn't sure if it was the laughter or the kicking that was hurting him more, and that only made him laugh that much harder. "You're... what's amusing," he finally announced, panting and giggling.

Aleks shifted his foot, preparing to kick him again, but held. He was waiting.

"I've got a pretty good idea what to expect from you based on the abilities your mom exhibited," explained Xander. "The boundless shapeshifting, the insane speed and strength, the terrifying auric control... like you both keep preaching: god-like." Xander nodded, smirking, "See, I don't doubt that you're stronger and more powerful than me"—*For now, at least,* he thought, making no effort to hide the thought from Aleks' prying mind's eye—"and, even though we *both* know that's the case, you *still* want to be me!" He started laughing again.

Aleks stared down at him for a long, sustained moment of stunned intrigue. "What?" he finally coughed out. "What are you—"

"My gun? My mom's necklace? My city? I mean... *fuck,* Aleks, you were *free* from the castle for—what?—a day-or-so before you started making your way out here? And before that you had those psycho-Nazi hybrid brothers that Zoey and Isaac were chasing cutting through the country to get to my door. I get that Lenuta was totally obsessed with my family's bloodline due to the curse on the castle—if I knew I needed a specific person's blood to free me from a prison, castle or not, I'd be obsessed, too—but once you were free you had an entire planet available to you! You could've started this stolen mission to take over the world from Europe! Or, maybe you didn't want to set up shop too close to The Council. That's fair logic. Or maybe you were just *dying* to travel. Fine. Whatever! You could've gone *anywhere-fucking-else* on the globe! Asia? Africa? South America? The Antarctic?" Xander dared a scoff then, "God-damn, Aleks, you coulda still come to the US and planted yourself in LA or something—gotten a genuine foothold and done some real damage with a bunch of know-nothing nobodies to stop you. After all, nobody else in the world knows how to handle your kind—only a handful of people even know your kind exist!—and y-you... you..." Xander was starting to laugh again, "You...

heh—after a *lifetime* of entrapment and starvation and neglect —*heh heh,* you *literally* haul your obsessed ass halfway around the world and start shit right next door to the only two people who could stop you!"

Fresh laughter erupted.

So I'm not going to say that Xander's being real smart, Zane announced in private to Zoey, working to stifle the urge to laugh from behind his tombstone, *but the goth-loving son-of-a-bitch has definitely found his sense of humor.*

I can hear him, Zoey informed him. *And what you're calling humor I call suicidal. Estella would kill him if she knew what he was doing.*

I doubt it, Zane countered. *Either he knows what he's doing and his woman would support it... or he* is *being suicidal, and what good would killing him do to punish* that*?*

There was a pause as Zoey likely considered this. *Fair point,* she said.

Speaking of fair points, why do you think Aleks chose to come here? Xander makes a good point: seems stupid to start a campaign in the one place you're most likely to be stopped, right?

Not necessarily, Zoey said. *I won't say that Xander's insults don't carry a bit of truth. Aleks* does *seem to have a fixation on him, after all, but not in a way that's any different than Xander's fixation on the subject of his own parents or even Estella's safety. Those things all represent what he has to fight for, his passions. From the sounds of it, Aleks' passions are a bit more finite: revenge against Xander and world domination. A clever tactician would surmise that finding the fastest, most effective way to do both would be anything but stupid.*

Zane frowned, glancing out around the corner of his cold, stone hideaway. He saw Aleks, still glaring down at Xander, open the hand that held the gun; keeping his trigger finger hooked within the guard. The gun spun free, swinging in the varcol's palm. Rotating it in mid-turn, Aleks came to grip the barrel, holding the grip out towards Xander.

Xander's laughter caught in his throat and seized to an abrupt stop at this, and Zane got the distinct impression that something bad was about to happen.

Sometimes I hate it when you make sense, Zoe...

CAN *you hear me in there, Stryker?* Aleks' voice tolled in Xander's head. *Your laughter seems much quieter, much less boisterous, in here—where it matters most—so I imagine you can hear me just fine.*

Xander forced himself to keep laughing, pretending he couldn't even hear the crystal-clear psychic connection.

I did not come here to kill you, Stryker, he went on. *I told you that I was disappointed when I thought you'd died, didn't I?*

Still Xander went on laughing. He had to. For Zane's sake, he had to.

I also told you that I was your opposite—Yin to Yang, yes?—and, among the many reasons that that is clearly the truth, I also told you that I chose life. With that, he let his grip on Yin loosen and turned the revolver on itself, holding it out as an offering to Xander.

Xander couldn't force himself to laugh any longer.

"No," Xander whispered back to him. "I'm not going to do that."

"I think we both know you will," Aleks said.

The vision of Xander and Aleks struggling over the gun replayed in his head; of a decision he'd yet to make being made. The vision ended with the gun going off in Xander's face—him *letting* it; him *choosing* it—and his head...

"No," Xander said again.

He didn't care what the Great Machine showed him.

That wasn't happening.

Not here... not now.

"Guess you're just going to have to kill me," Xander muttered. Even as he said these words, however, he'd begun thinking of Estella and their child, thinking of Zane and Serena cursing one another out, thinking of sex on a private island, watching his mother getting beaten and raped, racing through Lenuta's castle. Xander forced himself to think of anything and everything that a person would think of in their last moments of life, because Xander needed Aleks to see those thoughts and believe he was thinking them for that reason.

And, as he forced himself to think those thoughts, he worked to trace a pattern in the upturned soil with his fingertip.

"That's not how I want this to work," Aleks declared. "I want to see you do it yourself. Like you were meant to all along."

Xander caught himself thinking about how the Cebourists had crippled Ruby, stolen her vampire strength and speed from her, and he cycled the thought to reflect concern for the young vampire's wellbeing. Estella had told him that it was Aleks who'd saved Ruby that night, something he'd done to earn their trust while getting to freely slaughter dozens of human activists in the process, so he knew that the memory would resound with the varcol, as well.

"No," Xander said again, then, hoping he'd gotten the blindly drawn symbol right, he called upon the necessary energies, pumping them into the etching and rolling free of the resulting blast.

The light that burst forth shone like a tiny, homemade sun for a single instant. In Xander's mind's eye, he watched Aleks' eyes roll back against the glare—the bloodshot whites wavering behind fluttering eyelids—as he was knocked off his feet by the force of the spell. Xander had been considering the moment the Cebourists had robbed Ruby of her mythos strengths because he was hoping to remind himself how to do the same. Allen Carrey had taught him and his growing community much, but the ability to take all the speed and strength and power that made a "superior" race like the mythos and leave them on par with humans was undeniably one of his greatest lessons.

Though he'd never been very good with it, Xander took a leap of faith that he'd gotten it right.

This one's for you, Tennesen!

HOLY SHIT! Zane wasn't sure if he wanted to scream, clap, or brace for the End of Days. *ALEKS IS DOWN! ALEKS IS—oh... wait, he's back up again...*

XANDER CURSED as he watched Aleks begin to drag himself back to his feet. He'd barely managed to pull himself up, was still too battered to close the distance with any real swiftness, and already his opponent was recovering from the...

But he *wasn't* recovering, Xander realized.

He was only standing.

Xander considered this, realizing that he had no idea *how* Ruby had been affected by the Cebourists' spell. There were no accounts on whether she'd been knocked out, injured, or if she'd even been aware of the effects of the spell until she'd actually tried to use her vampiric abilities; it simply had never come up—the *"how"* taking precedence over the *"what"* in regards to what had happened.

Deciding that faith had carried him that far, even if it *was* only to his feet, Xander committed to going further. He charged at Aleks, pushing his tortured body into overdrive. He saw Aleks watching him, saw the varcol's eyes adjust to follow him as he shifted speeds, and he could even see the yellowish-green and red tendrils of his auric layers beginning to adjust for whatever he had planned. It was obvious at that moment that the spell hadn't stripped him of all of his abilities...

But, too committed to his attack, Xander couldn't stop...

And, despite the many times he'd easily evaded faster attacks prior to that moment, Aleks didn't move.

Xander wasn't sure which of them was more shocked by his fist's impact on the varcol's face, but Aleks was certainly more shocked when a voice rose from across the cemetery:

"FUCK YEAH, STRYKER!"

ZANE, YOU IDIOT! Zoey roared in his head.

"You're an idiot, Zane," Xander's expression said.

And Aleks? Well, Aleks' face, the parts that weren't swelling with fresh bruising, seemed to say, *"How'd that idiot get here?"*

"Yeah," Zane groaned to himself, "that was pretty idiotic."

Aleks rolled to his feet, still dazed—catching himself in a stumble—from Xander's attack, and turned so that he had the two of them on either side of him. The weakened varcol's head swiveled between the two, working to keep a bead on both of them.

"You gonna tell me how you did that?" Zane called out to Xander.

The two of them had begun to cycle around Aleks, forcing the disoriented varcol to keep rotating in an effort to maintain his view of the two of them.

Xander smirked around his labored breathing and shook his head. "It'd require you closing your mouth and opening your ears, I'm afraid."

"Hey! It's my wife that has trouble closing her mouth!" —*And everything else,* he thought to himself before realizing that Zoey could still likely "hear" him in his mind.

Yes, Zane, her voice chimed, *I'm still here. And I should warn you that Serena very well could be, too.*

Zane didn't have a response to this as he saw Aleks beginning to make a lunge for Xander, putting Zane in his blind spot in the process. Jumping into overdrive, Zane tried to get the drop on the distracted varcol, only to have him turn back on him at the last moment and steer him back with a wide, furious strike.

Catching his breath, certain that he was about to lose his head and relieved to find it still attached, Zane chuckled nervously and said. "This fucker's still got some spark in him, but he ain't what he was, that's for sure! You sure I can't convince you to teach me whatever it is that did this?"

"I could try," Xander offered, "but it's a studying-thing, not a barbell-thing."

Zane rolled his eyes. "I'll have you know I had straight-As when I was a human and still in school."

"Oh yeah?" Xander challenged, "What subjects?"

The twisting, darting dance between the three continued; all of them working to keep a distance from the other.

"Phys-Ed," Zane confessed with a laugh. "Though I aced Health Class my Junior year."

"How'd you manage that?" Xander called back.

Zane grinned at their dialogue, not just for the casual nature of it given the severity of the circumstance, but also for the very obvious impact it was having on Aleks. The weakened varcol, still reeling and looking confused about whatever had happened to him, was actually beginning to shake!

"Let's just say I proved to the teacher I had an advanced understanding of the female anatomy," he said with a laugh.

"SHUT UP!" Aleks roared, flexing his body like a character Zane had seen in a Japanese anime once. An anime where the character...

Oh shit... Zane thought, realizing he couldn't see the aura that was likely coming his way.

Xander wasn't sure if the abilities that Aleks had retained was due to an imperfection in the spell or due to the heightened levels of strength he was working to strip away. From what he could tell, Aleks was no longer able to move beyond standard overdrive, and his auric control, though still present, was nothing beyond the realm of what any other auric vampire would be capable of. He could imagine Estella, with all of her logic and reason, deducing that the spell must knock a mythos' strengths down what could be called a "peg," and if most mythos breeds were one "peg" above humans, then it was a good spell to reduce most mythos breeds to human-level. This, Xander supposed, was a good example of what it looked like when a varcol, who must stand on a metaphorical second "peg," was knocked down to the first.

Or maybe he'd just botched the spell and it was better to leave logic and reason to more logical and reasonable minds like Estella's.

With the word "peg" still cycling around in his head from all the mental repetitions, Xander lowered his auric shield and dared to look away from Aleks to make sure Zane had managed to stay alive after the auric attack he'd taken head-on. A groan and a few cycles of the word "fuck" gave him confidence that his friend—his *bro,* as Zane would call it—was going to make it.

Aleks appeared in front of Xander, dropping out of overdrive mere inches from him, with Yin's barrel already jammed against his temple. Xander knew this move well, but that meant that the trigger had already been—

Though the Great Machine's visions were typically obscure and distant, this one resounded with enough clarity and proximity for Xander to understand that what he was seeing was practically already happening. His moment of distraction to check on Zane *had* registered with Aleks, and he *had* made his move. Xander didn't even have time to jump into overdrive to brace for what was coming, he simply had to act based on what amounted to a very precise calculation.

Vast cosmic insight and an understanding of quantum mechanics that he *did not* understand all came together in a single instant and Xander...

Dropped backwards.

ZANE WAS in the process of using the edge of a nearby gravestone to pull himself to his feet when a flicker of motion caught his attention. It was a familiar sort of motion, that of something that *wasn't* there one moment suddenly *being* there the next. To an untrained eye it could be disorienting—some minds even going so far as to create false memories that they'd seen nothing odd; that that person had been there all along—but, when it was a typical day-to-day sight, one got used to it.

Except when the person that *wasn't* there is an enemy and the *there* in question was directly in front of one's bro.

That was something one didn't just get used to.

Though he couldn't see what Aleks had done from his angle, Zane watched Xander's body, stiff as a board and gazing off at nothing, start to fall back. It was almost funny, Zane thought—kind of like those videos online of the "fainting" goats that just kept toppling over—except that, no, there was nothing funny about it.

Especially when, still in mid-fall, the black revolver that Aleks had been toting fired a shot.

Zane was charging towards the varcol's back in overdrive before Xander's body had even touched the ground. Aleks, either sensing his approach or preparing to get the drop on him, began to turn in a slow-mo crawl.

Only halfway into overdrive, you murderous fuck! Zane thought, fists clenched and right arm hauling back to deliver the ultimate "FUCK YOU" into Aleks' chest. *And I'm already halfway through your ribcage!*

I'm not dead, Zane, Xander's voice sounded like an angel's chorus in Zane's head.

Distracted, the "FUCK YOU" he'd intended to deliver on Aleks' doorstep wound up on his neighbor's... unsigned and left unattended to be stolen by—

Zane realized this metaphor had gone too far in his own head when his intended target had managed to not only duck the punch, but use his own momentum to launch him skyward.

Fuck... you... Stry-ker! he thought-crawled, half-in and half-out of overdrive.

It really was such a beautiful night if one slowed down to appreciate it.

Id-i-ot, Serena's voice chimed in his head.

Told... you... she... was in... here too, Zane, Zoey gloated.

The fact that the psychic voices in his head had begun to speed up *should* have been an indicator that his fall, too, would be speeding up. But, as a lot of people had been telling him all throughout the night, Zane was something of an idiot.

He was unprepared for the impact that shot up to meet him, and wound up breaking through a marble headstone and dislocating his shoulder in the process.

Xander's "faith fall" had allowed him to avoid losing his head as Aleks, already in the process of dropping out of overdrive, tried to use one of Xander's favorite time-tested attacks against him.

He could still feel where the heat of the bullet had grazed his nose.

Once in mid-fall, he'd jumped into overdrive, spotting Zane in mid-sprint towards Aleks with his mind's eye. His friend, all fists and fury, was certain he'd just watched Xander die. He thought it only right to inform him that he wasn't.

It hadn't exactly worked out for Zane, but, with things

time-slowed and Aleks distracted, Xander had an opening to retrieve Yang and squeeze off a shot of his own. He would have been happier with a headshot, but at that point he'd be happy just to get out of the cemetery.

More and more he had been beginning to worry that he'd just gone and saved someone a great deal of trouble by delivering himself inside those time-warped iron gates before getting himself killed.

Coun-cil's... on... their... way, Zane announced, already out of overdrive and sounding sluggish in Xander's mind as a result.

Xander rounded his shoulders and worked to kick his feet up and over his head as he braced for the long-awaited impact with the ground. Despite how the night had been going, he managed to time the maneuver right, and he rolled with the landing, performing a backwards summersault that carried him into a bow-legged kneel a few feet from Aleks.

The varcol was hissing and seething, toppled back and clutching at a bloody stump where his left leg should have been. The flesh around the charred leg oozed and writhed, twisting and thrashing as the varcol's weakened shapeshifting abilities struggled with the dilemma. During the fight with Aleks' mother, Xander and Estella had watched her transform her body in ways they hadn't thought possible—it seemed if the varcol mind wanted a part of their body to exist as something, *anything,* else, that alone was enough to make it happen. Hands became claws, eyes turned to mouths, tongues turned to tentacles...

Xander nearly retched at that memory.

Now, however, with Aleks' abilities weakened by Xander's Cebourist spell, the destroyed limb seemed unable to communicate with itself. Rather than one cohesive transformation, small bits of singed flesh began to turn into tiny, flexing fingers. The jagged end of exposed bone seemed to yawn before stretching outward, "testing" the air, and then beginning to withdraw back into the mass of shredded meat.

Xander watched, entranced by the sheer morbidity of the sight, as the bottom half of Aleks' demolished leg stretched, pinched, and then widened to become a mouth that opened, closed, appeared to draw in a breath, and then began to shriek like a wounded animal. Seeming more annoyed with his own body's response to the injury than actually pained, Aleks began swatting at the bloody meat-mouth, actually tearing a portion of the muscle in the process. The now-silenced length of ripped thigh muscle, seeming fed up with the treatment, elongated, twisted, and turned itself into what looked to Xander like a bald, fibrous cat's paw that went about trying to drag itself away from the rest of the horror show.

"That..." Zane, clutching his arm, groaned, "... is some next-level fucked up shit!"

Before either of them could think of taking advantage of the situation, Xander saw Aleks turn away from his injury and begin to issue an auric call to the opposite side of the cemetery, the limited-yet-still-far-reaching strands of his aura breaching the far gate and vanishing into the night.

A moment later a series of rapid auric blips registered in the distance.

"Shit!" Xander growled, moving to stand. "Stop them!"

"'Them'?" Zane repeated, confused, "Them—who?"

Xander could sense their auras arrival before they were visible, but he kept himself from saying *"THEM!"*—knowing that Zane wouldn't be able to do anything until he had a visual. Unfortunately, this left Xander struggling to juggle the arrival of five... no, six freshly fed sangs. They flashed into existence, creating a pyramid-like barricade between them and Aleks. In an instant, Xander and Zane were face-to-face with three hissing sangs with two more waiting behind them acting as backup. The sixth—easily the largest and, Xander was sure, the fastest—was already kneeling over Aleks and working to scoop him up.

"NO!" Xander roared and lunged, only to have to sacrifice the effort to dodge a strike from the nearest sang.

Growling at the interference, he took a long swipe at the new vampire's neck, tearing out a good portion of its throat. His death wasn't immediate, but Xander was pleased to see him change his priorities as he stumbled out of his way and began focusing on containing the ceaseless torrents of blood.

Zane, grinning at the opportunity to take on an opponent he knew he could handle, released his injured arm and used his freed fist to drive a punch into the face of the sang closest to him. A pained gurgle melded with a wet crunch and the vampire's jaw fell several inches, stretching his face into a startled grin. Sneering at this, Zane drove his forehead into the bridge of the still-whimpering vampire's nose, driving the cartilage back into its skull and sending it toppling back with a shrill howl into the chest of the reinforcing vampire that had been waiting behind him.

The last capable line of defense tried to make a grab at Xander, who lunged past him and worked to grab at Aleks as the hulking sang secured him in his arms and began to stand. Knowing that he'd never manage to stop the rescue effort and that, injured and exhausted as they were, they'd never manage to keep up in a chase, Xander shifted his focus but maintained his reach. Flexing fingers found purchase on their target and worked to secure the grip.

As his gaze locked on Aleks' own, Xander dared another reach, this time with his aura, and sent Aleks off with a message:

Happy healings, motherfucker!

A soft *clink* sounded as a familiar chain snapped, and Xander couldn't help but smile.

Glancing down at his open palm, he saw the ruby eye, inlaid in a silver diamond-shaped setting, glimmer victoriously back up at him.

CHAPTER 22
REVELATIONS

"The suicide arrives at the conclusion that what he is seeking does not exist; the seeker concludes that what he has not yet looked in the right place."
Paul Watzlawick (1921-2007)

Xander and Zane rode back in relative silence. They rode in Sawyer's car, but it was not Sawyer who drove it. Despite the agreement and all the screaming and cursing that it had taken for Sawyer to claim the car from Serena, it was Serena behind the wheel. Beside her, twisting around in the seat to all-but face Xander, was Estella. She looked uncomfortable, but Xander could tell it had nothing to do with her seat or Serena's driving.

You were watching... he thought-spoke to her, not looking up from his lap. He'd folded his hands there, cupped them lovingly around his mother's pendant, and they gave him something to focus on.

I had to, Estella replied. *I knew what Aleks had done to you the moment it started. I knew what he'd do the instant you said you'd lower your defenses. Powerful as you are, you are your own worst enemy, Xander. Giving a monster like Aleks an opening like that...*

Xander gently squeezed the pendant before forcing himself to look up at her.

Her blue eyes were bloodshot, the skin surrounding them puffy and red. She'd been crying, and the aftermath of that fact hurt him to see.

It was *stupid,* he admitted, *but it wasn't for nothing.*

He saw Estella's bloodshot, puffy eyes drift down to his hands, and a small curl tugged at the edges of her lips. *You got it back,* she sounded just as relieved by that as he had been.

Xander nodded and slowly opened his hands to reveal the pendant. The glare from a passing streetlight caught the ruby's eye and refracted its scarlet brilliance in that instant. Then another. And another. The rhythm of the passing lights and their glow off the gem made it look like a small heart pumping in Xander's hands. The sight made the breath catch in his lungs, and he had to cover it again before the reality of that metaphor grew powerful enough to break him.

I hurt him, too, Xander went on, forcing himself to change the subject. Though he was sure that it was just the residual insanity that had begun to slip by during his fight with Aleks, he thought he felt the pendant thrumming against his palms. *Used the Cebourists' magic to weaken him, and then blew off the motherfucker's leg.*

Estella looked happy to "hear" this, but the joy didn't spread into the realm of hope. *I'm glad for the small victory,* she started, *but we both know that he'll be able to heal from it.*

Xander nodded and looked out through the window at the passing view of the city. *I know. But it'll take time. Between reversing the spell's effects and putting himself back together, I've at least bought us a little extra time.*

How much? she asked.

Xander shook his head. *Not nearly enough, I'm sure,* he admitted.

"You two gonna quit passing notes and share with the rest of the fucking class?" Serena demanded from the driver's seat.

"Serena!" Zane growled, cutting a glare in her direction from behind Estella's seat. "Now's not the time!"

"No. It's a fair request, Zane," Xander sighed, looking at the rearview mirror and seeing Serena's purple eyes looking back at him. Early on in the drive, he'd caught her adjusting the mirror and now realized it had been to sacrifice her view of the passing road in exchange for one of him and her husband. "I'm guessing you two have already passed your own notes on what Zane saw?"

"Notes? Stryker, Zoey and I were practically watching everything from Zane's head while it was happening!" she informed them.

Xander frowned at that. "Then what do you want to know? If you saw everything then—"

"Whoa!" Serena interrupted. "Let's be clear about something: Zoe and I couldn't *see* shit, not like your wife was seeing things, at least. What we had was more like a fucked-up radio broadcast with a shit-ton of static and a bunch of random, blurred images. We got the impression that you used some spell on the cocksucker, and that this somehow slowed him down and made him weaker. We got the impression that you and Zane had a bit of a dancing match with him, that you did some weird shit that ultimately got Zane's shoulder fucked up, and that you sent that ingrown nutsack hair running—so to speak —in the arms of one of his bitch-boys after you shot off his leg, which, from what I've 'heard,' resulted in some sort of nightmare show the likes of which have genuinely unsettled my otherwise unshakable he-man. All of this, however, amounts to a cold bucket of piss when the reality of the situation is this: Zane has no fucking idea what happened back there, ergo *we* have no fucking idea what happened back there."

"What happened back there," Xander said with a sigh, "was I discovered a weakness in Aleks that's just as much a strength."

Serena glared back at him through the adjusted mirror. "That supposed to mean something, Riddler? How can something be both a weakness and a strength?"

"He's crazy, Serena. Totally and utterly batshit insane," Xander answered, returning his gaze to the window, but no longer looking at what existed on the other side of it.

Serena was quiet for a moment—everyone was; the only sound in the car the airy current and its rhythmic hiccups every time they passed something that interrupted the flow—as Xander's words were considered. Then she said, "And that's both a weakness *and* a strength?"

Xander nodded. "Trust me," he said, "I speak from experience."

Serena sighed and swerved to catch their exit. "Anybody ever tell you that you make pussies wet when you're cryptic like that?"

"Pretty sure you've said everything about pussies that can be said to a guy, Serena," he said with a groan.

"Yeah? Well, I ever tell you I like to grab my labia in the shower and flap them around like a little fleshy cunterfly?"

Estella's aura vibrated with embarrassment, but she couldn't keep herself from laughing at that.

Xander, realizing that he wasn't as reborn and open-minded about the subject of sex as he'd previously thought, delicately dragged the pad of his thumb across the pendant in his hands as he turned to face Zane. "Cunterfly?"

Zane shrugged and gave a dismissive roll of his eyes. "Would you rather she talked more about Isaac's cock?"

"Do you two ever talk about anything *except* genitals?" Estella asked, though her giggles betrayed that she wasn't as disgusted by the conversation as Xander.

"Sure do, Goddess," Serena said, taking a sharp turn that

had Zane falling against Xander and Estella falling against her. "Sometimes we talk about assholes."

"SANA'S STALLING THE COUNCIL?" Xander asked.

Estella nodded and said, "She told Serena that she could keep them occupied until dawn."

Xander regarded Serena with a suspicious eye. "She told *you* that?" he asked, certain there was more to it than that.

Serena shrugged, catching on. "I asked her to keep them away for as long as she could, yeah. So fucking what?"

Folding his arms across his chest, Xander said, "And I'm willing to bet that's *exactly* how you said it, right?"

Another shrug. "I might've said that I don't give a fuck *how* she stalls them, provided they were stalled for as long as possible," she admitted.

Xander raised an eyebrow back towards Zoey, deciding he trusted her judgement more for what he was about to ask next. "And what are your thoughts on how she's been stalling them so far?"

Zoey blushed and glanced back towards Serena, then flinched.

Xander turned back in time to catch the crazy blonde making throat-slitting motions at the blue-haired auric. Rolling his eye, he looked back at Zoey.

"She's... uh, well... So far she's tricked four of The Council's elders and two of their drivers into thinking they were either ill or in need of a rest stop. Eventually one of their more keen auric minds caught on to the invasion, and they boosted shielding everyone in their caravan. Then Sana began altering the signals on their GPS systems."

Xander raised an eyebrow at that. "Aurics can do that?" he asked, bewildered to hear it.

Zoey shrugged. "I guess so," she said, obviously just as

bewildered. "I honestly never thought to try something like that."

Sana really is something special, Xander thought. Then, nodding to Zoey, he said, "Go on."

Zoey nodded back. "So she started in with their navigations system, and up until recently that'd been working. Then somebody obviously realized that the path they'd been taking wasn't making sense."

"And?" Xander pressed.

Zoey shrugged. "That's it. Sana told me only a moment ago that their GPS signal had gone offline."

Xander smirked and shook his head at that. "Sons of bitches must have rediscovered maps," he mused.

"Maps?" Serena echoed with a scoff. "How archaic!"

"Can you even spell 'archaic?'" Isaac asked with a smirk.

"Sure can!" Serena boasted, turning to face him. "A-R-C-F-U-C—"

Isaac rolled his eyes and cut her off with, "I can already see that my point's been proven."

"Only point you've ever proven," Serena shot back, "was that Hefty should release a brand of prophylactics."

"Ah!" Isaac exclaimed, "Yet another word you probably can't spell."

"Spell?" Zane said with a chuckle, "I'm surprised she even knows what prophylactics are!"

"Are you fucking—whose fucking side are you on, queef-nugget?" Serena growled, smacking her husband in the chest.

"In this case?" Zane said, rubbing his chest, "I'm on *my* side, the side that knows that Donkey-Dick there probably laughs at Magnums and that you wouldn't be able to pick a condom out of a lineup between a sandwich bag and a hairnet."

Serena frowned at this and crossed her arms, pouting and looking away. "Not my fault I like the feel of—"

"MOVING RIGHT THE FUCK ALONG!" Xander yelled, clapping his hands for emphasis before turning back to Zoey and asking, "So is there anything else Sana can do to stall them? There's still another few hours until sunrise and, from the look of things, The Council can be here in an hour if nothing else is done."

Zoey nodded, smirking. "She just bought you some time, actually. Admittedly another trick I didn't know we had."

"Oh?" asked Xander.

Zoey giggled. "She just drained all their cars' batteries."

Serena began cackling.

Xander nodded slowly, trying to decide why he'd never even thought to try such a thing. "Well then," he finally said, impressed, "it seems like she has everything under control."

"So what happens if they get rolling again?" Isaac asked. "If one auric could drain their batteries there's nothing to say that one of theirs can't just charge them back up again."

"They driving newer models?" Zane asked.

Zoey nodded and said, "Of course."

Zane smirked. "So have the little mind-fuck prodigy go to town on the onboard computer systems. Everything—fucking *everything!*—on newer cars relies on that shit. If she can fuck with digital and electrical signals from this distance there's nothing to stop her from basically turning their no-doubt sleek and modern parade of authority into a row of 'ain't goin' nowhere soon'-steel buckets. They'd have to call on the closest clan to give them a lift—I certainly don't see the fuckers calling triple-A—and, since you guys aren't on their payroll anymore, that leaves them relying on—what?—a clan that's at least an hour-or-two out? Assuming that clan's even got the time and resources to spare them an immediate lift, that'd buy us the time we need to secure the area and brace for what's coming. It'd certainly give me and you a chance to heal and maybe get laid in the meantime, Stryker."

Xander considered this for a moment, then let the Great Machine show him the sequence of events that would pass if they tried things that way:

He sees anger. He sees irritation. He sees their aurics reaching back, searching for the one who's been interfering and—

Xander smiles and nods. "Good for you, Sana," he caught himself saying aloud; the auras of those around him shifting with curiosity, wondering what he meant.

He sees The Council, desperate and thinking themselves clever for calling upon backup given their growing eagerness to kill Xander, issuing a call to the Daius Clan. Though, true to Zane's predictions, they're still several out of range, they have been noticing a decrease in activity—they not only have the time and resources to aid The Council, they're eager to do so. Not about to make the same mistake twice, the members of The Council warn their Good Samaritans to guard against Sana's efforts. With the exception of beginning to drop entire buildings in their way, their journey from there will be uninterrupted...

And they'll be arriving with backup.

Whether or not they have Elder Luis with them—Why can't I see if you're there?—*there is no chance for a peaceful negotiation. And while the potential for loss is still minimal, limited only to a family of new arrivals if they choose to make the journey tonight, Xander and the others still won't have to kill any of The Council, but with a small battalion of Daius warriors ready to take on Xander and anybody supporting him the possibility of death increases quite a bit on both sides...*

Of the increasingly limited paths that don't compromise the endgame, Xander sees, only a few of them are ideal. Except for the...

Xander cocked his head in Estella's direction, but he wasn't seeing her in the here-and-now. Grinning, he said "Zap-trap," and gave a nod before taking a step and...

He saw where he was—back in the conference room with Estella, the Vaileans, and Zoey and Isaac—and realized he'd lost track of time...

Literally.

"Sorry," he muttered.

"The fuck was that?" Serena asked, beginning to laugh, "And what the fuck is 'zap-trap?'"

"It's... uh," Xander blinked, not sure how to answer that.

"It's a fighting tactic that we'd been working on before... well, before all *this* happened," Estella explained, keeping a questioning gaze on Xander.

Xander bit his lip, nodding his thanks for her for explaining it. He realized then that he was absently stroking the ruby of his pendant and he glanced down at it, eager for a reason to not have to look at the others.

"Okaaayyyy..." Serena said, stretching the two syllables into well over five. "So what is it?"

Xander felt Estella's gaze on him. Then, after a brief silence, she said, "I think you're going to find out soon enough."

AFTER HAVING BEEN force-fed the stuff by what had felt like the gallons prior to his reawakening, Xander was committed to never drinking synth-blood again. Though he couldn't come up with a decent comparison to brace the new vampire recruits for the experience—the Vaileans certainly had all sorts of colorful ways of describing the taste, none of them even remotely pleasant—he couldn't help but feel that the awful experience was more than just a matter of taste. It was, when all was said and done, an all-out assault on all the senses. A vampire that ingested the enchanted, synthetic blood substitute would taste something vile, and, with this, experience a smell to match—something in the league of, but not quite as basic as, trying to ingest cold, clotted skunk's blood tapped directly from its backside. Drinking such a thing, unsurprisingly, had an almost surreal effect of having one seeing and hearing their own body's conflict with what it was dealing with: on the one hand being so eager to outright reject something so awful while, at the same time, trying to figure out where it could get more. All of which, of course, made for a terrible sort of ache...

Only not.

Because, heinous as the stuff was, synth-blood *worked.* Aches, pains, lacerations, breaks—*everything!*—began to heal the moment the system began to absorb the wonderful fusion of science and magic.

And, best of all, it replaced the need for actual blood entirely!

Provided everything worked out, Xander was hopeful that it would help to lessen the negative stigma surrounding vampires in the eyes of humans. It would cut out the *need* for living blood, which would, after the murder-happy rogues were weeded out and dealt with, allow for the public outlook to shift. After all, no blood-hunger meant no blood-hungry monsters; one of the most prevailing dividers between mythos and humans would be a thing of the past.

But—*gods above and below!*—it still tasted awful!

Three thermoses later, Xander was having a hard time deciding which he'd prefer most at that moment: the sweet taste of the real thing or the sweet release of death.

He decided that *both* of those thoughts were counterproductive to two very different convictions he was working to hold to and promised himself never to think them again...

Until I have to swallow another drop of that stuff! he thought-muttered to himself.

I heard that, Estella chimed in his head. Then, *I heard* all *of that.*

Xander cringed and looked back towards her. After wrapping up their second meeting for the night—"T*wo meetings too much, in my opinion,"* as he'd said to Estella on their way out—she'd helped them back to their room, already toting a bag in her free hand. The bag, courtesy of Zeek, had been waiting alongside another like it in the conference room. One for Xander and one for Zane. Both of them, knowing what was in store for them in those bags, opted to suffer through the pain of their injuries until they could retch over the stuff in the privacy of their respective rooms. Admittedly, neither of the two had suffered any real extensive injuries. Enough to prevent them from pursuing Aleks, yes, but nothing compared to the horrific states that Xander had emerged from in past battles. Zane had, prior to Serena and Estella's arrival at the cemetery and with Xander's help, reset his shoulder, and, with the joint back in place, the two looked more scuffed and embarrassed than mortally wounded.

All the same, Zeek, knowing that The Council was on their way—and, in his own words, "not taking any chances"—had "prescribed" them what they both agreed was a ridiculous amount.

Though he'd never admit it to the anapriek, Xander *did* feel like he could take on The Council. In fact, he felt like he could take on the entire world. Whether or not he would *live* through it, however, was an entirely different story.

He caught himself laughing at that thought.

Then he realized that Estella had caught him laughing at that thought, as well.

Fuck... he thought, seeing how angry she looked.

"Aren't you afraid?" Estella demanded.

Though she didn't like the idea of *wanting* Xander to be afraid of anything, especially when his strength and confidence seemed to be the only thing keeping everything from unraveling, she worried what it would mean if he'd risen above such a fear.

She would have imagined that, after the last time Aleks had lured him into a trap, he'd know better than to be so reckless. Granted, the trap that had been set this time around *had* been a truly awful one—one that even Estella had nearly gone rushing into once she'd seen what Aleks was doing—but...

But she would have at least gone into that cemetery *afraid.*

Xander had just seemed...

She shivered.

Eager. Xander had seemed *eager.*

"Doesn't death scare you anymore?" she pressed on.

"Some deaths scare me, I suppose, but..." he sighed and seemed to resolve to a thought that he didn't like; Estella saw his aura shifting in the same way it had plenty of times when he was upset about how things were going. "There are good deaths, too; deaths that can make a huge difference to how things turn out." He looked away, almost looking embarrassed. "Death is like love, 'Stell. And... and for the sake of certain outcomes, I have to be prepared."

"Prepared? Prepared to *die*?" Estella shook her head, her voice straining. "Xander, what on earth could justify you *sacrificing* yourself when..."

The way he was looking at her answered the question before she even had a chance to finish it. "Xander..." she drew in a difficult breath, "Wh-what's going to happen? Have... have you seen me die?"

Estella felt like she was taking a step into forbidden territory; like she was looking in the single direction no living being was meant to look in.

Was she truly prepared to face the possibility that she might...

But Xander pulled her back; turned her away; refused to even offer her that possibility.

"No," he said flatly, but there was no relief—no satisfaction—in that answer. "Because I refuse to watch it."

Estella stared back at him. "Refuse to...?"

Xander gave a single nod. "I've watched the others—*all* the others; even ones I haven't even met yet—die in hundreds—*thousands!*—of different ways. I've watched my own death, too;

probably with more fascination than you'd like, but I'm only admitting that because, with all the things I have to keep from you, I feel you still deserve that truth. But when it's *yours*—" his voice caught and he shook his head, "I don't allow the vision to finish."

"Vision?" Estella repeated. "You've seen *thousands* of potential deaths for everyone else... but only one for me?"

Xander shuddered, paused, dared a look at her, and then nodded.

"Always the same?"

Another nod. Estella could see tears welling in his blood-red eye.

Strangely enough, she found herself worrying most for him at that moment. "A-and you think that sacrificing yourself will..."

Xander tensed, his eye wavering across her face—watching something that nobody else could see—and finally let out a heavy exhale. It did nothing for his tension this time. "If that's what it takes," he finally said. Then he turned his back on her. "And you can't blame me for that decision, 'Stell; not this time. You're more than *you* now, and I would have died a million times to keep you alive *before* you were pregnant. Now..." she saw him raise a hand to his face, wiping at it. "I have to be braced for *everything*—*all* of the potential rises and *all* of the potential falls—but, ready as I am for everything else, I can't face that single reality. In every possible scenario we'll make mistakes, terrible ones, and, no matter what, we'll be broken... I can't do a thing to stop all of what's coming, and there's no instruction manual on how to do what I'm trying to do. Stan didn't go that far, I'm afraid. I'm going to do everything in my power to keep from crossing that path—do everything to divert from it ever happening—but if it should come to pass... then, no, I'm not afraid to die to alter its course. But..." he sighed, seeming to relieve himself of a great deal of stress in doing so and gave Estella a smile, one that took great effort but didn't seem insincere for it. "But I've got you," he finally said, "I've got you, and we have our baby, and..." he nodded, and Estella felt like he was, at that moment, answering a question that only he could hear, "And I believe that will be enough to make it work."

"But..." Estella suddenly understood how Xander felt, because the possibility of him dying was driving her to consider any possible means to prevent it. "But what if neither of us had to die?"

Xander shivered and, slowly, he turned back to look at her. "'Stell?" he asked, obviously sensing that she was going somewhere with all of this.

She nodded, frantic. She wanted to believe she was being logical and reasonable, but, as Xander had proven on countless occasions, passion had a cruel way of skewing logic and reason. "The Council knows about Aleks now, right? His intentions, his abilities, and they know all that he's been gaining followers..." her voice pitched as she felt her sinuses tighten; she struggled to fight the wave of tears. "Isn't there some path where all of that handles itself? Can't there be at least one path where we don't have to fight?"

Xander's face reflected the rawest image of sympathy Estella had ever seen. "Estella..." his tone hugged her name.

"No!" she protested. "There must be! There has got to be some path where all of this happens *without* you having to put yourself out there!" Rage, genuine rage—the sort that she'd only ever seen in him—boiled within her; her fists, balled and already aching, shook at her sides. "Haven't you done enough for the world? The Council's here now! This is *their* job! Why can't they all just fight it without you? Why can't we just get away—you and me and our baby—and find someplace quiet, someplace safe?" the tears were beginning to fall as Estella asked this.

Xander drew in an uneven breath. "That's... it's a possibility, yes. But every path where we run—any reality where we hide, whether it works or not—ensures that Aleks wins. The world—"

"The world doesn't appreciate you enough to deserve your visions!" she growled, closing the distance between them in an instant and pulling herself into him—claiming him as hers and hers alone. She was hoping she could hide her tears from him but knowing she was trying to hide herself from the truth. "We're strong enough to protect ourselves if we need to, but... but you shouldn't have to protect them anymore, Xander; you don't need *this* to be your legacy. You... me... *this*"—she moved one of his hands to her stomach then—"*this* could be enough, couldn't it?"

Xander blushed, and Estella couldn't tell if he was staring at his hand or past it. A part of her liked to believe he could see more, and another part knew that he could. Then he frowned and looked down, saddened. "Could you take any joy in being the wife of the man who let the world fall?" he asked.

"I'd take you in being *your* wife!" she shot at him, hurt and angered by the question. "Dammit, Xander, look around: that we've gotten this far—that we're still alive—is nothing short of a miracle!"—she heard his voice say "*You're the miracle, 'Stell"* and wasn't sure if it was a memory or a psychic reminder—"And... and this baby," she forced herself to go on, "Xander, *this* is all we need! After everything you've been through..." she caressed his cheek, "You don't owe them anything; any of them. If I knew that you'd finally have a chance to be free of all this pain, I'd turn away from this—all of this—and love you no less for it."

"Estella..."

She could see Xander struggling with the idea. That was good, she thought; it meant that he was considering it. But she could also see a familiar look of guilt growing on his face. She could see that something was pushing him to take action like he had so many times before.

"What about—"

"About what? The world? *Fuck the world,* Xander!" she saw him stagger at her words—at the weight of them—and knew that he'd never have expected to hear such a thing from her. "I've watched the world hurt you for too long, and I'm frankly tired of doing it any favors! You nearly got yourself killed trying to save the entire mythos community, and now most of them want you dead for it! Why should I want to do *them* any favors? Let The Council and Aleks have their own war; let them kill each other once and for all! And I'm not sorry for saying that, either; I'm not going to pretend that peace is an option when I've had to listen to everyone talking about how much you deserve to die. This world has been taking from you from the start, and you've never stopped pushing yourself to the breaking point for them."

Xander shook his head. "You don't understand, 'Stell."

"No, Xander," Estella hissed. "*You* don't understand! You dropped a bomb on me with that 'You could die and I'm prepared to sacrifice myself to stop it'-speech, and—guess what?—maybe I'm prepared to sacrifice myself to stop your death! Now what? Are we going to argue in an eternal circle over which of our sanctimonious sacrifices is more justified? Because the world needs you and your powers more than it needs me! And now that I've offered a third alternative, one that saves *both* of us and leaves the rest of the world to fend for itself, you're acting like that's not good enough. I'm sorry that I have to add to the already monumental burden that you're carrying, but you're going to have to accept in this situation that you have to choose between saving the world and saving me—saving all of us!—and I'll tell you right now that, if you choose the world, your death is not an option! Now, that's a big decision to make, and I can't imagine ever having to make it for myself... but I want it known that, if you feel you owe the world any favors, you haven't been paying attention. I'm tired of watching you push yourself for the sake of—"

"You *are* my world, 'Stell," he blurted out. "I've only ever pushed myself like I have for *you!*"

Estella blushed at that, remembering Zane's words—*"Simply put, I don't think there's much of anything Xander couldn't do—or wouldn't try to do, at least—if he knew he was doing it for you."*—and she realized how right he'd been.

Xander blushed, looking like he'd just confessed to the worst kind of sin, and gave a slight nod. "I didn't even want to survive the fight with Kyle after I was first turned, remember? Lenix, the hunters... hell, every one of them—all of *this*—I did because I was afraid of seeing you hurt." He blushed and then smiled, "That, or because you seemed proud of what I was doing."

"Oh, Xander," she whispered, planting a loving kiss on the top of his head. "Sweetheart, I *am* proud of you—I have *always* been proud of you—but... but not because of what you've done for me or what you've done for the world. All of that has been spectacular, don't get me wrong, but there's more to you than all of that, and I'm telling you that you don't have to keep putting yourself at risk anymore, baby. Not for me or anybody else. We can leave; run out that door tonight and be free of this, of war and blood and fear, and just be together. That would be enough for me! It would be enough, and I would not blame you for leaving all of this for somebody else to deal with!"

"I... I can't do that. Much as I want to—beautiful as that all sounds," he whispered.

"Why not?" she demanded.

"Because it's not just about you and me anymore. If it was, we could probably have killed Aleks already, and even if that wasn't the case we could live out our lives—just you and me—with relative ease. Like you said: we *are* strong enough to survive in whatever world Aleks might create. But..." he shook his head. "When my mother was pregnant with me, my father set out to kill Lenuta. He caught wind of what she intended to do and sought to stop it. I'd been blaming him for it ever since, but now..." he stared down at Estella's still-flat stomach. "Now I understand. I can't let *that* be the world our child grows up in."

Estella's breath caught as she considered this, then she, too, glanced down at her stomach. She saw her hands move to frame either side of it, strangely embarrassed at how small and insubstantial it seemed given all the attention it was getting.

Their child—hers and Xander's...

If that child shared a shred of Xander's power or even an iota of his audacity then she would feel sorry for anybody who dared to cross them.

But, once again, passion was skewing logic and reason. This time, however, there was no cruelty to it; she already loved her baby, and she could see that Xander felt the same. There were dangers ahead that Xander was struggling to weave through, but he was doing all of it for the sake of her and their unborn child.

"I would have died a million times to keep you alive before you were pregnant."

"It was never my story."

Something between a chuckle and a sob coughed out of Estella at that moment, and she shook her head. "Gods... what does it say about me that I keep forgetting?" she asked.

Xander's lips curled in a gentle grin. "This early on, with everything else that's happening? If it weren't for all the constant reminders of the future, it'd be slipping my mind, too; especially when presented ugly decisions like this one. Let's be fair, 'Stell, if you had these powers and you were telling me what I'd just told you, I wouldn't give you the option—I'd just take you! We'd be gone—'fuck the world and everyone in it,' just like you said."

Estella blushed. "I didn't say it like *that*."

"Whatever," Xander shrugged. "The point is you're not wrong. What it says that you keep forgetting is that you're a pregnant woman in an unfortunate circumstance to not be allowed to focus on *just* being pregnant. But you *are* pregnant, and the world *is* at stake, and I *am* the only one that can do something about it. So I have to stay, and I have to fight. And if I see things headed in the direction where you and our baby are at risk, I'm going to choose a good death—a death that will offer you two the life I'm stuck here fighting for already—but know now that I'm going to be doing everything in my power to keep it from happening that way."

"You promise?" Estella demanded.

Xander smirked at that and nodded. "I already made that promise a long time ago, and I've never stopped making it."

Blushing at that, Estella took his hand. Reassured and feeling that Xander deserved a distraction before his confrontation with The Council, she started towards the bed. "Come on," she said. "Zane said that you two should heal and get laid... and it looks like you're all healed."

LESS THAN AN HOUR BEFORE SUNRISE, and Sana had been forced to drop a building in The Council's path. When Xander had seen that as a possible scenario through the Great Machine it had seemed like such a surreal, nearly comical path that he'd never truly considered it as a possibility. Coming to grips the magnitude of the action—how absolutely ludicrous it was to even *imagining* it—was nothing compared to what it truly reflected when Xander was forced to give Sana the order.

Because, on top of feeling that the possibility of weaponizing entire buildings was too farfetched to ever actually happen, Xander had overlooked one of the details surrounding the few paths that deemed that farfetched reality a necessary step:

They were expecting a family of new arrivals.

And, had Xander slowed down and diverted from the single path of dominos that represented The Council's journey to their doorstep, he'd have had a good reason to reconsider his options.

It hadn't occurred to him that the possibility—and it *had*, at that time, only been a marginal one—of a small group of newcomers to their growing community should, in any way, motivate a shift in his plans. The way he'd seen it, once he and Zane were healed and the area was secured, it didn't matter if The Council arrived a little ahead of schedule. Xander *had,* after all, been given enough time to get back, get healed, and even get laid.

Except that he *knew* the family, and he would have *known* that he knew them if he'd just...

Those damn dominoes, he thought again as he assured Sana for the fifth time that, yes, he meant what he said. *How in the hell did you handle this many simultaneous paths at once, Stan?*

What's that? Sana called back, and Xander realized that she was picking up on his private thoughts.

Doubling up on his auric shields and once again marveling at the young girl's powers, he thought-spoke back, *Nothing. Just wait until they're somewhere secluded. And* no *fatalities, got it?*

I wouldn't be doing this if I thought you wanted me to kill them, she told him. *I didn't join you to be a killer.*

Xander kept himself from asking what she'd intended to do as a warrior if she was unwilling to kill. In that instant, he'd nearly forgotten that he was *married* to a warrior with the very same policy.

Right, he finally said. *Then I guess we're in agreement.*

"Holy shit!" Serena almost seemed giddy. "So this is really gonna happen? Like, really-*really?* We're *really* about to drop a building on *The*-motherfucking-Council?"

"We're going to drop *parts* of a building *in front of* The Council," Xander clarified with a sigh. "But—yes, Serena—we're really going to do it!"

"Fuck yeah!" she screeched, punching into the air. "Oh god! This is so fucking awesome! I think I just flooded my panties!"

Well, Xander thought, *I hope you get a chance to wipe up before they get here, 'cause otherwise you're fighting them wet.*

Though Xander almost felt that there would have been some sign of the calamity—a rumble felt as the barricade fell into place, a roar of screeching brakes and cursing mythos elders, or maybe a flash of outrage in the distance—the event came and went. The others, those who could watch through their minds' eyes, did so with emotions ranging from skepticism (Zoey) to patience (Xander and Estella) to outright elation (Serena). Zane and Isaac, unable to watch, had to gauge what was happening through the reactions of the others. Even then...

"So..." Zane looked around the room after a long, silent moment had passed. Obviously he, too, had been expecting something more. "Is that it then?"

"I guess so," Xander said as he closed his mind's eye to the vision of the Daius Clan's cars getting boxed into a stretch of road lining a since abandoned portion of the city's ghetto.

"Tell me why we had to do that again," Isaac said. "It seems an awful big investment for one family of three."

"I already told you," Xander growled as he moved to leave the room. "I *know* them. One of them, at least."

Estella was already following him. "You're sure that it's him?" she asked.

Xander nodded. "Yes. I'd have known earlier if I was actually paying attention, but he..." he smirked and shook his head, "He called ahead."

"I'm sorry," Zane said, "but did you just say that a *human* family called ahead? How in the hell could they have done that? How long you been advertising our kind?"

"Not since before the broadcast, I promise," Xander told him.

"Long enough for one of them to get your number, apparently," Zane shot back.

Xander almost laughed at that. "I didn't say that they called me by phone."

This actually stumped the tattooed vampire long enough to earn a few seconds of silence.

"Then how in the holy fuck did they manage to call, Mister Wizard?" Serena asked.

Figures she'd be the one to break the silence, Xander thought, turning back. "Funny you should say it that way," he answered, "because the one that I actually *know* just so happens to be magically inclined."

Isaac folded his arms across his chest, his aura shifting with suspicion. "How convenient," he said in a flat tone.

"Not really, no," Xander admitted with brazen openness. "Because I'm the one that unlocked his brain's psychic receptors and put him on that path."

"You can do that?" Zoey asked.

"Not right now. Not yet, anyway," Xander answered.

"But you managed to do it at some point in the past few weeks?" Isaac pressed. "Otherwise you *would* have been, as Zane put it, 'advertising' prior to the broadcast."

"Nope," Xander replied, crossing his arms over his chest and leaning back against the wall. It was obvious they weren't about to let him leave. "It was a while ago, actually. Before Estella and I got engaged, in fact. And it wasn't 'advertising' or anything like that, either." He shrugged, "I just saved the kid one night—needed him to be able to shield himself from a pretty substantial threat—and figured I'd let him keep the powers and the memories."

"You do realize how many laws that would have broken, right?" Zoey asked, actually sounding surprised.

Xander gave her a look.

Zoey blushed and looked down, catching on to what she'd just asked and to whom she'd asked it.

"So there's been a human kid just running around the city with memories of *you*—basically an awareness of our kind—and a magical skillset that *you* enabled within him," Zane clarified, "and you never thought to mention this in a report or anything."

"A report?" Xander laughed. "Now *that* would be advertising, wouldn't it?" He nodded towards Zoey. "Like she said: I broke *how many* laws that night with that act alone? And, let me tell you right now, I went royally overboard that night—best to just say I wasn't' in my right mind and leave it at that—so *that* was likely not the worst offense I committed that night."

A long silence followed.

"Just out of curiosity," Zane finally said, "what would have been the worst offense?"

Xander gave him a long, challenging stare; a stare that seemed to ask, *"You really want to know?"*

Zane stared back, unflinching.

Xander sighed and shrugged. "Setting fire to the sky and destroying most of the city," he answered. "And scaring the shit out of the family that lives in my old house. I doubt The Council would have cared much about that last one, but I felt worse about that than I did about the other stuff."

Another silent moment passed.

"And we're just supposed to believe all this shit went down without anybody saying anything about it? Not to mention—*HELLO!*—you still got a fucking city out there! Kinda hard to believe you destroyed it a while back when it's doing alright now. Been better, I'll admit, but the same can be said for anyplace on the planet right now."

"Our friend sort of fixed it all afterwards," Estella explained.

"Fixed?" Isaac asked. "Your friend *fixed* a destroyed city?"

Xander and Estella both nodded.

"I can only imagine you're talking about that Stan-fellow?" Zoey asked.

They nodded again.

"Shit..." Zane groaned, wiping his face. "And now that power's inside you?"

"More or less," Xander said. "Though most of it's yet to be unlocked."

"And the last time you had it—all unlocked and available in

its full potential—" Isaac said, "was the night you did all these things?"

"Yes," Xander said.

Isaac looked at Zoey, and then over between the Vaileans. "Pardon me for saying so," he said with a heavy sigh, "but I don't think I like the idea of you getting those powers back."

"You and me both, Isaac," Xander said. "Unfortunately, all of our lives and the lives of most of the people on this planet sort of depend on those powers showing up. Preferably sooner rather than later."

Zoey bit her lip and took a step towards him. "How do the powers work?" she asked.

Xander, disarmed by the question, unfolded his arms and pulled himself away from the wall.

You think it, a distant voice echoed in his mind, *and the Power makes it happen.*

"I'm not sure, honestly," he said. "It just sort of... *works.*"

Zoey's eyes drifted to Xander's torso. She paused, seeming to study his chest, then his abdomen, then her eyes shifted to his right arm before traveling to his hand. Then, furrowing her brow, she reached out with a shaky hand.

"Zoey?" Isaac called after her.

She didn't seem to hear him.

"What is it, Zoey?" Estella asked, seeming just as unnerved as Isaac by her unnerving fixation.

She still didn't answer.

The auric's small hand took Xander's, then turned it so that his palm was facing up at them. Xander's pendant still rested there, but Zoey's eyes seemed to be looking past this. Then Xander realized she was studying the large, eye-shaped scar that had been carved into his palm after Aleks had attacked him during his broadcast. Reaching for his other hand, she found a similar marking there, then turned his hands so that the combined message "ALWAYS WATCHING" stared back up at them.

"Zoey?" Estella called out again, this time setting a hand on her shoulder.

Zoey jumped at the contact, so deep in her own thoughts that she'd been distracted from everything else.

"I... I'm sorry," she said, still blinking down at the scars, "but I think the powers might be more unlocked than you think, Xander."

Xander frowned at that. "What do you mean?" he asked.

She nodded towards the scars again. "Not to get personal," she turned to look at Estella, "but I'm guessing the scars on the rest of his body are still present, too?"

Estella nodded.

"What is it, Zoey?" Isaac asked, stepping up behind her.

Zoey looked back, seeming relieved to see him there, and smiled as she took his hand into hers. This, Xander saw, was enough to ease Isaac's tension.

"We saw your body, Xander," she explained. "The day after all this started—after you... well, *after*—we all saw what had happened to you. Your body was... I mean, I'm no doctor, but even Zeek seemed certain you weren't going to make it. You were as good as dead. And, what's more, you had injuries that were so bad—so extensive!—that you shouldn't be able to be walking right now, let alone fighting and flying and..."

"And fucking!" Serena offered.

Zoey rolled her eyes, but didn't turn away from Xander. Then she looked back down at the scars on his hands and shivered, shaking her head. "Everything that Aleks and his followers did to you that night—all the injuries that should have left you crippled or disfigured—just miraculously healed the instant you woke up. And yet..."

Xander sensed Estella's aura flare with realization.

Isaac's eyes widened beside Zoey.

Zane hugged his arms across his chest, suddenly seeming cold.

Serena clapped her hands over her mouth, a muffled "oh shit" breaching past her palms.

He felt Estella's hands against his chest as she moved to look up at him, but his mind was somewhere else.

"IT IS NOT FAIR TO DO THIS TO YOURSELF!" his father's voice echoed.

Xander remembered the pale scars on his forearms, remembered the nights as a teenager that had put them there. Visions of razor blades and blood.

"No..." he heard himself whisper. "No. I wouldn't do that."

But even he didn't believe that.

He'd remembered the entire beating—relived it all from start-to-finish—before waking up. He did not remember how he'd gotten the scars, though; couldn't remember how he'd lost his eye. He looked at his hands—*"ALWAYS... WATCHING"*—and he knew if he turned them around there'd be a pair of crude eyes carved there to look back.

"Xander... baby?" Estella was whimpering beside him. "Is that it? Did you..."

"Did I..." he moved to pull his jacket and shirt from as much of his left shoulder as he could.

He managed to uncover *"how many deaths will yo"* before the clothes would stretch no further. But, he knew, they didn't need to stretch further. That was all there was to that message. To most, he knew, it would appear as an unfinished message...

But to somebody with cosmic powers of deductive reasoning—somebody who could look ahead and see this moment, this revelation, unfolding—it was all the message one would need to prove a very horrible point.

The message wasn't finished, Xander realized, because when he first saw the vision of what he'd do to himself that was all there was to see...

Xander trembled.

He'd escaped Aleks' efforts to kill him with Stan's powers; been carried off into the sky beaten, battered, and near death...

But without a mark on him.

It had been Xander's guilt at nearly letting himself die without even recognizing Estella's pregnancy that had motivated the Power to keep him alive, but that same guilt—all of that self-hatred—and twisted inward, and he'd forced himself to forget.

What if something else had twisted inward with it? Something like a dormant self-destructive urge eager to punish him?

"die die die STRYKER die di die"

"WEAK"

"WHERE IS TREPIS NOW?"

"ODIN"

"traitor"

He'd gone up there, knowing that the eyes of the world—*"ALWAYS WATCHING"*—had just witnessed him commit the worst sin he could imagine. He was a monster in their eyes, and, at that moment, he'd been a monster in his own...

It only made sense to take out his human eye.

It had been the Power, acting on his own subconscious, that had scarred him as it had. That was, after all, how it worked:

The Power makes it happen.

So why, when it finally managed to bring him back—to once again make the impossible possible by healing everything Aleks had done to destroy him—would the Power bother to heal what it had done to itself?

"Oh god..." Xander dropped to his knees.

Estella dropped down beside him, wrapping her arms around him as he began chanting "I'm sorry" to her.

Though it was hard to see through his blurring vision, Xander could see four other silhouettes standing around him.

Their auras all shone with compassion.

Xander was far—*FAR!*—from pleased by this latest revelation, but it did help to clarify a few things and affirm a few others. While he wasn't happy to know he was wearing a body adorned with so many testaments to his own self-hatred, he'd at least come to peace with the fact that, though they hadn't been nearly as elaborate or scattered, he'd been wearing scars like that for most of his life. However, what these scars meant—beyond the obvious, of course—was that the Power was more active than he'd thought. This, he realized, explained why the extra sense that had come to be known as the Great Machine seemed to be operating independently and why he kept slipping in-and-out of awareness. In short: it explained why he'd been acting so strangely.

He wasn't possessed. He wasn't channeling dead spirits or sharing a body with the recently deceased. He was once again in possession of the Power, and he was once again doing a shitty job of keeping it under control.

Well that stops now! he told himself, starting down the stairs from the conference room. Eager to be there when Joseph and his family arrived.

"Xander!" Estella called, hurrying to follow him down.

He stopped to wait for her.

"Are you..." she stopped in front of him, one step taller for it, and looked at him with raw, aching concern. "Are you okay?"

"No," Xander answered, wrapping his arms around her and resting his forehead against her chest. It felt good to be close to her then, and, taking in that radiance, he said, "But I will be. Provided you don't hate me for doing this to myself, I will be."

"Dummy," she whispered into his hair before kissing the top of his head. "I could never hate you."

Hearing this, Xander realized that, for the first time, he believed it every bit within his heart—his soul—as he thought he'd believed it in his mind. For the first time it felt real, and that resonated within him; strengthened him.

Drawing back from Estella, he looked down at the pendant

in his hand, at the length of chain that had been broken when he'd torn it from Aleks' neck. Then—deciding that, whether or not it existed within him at its full potential, the Power was going to begin working entirely *for* him rather than casually *around* him—he pinched either side of the broken links between the thumb and forefinger of his opposite hand.

Whole, he thought.

And the Power made it happen.

Moving his hand away, Estella saw that he'd fused the links together in the brief instant he'd held them. They regarded this simple-yet-marvelous feat for what it represented at that moment, smiling at one another.

Then, slipping his ruby pendant around his neck—returning it to where it had always belonged—Xander took his wife's hand and started down the stairs to meet their community's newest members.

CHAPTER 23

ALL MY FRIENDS ARE HEATHENS/IF WE GO DOWN, WE GO DOWN TOGETHER

"Any intelligent fool can make things bigger and more complex. It takes a touch of genius and a lot of courage to move in the opposite direction."
E. F. Schumacher (1911-1977)

"I... err, suppose you're this Xander I've been hearing so much about."

"That'd be me."

"And you're... uh, well... one of, you know... *them*, right?"

"Dad!"

"Honey, I don't know that it's such a good idea to..."

"It's fine, Missus Wilson," Xander could see Joey's mother's lip beginning to tremble as her husband, looking battered and breathless, tried to remain calm under the circumstances. Behind them, looking a lot taller than he had the last time Xander saw him, was Joey—wearing the now too-tight red leather jacket he'd sent him and carrying three backpacks, one cinched over his shoulders, another dangling in his left hand, and a third clutched to his chest. With the exception of the teenager, the family of three looked certain they were about to die. Unfortunately, if Xander didn't get them out of eyesight and out of the way, they would prove themselves right. "I can understand how hard this must be. It looks like you've had a rough night already, and now to uproot and come *here* of all places, right? Mister Wilson, to answer your question: yes, I'm one of *them*—probably the one that you've been hearing the most about, actually—but there's lots of other '*them*'s here, as well. We've also taken in other humans, so you and your family don't have to feel too left out. How about I show you to someone who can help you with your injuries and—"

"My son tells me that you helped him through a bad spell a while back," Mister Wilson chimed in. His lip was bleeding, and his shirt was torn; his aura was shaking, but his body was rigid. He was a man fresh from battle and living through another one: a battle *not* to break down when he was expected to keep it together for his family.

Much as he felt for the man, Xander didn't have time to finagle the situation with any semblance of delicacy.

Offering a polite smile to the man, Xander nodded and said, "I like to think that we helped each other that night."

Mister Wilson's aura trembled and Xander watched his mind waver between anger and sorrow. He teetered there, wavering first towards breaking down and sobbing over the events of the night and then towards deflecting all the pain and confusion and converting it to rage.

He chose the easier of the two:

"But I doubt anything my son did to help turned you into a *freak,* right?" he shot through clenched teeth, taking a step towards Xander.

A few passersby, pausing to take in the curious scene of the human newcomers to their makeshift community, gasped at the sight of a human making a threatening move towards Xander Stryker. Nobody thought to intervene. Nobody knew the newcomers well enough to step in on their behalf, and nobody thought for an instant that *the* Xander Stryker would need help handling a human who already looked to have been on the losing end of a fight that night.

When Xander didn't waver from the man, Mister Wilson's bold step turned into a stumble. Where he'd obviously expected some reaction—a move to put distance between them or an act of violence to justify his doubts in coming there—he'd been met with a brick wall in the shape of a young man who looked roughly half his age. He was older and, at a glance, nearly two inches taller with likely fifty pounds over the red-eyed stranger. His fumbled advance was halted by Xander's left hand as he moved to stop it, more catching the man than holding him back. The moment his palm found the man's chest, Xander began to draw in some of his rage.

Mister Wilson, Xander projected the thoughts directly into his head, *I understand that times are tough and that you are scared —I understand that you need to stay strong for your family and that you do not want them to see how broken you are—but I am not your enemy and things can get a lot worse if you do not do as I say. There are dangerous vampires coming, and I need to work to keep them from killing me and everybody else seeking the same peace and shelter here as you. Quite frankly, you could not have chosen a worse time to have arrived, but I'm being accommodating all the same.* He let his lone eye catch Mister Wilson's widening gray-blue gaze and he saw a flash of genuine terror. *I am not typically the accommodating type, but I have a great respect for your son—enough to not just do him the disservice of letting my entire community watch me render his father unconscious moments upon their arrival—and I'd rather come to learn to respect you, too.* Xander gave a single, subtle nod that told the man that he meant business at that moment. *Now, I'm going to give you the opportunity to retain the dignity you're working so hard to protect, and you're going to work with me to accomplish that. Otherwise I* will *use this connection to your mind to put you to sleep, and then your family will have to watch you be carried to a safe place so that I can make sure that Joey stays safe while I handle this. Do you understand? Just think "yes" or... well, just think "yes," got it?*

Though it was a sizable rant, Xander managed to feed the entire psychic transmission into Mister Wilson's mind in a matter of a few seconds. To everybody else, it appeared to have been just a tense stare-down. Realizing this, the man drew in a breath—a deep, meditative breath that, Xander saw, did wonders for his aura's stability—and gave a similar nod back to him.

He prefers "Joseph" now, he thought back to Xander. *He's my only son... and I don't want him to think his old man's weak.*

He watched his old man stand up to a vampire who broke into his home, Xander offered with a smirk, taking a peek into the events of that night. *Trust me, you're a hero to him right now.*

He's the one that stopped the damn thing, he explained.

Because he could, Xander reminded him. *Not because he's a freak, but because he's gifted with the control I unlocked within him.* Then, content with the diminished levels of rage in the man, he withdrew his hand and said aloud, "Us freaks gotta stick together, right?" he held out a hand—what the others and his family would all see as a sign that there was never any hard feelings between them—and, seeing what he was offering, Mister Wilson took it and gave it a firm shake.

"Y-yeah," he said, his voice wavering but otherwise strong. Xander thought he saw a faint trace of a smile begin across the man's face, but it was burning brightly on his aura. "Yeah!" he repeated, this time with more gusto, "I suppose they do."

Nodding at that, Xander motioned towards the storage facility, where Zeek was already waiting in the opened garage doors. The light spilling out from inside backlit the anapriek and created a silhouette that was all lanky limbs and unnaturally long ears. "See that gangly-looking elf over there?"

Mister Wilson stared, blinking in astonishment at the sight, and gave a slow nod.

Oh man, Xander thought, *if long ears are enough to freak him out I'd better warn Satoru to keep a low profile for a few days.* Clapping a hand on his shoulder and gently guiding him in that direction, Xander said, "He might not look it, but he's actually a very good doctor. Let him take a look at that lip and make sure that everything else is where it should be, okay?"

"Will we be safe?" Mister Wilson whispered back to him. "The only reason I agreed to come here was because Joseph said—"

Joseph wasn't wrong about the place, Xander explained in thought-speak, still working to avoid embarrassing him in front of his family. *Just about the day. Tonight seems to be the day for unwelcomed and violent intruders, wouldn't you say?*

Mister Wilson's aura shifted uncomfortably at that. *I am sorry...* he thought.

I didn't mean you, Xander said.

As they passed Missus Wilson and Joey, who apparently now preferred Joseph—Xander smiled knowingly at this—they began to follow. Missus Wilson set a pair of trembling hands on her husband's arm, her eyes all questions and concerns. Mister Wilson set one of his own hands over hers, gave her a reassuring smile and a nod, and took up the effort of walking with confidence towards Zeek and the storage facility. Watching this, Joseph fell back a pace and let his eyes glance in Xander's direction.

Sorry about him, he thought-spoke.

For what? Xander asked, smirking back at him. *A father's gotta look out for his family, right?*

I suppose, Joseph replied with a subtle shrug. *He just gets that way when he doesn't understand something. Nearly threw his new smartphone out the window after we finally got him to upgrade from his ancient flip-cell thingy.*

Xander shrugged. *In his defense, those things can be complicated for old fucks like us.*

Old? You're, like, ten years older than me, right? Joseph thought back with a sneer.

Exactly, Xander boasted, shooting him a grin. *Like I said: "old."*

Joseph laughed at that, and Mister and Missus Wilson glanced over their shoulders, curious.

Both Xander and Joseph beamed with "nothing to see here"-smiles.

Joseph's parents shared an uncertain glance with one another before stepping through the threshold of the storage facility's garage and regarded Zeek. Mister Wilson tried to maintain his composure in front of the tall, elf-like creature while Missus Wilson seemed to be struggling to *not* reach out and touch his ears.

Xander and Joseph watched and waited a moment.

"So you actually fought the vampire that broke into your home?" Xander whispered to him.

Joseph gave a dismissive shrug. "I wouldn't call it 'fighting,'" he confessed. "I was using my psychic powers to scan for you. Sometimes I catch you in the middle of one of your fights and it gives me ideas for my comic books. Anyway, I think the other vampire must've, like, picked up on my scans or something, 'cause that was when I heard the door get kicked in. Guy was screaming your name and flashing his fangs—would've been really cool if it wasn't, y'know, in our house and all real and stuff."

"That does have a way of fucking things up," Xander agreed.

"Honey?" Missus Wilson called out after Joseph. "Come on in, okay? Leave Mister Stryker to his work, alright?"

"He'll be right in, ma'am," Xander called back. "We're just catching up."

Joseph's parents considered this for a moment. It was Mister Wilson, however, who turned away, committed to the role of dignified confidence that Xander had offered him, and led his wife inside with Zeek beside them.

"So this vamp that honed-in on your psychic scans and broke into your home?" Xander started. "He say anything else?"

Joseph shook his head, and Xander was sure that was the end of it. "He only screamed your name," he repeated, and then gave a coy smirk, "but he was *thinking* all sorts of stuff."

Xander raised an eyebrow at that. "Oh?"

Joseph nodded. "The word 'Messiah,' for starters. Just kept thinking it over and over, kinda sounded like the thoughts of a crazy person with how much it was going through his head. I thought maybe it had something to do with those church-folks you've been fighting lately, but then I remembered that they don't get along with vampires, so that seemed stupid."

"The church-folks?" Xander folded his arms across his chest. "Oh man, you really *have* been watching me, huh?"

Joseph flinched at that. "Is that bad?"

"Well, bad for me, I suppose," Xander laughed. "I shield myself pretty heavily whenever I'm out, so it doesn't say much for me that you can just *spy* on me from your bedroom for the sake of writing a comic book. How're those coming along, by the way?"

"Good. Good," Joseph nodded, blushing. "I used the money you sent to put out a graphic novel based *loosely* on what I saw between you and that crazy dude the night we met. Sort of like Dragon Ball Z, but with more fangs and F-bombs. I didn't feel like it really captured *you*, though, so that's when I started scanning for inspiration. At first I was writing the new series with a character named 'Xavier Steeler'—*gah!* It sounds so stupid out loud now—but, well, after you went on TV and basically gave away everything I figured I didn't have to worry about changing your name. In my defense, though, I thought you were dead at first, so those first few issues were going to be to honor your memory—a sort of 'in memory-um'-thing or whatever—but then I started getting blips of your psychic energy again—'cept it was all different; stronger or whatever—and that's when I started 'watching' you fighting with the church-people."

"Says a lot that you *could* watch all that," Xander said. "Means you're stronger than I would've guessed. I wouldn't be surprised if you were naturally inclined. Maybe, even without me unlocking anything in your head, you would've come about them on your own."

"You think so?" Joseph asked.

Xander nodded.

Seeming pleased with this, Joseph grinned and nodded. "That's cool, I guess. Though I could never see what the church-folk were called. They were always sort of blurry in my head, so I had to draw them with, like, heavy robes and shit—real cryptic, old-skool 'crazy religious kooks'-sort of illustrations, you know?"

"I don't," Xander admitted, "but I was never the artistic type. Then again, those assholes—they call themselves 'Cebourists,' by the way—probably *would* rock the 'old-school' robes if they had any sense of fashion."

"Says the vampire who was wearing a jacket straight out of the eighties to fight a crazy flying man," Joseph laughed.

"Hey!" Xander defended, "Look who's talking, Mister 'Wearing-That-Same-Jacket' even though you've clearly outgrown it."

"Yeah, well..." Joseph gave the collar of his own jacket a tug and smirked. "I guess you made them cool again. Then you show up wearing this kickass new thing," he nodded towards Zoey's gift. "Looks like someone crossed 'The Matrix' with something out of 'Hellsing.'"

Xander chuckled and shook his head. He didn't want to admit that he'd only ever heard of 'The Matrix.'

"I would've thought a guy like you would be all about anime," Joseph absently said.

Xander blinked over at him. "You can read my mind right now?"

Joseph flinched again and nodded, looking like a kid who'd just been caught with his hand in the cookie jar.

"Damn..." Xander smirked and shook his head. "You *are* powerful."

"I guess so," Joseph said. "Enough to catch the 'Messiah'-crazed vampire off guard. I was running downstairs to see what was going on when I saw him throw my dad across the living room into the TV. It looked like he was about to do more—like, bite him or something like that—so I threw him through our living room wall."

Xander gaped at him. "You... *threw* him? Threw him *through* a wall?"

Joseph nodded, glancing back at him. "Yeah. Why? I'd seen you do it all the time. 'Hit hard, hit fast, and make it the hit you're remembered for,' remember? That's what you told me, at least, and I figured it was the best way to deal with him. I mean, I *thought* it was. Obviously you do it better, 'cause he just growled a lot and stood right back up. Between him and my dad flipping shit over everything—the vampire showing up and then me using my powers in front of him—I decided it was better *not* to try to be you and just, like, put him to sleep."

Xander stared.

"What?" Joseph demanded.

"You were able to use your powers to *lift* the intruding vampire, *throw* him with enough force to break through a wall of your home, and then *casually* render him unconscious?"

"Well... *yeah!*" Joseph said with a shrug. "Like I said, I'd seen you do stuff like that all the time, so I just figured... well..."

"Damn, kid," Xander chuckled and shook his head. "You really are powerful. Little bit of formal training and you might even—"

XANDER! Zoey's voice was loud enough in his head to make him flinch.

Joseph, seeing this, started to reach out in concern.

Xander waved him off with an "I'm fine," before focusing back on the connection with Zoey. *They're here?* he asked.

The first car was just spotted, she confirmed.

Xander nodded to himself, closing the connection, and motioned towards the storage facility.

"The Council's here?" Joseph asked, already starting to take a few steps towards the building.

Xander tried not to feel surprised at that—the kid *was* consistently proving himself, after all—but it caught him off guard to hear him speaking so casual of the mythos government, which he wouldn't have imagined Joseph ever gaining insight to.

"Seriously," he called back to the wizard prodigy, "formal training when this is all behind us."

"Really?" Joseph asked, his aura spiking with excitement. "You promise?"

But Xander had already turned away and started back. He was glad for the break, though; he wasn't sure he felt confident making that sort of promise just yet.

Make sure everyone else is hidden and secured, he cast out across their territory. Though he was directing the message to those with the power to carry out the command, he figured it was worth it to emphasize to everyone else how important it was to keep a low profile for what was coming. *Estella and I are going to shield everyone as best we can, but anybody else who* can *shield themselves and others be sure to do so. There's some very powerful, very dangerous aurics inbound, and I don't want them picking up on any stray signatures that they can target while I try to negotiate with them.*

Xander already knew full-well that the chance at peaceful negotiations was no longer an option. Everybody else, however, didn't need to know that just yet.

Over the next few seconds, he could sense auric signatures all around him flaring up, enveloping their immediate surroundings, and then winking out of existence. Though he hadn't been expecting much when he'd said it, Xander actually found himself impressed. He and Estella had yet to shield the compound against the approaching threat—against distant threats, sure, but once the veil of those shields were penetrated everything within it would be accessible to a strong enough mind—and already the combined efforts of "Stryker's Vagrants" had dimmed the combined auric mass a great deal.

Zoey, Xander called out, jogging towards the clearing that fed out to the main roads. The Council's caravan would have to pass through there, and Xander had no intention of letting them get further than that before he was certain they were no longer a threat. *I need an ETA.*

Zoey was two words into *"They're already here"* before Xander was sending out another order to Sana:

Stop their first car!

Xander could already hear the squeal of brakes as he jumped into overdrive to clear the distance.

ESTELLA WAS at Xander's side while he was still in overdrive. It caught him off guard—seeing somebody suddenly explode into existence beside him while he was otherwise surrounded by a time-frozen world—but only for an instant.

That varcol speed still freaks me out, he confessed in thought-speak to her.

Everything you can do, she thought back, *and a little bit of speed gets to you?*

Xander wanted to laugh at that. *We're going to have to discuss what 'little bit' means when all of this is over,* he promised her.

They were silent a moment as they cut through the area, weaving between buildings.

There's definitely going to be a fight now, isn't there? she asked.

Xander let his gaze drift over to her. *Did you read my mind?* he answered with his own question.

Estella shook her head, looking almost insulted, and said, *You're not the only one who can apply deductive reasoning, sweetheart. We* did *drop a building on them. I have to imagine we'd exhausted any chance of them being patient at that point.*

Xander nodded, smirking. *Deductive reasoning: the new super-power,* he quipped.

With how the world behaves, Estella thought, *it might as well be considered one.*

Well, fellow super-deducer, you guessed right. There will most certainly be a fight, he told her. *Just don't let the Vaileans in on it just yet. I need them to come into it naturally, which means you—*

Need to react to what comes naturally, I know. Honestly, I'm just going to go through the motions as though there's still a chance to avoid a fight. I'm still not sure I believe that we can go through all this and still have a shot at gaining their support, she confessed.

Oh, ye of little faith, Xander quipped, then immediately wondered why. Then he remembered that he still had bits of Stan's auric traces lingering within him. *If I start quoting sonnets...* he thought to himself, and then immediately wondered when he'd last used the word "sonnet."

Faith, Estella responded with a chitter of psychic laughter riding along the word. *Never would I have believed I'd be told to have faith that Xander Stryker, love of my life and soon-to-be-father of my child, would* not *be killing, maiming, and otherwise un-aliving somebody he* knew *he was going into battle against.*

"Un-aliving," he repeated. *You just make that up?*

It was in a comic book I read, she confessed. *Remind me to thank Joseph for getting me into them when all this is over. I'll be honest: it's nice knowing that he's here. That boy really looks up to you.*

Yeah, Xander thought-spoke with an internal groan. *That's what I need right now: hero worship.*

The conversation lasted a fraction-of-a-second as they crossed the distance, effectively sprinting from the far side of the harbor to the opposite end of the territory they'd claimed. This, Xander figured, was roughly the size of three square city blocks, but, because it all existed as a private lot of land that had once served as a bustling portion of the harbor's business district, existed almost privately from the rest of the city. As the buildings broke away and became the main entrance—a graffiti-laden sign by the offshoot from the main road declaring "SEASIDE OFFICE PARK"—Xander could see a black BMW that appeared to have broken down in mid-turn. This, he realized, had been the first car in The Council's recently borrowed caravan, and it was effectively blocking the rest of their cars from entering. Sana, upon hearing the order to stop the leading car, had forfeited all subtlety and, with no buildings to drop in front of them, had gone and smashed in the hood. Black smoke hung in a time-frozen swirl over the cratered metal, and a few members of The Council and their Daius escorts were suspended in mid-step from that car. Others, equally as frozen, had begun to emerge from the halted ones behind it.

Except, Xander noticed, for one of the cars. Though all four doors hung open, there was nobody in or around—

Incoming! Estella warned, then flashed back out of sight as she used her varcol speed to slip out of Xander's already time-enhanced perception.

He spotted the four Daius warriors sprinting back his way, guns holstered at their hips and matching combat knives drawn.

They were already prepared to kill him then and there in overdrive.

That, he thought, *would put a damper on negotiations...*

Then, in a sudden burst of motion, two of the warriors who'd been standing closest to one another were thrown off their feet. No longer able to sustain their superhuman speed, the two vampires hung, suspended in midair—their bewildered eyes still darting about in confusion; their arms and legs flailing to find a grip—with Estella, just as time-frozen but nowhere near as bewildered, drifting between them, her aura binding one as she braced her elbow at the throat of the other.

That, he thought spoke to her, *is going to suck when you land.*

For these two, maybe, she responded.

Xander would have said more, but as the closest of the

remaining two warriors closed the distance he was forced to side-step to keep from getting cut. Sent off balance, he worked to pivot, hoping to maintain his hold on the ground and not stumble out of overdrive. He overcompensated, however, and began to topple in the opposite direction.

On your six, Stryker, he "heard" Zane behind him.

Though he didn't have the auric control, Xander realized that he'd learned to project his thoughts in a way that was easily picked up by auric minds. A perk, he supposed, of working so closely with a high-level mind like Zoey's and being married to an auric-sang hybrid. Confident that his friend had the last warrior covered, Xander cast out his aura and ensnared the Daius warrior who'd thrown him off balance.

Turnabout's fair play, asshole! he thought, not caring if the warrior could "hear" it or not.

Xander exploded out of overdrive and skipped violently across the pavement, his new coat absorbing the impact and, without the interruption of pain stalling his movements, he tucked into the fall and rolled to his feet. The Daius warrior, still being towed by his aura, crashed to the street with the same violent force. Neither armored against the impact nor expecting it, however, the other vampire's fall had him crying out in pain as his arm snapped from trying to catch himself. As he came to a lurching stop, howling in pain and clutching his arm, Xander reached out with an auric probe and disabled the firing pin in his sidearm. Ahead of him, Xander spotted Estella, shielding her own impact with the road by using the two warriors she'd knocked out of play, and rolling with a similar maneuver to her feet as her own opponents writhed from what he had to imagine was the worst set of friction burns across their backs and arms. Beside him, not far from where he'd seen the last Daius warrior, Zane stood, already out of overdriving and holding his own opponent by the bottom of his jaw in a choke-hold that had the warrior's feet dangling nearly a foot from the ground; the wrist of his knife-hand twisted backward and both of his weapons already slipped into the waistband of Zane's jeans.

"NO KILLING, RIGHT, STRYKER?" Zane called across the distance, though Xander could tell the volume was more for the sake of advertising to The Council that they were interested in a peaceful resolution.

Xander, considering this, figured it was better *not* to give them such a certainty. "NOT UNLESS THEY GIVE US NO OTHER CHOICE," he called back.

His aura flaring with excitement for a fight, Zane shook the warrior in his grip and growled, "Please, asshole! Give me no other choice!"

Though Xander knew it was just for effect, he had to admit that Zane could be quite convincing.

So I'm guessing you were referring to this when you brought up the 'Zap-Trap,' right? Estella asked in thought-speak.

Xander only gave her a slight nod as he spotted a few of The Council's elders begin to come around the blocked-in caravan. He'd been seeing the name "Luis" in every vision wherein a fight became an absolute certainty, so he wasn't surprised to see that one of the older-looking vampires—an auric—carried that name. He wasn't sure, however, if this meant that circumstances had been shaped as they had *because* Elder Luis was among them or if this simply represented one of the only possible outcomes and the elder's presence was purely coincidental.

This Great Machine-shit is going to be the death of me, Xander groused to himself, then immediately regretted his choice of words.

I imagine you know why we are here, Xander Stryker, a voice chimed in Xander's head, and he felt an auric connection tie him back to the elder he'd identified as Luis.

"I SHOULD HOPE I'D KNOW WHY YOU WERE HERE," Xander called back aloud, hoping hiccup the upcoming violence by getting at least a few of the other Council members interested in hearing what he had to say. "SINCE I'VE BEEN WORKING SO HARD TO MAKE IT HAPPEN."

Sure enough, that had a few of the auras surrounding the caravan shifting with curiosity.

Beside him, Zane tossed the now-gasping Daius warrior to the street, casually growling "Stay down" as he did.

A moment later Serena appeared beside him, her auric bow-and-arrow drawn and leveled down at the downed vampire.

"Just give me a reason, shit-stain," the blonde hissed down at him.

"Already said that, toots," Zane called back to her, then, though he didn't sound at all surprised, he said, "And I thought we agreed you were going to sit this one out."

Serena, already seething at hearing that her threat had been stolen—the term *"sloppy seconds"* echoing in her mind—jutted her chin in Estella's direction and said, "But she gets to fight," in a pouty tone.

Zane gave Xander a "you sure about that"-look.

Xander gave a "what else could we do"-shrug.

Offering an appreciative "wives, right?"-eye roll, Zane dismissed the matter and used his freed right hand to retrieve the stolen knife.

The Council elders—there looked to be seven of them present, Xander noticed—considered Serena's arrival for a moment, one of the younger-looking ones shifting his weight and seeming to come to some uncertain conclusion.

And you must be Damiano Moratti, he thought.

Around the seven, several supporting, lower level members of The Council stood, looking even more uncertain than the elders and, surrounding them, almost a dozen Daius warriors, looking even more confused. As the growing doubt in the crowd of invading mythos reached a crescendo, they all turned their questioning gazes on Luis.

Elder Luis stretched his shoulders, appearing shrug off the rising doubts of the other Council members. "That claim," he spoke in a low tone, but his aura carried it across the distance, "almost seems to imply that you *meant* for this to happen."

"BECAUSE THAT'S *EXACTLY* WHAT I'M IMPLYING!" Xander shouted back, still wanting the others to hear it.

More confusion. More doubt. More increasingly unsteady nerves.

Xander saw that nearly half of the Daius warriors who'd escorted them were no longer as committed to their cause. Though they'd still carry out their orders—they *were* clan warriors and, as such, enforcers of Council law, after all—this shift would allow Xander and the others to claim an immediate upper hand.

"Interesting," Luis mused before wetting his lips and taking a single step forward. "I had my suspicions. Certain... *details*"—he claimed the word after a brief pause with a ferocity that almost seemed to hum, the resonation of which seemed to echo through the air itself—"seemed a little too perfect; a little too compelling. But..." he took another step, "It *does* beg the question of *why*. So, Xander Stryker, son of Joseph Stryker, *why*—knowing what you know, having done what you did, and understanding all that you do of our ways—would you *want* us to come to you?"

"TO SAVE THE WORLD," Xander announced.

"Oh, I have every intention of it," Luis informed him. "Starting by ending the life of the one who worked so hard to destroy it." Then, glancing back at the others, he moved to give an order.

"Kill them," Xander heard the words before Luis spoke them, the Great Machine slipping forward by mere seconds.

BRING THEM DOWN! Xander ordered, already beginning to jump into overdrive. Then, to Estella, he finally confirmed the plan: *Zap-trap!*

Elder Luis still hadn't gotten the words out before the four were closing the distance in overdrive. Even the sangs in their group, Xander realized, hadn't registered their movement yet.

It's a good thing I don't want you or your crew dead, Xander planted as a psychic message within Luis' head. Though the auric vampire wouldn't be able to "hear" it at that speed, it existed in his mind now as a seed that would blossom when they returned to normal time.

Instructing the Vaileans to handle the able-bodied fighters to the right of Luis, Xander darted off towards the left with Estella by his side. Already their auras were slipping ahead, sweeping the nearest Daius warriors off their feet. Passing between another two, Xander knocked their knees out, leaving them in a time-frozen topple. Estella, sweeping out with her own aura, left another three in mid-fall. Another Daius warrior, this one a perfect, Xander slammed down on the caved-in hood of the nearby car, hoping to daze his auric senses when they dropped back out of overdrive long enough to let the second part of his and Estella's plan come to fruition. Targeting another perfect, Estella drove her elbow against his forehead, slamming his head abruptly back and casting his gaze skyward.

That one's gonna have quite a headache when he comes out of it, Xander called out to her.

Let's just say I'm not thrilled with what he had in mind for you if Luis gave the order to kill us, she called back.

Realizing that she'd "overheard" an unpleasant intention on the mind of one of the few warriors *not* hindered by Xander's words, he decided he likely had it coming. *Should have known better than to piss you off,* he thought back.

The chittering of his wife's psychic laughter resounded in his head as he continued taking The Council's fighters out of commission.

So we're just supposed to knock 'em down? Zane asked.

Yeah, Serena chimed in, sounding disappointed. *No offense, Stryker, but this shit's almost too easy. We can't, like, break a few femurs or punch a few of them in the dicks or something?*

We've already broken four of their more eager entourage, Xander explained. *It'll be tough to maintain the "we meant well"-*

argument if we take advantage of this situation and do any more damage than what's necessary.

But the fuckers are just gonna bounce back up! Zane argued.

No, Estella informed them. *They are not.*

Guess we're gonna take the goddess' word for it, Zaney-poo, Serena, still sounding disappointed, mused. *But I'm still punching... this one*—there was a brief pause in her psychic message —*square in the baby-maker.*

Was that really necessary? Estella demanded.

Is anything that I do necessary, *Goddess?* Serena asked, actually going so far as to try to sound innocent. *Of course it wasn't! But it* was *funny. You should try it.*

Nobody punch anybody else in the dick, Xander ordered. *For fuck's sake, Serena, we're trying to gain their support!*

So tell them it was a "WHOOPSIE!" or something. We're darting around like lubed-up lightning, after all; a nut-tap is bound to happen at these speeds.

Good luck selling "nut-tap" to the guy whose dick you likely just turned to putty, Zane pointed out.

Oh, bah! It was a love-tap at best! Serena defended.

Are you two finished yet? Xander demanded.

Huh? Serena sounded confused by the question, actually seeming to have forgotten what they were doing. Then, *Oh, that? Yeah! I think we got 'em all. They don't* know *they've been gotten yet, but—yeah!—all ours are good and gotten.*

Rolling his eyes, Xander grabbed the nearest of the mid-falling opponents—this one a lower-ranking Council official—and planting him at Luis' feet to be certain the message they were about to send was clearly received.

Then, satisfied, he called *"fall back"* and left Estella to do her part.

She was already beginning the chant to focus her energies as she dropped out of overdrive beside him.

Time lurched back into play, and the scene before them burst into a wave of motion as all but a few of the oldest

Council elders, Luis included, began to collapse. The instant their bodies made contact with the ground, Estella's magic flared like bright-orange electricity that snaked and coiled around their bodies and shackled them where they lay.

"HOLY SHIT!" Serena cried out with a burst of laughter at the sight.

Zane, who could only see the fallen vampires thrashing against invisible binds, considered what he saw and muttered "Zap-Trap?" to Xander.

Xander only nodded as he kept his gaze fixed on Luis as a psychic seed—*"It's a good thing I don't want you or your crew dead"*—sprouted in the elder's mind.

Then Elder Luis surprised Xander by smiling.

"I thought Stanley's magic might have something to do with all of your tricks," he said with an amused chuckle. Then, giving another glance about at the scene surrounding him, he gave another of his shrugs and said, "Alright, Stryker. Let's hear what you have to say."

SIX OF THE seven elders still seemed uncertain as Xander and Estella led them up to the conference room. Four of those six were certain that it was a trap and that the Strykers were preparing an attack; that they were going to try to seize power of the mythos government for some nefarious plot. Two of those four, moreover, were already preparing to seize Estella's mind in the hopes of gaining a hostage should Xander show any sign of treason. Much as it angered Xander to "see" anybody planning harm on his wife, he also knew that Estella could see into their minds as clearly as he could.

And he knew that, should any of them try to capture her mind—or any part of her, for that matter—it wouldn't be Xander they'd have to worry about.

The two shared a knowing glance and a smirk at this

mutual thought as they entered the room. They made no effort to stop and invite the elders to pass through first, they already knew that they wouldn't feel comfortable putting a Stryker at their backs, and so they passed through with the seven following close behind. Six of the seven auras behind him shifted with uncertainty as they saw the demolished table occupying the center of the room and the gaping hole yawning above that.

Deciding he had an opportunity to not only show the seven some hospitality but *also* show them a display of his powers, Xander, not breaking his stride towards what looked like a warzone, reached out with his aura.

You think it, he recited to himself, *and the Power makes it happen.*

Even Estella stared, awestruck, as the ten-sided table reassembled itself before their eyes—wood fibers that had been reduced to splinters coming back together and reforming in ways that no auric mind could achieve. An aura could move the pieces and even hold them together, but even the most accomplished auric vampire could not alter matter on a molecular level. Broken was broken, and even the strongest and most stubborn aurics in that room knew this to be true. But as Xander finished with the table and began rebuilding the roof, he was proving this limitation to be beneath him. Finally, with the table whole and the ceiling restored, nine chairs floated from where they'd been discarded and took their places.

Xander and Estella sat first, followed soon after by Elder Luis, who took the open chair closest to Xander. Still uncertain, the other six followed suit, being certain to leave a gap between the nearest elder and Estella.

Even then, with the exception of Luis, The Council was prepared to kill them and everyone associated with them.

Ignoring this, Xander finally began the overdue explanation.

He told Elder Luis and the other six Council elders everything. He showed them everything, as well, starting with his encounter with Ariel and the Cebourists the night he'd "attacked" the entire mythos community.

"Attacked." As though he'd done it with any intention *except* warning his fellow nonhumans the world over of a global threat to their very existence. He and Estella had some choice words for that—responding to the word "attacked" with a series of words that, on any other occasion, would have likely brought the metaphorical axe down on their heads—and the elders stared, wide-eyed and obviously offended, as they said them; though those words alone should have gotten them killed, The Council sat and listened.

Because, after the display we put on, Xander thought, *what the hell else are they going to do?*

Then, when there was nothing left to be said regarding the motives and intentions behind Xander's actions several weeks earlier, he told them about Aleks. Like with the first subject, the elders weren't eager to reconsider their stance on things; they certainly didn't want to acknowledge and allow themselves to feel concern over an entirely new problem. After Xander said the words "Lenuta had a son," however, any urge to interrupt was squelched.

And then Xander added, "And he wants to take over the world; wants to make it his. Lenuta's son, Aleks, wants to destroy everything."

This was all it took to shut up the arrogant old farts.

Nothing scares men of power more than realizing their power might be lost, a little voice in the back of Xander's mind chimed. For a moment he thought it was the lingering voice of Stan's aura getting in its two cents as it had been since his reawakening.

But then Xander caught sight of Elder Luis smirking knowingly towards him out of the corner of his eye, and Xander found himself wondering.

Then, like he had with the subject of Ariel and the

Cebourists, Xander showed them what he'd seen from Aleks. As he broadcast his fight in the cemetery earlier that night with Aleks directly into their minds—he tried not to smirk as the visions had some of the elders ducking and dodging blows that had already come to pass. Luis, however, didn't seem surprised —not by the display, anyway—but, then again, he'd already proven to know more—to understand more—than Xander had anticipated.

"I thought Stanley's magic might have had something to do with all of your tricks."

Just how much do you know about this, old man? Xander thought absently as he finished broadcasting his memories into the elders' heads.

More than you'd think, Elder Luis' voice chimed in his head, though his eyes still shifted about in his wrinkled face in response to the streaming visions of Aleks and the cemetery. *And less than I'd like.*

Xander stayed silent after that, both inside and outside his head.

One by one, with the memory fading on the sight of Aleks vanishing from sight in the arms of one of his followers, the elders began to murmur. What started as the contemplative mutterings of one turned into the hushed whispers between two, then the stifled debating of three. Xander let his eye circle the table as three was suddenly five, and then, finally, six. All were now actively deliberating on what they'd just seen

All but Luis, who only clasped his hands together and set them in front of himself on the table.

The deliberations went on for ten minutes between the six elders as the Strykers and Elder Luis watched them, occasionally breaking away to offer a glance at one or the other. With the words being spoken, Xander could "hear" everything that went unspoken, as well—the minds of even the most accomplished aurics around them little more than open books to him. Estella, with her varcol-like powers, was no different. And while

Xander was certain that Luis could just as easily read his comrades' thoughts—he'd been showing no sign of struggle in slipping inside Xander's head since their arrival, after all—it also stood to reason that the old auric was just as capable of deducing what they were thinking without prying. After those ten minutes passed, however, Elder Luis, letting Xander and Estella see him roll his eyes in their direction, cleared his throat.

It was a simple gesture—*not even a very loud one,* Xander thought—but the other six elders fell silent in an instant.

"It seems to me," Elder Luis said in a voice that wore the guise of a casual suggestion but carried all the weight of a command, "that Xander, his beautiful wife, and all of his supporters have been doing our job for us."

Six auras flashed with indignation, fizzled with shame, and finally settled once more.

Luis nodded at this and sighed, shaking his head. "But..." he turned his gaze and his heavy tone on Xander, "you *did* break the law. And I do mean *the* law—the very law by which practically every other law this Council has come to pass is based upon. Were there a hundred laws, a thousand, or even a million," he furrowed his wrinkled brow as though he smelled something foul, "I could say with absolute certainty that *ninety-nine percent* of those laws could be wiped away entirely and replaced with that single law: *keep... the... secret!* And you, Xander Stryker..." Elder Luis barked out a laugh that was more of an enraged bark, "you *did not* keep the secret. One could not even claim that you broke this law, in my humble opinion, for that seems to almost imply that it could be fixed." He trained his strong, old eyes on Xander. "This *cannot* be fixed; this law was not simply broken, it was destroyed!"

The other six elders murmured and nodded in agreement, their auras beginning to swell with anticipation for what was to come.

Beside him, Xander sensed Estella beginning to tense, certain that an execution was about to be attempted.

He moved his hand, careful not to alarm any of the elders and motivate a premature strike, and set it atop her thigh.

It'll be alright, he assured her.

But, Xander... she began.

Xander gave her thigh a gentle squeeze for reassurance.

Luis held his gaze on Xander for a long, long time. The silence stretched on for just as long.

Xander held the elder's gaze for every crawling second of it.

Then, finally, Elder Luis gave a slow, methodic nod.

"But perhaps," his words came out with quiet resolve, "it is better to destroy old laws than to let them destroy those who obey them."

"Elder Luis, you can't be—"

"He has endangered—"

"It is an unprecedented—"

"How will we—"

"SILENCE!" Elder Luis cut off the words of four elders and halted those of those who'd yet to speak with only one of his own. The table, still vibrating with the auric vibrations from his command, fell silent. "You have presented us with a great many troubling ongoings," he went on to Xander. "These Cebourists, it would appear, are not something to be trifled with, and with the power and numbers that they've acquired I have not a single doubt that they could have and *would have* used our very secrecy against us as you claim—forcing us into hiding while they tracked us down and hunted us to extinction. Though we weren't happy to see mythos the world over falling under the spotlight, it would appear that many had no other choice. I shudder to imagine what sort of losses we might have faced if not for your unorthodox warning. Obviously measures need to be taken against them, but..." he paused to rub at the corner of his chin, "But this varcol—this Aleks—presents a far more demanding threat. It will do us no good to work to brace against a world of empowered humans if the world has fallen; there would be nothing left to fight for and, what's more, no use for us"—he motioned to himself and the other elders—"if one blood-thirsty dictator assumes the role of the world's sole government."

"Then you'll help us?" Estella blurted, her aura swelling with hope.

Elder Luis smiled at her. It was not the sort of smile that tired, old men offered to beautiful, young women, though; it was the sort of smile that wise, knowing minds offered to those who gave them a glimmer of hope for the next generation. It was the same smile that the auric elder offered to Xander then, finally giving a single nod.

"On the condition," he began, raising an old, bony finger, "that you tell us who it was that has been making our lives so difficult on this night?"

Xander blinked at that, uncertain of what he meant. "Huh?" was all he could think to say.

"All night—ALL BLOODY NIGHT!—" Elder Luis snarled, "an infernal menace had been stalling our approach. Our navigations, our cars, and even our own goddam bladders:"—Xander had to struggle not to laugh at that—"all the playthings of an auric force that finally managed to steer us into Hell's sweet nowhere and begin dropping pieces of a god-damned building all around us! And all the while we could neither track nor shield against their tricks," he explained. "We know that the owner of that aura—that *pink* aura—is one of yours. And we want them!"

"Sana," Xander called out to the auric prodigy, leading the elders towards her.

Seeing them approaching, the color began to bleed from Sana's face. Then she saw Xander's expression—read his aura—and looked confused.

"Xander?" she offered a bow in his direction and then flinched as Elder Luis stepped around him to face her head-on.

"You?" Elder Luis said, doing nothing to hide his surprise. "You're the one who's been making our lives difficult?"

"I... uhm," Sana blushed and dragged her shoulders up in a slow, sustained shrug.

"SANA!" Tim's cry, and his aura, burst into existence between Sana and the elder, his fangs bared and his stance braced for a fight.

Xander didn't want to admit at that moment that his form was solid, and he wasn't sure how he felt about the swell of pride that came at seeing Elder Luis actually fall back a step. It took a lot of skill—*and quite a set of balls,* Xander thought—to catch somebody of Elder Luis' skills off guard.

All the same...

"Tim," Xander set a hand on the young vampire's shoulder and applied just enough pressure to remind him he could apply a lot more.

Tim maintained the snarl for another moment, not taking his eyes from Elder Luis.

Xander tightened his grip. "Tim!" he said with sharpened his tone.

The young vampire finally flinched and looked up at him, unspoken questions burning in his eyes.

"And who is this?" Elder Luis asked, folding his arms across his chest.

"This is Tim," Xander explained. "He's been with us since the beginning—since before the Trepis Clan had even come into being, in fact."

Elder Luis cocked his head. "His lineage?" he asked, though Xander could see that he wasn't curious about pedigree but, more simply, asking where his parents were.

"He came with friends, sir," Xander explained. "That's all I'll say about that. With all due respect, it's not my story to tell."

"Training?" Elder Luis went on, not seeming swayed by Xander's answer.

Xander shrugged, modest. "Informally with his father at a young age, but I've been training him ever since."

A bushy gray eyebrow raised at that. "You've personally trained this boy?"

"Yes, sir," Xander nodded.

Elder Luis lingered on this a moment, looking over Tim with an analytical gaze. Then, addressing him directly, the elder said, "I'm to gather that you have feelings for this girl?"

Tim's face turned red at the question, but he nodded.

Behind him, Sana's face softened; her pink aura swelling with affection at the confession.

Seeing the obviously familiar aura, Elder Luis' eyes gleamed with intent. Wetting his lips, the old auric's head bobbled—neither a shake nor a nod—and he said, "Well, son, we're—"

"I'm not your goddam son!" Tim growled at him, once again presenting his fangs.

Elder Luis flexed his hands, popping a few joints in the process. He seemed to be putting on a display, but his aura made no move to slip from his body.

Then again, Xander realized, *Tim would have no way of knowing that.*

The young vampire stood his ground, not even his aura betraying a hint of fear.

Elder Luis seemed to notice this, as well.

Nodding, he glanced back at one of the lesser Council members—Xander got the impression he was an assistant to Elder Luis—and said, "Him, as well."

Xander scowled and crossed his arms. "'Him, as well?'" he repeated, shaking his head. "I said I'd agree to giving her the *choice*, but I'm not about to—"

"And if we give him the same choice?" Elder Luis asked.

Xander paused at that, biting his lip. A part of him felt saddened by it, but he offered the old auric a nod all the same.

Estella had left Xander with the elders and the rest of The Council to do what they would. The idea of the decision that was about to be made was not something she felt she could emotionally handle at that moment. She'd kept it together through a great deal already; *that* was simply too much for her to stomach.

Word had begun circulating that Xander and The Council were, at the very least, *not* fighting—not within eyesight of any of the others, at least. With Estella walking freely towards the storage facility where Zane and Serena had gone to let them conduct their business, however, she began to overhear the increasingly optimistic thoughts and whispers of all who spotted her. Her being there, being *alive*, meant a lot on its own. Even those who didn't know much of the Strykers knew that Estella wouldn't have left Xander to handle a possible threat on his own if she could be there to prevent it, and if she *couldn't* be there to prevent it then she certainly wouldn't have been casually strolling about. That she *was* casually strolling about was a good sign that some sort of agreement had been made. Granted, it was not a sure sign—there were plenty of pessimistic minds around the area who knew that to be true and were not afraid to share that opinion—but it was enough to generate a rise in activity.

And it was enough to draw out Allen Carrey.

Having to jog to catch up, he finally fell into stride beside her winded and breathing hard. Estella was quiet while he caught his breath, but she did nothing to stop or slow. Then, drawing in a deep lungful of chilled night air, he spoke:

"That... was incredible!" he declared. His voice was an entirely different creature than it had been since he'd come to live with them; it was excited and hopeful. He sounded convinced.

"Big leap from 'this is crazy,' huh?" Estella asked with a smirk.

"I *would* be crazy if it weren't for... I mean, Missus Stryker, I've never seen anything like that!" Allen went on. "I've been fighting mythos for years. *Decades!* I've killed more than I could even begin to—" he caught Estella giving him a dirty look and stopped, clearing his throat before saying, "Look: all I'm saying is that, based on what I've seen—based on what *should* be—it *would* have been crazy. Mythos are powerful, I'm not about to argue that point —you've got the fast ones, the strong ones, the psychic and telekinetic, the... well, you catch my drift—but what all hunters, even the Cebourists, relied on was that they're still *limited!* Provided you knew the weaknesses and understood the nature of the creatures, it wasn't very hard to aspire to hunt them. The point is that I *know* mythos, and based on what I *know* this *was* a mission that was doomed to fail. Even without being able to take advantage of their secrecy—man, you would not *believe* how pissed everyone was about *that*—but even *without* that, you all might as well have been ice skating uphill; you'd have exhausted yourselves before—"

"I understand the metaphor," Estella said with a sigh, finally stopping and turning to Allen. "But all I'm hearing is you telling me that, up until now, you've been doubting my husband, which means you've been doubting my judgement."

Allen Carrey gave Estella a look before finally saying, "If you were in my shoes, would you have had blind faith in Xander? Would you have invested absolute certainty in the words of his wife?"

Estella didn't like that he had a point there. Turning away, she started back towards the storage facility. "I'm not about to disagree with you, Allen," she admitted, "but I still don't hear a point being made."

"My point is I've been holding back," he called after her, still standing where she'd left him.

She stopped and turned.

Allen Carrey was nodding as she looked back at him. "I came here because, after watching Dianna die trying to save that vampire, I realized that there was more to all of this than I'd ever thought. If a fellow hunter could be swayed to that degree—to love a nonhuman so completely as to be willing to sacrifice herself to save him—then vampires and werewolves and all the other critters out must have something resembling a soul, right?"

"You're skating on thin ice," Estella warned him, deciding to stick with his own theme for metaphors.

"Sorry. Sorry," Allen Carrey said, holding up his hands. "Anyway, while I *did* come here to figure things out and pay my respects to Dianna's sacrifice, I still wasn't sure about just handing over all my secrets. I figured that, if the shit hit the fan and you all proved to be the monsters everyone thinks of you, I'd rather have a few tricks to use; tricks that would give me the upper hand if I needed it."

Estella narrowed her eyes at that and started to storm back in his direction. "Like the sort of trick that robs a mythos of their strengths? *That* sort of trick?" she demanded.

Allen Carrey shrugged. "That one I taught, sure, but I'll admit that I only taught enough to take *half* their strength."

Estella closed the rest of the distance in overdrive, pinning the human against a nearby wall. "You nearly got Xander killed because of that!" she hissed in his face. "He cast that spell on a varcol and—"

"And if he'd been unable to fight a varcol at half strength," he strained around Estella's grip, "then I would've been right about him all along and this all *would* have been crazy!"

Estella hissed in his face, still enraged at his deceit, but finally flung him to the ground. "You'd better make a redeeming point soon," she snarled after him, reaching to the sheaths at her back and drawing Helios. The golden tonfa began to shine within her hand, responding to the magic of its owner, and she spun it in her grip, letting the longer half of the baton-like weapon come to rest against her forearm so that she was pointing at him with the shorter end. Sparks hissed and popped from the shimmering surface, illuminating the area for several meters.

Allen Carrey's eyes widened and he held up his arms, stammering. "I-I believe now. I BELIEVE! A-and, though I'm starting to wonder if I should, I t-trust you, too." Struggling to prove his point, he shakily began to lower his arms, remaining on his knees for the time being. "And I'd like to finish everyone's training—*all* of their training—and begin helping that blue-haired auric to create some weapons for what's coming."

CHAPTER 24
DON'T FEAR THE REAPER

"Death may be the greatest of all human blessings."
Socrates (469-399 BC)

If it had been up to Estella, she would have kept Allen Carrey's confession to herself. Sure, she would have told Xander, and she supposed that Zoey, who would apparently be working with Carrey, would have to know *why* things were changing all of a sudden. And maybe she wouldn't have minded sharing the details with a few of her more trustworthy sources...

Her more *sane* sources.

When all was said and done—if Estella was being wholeheartedly truthful with herself—she wouldn't have minded sharing the details of Carrey's deceit with just about anybody. She *was* fuming about it, after all, and talking to others about that sort of stuff had a way of helping.

But, if it had been up to Estella, she would have at least kept Allen Carrey's confession away from Serena.

Unfortunately...

"Did I hear this little choad-biscuit right?" the crazy, pregnant blonde was already standing beside Estella and glaring at the still-shaky human. "Did he actually send Xander out with a half-cocked spell to face off against Aleks?"

Estella saw Serena's aura creep out of her chest and began to take shape.

"Serena," Estella called out to her. "Don't."

"No, Goddess. You don't get to order me around. I'm Serena-fucking-Vailean, leader of the Clan of Vail and in no way obligated to take orders from you *or* even your husband. I'll take suggestions, and up to this point I've even humored those suggestions, but I still outrank you—quite frankly I still have an active clan—and, regarding *this* little scrotum-muncher..." she snarled and shook her head, drawing back her auric arrow, the arc of the shimmering purple bow thrumming. "As far as I'm concerned, he just confessed to committing an act of sabotage."

Serena loosed the auric arrow.

And suddenly Xander was there, standing over Allen Carrey, in time to catch it.

"Stand down, Serena," Xander said.

"FUCK YOU, STRYKER!" she hissed. "Y'all been tossing orders like I fucking work for you. I don't! I ain't one of your followers, douchebag; I'm your *friend!* I..." she roared and snapped her aura back, yanking it from Xander's grip and returning it to the inside of her body. "I *love* you two like family, dammit! And he"—she jammed an accusatory finger in Allen Carrey's direction—"could have gotten you killed by pedaling limp-dick fucking magic that he *claimed* would protect you against mythos!"

"And hasn't it?" Xander asked, voice still level and calm.

Serena was shaking with rage. "Hasn't it? HASN'T IT? Aleks nearly fucking killed you and Zane even after you cast the spell on him! You said it yourself: it didn't take away all of his strength!"

"No," Xander agreed. "It didn't. It took away *half* of his strength."

Estella watched as he turned, trusting Serena not to make another attempt on Allen Carrey's life, and held out a hand to help him to his feet.

"I..." Allen Carrey looked like he was about to cry in the face of Xander's generosity in the face of what he'd clearly overheard. "I am so sorry, Mister Stryker."

"I know," Xander said to him. "Just make good on your promise, okay? Help us to save the world and we'll forget all about this, okay? And—*please!*—don't ever call me 'Mister Stryker' again."

Allen Carrey, blushing, looked upon Xander at that moment as though he was a god.

Estella couldn't bring herself to disagree.

They watched the human retreat, darting on still-wobbly legs around a building, where Estella could sense him pausing to catch his breath. Though she was sure Serena could sense it, as well, having him out of their line of sight worked to bring down the tension on the blonde's auric pressure.

"You should have let me kill him," Serena finally said, sounding more hurt than angry.

Xander started towards the two of them. His focus was honed entirely on Serena, and Estella wondered for a panicked second if he was about to hit her. She tensed, seeming prepared for the same outcome. He surprised them both by hugging her.

"It's alright," Estella heard her husband whisper to her. "Zane and I made it out of there in one piece. That's all that matters."

Serena tensed and then, after a long pause, began to shake in Xander's arms. "But he... You could have killed that son-of-a-bitch—could have been done with Aleks for good!—if the spell had only worked right!"

Xander shook his head. "No, Serena. There was no path that would have ended with Aleks' death in that cemetery. Mine and

Zane's, maybe, but never his. Even if the spell had worked—even if he'd been rendered powerless—he had those vampires poised to make an appearance at the first sign of danger. A mind like his... Serena, even a human can learn how to cast a psychic call for help—Zane does it all the time. If I'd taken all his powers, he'd have just called for the backup and gotten away, probably with his leg *and* this:" he stepped away from the embrace and moved his hand up and gingerly lifted his pendant for show. "Things happened as they happened, and we can neither regret how they went nor hope they'd gone differently. We can only look forward now and make use of what we have. And what we have now is a great deal more than what we had only a few hours ago. But to kill Allen, especially now that he's prepared to dedicate to the training, would be a step in the wrong direction."

Serena looked down, her face red and tight with effort.

"Thank you for being such a good friend, Serena," Xander said then. "I know you don't get the credit you deserve for it, but you've done a great job watching over us and keeping us on track."

Serena's eyes, shimmering with tears, widened. A small, nervous laugh coughed out as she said, "Y-you... you weren't supposed to notice that."

Xander smirked and shrugged. "You hid it well, Vailean. Took cosmic powers of deduction to even catch a glimpse," he offered with a shrug.

A few tears finally betrayed Serena and began a slow crawl down her face. Despite this, Estella could see that she was smiling. "Anyo—" she hiccupped on the word and sucked in a breath, looking embarrassed, "A-anyone... ever tell you..."

"That I'm sexy?" Xander finished for her, glancing over at Estella and giving a casual shrug. "Yeah. I think I've heard that somewhere before. But you're sweet to say so."

"Even with the sex jokes?" Serena asked.

"Especially with the sex jokes," Xander answered.

"Everything okay?" Zane, still a short distance off, called out to the three.

Estella saw her relax her shoulders at the sound of her husband's voice, and she couldn't help but smile at the glimpse they were being offered at the real Serena.

Not too different from us, huh? Xander asked in her mind.

Estella, still smiling, thought back, *Like Yin and Yang.*

Xander seemed amused by her choice of words. *Read my mind, 'Stell.*

THE STRYKERS WATCHED Zane lead Serena off towards the water. The Vaileans didn't have any vulgarity or perversions to exit on, but Xander and Estella were happy to see that this was not an indicator that something was wrong. If nothing else, it looked as if things were finally going right.

Estella leaned against Xander once they were alone, still standing a short way's away from the storage facility. So much had changed in a few short weeks—some very much for the worst, but some also for the better. Not the least of which of the latter being that Xander was *still* changing things.

"But perhaps it is better to destroy old laws than to let them destroy those who obey them."

Estella felt confident against Xander as she considered all that he had changed, and she realized with a dawning sense of clarity that her phantom optimism—the positive outlook that she *might,* at some point, manage to see things with a positive outlook—was finally beginning to turn into a genuine, non-secondary optimism.

"Sana's leaving us, isn't she?" she finally asked, though she felt like she already knew the answer.

She felt Xander nod against her. "Yes," he confirmed, "and Tim, too."

Estella looked back at that, saddened to hear this but not surprised. "They didn't want to be apart?"

Xander gave a weak shrug, and Estella could see that he was sad to see the two go, as well. "Not like I would've just let you go if you were offered the same choice."

Estella smiled weakly at that.

Though she and Xander had thought that Elder Luis had intended to punish the auric who'd interfered with their caravan over the course of the night, it turned out that they'd been impressed enough by the display to decide before their arrival to attempt to recruit them. Xander *had* convinced Luis, and, through him, the rest of the elders, to forgive his offenses, but, as a gesture to help the mythos government save face when everything was over, they demanded a trade—a sign of humility and respect to earn back the faith of The Council.

"At least," Elder Luis had said, *"that's how it will be remembered on paper."*

Xander, not about to just hand over the teenage auric prodigy, told them that they were free to ask her if she'd be willing to join them. He was firm in explaining that, though she'd been formally inducted as a member of the Trepis Clan and was therefore in service to The Council already, the collapse of their clan and the subsequent charges filed against him and the rest of them was enough to—*"on paper, at least"*—make the Trepis Clan nonexistent and, as such, all of its members free from all prior regulations.

"You're in a community of rogues now, Elder Luis," Xander had told him. *"And rogues speak for themselves."*

Reaching an agreement, they'd set off to ask Sana if she'd be willing to leave with The Council when it came time to return to Europe. Estella, however, having become attached to the girl in the short time they'd known one another, couldn't bring herself to be present for that conversation.

She'd already known how it would turn out.

Though it still confused her, Estella had seen enough from

Xander—heard enough of his "seeing how the dominos fall"-speeches—to begin searching for her own signs of where things were headed. She'd gotten an inkling, just an itch in the back of her mind, while Xander had been pleading his case to the elders—the ten-sided table was missing a spot, and, subtracting the two of them, that left them in the company of seven elders. Before that, she hadn't really thought much of the number of senior Council members who'd arrived to kill them, but the empty spot beside her had gotten the gears of her mind moving with a series of thoughts that seemed to tick along on their own like clockwork. At that moment, the number seven had seemed so relevant, so familiar; it felt like something she'd somehow seen coming.

Except that she hadn't. She'd been told that it was coming.

Then Elder Luis brought up the auric, told the two of them that they wanted that auric to join them. An auric of that strength was exactly the sort of mythos that belonged in their ranks, and with the world headed where it was they would need all the strength they could gather.

And, even though all of the seven elders had been of varying views and degrees regarding almost everything else that had been brought up that night, all of them were of one sound mind when the subject of that auric and bringing them into their ranks came up.

Like the otherwise independent arms of an octopus suddenly reaching towards one goal, Estella caught herself thinking.

And then, just like that, she'd remembered the dream that Sana had told her about. She remembered the massive, world-changing fire-tiger that was Xander storming through the streets, demanding action. She remembered the horrible dragon that stood against the tiger, ready to burn the entire world. And she remembered Sana, as she braced to join the side of the tiger, being claimed by a seven-armed octopus.

It had never been about the Cebourists... she'd realized then.

And, at that moment—just like Xander with his dominoes

—Estella had known that Sana would be leaving them, in fairness to a better life than what she'd originally feared, but all the same...

And, as it turned out, they'd be taking Tim, who she couldn't help but still see as little Timothy, with them.

It was a bitter-sweet revelation, like something out of the combined minds of William Shakespeare and Bram Stoker.

"It'll be a good life for them, right?" Estella heard herself ask Xander.

Another nod. "Better than others, yes," he admitted. "And, if it makes you feel any better, Sana and Tim both said that they'd only agree on two terms of their own."

"Oh?" Estella perked up at this. "And what terms were those?"

"For starters," Xander said, a smile ringing on his voice, "The Council had to agree to support and fund our little community here. While we agreed that we don't want this to be registered as a formal clan, we'll have access to their resources, their protection, and once again entitled to all the perks that comes with their support, which is all a very diplomatic way of saying that we can go around blowing the heads off of evil mythos again."

Estella smirked and rolled her eyes at that. "So why stop there? Why not just have the Trepis Clan reinstated formally?"

"Because a clan would serve only the mythos community—would only act in the interests of The Council—" Xander explained, "but, since I've already gone this far to bring humans and mythos together, I figured it would be better to operate as a neutral site that protects the interests of *both.*"

Estella raised her eyebrows at him. "That's... surprisingly diplomatic of you."

Xander shrugged.

"How'd the elders take that?" she asked.

Xander chuckled. "About as well as could be expected, but it *was* one of the conditions that they had to agree to in order to get Sana and Tim to go along with them."

"I suppose it was," Estella said with her own chuckle. "So what was the other condition?"

"That one was a lot simpler: they both wanted to maintain contact with us whenever they wanted. Sana described it as a 'direct Council line' to any of our needs, but really she just didn't want to lose touch with us. So not only do we not really have to say 'goodbye' to them—not for good, at least—we'll also now have friends on the inside," he grinned down at her. "So to speak."

"You know what? That *does* make me feel better," Estella said with a smile.

Xander smiled back at her. "I figured it—"

Stryker, Elder Luis' voice rang out in his head, cutting off his words. *I'd have a word with you, if you'd be so kind as to grace me with your presence."*

"You alright?" Zane asked as he sat down with Serena on the edge of the dock they'd found themselves on.

They had walked in relative silence, forcing a line occasionally when something presented itself, but only for the sake of having a silence to slip back into. This, Zane realized, was a strangely romantic notion in and of itself: breaking a moment of quiet so that they could create a new moment of quiet to ease into. Like a moment of deep sadness, one could appreciate it if they recognized that it made the peaks of happiness on either side all the sweeter. Quiet, like joy, could only be measured against the moments where one didn't have it. And, like the stars that had begun to come into view overhead as they walked further and further from the lights and sounds of the "Stryker's Vagrants" community, silence could be as easy to forget about until it finally presented itself.

Zane didn't have an auric bone in his body. When the Maledictus curse had been active within him, the monster he'd become had been able to do all sorts of auric tricks. Being a creature of raw destructive force, any and all possible means of bringing pain and despair and ruin and, most of all, death were at that *thing's* disposal. It could read thoughts if only to manipulate and torment the thinkers, and it could use its aura like the best auric as a means of tearing and smashing and generally tearing everything and everyone to pieces.

And then Serena, the crazy fucking bitch, came into his life —*their* lives—and won over both the man and the monster. Through a fluke in the taroe's curse and an admittedly fucked-up act of passion that had turned Zane's body into little more than a living bridge for Serena and her dead ex-boyfriend to screw, Maledictus—always watching, as it turned out—had received something it was never meant to:

Passion.

Beauty.

Love.

Ironically, *because* of the Maledictus curse, Zane wasn't meant to get those things, either. And while he hadn't woken up beside Serena after that night in the best of moods—hot as the naked blonde was, Zane couldn't remember a damn thing and, to be fair, fucked up was fucked up no matter how great a pair of tits might be—he'd be lying to himself if he said it wasn't a more welcome sight than the whores he typically had to resort to buying when humping his fist proved to not be enough. Whores didn't love, though, and they certainly didn't include passion on the menu. That Maledictus had only butchered a few of the whores Zane had fucked over the years seemed now like a twisted act of charity on the monster's behalf, but—*who knows?*—maybe the crazed death-mongering curse enjoyed a good nutting as much as Zane did.

But the moment Serena entered the scene, Maledictus was putty in her hands. And *only* her hands.

And, as far as Zane was concerned, a girl who was batshit crazy enough to tame the absolute most batshit crazy monster on the planet is worth holding onto.

Eventually, with the help of his new love and his friends, Zane had finally gotten rid of curse that had been fucking up his life for so long, and, as an added perk, he'd even managed to get his best friend back. That Raith managed to get Nikki back into his life was cool, too, he supposed (even though Nikki was a royal pain in his ass), and Zane, even in losing the strength and auric control that the curse granted him, honestly couldn't have been happier.

Especially since he came out of it with a hot-as-fuck and crazy-as-shit blonde who somehow managed to be even hornier than him and was actually willing to let him put babies in her. He knew he didn't say it out loud enough, but one of the benefits of having a psychic wife was knowing that she could just check into his head each and every time she wanted to hear "I love you."

And he knew that, no matter what they were going through, that was *exactly* the words she'd find waiting in his skull when she did.

And possibly a crude thought about her vagina and future intentions regarding it—BUT WHO COULD BLAME HIM?

No, Zane didn't have an auric bone in his body, but he'd managed to sense something from Serena all the same. It had started as anger and sadness, which, when Serena was concerned, were often one and the same. But then it had slipped into something new: just sadness. Stepping out, asking the anapriek to watch Gregori for him, he'd spotted Xander hugging Serena and, not the least bit jealous from the sight, could tell that he'd done for his wife what he'd hoped he'd done for Estella several weeks earlier.

He felt in his heart that she was alright, but the urge to hear her speak the words had driven him to ask anyway.

"I am, Zane," Serena said, sounding surprisingly *not* loud.

Though he'd never been bothered by the front his wife put on to others—quite the opposite, in fact; she never failed to keep him on his toes, and he was never far from a laugh since finding her in those woods all those years back—it was a pleasant surprise to see her not trying so hard

"Stryker really is something else, huh?" he asked.

Serena hummed at that, smirking. "Yeah, I guess so. If you're into that whole sleek-and-sexy punk-rock thing. But me..." she sighed longingly and leaned back on the dock, letting the canopy of stars fill her vision. "I'll always have a place in my heart for big, tattooed gorillas."

Zane smirked at that and said, "You must really miss Harambe."

"Like you wouldn't believe," she replied without missing a beat. "Best lay of my life, and great with kids."

"Ouch..." Zane cringed. "That one stung even me."

"Yeah..." Serena pouted. "I feel a little dirty for that. Sorry."

Zane raised an eyebrow, taking in the sight of her heaving chest and the early swell of her pregnant belly. "Mind if I make you feel a little dirtier?" he asked with a grin.

He didn't wait for an answer.

Elder Luis had made it clear that he wanted to speak to Xander alone. After clarifying that "alone" meant no company for both of them—not wanting to walk into an ambush—he agreed. Though neither his aura nor the Great Machine detected any further threat from the Council elder, the fact that he'd managed to elude so much of Xander's scans *and* the fact that he was able to not only shield his own thoughts from Xander, but actually *read* Xander's shielded thoughts in turn made him very uncomfortable.

He found the old auric in the conference room, sitting at the table and staring expectantly at the door. Xander stood at the threshold, staring back, and trying to size up the nature of this private meeting.

Then, still not making a move, he asked, "How do you know about Stan?"

"He was close with your father," Elder Luis answered, sounding like it was the most obvious thing in the world. Xander supposed it was. "You think your father could have all the eyes of the world on him and keep those same eyes off of somebody like *that?*"

"That's fair," Xander conceded, taking a single step inside, "but there were plenty who wouldn't have understood what they were seeing when they looked at Stan. Hell, there were plenty who knew Stan personally who didn't understand him."

"That's fair," Elder Luis parroted. "Then I suppose I should add that I had a particular interest in knowing all I could about Stanley."

"And why was that?" Xander asked.

"Why wouldn't I? He was born a human but somehow managed to turn himself into a being of seemingly limitless power and potential who made the efforts of even the best of ours look like cheap parlor tricks. Before you and your wife, he and your father were the only ones on record who'd ever stood against a varcol. Before that, the earliest documentations of their kind were... well, they might as well have been chiseled into stone. Let's just leave it at that. They were a mysterious creature back when the world actually knew of their existence. Then your father and Stanley barreled into Lenuta's castle, stirred up a crazy night for themselves, and somehow managed to not only escape but actually *trap* their target up in those mountains."

"They had help, you know," Xander said.

Elder Luis nodded, but looked otherwise unconvinced. "I suppose they did, but it was Stan's magic and your father's seal that won the night. Everyone else was along for the ride."

"Serena's parents were there," Xander reminded him,

folding his arms defiantly cross his chest. "I don't think she'd appreciate you making their efforts sound so unnecessary."

"Then I suppose I should be glad that she is not with us to hear me say it," he replied in a low, unimpressed tone.

"How's this:" Xander challenged, "*I* don't appreciate you making their efforts sound so unnecessary."

"Fair enough," Elder Luis said again.

Xander advanced another step.

"Why do you defend the others' efforts rather than accept the praise I direct towards Stan and your father?" the auric asked.

"Because I spent most of my time as a vampire believing my father was something he wasn't," Xander said.

Elder Luis looked intrigued by this. "And what would that be?" he asked.

"God-like," Xander said. "Maybe not like Stan, but everyone seemed so eager to make it sound like flowers blossomed in his footsteps and that everything he touched was gold; that he was some great and powerful, 'do no wrong'-auric blessing on the world. You all still talk about him like he was the Jesus of all nonhumans."

"And this bothers you?" Elder Luis challenged him.

"As a matter of fact, yeah, it does!" Xander said, taking another step closer to the table. "See, somebody like that—a 'do no wrong'-auric blessing who farts happiness and shits perfection—isn't really such a wonderful thing. That's what they're there for, after all. My father had to fight through fear and doubt, same as the rest of us. What made Joseph Stryker special wasn't that he was special, it was that he forced himself to be something special to so many. He hand-picked the warriors he went in with that night, and when all was said and done they all had to run—my father and Stan included. Take it from somebody who's been a god *twice,* Elder Luis, there are no gods but the ones willing to do godlike shit."

Elder Luis regarded Xander for a long, silent time. Though

he didn't seem to be changing his mind about anything, he did appear to be intrigued by what he had to say. "That, too, is fair enough," he finally said, followed then by, "Please. Sit."

Xander did so, picking a seat beside the old auric.

"You seem to have quite a decided stance on who your father was despite having never met him," the elder said as Xander was still getting settled in.

"Let's just say he hasn't been as dead to me as most dead folks have a way of being," Xander said with a grunt. "I hate this table, by the way. Me putting it back together was a courtesy that I've since been being punished for, it would appear."

"It would be dishonest of me to say I'd never seen a trick like that before," Elder Luis said, "but it doesn't change the fact that it was an impressive feat. You seem to be doing well with our late Stanley's powers."

"Hardly," Xander said. "Still haven't been able to unlock their full potential. Last time Stan gave the powers to me I made a pretty big mess that he had to clean up."

"I'd heard rumors," Elder Luis said, seeming to dismiss the confession as quickly as it was offered. Then, clearing his throat, he set one arm across the table so he could lean closer to Xander and asked, "You say that your father's appeared to you? How, exactly?"

"Dreams mostly. Like, trances and such—needs a bit more effort than just closing my eyes, I guess," Xander explained with a shrug. "He likes to appear to me when I'm close to death, or, better yet, when I'm in the process of dying. That's a good way to earn a visit from my old man: getting shredded and lingering on the brink."

"And you're certain that this is truly him? That these are, in fact, genuine visits from *the* Joseph Stryker"

Xander only nodded.

Elder Luis' forehead creased, but Xander didn't think it was from doubt. "How can you be sure?"

"How can you be sure that I'm in front of you now?" Xander quipped.

Elder Luis smirked at that and said, "You're implying that you're not."

Xander shrugged. "Plenty of your informants had stories about me being in places that you know for a fact I couldn't have been. Ask them and they'd be certain they saw me: flying around, demolishing this-or-that, being a general badass of, dare I say, *godlike* proportions. If I told you that, almost every time they had those visions, I was sitting off somewhere in this city in a trance, projecting what they were seeing into their heads while they stood around and drooled on themselves. But you already knew that, and, because you know that, you also know *why* I didn't try that trick with aurics, right?"

Elder Luis nodded, smirking. "Because we'd catch on to the illusion," he admitted.

"And so you know that I am, in fact, here with you now," Xander clarified. "In much the same way I know when there's another auric presence appearing before me. 'Cept my dad doesn't stand before me, he just 'wakes up' in my head."

"And why would your father be sleeping in your head?" asked Elder Luis.

"Because," Xander said, leaning forward in much the same way the old auric was, "that's where his aura buried itself after he died. He's not as active as he was, but I guess there's still some bits and pieces bouncing around up there. And, contrary to all the stories about him, he's been pretty open about how hard things were for him."

"And that brings you more comfort than the stories?" the elder asked.

Xander shrugged and nodded. "Makes me feel like I'm not such a fuckup for getting my ass handed to me or being scared shitless, at least."

Elder Luis seemed to be stunned into a genuine silence by this. Xander could practically hear the seconds of a nonexistent clock tolling as the auric worked to process this—his mind still every bit the impenetrable fortress it had been all night.

Then the elder did something odd.

He looked suddenly sad.

A crippling sort of sadness—the sort that only one so old could manage to hold onto; the sort of sadness only the elderly could tame—and, despite this, he smiled.

And then he laughed.

It was a laugh that erupted with such suddenness and violence that it made Xander jump. Unsettled, he tried to decide if he should help him—though how to begin to help he couldn't begin to imagine—and then, resigning from that idea, he wondered if the old Council leader had lost his mind.

"Wh-what—*heh haha... heh*—what do you know... of your father's death?" he finally asked, his words struggling around dying bouts of laughter and heaving pants for breath.

It took a moment for Xander to fully grip the question. He had to turn it around in his head, consider the wording, making sure he wasn't being challenged with some sort of riddle. Then, finally, he wet his suddenly dry lips.

He made it as far into his response as "I'm not—" before the elder spoke again:

"And I don't mean the..." he cleared his throat then, seeming to remember not only his otherwise dignified composure, but also the nature of the subject. Silence passed for a moment, and the sadness crept back like ivy, covering up any lingering signs of the manic humor. He took a deep breath, cleared his throat again, and then said, "And I don't mean the details surrounding his death. No, I'm sure you know all of that—the 'who's and the 'what's; the 'how's and 'why's—and I'd hate to make you recite them almost as much as I'd hate to have to listen to them. Especially since..." he cleared his throat again, "Especially since I was the one that wrote the report on his death." He shook his head and then craned forward, bringing himself closer to Xander and leaning against his legs as though they were suddenly discussing deep secrets.

As if there's any secrets left in the world, Xander thought.

If the elder "heard" this thought, however, he did bother to acknowledge it. "What I'm asking," he said, not whispering but certainly lowering his voice, "is if anybody's ever told you the details surrounding your father's death? If you know what sort of time it was, what sort of impact it—Joseph's death, I mean—had on us; had on the world?"

It felt like a saying anything then might dirty the moment. The elder's raspy voice seemed to be demanding some degree of silence, and Xander couldn't think of how to maintain that air of silence and still manage to speak. Uncertain and more than a little uncomfortable, he shook his head.

The Elder Luis' sadness shifted, tightening his face and turning the wrinkles and creases into a map of pockmarked valleys and weathered mountains. He said, "Well, I hope you won't take this the wrong way, Xander, but your father's death saved us. Saved all of us, in fact."

Xander stared at him, resisting any number of urges at that moment. "And I'm sure he was just thrilled to be of service," he finally said, making sure to clasp his hands at his lap before doing so. "Tell me, you Council guys get out much? Sample the life? Maybe engage in a little socializing? I only ask because you—"

"Yes, yes," the elder grunted and looked away. "'The delivery sucks,' I know."

Xander kept staring, not surprised that his exact thoughts had been recited back to him.

"You'll have to forgive me, Stryker. It's... this is uncharted territory. Your family—your father and your father's father especially—had a knack for... eh, well, 'twisting our tits' is, I'm sure, a suitable enough way to put it—a turn of phrase that's proven to be a true gem; a true magnum opus of this day and age."

Still trying to get his head around the mention of his grandfather, Xander could only offer a halfhearted, "Uh-huh." He didn't feel like breaking the old vampire's heart and pointing out that his opinion of what defined a generation seemed a bit off.

"Uh-huh," it seemed, was enough to keep the old vampire talking.

"In all fairness," his voice lowered even more, "things had always been bad. Humans and mythos..." he made a dismissive sound. "Evolution might have divided us with a heavy hand, but it went soft when it came to brains. Gifted all of us with... well, shit." He nodded and let out a dry cough. Xander thought it sounded forced. "'Shit-for-brains,'" he muttered, "another gem.

"So things were always bad," Elder Luis went on. "Tensions were high, doubts were higher. Mythos, by and large, had begun to lose hope in not only The Council, but they'd also begun to lose hope that any of us would survive much longer. Even those who didn't live badly were beginning to feel that fractured lives spent clinging to shadows were not the sort of lives worth living. Imagine, if you will, what the weight of the secret that you saw fit to reveal to the world after only a few years as one of us must have felt like to those who'd been living far longer. Ten years? Fifty? A hundred? A thousand? And, not to rub at any sore spots, but you've enjoyed quite a number of luxuries since your rebirth that many never do." He sighed and shook his head, "Ours has always been a lonely, fear-filled life, Xander. But at least, early on, we might be allowed to at least *live* with our secret—leave it unspoken and rarely even considered. But times changed." Elder Luis let out a tired groan. "There'd always been legends," he explained, "stories that humans passed around of bloodthirsty beasts or beings who changed shape. Mermaids, trolls... ah, the stories were great. But, back then, they were all just spoken. Passed around at campfires or told to children to scare them into behaving. A storyteller would be lucky to reach maybe only a handful of willing ears to listen. But times kept right on changing. A spoken story to a few became a handwritten text for several more, then a printed book for that many more. And on-and-on it went. Audiences grew, and the secret became harder to maintain; suddenly it wasn't about simply living lonely lives, but *working* to do so. And still things changed, Xander. By the eighties and nineties, there were so many books and movies and other readily available commercial fictions available to the masses that there was no way for our kind to hide the reality of what we'd allowed our true selves to become. Tales of vampires and werewolves were everywhere, fetishizing our kind and turning us into global obsessions that practically mocked the truth—there was no glamour or romance or power for our kind to loom over humans, not in the long run, at least.

"Now, those like myself—" the auric boasted, "those who'd been around the longest, mind you—we weren't too worried. We weren't happy to find that a few of our own were responsible for some of the biggest books and movies to come out, but..." he gave a "what are you gonna do?"-shrug. "We had to issue a few executions, yes, but it was all just the same sort of work—just more of it. We thought nothing of it, Xander, but what we thought and what the rest of the world thought: two very different types of animals. And, yes, human intrigue in the supernatural was on the rise, there was no denying that. They weren't exactly believing—I wouldn't lie and say it was a threat to our secrecy; not so much as a constant reminder of it—but the fantasies had a way of working on both humans *and* mythos. More and more humans were beginning to *want* to believe, and more and more mythos were beginning to *want* the glamorous lives of the creatures depicted in those fictions."

Elder Luis paused and shook his head, sighing. "We saw the highest rise in rogue activity during that time, acting out the violence and the sex and the fame depicted in the stories. This, of course, made the law-abiding mythos community very nervous and, for the humans, it only served to create more. They created more art, more trends—games, fashion, even sexuality—" he gave an old man snort at that, "and the cycle repeated, bigger and badder; over and over. And this was back when the concept of the internet was still just a phantom!"

Xander had begun to lose track, or maybe just interest, in what the elder had to say. He was forcing himself to listen at that point solely to figure out how his father—or, more specifically, his father's death—fit into this grim depiction of the not-too-distant past.

Likely reading his mind, Elder Luis grunted and nodded. "And then your father died," he said the words, Xander supposed, to bring the story to its point, but it still felt like a punch to the gut. "It was a 'shot heard 'round the world'-sort of moment. There weren't many at that point who *hadn't* heard of your father, and, whether you loved him or hated him, there was no denying that he stood for something; he *represented* something to all of those scared, jittery, uncertain mythos. And, to those who'd taken to acting out there fantasies at the expense of others, he represented a clear and real threat."

Elder Luis paused then, seeming to get lost in the memory and the pride he'd felt for that time. Then, leveling his gaze on Xander again, he said, "When people like your father, people who've become more of a symbol than a person—when people like *that* die—their death becomes a symbol, as well." He gave an innocent shrug. "You don't need to look too far back in history to know that tragedy has a powerful way of uniting people, Xander, and your father's death was exactly the sort of global mythos tragedy that we all needed to calm the waters, get everyone seeing a bit more clearly. Even we at The Council, myself included, were forced to reevaluate some things."

Xander raised an eyebrow at him.

"Okay," the elder rolled his eyes, "we had to reevaluate *a lot* of things. Including any number of laws, regulations, procedures, yammah-yammah-yammah, etcetera and etcetera." He smiled then, one that almost cleared all the ivy of sadness that had been lingering in his face in one pass, and gave a nod. "Your father, even in death, inspired and motivated a degree of change that, pardon me for saying so, he'd have *never* achieved in life. *Never!*"

A long silence passed then. At first it seemed to stem from a mutual assumption that the other would have something to say at that moment, but when neither of them came to occupy it and it had evolved into a full-scale awkward silence, it became that much harder to break.

But a question had begun to blossom in Xander that was threatening to grow into something he couldn't contain:

"Why are you telling me all of this?" he finally asked, shattering that cursed silence.

Another ivy of sadness began to spread. Another nod tilted the elders sinking expression into shadow.

"A couple of reasons, actually," he confessed in a suddenly raspy, tired voice. "You see, Xander, a lot of us might not have agreed with your father's methods or the decisions he made, but, in death, he taught us a great deal. Among those lessons was a rather harsh and unforgettable one: don't question a Stryker on a mission." The old auric let that statement hang in the air; let it sink into Xander's bones. "I'm not going to pretend to understand just what the hell you were thinking when you stepped in front of that camera, and I'm not about to smile pretty and say that things are going to work out all finely-wrapped and pretty like one of those movies or storybooks..." he shrugged and looked away, smirking a humorless smirk, "but I won't question it. Like I said: you have our support—I'm not about to make the same mistake twice. We'll stand beside you, do what we can to get others to do the same, and trust that you know what you're doing." He grinned then, wheezing out a chuckle, "And maybe in doing so we'll get a little of that hero glory that we missed out on the first time around."

"That's only one reason," Xander pointed out with a sigh, "and a pretty lame one, at that."

The wheezing chuckle came to an abrupt end, and the elder's voice finally slipped into a whisper. "The other reason isn't such a pretty one, Xander," he warned. "You see, you, your charming wife, the Vaileans and their... uh, *unconventional* entourage—all of you—have sparked a rather aggressive shift. You more than any of them, absolutely, but you've all become symbols now in the same way that Joseph was a symbol." He cleared his throat, and his gray-blue eyes shifted away, no longer able to hold Xander's gaze. "I wanted you to hear this, Xander, because sometimes the best thing a symbol can do to motivate the masses..."

The elder's words faded out as a recent conversation with Estella echoed in Xander's mind. With the subject of sacrifice and "good deaths," bubbling in his brain, he saw an increasingly familiar vision of him struggling with Aleks over a revolver—the barrel creeping closer and closer to an all-deciding moment—and a decision that would resound with greater force than the gunshot itself.

Feeling a nauseating sense of repulsion and, oddly enough, inspiration, Xander realized that Elder Luis must have had the same vision. Finally getting a glimpse into the Council elder's head, he was offered clarity to finish his sentence for him:

"Is to die," Xander whispered.

"Precisely," Elder Luis whispered back.

Gulping, trying to stave off his rapidly drying throat, he dared to dig further:

"How can you know all of this?" he asked, "How can you recognize Stan's magic? And why can't I read you like I can everybody else?"

"Because Stan was like you, Xander. He saw many things, and he had to be sure that things happened as they were meant to happen. I can't say that he got everything right, and I'll admit that there was much that he missed," he held his arms out as if to illustrate everything that was happening around him, "but he knew enough—*saw enough*—to know that one day I'd have to be having this conversation with you."

"He showed you my death?" Xander asked. "The struggle over my father's gun? And the decision to take my own life?"

The ivy of sadness had officially begun to strangle the rest of the old auric's features. His jaw worked to open, trembled, and then fell still. Tired, gray-blue eyes sank behind heavy-looking lids.

And then Elder Luis gave a single nod.

Alright, little guy.

You all set? Fangs brushed? Hair combed? Ass wiped? Well, then let's get you tucked in!

There's my little ass-kicker!

What?

No. No... Mommy's not sad, not—y'know what? No! I ain't gonna fucking lie to you, Gregori; shit wouldn't be right. But I'm not sad, okay? I'm scared.

I'm scared...

WHOO! That is not an easy thing to say, even to a little bed-wetter like you.

Huh?

Oh, yes you goddam do, you little liar! But it's okay, 'cause Mommy wets the bed, too.

Hehehe!

Huh?

No. Nothing. I'll explain when you're older. Don't ask dirty questions, ya little perv!

"Why"? Why is Mommy scared? Hmm... I'm not sure if I should talk about that, bud.

No, I am *not* lying to you! Lying is *saying* something that isn't true, dummy; I'm saying I'm *not* saying something that is true—see? Not lying!

Really? Quit your pouting! Gah! Such a fucking con-artist. You take after your dad more than you'll ever know!

Okay, okay... just let me think for a moment, kay? Gotta make sure this shit's appropriate for a kid...

Hmm...

Fuck! Being creative ain't as easy as those fairies at Netflix make it look...

No, Greg, not real fairies! Don't be a dumbass!

Okay...

So you know how a few weeks ago those old bastards showed up and Mommy, Daddy, and Uncle Xan-Xan and Auntie 'Stella had to kick their asses and make 'em mind their manners?

HA! Yeah! When Mommy punched that one douche-canoe right in the wiener! You got it, champ!

Anyway, Uncle Xan-Xan actually *made* them come here. Sounds like some crazy shit, I know—inviting a circus of ancient turds in overpriced, ugly suits who want to kill you to pull up to your doorstep in their Men-in-Black cars—but Uncle Xan-Xan is kinda like Mommy and Daddy: he's nutso in the head! But, like, good nutso, you understand? Like... crazy in the same way that God must be crazy.

I don't know if I believe in God, I don't think about crazy shit like that.

Sure, buddy, you believe whatever you want. Mommy ain't gonna stop you from being you. Not ever. Anyway...

So, nutso as Uncle Xan-Xan is, his little My Chemical Romance-ass actually went and got those old fuckers to play nice. Didn't even have to punch any other wieners to do it, either. Like I said: nutso. And, 'cause they're all playing nice, those cranky old Council-kooks are pretty much giving Uncle Xan-Xan whatever he needs to fight this... uh, well—fuck it! Let's just call it what it is—a monster.

Yeah, kiddo, a real one!

No! Not like us, ya little 'tard! We ain't fuckin' monsters!

I don't care what the cartoon said. The cartoon's nutso, and not the good kind. Got it? We ain't monsters! I wanna hear you say it for Mommy, kay: say "We ain't monsters."

Yes, Greg... I know what grammar is.

No, Greg... I don't need to hear about what Aunt Zoey said.

Yes, Greg... I say bad words, but am I a bad mommy?

Aww, thanks, kiddo. You kick ass, too. And, remember: we're *not* monsters. 'Specially not you. No matter what you hear out there. The real monsters—the ones like what Uncle Xan-Xan and everyone are getting ready to fight—are the ones who wanna hurt people. Like, *a lot* of people. Got it?

Yeah, I guess it is kinda like in the cartoons. 'Cept we're the superheroes and *they're* the monsters.

Exactly. You got it, bud. So that's why everyone's been so busy lately—that's why Nikki and Raith came here, why Aunt Zoey's been working so much with that human creep, and why Daddy's been stockpiling weapons like Mommy does with candy bars.

No. You just brushed your fangs, Greg, you can't have a candy bar. I ain't letting you go to sleep with shit-colored fangs.

Anyway...

So Uncle Xan-Xan told me earlier today that it won't be long before they have to fight the monster, and I guess he's been working just as hard as we've been, 'cause he's got *a lot* of other monsters on his side.

Yeah, Greg... an army.

No. No tanks. Least I hope not.

Nope. Mommy and Auntie 'Stella can't go, 'cause we both got knocked up.

It means we're fat with a baby, sweetie.

Ask your father how it got there; I'm already telling you a fucking story.

So... yeah! Mommy's scared because Daddy and Uncle Xan-Xan and everyone else we love are going to have to go out soon and face a whole lot of monsters who want to hurt us all real bad. It's scary stuff, you know?

Thanks, bud. I feel better knowing you'll stay here to protect us knocked-up fatties.

Yes, Greg... I know Auntie Stella's not as fat as I am. Jeez, you're a little fuck!

Ha! Yeah, I still love you even though you're a little fuck.

No, sweetheart. I won't let the monsters get you; not ever! That's a promise.

Love you, too. Sleep tight... and don't wet the bed.

HA!

"We love life, not because we are used to living
but because we are used to loving."
Friedrich Nietzsche (1844-1990)"

"Tradition, thou art for suckling children,
thou art the enlivening milk for babes,
but no meat for men is in thee."
Stephen Crane (1871-1900)

The Great Machine finds itself tamed once again.
The Great Machine finds itself in the reigns once again.
But this time—with this rider—there is more:
More strength,
More determination,
More potential.
But, as the world spins and teeters—dipping and shifting—
The Great Machine works on a narrow wire of time.
So much lies ahead...
So much to see...
But the rider, just as unbalanced as the world he strives to save,
Guides his new toy back-and-forth...
Back-and-forth...
Tolling tirelessly on a single point in time—
A single note played over and over on a piano with infinite keys—
And the Great Machine grows tired of the tune;
Tired of the monotonous obsession;
Tired of the one-worded chorus it follows:
Estella...
Estella...
Estella...
The song's unfinished, but the rider can't hear, the second stanza:

Ruby…
Ruby…
Ruby…

"Let me dedicate my life to proving how much I love you."
Xander Stryker

CHAPTER 25
NEW DAWN

"The cold passed reluctantly from the earth,
and the retiring fogs revealed an army stretched out on the hills, resting.
As the landscape changed from brown to green, the army awakened,
and began to tremble with eagerness at the noise of rumors."
Stephen Crane (1871-1900)

"There's greatness in you, Xander, the kind of greatness that can overpower any monster.
Some might even say the kind of greatness that can change the world."
Emily Stryker

Dawn crept through the city like a sickness. It was more than just light, more than just an orange glimmer in the distance, though; those first rays of sunshine were the last grains of sand in an hourglass. The past few weeks, all seeming like a blur now, had existed for Xander and so many others solely as a means to prepare for this moment. And, as the UV assaulted the skin of Xander's hands, neck, and face, the flood of rage that came with sun poisoning seemed more appropriate than ever before.

"Come on, Aleks," he muttered under his breath, thumbing back Yang's hammer and flexing against the kukri he had sheathed at his back. The firmness that his shoulder blades were met with, the heft of the short, curved sword that rested between them, brought him a sliver of comfort. "Come on," he repeated, "you son-of-a-bitch!"

Never had he meant those words so strongly.

Beside him, on his right, Zane bounced on his feet and rolled his shoulders in their sockets. Xander thought he looked like a fighter preparing for the toll of a bell, but then, throwing his head first one way then the next—earning a few hearty cracks in the process—he moved to retrieve his own weapons: the short axe that he'd brandished in the hotel battle—sporting a new, rust-free head—and a sawed-off, lever-action shotgun that hung casually at his side by a long strap. Both the axe and the shotgun's shells had been enchanted with Cebourist magic by Allen Carrey, himself.

In fact, just about every weapon and all the ammunition that they were armed with had been enchanted by Allen Carrey.

Considering the former hunter-slash-Cebourist, Xander let his mind's eye drift back to one of the skyscrapers a few blocks behind him, where he knew Allen Carrey had set himself up with a good view of the city through the scope of his sniper rifle. Each of the rounds in his gun, like the shells Zane carried for his shotgun—and like the rest of the ammunition that Xander's army carried—were laced with anti-mythos magic.

Xander tried not to feel dirty about that fact.

Beside Zane, Nikki and Raith took in the sight of the sunrise. Nikki, clutching a pair of glowing sai and letting her taroe tattoos seem to "breathe" in time with her—growing brightly before dimming almost back to flat-black before flaring up again—looked almost impatient as she spun her forked daggers first clockwise, then counterclockwise in her hands. Her dark, exotic face studied the horizon as if it was an enemy with a weakness she was eager to exploit. Raith, already contradicting Nikki's looks with his own—sporting a round, pale face with a messy splattering of dirty-blond hair all perched on top of a strangely soft-yet-athletic body—seemed almost comfortable with the wait, even going so far as to lean against the handle of the giant mace he'd chosen to drag into battle. Xander caught himself studying the weapon again, noting the large, bowling-ball sized head lined all the way around with seven-inch long steel spikes—all of which perched at the end of a nearly five-foot long length of dark, dense wood. Looking like it weighed well over a hundred pounds, that weapon, compared to Nikki's small, sleek sai, seemed to almost visually represent the pair of lovers on its own.

And yet, based on what he'd seen from them since their arrival almost a week-and-a-half earlier, they couldn't have been more perfect together.

Guess opposites really do attract, Xander thought of the two for likely the hundredth time since meeting them before catching sight of a familiar blue aura as it made a pass around the immediate area.

"Still nothing," Zoey said in a low, professional tone as she withdrew her aura back into herself.

Xander nodded to her, and, as he did, noticed that the holster she was wearing had kinked. He realized that it was likely the first time that she'd worn one, which, though not surprising—she'd never seemed the sort to fire a gun when she could use her aura instead—still worried him in the long run. Isaac, however, had gone to great lengths to strap all number of various styles of guns to himself. All of his holsters were fitted loosely, as well, but this didn't surprise Xander at all. Wanting loose-fitting holsters on a body that could nearly double in size was just being practical. What *wasn't* practical, however, was covering oneself in guns that they wouldn't be able to use once their hands were too big to properly grip them.

Not about to question the logic—admitting that he wasn't the logical mind; *She isn't here,* he reminded himself—he chose to leave the subject of Isaac's weaponry as his own business and, instead, alerted Zoey of the kink in her own holster.

Groaning at this, Zoey went about trying to locate the problem before Isaac finally started to readjust the strap for her.

And still the dawn crept on; still the sickness spread.

Behind him, the rest of Xander's immediate comrades readied themselves, as well. All around them, the vast army that The Council had managed to amass for him for this moment prepared—checking their own weapons, adjusting their own equipment, and otherwise mentally bracing for what they were all there to do.

And then there was Ruby...

She stood beside him, her body poised and ready in her black cargo pants, matching turtleneck, and her form-fitted red leather jacket. She wore a pair of second-generation Yin-Yang pistols at either hip, the guns modeled after the original set's black-and-white aesthetic but following a clan-issued Beretta design, and had borrowed one of Satoru's katana-like short swords to wear at her back. Xander wasn't sure whether he should feel honored or violated by the obvious imitation. But, in Ruby's defense, she was doing everything to present herself as a capable warrior at that moment—despite the raging worry on her aura—as she took in the same dawn that was unnerving everyone else.

It was, Xander thought, exactly what she'd promised to him, after all.

Her promise...

~Four days earlier~

Though the area making up the territory for "Stryker's Vagrants" had already been bustling with activity ever since The Council's arrival, it had become an outright madhouse since Aleks' messenger had arrived.

It wasn't an unusual thing to see a human wandering into their community. Since the first day of Xander's reawakening, they'd been willing to take in any and all who arrived. So it hadn't come as any real surprise to see another strolling with calm-yet-purposeful steps past the graffiti-laced sign and the demolished Daius BMW that had been dragged out of the main entrance way but left otherwise unmoved. She hadn't looked suspicious, hadn't looked dangerous, and certainly hadn't looked out of place. Her aura, however, had clearly been all of those things, and Xander had known it for what it was the moment he'd spotted its approach.

He'd done everything he could to avoid arousing suspicion from the others, not wanting to start a panic, but he *had* told Estella of what was coming. Despite his best efforts, she'd joined him in meeting the newcomer.

The human, they could see, was already *mostly* dead. A small part of her original self lingered, however; the part that remembered Xander and how he'd saved her and her friend. She'd been conflicted about what to do since that day, but, with her friend running into another unfortunate circumstance with another rogue, she'd decided to track down Xander and seek his help yet again. The attack on her friend, as it turned out, had been a calculated move, and her decision had been "the fish taking the bait."

Those, at least, had been Aleks' words. And it had been Aleks' words that continued to spill from the poor, already dead girl's lips. Using her body and the information in her brain to track down their headquarters, Aleks had no trouble steering his "momentary plaything" to their front door.

"It looks like you're already preparing," he'd said through her, grinning in a way that would have hurt the girl if there was anything left of her to feel pain. "That's good, Strykers. Very good. Because I'm preparing, too—have been preparing for quite some time—and I feel the time is nearly upon us. You feel the same I imagine, yes?"

"Time and place, asshole," Xander had growled back at the leering creature hiding behind the face of a dead teenage blonde.

And a time and place had been given. Then, as the already impossible grin widened that much further, the already dead girl began to laugh and slowly turn her head, working as if to look behind her. The laughter warped, strained through a stretched windpipe, but maintained as she began yanking her head further and further, seeming to throw everything she had into the violent, jerking motions, until finally, with a loud snapping sound, the laughter had gone silent and the body had fallen to the ground.

After that, all of the work that had been done seemed suddenly insubstantial, and all of the hypotheticals that had been motivating future intentions became certainties motivating a sense of "why haven't we done this yet?"

That was why, with only a few days until they were all supposed to go to war, the subject of who was (and who wasn't) going to be present at that war became a very relevant issue, and Xander found himself marveling at the fact that it took less effort to convince the "too old" members of The Council to sit out the coming war than Estella and Serena. While he was prepared to handle the protests from both of the pregnant vampires, he'd been just as prepared to ward off the outrage that the elders—those who truly lived up to the word, at least—would feel at being told that they would not be joining him on the battlefield. Instead, he only had to deal with a few indignant grumblings, one halfhearted claim that "there's still some fight in these old bones," and, unsurprisingly from Elder Luis, a rather pompous-sounding "Of course not!"

Whether the old auric's eagerness to avoid the impending battle was due to the conversation they'd had almost a week-and-a-half earlier or simply because he felt he'd already paid his dues was something Xander neither knew nor cared to know.

Though it had already been discussed countless times, Estella was still unhappy with the reminder. Unhappy, but not argumentative. Serena, on the other hand, had obviously taken all those prior conversations as either a series of very consistent jokes or a bunch of halfhearted commitments that she'd be able to break when the time for action was at hand. At the first hint of protest, however, Xander pointed out that he needed somebody powerful and capable to keep an eye on their compound and on everyone that had to stay behind.

This, Xander knew, Serena would take as a personal mission to watch over Estella. Whether or not Estella *needed* to be watched over was an entirely different issue and, quite frankly, one that Xander didn't feel needed to be brought up. As it turned out, Serena was more than willing to stay behind after this request was made.

Satisfied that he and Zane could go into battle with confidence that their pregnant wives wouldn't be endangering themselves or their unborn, Xander went to the storage facility to check on Zoey and Allen Carrey's progress.

The dilemma when it came to making weapons infused with Cebourist magic was to make sure that the weapons weren't just as deadly to the mythos *using* the weapons as they would be to the mythos they were being used against. Something like a gun, something that could be aimed, was simple enough—it was just a process of enchanting the ammunition while making certain to provide a counteracting shielding enchantment on the magazines. By the time the bullets were out of the chamber and of any danger to a nonhuman, they were already too far from the person firing the gun to represent a danger. With any other kind of weapon, however, the conundrum of how to make an enchanted weapon, something that radiated anti-mythos magic, that wouldn't irradiate the wielder just as much as its intended target.

As it turned out, however, Xander wound up giving them the solution.

That was not to say that he provided a solution—this, Allen Carrey was quite eager to point out with a laugh—so much as his arrival at that moment had inspired the solution. As he walked in, Zoey and Allen Carrey were discussing the problem. Not wanting to interrupt, Xander leaned against the table where much of their projects lay, unfinished, and began fidgeting with one of the loaded magazines. Not really listening to what they had to say—certain he wouldn't understand most of it, anyway—he absently went about ejecting the topmost bullet with his thumb, catching it in his opposite hand, and loading it back into the magazine. This went on for over a dozen passes while the two continued to provide "what if"s to one another before both, growing irritated by the rhythmic *click, whump, click* of Xander's process, turned their attentions on him. Caught in mid-ejection, the enchanted round slipped from Xander's grip, landed on the table, and started to roll towards Zoey, who began to falter on her feet under the weight of the unobstructed magic. Xander was quick to scoop up the fumbled bullet then and returned it to the protection of the shielded magazine.

Zoey's recovery was almost instantaneous.

Allen Carrey, having watched the entire process, nodded slowly.

"What if the solution doesn't lie with the weapons?" he asked, "But, rather, the people wielding them?"

Zoey, still rubbing her head, gave him a questioning look.

Nodding back towards Xander, he pointed out that, because

he was an adept user of magic, he was able to shield himself against the effects of the anti-mythos enchantments.

"It's like a vaccine," he explained. "Because his body knows how to use the Cebourist's magic—understands its workings—he's able to shield himself against the dangers it would normally represent."

"It *does* seem to have a lesser effect on the ones who've been attending your lessons," Zoey mused, mentally kicking herself for not attending what she'd referred to before as "mythos cursing classes."

"Right," Allen Carrey agreed, "but none of the other mythos taking the class ever had a reason to practice magic before. Xander and Estella, on the other hand, *have;* and that experience allowed their minds and bodies to shift in order to accommodate the necessary strain and focus needed to channel those energies."

The arts have tainted you, Xander thought when he heard that, remembering an old line he used to use.

With this revelation, Allen Carrey was able to begin work on what he referred to as an "inverted enchantment." True to his vaccine metaphor, the end result basically entailed placing a spell on each and every nonhuman warrior who would be on the battlefield—one that recognized the spells laced throughout their weapons and refocused the negative effects away from them.

After that, because Zoey and Allen Carrey no longer had to worry about those on their side falling victim to any possible spill-off of the enchantments, they were able to begin developing new weapons and tactics that had previously been too dangerous.

Content with knowing that he had (sort of) helped, Xander's next person of interest was Sawyer. The vampire warrior, who'd managed to isolate himself enough that most of the newer arrivals didn't even know he existed, had been holed-up in his room. Though it wouldn't have been impossible for Xander to check in on his old friend—even without him realizing it—there were any number of reasons that he didn't. Xander kept himself convinced that it was out of respect for Sawyer's privacy that he didn't go snooping with his mind's eye, but the unavoidable truth was that Xander knew what was happening to his friend. Sawyer had lost Dianna. Worse yet, he'd been forced to watch it happen. And, while Sawyer didn't know the details surrounding her death, the guilt that Xander felt about motivating the events was enough to keep him from digging any further into the warrior's affairs. If nothing else, the guilt of knowing that Sawyer's suffering had yet to end certainly was enough to force him to keep away.

However, with the battle drawing nearer and Sawyer still having a role to play in it, Xander could not avoid him and the guilt surrounding him any longer.

Before he could make it to Sawyer's chambers, though...

"Xander! XANDER!" Ruby called, already jogging to catch up with him.

Realizing he wasn't expected to stop nor wait, Xander did neither and allowed her to walk beside him. "What's up, Ruby?" he asked.

"I just w-wanted to..." Ruby began before catching herself in a stammer. Then, after sucking in a breath of air and working to steady herself, she said, "I just wanted to apologize again."

Xander frowned at her, confused. "Apologize for what?"

"For, well... you know," Ruby sounded surprised at that. "For failing before. With the Cebourists."

Though Xander had never viewed what had happened to Ruby as a failure—though he continued to not view what had happened to her as a failure—he realized that this didn't change the fact that Ruby viewed what had happened to her as a failure. Pausing to look at her, he decided that her believing it was the case was enough to make it true for her. No amount of "you didn't fail"s was about to change her mind about that.

Taking a breath of his own, Xander instead decided to refer to some of his own more recently acquired wisdom:

"We're allowed to fail, so long as we don't allow those failures to define us," he said, then added, "What happened to you before won't define you. I won't let it."

Ruby's aura exploded with elation at that, and she'd thrown her arms around him with a squeal of thanks and praise that was all mashed together in one, long, incoherent sentence.

Finally, thinking he was finished with the conversation, Xander managed to shrug Ruby off of him and once again started towards the office building where Sawyer had been staying.

"Then you'll let me join?" Ruby asked, following after him.

"Let you join... what?" asked Xander.

"Th-the battle..." Ruby's voice had started shaking again, Xander's confused tone sending ripples of doubt through her aura. "The battle against the varcol!" she clarified, "You... you'll let me go, right?"

"Of course I will, Ruby," Xander said. "We need as many able-bodied warriors as we can get. And your body's able, right?" he challenged, knowing it would get her excited—get her confident—once again.

It wasn't until the words were out that he realized the connotation

Ruby, thankfully, didn't seem to notice. "Yeah!" she boasted, proving him right. "I'm definitely able! And I'm going to prove myself useful this time around!"

Xander nodded as he reached the building, already beginning to consider what he intended to say to Sawyer. Hoping to wrap things up with Ruby, he said, "Glad to hear it. I need you out there."

It wasn't until he felt the swell of her aura in response to his words that he caught on to what he'd said.

"I need you out there."

"I..."

Blinking at himself, lingering there in the doorway, he asked himself why he'd said "I" when what he'd meant to say was "we." He was certain—*positive!*—that what he'd meant to say was "*We* need you out there."

But with Ruby already gone and his intended destination mere steps away, he wasn't really in a position to dwell on it.

And he hadn't had a chance to consider it again since.

By the time he was at Sawyer's door, knocking for the fourth time with still no response to show for his efforts, he'd already forgotten about everything else. Finally, tired of making himself feel like a fool, he reached through the door with his aura to unlock it from the other side.

"Sort of defeats the purpose of knocking if you're just going to let yourself in," Sawyer grumbled.

Xander stared at him, seated on the floor of the room over a heap of dismantled gadgets and a few photocopied pages of Allen Carrey's notes. He made no move to get up, to hide his work, or to even look away from his project as he worked on unscrewing the plating from something that looked dangerous on its own.

"What's the point in knocking if you're not going to answer?" Xander challenged him.

Still not looking away from his work, Sawyer said, "The point of not answering is to get the knocking to stop."

"Technically it did," Xander offered before taking a seat on the unused chair in the corner. "So what are you working on?"

"Don't worry about it," Sawyer dismissed, finally removing the last screw and yanking the plating off of the device. A series of wires of varying hues snaked in every conceivable direction beneath the smooth, discarded surface. Sawyer began yanking these out with total abandon, and Xander couldn't help but imagine a madman tearing out his own hair. "You aren't supposed to be seeing any of this anyway, so just pretend you didn't and go on with your business."

"You are my business," Xander pointed out, realizing that

the skin around Sawyer's fingers was red and blistered. He let his eyes drift back to the copies of Allen Carrey's notes. "And I'm not sure I should be letting you fool around with the Cebourist's magic. You're not immune to that, you know."

"I can handle it," Sawyer said, finally discarding the last of the wires and beginning to pry a security cap free from the area he'd uncovered. Discarding this, he finally looked up from his work, saying, "And you can rest easy, Stryker: your loyal lapdog will be there on the battlefield bright and early."

His face was sickly, pale and sunken from malnourishment.

Staring at him for a long moment, unsure of how to respond, Xander finally shrugged and pulled himself from the chair. "I didn't come here to treat you like a lapdog, Sawyer; I came here to check in on you."

"Consider me checked in on, then," Sawyer said before turning back to his work while muttering, "And the next time you find my door locked, leave it that way."

"Get some synth-blood in you before tomorrow and you can consider that a deal," Xander said, heading for the door.

He suddenly felt like he was going to be sick. The thought that he'd had anything to do with letting his friend turn into *that* was...

But what else was he supposed to do?

He was staring at any number of potential realities where Aleks ruled over everything, and his first order of business, assuming he hadn't already killed them, was to target anyone and everyone Xander had ever known. How could he justify trying to save somebody who was already doomed at the expense of everything else?

It wasn't fair!

It wasn't fair!

It wasn't...

Xander managed to put enough distance between himself and Sawyer's door to feel safe with the sickness that burst past his lips. Bent over and sucking in foul-tasting air, he promised himself that it was not all going to be for nothing.

He wouldn't allow it to happen that way!

Needing to get away from business, deciding that he could only handle so much in one day, he scanned for Estella's aura and worked his way to one of the larger office buildings. He found her, along with the Vaileans and Nikki and Raith, inside the cafeteria that took up nearly a quarter of this building's first floor.

As he walked in, he caught sight of Estella pushing a small box of peanut butter cups across the table towards Zane, who stared at the gift through a mask of confusion.

It was Serena who asked, "What's that for?"

Estella, shrugging, said, "I think you phrased it as 'thrusting and grinding,' but, really, I just figured he'd earned some candy of his own for everything he's been doing more recently."

Gregori, locking his wide, hungry eyes on the box of candy, screamed, "GREESE'S!" before clapping his hands on either side of it and vanishing from the table.

"SON OF A—" Zane started, watching his gift vanish in a flash.

Serena and Nikki both began cackling.

Raith, chuckling, said, "Tough break, bud."

Estella stared at where the box had rested. "Easy come, easy go, I guess," she mused before looking up at Zane. "What'd he call them? 'Greasy?'"

"'Greese's,'" Zane clarified.

"Why does he call them that?" Estella asked.

"Because he can't read yet," Serena explained, still giggling. "Probably misheard somebody else, so now they're 'Greese's.'"

"Are none of you worried about where Gregori might have gone?" Nikki pressed, looking around between Zane and Serena.

"He just stole a box of candy," Zane growled. "I doubt he's gonna start crossing borders anytime soon. More than likely he hasn't even left the building—probably hiding around one of these corners and already smeared in chocolate and peanut butter. Little bastard! I'd better get at least one of those things!"

Sighing, Serena took her husband's hand and led him to his feet. "Come on, then," she pulled him along. "Let's go see if we can catch the little hummingbird and save your fucking treat, you big woman!"

The Vaileans vanished into overdrive to track down their thieving son, leaving Estella alone at the table with Raith and Nikki as Xander approached.

"It was a nice thought, at least," he offered.

"Too bad Serena will probably finish whatever Gregori doesn't," Raith said with a laugh.

Nikki giggled and nodded.

"You two having any trouble settling in?" Xander asked, sitting down across from Estella.

Raith shook his head and took a sip from a bottle of Coke before saying, "No complaints here."

"The accommodations are fine," Nikki said, "I'm just not sure about this whole varcol-thing, to be honest. I mean, we sort of already did the earth-threatening monster-thing. I sort of thought that was a one-time fiasco."

"Yeah," Xander sighed. "Sucks that monsters keep popping up to threaten everything."

"Says the guy who advertised the existence of monsters to the whole world," Nikki challenged. "You sure you didn't make this happen with that little stunt? You sure this Aleks-guy isn't just rising to the challenge of being top dog?"

"Nikki..." Raith frowned and set a hand over hers, shaking his head. "I thought we were over this."

"No, it's fine," Xander said with a sigh, surprising even himself at not getting riled by the taroe woman's words. "Granted, I'm sure there's plenty of 'top-doggers' out there—hell, maybe Aleks even recruited some of them—but all this was a long time in the making, I'm afraid."

"And you know that for a fact?" Nikki asked. "We're not here to help clean up one of your messes?"

"No," Xander said flatly. "Aleks has a personal vendetta against me, sure, but he'd be doing all this whether or not his psycho-mother had killed me the night he broke free."

"That's good enough for me," Nikki said, standing up. "Good to know that this ain't another Zane-Maledictus shit-show."

Raith flinched at the name of the curse that had afflicted him and Zane for years.

"Even though Zane's curse was sort of your peoples' doing, as well, right?" Xander challenged with a quirked eyebrow.

Nikki paused and shot him a look.

Xander, holding his smirk, psychically added, *Just because we're tied to something doesn't make us responsible for it, right?*

Nikki's face shifted, and she seemed eager to challenge the claim. After a tense silence, however, her aura shifted—her taroe tattoos lighting with an abrupt fury and then dimming back to normal—and she smirked, nodding.

"You're alright, Stryker," she said, taking Raith's hand into her own. "An undeniable punk... but still alright. Come on, Raith, I wanna see if we can't steal some of Zane's candy, too."

As he was dragged off by his taroe lover, the goofy therion waved his Coke to Xander in an awkward farewell. "Thanks again for letting us stay," he said.

"Least I could do," Xander balled back.

And then Xander and Estella were alone.

Free of the entrapment of socialization, he let out a heavy breath and leaned back.

"All that power and you still get so tense around other people," Estella said with a giggle. Then, seeming to see something on his aura—or maybe just smelling his breath—she asked, "Is everything okay?"

Xander nodded and shrugged, just saying Sawyer's name.

It was explanation enough.

Estella chewed her lip for a moment, sighed, and then offered a shrug. "I know it's tough," she said, "but I believe you're doing the right thing."

"Yeah, I know," Xander said with a sigh. "It all makes sense in the long run. It's just... fuck, 'Stell, you didn't see him. He's... he's not doing well."

Estella frowned and nodded. "And who could expect him to. It's unfair: both what happened to him and that you're the one forced to shoulder all of it. But I don't think it's fair to blame yourself. If anything it's Aleks' fault," she explained.

"Even that doesn't feel right. Not saying Aleks is innocent in all this—far from it—but I just can't funnel all of it back on him," Xander said, remembering something Stan had said to him.

Estella nodded and gave him a warm smile. "It's war," she said, "And war is hell."

Between everything that had transpired that night—Zoey and Allen Carrey's breakthrough, Sawyer's condition, and the band-and-forth with Nikki and Raith—Xander had all but forgotten his encounter with Ruby. Even then, with everything on his mind, he'd barely registered Ruby, her promise, or his words to her.

But now she was standing beside him on the frontline of a war to decide the fate of the world, and all he could suddenly remember was *"I need you out there."*

Just like his uncomfortable blunder with *"Is your body able?"* he wanted to pass it off as something that had come out wrong. But, with her standing there and looking more ready than many of the seasoned warriors around them, there was an increasing sense of purpose. Ruby's promise and even Xander's words felt right, and suddenly nothing else seemed to matter.

None of the preparations, none of the scouting that Xander

and his team had done to over the past few nights to set traps and plot attack points, and not even the vast numbers they'd been able to amass in such a short time seemed to matter at that moment.

Because Ruby was there beside Xander, and she was ready to keep her promise.

What's more, the raging worry on her aura, unlike the worry on everybody else's, wasn't about the war that was to come. Even then, waiting for the varcol and his own army to arrive, there was no fear for what was coming. No. Ruby's fear, powerful as it was, had nothing to do with Aleks or his army or even the world. It was all about proving herself to *him*; proving herself to Xander.

She'd meant what she said, truly meant it; turned it into her very own religion and been worshipping and praying on it every second since the moment she'd made that promise.

And now that the moment was upon them.

Now that the chance to redeem herself had arrived.

And Xander, for whatever reason, valued that more than the thousands of mythos warriors surrounding him, prepared to charge into the single greatest threat that they and the world would likely ever know. Then, just as obvious but no less surprising, he realized that, even though he'd been certain that he had misspoken at the time, he meant exactly what he'd said, too.

"I need you out there."

It seemed a strange thing to feel so personal about at a moment that was neither about him nor about her—it was, after all, a battle for the sake of the entire world—but he couldn't feel that, when all was said and done, he truly had not misspoken.

Then...

There you are...

"Xander..." Zoey's voice was a whisper.

He nodded, feeling his fangs extend in response. "I sense him, too," he told her. "I can sense all of them."

It was like a dark cloud rising to overwhelm the sun. A mass of auras in the distance—*"Messiah"* echoing on every one of them—charging through the city towards them. The vibrations of their approach could be felt through the street, and Xander felt an unsteady wave ripple through his warriors. Though he knew that not all of them could sense the numbers that Aleks was bringing to the fight, there seemed to be an understanding from the sheer impact they were creating that they were already outnumbered.

Close to five times over...

Xander... Zoey called to him.

I know, he thought-spoke back.

"So where's Aleks?" Zane demanded.

And then, as if waiting for one of them to say his name, the varcol appeared at the end of the street.

"THE DAY IS UPON US, STRYKER!" his voice echoed all around them and in their minds, leaving not one with Xander's army unaware of his arrival.

"You're a lot like your father," Xander said back, not bothering to raise his voice. "You talk too fucking much."

"AND SOON," Aleks roared back at him, ***"YOU'LL BE LIKE YOUR FATHER, AS WELL!"***

No sooner had the threat been bellowed from Aleks' lungs than his stampeding army reached him and charged past. The order, Xander realized, had already been issued, and it fell on him in that instant to lead his own side forward or allow them to be swallowed by the horde in the next.

They charged.

Auras slipped ahead of them, forming a multicolored wall that trembled against the force of the first wave of Aleks' army crashed into it. Some of the enemy mythos tried to fall back, seeing the barricade coming their way, only to get swept up in the current of snarling bodies. As they fell back, creating a sizable hurdle for the second wave, Xander issued a psychic call to all the available magic-users.

In preparing for this moment, Xander and Allen Carrey had personally worked to lay as many traps as possible throughout the city. With all the mythos on their side immune to the magic's effects, they had a chance to gain the upper hand early on in the fight by weakening—if not totally incapacitating—their enemies. This, Xander remembered, had been one of the Cebourists' most powerful tactics—littering the city with what appeared to be simple graffiti until unsuspecting nonhumans got too close.

As the call to charge the traps that had been set throughout the battlefield was cast, Xander felt a swell in various auras all around him. Allen Carrey's own aura billowed, his control of the magic still outweighing all others', and the symbols that had been laced throughout the streets sparked to life.

Startled cries and shrieks of pain erupted in a deafening roar—the city acting as an echo chamber as almost all of Aleks' army were staggered in a single instant—and the already stalled horde charging against the buckling auric wall fought to remain on their feet. The aurics finally withdrew, the wall fading from view, and the sangs occupying Xander's army began slipping out of view as they jumped into overdrive.

Staggered enemies dropped around them, limbs seeming to jump from their bodies as Xander's warriors raced ahead and cut down the opposition. Seeing this, a few of the more resilient sangs of Aleks' side, struggling against the magic's crippling effects on their bodies, worked to push themselves forward, as well. Most were overworked by the process—their bodies giving out under the strain and collapsing out of overdrive as corpses—while a few managed to tackle their would-be assassins, only to be shot or skewered a moment later in their exhausted haze.

Still standing where he'd first presented himself, Xander spotted Aleks. The varcol, sneering at the immediate turn the battle had taken, began to work his aura throughout the city, seeking and destroying all the enchanted symbols he came across.

Allen, Xander called back with his aura, *I need you to pump as much energy as you've got into the remaining traps.*

That's a tall order for just one guy to fill, Stryker, Allen Carrey shot back. *Maybe if you hadn't benched your wife we could—*

JUST DO IT! Xander roared, taking out his immediate aggression on a perfect vampire he'd caught in mid-leap with a kukri thrust between the ribs and a shot from Yang in the side of the face.

Xander "heard" *"asshole"* muttered over the psychic connection as it was severed, but a moment later Allen Carrey followed through with the order. The morning flashed that much brighter as the still-active Cebourist symbols peppering the city shone like their own suns. The glare, bright enough to make even Xander's immune warriors flinch, sent another wave of howls ringing through the streets. Several hundred auras blipped out of existence as more lives were lost—*Only got three for every one of ours now, Aleks,* Xander thought to himself, though he was sure the varcol could "hear" it all the same—and Xander saw through his mind's eye as more of his own warriors managed to slip past the opposition's defenses.

I don't mean to be a downer, Zoey admitted through thought-speak, *but we're still outnumbered... and Aleks is—*

Xander could have made any number of guesses as to how Zoey was going to finish that sentence. It might have been a warning or a theory. It might have had something to do with the fact that, with him somehow immune to the Cebourists' magic and able to work around the spells bursting around the city, he'd finally managed to neutralize the last of their traps. Or it might have reflected the simple observation that the varcol was really living up to his role as Xander's opposite by showing up in a long, royal-looking purple jacket and clutching Yin's opposite at his side.

Zoey could have been preparing to say any one of those things, Xander thought, or perhaps any number of other things.

But he couldn't be sure.

Because, though Xander could have made any number of guesses about what Zoey was *about* to say, as the varcol shot forward and threw him off his feet, he came to his own conclusion:

Aleks is pissed!

THOUGHT YOU WERE CLEVER, *Stryker?* Aleks snarled in Xander's head, driving a fist into his face. *Thought you would win the day with the same trick as before?* Another series of punches rained down, and then Xander felt the barrel of his stolen gun under his chin.

He yanked his head free of the trajectory as the shot was fired. Ears ringing, he worked to squirm free; Aleks' grip held as he brought the side of Yin's barrel across his face. This was enough to rip Xander from the iron grip—*Or maybe he just decided to let me go,* Xander morbidly thought in that instant—and send him careening through the open air and then crashing to the street. The sounds of battle were everywhere, and as he used his aura to push himself back to his feet Xander was forced to duck as the massive fist of a tergoj. The nine-foot behemoth's swing dragged it in a stumbling arc, the mythos grunting and whining—large, hooked nostrils flaring on its eyeless face as it tried to sniff out Xander for another attack. The troll-like creature caught its balance, steadied itself, and then charged. With his mind's eye, Xander could see Aleks waiting on the other side, preparing to catch him off guard should he manage to dodge the attack or ready to stomp on the aftermath if he didn't.

Xander, resisting his vampiric instincts to hiss at the challenge, sheathed his kukri and threw himself into a one-handed vault over the five-feet wide mass of rock-hard muscle and roped the gargantuan mythos with his aura. Spotting Aleks preparing to catch him in midair, he dragged the tergoj off its massive feet and yanked it over his head. The makeshift catapult sent the flailing, car-sized creature into Aleks' path and forcing him to pull himself free with an auric tendril.

Spotting his intended route with the Great Machine, Xander had a shot lined up and fired before he'd landed. Not expecting the attack to end the fight, he started at a human sprint across the street as Aleks was forced to deflect the enchanted round with his aura. Halfway up the road, the tergoj crashed down, tearing up concrete and catching a small cluster of warriors off guard. They, like Xander, were just as stunned to see such an elusive and typically docile mythos rampaging about in the city. It was a curious sight, but, from the looks of things, Aleks had been hard at work recruiting just about every breed of mythos he could find.

And, with his power and outreach, Xander imagined that Aleks could find anything and everything he wanted.

"YOU DON'T KNOW THE HALF OF IT, STRYKER!" Aleks roared, his voice rattling in Xander's ears and in his brain as he ensnared him in a vice-like auric grip and threw him down another street and into a large, concrete slab that had seen better days. ***"I NOT ONLY* COULD *FIND ANYTHING AND EVERYTHING... I* DID!"**

Growling, Xander worked to pull himself from the already crumbling mass of...

He looked down, curious as to what he'd just been thrown into, and found himself looking at a half-destroyed, four-foot tall concrete anchor set into the center of the road. Several feet ahead, he saw another—this one whole—and, beyond that, another. Glancing up, he saw that each of these anchor points supported a metal pillar that served to support the track of the monorail system that circled the outer rim of the city.

What the hell could have done this? he asked, marveling at the already shattered portion of concrete that he was half-embedded within.

"Your wife did this!" Aleks seethed, standing uncomfortably close beside him in that instant.

The varcol's fist crashed down on Xander's chest, pummeling him further into the crumbling mass, and again Yin's barrel flashed in his vision. Xander dodged, once more narrowly avoiding a shot from his own long lost gun, only to have Aleks grab him by the throat and yank him free from the concrete. Though he struggled against the hold, Xander still felt like a ragdoll in his enemy's grip as he was swung around and into the steel support, caving a portion of the metal around his hip. Despite much of the impact being absorbed by Zoey's jacket, Xander still felt something crack in his midsection. Not ready to test the coat's resilience any further, he yanked the kukri free—feeling the heat of the Cebourist magic radiate from its blade—and swiped it at the arm holding him.

Aleks roared as his arm was cut free from his body.

Xander, landing hard on the street, rolled free as the varcol drove a foot down where his head had been an instant earlier. By the time he'd gotten himself turned around to face him, Aleks had already retrieved his severed arm with his aura and secured it to the stump just below the elbow. Though the wound didn't heal immediately, Aleks didn't waste any time with waiting—simply holding the limb in place with his aura as the bone, muscle, and flesh fused back together—and jumped forward, making a note of slapping Xander with it before taking another shot with Yin.

Bullets, Xander admitted to himself, were easier to dodge than varcols.

"See how well you dodge *this,*" Aleks hissed, snatching him by the ankles with his aura and flinging him with breath-stealing force against one of the monorail supports.

Though the pain was excruciating, Xander found himself dreading an entirely different sensation at that moment. There, deep beneath the intense pain of the impact, was a steady vibration. A growing one. Ahead of him, the shattered concrete of the first support anchor began to crumble further. Above him, the track was beginning to show the slightest sway of distant use.

The morning commuter train...

Eyes widening, Xander remembered one of the Great Machine's reminders—*Nikki needs to reinforce the monorail support*—and, along with that memory, the realization that he *hadn't* followed through with it. With so many visions and so many possible realities, there was no way to ever be certain which ones were the most pressing. Thinking back on it, Xander couldn't even be certain he would have known what the warning even meant!

But it was only the one support! And, even shattered, it had survived for *how* many weeks without any—

Aleks' aura came around like a giant hammer, connecting with the twisted length of metal where Xander's body had just dented it, and the tortured concrete finally gave out. Unsupported, the steel support bowed one way, pitched the other, and finally began to fold under its own weight. Above them, the track began to sink, then lurched as the supports on either side halted the process. Aleks paused then, leering back at Xander, and gave a wide, showy grin that was filled with serrated daggers.

Then his aura barreled straight up at the track as the train worked its way forward.

ALL AROUND HIM, Xander was aware of the war.

He was aware of suffering, of pain, and of death. He was aware of, in each and every second that passed, the hundreds-upon-hundreds of auric flashes—flashes that spanned from a glimpse at a possible opening to attack to the panic at being caught off guard with an attack; flashes of victory and flashes of defeat. Xander was aware of everything happening around him, but it was the sight of Aleks preparing to drop a train filled with human commuters onto their battlefield—not a sight the Great Machine fed into his mind, but the one framed with painful clarity right in front of him—that had him forgetting everything else.

Aleks' aura was working the length of track, yanking it in either direction as more and more tendrils shot out towards the remaining support pillars around them. Seeing one of these tendrils rocketing towards his head, Xander threw himself free of its trajectory and rolled to his feet a short distance away. Through his mind's eye, he saw the train taking the bend a short way's back, its approach shaking the track that much harder and causing the sinking portion to drop several more feet. Aleks, too consumed in his mission to tear the track free, didn't even seem to notice that Xander had moved.

And, at that moment—surrounded by war and aware of the struggles of every other warrior occupying the city—Xander was faced with a choice: allow a speeding, runaway train to be thrown into the fray so he could take advantage of an opening on Aleks *or* do whatever he could to stop the train and leave Aleks to his devices. His teeth clenched and his breath caught as the track dipped another few feet, swaying more and more from the approaching train, and, in the back of his head, Xander heard Stan's voice:

"There are boundaries I can't cross that they won't hesitate to, and that gives them the upper hand."

Xander wanted so badly to be willing to sacrifice human bystanders and warriors alike—*And when have I ever stopped to worry about property damage?*—but with the changes he'd set into motion, he knew that he'd only be hurting his own cause. Turning the entire city into a warzone on its own was going to make convincing the humans that they weren't monsters that much harder, he knew. However, if he allowed Aleks this one act of wanton destruction then he was practically proving their fears accurate right then and there.

Decisions, decisions, Aleks taunted in his head. *Now decide, Stryker!*

Growling and cursing Stan's infernal and undying logic under his breath, Xander turned his back on Aleks and started at a sprint towards the nearest support beam that had yet to be torn down. He jumped into overdrive, working to gain momentum before taking his sprint vertical and racing up its length. Halfway up, reaching the most strained point on the support, Xander used his aura as a makeshift brace before pushing off and dropping out of overdrive. The leap carried him through the air and nearer to the dipping track.

The roar of the approaching train had Xander's fangs rattling in his skull as he roped the track's ledge with an auric tendril and swung himself onto its surface.

"Good job, Xander," he muttered to himself, staring up the length of dipping track, "you're now standing in the path of a soon-to-be runaway train. What a productive use of—"

Though his auric brace remained in place, the support it was wrapped around finally gave out entirely and the track sank yet again. Glancing at the aggressive dip, Xander realized that, even if he managed to keep the track from giving out entirely, the train would never be able to maintain its course. One way or the other, it would be derailed.

Still in the process of solidifying what he was certain wouldn't be able to work, Xander flung himself over the side of the bowing monorail track towards a neighboring office building. Once in midair, he pushed himself to slow time through his eyes in an effort to calculate his steps:

Behind him, he cast out a pair of auric tendrils and captured the sinking track at its lowest point.

Below him, he retracted the auric brace, letting the final support beam begin to collapse.

Ahead of him, he fired an explosive round from Yang and braced an auric shield around himself, hoping that Zoey's claims about the jacket's resistance to heat hadn't been an exaggeration.

Then, operating on little more than faith and momentum, Xander dropped out of overdrive.

The track dropped, snapped, and was immediately dragged by the auric tendrils after Xander's Hail Mary leap. Feeling the heat of the explosion on his face as it went off against the building, Xander clenched his eyes and focused his aura's hold as he felt himself crash through the wall. Glass and steel wailed around him as he tumbled to the floor, rolled to his feet—the tethered track whining behind him as it bent—and jumped into overdrive so that he had a fair chance of outrunning the train he was now steering. Once satisfied that the redirected track was set enough within the building to remain secure, he released it and hooked back around, starting back the way he'd come.

Come on! Come on! Come on! he chanted to himself, willing the Great Machine to show him the possible outcomes of this course...

And immediately saw the runaway train crash down over him.

Redirecting his course, he found himself running towards one of the still-intact windows neighboring the furious-looking chasm he'd barreled through moments earlier. New course:

He saw the train banking off the track and shooting out into the street, defeating the purpose of...

Everything! Xander finished, deciding that he'd have to personally keep the train on its track.

Cursing Aleks, Lenuta, Stan, his father, and just about every other name he could think to curse at that moment, he threw himself through yet another window and pulled himself to the roof of the train with an auric tether. Perching on the sleek, silver surface, Xander fought to maintain overdrive as he cast his aura out around the entire structure before working to secure it to the track. When he was certain he had a hold on both, he dropped out of overdrive and braced himself.

The train's mechanisms were already shrieking as time exploded into play around him, and he struggled to focus through the sound as he worked to keep it on its track. Inside the train, he felt the panic of the passengers begin to grow as they felt the sudden dip begin to drop them. Some of the people, he saw through his mind's eye, were quick to secure themselves—grabbing for whatever they could to support themselves or gripping the edges of their seats—while some unfortunate others were thrown by the force. A few of these unfortunate passengers were killed in that instant, and one in particular, Xander realized, did not die from the impact of being thrown...

But by an aneurism that was triggered by the stress.

Though he couldn't be sure of the details, Xander was suddenly very aware that a bad man who'd yet to die would have no one to mourn him at his funeral.

There was nothing you could do for her, something that was either a thought or Stan's voice rang out to him, and this was enough to keep Xander fighting to keep the train secured on its track as it derailed and began to barrel through the hole he'd put in the side of the office building. Satisfied that the train had reached its not-so-intended destination, he rolled from its surface, leapt back through his secondary entrance, and, beginning a partial overdrive-sprint beside it, used his aura to drag it to a stop.

Though it was dented, smoking, and "parked" in the middle of the the evacuated depths of a cubicle-riddled office building, the train was saved.

And all it cost me was a shot at that psychotic son of a... Xander's thoughts trailed off as another one occurred to him. That entire process—one that Aleks had worked at great lengths to throw into motion—had gone uninterrupted by a creature that had the power and drive to do just that if he so desired. *So where the fuck is he?* he found himself dreading.

CHAPTER 26

ON THE LOSING SIDE

"A learned man came to me once.
He said, 'I know the way, --come.'
And I was overjoyed at this.
Together we hastened.
Soon, too soon, were we
Where my eyes were useless,
And I knew not the ways of my feet.
I clung to the hand of my friend;
But at last he cried, 'I am lost.'"
Stephen Crane (1871-1900)

"Faith is not about hoping that we'll be handed what we want; it's about knowing that we have the strength to find what we need."
Father Tennesen

Aleks was not pleased. He was not pleased with Stryker's sudden acuity. He was not pleased to have lost so many of his followers so early into their battle. And he was not pleased that all of his attempts to break the little piglet's mind were getting him nowhere. He had grown up dreaming of this moment—*his* moment against Joseph Stryker's son—and, since the night he'd first heard of Xander's suicidal tendencies after his mother's death, he'd *wanted* to make that suicide happen!

To be rid of the object of his mother's ceaseless obsession—rid of the piglet his father had been cast off to babysit—and see the glorious memory of the Stryker family legacy fizzle out with a premature and self-inflicted end...

The thought of it, how it would play out and what it would represent when held against the seemingly endless stories of Joseph Stryker, had been enough to give Aleks something to live for. He certainly wasn't getting such motivation from his mother!

Mother...

Oh, how that marvelous, awful, beautiful, twisted creature still managed to stir up such thoughts in him; such... confusing thoughts.

They will know such pain and torment in their last moments that death will be a blessing. They will rue the day they extinguished your light.

There will be no mercy for them; for any of them! I will tear them apart! Starting with the Stryker-spawn I will finish what Father started, and then I'll show the world a new order.

Aleks considered his final words to Lenuta as he dragged himself from the crumbled remains of their home—their prison—and sought the first source of blood his parched fangs could find. His mother, like that castle, had managed to be both the greatest and the worst parts of his life.

He'd wanted her approval, her love, and all he ever got was

tales of how great things would be as soon as Xander Stryker was in their possession. She spoke so highly of the world beyond the impenetrable walls of their cursed castle, when the only world that Aleks had ever known had been her and everything within those walls. How little she thought of him and how much she expected from him; he existed to her as a she existed to him: a paradox—something that offered nothing to her in those moments but represented too great a resource to simply eat like the rest of the living things that had been trapped in there with her.

The only time she ever seemed to love me, Aleks thought with a pang of realization, *was the moment Stryker's plane was within their reach.*

"Look, my darling child!" Lenuta had boasted at that moment, cooing and swooning over him and urging his own aura out, stoking it like she had before with his flaccid penis to take action and strike the object of her true desire out of the sky. *"Look! Our future has arrived! It hangs there like a piece of ripe fruit for us to claim, all we have to do is pluck it!"*

Never before had she spoken to him like that. Never before had Aleks truly felt useful—truly felt *cared* for—to the proud goddess, Lenuta. But, he supposed, decades of plotting and planning come to fruition would motivate such emotions, and she'd at least cared enough to tell Aleks to remain hidden should all else come to fail.

She'd told him to never let them see, and he supposed he hadn't. He'd caught himself wondering more than once why he hadn't taken his revenge on the Strykers the moment that they'd tricked his mother into unknowingly accepting her own death, but had dismissed it with the firm conviction that he'd known Xander would remove the spell on the castle if he let him live. And, as for the reasoning behind letting the Strykers escape those mountains with their lives once the spell *was* lifted...

Well, Aleks *had* just watched the two of them kill his

mother, a far stronger and wiser varcol than himself, hadn't he? What good would it do his mother's dream—his new legacy—if he went and got himself killed?

It certainly had nothing to do with the elation Aleks had been feeling upon Lenuta's death or the freedom he could celebrate with those damned castle walls cascading as rubble down the mountainside. Because surely no elation or freedom was felt.

Or so he'd been trying to convince himself.

"Sounds like I did you a favor," the Xander-piglet had said, and—*DAMN HIM!*—a part of Aleks could not help but to agree. And yet there was another part, the part he'd been drawing strength from since the start, that insisted that Stryker had taken everything from him.

Aleks did not like admitting that he hated his mother—his mother had not taken kindly to the times that she'd sensed such thoughts in his head—and, dead or not, it was hard for him to allow those thoughts to go unpunished.

Such confusing thoughts...

He looked back on the memories of his time with his mother, locked away in that castle—just the two of them—and could no longer make sense of the feelings they conjured. Xander looked upon the blood-witch—the one who'd dared to feed off his mother—with the sort of worship and affection that Aleks believed he felt for his mother. Xander and his blood-witch shared a bed in the same way that his mother had shared her bed with him, and yet those moments with his mother had not always...

He shuddered with phantom pains; old horrors racing through his memory as nightmares he'd long since awoken from were reborn anew.

"Your mother fed from you, raped you, let you starve, and all the while tormented you with her obsession? So why hate me for freeing you from that?"

"BECAUSE SHE WAS MY MOTHER!" Aleks roared out in a rage.

The road that he stood upon was scorched with the fury of his aura in that instant, and a nearby sign—one that he had been steering himself towards while Stryker stayed behind and played with trains—was torn from the ground and cast on its side in the middle of the concrete.

Aleks was still feeling conflicted about whether he had loved or hated his mother. He couldn't decide if he should look upon her memory as one would a monster, or if she had been to him what Estella was to Xander. After digging in his head, Aleks at least felt certain that he had never known anything like what Emily Stryker had been. Lenuta had *never* been a mother to him; only a monster or a lover.

And, suddenly feeling that this wasn't right—that it was the worst kind of injustice that a pathetic, weak, insipid little being like Xander Stryker should have a legendary father and a loving mother to look back on—he marched forward.

He could not target Xander's own mother—*My father already saw to her,* he mused with a gaping smile—but Aleks supposed that his lover was a decent enough compromise.

Thinking of how delicious it would be to make Xander watch what was coming, certain this would earn the suicide he'd been living for all this time, Aleks stepped over the fallen sign—"SEASIDE OFFICE PARK"—and started towards the blood-witch's auric signature.

Zoey's aura shot out in four parts, ensnaring and yanking just as many parking meters out of the street and spinning them in blurring arcs like top-heavy fan blades around her.

A group of three alv were beaten into a pulpy mess in the blink of an eye.

A panting, weasel-like therion wearing a large, beaten leather vest lost a portion of its head.

An anapriek with dark, malicious eyes and a complex row of silver rings lining one elongated ear seized in mid-attack, rapier still held at the ready, as a coin-spilling length of rusted metal was driven through his back.

And still the varcol's battalions raged onward. Though she wasn't curious enough to dare looking into their heads—still having nightmares from the last time she'd gone poking inside the minds of those who'd decided to follow the one called "Messiah"—Zoey couldn't help but wonder just what was motivating them. Fear? Riches? Or had Aleks just outright lied and offered them some sort of claim to the world he aimed to take as his own? Could mythos who, themselves, existed for such selfish, monstrous means truly bring themselves to take the word of such a powerful-yet-equally-selfish creature?

Beside her, Isaac roared and caught two of the parking meters in his large, clawed hands. He lunged ahead, bringing the makeshift hammers down on an ykali's head—reducing the lizard-like creature's skull to a pulpy mess in a single pass—before plunging the jagged end of the other down a chittering gerlin's throat. Kicking the gray, winged mythos away, Isaac snatched up one of the fallen alv corpses and threw it at an oncoming crowd of the varcol's followers.

Zoey watched this through her mind's eye, mesmerized by her usually sweet and wise lover's brutality as she spun, jumped, and wove like a deadly dancer through an oncoming horde. Her own weaponized parking meters spun after her, trailing her swirling path in a pair of blurs, as more auric tendrils shot out to behead a pair of sangs bracing to jump the two of them from a neighboring rooftop. As she closed in on Isaac, she allowed several smaller wisps of her aura to retrieve several of the holstered guns littering her lover's body. More alvs vaulted out from a side street, baring their shark-like teeth at the pair, and then froze as three of Isaac's guns—

seemingly hovering in front of them—went off at once in their faces.

Spotting another anticipated aerial ambush being prepared, Zoey spun to meet the challenge, hurling both parking meters like a pair of spears through the chests of their would-be attackers.

In that instant, sacrificing her view through her mind's eye in exchange for a genuine look, a therion roared and threw itself at Isaac, its claws sweeping at his face.

"ISAAC! NO!" Zoey cried out.

FIGHTING, Zeek realized, was like riding a bicycle. It was a bicycle with a missing seat, a sword tip in its place, and ridden along a course buzzing with bullets, but was anything in this crazy, twisted world ever easy? Taking the role of a fancy clan doctor or training doe-eyed recruits how to swing a stick was cozy work, and there was more pride to be taken in saving a life than taking one, but one that has seen battle could never be blind of it. Zeek considered this in a state of passive contemplation as he swept the feet out from a dazed auric vampire with his bo staff, planted the opposite end into the fallen enemy's chest, and used the added leverage to launch himself into a flying kick that had a particularly cocky-looking therion wondering which way was up. As Karen dove in on the auric before they could get their bearings, Zeek got the bo spinning, built up his momentum, and then carried it in a swinging arc with vertebrae-splitting force down on the back of the whimpering therion's neck.

It did not die, but it did not get up, either.

Zeek considered the sight of the beast, its left side rigid and still while its right flexed and flailed. Supporting himself on his weapon, he reached with his free hand to retrieve the nine millimeter Stryker had forced him to carry. Though he'd never been a fan of guns—being chased down by an automatic's spray of bullets had a way of doing that to an anapriek—Stryker had been insistent that, unless one could move faster than the bullets, it was better to have bullets on one's side. Much as he hated to agree with him (on most things, in fact), Zeek had been unable to argue with him on this point. And, as it turned out, at least he could use the damned thing as a tool of mercy.

And then Karen stomped a heavy foot down on the crippled therion's skull, sending blood and chunks of... chunks through its ears.

Blinking down at the mess, Zeek begrudgingly returned the gun to the holster at his side.

Beside him, realizing what he'd been preparing to do, Karen offered an apologetic whimper.

Zeek shrugged and offered his love a smile. "Better to save the bullets, right?" he asked as an offering to make her feel better.

Karen shrugged.

Zeek had equal love for both of her forms, finding the sleek, fox-like creature and the strong, dark-skinned woman that shared a single body equally beautiful in their own way. He did, however, always miss hearing her voice when she transformed.

Beauty, brains, and a wit to match.

How could an anapriek get so—

Karen's eyes widened as something caught her eye over Zeek's shoulder.

Realizing he was blind to an ambush, he dove to the side, trusting that she would handle whatever was coming his way.

He was right.

Hitting the ground, he rolled and pushed off with his bo staff, righting himself and landing several feet away as the airborne sangsuiga who'd been aiming for his head with a claymore met only air...

And Karen.

The sang's claymore arm rested in a pool of blood a moment

later, and, as a few other parts of him started to get added to the pile, Zeek allowed himself to draw a breath.

Before he could inhale, however, he found himself falling to one side, hitting the ground with enough force to knock the stale air from his lungs and the bo staff from his grip. Looking up from his suddenly damp, sticky plot on the road, he spotted the second claymore-wielding sang crouched over a freshly severed leg.

Zeek's freshly severed leg...

SATORU STARED in stunned horror at the bloodied heap that had, only seconds ago, been Sasha's body. In that briefly-yet-infinitely distant moment, they'd been back-to-back, watching one another's flanks and cutting down waves of their enemies. It had not been a thing of beauty—Satoru could find no beauty in such a thing—but they had been together, and they had been functioning as only two warriors who paired as wondrously as the moon's glow and a still pond could.

Sasha...

Wild, untamed beauty.

This injustice, I'll avenge

To you I fly now.

Satoru was aware of the sharp tug at the small of his back as one of Sasha's killers planted a bullet there. Like a salted field, however, the seed of death would find nothing fertile there to take root. Howling, cat-like muscles flexed and sprung, sending Satoru across the pavement in sprint that caught even the blood-suckers off guard.

Shurikens hissed through the air.

A tanto was freed from its shallow sheath and buried between widening eyes.

Bodies fell, splaying in Satoru's wake as he hacked and slashed a bloody path from Sasha's body. His katana clicked free from its hilt with the flick of a clawed thumb, his free hand snatching a nearby foe and dragging him into the path of fresh gunfire. The body danced in the nejin's grip as he closed the distance. Tossing aside the dead mythos, Satoru drew his sword and swiped out with it—a fluid and practiced motion that had the nearest gunman's arm clattering to the street—and then drew back once more, thrusting through the dishonorable wretch's heart.

He panted, finally taking notice of the many bullets that had joined with that first all over his body.

He would be dead soon, he knew, but not before he saw to it that every last one of Sasha's killers met the same fate.

Throwing the corpse from his blade, he sucked in a painful breath, inflating his one good lung for his final act, and fought away the creeping darkness.

Shots fired.

Enemies howled.

Death claimed them.

Like a rain of cherry blossoms their blood fell, turning the ugly black road red in Satoru's wake. More and more of the varcol's lapdogs took the raging nejin into their sights, and none prevailed. Knives and swords followed the bullets, and before long Satoru had lost count of the weapons jutting from his body.

And still he staved off death.

A spear was thrust into his shoulder, twisted, and then snapped off; the weapon's head left jutting from a slowly oozing wound as its wielder moved to strike Satoru in the face with the splintered remains. He caught the attack in his free hand, sank his katana into the attacker's belly, and tore out his throat with his teeth.

When the body fell, it managed to pull Satoru's sword with it.

He was sad to see the katana leave his grip, but he decided that it was fitting that he should have to part with that, as well.

Huffing out a heavy sigh, deciding he could go on no further, he turned back.

Three more bullets tore into his body—he barely felt them.

Tired.

So tired.

He locked his fading vision on the bloodied heap that had, only minutes ago, been Sasha's body.

An alv hissed and leapt at him.

Satoru retrieved the spearhead from his shoulder and plunged it into the ugly creature's heart.

Closer now.

Sasha...

To you I fly now.

None could stop my love's fury.

We go. Together.

Satoru's final step was taken with blind eyes, but when he fell to his knees he fell with confidence that he'd manage to take his wolf-like lover's body into his cat-like arms.

Maybe there'd still be time to compose a haiku in...

"FUCKING SHIT! WHAT WAS—NO... NO!" Serena was on her feet and sprinting in Gregori's direction as the roar of another collapsing building thundered in the distance.

Estella was already by her side, sending out a psychic call to everyone on site to find a place to hide.

There wasn't a shred of irony in her voice as Serena asked, "How much good will it do?"

Estella tried her best to ignore that question.

Catching on to this, Serena finally asked, "How many are there?"

More willing to answer this, Estella let her mind's eye trail back and shuddered. "More and more every second," she whispered.

"Fuck!" Serena growled, scooping up Gregori in her arms and continuing to sprint alongside Estella through their compound. "What does it say that Aleks is here and... well, our side isn't?" she demanded.

"It says that Aleks wasn't satisfied with how the battle was going in the city," said Estella, relieved to sense Xander's aura still active.

Serena considered this for a moment before thrusting Gregori into Estella's arms and turning back.

"MOMMY!" Gregori cried, reaching after her.

"SERENA! STOP!" Estella called after her, starting to follow.

Don't you dare come after me, Stryker! Serena's tone was harsh enough in Estella's head to have her flinching. *You get my boy somewhere safe and you keep your cute little ass out of sight, got it? That motherfucker is after you—you know it, I know it, and I know that you know it—and I'm not about to give him what he wants!*

What do you think Zane would have to say about you risking yourself like this? Estella asked.

A long silence followed before Serena finally said, *Zane ain't here, Goddess. Now protect my son.*

Hurry, Missus Stryker! Elder Luis' voice rang in Estella's head before she could protest. *Bring the boy to me! I can shield our whereabouts!*

The old auric projected his location, and Estella was startled to find that he'd discovered a concealed passage beneath the original storage facility that fed into the boiler room. This, she imagined, was the access passage that maintenance crew must have used to get to the pipes. That nobody else had discovered the small doorway in the floor (or even been curious enough to look) gave her hope that it would suffice to keep them hidden while Aleks and the sangs he'd brought with him raided the area. Provided, of course...

"Are you sure you can shield this area from Aleks?" Estella demanded, "Do you swear you can—"

"Hush-up, girl!" Elder Luis snapped. "Give an old man *some* credit!"

"An old man *and* a young lady," Estella heard a familiar voice chime from further into the passage.

Craning her neck to see past Elder Luis, she spotted Sana and, with her, Tim. A moment of relief came at seeing the two of them safe, and Estella's confidence climbed with the knowledge that the gifted young auric would be available to help shielding the location.

"I'm giving you more than *some* credit," Estella told them, thrusting little Gregori into Elder Luis' arms. "I'm giving you the firstborn son of Serena Vailean. If something happens to him, you'll wish Aleks had gotten to you instead!"

Then, before the elder could try to stop her, she left him.

At the varcol-level speed, it felt more like the world was moving around her in a particle-haze. Through this perspective, Aleks almost appeared to be rushing towards her. This, Estella realized too late, was actually half true...

~Ten seconds earlier~

SERENA HOWLED with laughter as she yanked back her auric bow and loosed over a dozen purple bolts through the air.

"CATCH YOU FUCKERS WITH YOUR DICKS OUT? COME ON!" she taunted, watching as just as many sangs dropped where they stood. Beyond them, more of Aleks' lapdogs emerged out of overdrive, eager to take their place. "MORE?" she cheered, drawing back on her aura and preparing another shot, "I THOUGHT YOU'D NEVER..."

A dark, heavy dread sank into her core as something appeared behind her.

"... ask," her voice slipped out as a nervous squeak as she turned.

Before, whenever she'd seen Aleks, Serena couldn't help but think he looked like a pathetic, sniveling turd of a vampire. If she had ever been so bold—so thoroughly and completely fooled by the act the varcol had been putting on—she would have even said he looked like a pussy.

Maybe he'd gotten taller since then.

Or maybe he'd been hitting the gym.

Or, more likely, she caught herself thinking, *I was just a dumb blonde looking at a shapeshifter who could make me see and think whatever he damn-well pleased...*

"Would you look at that," the varcol seethed, moving a hand that was gradually becoming something else towards her face, "the slut found her brain." Three somethings that had, moments earlier, been five fingers elongated, flexed, and then closed in on Serena's jawline—two of the rough, leathery things hugging either side of her chin as the middle grazed her bottom lip. "What do you say, slut?" Aleks' voice rasped, seeming to be working through something that was no longer a throat, and Serena saw that his tongue was swelling and throbbing; reshaping into... something else. "Feeling slutty?"

"Oh god..." she whimpered, trying to pull away but finding herself unable to slip free of the hold. The middle *something* began to worm its way past her parted lips, suddenly bifurcating and working to pry her mouth open in slow, jerking pushes.

And then that awful not-tongue started to creep out from Aleks' mouth.

Wanna see a trick? his voice echoed in her mind as he closed the distance.

Then...

Nothing.

Serena dropped, sobbing, onto her knees. Her jaw ached.

Her lips itched. She felt herself heave and pitched herself forward to keep from being sick on herself.

She couldn't remember the last time she'd been so happy to puke.

Then, catching a glimmer of what had convinced Aleks to spare her, she began to swear like she'd never sworn before.

But before she could bring herself to get to her feet, track down Estella, and hand the Stryker-woman her own ass on a platter, eight of Aleks' bitch-boys got the jump on her.

SEEING ALEKS RUSHING TOWARDS HER, Estella remembered Xander taking Lenuta down with a move that was, simply put, not the most graceful. At that moment, however, knowing the nature of the beast she was up against and having some notion of what he had in mind if given the chance, she couldn't bring herself to worry about grace. Working to guard her stomach, she threw herself off of her feet and braced for what a landing coming out of this speed had in store.

She could see it playing out in her mind as it had played out for Xander against Lenuta: their high-velocity bodies suddenly becoming a tumbling mass of unpredictable, leg-sweeping chaos. Any attacks that their opponents had in mind were rendered useless, and any hope of staying on their feet was—

Estella, wracked with pain from the impact, sensed Aleks clear her barreling body with a vertical leap that carried him out of her path. Cursing and working to get to her feet, Estella cried out as Aleks' aura clapped around her and moved to throw her against a neighboring building. Snarling, she used her own aura to break free of the hold and sent a series of auric bolts in his direction.

Do you know what I'm going to do to you? asked Aleks as he sprinted around the attacks and jumped up to meet her in midair. His grinning face gave much of his intent away.

Estella didn't answer him. As his fanged leer drew near enough, she moved to punch him.

Rolling his head free of the attack, he roped his aura around her and, as they began to fall, he moved to throw her back towards the earth. *I think you have a good guess. I'm sure you have many good guesses, in fact. But I wonder if you know that I'm going to do all of those things to you* after *I've killed you.*

Estella threw her aura out below her, buffered the landing to one she could control, and, taking a page out of Serena's playbook with a touch Stryker style, shifted into varcol-level overdrive and aimed an imaginary gun up towards the varcol.

Bang, she thought, imagining Xander with his revolver.

A spark of auric energy pierced the air, closing in on Aleks faster than any bullet had ever traveled before.

The auric-bullet collided with the still-falling Aleks in a flash of light that had Estella thinking of words like "supernova" and "apocalypse."

A mass of thrashing meat and bones surrounded in a burning light of auric energy crashed with a loud, thick *SPLAT* onto the pavement a short distance away.

And then Aleks began to rebuild himself.

Disgusting creatures! Estella thought, deciding to take her borrowed trick a little further and letting her aura form into a pair of tonfas in either hand. Though she missed the weight of Selene and Helios—missed the *realness* of them in her hands—she found the act almost comforting in their absence. *Can see what Serena sees in this...*

A wad of writhing muscle twisted, gaining height and width as it built upon itself. The mass heaved, splayed open, and a series of bones began to erupt from the surface like a time-lapsed video of new trees bursting up from the earth. What Estella at first thought was a ribcage began to elongate further outward, and the tubular skeleton rolled forward as it took shape. The spiral of muscle, now beginning to show a patchwork of flesh spreading across its surface, stretched and flattened as it fell across the still-growing network of new bones. As Estella watched, she recognized the base shape of the organism as looking almost snake-like.

Just as this thought birthed itself in her mind, the tail-like appendage gave a hard, slithery "kick" and started towards her; the open-ended mass flaring and letting the unfinished bone-juts become teeth as a series of eyes began to open along the inner walls of its gullet.

Crying out at the monstrous creature slithering towards her, Estella moved to roll free of its path. Narrowly avoiding the gaping maw of the man-sized, visceral cyclone-snake, Estella twisted around to strike with one of her auric tonfas.

A new arm erupted from the side of the Aleks-creature, gripping her wrist and pulling her back towards it. Another arm jumped forth to claim her as the varcol rose up on its coiled tail, "standing" before her as its upper "body" began to build itself anew. The tooth-and-eye lined gullet puckered, belched wetly, and then prolapsed on itself, birthing a shiny, blood-streaked head.

Estella screamed.

The horrible thing had no face!

"LET ME GO!" she demanded, moving to throw her aura out at the monster.

Even without eyes, Aleks' aura appeared to first deflect and then bind her own.

As the upper body finished constructing itself—the new flesh stretching out over the freshly knitted framework of bone and muscle and then seeming to "breathe" in on itself, fitting to its new body with only a few squirming bits still poking out here-and-there—the faceless head began to pulsate. Estella whimpered and fought to pull back, but the new hands held her firmly. An area roughly set where Aleks' mouth *should* have been bulged and then stretched, warping the skin there as it did. With the flesh pulled taut, something—*Merciful Earth Mother,* Estella pleaded, *please just be a tongue!*—on the other side pushed against its surface, testing it. Seeming satisfied for a moment, the probe receded, and Estella could practically hear her heart beating in her throat as she waited for whatever would come next.

Then, following a violent lurch from deep within its chest, a pair of fang-like protrusions stabbed through the flesh and, in a sweeping motion, began to tear out a mouth-shaped hole. Torn flesh curled in on itself, seeming almost to rot in an instant, and darkened—becoming lips that flexed and pursed around a long, flat tongue-like appendage that still wore the two fangs at its tip. This, after a victorious stretch from its new, yawning mouth, sprouted a series of teeth that cycled around the original fangs. As the mouth worked to construct itself, Estella saw a pair of dark, sea-colored points drill out from the head's middle; carving a wide set of vacant cavities and then flaring out with pride—the small, blue points inflating into a pair of eyes that were just as suddenly occupying a pair of lids that narrowed at her. The mouth-tongue, finishing its reconstruction, allowed itself to be swallowed back—the new teeth moving to occupy their rightful place as a blood-colored tongue ripped free from the gaping maw, gave a sample wag to test its new existence, and then moved to form words:

"THAT... HURT... BITCH!" Aleks roared in Estella's face, giving her body a violent shake.

Joseph shook with every resonating impact that his father took. Beside him, neither understanding nor feeling what he was going through, his mother did what she could to comfort him. He could see in her mind that she knew that, in some way, he was helping her—helping both of them—to remain hidden. She could not see auras, and she definitely couldn't read minds, but Missus Wilson was at least aware that her son, who could do both (and so much more), was straining to keep them concealed from the vampires that had appeared.

Estella's psychic call had startled both of his parents. They'd been forcing themselves to eat—or, rather, putting on a show for one another of *trying* to eat—in one of the office's cafeterias when it happened, and while Joseph was still working to scan the area to understand what was happening, his father began pushing him and his mother towards the adjacent kitchen.

"Find somewhere to hide," he'd told them, repeating Estella's words. Pushing his wife further ahead, he'd taken a moment to pull Joseph close to him so he could whisper, "Protect your mother, son. I know you can," before turning away.

"Dad!" Joseph cried, "Where are you—"

Mister Wilson didn't turn as he said, "You heard me, Joseph. Do me proud, alright?"

And so Joseph did. At least, Joseph did what he hoped his father would be proud of. Picking up where he'd left off, he grabbed his mother's hand and pulled her further into the kitchen, navigating past rows of prep stations and supply racks before arriving at a wall lined with ovens. Joseph paused at this, curious about the likelihood of something horrific befalling the two of them if they tried to hide in one of the carbon-caked depths. Then, with visions of their charred remains baked into the back of his mind, he decided it was risking too much and steered the two of them towards a door marked "DRY STORAGE." Inside here, he discovered several rows of tall, wide metal shelves stocked with cans, jars, and condiments. After a moment of frantic searching, he spotted several large sacks of rice stacked on the bottom row of the nearest shelf and began pulling these aside to make room for the two of them to hide. Once painfully fitted against the wall so that he could pull the sacks back into place to cover them, Joseph set up a psychic shield and then, sucking in a strained breath, dared to scan for his father's location.

Unfortunately, he'd found him.

Though his mother didn't understand, he could see that she knew what his violent spasms represented. As she worked to hold him—to comfort him—within their confines, she began to weep and chant her late-husband's name.

"F-FUCKERS!" Serena snarled, snapping at a leg that had gotten too close to her face for the owner's own good.

The leg drew back, its owner hissing down at her, and then kicked her in the face.

"Fucking cunt!" a voice from overhead—*likely the owner of that leg,* she distantly mused—spat down at her.

More kicks followed.

Serena fought to shield her body with her aura, but another hybrid vampire tore through this effort over and over again. And still Serena worked to build a new shield. As long as she continued to convince them that her aura was busy trying to protect her body, she knew, none of them would stop to consider the auric shield she'd built around her womb.

You pig-fuckers... ain't gonna get... my baby! she chanted to herself, keeping up the show while looking for any chance to take a piece out of one of her attackers. *You fuckers... ain't gonna get... my baby!*

Somehow, even through the beating, she could sense the moment when a familiar aura—a very special aura that she'd spent the past month growing more and more fond of—vanished. Estella, she knew, had been taken. She'd saved Serena from a fate worse than any she could even imagine, and then she'd been taken. Despite everything Xander had done to keep his wife out of that disgusting fucker's clutches, he'd...

Serena screamed, fueled by pain and anger and fear, and lashed out. She drew on energy she didn't realize she'd managed to hold onto, and her manicured hand caught one of her attackers in mid-kick and dragged him, crying out in shock, to the floor beside her. The kicks intensified, and some of the sangs even went so far as to try pulling their comrade from the crazy, pregnant blonde's grip, but all they earned for their efforts was a series of bites.

"Y'ALL MOTHERFUCKERS LOOK LIKE SNICKERS TO ME!" Serena shrieked before sinking her fangs into her first meal.

Half her attackers recoiled, turned, and tried to high-tail for saner prey. A series of purple tendrils snapped out like bullfrog tongues claiming flies from the air and dragged them right back to her.

Didn't your mommas ever tell you cocksuckers it's rude to leave a lady dissatisfied? she chided in their heads as she gulped down another mouthful of blood. Then, deciding not to fill up on the appetizer, she snapped the sucker-punching little taint-monkey's throat and jumped onto the second course.

Hold on, Goddess, she thought, hissing in this new victim's face and slamming his head back, cracking his skull, *I'm coming!* Then, giving the sang another violent introduction with the street, she called out to the others: "REMEMBER, BOYS: I'M KILLING FOR TWO!"

Allen? ALLEN! I... I need cover! Please! Cover me! Zoey pleaded, sending up an auric flare to steer the magic-trained sniper to her location. *Isaac's hurt,* she explained, *I... I need to—*

Z-Zoe? Oh god... Zoe, please tell me that's you? I... I can't see! Isaac's thoughts carried out in a panic as he flailed on the street.

Zoey fought to keep her tears from robbing her of her own sight. She'd managed to put up an auric shield around the two of them—one that was under a barrage of attacks from enemy mythos—and had to fight to control her emotions in that instant to avoid having it collapse and invite certain death upon them.

His eyes!

The therion that had jumped him in that instant had gone straight for his eyes!

It's me, baby! she assured him, clasping one of his large, bestial hands in both of hers. *It's okay. It's going to be—oh god! ALLEN! ALLEN, PLEA—*

I gotcha, Blue, the human's thought-speak was faint; distant and weak from infrequent use.

Zoey hadn't heard the shot—Allen Carrey was set up too far away for that—but she knew that her cries had been answered as the first of the hazy bodies pounding on her auric shield dropped away. Then another, and another.

One by one the onslaught against her small, dome-like shield was whittled down to only three. But then the rescuing shots stopped...

Allen? Zoey called, certain he was reloading.

But nothing else happened.

Reaching back with her mind's eye towards the building Allen Carrey had stationed himself inside, Zoey only sensed another auric. One of Aleks'. One of theirs had tracked down their sniper and...

"Oh Allen..." Zoey groaned, tightening her hold on Isaac's hand.

Isaac squeezed back as he swallowed back his pain, his teeth clenched against any further whimpers, and he thought, *You're going to have to leave me...*

"NEVER!" Zoey screamed, jumping as a large body crashed against her auric dome. "Isaac... please, no! There's... there's gotta be..."

Then Zoey got an idea.

It was crazy, sure, but with the world being what it was—a place where someone like Xander could not only avoid extermination for breaking the most sacred of mythos laws, but actually win over The Council and organize *this* sort of mayhem in only half-a-month—crazy seemed to be what worked!

"Isaac, I need you to focus, alright?" she told him. "Just like when we're talking with our minds, got it? Imagine you're pushing to tell me your deepest, most private thought!"

The hum of Isaac's subconscious sounded like distant ocean waves in Zoey's mind; like hushed static on either side of the world's most beautiful radio station.

It came in...

Then faded out.

It came in louder, more clear...

And crept to a nearly nonexistent murmur.

"Focus, Isaac!" Zoey pressed, squeezing his hand harder. "I can only meet you halfway with this!"

Then, like a key fitting into its assigned lock, the notches of Isaac's mind came to match the tumblers of Zoey's and she began pushing a feed from her mind's eye back into his brain's vision centers.

Yelping, Isaac jumped and yanked his head back before swiveling it around; his mangled face aiming itself in various directions before reluctantly going still.

Zoe...? What'd you do? he thought.

"D-d it work?" she stammered. "Can you see?"

I... I think I... he began to reach out with his opposite hand, flexing it several times. His head dipped, no longer aimed in any particular direction, and he flexed his hand again before bearing his teeth in a therion smirk. Then, not moving his face towards her, he navigated the hand with perfect, gentle precision to cup her cheek. *Who knew you could see so little and so much all at once?*

The two paused suddenly, regarding his words with a sense of eerie awareness, and then worked to stand.

"Do you think you can fight like this?" she asked him.

Isaac gave a single nod, flexing his back and cocking his head to one side, seeming to regard their surroundings from all angles. Zoey watched in astonishment as his aura drifted with perfect accuracy in the direction of the enemies surrounding her auric shield.

Honestly, he thought back to her, *I'm not sure how I ever fought without this. And this is what you can see all the time?*

Zoey let out a laugh that carried the last traces of her cries. "Y-yeah. I guess it is," she offered.

KAREN STOPPED herself from wiping her eyes, knowing that the tears wouldn't obscure her vision nearly as badly as the blood on her hands.

Zeek's blood! This is Zeek's— she fought to slam the doors of her mind on the thought before it could send her spiraling out of focus.

She needed her wits about her; needed to focus on being the level-headed nurse she'd been working as for the past couple of months.

Except that she'd been working beside Zeek for those past few months. Now she was working *on* Zeek...

And the color was beginning to leave his face.

"No, no! Zeek! ZEEK!" she gave his cheek a few gentle taps, watching his eyes work to respond to the impacts. "Come on, honey, don't go to sleep on me now, okay? I need you. I—"

Zeek smiled weakly at that and reached for her hand. "Do you... know how happy... hearing that... makes me?" he asked in between uneven breaths.

Karen accepted his hand and giggled nervously. "That's why I said it," she offered. "And I'll keep saying it for as long as you stay with me, alright?"

"Did you... know..." he puttered out, "... that... you're naked?"

She couldn't help but laugh at that, but the effort betrayed her halfway through and she began to sob. "J-just to get you to stay with me, Zeek..." she whimpered.

The memory of getting Zeek into the neighboring building —what turned out to be an old movie theater that appeared to cater strictly to films released in the sixties—was something of a blur to her. She remembered tearing a vampire who'd been working to skewer him with an old-timey sword to pieces, only to see a second with the same type of sword taking off his leg. The events that followed felt rushed and hidden under what Karen felt was at least a hundred gallons of blood, but she'd finally managed to get them both inside and hidden behind the concessions stand. Then, knowing she'd be of no use to her lover as a seven-foot bipedal fox with razor-sharp claws, she'd abandoned all modesty and transformed back into her human form.

True to his observation, this left her wearing nothing but her birthday suit as she started taking inventory of whatever could be of use to her and began working to stop the bleeding.

"I..." Zeek cleared his throat and moved to push himself up. "I think..." he faltered and started to slump back down again.

Karen caught him, held him, and whispered, "Please, Zeek... I don't want to go through this without you."

Clenching his jaw and his eyelids for a moment, the anapriek sucked in a breath through his nose, held it, and then let it out in a slow, controlled exhale. "You won't have to," he promised her. "Just stay—"

The doors to the theater slammed open, and the two hears a loud, furious snort echo a few feet from the gold-painted box office booth. Shivering, Karen moved to peek through an empty display case that offered a blurred view of the opposite side of the concession stand. A dark, bear-like creature lumbered a few paces further into the lobby, grunted, and then rose onto its hind legs. Jutting its wide, shallow snout into the air, Karen heard it snort up a heavy, scent-laced dose of air.

Then, letting out a satisfied huff, the mythos bellowed.

Zeek flinched and then immediately after started to swoon as if he might faint.

Karen, moving in a low crouch, motioned to him to wait.

His eyes widened, life flaring back into him as worry overrode everything else, and he mouthed "NO!"

But Karen was already beginning to transform again, clenching her teeth to keep herself from crying out as her body underwent the change.

It always hurt more when she tried to make it go faster...

Zeek was still trying to silently protest his case as Karen, now fully shifted back into her more capable form, threw herself over the countertop and landed on the other side on all fours.

The therion that had entered the theater—she was certain he'd followed the trail of Zeek's blood—was massive. Still standing, it was forced to hunch, its broad, blocky shoulders stooped and its head dipped to avoid the ceiling. A wide, short snout stretched and curled to reveal blood-stained teeth as it grinned at Karen. She was sleek and long, poised low; he was vast and sturdy, towering over her. She could see that he was already celebrating his win.

She could only hope that he was wrong.

Giving a curt snort, the therion barreled towards her. She yelped at the movement, startled by his speed in the confined lobby. In three lumbering steps he was upon her, giving her only enough time to try to lunge for his throat. With the distance closing fast, however, she only managed to throw herself into its chest, missing her mark by nearly a foot. It was like throwing herself into a boulder. Head spinning, Karen reeled away and worked to force her body to remain upright. She failed. Too late, she realized that her equilibrium's understanding of "up" was far from accurate, and she toppled to the floor. As her head sank into old, faded carpeting, the room seemed to tilt to one side—she was certain she'd begin rolling along the increasing slant at any moment—and she shut her eyes against the dizzying effect.

Her ears twitched as she heard the therion take a step towards her. She remembered Zeek, weak and incapacitated on the other side of the concession stand and worked to push herself back up. The world might not have righted itself in her eyes, but she had to protect Zeek.

Had to...

The therion's fist drove into her belly with a force that seemed to transcend pain. Karen found herself more aware of the sheer force, which was enough to throw her back several feet and topple her onto her side. The room shifted first to one side, then the other; her stomach knotted. Then the pain came. Yelping at the sharp, burning agony that erupted in her guts, Karen folded herself around the pain—worshipping it like a lover—and fought to get it under control.

She had to stand...

Had to...

The floor drifted away from her, and, through the heavy curtain of pain in her stomach, she felt the pull at her nape where the therion was lifting her. Blinking against the suddenly nauseating glare of light, she found herself eye-to-eye with the towering beast. He grinned again, no less knowing regarding his victory this time around, and moved to hold her at an arm's length from his body. An arm's length, Karen realized, was a long way to travel.

Then, brandishing the claws of his opposite hand with a mocking wave of gorilla-like fingers, he slashed her throat.

The breath slipped from Karen's lungs faster than the blood from her wound, which seemed to pour down her chest by the gallons in a single instant. She wanted to whimper but found herself unable. She wanted to kick, but she couldn't find the strength. She felt herself dying, and—*Merciful god... no!*—she was doing it in the grip of a horrid enemy when the arms of her anapriek lover waited only a few feet away.

Worst yet, she couldn't even *try* to form the words to apologize to Zeek in that moment...

Thunder clapped within the lobby, and Karen found it odd that such a clear morning should turn so stormy so fast. Then, taking too long for her liking, she found herself wondering why a storm should be growing *inside* the safety of the theater.

And still the thunder rolled on...

Karen's world tilted again, this time with a distant sense of vertigo as she dropped...

And dropped...

And dropped...

The floor seemed softer this time around, and she watched through fluttering lids as the old, faded carpet began to turn red in the part of her vision that had yet to go blurry.

Zeek...?

She didn't know why she thought that, what she hoped would come from it, but, by some strange miracle, the thought seemed to earn a response.

Feeling a hand clasp around her throat, she moved to look and caught sight of a sleek, beautiful creature. Statuesque and regal, Zeek worked himself into a lopsided kneel on his remaining leg, using his staff to support his other half as he held the gun that Xander had ordered him to carry in his free hand. Smoke rolled from the end, and Karen thought of thunder. Daring a glance, she saw the towering therion, still standing, as it staggered. Karen thought he looked like a drunk bear, and she began to giggle.

"*st**a**Y...* ***w*****I**t*H...* **m**e***!***" she heard Zeek's voice—rolling and dipping and fading in and out of focus—calling to her...

And, hard as it was to capture the words and make sense of them, she heard him; she held them.

Though Karen could not speak, she nodded, promising Zeek she'd stay as best she could.

It was only fair...

He'd made the same promise to her, after all.

Two minutes. Two goddam minutes since he'd pulled a rescue mission on a potentially runaway train out of his butt! One-hundred-and-twenty "blink and you miss them"-seconds, and Xander hadn't managed to catch sight of Aleks anywhere. He'd shot, hacked, pummeled, and torn his way through *dozens* of Aleks' warriors, but all with no sign of the monster leading them.

Two minutes... Xander thought again, snarling and burying his kukri into the skull of a perfect vampire while he unloaded three enchanted rounds first into and then through the chest of an auric, taking out another that had been waiting behind him. *A varcol could do* a lot *with two minutes.*

"WHERE THE FUCK ARE YOU?" he roared at the rapidly diminishing crowd of enemy mythos.

Zane was doing pretty well, all things considered. He'd taken a few good hits—nothing to write home about, but he'd probably be feeling sore for a few days—and had even scored a few decent nicks and scratches to flash at Serena when all this was over. The only real prize-winning injury so far, he thought while giving his gray muscle shirt a quick glance, was just above his collarbone. There, though shallow, was an inch-and-a-half slash that a particularly mouthy sang had put there with the chaotic sweeping of a sad little pig-sticker in desperate need of sharpening. The sang had been all "GET SOME"-this and "COME AT ME"-that, but, when Zane decided to come at him and get some, the bratty fucker went chicken-shit on him.

Granted, it wasn't easy to be ballsy when one's balls were being punted halfway up their stomach. Feeling bad for the shrill-voiced little piss-ant, Zane had driven the broad side of his shiny new axe blade down on his head. He'd been working to send his head down through his neck, thinking it'd be nice to reunite him with his balls somewhere around his midsection.

Unfortunately, he only managed to cave in the fucker's skull, rupture one of his eyes, and leave him with a particularly nasty nosebleed.

The vampire had been a sniveling punk, but he'd managed to give Zane his most memorable wound of the day (so far). It was enough to bleed across most of his chest and, in the process, soak into his shirt. This, though the bleeding had since stopped, made it look far worse than it actually was.

He decided to give the dead vampire an 'A' for effort and a 'D' for effectiveness.

He was about to start down another street towards a cluster of gerlins who looked to be in desperate need of an ass-kicking when—

"ZANE!"

His heart skipped, paused, and then pounded with rage.

Serena!

After everything he and Xander had done to secure their...

She'd left the compound and...

Praying to whatever god might be listening for the patience to *NOT* beat his pregnant wife within an inch of her life for risking...

Zane groaned, whimpered at what was an obvious punishment for jerking off to too many Bonnie Rotten videos.

Not like Serena wasn't right there beside me buried up to her...

Then he turned and caught sight of her.

"Oh my... Serena? What—"

Caught off guard by the sight of his bruised, bloodied, and generally beaten wife, Zane roared in pain as his entire body seemed to catch fire. For the first time since he'd finally rid himself of the Maledictus curse all those years back, he caught sight of his taroe tattoos glowing. His body throbbed, searing itself, and the complex network of tribal designs flared like a hot brand. Bad as the pain was, Zane was that much more tortured by the discovery that, with his wife in obvious need a short distance away, he couldn't move. His legs worked, straining to push the rest of him forward, but the soles of his boots just scraped uselessly at the street. Groaning with strain, he moved to look around, certain that this was an attack of some kind.

And an attack... must include an attacker!

Craning his neck, Zane caught sight of their glow before he caught sight of them.

Three of them!

Taroe!

Struggling against the three's hold on his tattoos, he growled, "So how'd... the varcol... manage to... buy you?"

They didn't answer.

"So much... for taroe pride... eh?" he mocked, forcing a laugh through the pain.

One of the tattooed wizards seethed from his words, marching ahead of the other two—much to their disapproval—and planted himself one pace from Zane.

"I lost family when you attacked our kin, *Maledictus!*" he said, spitting out the name with a disgusted hiss.

"I don't go by that name anymore," Zane muttered, forcing the glaring taroe to inch forward to hear.

"It's not the sort of title one just—"

Zane drove his forehead into the taroe's face. It might have only been a head-butt, but he was still only human. The taroe's glowing tattoos sputtered as he staggered back, his face cratered in around his now-sunken nose. He rose his hand, finger extended, as if about to make some profound point, and then dropped.

The hold on Zane's right arm faded, the glow diminishing from the tattoos adorning the limb, and he beamed at the other two. Their faces sank with worry as he yanked his shotgun from his side and put a magic-laced slug in one's chest. It took an embarrassing moment to realize *why* the Cebourist magic wasn't putting on any sort of light show, and he rolled his eyes at himself.

Human. Right!

The last taroe, still keeping hold of Zane's left arm, jumped back and worked to reclaim his hold across his captive's upper body. Tattoos glowing that much brighter, Zane watched as the lone taroe strained. The pain in Zane's left arm diminished as the tattoos there dimmed, the effects starting to spread across his chest and across to his right arm. Though this seemed to reclaim his entire upper body, Zane found the pain and the weight of the overall hold compromised. One single taroe, he realized, wasn't enough to hold all of him back. Growling, he began to push towards the final attacker. Each step was a labor, but he was at least moving. Grinning at the otherwise simple achievement, he moved to pump a fresh slug into the chamber of his shotgun and worked to raise it.

Eyes widening at the sight of the weapon being leveled at him, the taroe focused all of his magic to Zane's right arm, halting the weapon's progress and forcing him to drop it.

Roaring, Zane lurched forward with his freed left arm and upper body, struggling against the anchor of his own arm in an effort to reach the last taroe holding him back from Serena.

"You're gonna die, ya fucking ink-wizard!" Zane threatened.

"Y-you'll have to lose your arm f-first," the taroe stammered, struggling to sound confident.

No, Zane thought. *Not the arm...*

Shifting his focus into overdrive, he reached to his axe. Though it wasn't much to look at, he'd managed to fashion a decent "holster" for the weapon with, of all things, a ripped boot strap. Looping the strip of leather through one of the belt loops of his pants and fastening it to itself, it was just the right size to fit the axe handle and keep it by his side. Though the reach was awkward with his opposite hand, Zane managed to yank it free and turned the freshly sharpened blade on himself.

"The world's worst tattoo removal will be a good thing..." he mock-thought, remembering Xander's disembodied words to him at the hotel. He wasn't normally one for remembering

what people said after so much time—especially when it was cryptic hoo-haw—but something about that line had stuck with him. *Go figure,* he mused as he gritted his teeth and began to drag the blade from his shoulder down to his wrist.

He cringed, cursed, and watched as the time-frozen world started to creep back to life as his focus waned. Clenching everything he could and reclaiming his control, he locked his gaze on the still-leering, still-confident taroe in front of him.

You have no idea how dead you are, fucker! Zane thought, using his soon-to-be target's smug face as a focal point as he continued to work the axe.

Serena wished she could have taken some degree of pleasure out of disobeying both Xander *and* Zane and finding an excuse to get herself onto the battlefield.

She *wanted* to claim some sort of victory in that moment of defiance...

But, under the circumstances, there was really nothing to celebrate.

Then, watching some sneak-attacking taroe shit-fucks get the jump on Zane and put him through obvious torture while trying to get to her, she felt nothing but rage at being forced to be there.

She'd been preparing an auric bow with a three-time "FUCK YOU" for the taroes when she was swept off her feet, carried through the air, and slammed with an alarming force against the stone steps of a library.

Thank fuck I never stopped shielding the baby! she thought with only a twinge of sarcasm as she felt something pop in her lower back.

At least she'd managed to feed before hoofing it back into the city.

Not that making that trip in overdrive had left her much in the tank.

A string-bean of a perfect vampire—close to seven feet tall but all limbs and no meat—planted a bony knee between her tits, bound her arms with his vegan-shit colored aura, and began wailing on her face with a series of overdrive-fueled fists.

"Not... my... cocksucking... lips!" Serena groaned. She was ready to tell him that her mouth was insured and that her insurance would make him regret what he was doing, but then she heard Zane.

Heard the pain in his voice.

Serena loved a good dick-sucking joke—she loved it almost as much as she loved sucking dick—but she didn't love either of them as much as she loved Zane.

Brace yourself, Onyx, she warned her unborn as she willed the auric shield she'd been maintaining in her guts to shoot upward, phasing through her stomach and barreling straight up through the string-bean's ass.

Serena was sure the baby hadn't felt a thing—maybe a little tug as his secondary womb slipped away—but the string-bean...

"Makes a prison-rape look like a prostate exam," she muttered, watching the vamp's remains crash onto the steps.

She realized with only mild amusement that his lower body looked like one of those blown-out, exploding prank cigars.

"Yeesh..." she cringed as a length of the vampire's bowels slipped free and began a morbid Slinky impression down the rest of the stairs.

She was climbing to her feet, preparing to handle Zane's taroe problem, when she saw the last of the three tattooed wizards fall to the street, Zane's axe buried into his face. Scanning the street for any sign of her husband, she spotted only a bloody mass of tattooed—

"Oh no..." she whimpered, wondering if the taroe had

somehow managed to reduce her husband to a small wad of inked flesh in the brief time she'd been distracted. "Za—"

"WHAT THE FUCK ARE YOU DOING HERE?" a beautiful voice roared at the bottom of the library steps.

Serena's breath caught and she sobbed with joy at the sight of—

"Z-Zane! Your arm!" she gaped. From his shoulder to his wrist, Zane's right arm was nothing more than a network of thick muscle fibers. Blood seeped across the hunk of meat and veins. "What'd you—"

"Had to get to you," he growled, starting up the steps. "Just like peeling off a condom. Not that you'd know. Little help." Seeing what he meant, Serena threw out her aura and wrapped it around his butchered arm. A semi-transparent purple sheen glimmered over its length, acting as a second skin for the time being. Zane, unable to see it, could still feel the pressure as it began to stop the bleeding. Nodding his thanks, he investigated her body, making an inventory of her injuries. "What happened?" he demanded. "Why would you come here? Dammit, Serena, the baby!"

"The baby's fine, Zane, and I'm... well, I'll be fine—looks worse than it is, I'm sure," she explained. "But... Estella! Zane, that fucking monster got Estella!"

Zane's eyes widened at this. "We... we gotta find Xander!"

CHAPTER 27
ON COURSE

"Perhaps an individual must consider his own death
to be the final phenomenon of nature."
Stephen Crane (1871-1900)

"Whoever fights monsters should see to it that
in the process he does not become a monster."
Friedrich Nietzsche (1844-1900)

"I will say this, though:
bad or not—whatever you want to call it—
the world needs people like Serena and the Strykers,
whether it's the crazy dead one that sparked all those changes in the
world

Two minutes had come and gone. Then three. Five. Xander fought on, mowing through enemies with Yang, his kukri, and his aura. It was easy; easy enough to let his mind slip—steered solely by his mind's eye and the Great Machine—and dwell on far more ominous thoughts than simply what sort of crazed, murderous creature was preparing to kill him at that moment.

Duck. Evade. Shoot.

Dart. Roll. Cut.

Slash. Shoot. Jump.

Mythos fell, blood spilled, and still Xander's mind wandered.

He felt uneasy. A terrible sense of déjà vu had begun creeping across the forest of his mind, turning lush, fertile land into a barren, hopeless landscape where nothing good could grow; the only constant was a cold wind that whispered a dreadfully familiar line:

On course...

And that—those two words, without context or purpose—meant more to Xander than all the enemies rushing at him or all the enemies he'd left dead behind him.

On course...

On course...

On course...

He roared, hacking away at the next unfortunate mythos to find itself in his path. His kukri chopped nearly halfway through the watsuke's scaly side, a reek of entrails and sea water filling the air as its insides spilled out across the street. The mythos shrieked, gnashed its piranha-like teeth, and hummed with a residual electric current that would do it no good at that moment. Watching the fury and murderous intent fade from the creatures bulbous, dark eyes, Xander set Yang's barrel to the side of its head and pulled the trigger.

At the end of the street, a small cluster of mixed mythos

breeds considered what they'd seen. Xander regarded them passively, opening his revolver's cylinder with a flick of his wrist and dumping the spent casings before retrieving a fresh moon clip of eight enchanted explosive rounds with his aura. The enemy mythos watched him, the previously rigid fortitude beginning to go flaccid. There was an auric in the group, Xander saw, and they were insisting that it wasn't worth it to try anymore; that Xander was proving all the rumors right—that he *wasn't* a normal vampire anymore—and, finally, that they stood a better shot of avoiding Aleks for the rest of their lives than taking a shot against what they'd just seen.

Coming to a decision—one that Xander had already seen coming through the Great Machine—they turned and ran.

Xander let them run. He couldn't bring himself to care about what they'd done or what they might eventually do, and he was reminded of a similar decision his father had made many years ago at the entrance of a terrible castle he'd just cursed the inhabitants of.

Lesson learned, he begrudgingly thought.

There was no response. Nothing new, at least.

On course...

On course...

On course...

Cursing under his breath, he moved to scan the city once again for Aleks' auric signature, already prepared to once again come up empty.

But he didn't...

Shining like a beacon, he felt the varcol's aura swell with pride as he heard his voice thunder through the streets, beckoning him.

"STRYKER!!"

And there, at the end of the vast stretch of city street—separated by four blocks and a small army of Aleks' warriors—Xander's enemy stood...

With his stolen revolver leveled at Estella.

On course...

On course...

On course...

"No..." Xander heard himself say, staring in utter horror at a sight he'd seen too many times to count.

Those damn dominoes...

That fucking Great Machine...

He'd worked so hard to—

I'll see you die by your own hand, Xander Stryker, Aleks' voice chimed in his head. *I just have to give you a reason.*

Xander didn't have time to think the words to bargain with Aleks before he pulled the trigger.

ESTELLA...

His Estella!

His *everything*!

The streets, alive with more chaos than Xander had ever thought possible, seemed to bleed away and leave only the two of them. Even without the rest of it—the death and mayhem all around them—the distance seemed unbearable. Somewhere far off in his own mind, he knew he was screaming out to her.

Sound didn't matter to him, though; nothing else mattered at that moment.

He wasn't quite in overdrive, not yet—not fully—but the roaring hum that all sound bled into through his warping senses was, if nothing else, easy to ignore. Much of the chaos, too, had become easy to ignore, but he still spotted others around him, friend and foe alike, already in overdrive. He felt torn between two worlds: that of the not-quite-frozen and that of the already there.

All around him, what should have been a time-frozen world proved itself to be otherwise. Warring bodies crept ever-so-slightly. Those who had died but did not yet know they were dead drifted in mid-fall. One could almost believe they weren't moving at all, but it was the sight of another stream of bullets —this one mowing down a sang who'd been caught off guard —that gave away just how far from overdrive Xander still was. Each round crept through the air, a lazy, hovering creature working at a confident pace that, yes, it would get to where it was going to deliver death.

The bullet in Aleks' stolen revolver no doubt thought the same...

Of Estella.

And then, of course, there were the sangs darting around the scene—those active in overdrive and creating the illusion that they existed in fast-forward—and seeming to taunt Xander's stagnancy in that moment.

The single moment when he needed that speed—*their* speed—most of all.

On course...

On course...

On course...

The Great Machine, over and over and fucking over again, had been pushing him to see this moment, and every dragging step he took was a nightmare of reliving it. He'd stood this ground, run this course, and made every conceivable shift that he could think of.

Thousands of passes...

Dreaming and dreading of nothing but this moment.

And Aleks, that sick fucking son of a bitch...

Had aimed for Estella's stomach!

His eyes were locked on Xander, his face beaming—triumphant!—and his mouth peeling back painfully slow into a horrific grin.

... make you do it, Stryker! he whispered in his head.

Xander saw the bullet breach the barrel of Aleks' stolen revolver, and he roared again; pushing that much harder. He could feel his body breaking under the force, and he invited it to happen.

Let me come apart at the seams, he prayed. *Take me apart piece-by-bloody-piece. Just please*—PLEASE!—*let me get to her before it's too late!*

Aleks' bullet lurched and then stopped, held at the threshold of the barrel. He'd reached overdrive! He'd—

A sang's aura flared with malicious intent as he came at Xander from the side, moving to tackle him off course. Xander's aura struck like a sickle blade, cutting him in half at the waist. The legs staggered and dropped, threatening to tumble into Xander's path. He shifted to evade them, stumbled, and used his aura to stabilize in mid-sprint.

Time jumped into being for an instant, and Aleks' bullet celebrated another inch. Xander could see it hanging in the air between the barrel and Estella's belly.

Push! Push! Push! he chanted to himself.

She will die, a voice chimed in his head. *She MUST die!*

He prepared to curse at Aleks before realizing it hadn't been the varcol's taunts he'd heard. The Great Machine, he realized, was trying to preach the same garbage it had been from the start.

Bullshit! he thought. *I won't—*

You will not reach Estella in time! the voice said, and this one sounded more like his own voice inside his head. *You must save Ruby!*

What does Ruby have to—

She must die!

Xander nearly faltered at this.

More of Aleks' sangs moved to converge on him, likely acting on their master's orders. Again and again Xander's aura lashed out, fighting to keep the incoming swarm away from him. They didn't even need to work on killing him, Xander considered with a flurry of rage—they only had to slow him down; only had to stall him.

They only had to let that time-frozen bullet finish its journey.

And then they'd all be able to celebrate knowing that they'd destroyed Xander Stryker without having to spill a single drop of his blood.

Estella...

You WILL NOT make it! the voice told him again.

Then, with the gears of the Great Machine whirring like the grinding teeth of an enraged creature, Xander remembered something Stan had said:

"That wife of yours, Xander, has kept you alive at every turn. I could not have foreseen her at any point prior, but, without her, every step you've taken since your reawakening could have been your last!"

Ruby!

His aura whipped and thrashed, reaching out for Estella—aiming to pull Aleks' damned bullet right out of the air—only to be knocked away by the varcol's own.

But his efforts seemed lagged somehow; his aura—everything about Aleks, in fact—seemed weaker.

"Starting from the suicide mission in Maine—when Estella demanded that you come back to her despite your initial plans—and everything ever since; it's been her keeping you alive and ensuring the next victory could even have a chance of coming to fruition. It was your rage at Lenix for what he'd done to her that pushed you against all odds, it was the chance that she was out there after that fact that kept you driven to find her, and it was she who brought you back from the madness my powers had dragged you into."

Save Ruby!

Xander threw the kukri out ahead of him, watched it spin through the air before it embedded itself in the gut of a sang working at a high-sprint directly for him. The force threw him off his feet and held him in midair. Passing the time-frozen corpse, Xander yanked his blade free, snatched the dead vampire in his aura, and worked to hurl it into the path of Aleks' bullet.

Only to have another sang sacrifice his would-be attack to tackle the weaponized corpse off course.

"And, like you said yourself, you'd have never survived against Lenuta without her—without her new strength or without the drive to push past your own limits to protect her."

SAVE RUBY!

Xander rolled around an incoming sang, ducking the punch from another, and threw out his aura in a cyclone to throw them both as far from him as possible.

He was close!

So close!

"You must be prepared, no matter the circumstances, to see her as the key to everything—"

SAVE RUBY NOW!

Closer now, Xander could almost reach out and—

He watched in horror as a sang wielding a bloodied sword brought his weapon down on Xander's outstretched arm; watched as the blade passed through the limb with a spurt of blood and a sharp, awful pain.

"—be prepared to disarm yourself and just as quickly arm yourself at a moment's notice—"

Xander pushed his mind, ignoring the pain and watching as the frozen world's gravity claimed his severed arm and, holding it where it had been cut free from his body, carried it away.

"—and, through it all, understand that you have never been the man with the gun; you have always been the gun and she has been the one keeping you aimed in the right direction. You keep her alive, Xander; no matter the cost, you... keep... her... alive!"

NOW!

And then Xander saw the last few dominoes set up in the row. Saw the truth.

He *wouldn't* make it to Estella in time.

He *needed* to save Ruby.

And she *would* die...

To his right, out of the only periphery he had left, Xander

saw a crimson shadow, unobstructed and unexpected, closing the distance.

And then he heard a not-too-distant memory chime—knowing now he hadn't misspoken:

"I need you out there."

Once more the Great Machine commanded him:

SAVE RUBY NOW!!

ESTELLA HAD HURT THE MONSTER. His words after he'd finally pulled himself back together—*literally*—hadn't just been a statement made out of anger. Like it had with Lenuta the night of their wedding back in her castle, the trauma of an injury like that—one that forced a varcol to reconstruct itself to that degree—weakened them. This, however, was only a temporary state. Aleks' new leg and the return of his powers was evidence that no injury was permanent for their kind.

He hadn't wanted her to know how badly she'd hurt him, but it was clear in the way he moved and the intensity of his aura. Aleks *was* weaker.

After putting himself back together, he'd seen fit to feed from one of his own warriors—ripping the sang off his feet, draining his body and his mind, and then, seeming in that instant to remember that he'd been left naked after the ordeal—stolen the pants off the corpse.

The blood, however, didn't seem to be enough to bring him to full strength.

The trip back to the city—though Estella was sure that her struggling and fighting every step of the way was partially to blame—had taken longer than it should. The process of binding her with his aura was slow, sloppy; he seemed to be tripping over his own efforts.

A few times, Estella thought she saw the flesh of his torso shift and crawl, as though his rebuilt body was nothing more than a sack of creatures that could no longer agree with one another.

She wanted to tell Xander this—wanted to tell Xander so much!—but, though slow and sloppy, Aleks' auric binds held more than just her body.

She wanted to tell him that she loved him, that she didn't regret a moment of what they'd had. She wanted to tell him that it wasn't his fault. She wanted to tell him, no matter what, not to let Aleks win; not to give him what he wanted.

And then she saw him lose his arm.

Eyes widening at the sight, she caught a blur of black-and-red to her left—just behind Aleks—and started to turn her head.

Ruby!

The fiery redhead sang's aura was a lightning storm of fury and intent—Xander's name cycling through her head as a mantra that seemed to push her beyond the very boundaries of their kind—as she closed in on them. Beside her, Aleks' aura sparked with realization. He'd been too focused on *just* her and Xander, Estella realized; his aura too weakened by their battle to sense the newcomer.

But he sensed her now, and Aleks' aura was shifting to stop her efforts.

Xander's aura spiked, and when Estella looked back she could see that he'd noticed this, as well.

Between him and Ruby, *she* was closest...

But Aleks' focus was shifting entirely to her now.

With the auric binds on Estella's mind lifting ever-so-slightly, she "saw" a single thought on her husband's mind:

SAVE RUBY!

And then his aura was a whirlwind of tendrils, scooping up scrap metal, debris, and anything else immediately surrounding him—floating the scattered mess of materials back to him as he redirected his focus to Aleks.

The bleeding stump of his arm lifted and drew back, a

phantom auric wisp creating a red-and-black ghost of an arm as he prepared to strike the varcol. Then, following through with the motion as he closed in—taking advantage of Aleks' distracted mind—he assembled the various components he'd collected into a makeshift arm with a heavy slab of iron making up the fist and drove it into the varcol's face.

Half of Aleks' brand new mouth tore out through the side of his cheek, and Xander threw all of the momentum he'd gained in crossing four blocks in a fraction of a second into a tackle that left a visible ripple in the air where the varcol had been standing.

The bullet that had been inching closer and closer to Estella and her still embarrassingly flat pregnant belly vanished in a blur of black-and-red as Ruby slipped around the chaos and yanked Estella out of its path, the impact of Xander's sonic boom knocking them both across the street and onto the sidewalk.

The breath exploded out of Estella, and she felt her lungs heave as she struggled to take in a breath. Her chest ached—her lungs burned—and, after a panicked moment of thinking that the bullet *had* hit her she realized that, no, she'd just been holding her breath too long.

Sucking in a lungful of air, she caught herself whimpering and rolled to check on Ruby...

The redhead was crying, face twisted in pain, as she worked a pair of shaky hands over a bleeding hole in her chest.

"Oh... oh no, Ruby..." Estella gasped, all of her aches and pains slipping into a distant part of her mind that made them seem nonexistent at that instant. "Oh no..."

"I-I did it," Ruby's voice was an airy whisper, but one so tightly packed with pride and victory that it became difficult to feel sorry for her. "I really did it, Estella; I... I kept my promise."

"Yeah, you did," Estella fought the urge to cry, trying to move her friend's hands to investigate the wound. "Here, let me—"

"Estella?"

"Yeah, Ruby?"

"Just... just stay with me, okay? It'll—"

"No! No, no, Ruby! Don't talk like that! I'll stay, but you have to—"

"I'm so sorry."

"For... for what? You *saved* me, Ruby; saved me *and* my baby! What could you possibly be sorry—"

"E-Estella... I love Xander; I always have."

"I..." Estella bit her lip at that and moved to run her hands through the girl's beautiful red hair. "I know, Ruby; I've always known. And it's alright! I know you care too much for us to... Ruby? Ruby!"

"Estella," Ruby's eyes drifted back, rolling behind fluttering lids. "I'm sorry."

"RUBY, NO!" Estella wailed, throwing herself over the girl's body. "NO!"

She felt Xander's arrival, saw through her mind's eye as he dropped to his knees across from her, and felt the shift in Ruby's body as he moved to cup her cheek.

"She... she had to die," Xander said then, seeming to hate the words as he spoke them but, at the same time, seeming committed to getting them out.

"You... you saw this?" Estella asked, looking up.

Xander shook his head. "I already told you: I... I was always too afraid to finish the vision. It just... it told me she had to die. It told me I'd never make it to you in time, and that I had to save Ruby. It just... it never made sense until..."

Tears were rolling down his cheek as he stared down at the dead vampire that had saved them both.

"She said that she kept her promise," she told him. "Does that... did that mean something?"

Xander stiffened and then trembled, nodding. "Yeah. Yeah, it did... but she already knew."

"Knew what?" asked Estella.

"That I needed her here with me today," he whispered.

Estella felt her lip quiver and a sob worked its way out.

Frowning, Xander moved to reach out to her. He caught himself halfway into raising the entanglement of clutter before letting it drop again and cupping her cheek with his left hand.

Estella's lips tugged in a phantom grin at the feel of his touch, but she couldn't complete the gesture as her eyes took in the sight of his injury. "Your arm..." she whispered.

Xander shrugged. "I'll figure out something prettier when all's said and—" He stopped and looked over his shoulder.

"Xander?" Estella called to him, catching his hand as it began to fall from her face. "Honey, talk to me. What's—"

"It's..." Xander stopped, seeming to consider something; his aura shifted from tense rigidity to withdrawing almost entirely. "It's Sawyer," he finally said. "He's about to..."

"He's going after Aleks?" Estella asked, realizing that seemed the most likely course the tormented vampire warrior would take.

Xander nodded.

"He's weaker now," she told him. "I... well, when he came to take me, I fought him."

Xander looked at her, his eye moving to investigate her more carefully as his aura scanned her. "Did he...?"

"I'm not going to lie and say he didn't hurt me," Estella said, "but he didn't hurt me enough for you to worry. More importantly, though: I hurt him. *Bad!* He's... his body isn't working right. Neither is his aura."

"Jeez," Xander said with a smirk. "Just what'd you do to him?"

"Same thing you do to everyone you fight: I blew him to pieces," she answered.

Xander paused at this, seeming stunned either by the answer or by the fact that, despite it, Aleks was still alive. "Damn..."

"So maybe whatever Sawyer has in mind will be enough?" Estella pressed, feeling hopeful.

"No..." Xander said, "but it *will*—" He growled and wiped his face before saying with a heavy tone of disappointment. "It'll help, but it won't be enough to finish him."

Xander considered this. Then, gazing off into the distance again, he seemed to recalculate the situation with this new information. Estella watched as his aura shivered with something that almost resembled hope, but he still looked withdrawn.

Estella could see there was something else. "What aren't you telling me?" she demanded.

Xander moved to stand. "Sort of defeats the purpose of not telling you if I answer that," he said, looking down at her sadly. "Please don't ask me to answer it. I already don't like having to lie to you."

Estella felt a tremor working its way up her spine, but she suppressed it and gave him a nod. She had a sick feeling that she knew what he was keeping from her; it was the only thing that he would struggle to keep from her.

"I need you to promise me that you won't die," she said to him.

RIDING out the momentum of her leap, Nikki used the makeshift hold on the mythos' head to stabilize herself and then wrap her thighs around its neck. Behind her, Raith swung his "Happy Hammer"—which she kept reminding him wasn't a hammer at all—into a crowd of the varcol's warriors. Clawed hands grazed Nikki's back, but she was already swinging her body around and clearing its reach. Her momentum continued to carry her, turning her bodyweight into a weapon that started to drag the blinded therion back. Then, now planted at the creature's back, she yanked her weapons free, began to gather the necessary energies for a spell, and completed the flip. Landing behind her towering opponent, she could *almost* hear his heart explode inside his chest.

Not realizing the therion was already dead, Raith bellowed on the other side of the still-standing corpse and swung his Happy Hammer into its head.

The dead therion's skull was turned to jelly, and the unnecessarily decapitated corpse finally fell.

"He was already dead, goof-ball," Nikki said with a sigh.

Raith cocked his head and looked down at the corpse.

"Yeah! Already dead! That was *my* kill!" she chastised him. "I'm not giving you points for knocking the heads off *my* kills!"

Raith grunted and gave her a silly dog grin.

"No! You're not gonna puppy-pout your way into *sharing* credit," she argued. "He wasn't "sort of"-dead or even "a little"-dead; he was "D-E-fuckin'-A-D"-*dead!* No heartbeat, 'cause he didn't have a heart!"

Raith whimpered, gave her the shimmering, wide eyes that always had her melting, and thumped his free hand over his chest.

Nikki sighed and groaned. "Okay... yeah. You still got a heart, right? And you *were* just trying to help me. Okay, okay..." She turned and sauntered off, "I'll give you... hmm, a *quarter* of that credit!"

Raith whined behind her.

She wagged a sai in his direction—a long, blood-soaked metallic extension of a lecturing finger—and said, "Nuh-uh-uh! You take that quarter or I'll take it all back! Now let's go! I can sense Zane and Serena no far from here and I'd rather be marching in this ungodly fucking parade with somebody I know."

Raith grunted, huffed loudly, and started after her, dragging the Happy Hammer loudly behind him like a child taking out his tantrum on a beloved toy.

Serena and Zane's panicked search for Xander to warn him about Estella's abduction had come to a tense-yet-relieving end when they'd heard Aleks' roaring call to him several blocks over. Things had moved too fast after that, and, by the time they'd managed to take the heads off of a pair of perfect vampires who'd decided to be the Vaileans new best buddies, Xander and Estella were reunited and in mid-mourning of a friend.

Much as she wanted to be there for them, Serena and Zane agreed that it was better that they leave the Strykers in peace for the time being. It had certainly looked like a shit-show through Serena's mind's eye, and she felt that the last thing Xander probably wanted was to see that *both* of the pregnant wives had gotten dragged into the fray.

And, speaking of the fray...

"Oh, Zane, darling," she cooed over her shoulder as she fired four auric arrows into the skulls of just as many enemy mythos ahead of her. "Your play-date is here!"

Zane's aura actually swelled with childlike excitement as he saw the mace-toting therion lumbering towards them.

Oh that is just too fucking adorable, she thought, reminding herself to thoroughly bust his balls about it when all this was over.

Where Zane and Raith had been tight for quite a while—and never more close than those years they'd shared a single body—Serena and Nikki's friendship, though still young by comparison, had been strained from the start.

Serena was so... well, Serena.

And Nikki was so... Nikki...

Unsure if there were adjectives in existence to serve the comparison, Serena just decided to put a tack in the idea and think back on it later. "Awesome" and "bitchy" didn't feel classy and, in Nikki's undeserved defense, they were too interchangeable in this case to do much good.

The point, the crazy blonde reminded herself, was this: tough as things had been between the two of them, Serena couldn't help but love Nikki and, as she saw her and Raith heading their way—Nikki setting an ykali on fire while Raith turned a pair of alvs into a single, coagulated mess with his mace—she couldn't help but smile.

The four convened, shared a silent-yet-relevant moment at their reunion, and then began kicking sweet ass as a unit. It was almost enough to get Serena nostalgic—though she was happy to *not* have the lyrics of "Buttercup Baby" being snarl-sang all throughout—except that something was still missing.

No, not some*thing*—a pair of some*ones*.

Not far off—at least, not far off by overdrive standards; *Blue-Bush and Donkey-Dick will still have a bit of a hike ahead of them,* she thought—she sensed Zoey and Isaac.

Grinning at herself as she ducked a broadsword swipe, Serena drove her foot into the attacker's balls—*Nothing like fresh guacamole!*—and sent out a call to the pair:

Yo, Twinkle-tits! Get you and Isaac's tight little buns out here and say "hello!" The gang's all here, and I wanna see which is bigger: Raith's mace or Isaac's—

After the day I've been having, Zoey cut her off, *I think it'd be only fair to ask that you* not *finish that sentence.*

Something in her psychic tone had Serena frowning. *Everything okay?* she asked.

It is now. Sort of, Zoey said. *But Isaac was blinded in—*

Whoa! WHOA! Blinded? *As in, like, blind-blind?*

As opposed to the "Help me! I can't hear!"-blind, Serena? Zoey quipped.

Humor, huh? Guess it can't be that bad if you can crack jokes about it, Serena challenged.

He's seeing through my mind's eye. It's... Serena, it's incredible! He's fighting better than I've ever seen, Zoey marveled.

Serena chuckled and said, *I bet it's better than he's ever seen, too.*

Subjects Serena's not allowed to joke about: Zoey started, *Isaac's penis, Isaac's blindness, and my pubic hair.*

Serena pouted, evaded an attack, and put her aura through an enemy's chest. An alv fell with a hole large enough to look through. *Alright,* she resigned, *that's all fair, I suppose. There's just one thing I'm curious about...*

And what's that? Zoey asked, already sounding impatient.

Do you think Isaac will be able to use his monster cock as a cane to bumble his blind ass towards your sky-blue beaver?

I'm going to hit you when we get there, Zoey informed her.

Kay! Serena chimed excitedly, *Love you too, doll. Bye-sies!*

Zoey promptly closed the connection, what Serena was sure she wanted to serve as the psychic version of slamming the phone down to hang up.

Returning her focus entirely to the fight, Serena fired an auric arrow through the back of an auric vampire who'd been about three seconds from catching Zane in an attack he wouldn't have been able to see. Beside him, Raith tore the winged arm off a gerlin, then silenced its shrieks by planting its arm-stump into its gaping maw.

Serena was strangely proud to say that the sight of the mythos' distended throat turned her on a little.

Nikki's tattoos flared, turning the ground beneath the feet of a pair of sangs into a liquid that swallowed them up to their ankles. Then, as they fumbled from their lost footing, the street beneath them became solid once again, trapping them in place, and the grinning taroe bitch turned away from them, leaving them to Zane and Raith's devices.

Their "devices," in this case, being a huge-as-fuck mace and a blood-streaked axe.

Serena thought that the screams that followed were like something from an Enya record.

And then she sensed something—a powerful and demanding auric call—and Serena turned to look up.

Though she still wasn't sure exactly what she was seeing at that moment, she couldn't help but think, *Xander...*

~Several seconds earlier~

XANDER STARED at Estella for a long moment. It was an ugly moment, but—*god-damn!*—she was so beautiful.

She was alive. Their baby was alive. And that was all that mattered.

Living through the moment that he'd been dreading for nearly a month and seeing it play out in a way he could have never predicted—coming out of it with his family intact—was enough for him. However, it cemented a theory he'd had that such a vision could be altered or somehow avoided. He'd come to understand that the visions were like the outcome of an equation, certain variables could be adjusted to alter specific outcomes, but it did not change the events as they existed within the system.

But that meant that everything he'd seen would, in some way or another, come to pass. Which meant there was still a showdown against Aleks with a revolver that was certain to end with...

He sighed and forced himself to look away. Then, hating himself for it, he left Estella beside Ruby's body; left her request unanswered.

The danger on Estella's life *was* certain—had always been certain—and Xander, no matter the circumstances, would not have been able to reach her. That was fact. That was a variable the Great Machine could land on—could *see!*—because *that* was something that all the parts that had been set into play turned into a certainty. What the Great Machine showed Xander *were* absolute; they were not predictions or possibilities provided the necessary components—the parts of the equation—remained unaltered.

Between this and the conversation Elder Luis had had with him several weeks prior, Xander wasn't proud of what he was prepared to do. He'd yet to understand *why* he would make the decision—he was certain that the old auric's words would have something to do with it, but he wasn't committed enough to accept self-sacrifice as a surefire solution. What would happen if he did it wrong? What if the sacrifice went unnoticed or if it didn't resonate the way they needed it to? Then Xander would have condemned the world, his friends, and his family to a future where Aleks ruled—a world where they'd likely be hunted down and slaughtered in the not-too-distant-future.

Not far ahead, Aleks and Sawyer struggled. It was a twisted game of Cat-and-Mouse that played out atop one of the city's tallest buildings—the same building Allen Carrey's body now lay within, where his efforts to save Zoey while she'd worked to share her mind's eye with a freshly blinded Isaac were halted. Not far from that building, Zeek and Karen had fought valiantly before both were crippled and forced into hiding within the Classic Debut Theater, where even then they struggled to keep one another alive. Only two blocks over from the CDT, on the steps of a library, the Vaileans had, mere seconds before Aleks had set Xander *On Course,* Zane had spilled his own blood in a rather gruesome tattoo removal. And this, he saw, was not far from where...

Oh no... he grimaced, seeing Estella and the Vaileans witness the truth of what would come to befall Nikki and Raith.

He contemplated going back—considered turning away and working to stop that vision; to try to save at least one of his friends from the horrors of what this war was threatening to do to them—but he couldn't. To steer away now was to give Aleks an opening, a chance at victory.

And there's another monster coming. Isn't there, Xander? a voice tolled within his mind, echoing with malicious laughter.

Gritting his teeth against the laughter, Xander worked to get to the top of the building in time to take advantage of the opening Sawyer, in his grief, was about to provide.

HE'D BEEN WATCHING, waiting, eager for an opening. But when the varcol finally presented himself—standing as an open and easy target in the middle of the street—he'd done so with Estella as a hostage.

It would have been easy, and it would have been fair.

Why should Dianna be the only loved one to perish in this fresh hell the world had become, after all?

But, no, that wasn't... wasn't right. Xander was a friend, and Estella was...

Innocent.

Dianna's history should not have defined her—he fought so goddam hard to keep it from defining her—but there was blood on her hands that he could never come to wash from her. He hated himself for feeling this way. She'd suffered, too. Her brother... that sick asshole was to blame. Dianna could hardly be viewed as the monster he'd been, but the life she'd lived—whether she'd managed to be cleansed and reformed of it—had followed her all the same. And, god-fucking-dammit, that old life and her new love had come crashing together to get her killed.

He couldn't let that awful, terrible truth allow him to believe that Estella deserved a similar fate.

And so he fought the urge to take the varcol then. He trusted that somebody—perhaps Xander, himself—would handle that *moment and, when another one presented itself, he would be there.*

And, sure enough...

Stryker had pummeled the monster something fierce, and he'd almost worried that he'd miss his chance—almost worried that he'd come to survive all of this and be forced to dredge on further—but then, overwhelmed by Xander's enraged barrage, he'd slipped free and bee-lined for a place to collect himself.

It only made sense he'd seek high ground. Safe; isolated; clear visibility. It narrowed down the options.

All he had to do was scope the obvious choices.

And, sure enough...

Then, arming the weapon he'd spent the past week rigging together, he fastened his jacket around the payload, said a little prayer to Dianna, and made his move.

And now he was getting his ass handed to him; getting thrown and smashed across the rooftop like he was a toy in the varcol's grip.

This hurts. Absolutely it hurts. But it's also a part of the plan.

Hurt me, *he thinks. And then he thinks,* For Dianna. For Dianna. For Dianna.

This, he finds, is his favorite thing to think.

And so he keeps thinking it.

Up until the moment the varcol throws a punch that tears through his back and erupts out of his stomach. Suddenly it's harder to think much of anything.

But still he wills his body to move, to act out the final stages of his plan.

He grabs the exposed wrist of the varcol, making certain that he can't pull free.

And then, with his other hand, Sawyer triggers the enchanted bomb strapped to his chest.

For Dianna, *he thinks as things begin to go dark.* For Dianna.

Then, before everything goes black, it goes white.

XANDER JUMPED out onto the rooftop with the vision from the Great Machine playing out a whole two seconds ahead of real time.

He saw Sawyer, his aura struggling to hold onto life despite every demand to fade out completely, holding fast to Aleks' protruding fist. He saw a soft glow emanating from behind the sang warrior's jacket. And he "heard" *"For Dianna"* toll like a funeral bell as an explosion swallowed the two of them.

Aleks shrieked as the fire enveloped him. Xander had seen that the varcol had begun to form a resistance to the Cebourists' magic since their last encounter—the traps they'd laced throughout the city had represented little more than an irritating itch to him—but the work that Sawyer had put into that last project and the raw, focused potency of the magic was enough to make even Xander, standing well out of the explosion's range and entirely immune to the anti-mythos magic, feel a phantom burn from it.

This was the opening he'd been racing to take advantage of!

But seeing Sawyer in his final moments—seeing the pain and anguish and hearing Dianna's name on his thoughts—was almost enough to push Xander over the edge.

The laughter in his head intensified, and Xander trembled, fighting the urge to echo the cackles aloud.

"No..." he stifled the instinct and pushed himself forward into overdrive.

Through the fire and flames—through the madness—and into the still-shrieking varcol. Aleks was trapped in his own personal hell in that instant, Xander knew. He'd been there before; been cast into that awful enchantment where all he knew was fire and pain and suffering for a time beyond time. He recalled a few seconds that felt like an eternity.

He hoped to have Aleks dead before that eternity of torment ended for him. He *wanted* that to be how things happened, but he knew that it wouldn't be.

Fucking Great Machine! he groused as he started pummeling Aleks in the face, resuming the onslaught he'd begun down in the street.

The barrage of attacks carried the two of them nearer and nearer to the edge of the roof, and as they came to stagger at the ledge Xander drew Yang in his left hand and...

Started to laugh.

Now? he growled. *I've* begged *and* pleaded *for you, and now —NOW!—you finally come around... only to threaten it all?*

Madness moves us, Xander, he offered with a giggle. *Didn't you learn anything last time?*

Xander growled and considered this; considered all the mayhem, the pain, the loss—considered watching his friends die and suffer through the Great Machine, considered the elation of watching Estella live while watching Ruby die, and then he considered the final straw of watching the weight of decisions since the beginning *literally* blow up in his face, taking one of his friends along with it.

Granted, it *was* enough to make a guy go crazy.

And Stan's Power just *loved* Xander's breed of crazy; loved it enough to reach through the door from the other side and turn the key for him.

At the very moment he *didn't* need it breaking through!

He had Aleks in a good place; could possibly end it in that instant if he just...

The laughter welled up, threatening to boil over and send him into an uproar of laughter.

It *wanted* him to kill Aleks; it saw that instant as an opportunity to snap through Xander's mind and terraform it into something for itself. Xander remembered all the homicidal fury and rage, remembered the Power trying to convince him to kill Estella and remake the world as he saw fit.

Xander remembered the Power trying to make him into what Aleks strove to be.

And it would be so easy for a creature like that...

Another monster...

Everyone had been right.

Xander *couldn't* handle the Power. Not as he was. It was enough to fight Aleks, even enough to stop him. But Xander was still too weak—even after everything he'd been through—to become what he needed to be to handle that sort of power. Even with the Great Machine and his enhanced abilities, he was still trapped in the confines of himself, surrounded by the ghosts of his past and catching himself with a metaphorical gun barrel jammed into his mouth.

He couldn't allow such an unstable mind to come to such power, no more than he could simply allow Aleks to claim the world as he intended to.

Either way he was handing everything—*everything!*—over to a monster who'd destroy it all.

He stood there, beginning to chuckle uncontrollably under his breath as the Power he'd yearned for so long to come to him threatened to turn him into something even worse than what he aimed to kill. Then, forcing the laughter to subside and his hand to pause, Xander stared out at the familiar view.

He saw himself...

Struggling against Aleks...

up there...

with his gun...

He saw the streets, littered with the dead and clamoring with the waging war.

And then he saw the blood. It was everywhere; was covering everything; was threatening to *become* everything.

And Xander liked the idea.

More and more he wanted to see that.

More and more he wanted to make damn sure it happened.

Then, content in the blood-world he—a GOD!—had made, he'd rule.

Aleks thought too small. Hell, the self-righteous son-of-a-cunt wasn't thinking at all if the death of only half the planet was the best he could come up with. There'd be nothing left to die if the blood of all was overflowing the seas.

More and more he was liking the idea of it.

More and more Xander wanted it...

And...how did it go?

You think it... and the Power makes it happen!

All he had to do was—

No. The calmness of the thought shocked the growing portion of Xander that ached to lose control.

But it did not shock the rest of him.

No.

The rest of him knew...

The world didn't need *any* monsters.

But, as there were plenty of monsters out there in the world, it *did* need those willing to fight them. And, out there—across the vast battlefield that his city had become—there were many willing to try, but, in the face of all that blood and death and seeing the unstoppable lengths that monsters were willing to go, they were losing hope.

His army *was* failing. His *was* the losing side. And, sensing that loss with greater and greater certainty, it wouldn't be long before they allowed themselves to succumb to the reality they'd come to accept.

But it wasn't too late!

He just had to give them something to fight for!

He had to be what Joseph Stryker had been to so many: a symbol; an inspiration. Joseph Stryker had achieved what many had thought to be impossible solely by doing what he knew was right. It had an ugly way of pissing people off—*twisting their tits,* Xander thought with a grin and a giggle—but what had come of it had made it all worthwhile.

Even in dying.

Because not only had Joseph Stryker moved the world to look beyond their sinking hopes and selfish views to construct a new future for their kind, he'd managed to do the unthinkable and live on past death. Even Elder Luis had been stunned to hear of Joseph Stryker's journey beyond the veil of his body; how he'd focused his aura and everything he'd been into the mind of his unborn son. And, in doing so—in becoming the disembodied voice known as 'Trepis' and helping to guide Xander through a life of chaos and blood he'd unknowingly been born into—he'd helped steer things to this point.

Xander blinked with realization as he realized all of this—realized he stood at a crossroads where he would either be like his father or be like Aleks—and he finally understood the 'why' behind a decision he'd seen himself make weeks ago.

Aleks slipped free from his personal hell at that moment, groaning as his aura sparked back into focus.

"Wanna see a trick?" Xander whispered to the stunned varcol as he cast out an auric call across the city.

It was unlike anything any of those battling in the streets had ever felt. Even in the throes of a war to decide the fate of the world, not a single living being could resist that call.

All at once, Xander and Aleks were all any of them could see.

And, there, Xander saw—honing in on an aura he'd always return to—was Estella, her eyes wide and knowing and scared.

I need you to stay strong for me, he called out to her.

He could practically hear her crying from there. *Xander, no...* she pleaded, *There's got to be another way!*

But there was no other way. This was the way.

And it was good.

Who needed a body anyway?

My father showed me what to do. Then, feeling it was only right, he added, *Trust me.*

Though it was a defeating notion that it would all come back to this, it seemed fitting that it end the same way it had begun: with one of his father's guns.

At least it's the white one this time, he thought as the last domino fell.

And then Xander, leaning his head back and accepting what was to come, shot himself in the head.

CHAPTER 28

XANDER'S WITH US/DIVINATION

"He vaguely desired to walk around and around the body and stare; the impulse of the living to try to read in dead eyes the answer to the Question."
Stephen Crane (1871-1900)

"That which does not kill us makes us stronger."
Friedrich Nietzsche (1844-1900)

"You manipulative witch."
"There's no better kind."
Xander & Estella Stryker

The headless body of Xander Stryker slumped against Aleks, spurting blood across his chest and leaving a hot, limp weight that he found himself struggling to keep upright.

Why...? he caught himself thinking in that instant. *Why did he do that?*

It was all he'd ever wanted. It was what he'd lived for—everything he'd lived for!—and the only thing that he'd known to be *his*. He stared out at the city, saw the eyes of every conceivable breed of mythos staring up at him. Some stared in awe and elation. Others stared in shock and horror. As he let the body fall, he saw all their auras rise.

The 'why' behind their auric responses varied, but what intrigued Aleks most was what these responses meant for either side:

Those with "Messiah" in their minds, awestruck and elated as they were, no longer possessed the drive they had only moments ago. The day was won. Stryker was dead. And that, Aleks saw, was enough. Like a mighty ship after coming upon land, there was no need for any wind in their sails.

But for those who'd been fighting with Xander...

Fear.

Anger.

Indigence.

Resentment.

And, with all of this, a rising drive—a shared and unanimous demand—for vengeance.

Xander Stryker had died fighting for them, the very piglets that Lenuta and, by extension, Aleks were set to slaughter and enslave. This sacrifice, Aleks saw, was doing for Stryker's side the exact opposite of what it was doing for his.

They actually seemed to be *rising* as a single force while his own settled into lazy contentment.

That WILL NOT do!

Aleks roared, loosing his aura across the city and sweeping up the hundreds-of-thousands of gallons of blood—blood from every conceivable breed of mythos—and began to carry it upward.

"THE DAY IS OURS!" he bellowed, making a show of shaping the blood into a vast, crimson orb that continued to rise higher and higher. ***"WITNESS!"***

Soon, carrying the accumulated mass of mythos blood that had been spilled for this moment, it came to slip in front of the sun. The sky turned red and angry, and Aleks howled in triumph for his servants to admire. And admire they did. But the bloody eclipse was quite far, and the roaring chant was very near.

Then, hellbent on making a name for themselves so that they might be remembered as fondly as Xander Stryker, his warriors grew tired of chanting and began to fight.

Like Xander, they fought with raw fury and utter determination. Like Xander, they thought of who they fought for and dedicated every attack to their names. Like Xander, they fought as though they were ready to die for what they fought for.

And—*Damn them all!*—it was working for them!

Staring out at the new scene as it unfolded, Aleks found himself feeling empty and lost.

Why did he do that? he thought again.

ESTELLA COULDN'T BE sure of exactly what she'd seen. Her keen vampire eyes had seen Xander, struggling with Aleks over his gun. For a time, it had seemed that Xander had the upper hand —that he might manage to end it then and there—but then, as Aleks' aura began to thrash about and his eyes took on a fresh fury, something had gone wrong.

At a glance, it *appeared* as though Aleks had managed to set the gun off in Xander's face. Everybody else, friend or foe, seemed certain that the varcol had taken the winning shot soon after Xander sent out a call.

Nobody else seemed to question it. They just took it for what it was, dug no farther, and committed either to an early victory *or*, in their case, to raw, animalistic fury.

In a single instant, Estella watched the tides of the war turn around. All at once it was their side gaining the upper hand, driven by a series of emotions Estella had come to know well.

But she couldn't bring herself to care about any of that.

Like she had that first night after watching Xander's broadcast—after she was certain that she'd watched him die—she felt herself overtaken by a deep and terrible rage. While mythos warred around her, Estella's eyes remained fixed on Aleks' silhouette against the blood-red sky. His aura stretched across the sky, working to maintain the spectacle.

Estella thought he looked scared.

He fucking should be!

The thought swelled and, with it, a sense of power and drive inflated within her. It seemed to be the same sort of motivation that the sight had inspired in the others of their army, but where their drive aimed them at any who fought for the varcol, Estella's was far more specific.

A few of Aleks' warriors, retreating from a cluster of Daius warriors who'd joined Xander upon The Council's request, started towards her. She saw in that instant—reading their minds with the same casual ease as she had before—that they'd consider "offing Stryker's whore" as a personal victory. They seemed certain that they could, in a passing blow, reclaim a bit of their lost dignity before fleeing from the city and, with it, "that psychotic varcol."

They were still half-a-block away before Estella's aura lashed out and crushed them in mid-sprint. Of the group, a perfect vampire was keen enough to spot the approaching auric attack and jumped into overdrive to evade. As he cleared Estella's aura, however, he discovered the recently widowed Missus

Stryker standing only several paces in front of him. A small, pale hand had him by the throat before he could figure out how such a thing was possible.

And then Estella was pumping every conceivable Cebourist spell Allen Carrey had taught her into his body at once.

The vampire combusted in her grip, turning into a shriveled husk in a matter of seconds.

Dropping the remains of the one who'd dared to call her a "whore" to his friends, Estella turned and aimed her sights back on Aleks and his blood-red sky.

I'm coming for you, you murderous son of a bitch!

Before, when she'd carried this rage within her, Estella had almost been nervous. Like then, she felt that a part of Xander was growing within her—more than just the baby in her belly, but the very essence of Xander, himself—and she refused to let that scare her this time. That first time, she figured, she'd been afraid to nurture that essence out of fear that it would mean that she was accepting his death.

But there was no question of whether or not Xander's death should be accepted now.

She had *watched* it happen.

Now she was proud to carry Xander within her, and if that made her a vulgar, violent creature then so be it—Aleks was long overdue for an ass-kicking and a "FUCK YOU!" as far as she was concerned.

"I'm not afraid to carry you within me, Xander," she whispered, not sure *why* she said it but loving the sound of it.

NIKKI MARVELED at how everything had changed in a single, awful moment; an awful, terrible, wonderful moment. She couldn't say that she'd *liked* Xander Stryker. Like many, with all the rumors and stories of how the son of the late, great Joseph Stryker seemed to be manipulating and using the system to do as he wanted while playing out selfish and psychotic fantasies, she'd have even gone so far as to say she hated him. Nikki had been forced to face a very harsh reality. Her entire tribe, however, had faced a far harsher reality. Zane? Raith? Hell, even Serena had to struggle to play within the confines of The Council's rules while trying to stop her power-hungry, Council-ranking brother. That crazy, blonde bitch had walked a tightrope of razor wire to *help* the very government that was at risk, but Xander Stryker could blow up buildings, paint the streets with blood, and even live-broadcast his own video confessional at the expense of every other nonhuman the world over and not even face a slap on the wrist for it.

Fuck a slap on the wrist, Nikki had caught herself thinking early on. *The Council went and gave him an army for what he did!*

She couldn't have cared less about what Xander had done under any other circumstances. As a human—enchanted tattoos or not—she could have just slipped back, committed to never using her magic, and let the species war wage itself to extinction. Under any other circumstances, that's *exactly* what she would have done.

Except that she'd gone and fallen head-over-tattooed-heels in love with a therion. Her infatuation with a mythos—that big, beautiful, goofy bastard—might as well have made her a nonhuman, as well. Because his world was her world; his war for survival was hers. She'd *wanted* to hate Xander Stryker and, with that hate, convince Raith to point themselves in whatever direction he *wasn't* and keep on going until they could put no more distance between them and the world-destroyer without putting themselves closer to him at the opposite side. But then Raith—that big, beautiful, noble bastard—heard that Xander needed help. Moreover, he heard it from his best friend, who, being just as crazy as his crazy wife, was *of course* already at the front lines and "good friends" with Xander by that point. That argument was lost before it could even begin; the normally carefree, grin-wearing lunk would, under no circumstances, take "no" for an answer.

And so, hating Xander Stryker all the more for it, Nikki agreed to help.

Come to find that the object of her hate wasn't at all what the rumors and stories said he was. Come to find he was, in his own way—in a distant, shadowy, "I can barely see it"-sort of way—actually a pretty okay guy. Nikki could almost—*ALMOST!*—see herself coming to even *sorta* like Xander Stryker, maybe even aspire to someday consider him a friend.

So, of course, he'd go and get himself killed.

And, because it seemed the very legacy of Xander Stryker to wipe peoples' faces in the steaming pile of "YOU WERE WRONG" that they'd been dropping all around themselves, he'd proven that The Council was right to give him that army. Because now, having seen him die for them, that army was going utterly and entirely batshit crazy in his name. And even Nikki, who still couldn't even say with any conviction that she'd even come to *like* Xander Stryker very much, couldn't deny that what she'd just witnessed *had* birthed within her a powerful drive to do *something* about it.

Glancing around, she saw that *everyone* seemed to feel the same.

Especially Zane.

Not long after everyone had witnessed the death of the mythos that was already proving to be a legend, Zoey and Isaac arrived. It was a tense and morose reunion, not at all what it might have been only a few seconds earlier, but it felt good—felt right—to be back together as a team. Though they were far and fewer than they'd been when they'd fought as the Clan of Veil, something about the six of them, together, seemed to not only strengthen their renewed efforts but also offer them a sort of comfort.

Zane roared, hacking away at an already dead vampire with his axe. Nikki could see tears in his eyes, and the threat of madness seemed to alleviate only when Raith set a large, clawed hand on his back. Pulled back, Zane stared down at the mass of bloodied meat he'd been working on, spat on it, and gave Raith a thankful nod before turning away.

Behind him, Serena, who'd gone eerily quiet after the event, stared after her husband with sympathy. It took Nikki a moment to understand that the shimmer in the crazy blonde's normally fiery purple gaze were tears. It was a rare sight, and one that Nikki didn't think she'd ever get used to.

They fought on, driven solely by their inexplicable urge to put as many bodies on the ground in Stryker's name as they could. This goal—their new mission—had started rather simply; the varcol's army had gone stupid, seeming to think that the fall of the one who'd organized them would somehow motivate everyone else to just give up and walk away. They did not give up; they did not walk away. Those who had gone in willing to fight *with* Xander turned on the varcol's army, now ready to kill *for* Xander, as the fools began their premature celebration—treating the varcol's bloody eclipse like some sort of disco ball hanging over the party their lives had become.

Many of Aleks' warriors died in the seconds that followed. Some abandoned the battlefield, realizing it was far from over. And those that remained—those that survived the shift and stood their ground—were forced into a simple decision: do or die; kill or be killed.

And the ferocity of the war doubled in an instant. The divide between sides that much larger. No longer were any of them fighting out of a hypothetical outcome. There was no more *"Maybe the world will be what I want it to be when the dust settles,"* no—now it was the difference between *"This was enough for Stryker to DIE for!"* and *"If I don't cover my ass then I won't have an ass to cover."*

Considering this, Nikki took very little humor out of the ironic scene of Serena tearing the lower half off of a fleeing auric vampire with her makeshift bow. The blonde's purple aura flared, abandoned its shape, and shot off in either direction to hoist a pair of cars that had been parked on either side of the street. Bracing herself, Serena hurled them towards the end of the street, blocking off a small horde of retreating mythos.

Zane appeared behind them an instant later and began furiously hacking away at them.

Zoey and Isaac weren't far behind, forced to follow at a quick-yet-still-human pace.

Raith stared out at the carnage and then gave Nikki a questioning glance.

Nodding, Nikki nodded for him to go ahead, nodding towards Serena as explanation for holding back.

Raith gave her a single nod of his head before galloping off to join the others.

"You alright?" Nikki finally asked.

Serena was panting, hunched and glaring off at no one particular point. "No," she said in a low growl. "I'm pretty fucking far from alright." Then, shrieking in rage, she pulled back her arms, constructed an auric bow that was nearly twice its normal size, and sent wave after wave of monstrous auric bursts into the air. The purple bolts cut upward, hung in the air for a moment, and then began rocketing downward in various directions, crashing with enough force at various points across the city to shake the ground. "I'M NOT FUCKING ALRIGHT!" she roared, sending another wave of the city-pummeling auric arrows into the air.

Nikki watched the display, awestruck, and then glanced back towards the others. They'd finished with the opponents that Serena had trapped behind the two cars, and were now starting with another wave of enemies who were forced to climb over the wreckage.

"I wish I'd gotten to know him better," she admitted to Serena, witnessing firsthand how much he'd meant to them. "I wish everyone had gotten to know who he really was."

Serena seethed, shaking her head, and released her auric

bow. It fizzled and receded back into her chest as she wiped at her eyes. “He deserved better...”

“Yes,” a small-yet-awesome voice chimed behind them. “He did.”

Nikki and Serena turned, saw Estella Stryker standing there.

She looked...

Nikki stared, confused.

Estella Stryker looked different. Not on the surface, at least—that seemed unchanged, save for an expression of raw fury that Nikki wouldn’t have thought possible for her—but something...

Deeper.

“Estella...” Serena’s voice cracked and she put her arms around the girl.

Estella’s lip trembled as she weakly returned the hug, but her expression went otherwise unbroken. “I’m going up there,” she told Serena. “I need to get to Xander.”

Serena blanched. “What? Estella... no! You can’t! You saw what that monster did! There’s nothing to go up there to!”

Estella seemed to consider this, staring out towards where everyone had just watched Xander Stryker die; where the varcol continued to stand, arms outstretched, maintaining his blood eclipse. Then, taking a step past Serena, she said, “I’m going to Xander.”

Serena moved to follow. “Then we’re going with you!”

And Nikki, who still couldn’t even say with any conviction that she’d even come to *like* Xander Stryker very much, found herself following, as well.

Two sangs in overdrive coming in from the left, third hoping to flank from behind. Therion on the rooftop. Six alvs in the alley.

Estella’s mind’s eye was more keen than ever. The thoughts flowed through her mind with no effort, warning her of dangers she didn't even know to look for. Her varcol speed and reflexes acted, caught the first sang out of overdrive, ripping out his throat in a flash before crushing the other's skull with her aura before he'd even reached her. Pausing, she hurled the first sang's corpse into the third just as he moved to grab her. Panic and confusion flared as he crashed to her feet, then snuffed out completely as she stomped down on the back of his skull.

The therion on the roof, thinking he'd caught Xander's "blood-witch" off guard, threw himself down at her. A weak yelp belched from his throat as his fall stopped halfway down. Not seeing Estella's auric hold on him, he didn't see what began to take him apart piece-by-piece as she turned and continued past the alley.

Three alv got a total of five steps from the alley before there was nothing left for them to take more steps with. The last three alv decided that the crazy varcol and his dreams of world domination weren't worth the effort and ran.

"Jee-zus......" Zane muttered, staring in astonishment at the aftermath.

"You don't have to follow," Estella told the others again, starting into the building and heading for the stairs.

Push! You can do it! Don't break now, her mind urged her on. *Close, so close. Just a little further!*

"We're not abandoning you now, Goddess," Serena said. "That was just..."

"Impressive," Zoey finished for her.

How can she see them all like that? Isaac thought to Zoey.

I'm not sure, she answered, *but I think it has something to do with the varcol blood she drank.*

Estella didn't want to confess to them that their thoughts weren't as private as they would have liked. Like they had before, her senses had shifted to a state of sensitivity that she couldn't figure out how to filter.

Then, seeming to challenge this, a horde of Aleks' soldiers—

ones that she could not sense coming before—started stampeded down the narrow stairwell towards them.

"INCOMING!" Zane called out as the sudden thunder of steps echoed through the corridor.

The wave of mythos bottlenecked around the bend, and some of them took to vaulting the railing. Estella and the others quickly found themselves surrounded on both sides. Though Estella was certain she could force her way through, she found herself at an impasse.

To evade the wave of enemies would be to leave the others...

They need you! Fight, Estella; fight!

And, somehow, that thought was enough.

"Fuck," she muttered under her breath, startling herself once again at how easily she slipped into the anger and profanity.

Just like Xander...

Estella shrugged off this thought as she used her aura to break through the doorway leading to the eighth floor, the horde rushing after behind them. Zoey and Serena used their auras to repeatedly knock the clamoring horde away, but they managed to gain all the same.

Estella turned, preparing to face the horde with the others when—

He's coming! Aleks is—

A blur smashed through the ceiling. Heeding the warning thought, Estella rolled free in time to save herself as the varcol's bullet-like trajectory took it through the floor. An instant later, his aura snaked back through, yanking him back and sending him careening at Estella. Forced to dodge yet again, she managed to reach out this time and hook an auric bind around Aleks, spinning him off course and throwing him through several walled-off offices. Behind her, the others worked to take on the horde as it continued to spill out from the stairwell. The room flashed purple and blue with Serena and Zoey's auras as twin roars from Isaac and Raith. Zane snarled, snatching a bulky monitor from a nearby desk and bringing it down onto the skull of another vampire before using the trailing power cord to strangle him.

DOWN!

The thought was enough to startle Estella, but she managed to duck her head before losing it as Aleks' aura whipped over her like a blade. Twisting around and pushing off towards the varcol, Estella caught him at the waist, drove him back several meters, and then used her aura to propel them upward, using his body as a battering ram to clear five floors in an instant before throwing him through a window.

"DIE!" she roared after him, watching him plummet out of view.

An instant later his aura shot through the opening, securing his fall, and she heard him crash through one of the lower level windows. Growling, she stepped through the hole she'd just made and allowed her body to drop, scanning each level as she fell through. Aleks caught her two floors down, nearly catching her in the stomach with a punch that, even deflected, was enough to throw her back. Managing to catch herself, Estella caught sight of him charging at her again and managed to dive clear of attack.

Several floors below, she heard a series of gunshots followed by a pained howl that she recognized as Raith's, and, through her mind's eye, Estella saw that the amassing horde had begun to get the better of the group. Certain that she'd just heard the therion getting shot, Estella was startled to "see" him unhurt—Zane holding him back—as Nikki collapsed with several blossoms of gore blooming across her chest. The taroe woman's magic flared and then went dim, and Raith howled in anguish, throwing Zane off of him and beginning to barrel through their enemies with total abandon to get to his lover.

"RAITH, STOP!" Zane shouted after him.

Estella watched on in horror as Serena was forced to pull him away from the small army with his aura moments before the shooter responsible for killing Nikki began opening fire on them.

Don't worry, Aleks' voice rolled through Estella's mind as he charged back at her, "they'll all be dead soon enough."

"AND YOU WON'T BE AROUND TO ENJOY A MOMENT OF IT, ASSHOLE!" Estella shrieked, catching the varcol by the head and driving her knee straight up into his chin.

He popped up, hit the ceiling, bounced back towards Estella, and then barreled off the side as she struck him with an auric blow that had half his recently reconstructed face in dire need of another reassembly. He crashed to the floor, gurgling and roaring from mouths that were tearing open across his entire body.

"STRYKER!" his voice seemed to shake the entire building, and the sky rolled from blood-red to clear as the hold on his gory eclipse faltered.

Taking advantage of the opening, Estella threw the entirety of her energy into sending the full mass of her aura down to the lower levels. She felt her body grow weaker and weaker by the instant as she used her heightened speed and auric control to seek out every one of Aleks' warriors and struggled to rip the life from them.

Feed! Feed! Feed!

The act made her feel dirty—using her grip on all those minds to invoke heightened levels of fear and pain so that she could just as quickly siphon the spike in energy back into herself—but these, she decided, were dirty times.

At that moment, Estella decided that psychic energy *could* taste as awful as Zoey's synth blood.

Aleks growled in the distance, and Estella barely had enough time to pull her aura back to herself before a fleshy mass that looked to be an amalgamation of the varcol's left arm and both of his legs crashed down where she'd been standing.

"WHY?" he shrieked, slamming the massive, writhing

appendage around and working to crush Estella again and again. ***"WHY? WHY? WHY?"***

Serena, she called out, jumping free of another attack and jumping through the overhead opening. *I'm heading for the roof! I can't say for certain—Aleks might still have shields up—but I think it's clear.*

On our way, Goddess! Serena answered. *Do we have you to thank for all the dead motherfuckers down here?*

With the exceptions of the ones you all put there, she offered.

Yeah, Serena scoffed, *because you're not upstaging us or nothing, Miss I-Grew-Up-To-Be-A-Varcol!*

Estella ignored this, closing off the connection, and began climbing through the holes that Aleks had put through the building in his effort to catch her off guard. Her aura worked, reaching and pulling her higher and higher.

That's it! That's it! Almost there! Almost—WATCH OUT!

Estella darted free and steadied herself with her aura before corkscrewing back, using her varcol speed to gain momentum over the short distance while putting up an auric shield and slamming into Aleks as he came up through the opening. He staggered back, stunned, his body still writhing and struggling to maintain a single form.

He's hurt... bad!

Good!

Now's your chance. Get to the roof!

Estella paused, confused by her own internal dialogue. With Aleks down here with her, what was there on the roof for her to—

He's getting up! Go!

She couldn't argue. What use would there have been in arguing with herself? Her instincts had gotten her this far! All throughout the city, warriors had been inspired to carry on the fight. They all carried a bit of Xander's spark in them, and it was making them stronger and more deadly.

Estella could feel it, as well. She'd made it this far with these new instincts. Why not see where they'd take her?

Grinning—actually *grinning* after the shrieking mass that Aleks was being reduced to—she paused to aim an imaginary gun in his direction. In her mind, she saw it as Yang, and she moved her thumb to cock back the nonexistent hammer.

Bang!

Bang!

Twin thoughts, twin shots. The auric bolts crossed the distance at varcol speed, and Aleks once more roared the question—***"WHY?"***—as they found their mark.

Estella didn't wait to see what effect the shots had. She didn't believe that Aleks was dead, but he was most certainly regretting being alive. Finally reaching the rooftop, Estella paused in mid-step as she caught sight of Xander's headless body slumped at the edge of the roof where it had fallen.

Seeing it—seeing *him*—like that made the breath catch in her lungs. She took a step, faltered, tried for another, and fell several paces away from him. She couldn't bring herself to look at him. It hurt too much to see it; hurt too damn much to see him like that.

"I'm... I'm here," she whispered.

I'm here.

"I'm so sorry."

I'm sorry.

"I wish there was..." Estella paused and looked down.

Her mind was a jumble, uncertain of whether she was saying what she was thinking or thinking what she was saying.

Focus...

Focus?

Look—

The doorway to the rooftop swung open and the Vaileans and Zoey and Isaac stepped through. Raith, Estella could see through her mind's eye, wasn't with them; a quick scan showed her that he'd chosen to stay behind—chosen to stay with Nikki's body.

"Oh god..." Serena sobbed.

Zane's aura flared, and Estella "heard" him think, *Dammit, Stryker...*

The four stared at Estella, solemn and confused.

They'd all fought so hard to reach this point, and none of them—not even Estella—could be certain why.

Above them, the bloody eclipse had begun to sink over the city. Droplets of mythos blood started to come unbound from the mass, and a thick, red rain began to pour over everything.

Look... Estella heard herself think. *'Stell, I need you... to look. I just need you to focus, baby. You've come this far, carried me this far. Now let me do the rest.*

Estella blinked and moved to look up at the corpse. "Xander?"

Four auras spiked with confusion behind her.

"Estella?" Serena called, "Goddess, what are you—"

Too engrossed to answer, Estella reached out—distantly aware that the hand she reached with was swirling with an auric mass the color of sunrise: a mass of orange from her own aura...

And swirls of red laced with black.

As this observation took weight in her mind—as she began to realize what it could mean—the sunrise jumped from her fingertips.

The sinking blood eclipse seemed to take on a life of its own, slipping out of the sky and slithering down in a winding spiral; the wave of red-and-black auric energy seeming to call it down towards the rooftop. Estella fell back, certain that the torrent of blood was about to crash down and drown them all, but it only reached out further, snatching Xander's body and the red-and-black energy and sucked both into its mass.

Estella and the others stared, horrified, as the bloody orb bobbed over their heads. It rippled, darkened, and began to turn in on itself. Then, seeming to digest both Xander's body and the aura that Estella had unknowingly been carrying with her, it formed a dark, black center—looking like a pitch-black pupil in the center of a giant blood-red eye...

And, within its depths, they saw a figure begin to emerge.

Though none of them could begin to understand what they were witnessing, not a single one of them was uncertain of who they were seeing.

"Now *that,*" Serena crooned, "is a Crimson Shadow!"

CHAPTER 29
(RE)BIRTH/TWO HEARTS AS ONE

"Courage is knowing what not to fear."
Plato (427-347 BC)

"Just as a candle cannot burn without fire,
men cannot live without a spiritual life."
Buddha

"We are the scars we wear."
Xander Stryker
(The Crimson Shadow)

"It's..." Estella struggled to speak, gasping and sobbing around excited breaths, "It's a miracle!"

"You're the miracle, 'Stell," Xander called as he floated free of the mass of mythos blood and let his feet touch down gently where his body had been lying moments before. He wore a long, red jacket that shined wetly and seemed to move around his body like a living thing, and, though it was a stunning thing to behold, Estella couldn't say that she hadn't seen something like it before.

Only it had been a black jacket when she'd seen Stan wearing it.

A pair of familiar hazel eyes regarded her with all the love and adoration that Estella had come to expect from him, but they held within them all the confidence and power that he'd come to show over the past few weeks. Taking a step towards her, he held out a hand—one free of the scars he'd put there—and, as she took it, Estella felt the warmth she'd come to crave from him radiate through her.

"You're... alive?" she stammered. "But how?"

Xander shook his head. "I never really died, 'Stell. Not completely, anyway. Just like my father lived on inside me, I just traveled through my aura to you."

"Then you *allowed* yourself to die?" Estella whimpered.

Xander frowned and shrugged. "More like I allowed a body that wasn't strong enough to handle what was coming to be destroyed," he said. "Stan's powers were coming back—doing to me what they did the first time around."

"And now?" she pressed. "The Power isn't too much for you now?"

He shook his head, grinning, and held up his hand, letting Estella watch as a red-and-black flame began to dance across his palm. "We are the scars we wear," he said, finally snuffing out the flame in a clenched fist. "Something that Aleks is quickly learning."

Estella gave him a sharp slap to the chest. "And you decided to do this by *sacrificing* yourself?"

Xander flinched at the impact and offered a sheepish grin. "H-hey! It makes sense if you think about it! I needed Aleks off guard, I needed our warriors to have something to fight for, and I needed a new body that could handle the Power!"

"And you did all that by making me think you'd died?" Estella growled.

Xander bit his lip and looked away. "I needed you to believe the worst so that you'd push to do the unthinkable. The same way believing that you were about to die pushed me to be where I needed to be to save Ruby so that she could save you."

Estella considered this, blinking in astonishment at what she'd accomplished while "carrying" Xander through the city. "Oh my..." she chuckled nervously. "It was all—you mean that this was how it was meant to happen all along?"

Xander shrugged. "More like this was the best way for us to get to where we are, but—yeah—I like your version better."

"And you're..." she paused to look him over, "Are you still Xander?"

He laughed at that and nodded. "Yeah, 'Stell, I'm still me. I've just upgraded a bit by rebuilding myself in all that mythos blood."

"Upgraded?" Estella repeated.

Still grinning, Xander's right eye darkened and turned to his more familiar blood-red counterpart as his jacket began to reshape itself, suddenly resembling the old leather jacket that had once belonged to his father. Raising both hands, he made a show of turning them into a pair of therion claws and then back again, then tilting his head to allow his ears to grow into a pair of anapriek points before shifting back again.

"How... how did you do that?" Estella coughed out, her chuckle turning to nervous laughter. "How did you do that?"

"The Power," he said, and then added, "plus I just rebuilt a vampire body out of the blood of different species of mythos."

Estella studied him, sensing within him a new level of strength; his aura was stronger, bolder.

But, true to his words, he was still Xander.

"Oh gods!" Estella cried out with joy, throwing her arms around him. "You manipulative blood-sucker!"

Xander laughed, holding her back, and whispered, "There's no better kind."

A moment passed before an uneasy aura spiked behind them and Zane called out, "So I... uh, guess this means I won't be providing any tear-filled eulogies at your funeral?"

Xander laughed and shook his head. "Not yet anyway... *bro.*"

Zane stared at him. "'Bro?' Did he just 'bro' me? No! No way that's Xander! I call bull! No way the real Xander would 'bro' me!"

"Oh no, no, no," Serena mused, crossing her arms in front of her chest, "*That's* Xander, alright. I'd recognize that hot-as-fuck physique *anywhere!*"

"Incredible..." Zoey remarked, studying him.

Isaac smirked and said, "Looking good, Stryker."

Xander blushed at the compliments, proving to Estella that, new body or not, he still wasn't tough enough to handle the praise of his friends.

Then, rolling his eyes—*Gods! It feels good to be able to look into both of them again!* Estella thought—he said, "There's some unfinished business heading our way."

"Aleks?" she asked.

Xander nodded. "What's left of him, anyway," he said, sounding more annoyed than worried.

Though she couldn't boast his cosmic powers of deductive reasoning, Estella took his calmness as a good sign.

Bracing for what was to come, Estella took Xander's hand into her own.

~32 weeks later~

Bracing for what was to come, Estella took Xander's hand into her own.

"That's it, 'Stell," her husband whispered to her. "Just a little longer."

"Okay, Estella," Zeek said, still breathing in time with her to keep her on track. "You can do it! Don't give up on me now. Push!"

Motivated by the anapriek's words—feeling a strange nostalgia arise from them and driven that much more by the memory—Estella breathed and worked through the pain. She considered all she and Xander had struggled through to get to this point. Only eight months earlier they'd fought a war to decide the fate of the world, all so that they could have this moment.

All their struggles. All their pain. And all that they'd had to push themselves through.

All for this moment.

Zeek looked up, nodding to Karen and signaling with a free hand towards his brow and stepping back onto his prosthetic leg. A moment later, his nurse—and more recently his fiancé—stepped up beside him to wipe the growing sweat from his brow. Just below the collar of her sterile button-up, right at the base of her throat, a crescent-like scar grinned.

A short distance away, Serena stared on in morbid fascination and chanted, "That's it! Get out of my sister's snatch, you belly-bulging bastard!" In one arm she held her and Zane's second child, Onyx—the black, diamond-shaped birthmark beside his right eye catching the light as he cooed and burbled; his wide, intelligent eyes taking in the various wonders around him—while, with the other, she slapped at her husband's leg.

Zane, averting his gaze, allowed his wife to beat on his thigh in rhythm with her chants. Eager to make himself look busy without having anything to do, he began to tap away at an itch that had begun to grow on his otherwise barren-yet-fully-healed. Several days earlier, eager to "decorate" the blank canvas, he'd gotten a new tattoo, one that little Gregori had picked out for him:

A grinning fox.

Just outside of the room, Zoey and Isaac and Raith waited with little Gregori. Beyond those walls, the renovations on their sea-side property went on.

The "Stryker's Vagrants" community already needed some more dormitories.

They'd all come so far. They'd all been through so much.

Welcome to the world, little Ruby, Estella thought, straining to bring hers and Xander's daughter into the light. *It might not be perfect, but Mommy and Daddy and a lot of other heroes went through hell to save it.*

"Learn from yesterday,
live for today,
hope for tomorrow."
Albert Einstein (1879-1995)

"Each time a man stands up for an ideal, or acts to improve the lot of others, or strikes out against injustice, he sends forth a tiny ripple of hope, and crossing each other from a million different centers of energy and daring, those ripples build a current that can sweep down the mightiest walls of oppression and resistance."
Robert Kennedy (1925-1968)

Balance.
The world, the Great Machine, and even its host have found balance.
Much is left undone—much still is left unseen—but for now...
Peace—peace of mind, peace of heart,
And, yes, even the ever-constant march for peace on earth.
The gears of the Great Machine groan, getting tired and old.
But there is another, young still, with great potential.
And only time—
The proverbial dominoes, as one host called them—
Can tell for certain what is in store for this gem...
This new Stryker...
This...
Ruby.

"Come a long way, I see."
Joseph Stryker

EPILOGUE

DREAM COME TRUE

~Five years later~

Xander couldn't help but feel like he was in a dream; in a perfect dream.

It was so beautiful.

She was so beautiful.

His little girl.

His Ruby.

Ruby Grace Stryker.

Named for a fallen hero, a powerful lesson, and a title that had inspired hope and fear for generations. And if the flame-colored tantrums of the little hellion were to serve as any early indicators, the legacy of the Stryker name was preserved for another generation still.

"Saved the world from one terror just to bring a whole new one into being," Xander had said, groaning, as he'd pulled himself out of a hole he'd made in the wall after his two-year-old daughter decided she didn't like synth-blood.

She ran beside him now, little feet pumping and leaping

with a swiftness and agility that filled Xander with both pride and terror. It was hard *not* to feel pride every time he set eyes on her, seeing hints of himself or Estella in her movements and her mannerisms while, at the same time, claiming an identity all her own with each passing day. But, shadowing that pride, was the terror of knowing that, yes, she *was* just like her parents—her mother's brilliance and her father's reckless arrogance—and if there was anything the Strykers knew with absolute certainty it was just how dangerous being like *either* of them could be.

But, at that moment, sprinting across through their city, laughing and screaming with excitement every time their feet left one rooftop and touched down on another, Xander felt that terror could wait. Now was a time only for pride and joy.

Another leap, more laughter, and they landed. Ruby stumbled, toppled, rolled, and was once more on her feet in an instant; her laughter doubling as she pumped her little legs that much harder to make up for lost momentum and returning to her father's side.

"Couldn't stick the landing, brat?" Xander teased her.

Ruby giggled as she said, "Better than you, Daddy!"

Xander didn't have a chance to question her before a flame-like aura kicked out from her body and tripped him. He was laughing before he hit the rooftop, and laughing still as his red-and-black aura slipped free, carried him into a crouch, and pushed him into the air. His laughter called his daughter's attentions to his game, and he felt her mind's eye spot him at his tricks.

"Hey!" her small voice scolded. "No flying!"

"When was that a rule?" he challenged her, but still let himself drop out of the air and resume his sprint beside her.

"Doesn't need to be a rule. It's *physics!*" Ruby countered.

Xander raised an eyebrow at that. "Physics, huh? Has Mommy been getting ahead of herself with your lessons again?" he asked.

"Mommy hasn't had the chance," Estella chimed in, dropping in beside them. "She's been getting ahead of herself with her own lessons!"

Ruby, leaping up and throwing her arms around her mother, screamed "MOMMY!" with excitement. Then, doing her best to glare at Estella, she said, "You were late! So me and Daddy started our run without you!"

Xander scoffed, feigning shock at this. "Daddy did no such thing," he defended himself. "Mommy was late, so this little punk took off without *both* of us. It was either wait up for you or let the little terror have her way with the city!"

"Might the planet never have to know of such horrors," Estella said with a giggle as she carried Ruby a bit further, jumping alongside Xander to another rooftop before setting her down and letting her continue on her own between them. "So do we have a destination in mind?"

"I've got one, yeah," Xander said. "But it's going to be a challenge." He smirked down at Ruby, quirking a brow. "You up for it?"

Celebrating the chance to do more, Ruby surprised them both by sputtering ahead several feet in overdrive. Realizing what she'd done, the little vampire let out a wail of victorious laughter before leaping for the next rooftop.

Estella's aura spiked a bit as she saw that their daughter wouldn't cross the entire distance. "Xander," she pushed.

But he was already halfway into overdrive and diving off the rooftop. Twisting in midair, Xander gazed up at the purple-black night sky, saw the slowly pumping feet of his daughter as she began to realize she'd undershot the jump and began mock-sprinting on the air in an effort to outrun the rules of physics.

Grinning at this, Xander thought-spoke, *Can't fight physics yet, kiddo,* and then used his aura to boost her the rest of the way to the next rooftop. Then, half-flying and half-gliding, he steered himself to the side of the building, sprinted up its side, and hooked an auric tendril over the ledge to launch himself into a flying summersault onto its surface.

Ruby laughed, seeming to find the process of being rescued an entertaining one, and, at the next jumping point, she simply let herself drop over the edge.

"Great..." Xander groaned, "She's discovered the joys of suicide."

"Xander Stryker!" Estella hissed.

"I know, I know," he said, still chuckling. "Not funny."

Not even a little, Estella finished in thought speak, making certain to get the last word as he leapt over the edge, hooked his daughter with his aura, and tossed her into the air above him before flying back up again.

Estella twisted through the air, catching the cackling child and holding her to her chest as she used her free hand to catch the next rooftop and land on her feet. "Ruby Grace!" Estella was struggling to sound stern despite the obvious waves of joy in response to her daughter's laughter, "Don't you *ever—*"

"AGAIN!" Ruby demanded. "AGAIN! AGAIN!"

Estella sighed resigned to her daughter's play, calling out to Xander, *Honey?*

Give the kid what she wants, he thought back. *It's nearly her birthday, anyway.*

The kid wants to throw herself off rooftops, Estella reminded him, *And we're only in the first week of July! The sixteenth isn't for another—*

Oh, cone on, 'Stell! Please? Xander pleaded.

Yeah, Mommy! Please! Ruby startled them both by barging into their psychic connection.

Estella sighed, groaned aloud, and muttered, "You two are gonna turn me gray," before throwing Ruby into the air.

"Up we go!" Xander sang as he caught Ruby out of the air, corkscrewing and scream-laughing with her as he created her own personal rollercoaster ride.

Then, waiting for Estella to land on the next rooftop, he

dropped her, letting her careen through the air—leaving wails of frantic laughter as she did—before being swept up once again in her mother's arms.

Still flying over the two ladies of his life, Xander took a moment to survey the city, considering how things had changed. Ruby was growing up in a world where mythos were recognized for what they were. Whether this was a good thing or a bad thing still depended a great deal on individual opinion, but his work with both The Council and the more open-minded human politicians the world over had begun to open doorways that had been, only a few short years ago, considered unheard of. It was, admittedly, far from a perfect world, and on most nights Xander was confident that he would likely never see a perfect world even if by some bizarre turn of fate he *did* manage to live forever.

But, despite what some humans still chose to believe, mythos weren't immortal.

Perfect or not, though, it was *their* world, and it was undeniably better than the alternative. And, best of all, he could see that things *would* get better.

This, however, he did not need the Great Machine for.

To know this truth, Xander only had to look down at his family.

Smirking, he dropped out of the air once again, landed behind the two, and scooped them up in his aura before catapulting them an impossible distance to a distant and familiar rooftop. One that towered over the rest of the city. One where, years ago, he had died, been reborn, and then joined Estella in tearing into the chest of a monster to rid him of the burden of two hearts.

Both Estella and Ruby cried out with laughter, their auras flailing with equal doses of terror and excitement as they flew through the air, confident that Xander would catch them.

And he always would.

Time to pump those legs, Strykers! he announced in thought-speak. Then, to Ruby, added, *Just like I showed you, punk; time to show Mommy what you got!*

Ruby's aura flared with excitement at the chance to show off.

And then Xander eased all three of their feet against the side of the building.

With that, like a great machine, the three Strykers were in overdrive and sprinting vertically up the building's side.

HOW'S THIS FOR DEFYING PHYSICS? Xander cried out triumphantly.

LOOK, MOMMY! LOOK AT ME! Ruby boasted.

Estella's aura swelled with pride, not mentioning that Xander's aura was still supporting them in their "physics-defying" sprint. *Yeah, sweetheart! Look at you go!*

Finally they reached the top, bursting into the air and dropping onto the rooftop...

Just as the first rays of the morning sun licked over the horizon.

Ruby squinted at the sight, seeming conflicted by it. Her mind buzzed with astonishment at the beautiful view—and it was undeniably that—but, being smart as she was, she knew to worry about the dangers that sunlight represented to their kind. Taking her hand, Xander offered her a reassuring smile and showed her his aura, which he'd cast out before them to shield against the UV.

"Will it hurt us?" she asked, reaching out with her own aura to test her father's barrier.

"No, Ruby," Xander said, letting Estella take his opposite hand into her own. "I won't let anything hurt us."

"You promise?" she asked, squinting against the light and, seeming awe-inspired by it, finally gaping in raw wonder.

"Yeah," Xander said, promising to her, Estella, and to himself that he would never allow harm to befall any of them. "Yeah, I promise."

There was no question; no doubt.

It wasn't about fighting to find something worth dying for, not anymore. He wasn't so bold—so foolish—as to believe that his fighting days were over. So long as monsters, *real* monsters, lived to bring suffering upon the world he'd put so much into helping to save, he would never be done fighting.

But now, staring out at a new day as it emerged over the horizon, already envious of the trio's auric splendor, Xander Stryker knew that he'd never go another day without something to live for.

~THE END~

There will be more...

ABOUT NATHAN SQUIERS

Nathan Squiers, along with his loving wife & fellow author, Megan J. Parker, one incredibly demanding demon wearing a cat-suit, and a pair of "fur baby" huskies, is a resident of Upstate New York. When he isn't dividing his time between writing or "nerding out" over comics, anime, or movie marathons, he's chasing dreams of amateur body building.

His Crimson Shadow series has gained international recognition and has been a bestseller in urban fantasy and dark fantasy. His novel, Curtain Call, won best Occult & Paranormal Thriller in the 2013 Blogger Book Fair Awards. In 2016, he became a USA Today bestselling author and since then, has been on the list four times.

Learn more about Nathan's work at www.nathansquiers-books.com

Made in the USA
Middletown, DE
09 March 2023